# Murder on Main Street

# Murder on Main Street

## Small-Town Crime from

### ELLERY QUEEN'S MYSTERY MAGAZINE

### & ALFRED HITCHCOCK'S MYSTERY MAGAZINE

EDITED BY

## Cynthia Manson

BARNES
&NOBLE
B O O K S
NEW YORK

# Acknowledgments

GRATEFUL ACKNOWLEDGMENT IS MADE TO THE FOLLOWING
FOR PERMISSION TO REPRINT THEIR COPYRIGHTED MATERIAL:

MY FIRST MURDER by Steve Barancik, copyright © 1988 by Davis Publications, Inc., reprinted by permission of the author; THE DETTWEILER SOLUTION by Lawrence Block, copyright © 1976 by Davis Publications, Inc., reprinted by permission of Knox Burger Associates, Ltd.; TO KILL A CAVANAUGH by Brenda Melton Burnham, copyright © 1992 by Dell Magazines, a division of Bantam Doubleday Dell Magazines, reprinted by permission of the author; SOMETHING'S HAPPENING AT THE HALLIWELLS' by Jeffrey Bush; copyright © 1989 by Davis Publications, Inc., reprinted by permission of the author; ACCIDENTALLY YOURS by Ellane Caveney, copyright © 1985 by Davis Publications, Inc., reprinted by permission of the author, BEST OF LUCK! by Vickie Dubois, copyright © 1987 by Davis Publications, Inc., reprinted by permission of the author; THE WITCH OF WILTON FALLS by Gloria Ericson, copyright © 1967 by H.S.D. Publications, Inc., reprinted by permission of the author; THE SOUNDS OF SUNDAY MORNING by Augusta Hancock, copyright © 1987 by Davis Publications, Inc., reprinted by permission of the author; DEATH OF AN OTTER by Joseph Hansen, copyright © 1987 by Davis Publications, Inc., reprinted by permission of the author; AUGUST IS A GOOD TIME FOR KILLING by Joyce Harrington, copyright © 1977 by Davis Publications, Inc., reprinted by permission of the Scott Meredith Literary Agency; A SOUL TO TELL by Jeremiah Healy, copyright © 1990 by Davis Publications, Inc., reprinted by permission of Jed Mattes, Inc.; THE MAGGODY FILES: D.W.I. by Joan Hess, copyright © 1992 by Dell Magazines, a division of Bantam Doubleday Dell Magazines, reprinted by permission of the author; TALL BOYS by Rob Kantner, copyright © 1990 by Davis Publications, Inc., reprinted by permission of the author; FIRST WEEK IN SEPTEMBER by Jean Leslie, copyright © 1967 by H.S.D. Publications, Inc., reprinted by permission of Blanche C. Gregory, Inc.; A MAN AROUND THE HOUSE by Virginia Long, copyright © 1989 by Davis Publications, Inc., reprinted by permission of the author; SO LONG, LANA TURNER by William T. Lowe, copyright © 1990 by Davis Publications, Inc., reprinted by permission of the author; DARK PLACES by James McKimmey, copyright © 1983 by Davis Publications, Inc., reprinted by permission of Robert P. Mills, Ltd.; A FRIEND IN DEED by Don Marshall, copyright © 1992 by Dell Magazines, a division of Bantam Doubleday Dell Magazines, reprinted by permission of the author; DEAD STANDSTILL by Rex Miller, copyright © 1990 by Davis Publications, Inc., reprinted by permission of Richard Curtis Associates, Inc.; GOOD NEIGHBORS by Sharon Mitchell, copyright © 1989 by Davis Publications, Inc., reprinted by permission of the author; BRIDEY'S CALLER by Judith O'Neill, copyright © 1988 by Davis Publications, Inc., reprinted by permission of the author; SUMMER NOTES by Karen Parker, copyright © 1989 by Karen Parker, reprinted by permission of the author; WHEN GOD'S IN TOWN by J. A. Paul, copyright © 1991 by Davis Publications, Inc., reprinted by permission of the author; **EARLY SUMMER** by Jas R. Petrin, copyright © 1986 by Davis Publications, Inc., reprinted by permission of the author; **A DAY AT THE LAKE** by Ed Poole, copyright © 1989 by Davis Publications, Inc., reprinted by permission of the author; **THE YOUNG SHALL SEE VISIONS, AND THE OLD DREAM DREAMS** by Kristine Kathryn Rusch, copyright © 1989 by Davis Publications, Inc., reprinted by permission of the author; **A MATTER OF THIN AIR** by Lawrence Treat, copyright © 1982 by Davis Publications, Inc., reprinted by permission of Robert P. Mills, Ltd.; **THE SPRING THAT ELLIE DIED** by Stephen Wasylyk, copyright © 1983 by Davis Publications, Inc., reprinted by permission of the author; **JUST AN UNOFFICIAL INVESTIGATION** by E. N. Welch, copyright © 1986 by Davis Publications, Inc., reprinted by permission of the author; all stories previously appeared in **ALFRED HITCHCOCK'S MYSTERY MAGAZINE,** published by **Dell Magazines, a division of Bantam Doubleday Dell Magazines.**

**THE HEDGE BETWEEN** by Charlotte Armstrong, copyright © 1953 by Charlotte Armstrong, reprinted by permission of Brandt & Brandt Literary Agents, Inc.; **THE PERFECT VICTIM** by William Bankier, copyright © 1992 by Dell Magazines, a division of Bantam Doubleday Dell Magazines, reprinted by permission of Curtis Brown Ltd.; **MARY, MARY, QUITE CONTRARY** by George Baxt, copyright © 1983 by Davis Publications, Inc., reprinted by permission of the author; **HOW'S YOUR MOTHER?** by Simon Brett, copyright © 1980 by Simon Brett (first published in THE MYSTERY GUILD ANTHOLOGY, London 1980), reprinted by permission of the JCA Literary Agency, Inc.; **NATURAL CAUSES** by Dorothy Salisbury Davis, copyright © 1983 by Davis Publications, Inc., reprinted by permission of McIntosh & Otis, Inc.; **MRS. MOUSE** by Stanley Ellin, copyright ©1983 by Davis Publications, Inc., reprinted by permission of Curtis Brown Ltd.; **MIZ SAMMY'S HONOR** by Florence V. Mayberry, copyright © 1992 by Dell Magazines, a division of Bantam Doubleday Dell Magazines, reprinted by permission of the author; **MERCY'S KILLING** by Barbara Owens, copyright © 1991 by Davis Publications, Inc., reprinted by permission of the author; **STILL LIFE WITH ORIOLES** by James Powell, copyright ©1988 by Davis Publications, Inc., reprinted by permission of Scott Meredith Literary Agency; **THE DIVIDING FENCE** by Jeffry Scott, copyright © 1988 by Davis Publications, Inc., reprinted by permission of the author; **JUST THE LADY WE'RE LOOKING FOR** by Donald E. Westlake, copyright © 1964 by Donald E. Westlake, reprinted by permission of the Scott Meredith Literary Agency; all stories previously appeared in **ELLERY QUEEN'S MYSTERY MAGAZINE,** published by **Dell Magazines, a division of Bantam Doubleday Dell Magazines.**

# Contents

# Foreword

A murderer is not always recognizable, for the deadliest crime can be committed by a seemingly innocent next-door neighbor in a charming small town.

In *Murder on Main Street*, the darkest of secrets are hidden behind white picket fences, in deep, dark cellars, and in the blood-stained hearts of everyone from the casserole-bearing welcome committee and the bank president, to the sinister spinster in the decrepit Victorian house on Elm Street.

Yes, murder *is* on the mind of that friendly person who lives down the block—and whether it takes place in a country lane, suburban development, or backwoods cabin, it's still a fatal crime.

In Simon's Brett's entertaining tale "How's Your Mother?," neighborhood concerns unearth a strange secret about a reclusive man's mother and one of the most peculiar family relationships since *Psycho*. Neighborly intrigue is further outlined in Charlotte Armstrong's "The Hedge Between," wherein a teenage girl solves a seven-year-old murder that took place next-door. Rex Miller, critically acclaimed author of *Frenzy*, investigates domestic sabotage and scheming in "Dead Standstill," and Lawrence Block describes a scam that backfires badly in "The Dettweiler Solution" as two brothers plot each other's murder.

Joyce Harrington explores a classic feud between neighbors in "August is a Good Time for Killing," when a New York divorcee and her two children move to the country; and Rob Kantner reveals the seamy underside of suburban life in "Tall Boys"—Ben Perkins' first case.

*Murder on Main Street* offers an abundance of entertainment in forty tales of envy, deceit, revenge, and murder—all situated in the most tranquil of settings. Would that nice elderly lady across the street actually commit murder? No? Are you sure? Have you checked out her garden and cellar personally? Better think twice before you read this book out on the lawn. . . .

—Cynthia Manson

# How's Your Mother?

## SIMON BRETT

t's all right, Mother. Just the postman," Humphrey Partridge called up
the stairs, recognizing the uniformed bulk behind the frosted glass of
the front door.

"Parcel for you, Mr. Partridge."

As he handed it over, Reg Carter, the postman, leant one arm against
the doorframe in his chatting position. "From some nurseries, it says on
the label."

"Yes—"

"Bulbs, by the feel of it."

"Yes." Humphrey Partridge's hand remained on the door as if about to
close it, but the postman didn't seem to notice the hint.

"Right time of year for planting bulbs, isn't it? November."

"Yes."

Again Reg was impervious to the curtness of the monosyllable. "How's
your mother?" he asked chattily.

Partridge softened. "Not so bad. You know—considering."

"Never seem to bring any letters for her, do I?"

"No. Well, when you get to that age, most of your friends have gone."

"Suppose so. How old is she now?"

"Eighty-six last July."

"That's a good age. Doesn't get about much?"

"No, hardly at all. Now if you'll excuse me, I do have to leave to catch
my train."

Humphrey Partridge just restrained himself from slamming the door on
the postman. Then he put his scarf round his neck, crossed the ends
across his chest and held them in position with his chin while he slipped
on his raincoat with the fleecy lining buttoned in. He picked up his briefcase and called up the stairs, "Bye, Mother! Off to work now. Be home the
usual time!"

\*   \*   \*

In the village post office, Mrs. Denton watched the closing door with disapproval and shrugged her shawl righteously around her. "Don't like that Jones woman. Coming in for *The Times* every morning. Very lah-di-dah. Seems shifty to me. Wouldn't be surprised if there was something going on there."

"Maybe." Her husband didn't look up from his morbid perusal of the *Daily Mirror*. "Nasty business, this, about the woman and the R.A.F. bloke."

"*The Red Scarf Case*," Mrs. Denton italicized avidly.

"Hmmm. They say when the body was found—" He broke off as Humphrey Partridge came in for his *Telegraph*. "Morning. How's the old lady?"

"Oh, not too bad, thank you. Considering."

Mrs. Denton gathered her arms under her bosom. "Oh, Mr. Partridge—the vicar was in yesterday, asked me if I'd ask you. There's a jumble sale in the Institute tomorrow and he was looking for some able-bodied helpers just to shift a few—"

"Ah, I'm sorry, Mrs. Denton, I don't like to leave my mother at weekends. She's alone enough with me being at work all week."

"It wouldn't be for long. It's just—"

"I'm sorry. Now I must dash or I'll miss my train."

They let the silence stand for a moment after the shop door shut. Then Mr. Denton spoke, without raising his eyes from his paper. "Lives for his mother, that one."

"Worse things to live for."

"Oh, yes. Still, it doesn't seem natural in a grown man."

"Shouldn't think it'd last long. Old girl must be on the way out. Been bedridden ever since they moved here. And how long ago's that? Three years?"

"Three. Four."

"Don't know what he'll do when she goes."

"Move, maybe. George in the grocer said something about him talking of emigrating to Canada if only he hadn't got the old girl to worry about."

"I expect he'll come into some money when she goes." When Mrs. Denton expected something, it soon became fact in the village.

Humphrey Partridge straightened the ledgers on his desk, confident that the sales figures were all entered and his day's work was done. He stole a look at his watch. Five twenty-five. Nearly time to put his coat on and—

The phone rang. Damn. Why on earth did people ring up at such inconvenient times? "Partridge," he snapped into the receiver.

"Hello, it's Sylvia in Mr. Brownlow's office. He wondered if you could just pop along for a quick word."

"What? Now? I was about to leave. —Oh, very well, Miss Simpson. If it's urgent."

Mr. Brownlow looked up over his half-glasses as Partridge entered. "Humphrey, take a pew."

Partridge sat on the edge of the indicated chair, poised for speedy departure.

"Minor crisis blown up," said Brownlow languidly. "Did you know I was meant to be going to Antwerp next week for the conference?"

"Yes."

"Just had a telex from Parsons in Rome. Poor sod's gone down with some virus and is stuck in an Eyetie hospital, heaven help him. Means I'll have to go out to Rome tomorrow and pick up the pieces of the contract. So there's no chance of my making Antwerp on Monday."

"Oh, dear."

"Yes, it's a bugger. But we've got to have someone out there. It's an important conference. Someone should be there waving the flag for Brownlow and Potter."

"Surely Mr. Potter will go."

"No, he's too tied up here."

"Evans?"

"On leave next week. Had it booked for yonks. No, Partridge, you're the only person who's free to go."

"But I'm very busy this time of year!"

"Only routine. One of the juniors can keep it ticking over."

"But surely it should be someone whose standing in the company—"

"Your standing's fine. Be good experience. It's about time you took some more executive responsibility. There's bound to be a bit of a reshuffle when Potter retires and you're pretty senior on length of service . . . Take that as read then, shall we? I'll get Sylvia to transfer the tickets and hotel and—"

"No, Mr. Brownlow. You see, it's rather difficult."

"What's the problem?"

"It's my mother. She's very old and I look after her, you know."

"Oh, come on, it's only three days, Partridge."

"But she's very unwell at the moment."

"She always seems to be very unwell."

"Yes, but this time I think it's . . . I mean I'd never forgive myself if . . ."

"But this is important for the company. And Antwerp's not the end of the earth. If something happened, you could leap onto a plane and be back in a few hours."

"I'm sorry. It's impossible. My mother . . ."

Mr. Brownlow sat back in his high swivel chair and toyed with a paper knife. "You realize this would mean I'd have to send someone junior to you . . ."

"Yes."

"And it's the sort of thing that might stick in people's minds if there were a question of promotion or . . ."

"Yes."

"Yes. Well, that's it." Those who knew Mr. Brownlow well would have realized that he was extremely annoyed. "I'd better not detain you any longer or I'll make you late for your train."

Partridge looked gratefully at his watch as he rose. "No, if I really rush I'll just make it."

"Oh, terrific," said Mr. Brownlow, but his sarcasm was wasted on Partridge's departing back.

"Mother, I'm home! Six thirty-five on the dot. Had to run for the train, but I just made it. I'll come on up!"

Humphrey Partridge bounded up the stairs, went past his own bedroom, and stood in the doorway of the second bedroom. There was a smile of triumph on his lips as he looked at the empty bed.

Partridge put two slices of bread into his toaster. He had had the toaster a long time and it still worked perfectly. Better than one of those modern pop-up ones. Silly, gimmicky things.

He looked out of the kitchen window with satisfaction. He felt a bit stiff, but it had been worth it. The earth of the borders had all been neatly turned over. And all the bulbs planted. He smiled.

The doorbell rang. As he went to answer it, he looked at his watch. Hmm, have to get his skates on or he'd miss the train. Always more difficult to summon up the energy on Monday mornings.

It was Reg Carter, the postman. "Sorry, I couldn't get these through the letter box." But there was no apology in his tone—no doubt he saw this as another opportunity for one of his interminable chats.

Partridge could recognize that the oversize package was more brochures and details about Canada. He would enjoy reading those on the train. He restrained the impulse to snatch them out of the postman's hand.

"Oh, and there was this letter, too."

"Thank you."

Still, the postman didn't hand them over. "Nothing for the old lady today neither."

"No, as I said last week, she doesn't expect many letters."

"No. She all right, is she?"

"Fine, thank you." The postman still seemed inclined to linger, so Partridge continued, "I'm sorry, I'm in rather a hurry, I have to leave for work in a moment."

The next thing Reg Carter knew, the package and letter were no longer in his hands and the door was shut in his face.

Inside, Humphrey Partridge put the unopened brochures into his briefcase and slid his finger along the top of the other envelope. As he looked at its contents, he froze, then sat down at the foot of the stairs, weak with shock. Out loud he cried, "This is it. Oh, Mother, this is it!"

Then he looked at his watch, gathered up his briefcase, scarf, and coat, and hurried out of the house.

"There's more about that Red Scarf Case in *The Sun*" said Mr. Denton with gloomy relish.

"It all comes out at the trial. Always does," his wife observed sagely.

"Says here he took her out onto the golf links to look at the moon. Look at the moon—huh!"

"I wouldn't be taken in by something like that, Maurice. Serves her right in a way. Mind you, he must have been a psychopath. Sergeant Wallace says nine cases out of ten—"

Partridge entered breezily. "*Telegraph*, please. Oh, and a local paper, please."

"Local paper?" Mrs. Denton, starved of variety, pounced on this departure from the norm.

"Yes, I just want a list of local estate agents."

"Thinking of buying somewhere else?"

"Maybe not buying," said Partridge, coyly enigmatic.

He didn't volunteer any more, so Mr. Denton took up the conversation with his habitual originality. "Getting colder, isn't it?"

Partridge agreed that it was.

Mrs. Denton added her contribution. "It'll get a lot colder yet."

"I'm sure it will," Partridge agreed. And then he couldn't resist saying, "Though with a bit of luck I won't be here to feel it."

"You are thinking of moving then?"

"Maybe. Maybe." And Humphrey Partridge left the shop with his newspapers, unwontedly frisky.

"I think," pronounced Mrs. Denton, focusing her malevolence, "there's something going on there."

*    *    *

"You wanted to see me, Partridge?"

"Yes, Mr. Brownlow."

"Well, make it snappy. I've just flown back from Rome. As it turns out, I could have made the Antwerp conference. Still, it's giving young Dyett a chance to win his spurs. What was it you wanted, Partridge?" Mr. Brownlow stifled a yawn.

"I've come to give in my notice."

"You mean you want to leave?"

"Yes."

"This is rather unexpected."

"Yes, Mr. Brownlow."

"I see." Mr. Brownlow swiveled his chair in irritation. "Have you had an offer from another company?"

"No."

"No, I hardly thought . . ."

"I'm going abroad. With my mother."

"Of course. May one ask where?"

"Canada."

"Ah. Reputed to be a land of opportunity. Are you starting a new career out there?"

"I don't know. I may not work."

"Oh, come into money, have we?" But he received no answer to the question. "O.K., if you'd rather not say, that's your business. I won't inquire further. Well, I hope you know what you're doing. I'll need a month's notice in writing."

"Is it possible for me to go sooner?"

"A month's notice is customary." Mr. Brownlow's temper suddenly gave. "No, sod it, I don't want people here unwillingly! Just go! Go today!"

"Thank you."

"Of course, we do usually give a farewell party to departing staff, but in your case . . ."

"It won't be necessary."

"Too bloody right it won't be necessary!" Mr. Brownlow's eyes blazed. "Get out!"

Partridge got home just before lunch in high spirits. Shamelessly using Brownlow and Potter's telephones for private calls, he had rung an estate agent to put his house on the market and made positive inquiries of the Canadian High Commission about emigration. He burst through the front door and called out his customary, "Hello, Mother! I'm home!"

The words died on his lips as he saw Reg Carter emerging from his kitchen. "Good God, what are *you* doing here? This is private property."

"I was doing my rounds with the second post."

"How did you get in?"

"I had to break a window."

"You had no right. That's breaking and entering. I'll call the police."

"It's all right. I've already called them. I've explained it all to Sergeant Wallace."

Partridge's face was the color of putty. "Explained what?" he croaked.

"About the fire." Then again, patiently, because Partridge didn't seem to be taking it in, "The fire. There was a fire. In your kitchen. I saw the smoke as I came past. You'd left the toaster on this morning. It had got the tea towel, and the curtains were just beginning to go. So I broke in."

Partridge now looked human again. "I understand. I'm sorry I was so suspicious. It's just . . . Thank you."

"Don't mention it," said Reg Carter with insouciance he'd learned from some television hero. "It was just I thought, what with your mother upstairs I couldn't afford to wait and call the fire brigade. What with her not being able to move and all."

"That was very thoughtful. Thank you." Unconsciously Partridge was edging round the hall, as if trying to usher the postman out. But Reg Carter stayed firmly in the kitchen doorway. Partridge reached vaguely toward his wallet. "I feel I should reward you in some way . . ."

"No, I don't want no reward. I just did it to save the old lady."

Partridge gave a little smile and nervous nod of gratitude.

"I mean, it would be awful for her to be trapped. Someone helpless like that."

"Yes."

Up until this point the postman's tone had been tentative, but as he continued he became more forceful. "After I'd put the fire out, I thought I ought to see if she was all right. She might have smelt burning or heard me breaking in and been scared out of her wits . . . So I called up the stairs to her. She didn't answer."

The color was once again dying rapidly from Partridge's face. "No, she's very deaf. She wouldn't hear you."

"No. So I went upstairs," Reg Carter continued inexorably. "All the doors were closed. I opened one. I reckon it must be your room. Then I opened another. There was a bed there. But there was no one in it."

"No."

"There was no one in the bathroom. Or anywhere. The house was empty."

"Yes."

The postman looked for a moment at his quarry, then said, "I thought that was rather strange, Mr. Partridge. I mean, you told us all your mother was bedridden and lived here."

"She does—I mean she did." The color was back in his cheeks in angry blushes.

"Did?"

"Yes. She died," said Partridge quickly.

"Died? When? You said this morning when I asked after her that—"

"She died a couple of days ago. I'm sorry, I've been in such a state. The shock, you know. You can't believe that it's happened and—"

"When was the funeral?"

A new light of confusion came into Partridge's eyes as he stumbled to answer. "Yesterday. Very recently. It's only just happened. I'm sorry, I'm not thinking straight. I don't know whether I'm coming or going."

"No." Reg Carter's voice was studiously devoid of intonation. "I'd better be on my way. Got a couple more letters to deliver, then back to the post office."

Humphrey Partridge mumbled more thanks as he ushered the postman out of the front door. When he heard the click of the front gate, he sank trembling onto the bottom stair and cried out loud, "Why, why can't they leave us alone?"

Sergeant Wallace was a fat man with a thin, tidy mind. He liked everything in its place and he liked to put it there himself. The one thing that frightened him was the idea of anyone else being brought in to what he regarded as his area of authority—in other words, anything that happened in the village. So it was natural for him, when the rumors about Humphrey Partridge reached unmanageable proportions, to go and see the man himself rather than reporting to his superiors.

It was about a week after the fire. Needless to say, Reg Carter had talked to Mr. and Mrs. Denton and they had talked to practically everyone who came into the post office. The talk was now so wild that something had to be done.

Humphrey Partridge opened his front door with customary lack of welcome, but Sergeant Wallace forced his large bulk inside, saying he'd come to talk about the fire.

Tea chests in the sitting room told their own story. "Packing your books, I see, Mr. Partridge."

"Yes. Most of my effects will be going to Canada by sea." Partridge assumed, rightly, that the entire village knew of his impending departure.

"When is it exactly you're off?"

"About a month. I'm not exactly sure."

Sergeant Wallace settled his uninvited mass into an armchair. "Nice place, Canada, I hear. My nephew's over there."

"Ah."

"You'll be buying a place to live . . . ?"

"Yes."

"On your own?"

"Yes."

"Your mother's no longer with you?"

"No. She . . . she died."

"Yes. Quite recently, I hear." Sergeant Wallace stretched out, as if warming himself in front of the empty grate. "It was to some extent about your mother that I called."

Partridge didn't react, so the sergeant continued. "As you know, this is a small place and most people take an interest in other people's affairs . . ."

"Can't mind their own bloody business, most of them."

"Maybe so. Now I don't listen to gossip, but I do have to keep my ear to the ground—that's what the job's about. And I'm afraid I've been hearing some strange things about you recently, Mr. Partridge." Sergeant Wallace luxuriated in another pause. "People are saying things about your mother's death. I realize, being so recent, you'd probably rather not talk about it."

"Fat chance I have of that. Already I'm getting anonymous letters and phone calls about it."

"And you haven't reported them?"

"Look, I'll be away soon. And none of it will matter."

"Hmm." The sergeant decided the moment had come to take the bull by the horns. "As you'll probably know from these letters and telephone calls then, people are saying you killed your mother for her money."

"That is libelous nonsense!"

"Maybe. I hope so. If you can just answer a couple of questions for me, then I'll know so. Tell me first—when did your mother die?"

"Ten days ago. The eleventh."

"Are you sure? It was on the eleventh that you had the fire and Reg Carter found the house empty."

"I'm sorry. A couple of days before that. It's been such a shock, I . . ."

"Of course." Sergeant Wallace nodded soothingly. "And so the funeral must have been on the tenth?"

"Some time around then, yes."

"Strange that none of the local undertakers had a call from you."

"I used a firm from town, one I have connections with."

"I see." Sergeant Wallace looked rosier than ever as he warmed to his task. "And no doubt it was a doctor from town who issued the death certificate?"

"Yes."

"Do you happen to have a copy of that certificate?" the sergeant asked sweetly.

Humphrey Partridge looked weakly at his tormentor and murmured, "You know I don't."

"If there isn't a death certificate," mused Sergeant Wallace agonizingly slowly, "then that suggests there might be something unusual about your mother's death."

"Damn you! Damn you all!" Partridge was almost sobbing with passion. "Why can't you leave me alone? Why are you always prying?"

The sergeant recovered from his surprise. "Mr. Partridge, if a crime's been committed—"

"No crime's been committed!" Partridge shouted in desperate exasperation. "I haven't got a mother! I never saw my mother! She walked out on me when I was six months old and I was brought up in care!"

"Then who was living upstairs?" asked Sergeant Wallace logically.

"Nobody! I live on my own—I've always lived on my own! Don't you see, I hate people!" The confession was costing Partridge a lot, but he was too wound up to stop its outpouring. "People are always trying to find out about you, to probe, to know you. They want to invade your house, take you out for drinks, invade your privacy. I can't stand it! I just want to be on my own!"

Sergeant Wallace tried to interject, but Partridge steamrollered on. "But you can't be alone. People won't let you. You have to have a reason. So I invented my mother. I couldn't do things, I couldn't see people, because I had to get back to my mother. She was ill. And my life worked very well like that. I even began to believe in her, to talk to her. She never asked questions, she didn't want to know anything about me, she just loved me and was kind and beautiful. And I loved her. I wouldn't kill her —I wouldn't lay a finger on her. It's you, all of you who've killed her!" He was now weeping uncontrollably. "Damn you, damn you."

Sergeant Wallace took a moment or two to organize this new information in his mind. "So what you're telling me is there never was any mother. You made her up. You couldn't have killed her, because she never lived."

"Yes," said Partridge petulantly. "Can't you get that through your thick skull?"

"Hmm. And how do you explain that you suddenly have enough money to emigrate and buy property in Canada?"

"My premium bond came up. I got the letter on the morning of the fire. That's why I forgot to turn the toaster off. I was so excited."

"I see." Sergeant Wallace lifted himself ponderously out of his chair and moved across to the window. "Been digging in the garden, I see."

"Yes, I put some bulbs in."

"Bulbs, and you're about to move." The sergeant looked at his quarry. "That's very public-spirited of you, Mr. Partridge."

The post office was delighted with the news of Partridge's arrest. Mrs. Denton was firmly of the opinion that she had thought there was something funny going on and recognized Partridge's homicidal tendencies. Reg Carter bathed in the limelight of having set the investigation in motion, and Sergeant Wallace, though he regretted the intrusion of the C.I.D. into his patch, felt a certain satisfaction for his vital groundwork.

The Dentons were certain Reg would be called as a witness at the trial and thought there was a strong possibility that they might be called as character witnesses. Mrs. Denton bitterly regretted the demise of the death penalty, feeling that prison was too good for people who strangled old ladies in their beds. Every passing shopper brought news of developments in the case, how the police had dug up the garden, how they had taken up the floorboards, how they had been heard tapping the walls of Partridge's house. Mrs. Denton recommended that they should sift through the ashes of the boiler.

So great was the community interest in the murder that the cries of disbelief and disappointment were huge when the news came through that the charges against Partridge had been dropped. The people of the village felt that they had been robbed of a pleasure which, by any scale of values, was rightfully theirs.

But as the details seeped out, it was understood that Partridge's wild tale to Sergeant Wallace was true. There had been no one else living in the house. He had had a large premium bond win. And the last record of Partridge's real mother dated from four years previously when she had been found guilty of soliciting in Liverpool and sentenced to two months in prison.

The village's brief starring role in the national press was over and its people, disgruntled and cheated, returned to more domestic scandals. Humphrey Partridge came back to his house, but no one saw him much as he hurried to catch up on the delay of his emigration plans which his wrongful arrest had caused him.

\*    \*    \*

It was two days before his departure, in the early evening, when he had the visitor. It was December, dark and cold. Everyone in the village was indoors.

He did not recognize the woman standing on the doorstep. She was dressed in a short black-and-white fun-fur coat which might have been fashionable five years before. Her hair was fierce ginger, a strident contrast to scarlet lipstick, and black lashes hovered over her eyes like bats' wings. The stringiness of her neck and the irregular bumps of veins under her black stockings denied the evidence of her youthful dress.

"Hello, Humphrey," she said.

"Who are you?" He held the door, as usual, ready to close it.

The woman laughed, a short, unpleasant sound. "No, I don't expect you to recognize me. You were a bit small when we last met."

"You're not . . . ?"

"Yes, of course I am. Aren't you going to give your mother a kiss?"

She thrust forward her painted face and Partridge recoiled back into the hall. The woman took the opportunity to follow him in and shut the front door behind her.

"Nice little place you've got for yourself, Humphrey." She advanced and Partridge backed away from her into the sitting room. She took in the bareness and the packing cases. "Oh, yes, of course—leaving these shores, aren't you? I read in the paper. Canada, was it? Nice people, Canadians are. At least, their sailors are." Another burst of raucous laughter.

"'Cause of course you've got the money now, haven't you, Humphrey? I read about that, too. Funny, I never met anyone before what'd won a premium bond. Plenty who did all right on the horses, but not premium bonds."

"What do you want?" Partridge croaked.

"Just come to see my little boy, haven't I? Just thinking, now you're set up so nice and cosy, maybe you ought to help your mum in her old age."

"I don't owe you anything. You never did anything for me. You walked out on me."

"Ah, that was ages ago. And he was a nice boy, Clinton. I had to have a fling. I meant to come back to you after a week or two. But then the council moved in and Clinton got moved away and—"

"What do you want?"

"I told you. I want to be looked after in my old age. I read in the paper about how devoted you were to your old mother." Again the laugh.

"But you aren't my mother." Partridge was speaking with great care and restraint.

"Oh, yes I am, Humphrey."

"You're not."

"Yes. Ooh, I've had a thought—why don't you take your old mother to Canada with you?"

"You are not my mother!" Partridge's hands were on the woman's shoulders, shaking out the emphasis of his words.

"I'm your mother, Humphrey."

His hands rose to her neck to silence the taunting words. They tightened and shuddered as he spoke. "My mother is beautiful and kind. She is nothing like you. She always loved me. She still loves me!"

The spasm passed. He released his grip. The woman's body slipped down. As her head rolled back, her false teeth fell out with a clatter onto the floor.

Sergeant Wallace appeared to be very busy with a ledger when Humphrey Partridge went into the police station next morning. He was embarrassed by what had happened. It didn't fit inside the neat borders of his mind and it made him look inefficient. But eventually he could pretend to be busy no longer. "Good morning, Mr. Partridge. What can I do for you?"

"I leave for Canada tomorrow."

"Oh. Well, may I wish you every good fortune in your new life there."

"Thank you." A meager smile was on Partridge's lips. "Sergeant, about my mother . . ."

Sergeant Wallace closed his ledger with some force. "Listen, Mr. Partridge, you have already had a full apology and—"

"No, no, it's nothing to do with that. I just wanted to tell you . . ."

"Yes?"

". . . that I *did* kill my mother."

"Oh, yes, and then I suppose you buried her in the garden, eh?"

"Yes, I did."

"Fine." Sergeant Wallace reopened his ledger and looked down at the page busily.

"I'm confessing to murder," Partridge insisted.

The sergeant looked up with an exasperated sigh. "Listen, Mr. Partridge, I'm very sorry about what happened and you're entitled to your little joke, but I do have other things to do, so if you wouldn't mind . . ."

"You mean I can just go?"

"Please."

"To Canada?"

"To where you bloody well like."

"Right then, I'll go. And . . . er . . . leave the old folks at home."

Sergeant Wallace didn't look up from his ledger as Partridge left the police station.

Outside, Humphrey Partridge took a deep breath of air, smiled, and said out loud, "Right, Mother, Canada it is."

# The Dividing Fence

### JEFFRY SCOTT

The children upset Peggy Ipswich. It wasn't their rudeness, or the covert hostility—uncannily mature and stressed by complete lack of youthful grace or vulnerability. What made her teeth grind and her hands shake was that she'd never done anything to them, hardly exchanged a word with the little strangers next door.

She could have borne amusement and derision. Peggy was aware of having a funny name. During World War II she had worked in the Women's Voluntary Service canteen at Dorminster Magna and the American bomber crews had grinned or sniggered and sometimes hollered with laughter when the vicar's wife called, "Miss Ipswich, Miss Ipswich, more cups!" as it might be, or, "Miss Ipswich, the urn's playing up again!"

No harm in that, she'd been flustered, perhaps flattered in a mild way —it came to the same thing. "*Ips*-wich, Is-*swich*, Swich-swach," the men would chortle, deliberately tangling their tongues, then dismiss the matter and herself. Peggy had a knack for being unobtrusive, mouse-drab, humble, quick on her feet, very grateful for the homely face and unremarkable figure that encouraged glances to slide on to prettier friends. Not that she had many of those, though everybody knew her.

She'd never done anything to the Marshall children. All Peggy Ipswich had done was live next door to the house Les Marshall bought in 1985. She lived alone in the only bungalow in Peartree Close, poor relation among half a dozen mock Tudor four-bedroom houses. Peartree Close had been a farm track, nameless and undeveloped, when Percy Ipswich bought his ground in 1919.

The Marshall children would have relished Percy Ipswich. He'd been gassed in Flanders—blown up serving in the Ypres Salient in '17. His face was the wrong color, stained rather than tanned, there was a perceptible dent in his skull, and he dribbled when he spoke, so he tried not to talk at all. Wanting to get off by himself, an ambition shared by his wife, Gladys, who decamped as soon as their baby was weaned, Percy Ipswich bought land from the farmer and built the bungalow.

"We lived in a tent that first summer, Little'un," he told Peggy. "By winter, there was one room that kept out the worst of the cold, and that happened to be the bathroom, so that's where we lived that winter." Percy would talk to his daughter by the hour, back turned, gazing out of the window.

Ipswich supported himself and his daughter by selling cartoons to trashy magazines. Somehow he gained access to paper offcuts from some packaging process, his for the trouble of taking them away in the sidecar of his motorbike. An ingenious man, he used the stuff for beer mats and cocktail coasters. He printed them in the shed behind the bungalow, with customized designs for a number of roadhouses and pubs. Somehow he made money right through the Depression. The local council never got to hear of the project, which was just as well, for it defied the Green Belt zoning laws by carrying on light industry of a kind in an area restricted to agriculture and housing.

Peggy grew up knowing that they were doing something vaguely wrong, though not, her father stressed, sinful. "If I didn't have you and the business and my hidey-hole here, I'd die," Percy Ipswich declared and she believed him. It didn't make for an outgoing, confident personality, though Peggy was happy enough.

Soon after the end of World War II, Peartree Close got its official name and the big houses. A little longer afterward, Percy died. Peggy was startled to learn that he'd owned the land on which those houses stood and had left her comfortably off. She could have sold the bungalow and gone to live anywhere—but where? So she stayed where she was, and in due time Les Marshall bought the house next door.

The previous owners had been a retired couple named Anderton. He'd been in insurance and his wife did needlepoint and called once a week to take tea with Peggy and show her the latest letters and snapshots from Jim and Susie in Melbourne and Brian in Toronto and Helen, married to a dentist in Scotland. Mrs. Anderton's brood always seemed to be up to something and Peggy considered them better value than those radio serials because they were true. She had watched them growing up and been their "Auntie Peg" in her day.

But Mr. Anderton died, it comes to us all—a blessing really, considering his arthritis and the heart condition—and the widow went off to Australia and Number Six was sold.

Peggy watched the furniture van arrive and gave it an hour, then she went next door with two cups of tea and a saucer of biscuits on her best tin tray.

Les Marshall turned out to be one of those wrong-footing men who enjoy jokes yet seldom share them. He was wearing jeans and trainers and a creaking leather jacket over a hairily bare chest and there were tiny, yellowish clots of sleepy-dust at the corners of his eyes. Peggy spotted them immediately and kept glancing away, itching to tell him.

"What's this, then?" Marshall demanded jovially, as if she had arrived bearing a severed head. "Nice thought, luv, but we'll need a few straws."

Peggy gaped at him and there it was, the sleepy-dust, big as boulders now. And why would he want straws—to put in his hair? Then he jerked his thumb over his shoulder and she saw that the hallway was packed with children, four or five at least, with a silent girl, grubbily barefoot, nipples perceptible under a sequined T-shirt, beyond the pack.

"We'll need six more cuppas," Marshall explained. "Gawd, missus, your face! Only kidding, these'll come in handy for me 'n Marie, but if we want tea the gas is connected and the water's running, eh? No, you want to know what the road's getting itself into, who we are and where we fit into things, right?"

Peggy shook her head. A small voice, hard as ice, observed, "Funny old woman, Dad, she keeps pecking like a chicken. *Chookie, chookie, chookie!*" Breathless giggles, then another cold little voice confirmed, "Yuh, peck-peck chicken, she does look like."

"Cheeky little sods," Marshall commented with more amusement than reproof. He dropped his voice in an aside. "I'm Les and that's my lady, Marie, and this lot is the rest of the tribe. Dean and Mikey and Cheryl are mine and Tracey and Roy are hers."

Marie, tone limply straight as her yellow hair, said, "For Christ's sake, fetch that tea down here, darlin', seeing as the old girl fetched it round, I'm dying of thirst." Marshall grabbed the tray, making the cups slop. "Yeah, ta, nice thought. Oh, who are you when you're at home, then?"

"Miss Ipswich. Peggy. I'm from the bungalow next—" But the man was turning away, the front door closing.

As Peggy reached the gate, she heard the clatter of the letter-slot on the door flap behind her and one of the children shouted, "Witch, witch, silly old bitch!" When she turned, the flap snapped shut. From an uncurtained upper window, a small face stared back at her, blank, watchful.

Next morning, when Peggy went to collect her milk from the doorstep, she found that Marshall had left the tea things there the previous evening. The tray was awash with rainwater and an earwig had drowned in the bottom of a cup.

*　　*　　*

Peggy had never touched Percy Ipswich's workshop at the foot of the garden. Machinery had never been her friend and the shed was devoted to it: male objects, her father's property.

About a week after Marshall and Marie arrived, she got a terrible fright while pegging out her washing. She let a sheet collapse back into the wicker basket and hurried down the crazy-paving path. She hadn't sorted out the names, but two of the boys and a small girl, naked except for an abbreviated pink vest, stood in front of the workshop. "What—what's the matter?" Peggy muttered, flinching from asking what they were doing there.

A boy, still rattling the door handle, grunted, "What you got in here? We stood on the fence, you can see stuff through the skylight. Motorbike, looks like—not a Jap one, an old crock of a thing." He was perhaps eleven years old.

His twin confided, "Mikey's good with bikes. Give us a play on that one, Miss."

"I—I can't, I haven't got the key, it isn't mine to let you have. How did you get in here?"

Recognizing the question as rhetorical—three slats of the boundary fence, old as the house, had been wrenched off the rail—the first boy complained, "You got to have a key. It's your shed, innit?"

"Go back to your own garden, dear, and take your sister with you. You mustn't just barge in here, your daddy would—"

Mutinous, disgusted, they retreated. Almost at once, she heard feet thudding on what had been the Andertons' back lawn and a unison-chanted "Silly ole witch, silly ole bitch, peck-peck chookie, sling her in the ditch!"

Les Marshall was changing the plugs of an elderly estate car in the drive of Number Six. He gave her a what-is-it-now? frown as she approached.

"I'm afraid your lads got into my garden just now, Mr. Marshall," she said.

"Not to worry. Little sods get everywhere but they never get lost, more's the pity. They'll come to no harm, luv—streetwise if nothing else." Barking his knuckles, he swore vilely.

Peggy tried again. "It's the fence, you see, Mr. Marshall. The side fence. Mr. Anderton kept meaning to repair it, but his health—"

"Yeah, bloody place is falling to bits. Still, I got nothing worth stealing, so fences are the least of my worries." He slammed the hood and nodded abstractedly. "Nice talking to you, but I'm late for work."

"See?"

Peggy looked around, then down. The little girl in pink was staring up at her mockingly. "See? You told on Dean and Mikey but their dad don't give a toss for nobody. See?" The tot put her tongue out with great deliberation, squinting to sight the tip.

"Ten balls?" Irritable, incredulous, Les Marshall kept the engine revving. A week had passed and Peggy Ipswich, finding him elusive, had been standing sentry at her front gate, grimly, tremblingly patient.

"They break my flowers, coming over, the balls. I've asked the children, asked them nicely. Yesterday, all afternoon—they must have bought some of them specially. When I went out last thing, I had to throw them all back, and I counted. There were tennis balls and the big hard plastic ones, the footballs and a golf ball. There were ten altogether and my poor little fir tree snapped in half."

Les cleared his throat, patently stifling a guffaw. "Little sods! Look, you're making heavy weather of this—kids will be kids and neighbors understand that, leastways they do where we come from. Keep the bloody balls, that'll stop 'em—serve 'em right." And to himself, "Bloody hell, life's too short." He drove away.

Marie appeared as soon as the car had turned the corner into the main road. "You want to watch yourself," she said listlessly. "Keep it up and I'll take you to court. There's laws about persecuting people."

It was so absurd that Peggy Ipswich cried out in protest. Marie, misunderstanding, turned gracious. "I shan't get my solicitor in just yet, mind. Just stay your side of the fence and stop poking your nose in."

He was as bad as them in his way, Peggy concluded. She heard him scolding some or one of the boys. "I'll beat your head in, keep going over there, teasing that old biddy. Can't you tell she's a troublemaker?"

"Only getting my *ball*, Dad. Only takes a minute." True, for at the bottom of the two gardens the dividing fence had been reduced to a brace of spaced rails—the slats had vanished and the children had only to step through. "It's *my* ball, Dad, I only *fetch* it."

Heavy sarcasm from Les. "Ever think of not booting it over in the first place, dummy?" But his voice changed. "Come on, get it past me . . . Whoops, where's it gone? . . . Now I'm off, streaking down the wing— tackle me, tackle, tackle! Play the ball, Roy, never mind the man . . ." Shouts, panting, the yelp of the pack aroused.

Finally Peggy paid Mr. Feather, the local handyman, to renew the farthest portion of the fence. The cost took her aback, but then again the slats were heavy, the new section six feet high. The work was completed on a Saturday morning and Les put his head around the slat before the last piece was nailed home.

"Now we'll all be happy, eh? You might have asked me—strictly speaking, I have a say in this fence. It's supposed to be mine." He spoke with sulky dignity, painstakingly polite and reasonable and reproachful. "Bee in your bonnet because the kids kick up a bit out of high spirits, but you never stop to think what an eyesore this is—different height, different color, all patched up like. And we got to live with it."

The balls kept coming over. The children merely threw harder or chose the older stretch of fencing.

They had other games. A favorite was to set a watcher at a knothole in the fence as commentator while one of the boys, in a ludicrously high, squeaky voice, relayed what Miss Ipswich was doing.

"Now I'm pushing my mower. Now I'm pushing it back. Now I'm stopping and scratching my nose."

"Picking it, Roy, bet she's picking it!"

"Now I'm going to empty the grassbox. Oh, dear, it's stuck. Silly old grassbox. Silly old mower. Silly old witch can't do it." They could maintain the game for as long as she stayed outdoors. Her lawns became shaggy and weeds flourished during the long summer holiday from school.

Sometimes there was a variation. Marie spent a lot of time on Number Six's patio that summer, sunning herself on a lounger. The oldest girl, voice pitched to reach eavesdroppers, would ask, "What's a spinster, Mums? Why does that loony next door have blotches all over her hands? Are they freckles? Why are they so big, then? Don't loonies get sent away? Why isn't she getting sent away?"

"Trash," said the milkman. "I'll knock in future and you take your bottle straight in. I saw that girl sneak round, saw her in my mirror from the other end of the street. They're playing nasty tricks on you."

"I—I thought it was the birds. They can peck the bottle caps, for the cream."

"Get away—birds nothing. Bird with grubby little fingers," he scoffed. Peggy's stomach turned, her throat closed. The milk had been tasting strange, of late.

Some six months after their arrival, the Marshalls had a row. The children were forever at odds with each other and at the tops of their voices, so Peggy—woken at 7:00 A.M. and drawn to the bedroom window—assumed that they'd started earlier than usual. But this was the adults, Marie on the front path of Number Six, screaming abuse and struggling to draw jeans up her knobby-kneed legs while Les roared and shook his fist from the porch.

The door slammed like a gunshot. Peggy, knotting the cord of her dressing gown, hastened downstairs. "D'you want to come in here, dear?"

Marie blinked at her, large breasts heaving, mouth shiny with spittle. "Piss off and leave me alone. You and your nagging, no wonder the pressure drives him potty." She turned her back and stormed off around the side of the house.

Les banged out of the place an hour afterward and minutes later Marie slipped indoors. At lunchtime, looking more presentable than Peggy had ever witnessed, she departed in a taxi. The driver had to make three trips to the front door for her luggage.

Unfortunately, she went alone. Les's temper worsened and his designer stubble darkened into a mangy beard and moustache. Peggy kept out of his way, but the children, wilder than ever, couldn't be avoided.

In the first week of September, Peggy waited for them to straggle off to school and then devoted a morning to inspecting the older portion of fence. She seldom threw anything away and now the bag of corks proved useful. Tapping them home with the edge of a trowel, she corked a dozen or more spyholes.

"Thought you were a bloody woodpecker," Les Marshall grumbled, making her start. He was leaning out of an upper window, looking dreadful. "What are you at now?"

"Just—seeing to the fence," she faltered, trying to hide the corks bag behind her back. He always made her feel guilty.

Screwing his face up, Les jeered. "The kids have a point. You must be dotty, touched in the head. Corks! Look, some of us have to earn our living, some of us work nights, know what I mean, luv?" The window slid down with a thump.

Peggy's heart raced and stammered. But the spyholes were blocked.

Oversleeping, Peggy was claimed by disturbing dreams. Rats scuttled, monkeys gibbered, a macaw screeched—she was captive in a bygone prison ship and lost in the jungle all at once. The rats chewed deafeningly, the wildlife chattered. She woke in a panic, sweaty, stale, temples pounding.

A drill clattered, giving the probable clue to the interlude. She recalled that roadwork was going on where Peartree Close joined the bigger street. Les Marshall would not be allowed much rest today. Peggy was human enough to experience spiteful pleasure at the thought.

After a belated breakfast, she went out to her neglected garden—and found the real foundation of the dream noises.

The patio and nearest area of lawn were scattered with corks. The children, active early, had hammered them all out again from their side of the fence. In several places, foliage poked through. They had scaled the fence, snapped branches from her miniature trees, and jammed them into every knothole. And as Peggy watched, a bit of branch wagged tauntingly. There was no wind, not even a breeze. In her head she could see one of the children crouched on the far side, grimacing with glee over vandalism piled on counterattack.

Snatching up a spade she'd abandoned when last put to flight by mockery (a corner of her attention noted it had been rusted by a few nights' dew, Dad would have frowned over such sloppiness), Peggy swung it against the protruding branch with a gasp of rage and frustration. The branch was a snug fit, but the spade was heavy and swung with the force of desperation. Leaves stripping, the fat finger of wood jumped three or four inches and lanced back through the knothole like a dagger.

Les Marshall, squatting on his side of the fence, peering at the torn end of the branch and giving it a tentative shake while wondering what the hell it signified, screamed and fell backward. Hands clapped to his right eye, he scrambled up, groaning and in agony.

Peggy heard something larger than a child, apparently berserk with rage, snarling noises unleashed by her blind lashing-out. Her foot hurt. She had dropped the spade on it. The noises did not stop, but they did subside, become distanced.

Terrified and baffled, she fled into the bungalow. Fingers laced so tightly that the bones ached, shoulders hunched, she waited in the hall. The front door had a pebbled-glass porthole, allowing her the distorted vision of a melting, wavering Les Marshall fumbling at the gate.

Go away! she screamed, though not aloud. And he did, in the sense that he was no longer visible. She waited until her lungs protested, remembered to breathe again, and waited and waited. Eventually, forcing her hands to relax, she opened the door a crack.

Marshall could be seen on his hands and knees through the sunburst spokes of the iron gate. He seemed to be crawling back toward his house. The side of his face was wetly red.

Peggy shut the door and snicked the lock home, praying he would not hear. Now she'd done it! She had done something to him, something to do with the spade and the branch and the fence and the corks hammered clear. Pale, shaken, lips and nostrils pinched with dread, she went out to the patio. Leaves on a flagstone marked the spot where she had done— whatever it was.

She grasped the battered end of the branch and tugged. It was wedged, but she levered and worried at it, gained a firm hold, set her toes against the base of the fence, and leaned back. Suddenly it came free and she sat down with a bump. The other end of the wood was fang-shaped and damply stained.

\*　\*　\*

The Detective Inspector asked, "Now you're quite sure you never saw any callers next door, Miss Ipswich?" Before answering himself, "But how could you, being such a devoted gardener?"

It was her fourth encounter with the police in as many days. Despite the delay involved, she had managed to mow all the lawns—late in the year, it might be the last cut of the season—cleared away many dead plants, and kept a bonfire smoldering. She had dug out the worst-damaged tree and transplanted a small hydrangea. Probably it would die, it looked unhappy. The Inspector, no gardener, found nothing odd in a single bush among so many ornamental trees dotting the shaven lawns.

"We didn't get on," Peggy explained, as she had done from the start. "The Marshalls weren't neighborly, we hardly spoke."

He nodded, hardly listening. It didn't surprise him that she didn't know Marshall's common-law wife had left him weeks before. Your typical old lady, spry as a sparrow but sadly free of the traditional nosiness. Marking time, he sniffed loudly and murmured, "Creosote, love that smell."

"Once every two years, else the wood perishes." Peggy worked the brush around another knothole in the fence. "But you have to be careful—if it drips on the patio, the stains never come out."

"I daresay you spend every daylight hour out here, weather permitting," the policeman said.

"Just about. Callers for Mr. Marshall, they'd be out the front. Frankly, I never knew when he was at home, even. He worked irregular hours."

The Inspector snorted. "Didn't work at all, not to say at a steady job." He bit back the rest of the comment: Need To Know and all that. Searching Number Six had been a challenge, since a man alone with a gang of kids had let it degenerate into a tip. All the same, there'd been traces of recreational drugs, as the saying went. Lots of traces, and if only they could find the common-law wife they might establish whether the house had sheltered one user or more. Even a pair of users hardly accounted for the forensic evidence. The Inspector believed that Marshall had been dealing, either as a trade or to support his habit.

The kids were no help—sulky, obscurely scared little brutes. Poor old Miss Ipswich would be mortified if she knew that the children had—until sharply reprimanded—tried to sell the police the idea that she must have killed their father, foster father, whatever he'd been to them. Only youngsters, and rather unpleasant brats at that, could evolve such a theory. Marshall had been a big fellow, six-feet-two and change, slack-bellied but powerful. Miss Ipswich was elderly, trim but relatively frail, and might achieve five-feet-nothing on tiptoe. The weapon was still missing, but the stab into and past the eyesocket had been delivered with great power, on a level track. If anything, the pathologist reckoned, slightly downward.

Peggy straightened and, hands at the small of her back, surveyed progress. "We didn't get on," she repeated thoughtfully. "Er, did he—was there much suffering? Did he—*linger?*"

"Don't you worry about that, he was dead before he knew it," the policeman lied. Marshall had lasted quite a while, but the snag was that he'd done so out of sight and earshot of witnesses. Marshall's phone had been cut off and Miss Ipswich didn't have one. After being attacked, Marshall had obviously set off to get help, collapsing at the side of the road where the lunchtime-delivery postman had found him long after the event.

"I'm glad he didn't suffer." Peggy was still worried, however. "What about those children?"

Bless her kind heart, thought the Inspector. "Oh, they're in council care until we find the mother. If we ever do. Between ourselves, I believe she doesn't want to be found. And no wonder—they're no prize package."

Peggy didn't respond to that. Instead she pointed out, "Not all the children are hers, you know. Some are his by a previous marriage, or so I understand. It's all a muddle, isn't it?" And she sighed.

The Inspector was reassuring, dismissive. "That's what orphanages are for, Miss Ipswich. They'll be cared for, there's no question of them being turned out on the street. After all, they can't come back next door, now, can they?"

Peggy dipped the brush into the creosote, biting the inside of her cheek. "I'm very glad of that," she said. "Very glad."

Nice old girl, the Inspector told himself. Wretched kids slandering her in that irresponsible, luridly fantastic fashion, and here their welfare was the main concern with her. "Very, very glad," Peggy mused in time with her brush strokes. And the Inspector, putting his virgin notebook away, was unaware of proving that a listener and a speaker can share the same set of words while dealing with wholly different meanings.

# Good Neighbors

## SHARON MITCHELL

**W**elcome to the neighborhood, dearie," she said, beaming under an explosion of bright, bottle-red curls and a little bubble of a nose. "I'm Dearie Claxton, your neighbor over the back fence." Advancing with a covered casserole, she backed me right up against the mountain of cardboard boxes in the middle of my kitchen floor. "Don't you just love it here? We have such a nice view perched way up here on the top of the hill the way we are."

"Oh, I—"

"But let me warn you right off, be careful driving downtown. Hillcrest Road can be real treacherous in bad weather."

"I wouldn't be surprised."

"I brought you a little something for lunch, dearie." She deposited the casserole on the stove and stripped off orange oven mitts which she stuffed in a pocket of her green cobbler apron. They made a bulge over the bulge of her stomach. She was a short woman of about fifty-five, I guessed, with skinny legs and a thick middle. Under the apron were a pair of pink shorts and a purple T-shirt.

"Thank you—"

"I know how it is, dearie. My first husband was in the army. Every three years, at least, we had to pack up and move on. Now, Homer—that's my present husband—he's real seventary and I like that just fine. I hope you folks are seventary. Jim and Clara Thompson, the folks you bought this place from, just about broke my heart when they moved to Arizona. We were real close."

"Oh, that's why—"

"Homer said they moved because they wanted to get away from me, but he was just teasing. I didn't believe it for a minute. I was closer to Clara than I was to Jim, of course, the both of us being homebodies. We were back and forth all day long. I'd be over here for coffee first thing in the morning and then, like as not, Clara'd come over to my place for lunch and on and on it would go."

"I wondered why there was a gate in the back fence."

"The Neighborly Gate, I call it. I don't hold much with fences, but Homer just had to have one—doesn't like cleaning up after other people's dogs, if you catch my drift—so I says to him, I says, 'There's already so damned many fences in this neighborhood I'll have to go clear around the block to get to Clara.' So he says, 'Okay, okay, I'll put a gate in it.' Where's your hubby, dearie?"

"What? Oh! David went to the hardware store."

"I saw the handsome devil earlier. Tall, dark, and handsome was always my weakness, too. My problem was I always went for men with looks without thinking too much about what they had between their ears. I guess," she said with a naughty twinkle in her big, saucery blue eyes, "that's why I'm on my fourth husband. Homer's a nice-looking man, all right, but he's smart too, so maybe he'll be my last."

I searched for the proper response. I'd never met anyone before who'd been married four times. "Divorce can be a painful experience," I said lamely.

She sighed. "Well, I wouldn't know about that. Say, that hubby of yours isn't down at the hardware store buying tools, is he? Homer's got every tool in the world you can think of and I loan them out all the time. You newlyweds, dearie?"

"We've been married almost two years," I said, congratulating myself for keeping up with her.

"New in town?"

"No, we had an apartment on the north side, but now that I'm pregnant—"

"A baby!" She squealed and lunged at me, smothering me in a fruit salad hug. I mean it. The woman smelled like fruit salad. "I can't think of anything I'd like better than a new baby just across the back fence. Fiona —that's my second daughter—she had a baby boy last year, but he was six months old before I heard about him. Kids! I could've wrung her neck! Said she didn't want me flying clear across the country—she lives in Baltimore—just to help her with the new baby, so she waited until he wasn't new any more. Can you beat that? Don't believe I caught your name, dearie."

"Brenda Tay—"

"My real handle's Octavia. I don't think I look a bit like an Octavia, though, do you? My chin's too weak for an Octavia. When I was a girl my friends called me Tavie, but my first husband started calling me Dearie because that's what *I* call everybody. Your husband's name is David?"

"Yes, and he'll be back in a few minutes so I really should—"

"If he wants to buy more tools, you just send him to me. No sense in buying tools when Homer's got more than he can ever use. He's only got two hands, after all."

"David went to get a couple of garbage cans, actually."

"Garbage cans!" Dearie cried, alarm edging her voice. "*We've* got garbage cans! More than we need. You can have a couple of ours."

"Well," I said with a little laugh and a little shrug, "too late now."

"If there's anything else you need—"

"I think we've got everything covered. Listen, I think—"

"Why don't you folks come over for dinner tonight?"

"Thanks, but we've already promised to have dinner with David's parents."

"His folks live right here in town? Well, isn't that nice. I wouldn't want to keep you from that! Kids should spend time with their folks even if they are all grown up and married and everything. I see precious little of my own brood. Homer says—"

"Listen, I think I'd better get back to work. I wish I could offer you a cup of coffee but—" I motioned helplessly at the mountain of boxes.

"Oh, sure. I understand, dearie, believe me. How many times have I been in the same boat? Hundreds! Well, not really hundreds, of course, but it seems like it. No, I wasn't expecting a cup of coffee. Why don't I help you?"

"It's very nice of you to offer, Octavia—"

"Just call me Dearie."

"—Dearie, but I'd rather do it all myself so I'll know where everything is."

"I can understand that—your first real home and all—but don't you go overdoing in your delicate condition. How far gone are you, anyway?"

"Four months."

"You're going to start showing pretty soon, a skinny little thing like you. I'm just tickled pink for you, dearie. The first baby is always so exciting. Well, I'd better toddle off now and see about getting Homer's lunch. He likes to eat at twelve noon on the dot. Creature of habit, that one. You enjoy that tuna casserole now, and don't be in a hurry about getting that dish back to me. I got plenty."

"Thank you," I said, moving toward the door, "it was very nice of you to think of us."

"Neighbors should be neighborly, I always say."

"Yipes," David said, "it's awful!"

I had cleared a space around the kitchen table and served Dearie's tuna casserole on paper plates. "You're kidding," I said. "She runs around in a cobbler apron and everything." I tasted and quickly washed it down with water. How did one scorch an oven-baked tuna casserole?

"I'll go get hamburgers," David said.

"Please, I'm starved."

I scraped the tuna mess into the garbage and put the dish in the sink to soak. I had unpacked our everyday dishes and made a dent in a box that held small appliances when David came back with lunch Burger King style. "What's this?" I said, looking at his solitary hamburger. "Are you on a diet or something?" He always bought three hamburgers—one for me, two for him.

"I ate one on the way home to get that awful taste out of my mouth. I may never eat tuna again."

"She's probably a wonderful cook, David. Everybody blows it from time to time."

"Yeah, well, at least we've got one friendly neighbor. Did anyone else drop in while I was gone?"

"No, and I hope they don't for a while. All I want to do right now is get unpacked and settled in."

There came a tapping at the back door like a woodpecker at work on the eaves, the same tapping Dearie Claxton had tapped not more than an hour ago. "Oh, no!" I cried. "It's her! Get this stuff out of here. She's a nice lady and I don't want to hurt her feelings."

David jumped up from the table and, chewing furiously, dumped the burgers and fries back into the Burger King bag. Clutching it in his armpit, he snatched the Cokes and made for the far reaches of the house while I went to open the kitchen door for a grinning Dearie.

"I don't know where my head is today," she said, advancing again and backing me up against the same boxes she had backed me into earlier. She wagged a thermos in my face. "Coffee! You needed coffee, but it didn't sink in when I was here before."

"That's awfully nice of you."

"Oh, think nothing of it. So how was the casserole? I hope you ate it before it got cold."

"It was delicious," I lied stoutly. "Ate it all up."

Her saucer eyes went to the sink and lit on the soaking dish. "As long as I'm here, I might as well get that out of your way."

"Just let me wash it for you."

"Nonsense! You've got enough to do. I'll just run home and pop it in my dishwasher." She was at the sink in a flash, dumping water, swathing the dish in paper towels. "Now, if you need anything, you just holler," she said on her way out the door.

I was sure I wouldn't need anything other than a little peace and quiet, and I had the feeling I wasn't going to get it. I was wrong. Dearie came tapping at my kitchen door no more that day. "I thought she was going to be a real nuisance," I told David later when we were getting ready to go out to dinner.

"There's tomorrow and the next day and the rest of our lives," he said. "She's got plenty of time."

David was right. She came tapping bright and early the next morning with a bandage on her forehead and a coffee cake in her hands. "Oh dear," I said, "what happened to you?"

"Darned if I didn't fall down the basement stairs." She put the coffee cake on the table and sat down. "If I told Homer once, I told him a thousand times, 'Don't leave your junk all over the stairs,' but does he listen? No, he does not. Now that he's retired—he used to be an insulation therapist down at the hospital—he's always got some project going to keep himself busy, but can he find the time to put his tools away? Can he find the time to change the light bulb over the basement stairs? No! Got six stitches in my forehead, thanks to him, and I didn't get home from the hospital until nine o'clock last night. Was I steamed!"

"Are you okay now?"

"Oh sure, I'm indespructable. I always bounce back real quick. It's a good thing we've got lots of insurance because I'm just an accident looking for a place to happen. Still, you'd think a grown man would know better than to leave BB's or ball bearings or whatever those little round things were scattered all over the stairs."

David chose that moment to come up from the basement with a shiny new wrench in his hand. Dearie eyed it but surprised me by saying nothing about Homer's tools. Instead, she arched her plucked and penciled eyebrows coyly at him. "So this is the hunk."

"This is David. David, Octavia Claxton."

"Just call me Dearie."

"Nice to meet you," David said with a noncommittal expression on his lean, handsome face.

"I hear you're a high school teacher. I wish I'd had teachers like you when I was in high school." She tittered as if that was an original notion. I wondered how she knew he was a teacher. Maybe the Thompsons had told her before they headed for Arizona.

David could think of nothing to say for a moment. Then he rallied. "Well," he said, smiling his Back-to-School-Night smile, "I've got to go work on my plumbing."

Dearie's blue saucer eyes followed his retreating figure until it could be seen no more. Then she gave me a conspiratorial grin. "Men!" she cried with fond exasperation, apropos of nothing I could fathom.

"I've got to get back to work, too," I said meaningfully.

"Oh!" she cried fishing in the pockets of her cobbler apron. "I saw an article in the newspaper this morning and I says to myself, 'Dearie, this is right down Brenda's alley,' so I cut it out for you." It was an article about homemade baby food. "And I can show you how to make cosmetics—you know, face cream and shampoo and things like that—out of stuff you already have in your kitchen. It's kind of a hobby of mine."

No wonder she smelled like fruit salad. "Thank you. I'll read this the first moment I *can spare.*"

Her saucer eyes scanned my kitchen. "You've made some progress since yesterday, I see. Oh! You found your coffeemaker."

I looked woefully at it. *Why* had I started a fresh pot moments before she arrived? A defeated woman, I sighed. "Would you like a cup of coffee?"

"Don't mind if I do. I love coffee in someone else's kitchen. Now, don't worry about entertaining good ol' Dearie Claxton. Just go ahead with what you're doing and I'll keep you company.

*Okay, lady,* I thought as I poured her a cup of coffee, *that's just what I'll do.*

"I wouldn't bother with that," Dearie said when I got down on my hands and knees to scrub the cupboard under the sink. "Clara's a mesticulous housekeeper. She has a faddish, if you ask me."

"Just the same—"

"Oh, I know. You feel better if you get off to a good clean start. That's what I keep telling Homer. He's in my kitchen right now putting new heating elegants in my oven. He's miffed at me because he figured he'd be done by now. 'Homer,' I says to him, 'we're not putting new elegants in a dirty oven. You're just going to have to wait until I get it spic and span.'"

Dearie chattered on and on like an ecstatic squirrel. I learned, as I worked, more about our neighbors than I ever wanted to know. Insisting that I take a break because of my delicate condition, she served up coffee cake that was incredibly dry and pumped me about our background. It was as if she was checking our references. Just as I was despairing of ever having a moment to myself, she glanced at her watch and sprang to her feet with a startled cry. "Eleven o'clock! Time flies when you're having fun. I've got to run home and pop your casserole in the oven."

"Oh, no, you—you can't be fixing lunch for us every day. Besides, isn't Homer working on your oven?"

"He'll be through by now. You've *got* to try my taco cheesedog casserole!"

She was off in a flash, galloping across our back yard and through the Neighborly Gate, her round little buns bobbing up and down inside tight mauve stretch pants. I rolled my eyes at the ceiling and sighed a heartfelt sigh, wishing I had my grandmother's infamous lack of tact. Grandma would have told Dearie quite bluntly that she'd sooner eat raw eggs than attempt another of her casseroles, but I had not her courage. I would give the taco cheesedog casserole a try and then I would go ahead and make ham sandwiches.

As it turned out, we didn't have to taste Dearie's casserole. When one o'clock rolled around and she hadn't come back, I made the sandwiches. David and I ate an apprehensive lunch, expecting her to come tap, tap, tapping at our kitchen door any minute but nothing happened. We counted ourselves lucky.

"Sorry about the casserole," Dearie said woefully when she came tapping that evening just as we were sitting down to dinner in our new dining room. I didn't budge when she tried to back me into my kitchen. I was determined that my pot roast would not get cold while she rattled on and on. "Darned if that Homer didn't go and screw up with those new elegants. When I went to put the casserole in, I got a shock that came close to frying my eyeballs."

"Oh, I'm sorry!" Feeling like a jerk, I stepped aside and let Dearie come in and sink down on a kitchen chair.

"Got a jolt that knocked me clear across the room. I guess that was lucky because it broke the connection. Well, it blew a fuse, too, so maybe that's why I lived to tell the story. Needless to say, I didn't get the casserole done. Oven caught fire. Now Homer's got to buy me a new stove."

"Are you okay now?"

She gingerly touched the bandage on her forehead. "Got one heck of a headache, what with the stitches and the shock and all. I don't know . . . Seems like every time I turn around I'm having some kind of accident."

"Have you had dinner? If your oven's not working—I mean, I've got a pot roast on the table. There's enough for four if you want to call Homer."

She reached out and patted my hand. "That's real sweet of you, dearie, but we stopped for dinner on our way back from the hospital. At least I got to eat out for a change."

"Is there anything else I can do for you?"

"Oh no, no . . . I just wanted to tell you why you didn't get your casserole."

"Don't worry about that. I'm just glad you're okay."

"Something's rotten in Dearieland," David said when I returned to the dining room to tell him about Dearie, who had hobbled home clutching her head.

"She does seem to have more than her share of accidents."

"Smells pretty fishy to me. Do you know how unlikely it is to have that kind of accident just because her husband put those elements in himself? On most stoves, all you have to do is plug them in. Besides, getting a jolt like that—well, I'd think she'd have some burns or something."

"I've heard of people getting real zaps without getting burned. What are you getting at, David?"

"I don't know. Just strikes me as real weird."

"How about BB's scattered all over stairs where a light just happens to be burned out?"

"Weirder and weirder."

We were in the living room watching the tail end of a movie on television when we heard tapping at our kitchen door. David looked at me. "Can't be," he said. "It's almost eleven o'clock."

"I know that tap. Relax. I'll get it." Resolving to turn out all the lights in the back of the house after dinner from then on, I went to the kitchen door.

"I don't know where my head is today," Dearie said cheerfully. She was wearing a fresh bandage and she carried a cooking oil bottle that was filled with some doubtful substance. "I meant to bring this over earlier, but I could see that you hadn't gone to bed yet and bedtime is when you want to use this, so I thought I'd dash over. This is my own homemade liniment. Moving into a new house always gives you sore muscles, doesn't it, and this is just the stuff you need."

"Oh . . ."

"Just rub this on all over and in the morning you'll feel like you've been lolling on a Hawaiian beach. Tomorrow I'll show you how to make your own baby lotion. Save you a bundle when the little one comes."

"Are you sure you're feeling up to—"

"Oh, yes, I bounce back real quick. I've got three big boxes of those squeezable ketchup bottles that I've been saving for something like this. I'll have Homer haul them over first thing in the morning."

"I've got some shopping to do in the morning and I—"

"We'll do it tomorrow afternoon, then. Well, I'd better toddle off now and let you folks get to bed."

I took the cooking oil bottle back to the living room and presented it to David. He took the cap off and winced when he smelled the grayish liquid inside. "If we put this stuff on, we'll have to sleep in separate bedrooms."

I sniffed. It smelled like a mixture of horse radish, garlic, and an unspeakable something long past its prime. "Let's don't and say we did. I'd rather have sore muscles. David, she insists that she's going to help me make umpty-million bottles of homemade baby lotion!"

Dearie put in her next appearance while we were eating breakfast in the kitchen the next morning. "Those ketchup bottles are out there on your patio. Homer brought them over at the crack of dawn. He's an early riser, that one. I wanted him to wait until later so I could introduce you, but he said he had to work on the car." She eyed the coffeemaker so wistfully that I felt I had to offer her a cup.

"Don't mind if I do. I love a cup of coffee in someone else's kitchen."

She made herself comfortable at our table and began flirting with David while I scoured my brain for an excuse to get out of the baby lotion project. I was certainly not going to put any of her homemade lotion on our baby when it arrived, so innocent and trusting.

"—his fault I slipped and fell."

"What?" I asked, snapped out of my reverie by the tail end of Dearie's sentence.

"Homer says it wasn't his fault I slipped and fell and conked my head on the bathtub," she reiterated, "but who else could have spilled shampoo all over the bathroom floor if it wasn't me and it wasn't him? I know it was an accident, but it wouldn't hurt Homer to apologize once in a while. All he did was get sarclastic. Asked me if I wanted a fingerprint kit for my birthday."

"Well," David soothed, "maybe he knocked it over and didn't notice."

"Could be, I guess. I'm always after him about leaving caps off things. And I'm always after him about enlarging the bathroom. It's so small that you'd just about have to knock yourself silly if you fell, which is just what I did. I was out cold for a few minutes and Homer is no good in an emergency. All he could think to do was get me a pillow. When I came to, there he was, standing over me with a pillow in his hands."

"So are you okay now?" I asked, sending David a meaningful look.

"I'm kind of sore from all the tumbles I've taken lately, but I'll be okay. I always bounce back real quick."

"When did this happen?" David asked.

"About six o'clock this morning, right after I got up. Helluva way to start the day, huh? Listen, you don't mind if I beg off the baby lotion today, do you?"

"I don't mind at all," I said—not too eagerly, I hoped.

"Kind of got off to a bad start, and I've still got to get groceries and pick cherries."

"Cherries?"

"Didn't you notice my cherry tree? Jam-packed with big, ripe pie cherries. The weather man says it's going to rain tonight or tomorrow, so I'd better get them picked. I already told Homer to set the ladder up for me."

"Do you think that's a good idea, Dearie? Climbing a ladder after all the accidents you've had lately? Why don't I come over and pick them for you?"

"No way, little mother. Can't have you climbing in your condition."

"Couldn't Homer do it?" David put in.

"He can't climb. He's got indigo."

"Vertigo, you mean?"

"That's right. Can't stand heights, either."

I shot David another meaningful look. "Well," he said, not exactly brimming with enthusiasm, "I guess I could do it."

Dearie arched her eyebrows coyly at him again. "If you really don't mind . . ."

When David went over to the Claxtons' to pick cherries, I got in the car and drove down Hillcrest Road to the supermarket that sat at the bottom of the hill. Hillcrest was a long, winding drive with the river tumbling down beside it over a series of stairstep waterfalls. It was a lovely drive but not a particularly convenient one. I told myself I was going to have to get better organized. I wasn't living in an apartment complex with a store on the corner any more. Dashing out for a loaf of bread wasn't going to be the same, especially after the baby came, but if that was the price I had to pay for living in a nice, peaceful hilltop neighborhood with a marvelous view, I was willing to pay it.

I spent more money than I'd ever spent before at one time for groceries, stocking my roomy kitchen and the new freezer. When I got home, David appeared in the back door of the garage, ready to lug groceries. "Through picking cherries already?" I asked as he got a couple of bags out of the back seat.

"Haven't started."

I grabbed a bag and hurried after him, through the door and along the covered walkway to the patio. "Why not?"

"Well," he said going in through the patio doors to put the bags down on the dining room table, "if Homer's up to something, he's a real cool customer. When I went over there and announced my intentions, he turned to Dearie and said, 'I told you I wanted to check that ladder out before you used it.' She looked like it was news to her. Then he gave the ladder a quick once-over and muttered something about rotten wood. Took it down and hauled it off to the garage. Said he'd go buy a new one this afternoon."

"I suppose he sawed halfway through the top step or something and didn't want to waste it. He can't collect insurance on you, Davey-boy."

"He told me *she* put the ladder up. And guess what else?"

"I haven't the foggiest."

"They've already got their new stove. I saw the crate it came in out in the yard and there was an order date written on the side. It was ordered three weeks ago. Looks a little suspicious."

"A little? Maybe we should talk to Dearie. She seems awfully dense sometimes."

"I don't know," David said doubtfully. "I mean, the lady's kind of dingy, don't you think? We only have her side of the story."

"So what's Homer like?"

"Nothing like I expected. I pictured a bald, pot-bellied brute in greasy coveralls. He's kind of a spiffy old guy. Trim, neatly dressed, good haircut."

"Dearie said he was an inhalation therapist before he retired. Not the greasy coveralls type, I guess."

"An inhalation therapist? Then if he's planning to do her in don't you think he'd be able to come up with something a little more certain and a lot more subtle?"

"Yeah," I said thoughtfully, "maybe . . ."

"Been grocery shopping, I see," Dearie said when she came tapping a few minutes later. She put a shoebox down on the table. "I was going to go myself a little while ago, but I wasn't halfway down the hill when the brakes went out on the Buick. Scared me spitless. I keep telling Homer we need a new car. Looks like we'll be buying Mrs. Tate a new phododendron hedge instead—she's got that brick house right at the end of that sharp curve—but I told Homer, I says, 'Well, it's better than going into the river,' which is what I'd have done if I hadn't had the pleasants of mind to plant the Buick in Mrs. Tate's hedge. Maybe I'll use a little of the money Felix—that's my third husband—left me to buy myself a new car if Homer won't. He doesn't want me to spend that money, though. Says I should save it for my old age, but if I keep driving that Buick around, I won't *have* an old age."

"Were you hurt?" I said, shooting David yet another meaningful look.

Her hand went to her bandaged forehead. "Oh, bumped my head a little, maybe loosened up a stitch or two, but nothing serious. Had to call Dr. Nussbaum about my prescription, though. Scared me so bad I had to pop the last of my heart pills."

"You have a heart condition?"

"Sure do. Had a cornea three years ago."

I pulled a kitchen chair out for her. "Well, sit down, Dearie. You've had quite a morning. How are you feeling now? Did you get your prescription filled?"

"Homer's going to do it as soon as he gets the brakes working again. He's real handy with a car, I will say that. He was really surprised when he saw how shook up I was. I says, 'Homer, you'd be shook up, too, if you'd come within inches of going for a swim in a two-ton bathing suit.' That river's deep this time of year."

"So," I said, not knowing what else to say, "what's in the box?"

"Popsicle sticks," she said, lifting the lid with a flourish. "Homer doesn't care for desserts, as a rule, but he does like his rootbeer popsicle every now and then. I'm going to show you how to make napkin holders out of these sticks."

"Oh, that's . . . nice."

"After I get rested up a bit."

"Of course. In fact, you shouldn't even consider it for at least a month."


"Wouldn't you think she'd be just a little suspicious after her fourth potentially lethal accident in two days?" I said when Dearie had taken her bandaged head home. "And we've only been here for two days. Who knows how long this has been going on?"

"I'm back to thinking that's just what they are," David said. "Accidents, real honest-to-goodness accidents. It's an incredible run of bad luck, I'll admit, but some people are accident prone. Homer's not a stupid man. If you were trying to do me in—and get away with it—wouldn't you be just a tad more subtle about it? Four accidents in two days?"

"Well, I don't know, but Dearie really is going to be dingy if she takes many more blows to the head."

We managed to get through lunch without Dearie. David left immediately afterward for the lumberyard and the paint store. We wanted paint for the nursery and lumber for the lattice we had decided to hang from the walkway and patio covers. Training a nice, dense-growing vine on the lattice would be a good idea, we thought. Maybe someday we'd be able to smuggle groceries into the house unobserved. Maybe we'd even be able to use our patio from time to time without drawing Dearie like a moth to a flame.

When David came back, he started his lattice project on the patio, cutting two-by-twos to proper lengths with a new saw. I worked on the few odds and ends of settling in that still remained. I was hanging my asparagus fern in the dining room window—the one that looked out on the patio —when I saw that Dearie was back and had paused to supervise a grimfaced David. I was glad he was a relatively eventempered man with no history of high blood pressure. Slipping quietly out the front door, I went for a long walk.

Dearie came tapping at dinnertime. Having seen us through the patio doors, she made a beeline for the dining room when I let her in and plopped a questionable cardboard box down on the table next to the scalloped potatoes. Half a chocolate cake was balanced on top of an odd assortment of old socks that I could use to make dolls or puppets for the baby. She'd show me if I didn't know how, but I probably did because didn't everybody almost?

"Please help me eat this cake! Homer'll have his rootbeer popsicle every now and then, but otherwise he doesn't care for desserts. If I don't get rid of this I'll eat it all myself."

I tried to smile. I really did. "Thank you, Dearie."

"Would you like to come over and play cards a little later? I got my new stove, so I can show you how to make cranberry fudge."

"No, thanks. We're going to turn in early."

"I can understand that, dearie. It'll take you a while to get completely rested up. Moving really wears you out, doesn't it? All right, I'll let you off the hook this time, but tomorrow night we'll make an evening of it—make fudge, play cards, show you the slides of our trip to Mount St. Helens—"

"I don't think—"

"I didn't forget about the baby lotion. I've got a hair appointment first thing in the morning, but we can do it in the afternoon." She left with the promise to show David how to make logs for the fireplace out of old newspapers which she could supply because she had a whole closet full of them. We shouldn't thank her because she really needed to clean that closet out anyway.

"I thought this was going to be our dream house," I wailed, "not a dumping ground for Dearie Claxton!"

"This has got to stop," David said. "It really does."

The chocolate cake was so stale it was practically petrified. It went in the garbage. Turning out all the lights in the back of the house so Dearie would think we had gone to bed, we tried to wind down by watching a little mindless palaver on television, but it was hard to concentrate.

"I wonder if Dearie takes those little heart pills that look like saccharin tablets," I said.

"Why?"

"Homer got her prescription refilled today."

"And you think he might consider that a golden opportunity?"

I shrugged. "I finally got a look at Homer, by the way, when I was out walking. I saw him in his driveway tinkering with the car again."

"Yes? And?"

"Dearie has a hair appointment first thing in the morning. It's supposed to rain. She'll be driving down Hillcrest Road."

"Dearie's an excitable person. She probably needs those pills several times a day."

"A fact that probably hasn't escaped Homer. If the brakes fail again, even if she doesn't go in the river . . ."

"Yes?"

"Do you think Homer'd be crazy enough to—"

"Homer's a sane man. Infinitely sane. Otherwise he'd be sitting in a rubber room strumming his lower lip by now."

"Let me put it another way. Do you think he's capable of the big M?"

"Anyone is, pushed far enough."

"Do you think he's been pushed far enough?"

"*I've* been pushed far enough."

"Shouldn't we do something?"

"Like what?"

"I don't know."

"Even if I saw him with a gun to her head, I'm not so sure I'd want to do anything about it."

"Now, David . . ."

"Okay, okay," he sighed. "Tell you what. Let's sleep on it. She'll be safe until morning, anyway."

Sirens woke us the next morning at seven-thirty. They seemed to be coming from the back of the house, so David and I scrambled out of bed and ran to look out the kitchen window. Red and blue lights flashed on the street in front of the Claxtons' house. We could see the rear end of an ambulance in the driveway behind the Buick. Uniformed people were milling about.

"Oh, no!" I cried. "Looks like he got her good this time. We shouldn't have slept on it, David."

"I'm going to get a closer look," David said. That sounded like a good idea to me. We hurried back to the bedroom, threw on some clothes, and went out back as far as the Neighborly Gate.

Dearie, her bandaged forehead standing out whitely in the midst of the black police uniforms that surrounded her, wept into a handkerchief. Paramedics, carrying a blanket-covered figure, came out the back door.

I looked at David. "Homer?"

"Must be."

Two police officers, one in uniform and one not, saw us standing there and came over for a little chat. Dearie had stabbed Homer in self-defense, she claimed. However, some of the evidence seemed to indicate that Homer had been sitting at the table eating breakfast when he got it between the shoulder blades. As the Claxtons' neighbors, could we shed any light on the situation?

Of course we had to tell them about all the accidents Dearie had been having and that we had been suspicious of Homer's intentions, that we had even discussed it the night before, wondering what we could do about it. That seemed to give some substance to Dearie's claim. After all, even though there was blood on the table, Homer had been found face down on the floor. What Dearie told them could be absolutely true.

Homer had backed her up against the table and tried to strangle her. She managed to break away long enough to grab a kitchen knife and plunge it into his back when he lost his balance and fell to his knees. The angle of the stab wound—well, it *could* be consistent with what she was saying.

David and I spent a rather pensive morning doing little things around the house, pausing frequently to gaze out over the Neighborly Gate. I whipped up a casserole to take to Dearie when she got back from wherever the police had taken her. That was the sort of thing neighbors did for each other. She, after all, had done it to—for—us.

Lieutenant Somebody-or-other came to see us. We told him about Dearie's fall down the basement stairs and her near-electrocution and her car accident and her fall in the bathroom. We talked about Homer and his ladder and his heating elements and his pillow.

A police car brought Dearie home about noon. I passed through the Neighborly Gate for the first time shortly after with a bubbly-hot ham casserole clutched in my oven mitts. Her kitchen door was open, so I tried a tentative tap on the screen door with the edge of the dish. When I'd had no response after several dainty taps, my imagination conjured up booby traps left behind as a parting gift by Homer. Now wouldn't *that* be ironic?

With the little finger on my right hand, I managed to release the catch on the screen door without dumping the casserole and shouldered my way inside. I was about to call her name when raucous music shattered the stillness.

Normally, I like to believe, I am not a snoop, but I couldn't resist the pull of the music, so incongruous a thing for one so recently widowed. I followed it through the kitchen and dining room, homing in on its source. And then, in the living room, I saw Dearie.

She stood with her back to me before a large, decorative mirror that hung over the couch. She had a bottle of baby oil in one hand. Swinging her hips to the beat of the music, she rubbed oil on the stubborn adhesive left behind by the bandage that had covered her unstitched, unscarred forehead. She spun around when she saw my reflection. Somehow, she didn't seem very glad to see me.

"Don't look so worried," I said. "You bounce back real quick, right?"

# Bridey's Caller

### JUDITH O'NEILL

When the mail came this morning, I walked out to get it. The letter from my cousin Nellie was full of chatty family news about her children and grandchildren and questions about mine. I smiled as I strolled back up to the house, reading. And then she casually mentioned, in relating current town happenings, that "old Bridey" had died. I had to sit down suddenly on the steps.

When I was very young, almost forty years ago now, I used to go and stay with my grandparents in Helenwood, Kansas, for long weeks in the summer. I loved it there. I was the oldest—by four years—of all my cousins who lived in or around Helenwood. So during the time I was there, I was Miss Queen Bee. My cousin Nellie and I were especially close. She lived on a farm just outside the tiny town, and during my stays she would be brought in to keep me company. She was an adoring little girl, with dark curly hair and big brown eyes. And because she was so very gifted at worshiping, she was, for years, by far my favorite cousin.

My grandparents did not live on a farm, but coming as I did from the "big city" of St. Joseph, just across the river, their place seemed very rural to me. These were my mother's parents—the sober, honest, almost severe side of the family—as opposed to my father's side, which is another story altogether.

The very order of everything in my grandparents' Helenwood home appealed to me. All of my remembering years, I had been a part of that old white house set back from the dusty street. Helenwood had only one paved street. Actually it was the highway that ran through town, but it was referred to as "Main Street" and housed the post office, a grocery store, and, farther along, the red brick school (kindergarten through twelfth grade). My grandparents' home was three blocks away from the highway, back where the houses were separated by huge, tree-shaded, flat lawns. There were no sidewalks anywhere in town. In winter when the snow melted or in spring when the rains came and the river rose, you stayed indoors as much as you could.

Summers were dry and hot, and my mother would drive me over the arched, narrow bridge from St. Joe and deliver me to my grandparents. Nellie would already be there, and we would set about exploring. We did a lot of "exploring" because there wasn't much else to do. We walked everywhere, from the creek to the Missouri River, up to the highway and the post office, talking, talking.

But our favorite place, only four houses up the street from my grandparents' house, was Bridey's. Bridget was her name, and I'm not sure we ever knew her last name; everyone referred to her as Bridey, and so did we. She was a tall, thin woman, with gray hair pulled back in a bun and gray eyes. I remember they were gray because she was one of the few people I ever knew whose eyes were exactly the same color as her hair. She had a small three-room house, and the front room she had set up as a country store. Straight back from that was her bedroom and then the kitchen at the back. The "bathroom" was out on the back path, surrounded by vines and trees. It was all very neat and clean. She had a door shutting off her bedroom/sitting room, but in the summer all the doors stood open to let a breeze through so that when you walked into her store, you could look right back through the bedroom and kitchen to the back porch.

But Nellie and I were not very interested in what Bridey had in the back rooms. What she had in the front room was what we went for—that long, oval, zinc washtub set up on short sawhorses and filled with huge chunks of ice and floating bottles of soda pop. Leaning against that icy tub, fishing around for your favorite soda, was the coldest you could get in Helenwood in the summer. It is hard for people now to understand the effort and energy we had to put into keeping cool in those days. Nowadays it is just as hot in Kansas, but you can escape into air conditioning. Then you couldn't escape the heat. Even at night, when breezes turn cool in other places, in Kansas a hot wind blows up across Texas and Oklahoma and fries you. It is a sweet-smelling wind, and if it doesn't blow you can poach in your own sweat, but it doesn't really cool you. No, in those days there was no way to escape the heat except to jump in the creek or the river, but there was always my grandmother's fear of polio. So mostly we just tried to find ways to bear it, and that led us to spend a lot of time at Bridey's, leaning against the soda tub. She was never short or impatient with us; she let us lean and play in the water. She didn't pay special attention to us and we, in our turn, were polite, not making a mess or noise. As "Emmitt and Louise's grandchildren," we were conscious of a certain amount of responsibility. We behaved ourselves so as not to reflect badly on our elders. I'm not sure how they managed that bit of psychological control. I don't think they ever *told* us that—it was something we just knew. Nellie loved grape soda above all else, and I was overly fond of cream soda. Even then, I appreciated that Bridey kept the tub well stocked. When my whole arm finally became numb, I would fish a bottle out and pop it open with the opener tied by a string to the tub handle. Then I would lean back against the tub and slug that first icy gulp down my hot, dry throat.

I always thought it was an oversized zinc washtub; but it was very long for that and when I thought about it later—and believe me I did think *a lot* about it later—I thought maybe it had been a trough for horses to drink out of at one time. I have seen them from time to time in antique shops since then, and they always make me a little sick at my stomach.

Bridey lived alone, and while there were all kinds of Sunday laws in Kansas in those days, she would open her door about ten in the morning on Sunday and, if you went by, she would sell you whatever you wanted. But in our eyes Bridey had a fault. This was her Sunday caller. Every Sunday, about two P.M., Bridey's caller would come. He drove across the bridge from St. Joe, down onto the shaded streets of Helenwood, and around to the back of Bridey's. He never parked in front, always in back, under the trees there. Why, I can't imagine, as everyone in town could see his car in back as well as if he had parked it in front. Then he would get out of his car—a short, energetic, good-looking man in a dark suit and hat —and walk to the back door and go in. Shortly thereafter, Bridey would close her front door and her back door and no longer be available for business. Somewhere about five P.M., her caller would depart the way he had come, out the back, into his car, down the streets, and out of Helenwood to the bridge, not to be seen again until the next Sunday. I had broodingly watched this coming and going from my grandfather's grape arbor countless Sundays.

Of course Nellie and I were affronted by this because Bridey's was *never* closed. If she was there, day or night, she was open and there was easy access to the soda tub. And it seemed that the hottest and thirstiest we ever got was between two and five on Sunday afternoons. I was vaguely aware that my grandmother was affronted by this, too; but I could not fathom her giving a whit about the soda tub and she rarely ran out of things just as she needed them, so I couldn't put my finger on the cause of her displeasure. She liked Bridey, I knew; Grandma had known her all of her life. She would sometimes go and sit on Bridey's porch when she was passing on her way to or from the post office and they would talk. But when the Sunday closings came up, she would frown and get testy. My grandfather got a big kick out of it. Once, as we sat at Sunday dinner, Nellie and I were again complaining, of course, and Nellie—being as blunt and repetitive as any six-year-old—asked, for about the five-hundredth time that summer, "Why does she close every Sunday like this?" and my grandmother snapped, "Because she has a caller, you know that, now eat those mashed potatoes."

I was a little perplexed by this behavior myself. We didn't go around closing all our doors and keeping people out when we had company. "But why does she close the doors?" I asked, musing. "It must be hot in there."

My grandfather laughed. "I bet," he said.

"Emmitt, Emmitt!" my grandmother warned sharply.

But my grandfather was enjoying himself now and teasing my red-faced grandmother. It was seldom that I had seen her blush. "I think," he said, laughing at her, "that Bridey takes a little after-dinner nap."

My grandmother threw her fork down on the table and glared at him. "Emmitt, that's just about enough!"

He was laughing so hard now he had to take his glasses off and wipe his eyes with a napkin. And while he was doing this, Nellie said in her self-righteous little way, "But isn't it rude of Bridey to take a nap while her caller is there?"

My grandfather started choking and had to leave the table, and my grandmother turned on Nellie and me and told us in no uncertain terms that other people's manners were not our business and we had plenty to do to mind our *own* manners, and it was *very* bad manners to be so nosy about other people's lives and how they conducted them.

That was my tenth summer. It stands out clearly in my mind for many reasons. For one, it was the most incredibly hot summer I have ever lived through. Everyone talked about nothing but the weather and the crops and the lack of rain, and Nellie and I consumed a prodigious amount of soda. Second, I was at my grandparents' all summer for the first time ever, and the reason for that is the third, but far most important, reason I remember that summer. At the very beginning of it, just after school was out, my mother had a nervous breakdown. Up until the previous Christmas, I had never suspected she had a nerve in her body. She was always a happy, fun person with laughing eyes. To this day when I think of her, I remember those laughing brown eyes. Well, they weren't laughing that year. My father had fallen in love with someone else, she had told me just before Christmas. Just like that, my happy-go-lucky, handsome, generous father was gone. Gone with someone else. There's a lot about that Christmas I don't remember. I remember my mother sitting very still at the dining-room table in our house in St. Joe, with the snow falling outside the window behind her, and telling me he had gone. I had never even heard them argue. We would get used to it, my mother said bleakly. We would go on with our lives and they would be different, but we would get used to it. I knew my mother must still reside somewhere in that body, but I couldn't see her at all in the dead brown eyes and the bleached white face.

I went to my grandparents' the day school was out, and my mother went to the hospital.

My grandparents were sick with worry. They didn't talk about it to me much, but they talked *to* me a lot more. They seemed to go out of their way, both of them, to explain the whys of things and idiosyncrasies of the people in town. "Look at poor Cynthia Jenkins," my grandmother would say, "she lost both her parents in a flood when she was very young, and she's turned out all right." That sort of thing. I learned a lot about people in Helenwood I hadn't previously known as my grandparents gently pointed out one survivor after another. And somewhere in that summer I learned that Bridget was one of these—her father dead when she was less than three years old, her mother had married a man with four children, and it came out (from my grandfather, I'm sure) that the Sunday caller was one of these stepbrothers, a *married* stepbrother, my grandmother snorted.

We all suffered into August, one brilliant, blazing day after another. We woke up drenched, unable to cheat nature out of even a few minutes' early morning coolness, moved sluggishly through the day, and sank exhausted into the already heated sheets at dusk. It was that kind of a day the Sunday I was hanging around the grape arbor waiting for Bridey to open up. It was about time for her caller to leave, so I strolled up through the three backyards separating ours from hers. Yes, the car was still there, under the trees at the back of her yard. The back door was still shut. Standing well away from the trunk of the tree to catch even the hot wind and feeling it dry the perspiration on my face and bare arms and scorch my eyes, I waited impatiently for Bridey's caller to leave. And, waiting, I went to sit in the thick, green grass along the stone foundation of her little house where the breeze always seemed cooler.

And I heard Bridey crying. I don't think I purposely sat right under her bedroom window. I was just searching for the coolest spot around and that looked like it, on the shady side of the house, the grass deep and green and bending in the wind. But there I was, right under her open bedroom window. I should have crawled away, but the sobbing was so close I was afraid she would see me. She cried out in a low, strangled voice, "Don't, please don't, Ray, don't say you're going for good." She was crying so frantically and wildly that I was mesmerized there, scrunched up against the rough stone of the foundation. I could hear his voice as he answered her, but not his words. She began to beg. I cannot, writing here, relay to you the utter desperation and grief in those low pleas, nor their effect on me. It was Bridey's voice, strangled and harsh in terror and hurt and desolation, begging, begging. It was my voice, and my mother's voice. And I, who had taken the news of my own father's departure stoically and my mother's breakdown grimly but dry-eyed, rose from the grass sightlessly and ran along the side of the house, back into the trees, and down into my grandfather's grape arbor.

I threw myself on the ground under the heavy green leaves and clutched the grass there in my hands and wrenched and tore it out of the ground and beat the earth with my fists. But none of it helped and, just like an earthen dam gives way, so did I. I shut my eyes as tight as I could, but I could feel the flood coming, the terrible bitter tears of irreplaceable loss ripping out my heart, and then the dam gave way.

When the weeping was all over and I had rolled onto my back to stare up through the grape leaves at the bright sky, I marveled that there could have been that much water in me. And then I thought about Bridey. Now I know that he must have been everything to her. For twenty years, she must have lived for those short Sunday afternoons. Three precious hours of his time a week.

My grandfather was asleep on the recliner on the front porch, his iced tea sitting on the porch floor, all its ice long melted. My grandmother and Nellie were napping, too, when I went into the house. Nellie in her white, little-girl cotton slip on the big bed we shared, her dark curls stuck wetly to her forehead. I went into the bathroom, washed my face and combed my hair, and wandered down to join my grandfather on the porch.

And then the young people from the Baptist church came swinging down the street, led by the new minister. They had been calling on the sick and widowed and just plain backslidden. Dressed in their Sunday best, they looked hot and bedraggled and sweaty. The girls' hair was wet and hanging down their faces. They frowned against the sun. The boys had on their suit coats and looked like they wanted to die.

"We'll stop for a cool drink at Bridey's," the new minister said. "We'll try to get her to open a little early."

So of course I tagged along. The minister, being new, had obviously not yet caught on to the significance of the car's being there, but everyone else in the group had, because they craned their necks to glance toward the back. It was still there; but the young people, looking uncomfortable as the new minister walked up onto the porch and banged on the door, weren't about to tell him. I didn't have the words to tell him with. I stood in the shade with the others while he knocked and called. He came back shaking his head. "Guess she's not going to open," he smiled apologetically. "Let's go back to the parsonage for iced tea." And they went off.

I stood there, loath to put forth the effort to get myself back to my

grandparents' house, loath to put forth any effort at all, and saw Sheriff
Mills come out of his house three houses farther down the road and start
toward me. Sheriff Mills had company every Sunday. Mrs. Mills had
brothers all over the place, and they all gathered with wives and families
every week. I knew them, but they didn't have kids my age.

"Afternoon, missy," Sheriff Mills said. He was a big, broad, older man,
and he called all women under twenty "missy." "Miss Bridey not open
yet?" he asked, surprised, consulting his watch.

I shook my head. He glanced around at the back. "Hmm . . ." he said.
Sheriff Mills was not new in town. He turned back to look down the street
toward his house. "Well," he said, "it's getting on toward six, and Mother
needs milk to get supper on." He glanced behind the house again, hesitated, and mounted the steps.

I guess she had to open when she saw who it was. She didn't look all
that different from the way she had earlier that day. Maybe her eyes were
a little puffy, but that was all. Her hair was in the bun, not a wisp escap-
ing, her plain face pale but calm.

"I'm real sorry about this, Bridey," the sheriff said, stepping into the
store and explaining his quandary. We both refrained from glancing into
the back room. As Bridey was getting the milk from the big white icebox, I
scooted past the sheriff and went to the soda tub. I was fishing around for
a cream soda and I could hear her and Sheriff Mills talking, but I wasn't
paying any attention, really.

The water felt so good. I was barefooted, and I remember there was a
lot of cold water on the dark wood floor. I found my cream soda and
clasped it as it bobbed among the huge chunks of ice and the other
bottles. Then the ice and the bottles floated apart, and I looked down into
the face of Bridey's caller. He had blue eyes, I remember—very blue. He
seemed to be gazing up past me to the ceiling. Then the ice and the
bottles floated together again and covered his face.

I thought for a second that I was having heat stroke. My grandmother
had talked about it endlessly and warned us time and again to stay out of
the sun. She had had it once, when she was young; and when we asked her
what it was like, she said you got sick to your stomach and dizzy and
disoriented. I thought "disoriented" must mean seeing things.

I clutched my cream soda and moved it slowly back and forth in the
water to clear some space. The ice and the bottles slid apart again, and
there he was. He seemed to be lying on the bottom of the long tub staring
up through the water, his curly hair waving gently over his forehead.

I took out my soda and let the chunks of ice float back together, and I
turned to look at Bridey. She was staring over the sheriff's shoulder as he
dug in his pockets and rattled on. We looked at each other. Sheriff Mills

turned and saw me and said, "I see you got your soda, missy," or some-thing inane like that and went right on talking to Bridey. Bridey just stared at me. I think now of all the things I could have done. She must have been waiting for me to scream or faint or just say, "Look here, Sheriff Mills, at Bridey's caller in the soda tub."

I didn't do any of those things. I just walked across the small room, laid my dime on the linoleum-topped counter, and walked out. I remember the tough burnt grass on my bare feet as I crossed the yards. I remember my grandpa still asleep on the porch when I came up onto it. I remem-ber going in and sitting on a chair at the kitchen table and drinking my cream soda while my grandmother moved slowly around in the heat, start-ing to lay things out for a cold dinner. I don't remember at all just when I started to breathe again.

I don't know what she finally did with him. I don't know how she killed him or got him in the tub. Now that I'm older and have thought of the details of it, one crazy question that keeps popping into my mind is: how did she keep him on the bottom of the tub? Bodies float, don't they?

I don't know how she got rid of the car or how she explained it all. They found the car way out by Krug Park in St. Joe across the river, my grand-mother told me. It was a big scandal in Helenwood—how Bridey's caller had disappeared. And Bridey went right on living there, running her little store. I can't say that she was especially nice to me after that. She had never been *not* nice to me. We were just more aware of each other. She had to know that I knew. I wasn't four or five. I was ten. She had seen me see him.

I wonder now at how she must have waited. Maybe she thought I would tell my grandparents, or my mother when she finally got well, or a school friend when school started. It's strange that it never crossed my mind to fear her. I could have easily disappeared down a well or in the river.

I didn't see a great deal of her after that summer. My mother took me back home in time to start sixth grade in September. My father moved up to Mound City, and I began to spend summers with him and his new family. Two years later we moved to St. Louis and my mother remarried. So when I was in Helenwood, it was usually en route to my father's or just coming back from his place, so I was there for only a few days at a time. And then, of course, I grew up and had my own life.

Bridey lived there all the rest of her life in that little three-room house. She never had another caller. She would sit out on her porch in the evenings and she didn't close anymore on Sunday afternoons. Sometimes, when Nellie and I were teenagers, before I could drive Grandpa's car over to St. Joe, we would stroll down to Bridey's.

Nellie would still get her grape pop, but I never drank another bottle of cream soda. I had switched to ice-cream bars; and if anyone noticed, they thought it was more nutritional, anyway.

Bridey would take our money and exchange pleasantries, asking me about St. Louis, how I liked school there, and how my mother was getting on. I answered politely. We kept our eyes neutral. I never saw anything in hers aside from the polite curiosity she had always had, and I kept mine bright and warm and empty.

Of all the questions I have pondered, there is one I never had to ask myself. Why didn't I tell? Why didn't I run screaming out of the store to my grandmother and fall fainting against her, babbling and hysterical? You must know the answer to that one.

Any other summer maybe I would have. But that summer, after all, I knew all about men leaving you.

# Natural Causes

## DOROTHY SALISBURY DAVIS

When Clara McCracken got out of state prison I was waiting to bring her home. We shook hands at the prison gate when she came through, and the first thing I was struck with was how her eyes had gone from china-blue to a gunmetal-grey. In fifteen years she'd come to look a lot like her late sister, Maud.

There'd been twenty years' difference in the ages of the McCracken sisters, and they were all that was left of a family that had come west with the building of the Erie Canal and settled in the Ragapoo Hills, most of them around Webbtown, a place that's no bigger now than it was then. Maudie ran the Red Lantern Inn, as McCrackens had before her, and she raised her younger sister by herself. She did her best to get Clara married to a decent man. It would have been better for everybody if she'd let her go wild the way Clara wanted and married or not married, as her own fancy took her.

Maudie was killed by accident, but there was no way I could prove young Reuben White fell into Maudie's well by accident. Not with Clara saying she'd pushed him into it and then taking the jury up there to show them how. She got more time than I thought fair, and for a while I blamed myself, a backwoods lawyer, for taking her defense even though she wouldn't have anybody else. Looking back, I came to see that in Ragapoo County then, just after giving so many of our young men to a second World War, Reuben White was probably better thought of than he ought to have been. But that's another story and the page was turned on it when Clara went to prison. Another page was turned with her coming out.

She stood on the comfortable side of the prison gate and looked at my old Chevrolet as though she recognized it. She could have. It wasn't even new when she got sent up, as they used to say in those Big House movies. The farthest I've ever driven that car on a single journey was the twice I visited her, and this time to bring her home. Then she did something gentle, a characteristic no one I knew would've given to Clara—she put out her hand and patted the fender as though it was a horse's rump.

I opened the door for her and she climbed in head first and sorted herself out while I put her canvas suitcase in the back. There were greys in her bush of tawny hair and her face was the color of cheap toilet paper. Squint lines took off from around her eyes. I didn't think laughing had much to do with them. She sat tall and bony in her loose-hung purple dress and looked straight ahead most of the drive home.

About the first thing she said to me was, "Hank, anybody in Webbtown selling television sets?"

"Prouty's got a couple he calls demonstrators." Then I added, "Keeps them in the hardware shop."

Clara made a noise I guess you could call a laugh. Prouty also runs the only mortuary in the town.

"You'd be better sending away to Sears Roebuck," I said. "You pay them extra and they provide the aerial and put it up. I wouldn't trust old Prouty on a ladder these days. I wouldn't trust myself on one."

I could feel her looking at me, but I wasn't taking my eyes off the road. "Still playing the fiddle, Hank?" she asked.

"Some. Most folks'd rather watch the television than hear me hoeing down. But I fiddle for myself. It's about what I can do for pleasure lately. They dried up the trout stream when they put the highway through. Now they're drilling for oil in the hills. That's something new. I thought coal maybe someday, or even natural gas. But it's oil and they got those dipsy-doodles going night and day."

"Making everybody rich as Indians," Clara said, and she sounded just like Maudie. That was something Maudie would have said in the same deadpan way.

What I came out with then was something I'd been afraid of all along. "Maudie," I said, "you're going to see a lot of changes."

"Clara," she corrected me.

"I'm sorry, Clara. I was thinking of your sister."

"No harm done. You'd have to say there was a family resemblance among the McCrackens."

"A mighty strong one."

"Only trouble, there's a terrible shortage of McCrackens." And with that she exploded such a blast of laughter I rolled down the window to let some of it out.

I felt sorry for Clara when we drove up to the Red Lantern. It was still boarded up and there was writing on the steps that made me think of that

Lizzie Borden jingle, "Lizzie Borden took an axe . . ." Having power of attorney, I'd asked Clara if I should have the place cleaned out and a room fixed up for her to come home to, but she said no. It wasn't as though there wasn't any money in the bank. The state bought a chunk of Mc-Cracken land when they put through the highway.

While I was trying the keys in the front door, Clara stood by the veranda railing and looked up at the Interstate, maybe a half mile away. You can't get on or off it from Webbtown. The nearest interchange is three miles. But one good thing that happened in the building of the road, they bulldozed Maudie's well and the old brewhouse clear out of existence. Clara'd have been thinking of that while I diddled with the lock. I got the door open and she picked up her suitcase before I could do it for her.

The spider webs were thick as lace curtains and you could almost touch the smell in the place, mold and mice and the drain-deep runoff of maybe a million draws of beer. You couldn't see much with the windows boarded up, but when you got used to the twilight you could see enough to move around. A row of keys still hung under numbers one to eight behind the desk. As though any one of them wouldn't open any door in the house. But a key feels good when you're away from home, it's a safe companion.

The stairs went up to a landing and then turned out of sight. Past them on the ground floor was the way to the kitchen and across from that the dining room. To the right where the sliding doors were closed was the lounge. To the left was the barroom where, for over a hundred and fifty years, McCrackens had drawn their own brew. I knew the revenue agent who used to come through during Prohibition. He certified the beer as three point two percent alcohol, what we used to call near-beer. The McCracken foam had more kick than three point two.

Clara set her suitcase at the foot of the stairs and went into the barroom. From where I stood I could see her back and then her shape in the backbar mirror and a shadow behind her that kind of scared me until I realized it was myself.

"Hank?" she said.

"I'm here."

She pointed at the moosehead on the wall above the mirror. "That moose has got to go," she said. "That's where I plan to put the television."

I took that in and said, "You got to have a license, Clara, unless you're going to serve soda pop, and I don't think you can get one after being where you were."

I could see her eyes shining in the dark. "You can, Hank, and I'm appointing you my partner."

\*    \*    \*

Clara had done a lot of planning in fifteen years. She'd learned carpentry in prison and enough about plumbing and electric wiring to get things working. I asked her how she'd managed it, being a woman, and she said that was how she'd managed it. Her first days home I brought her necessities up to her from the town. The only person I'd told about her coming out was Prouty and he's close-mouthed. You couldn't say that for Mrs. Prouty . . . It's funny how you call most people by their Christian names after you get to know them, and then there's some you wouldn't dare even when you've known them all your life. Even Prouty calls her Mrs. Prouty.

Anyway, she's our one female elder at the Community Church and she was probably the person who put Reverend Barnes onto the sermon he preached the Sunday after Clara's return—all about the scribes and the Pharisees and how no man among them was able to throw the first stone at the woman taken in adultery. Adultery wasn't the problem of either of the McCracken sisters. It was something on the opposite side of human nature, trying to keep upright as the church steeple. But Reverend Barnes is one of those old-time Calvinists who believe heaven is heaven and hell is hell and whichever one you're going to was decided long ago, so the name of the sin don't matter much.

I was hanging a clothesline out back for Clara Monday morning when maybe a dozen women came up the hill to the Red Lantern bearing gifts. I stayed out of sight but I saw afterwards they were things they'd given thought to—symbolic things like canned fish and flour, bread and grape juice, what you might call biblical things. When Clara first saw them coming she went out on the veranda. She crossed her arms and spread her feet and took up a defensive stand in front of the door. The women did a queer thing: they set down what they were carrying, one after the other, and started to applaud. I guess it was the only way they could think of on the spot to show her they meant no ill.

Clara relaxed and gave them a roundhouse wave to come on up. They filed into the inn and before the morning was over they'd decided among themselves who was going to make curtains, who knew how to get mildew out of the bed linens, who'd be best at patching moth holes, things like that. Anne Pendergast went home and got the twins. They were about fourteen, two hellions. She made them scrub out every word that was written on the steps.

During the week I went over to the county seat with Clara to see if she could get a driver's license. I let her drive the Chevy, though I nearly died of a heart attack. She had it kicking like an army mule, but we did get there, and she could say that she'd driven a car lately. I watched with a sick feeling while the clerk made out a temporary permit she could use until her license came. Then, without batting an eye at me, she asked the fellow if he could tell us who to see about applying for a liquor license. He came out into the hall and pointed to the office. Yes, sir. Clara had done a lot of planning in fifteen years.

It was on the way back to Webbtown that she said to me, "Somebody's stolen Pa's shotgun, Hank."

"I got it up at my place, Clara. You sure you want it back?" It was that gun going off that killed Maudie and I guess this is as good a time as any to tell you what happened back then.

Clara was a wild and pretty thing and Maudie was encouraging this middle-aged gent, a paint salesman by the name of Matt Sawyer, to propose to her. This day she took him out in the hills with the shotgun, aiming to have him scare off Reuben White, who was a lot more forward in his courting of Clara. It was Maudie flushed the young ones out of the sheepcote and then shouted at Matt to shoot. She kept shouting it and so upset him that he slammed the gun down. It went off and blew half of Maudie's head away.

I don't think I'm ever going to forget Matt coming into town dragging that gun along the ground and telling us what happened. And I'm absolutely not going to forget going up the hill with Matt and Constable Luke Weber—and Prouty with his wicker basket. Clara came flying to meet us, her gold hair streaming out in the wind like a visiting angel. She just plain threw herself at Matt, saying how she loved him. I told her she ought to behave herself and she told me to hush or I couldn't play fiddle at their wedding. Luke Weber kept asking her where Reuben was and all she'd say in that airy way of hers was, "Gone."

I couldn't look at Maudie without getting sick, so I went to the well and tried to draw water. The bucket kept getting stuck, which was how we came to discover Reuben, head down, feet up, in the well. When the constable asked Clara about it, she admitted right off that she'd pushed him.

Why? Luke wanted to know.

At that point she turned deep serious, those big eyes of hers like blue saucers. "Mr. Weber, you wouldn't believe me if I told you what Reuben White wanted me to do with him in the sheepcote this afternoon. And I just know Matt won't ever want me to do a thing like that." I pleaded her temporarily insane. I might have tried to get her off for defending her virtue—there was some in town who saw it that way—but by the time we came to trial I didn't think it would work with a ten-out-of-twelve male jury.

But to get back to what I was saying about Clara wanting the shotgun back, I advised her not to put it where it used to hang over the fireplace in the bar.

"Don't intend to. I got no place else for the moosehead."

I took the gun up to her the next day and it wasn't long after that I learned from Prouty she'd bought a box of shells and some cleaning oil. Prouty wanted to know if there wasn't some law against her having a gun. I said I thought so and we both let it go at that. Clara bought her television from him. The first I heard of her using the gun—only in a manner of speaking—was after she'd bought a used car from a lot on the County Road. It was a Studebaker, a beauty on the outside, and the dealer convinced her it had a heart of gold. The battery fell out first, and after that it was the transmission. She wanted me to go up and talk to him. I did and he told me to read the warranty, which I also did. I told Clara she was stuck with a bad bargain.

"Think so, Hank?"

The next thing I heard, she got Anne Pendergast and the twins to tow the Studebaker and her back to the used-car lot. The two women sent the boys home and then sat in Clara's car until the dealer finally came out to them. "Like I told your lawyer, lady, it's too bad, but . . ." He said something like that, according to Anne, and Clara stopped him right there. "I got me another lawyer," she said and jerked her thumb toward the back seat, where the old shotgun lay shining like it had just come off the hunters' rack in Prouty's. Anne asked him if he'd ever heard of Clara McCracken.

Seemed like he had, for when Clara drove up to where I was painting the Red Lantern sign she was behind the wheel of a red Chevy roadster with a motor that ran like a tomcat's purr.

"How much?" I wanted to know. Her funds were going down fast.

She opened the rumble seat and took out the shotgun. "One round of shot," she said. "That's about fifteen cents."

I didn't say anything in the town about the partnership I'd drawn up so that Clara could reopen the bar in the Red Lantern. For one thing, I wasn't sure when we'd get the license if we got it, even though Clara was moving full steam ahead. For another thing, I had to stop dropping in at Tuttle's Tavern. I just couldn't face Jesse Tuttle after setting up in competition, even though it was a mighty limited partnership I had with Clara. I didn't want to be an innkeeper and it riled that McCracken pride of hers to have to go outside the family after a hundred and fifty years. We wound up agreeing I was to be a silent partner. I was to have all the beer I could drink free. That wasn't going to cost her much. Even in the days of

Maudie's Own Brew, I never drank more than a couple of steins in one night's sitting.

The license came through midsummer along with instructions that it was to be prominently displayed on the premises at all times. Clara framed it and hung it where you'd have needed a pair of binoculars to see what it was. By then the rooms upstairs had been aired out, the curtains hung, and all the mattresses and pillows treated to a week in the sun. Downstairs, the lounge was open to anybody willing to share it with a horde of insects. Prouty had ordered her some of those fly-catching dangles you string up on the lightbulbs, but they hadn't come yet. What came with miraculous speed was a pretty fair order of whiskeys and a half dozen kegs of beer with all the tapping equipment. I asked Clara how she decided on which brewery she was going to patronize.

She said the girls advised her.

And, sure enough, when I spoke to Prouty about it later he said, "So that's why Mrs. Prouty was asking what my favorite beer was. Didn't make sense till now. We ain't had a bottle of beer in the house since she got on the board of elders."

"Didn't you ask her what she wanted to know for?"

"Nope. I wanted to be surprised when the time came."

I suppose it was along about then I began to get a little niggling tinkle in my head about how friendly Clara and the women were. Most of those girls she spoke of were women ranging from thirty to eighty-five years old.

Going across the street and up the stairs to my office over Kincaid's Drugstore, I counted on my fingers this one and that of them I'd seen up there since Clara came home. I ran out of fingers and I'd have run out of toes as well if I'd included them.

Jesse Tuttle was sitting in my office waiting for me, his chair tilted back against the wall. I don't lock up in the daytime and the day I have to I'll take down my shingle. I felt funny, seeing Tuttle and feeling the way I did about competing with him, so as soon as we shook hands I brought things right out into the open. "I hope you don't take it personal, Jesse, that I'm helping Clara McCracken get a fresh start."

Jesse's a big, good-natured man with a belly that keeps him away from the bar, if you know what I mean. It don't seem to keep him away from Suzie. They got nine kids and a couple more on the hillside. "I know it's not personal, Hank, but it's not what you'd call friendly, either. I was wondering for a while if there was something personal between you and her, but the fellas talked me out of that idea."

I don't laugh out loud much, but I did then. "Jesse, I'm an old rooster," I said, "and I haven't noticed if a hen laid an egg in God knows how long."

"That's what we decided, but there's one thing you learn in my business: don't take anything a man says about himself for gospel. Even if he's telling the truth, it might as well be a lie, for all you know listening to him. Same thing in your business, ain't that so?"

"Wouldn't need witnesses if it wasn't," I said.

I settled my backside on the edge of the desk and he straightened up the chair. I'd been waiting for it to collapse, all the weight on its hind legs. He folded his arms. "What's going on up there, Hank?"

"Well, from what she said the last time we talked, she plans to open officially when the threshing combine comes through." We do as much farming in Ragapoo County as anything else, just enough to get by on. But we grow our own grain, and the harvest is a pretty big occasion.

"She figures on putting the crew up, does she?"

"She's got those eight rooms all made up and waiting. She got to put somebody in them. I can't see her getting the cross-country traffic to drop off the Interstate."

Tuttle looked at me with a queer expression on his face. "You don't think she'd be figuring to run a house up there?"

"A bawdy house?"

Tuttle nodded.

I shook my head. "No, sir. I think that's the last thing Clara'd have in mind."

"I mean playing a joke on us, paying us back for her having to go to prison."

"I just don't see it, Jesse. Besides, look at all your womenfolk flocking up there to give her a hand."

"That's what I am looking at," he said.

Every step creaked as he lumbered down the stairs. I listened to how quiet it was with him gone. I couldn't believe Jesse was a mean man. He wouldn't start a rumor if he didn't think there was something to back it up with. Not just for business. We don't do things like that in Webbtown, I told myself. We're too close to one another for any such shenanigans. And I had to admit I wouldn't put it past a McCracken to play the town dirty if she thought the town had done it to her first. I certainly wouldn't have put it past Maudie. There was something that kind of bothered me about what was taking place in my own head: I kept mixing up the sisters. It was like Maudie was the one who had come back.

Clara drove eighty miles across two counties to intercept the threshing combine—ten men and some mighty fancy equipment that crisscross the state this time every year. She took Anne Pendergast and Mary Toomey with her. Mary's a first cousin of Prouty's. And on the other side of the family she was related to Reuben White, something Prouty called my attention to. Reuben's folks moved away after the trial. It wasn't so much grief as shame. I didn't like doing it, but it's a lawyer's job, and I painted the boy as pretty much a dang fool to have got himself killed that way.

The women came home late afternoon. I saw them driving along Main Street after collecting all the Pendergast kids into the rumble seat. Anne had farmed them out for the day. I headed for the Red Lantern to see what happened. Clara was pleased as jubilee: the combine crew had agreed to route themselves so as to spend Saturday night in Webbtown.

"And they'll check into the Red Lantern?" I said. Ordinarily they split up among the farmers they serviced and knocked off five percent for their keep.

"Every last man. Barbecue Saturday night, Hank."

"What if it rains?"

"I got Mrs. Prouty and Faith Barnes working on it—the minister's wife?"

"I know who Faith Barnes is," I said, sour as pickle brine. The only reassuring thing I felt about the whole situation was that Mrs. Prouty was still Mrs. Prouty.

I came around. The whole town did. Almost had to, the women taking the lead right off. Clara invited everybody, at two dollars a head for adults, fifty cents for kids under twelve. All you could eat and free beer, but you paid for hard liquor. I recruited young Tommy Kincaid and a couple of his chums to dig the barbecue pits with me. Prouty supervised. Mrs. Prouty supervised the loan and transfer of tables and benches from the parish house. They used the Number One Hook and Ladder to move them, and I never before knew a truck to go out of the firehouse on private business except at Christmastime when they take Jesse Tuttle up and down Main Street in his Santa Claus getup.

Saturday came as clear a day as when there were eagles in the Ragapoo Hills. Right after lunch the town youngsters hiked up to the first lookout on the County Road. It reminded me of when I was a kid myself and a genuine circus would come round that bend and down through the town. I'd expected trouble from the teenage crowd, by the way, with Clara coming home. You know the way they like to scare themselves half out of their wits with stories of murder and haunted houses. The Red Lantern seemed like fair game for sure. Maybe the Pendergast twins took the curse off the place when they scrubbed the steps, I thought, and then I knew right off: it was their mothers who set down the law on how they'd behave toward Clara. In any case, it would have taken a lot of superstition to keep them from enjoying the harvest holiday.

Along about four o'clock the cry came echoing down the valley, "They're coming! They're coming!" And sure enough, like some prefabricated monster, the combine hove into view. Tractors and wagons followed, stopping to let the kids climb aboard. Behind them were the farmers' pleasure cars, women and children and some of the menfolk, dressed, you'd have thought, for the Fourth of July. The only ones left behind came as soon as the cows were let out after milking.

There was a new register on the desk and one man after another of the harvesters signed his name, picked up the key, and took his duffle bag upstairs. They came down to shower in the basement, and for a while there you couldn't get more than a trickle out of any other tap in the house. By the time they were washed up, half the town had arrived. I never saw our women looking prettier, and I kept saying to myself, gosh darn Tuttle for putting mischief in my mind. Even Clara, with color now in her cheeks, looked less like Maudie and more like the Clara I used to know.

The corn was roasting and the smell of barbecued chickens and ribs had the kids with their paper plates dancing in and out of line. There were mounds of Molly Kincaid's potato salad and crocks full of home-baked beans, great platters of sliced beefsteak tomatoes, fresh bread, and a five-pound jar of sweet butter Clara ordered from the Justin farm, delivered by Nellie Justin. Clara sent her to me to be paid her three dollars, but Nellie said to let it take care of her and Joe and the kids for the barbecue. Neither one of us was good at arithmetic. Peach and apple pies which any woman in town might have baked were aplenty and you can't believe what a peach pie's like baked with peaches so ripe you catch them dropping off the trees.

It was along about twilight with the men stretched out on the grass and the women sitting round on benches or on the veranda, dangling their feet over the side, when I tuned up my fiddle and sawed a few notes in front of the microphone. I never was amplified before and I don't expect to be again, but Dick Moran who teaches history, English, and music at the high school set up a system he'd been tinkering with all summer and brought along his own guitar. We made a lot of music, with everybody clapping and joining in. Real old-fashioned country. You might say people danced by the light of the moon—it was up there—but we had lantern light as well. I'd called round that morning and asked the farmers for the loan of the lanterns they use going out to chores on winter mornings. And when it finally came time for these same farmers to go home, they took their lanterns with them. One by one, the lights disappeared like fireflies, fading away until the only outdoor light was over the hotel entrance, and it was entertaining a crowd of moths and June bugs, gnats and mosquitoes.

Most people who lived in town weren't set on going home yet. Tuttle had closed up for the evening, not being a man to miss a good meal, but he said he thought he'd go down now and open up the tavern. Tuttle's Tavern never was a place the women folk liked to go, but now they said so right out loud.

Without even consulting me, Clara announced I'd fiddle in the lounge for a while. The women took to the idea straight off and set about arrangements. The old folks, who'd had about enough, gathered the kids and took them home. The teenagers went someplace with their amplifying history teacher and his guitar. The men, after hemming and hawing and beginning to feel out of joint, straggled down to Tuttle's. By this time the harvesters, with their bright-colored shirts and fancy boots, were drinking boilermakers in the bar. I didn't like it, but they were the only ones Clara was making money on, and she kept pouring. Prouty hung around for a while, helping move furniture. I asked him to stay, but he must have sneaked away while I was tuning up.

It gave me a funny feeling to see those women dancing all by themselves. I don't know why exactly. Kind of a waste, I suppose. But they sure didn't mind, flying and whirling one another and laughing in that high musical trill you don't often hear from women taught to hold themselves in. A funny feeling, I say, and yet something woke up in me that had been a long time sleeping.

Clara came across the hall from the taproom now and then, hauling one of the harvesters by the arm and kind of pitched him into the dance. His buddies would come to the door and whoop and holler and maybe get pulled in themselves. I kept thinking of my chums, sulking down at Tuttle's. I also thought Clara was wasting a lot of the good will she'd won with the barbecue. Man and wife were going to have to crawl into bed alongside each other sometime during the night.

Along about midnight Clara announced that it was closing time. Everybody gave a big cheer for Hank. It was going to take more than a big cheer to buoy me up by then. I could've wrung out my shirt and washed myself in my own sweat.

I couldn't swear that nothing bawdy happened the whole night. Those harvesters had been a long time from home and some of our women were feeling mighty free. But I just don't think it did, and I'll tell you why: Clara, when she pronounced it was closing time, was carrying a long birch switch, the kind that whistles when you slice the air with it, and the very kind Maudie had taken to Reuben White one night when he danced too intimate with Clara.

I was shivering when I went down to bed. I thought of stopping by Tuttle's, but the truth was I didn't even want to know if he was still open. I'd kept hoping some of the men would come back up to the Red Lantern, but nobody did. I did a lot of tossing and turning, and I couldn't have been long asleep when the fire siren sounded. I hadn't run with the engines for a long time, but I was out of the house and heading for the Red Lantern before the machines left the firehouse. I just knew if there was trouble that's where it was.

I didn't see any smoke or fire when I got to the drive, but Luke Weber, our same constable, waved me off the road. I parked and started hiking through the grass. The fire trucks were coming. I started to run. When I got almost to where we'd dug the barbecue pits, something caught my ankle and I fell flat to the ground. Somebody crawled up alongside me.

"It's Bill Pendergast, Hank. Just shut up and lie low."

I couldn't have laid much lower.

The fire trucks screamed up the drive, their searchlights playing over the building, where, by now, lights were going on in all the upstairs rooms.

Pendergast said, "Let's go," and switched on his flashlight.

A couple of minutes later I saw maybe a half dozen other flashes playing over the back and side doors to the inn. By the time I got around front, Clara was standing on the veranda with the fire chief. She was wearing a negligee you could've seen daylight through if there'd been daylight. The harvesters were coming downstairs in their underwear. A couple of the volunteer firemen rushed up the stairs, brandishing their hatchets and their torches.

By then I'd figured out what was happening and it made me sick, no matter what Tuttle and them others thought they were going to flush out with the false alarm. Not a woman came down those stairs or any other stairs or out any window. They did come trooping down the County Road, about a dozen of them. Instead of going home when Clara closed, they'd climbed to where they could see the whole valley in the moonlight. The fire chief apologized for the invasion as though it had been his fault.

"I hope you come that fast," Clara said, "when there's more fire than smoke."

I was up at the Red Lantern again on Sunday afternoon when the harvesters moved on, heading for their next setup in the morning. Clara bought them a drink for the road. One of them, a strapping fellow I might have thrown a punch at otherwise, patted Clara's behind when she went to the door with them. She jumped and then stretched her mouth in something like a smile. I listened to them say how they'd be back this way in hunting season. They all laughed at that and I felt I was missing something. When one of them tried to give me five bucks for the fiddling, I just walked away. But I watched to see if any extra money passed between them and Clara. That negligee was hanging in my mind.

A few nights later I stopped by Tuttle's. I figured that since I'd laid low with the fellows I might as well stand at the bar with them, at least for half my drinking time. I walked in on a huddle at the round table where there's a floating card game going on most times. But they weren't playing cards and they looked at me as though I'd come to collect the mortgage. I turned and started to go out again.

"Hey, Hank, come on back here," Pendergast called. "Only you got to take your oath along with the rest of us never to let on what we're talking about here tonight."

"What's the general subject?" I asked.

"You know as well as we do," Jesse Tuttle said.

"I reckon." I stuck my right hand in the air as though the Bible was in my left.

"We were going to draw straws," Pendergast said, "but Billy Baldwin here just volunteered."

I pulled up a chair, making the ninth or tenth man, and waited to hear what Baldwin had volunteered to do. I haven't mentioned him before because there wasn't reason, even though Nancy Baldwin was one of the women that came whooping down the road after the fire alarm. Billy wasn't the most popular man in town—kind of a braggart and boring as a magpie. Whenever anybody had an idea, Billy had a better one, and he hardly ever stopped talking. The bus route he was driving at the time ran up-county, starting from the Courthouse steps, so he had to take his own car to and from his job at different times of day and night. By now you've probably guessed what he'd volunteered for.

I made it a point to stay away from the Red Lantern the night he planned to stop there. I got to admit, though, I was as curious as the rest of the bunch to learn how he'd make out with Clara, so I hung around Tuttle's with them. The funny thing was, I was the last man in the place. Long before closing time, Pendergast, then Prouty, then Kincaid, all of them dropped out and went home to their own beds. Tuttle locked up behind me.

The next day Baldwin stopped by the tavern on the way to work and told Jesse that nothing happened, that he'd just sat at the bar with Clara, talking and working up to things. "The big shot's getting chicken," Pendergast said when Tuttle passed the word.

None of us said much. Counting chickens. I know I was.

Well, it was a week before Billy Baldwin came in with his verdict. As far as he could tell, Clara McCracken might still be a virgin, he said. He'd finally come right out and slipped a twenty-dollar bill on the bar the last night and asked her to wear the negligee she'd had on the night of the false alarm. At that point, Clara reached for the birch stick behind the bar and he took off, leaving the money where it was.

"You're lucky she didn't reach for the shotgun," Prouty said.

We all chipped in to make up the twenty dollars.

Things quieted down after that and I continued to split my drinking time between Tuttle's and the Red Lantern. Clara would get the occasional oiler coming through to check the pumps, and the duck- and deer-hunting seasons were good business, but she never did get much of the town custom, and the rumors about her and that negligee hung on. It wasn't the sort of gear you sent away to Sears Roebuck for, but the post office in Webbtown was run by a woman then and I don't think any of us ever did find out where that particular garment came from. Maybe she'd sent away for it while she was still in prison. Like I said early on, Clara had done a lot of planning in fifteen years.

Now I just said things quieted down. To tell the truth, it was like the quiet before a twister comes through. I know I kept waiting and watching Clara, and Clara watched me watching her. One day she asked me what they were saying about her in the town.

I tried to make a joke of it. "Nothing much. They're getting kind of used to you, Clara."

She looked at me with a cold eye. "You in on that Billy Baldwin trick?"

I thought about the oath I was supposed to have sworn. "What trick?" I asked.

"Hank," she said, "for a lawyer you ain't much of a liar."

"I ain't much of a lawyer, either," I said. Then, looking her straight in the face, sure as fate straighter than I looked at myself, I said, "Clara, how'd you like to marry me?"

She set back on her heels and smiled in that odd way of having to work at it. "Thank you kindly." She cast her eyes up toward the license, which I'd just about forgotten. "We got one partnership going and I think that ought to do us—but I do thank you, old Hank."

I've often wondered what I'd have done if she'd said yes.

But I've come around since to holding with the Reverend Barnes. Everything was set in its course long before it happened—including Clara's planning.

September passed, October, and it came the full, cold moon of November. You could hear wolves in the Ragapoo Hills and the loons—and which is lonesomer-sounding I wouldn't say. I've mentioned before how light a sleeper I am. I woke up this night to a kind of whispering sound, a sort of swish, a pause, and then another swish, a pause, and then another. When I realized it was outside my window, I got up and looked down on the street.

There, passing in the silvery moonlight—a few feet between them (I think now to keep from speaking to one another)—the women of the town were moving toward the Red Lantern. By the time I got within sight of them up there, they'd formed a half circle around the front of the inn which was in total darkness. One of the women climbed the steps and went inside. I knew the door had not been locked since I unlocked it when I brought Clara home.

I kept out of sight and edged round back to where I had been the night of the false alarm. I saw the car parked there and knew it belonged to Billy Baldwin. If I could have found a way in time, I'd have turned in a false alarm myself, but I was frozen in slow motion. I heard the scream and the clatter in the building, and the front door banging open. Billy Baldwin came running out stark naked. He had some of his clothes with him, but he hadn't waited to put them on. Behind him was his wife Nancy, sobbing and crying and beating at him until one of the women came up and took her away down toward the town.

Billy had stopped in his tracks, seeing the circle of women. He was pathetic, trying to hide himself first and then trying to put his pants on, and the moonlight throwing crazy shadows on the women. Then I saw Clara come out the door on my side of the building. She was wearing the negligee and sort of drifted like a specter around the veranda to the front.

The women began to move forward.

Billy, seeing them come, fell on his knees and held out his hands, begging. I started to pray myself. I saw that every woman was carrying a stone. They kept getting closer, but not a one raised her arm until Clara went down and picked up a stone from her own drive which she flung at Billy.

He was still on his knees after that, but he fell almost at once beneath the barrage that followed. One of those stones killed him dead, though I didn't know it at the time.

Clara went back up the steps and picked her way through the stones. She kicked at what was left of poor, lying, cheating Billy as hard as she could. The women found more stones then and threw them at her until she fled into the inn and closed the door.

Nobody's been arrested for Billy's murder. I don't think anyone ever will be. It ought to be Clara, if anyone, but I'd have to bear witness that the

man was still alive after she'd thrown the stone. She's never forgiven the
women for turning on her. She kept telling me how glad she was when
they came to take Billy in adultery. And I wore myself out asking her what
the heck she thought she was doing.

Along toward summer a baby boy was born to Clara. She had him
christened Jeremiah McCracken after his grandfather. At the christening
she said to me, "See, Hank. That's what I was doing." I'm going to tell
you, I'm glad that when Jeremiah McCracken comes old enough to get a
tavern license, I'll be in my grave by then. I hope of natural causes.

# Still Life with Orioles

JAMES POWELL

You've passed the sign and the turnoff a hundred times out there on the old highway. It's halfway between Merge and Falling Rock. Deer Xing, the town's called.

Maybe you've wondered how a place around here got to be named after an Oriental. Folks tell me he arrived in town one afternoon about twenty-five years ago—a small man, barely able to peer over the steering wheel of his modest car. The town was called Droverton then. He parked in front of the Drover's Bank, his quick, quiet step took him inside, and he was closeted with Chip Cullet for several hours. It was no secret that Cullet, the husband of old Charlie Drover's great granddaughter, wasn't interested in making a go of the bank and wanted to move back to Merge, where his family's business was. There had even been talk that the bank might close.

Deer Xing stayed at the Central Hotel for the rest of the week, taking his meals in the dining room—whose food I heartily recommend. He spent his days going over the bank ledgers. Evenings, you might come across him walking the town street by street. He must have liked what he saw, for pretty soon the word was out that the bank had found a new owner.

Everyone expected Deer Xing to live in the old Drover mansion, but instead he chose a cheery little place on the outskirts of town, which, along with an extensive apple orchard adjoining, had come to the bank through foreclosure. His arrival marked a kind of turnaround in the fortunes of the town. Most of those Deer Xing loaned money to prospered, and so, of course, did he. Over the next few years, he became active in the local service clubs and the Boy Scouts. Somewhere along the line he joined the Unitarian choir because it needed a baritone and he ended up marrying the church organist, one of those plain little women people always say will make some sensible person a fine wife one day. Well, people were right. They became a devoted couple and raised four fine smiling children.

Deer Xing was a kind of leaven for the town—congenial and modest, but at the same time a down-to-earth businessman happy to show would-be bank borrowers how better to structure their endeavor. He served three terms on the town council, and though he'd have been a shoo-in he steadfastly refused to run for mayor. The year he was Droverton Day chairperson, he turned the tired street fair into an event drawing people from miles around. All it took was renting a couple of circus calliopes to liven things up. From then on, they called it Calliope Day and it grew into a dueling pipe-organ and snare-drum kind of thing, with owners trundling their contraptions in from all over the landscape to battle for prizes offered by the Drover's Bank. And when some town booster suggested they put Droverton on the map by building a Circus Calliope Hall of Fame, it was Deer Xing who offered the seed money to get the project started and promised more where that came from.

Right after Deer Xing made this generous offer, he left on one of his regular business trips to Beltway, which is just about as close as we get to a big city out here. As she usually did when it was summer and school was out, his wife took the children to visit her mother, who lived in the mountains just this side of Donot Pass. That same night, at a special town meeting everybody had been secretly planning for some time, the mayor said, "Neighbors, why should we put Droverton on the map? What's the Drover family done for us lately?" Then he formally proposed that the name of the town be changed to Deer Xing in honor of their most beloved citizen. The motion was seconded and carried unanimously.

The next few days were a flurry of activity. The street signs and the name on the town hall had to be changed and the side of the police car repainted. I wasn't there when Deer Xing drove back into town and saw all the happy faces and the bunting and read the banner strung across Main Street that said WELCOME TO DEER XING, DEER XING, but considering what I know now I wouldn't wonder that he had trouble mustering a tired smile for everyone. That night the lights burned late at the bank.

The wire services picked up on the story about the town that changed its name to honor an Oriental model citizen, and because it was a slow news day many of the morning papers featured it prominently. A WMRG-TV crew arrived at Deer Xing's door early the next morning to find the house empty. The banker and his family had fled during the night. The bank examiners discovered a shortage of close to fifty thousand dollars, just about all the cash on hand at closing time, but considerably less than all the money Deer Xing had invested in the bank. So why run off the way he did? You tell me.

In all the confusion, few gave a mind to the two soberly dressed Oriental gentlemen who arrived in town that same afternoon asking polite questions, like did anybody see which way Deer Xing headed when he left town. Spud Horst, who ran the garage in town, swore one had a dragon tattoo wrapped around his wrist. As it happened, Deer Xing did, too. Whenever the town kids asked to see it, he'd smile and pull up his sleeve to reveal a long thin dragon that undulated down the forearm, wound around the wrist, and ended up with its head on the ball of his thumb. He told adults the tattoo was the result of a youthful indiscretion. So pretty soon after Deer Xing skipped, a story made the rounds that he had been the treasurer of some murderous tong, absconded with the fan-tan receipts, and come to Droverton seeking an oblivion which the town would inadvertently deny him.

I didn't start coming to Calliope Day until several years after Deer Xing's disappearance. When I retired, I started this little business. Give me a snapshot of your home and I'll build you a birdhouse for your back yard or a mailbox for out front that looks just like it. I work the small street fairs and flea markets, showing a few samples of what I do and taking orders. That's how I met Harvey Goodling's wife Nora, who had the stand next to mine one Calliope Day.

The Goodlings had rented Deer Xing's old house on the edge of town. Nora sold herb plants, which she grew herself, and oriole nests. The long-neglected orchard next door had become a terrible landscape of bramble, vines, and twisted trees by that time, wilder than wild, the way tame things do when you let them go. But several pair of orioles nested there. When she was a girl, her mother hung out bright strands of yarn in the spring for the birds to build their nests with. And so did Nora.

In early spring, she'd hear the first tentative calls and see flashes of color in the treetops. Soon the birds were making cautious sorties down to the wool. The particular creatures would sometimes build two or three nests before they were satisfied with their work, and each autumn when the leaves fell Nora and Harvey went through a gap in the chain-link fence and got the nests with a ladder. When she started bringing a few of the prettiest along with her when she set up her booth on Calliope Day, they were great conversation pieces. Somebody suggested putting them in with a swag of dried flowers to hang on your front door. Somebody else said Christmas-tree decorations. A cozy for a toy tea-set, said another. But when you come right down to it, I don't think people liked the idea of old birds' nests no matter how many bright strands of wool they had woven into them. Nobody ever bought one. Come to think of it, I never heard her mention a price. Maybe she didn't mean to sell them.

After Nora Goodling's headaches started, Harvey would handle the stand for her whenever he had the time. Harvey taught English at Falling Rock State College. If I was busy with a customer and he wasn't, he'd always have a book to stick his nose into. But if I wanted to talk, he'd close the book on his thumb quick enough. He had given up on his doctoral thesis somewhere along the line. I guess he'd never published anything. But I could tell he loved teaching. Mention Shakespeare and the poets and he'd talk your ear off. From what I heard, his students who liked such things liked Goodling and those who didn't said he made it all sound like they should. His courses at Falling Rock were usually freshman composition and remedial this and remedial that, with something fancier thrown in now and then when a colleague was off on sabbatical.

Goodling's life centered on his teaching, his wife, his bookish daughter Portia, and long walks along the river. He told me about this peeled log along the bank where he'd sometimes sit and read while he waited for the muskrat who had a burrow somewhere nearby to come swimming past, pleating the water with its nose, making a gentle grunting sound as it went, or he'd watch the kingfisher hover head high above the river. I liked Harvey. His point of view was a thoughtful one. He was fairly content at the way things had turned out for him. "I guess I'm a still life in a moving-picture world," he used to say. "But that's all right."

On the other side of the orchard, in a house trailer set up on a cinder-block foundation, lived Carl Baddish, his wife Malva, and their teenaged son Kyle. Baddish did a lot of the handyman work in Deer Xing, but he dreamed of turning junk into inventions that would make his fortune. The yard in front of his trailer was littered with old pieces of rusting machinery, cogs, and wheels he'd dragged home from the town dump. He spent his free time, rain or shine, sitting in an old overstuffed easy chair in a crude tepee made of tarpaulin and clothesline poles, looking out over this yard full of iron with his chin in his hand. Sometimes he'd go pick up a cog wheel here and walk over to a drive shaft there. For a few thoughtful moments he'd try to fit the two together like this and like that. Then he'd mutter, drop them both where he stood, and return to tepee and chair, to cheek and palm.

Kyle spent most of his time stripped to the waist, working on his car in the driveway. Malva had claimed the steep back steps outside the kitchen door as her own, and sat there to peel potatoes or crochet the pot holders she sold on Calliope Day or talk to Duke, their Lab who was chained to a dog box.

What bad feeling existed between the Goodlings and the Baddishes came mostly from Carl's notions about fuzzy-minded, stuckup college types. Harvey's few attempts at neighborly small talk hadn't changed

Carl's thinking one bit. Actually, Malva Baddish admired Nora. One year she decided to do oriole nests for Calliope Day, too, except with flashier colors. But Carl said, why waste good wool? Recycling's the ticket. Leave this one to me, he said.

Next spring, out on their sagging clothesline, he hung his accumulation of used dental floss, the spaghetti noodles from two nights before, a winter of bloody string from butcher parcels, worn and mended shoelaces, tape from the loudest of the loud rock-and-roll cassettes that Kyle played until they gave up the ghost, and things of like nature. Come fall, Carl collected his nests, which were easy enough to tell from the Goodlings'. He scratched his head while he looked at them like this and like that. Finally he decided to lacquer the nests, mount them on pieces of wood, and sell them as novelty wall plaques.

As it happened, one of the Calliope Day judges that year was Stanford Breeze, who taught contemporary-art history at Falling Rock. As he told the Deer Xing *Bugle*, "If architecture is frozen music, then surely transportation is frozen calliope music." (That kind of sounds like gridlock to me, but what do I know?) During his quick tour of the booths with his entourage, I heard Breeze express the hope that the abundance of pine cutouts of pigs, geese, and ducks decorated with calico ribbons represented the last dying gasp of the country-yuppie style. He paused long enough over the Goodling oriole nests to pronounce them "unrepentantly genteel." But he put on the brakes so fast he almost got whiplash as he passed the Baddish booth.

He called Carl's wall plaques the highest form of "found art," found art of the aided-and-abetted sort. He bought every last nest on the spot and promised to fix Carl up with a gallery to handle anything else he came up with. Then he threw his arm over Carl's shoulder and walked off with him, talking about how nature puts all artists to shame, except for those few whose talented eyes can discover and improve on the designs she has hidden all around us. Baddish must have bought it, for when I drove out of town I saw him out at the dump tossing a crushed thirty-gallon drum into the back of his pickup. (I later heard he applied some mother-of-pearl trim, entitled the thing "Carl's Concertina," and sold it for a bundle.)

After that, Baddish sold a lot of things—like the three river stones, See-No-Evil, Hear-No-Evil, and Speak-No-Evil, that are now on display in some big art museum out East. When spring came around again, he was paying farmers for the right to hang up his trash in their orchards and collect the oriole nests each fall. He even came upon Goodling's favorite tree trunk on one of his forays along the river and discerned in the tortured shape of the wood a naked man and woman twined together in passionate embrace. Didn't Baddish go and cart the damn thing off, polish and varnish it, and sell it to Falling Rock State College? And didn't they exhibit the damn thing right there in the quadrangle so that Harvey never had to go a day without blushing to remember what he'd sat on for years.

So, with Harvey looking on and shaking his head, half in wonder and half in disbelief, Baddish prospered and took to sporting a beret and an artistic swagger. He moved into town to live in the old Drover mansion. Not long after, he and some of the art faculty at the college launched the Baddish Correspondence School of Found Art. The venture was an immediate success and the next thing Harvey knew Baddish had bought the orchard, repaired the chain-link fence, and put No Trespassing signs all around.

About this orchard, did I mention how people started remembering things after Deer Xing disappeared? Like Coach Tawney recalling how he'd been in Beltway one afternoon getting a trophy engraved and saw the banker come out of a shop that bought and sold jade? Which reminded someone else how there'd always been a lantern moving in the orchard the night before each of Deer Xing's trips to the city. That started the story of a buried trove of priceless jade art treasures from mainland China that Deer Xing had been selling off piece by piece as the bank needed the money. This sure brought the diggers out for a few nights, in the hope Xing had had to leave the jade behind when he fled with the Red Chinese hot on his trail. But it was a big orchard and nobody ever found anything. I guess for Baddish, who was becoming a very busy man, buying the orchard was a way to make sure nobody stumbled on the jade before he got around to finding it himself.

The loss of the orchard would have been a bigger blow to Nora and Harvey Goodling if that spring a pair of orioles hadn't chosen to nest in the apple tree in their yard. The next time he saw me, Harvey insisted I come by for a look, swearing he was starting to see a pattern in the nests they wove. I stood with him and Nora in the yard, looking through binoculars at that windy tree, but I can't say I saw any pattern.

The year Baddish found the stain in the shape of North America on an old plaster wall and dreamed his dream of creating his now-celebrated Found Art Map of the World, Portia Goodling dropped out of college to run off and marry Kyle Baddish. Baddish, who had set his sights on the boy becoming an architect, never spoke to his son again. The couple settled down in Merge, where Kyle got a job with Culletco. Whenever Nora's health was up to it, Harvey took her to visit their daughter and son-in-law in their tiny apartment. He said he couldn't understand what Portia saw in young Baddish but it was clear to him that they were in love. Later

Harvey told me that even if he wished Portia had made something more of herself, he'd be the first to admit he hadn't set her much of an example.

When Baddish found the kidney stone shaped like the Rock of Gibraltar, a well known insurance company paid him a bundle to complete his Found Art Map of the World for the lobby of their international headquarters. That same year, Nora Goodling had her first fainting spell. The doctors diagnosed a small brain tumor. Her recovery from surgery was slower than expected. Portia was busy with her first child and expecting her second, but she gave as much help as she could.

All Harvey had time for now was preparing his classes, marking papers, and taking care of his wife. The orioles in the apple tree had to take the place of his walks along the river. He was very faithful about putting out the wool as Nora would have done. In fact, the next spring when I saw him outside the supermarket and remarked that for a still life he was moving pretty fast, he insisted that the new nests were definitely "plaidish." Inviting me to drop by sometime, he disappeared across the parking lot in a racket of shopping-cart wheels.

By the time Baddish got the last bit of geography for his map, a constellation of moles from the backside of an anonymous donor that was a perfect representation of the Scilly Isles, a blood clot sent Goodling's wife back to the hospital. When she came out again, Harvey had to hire a woman to help him care for her.

Things might have continued like this if the new president at Falling Rock State College hadn't decided to upgrade the place academically and get rid of the non-tenured faculty. Harvey's contract with the college wasn't renewed, and at the end of summer school he found himself out of a job. That winter he found part-time work teaching on the other side of Merge, although with what they paid I don't see how he kept going. Meanwhile, Nora's condition slowly worsened. Clearly she would soon need nursing-home care.

By spring there was a lot of talk about lantern sightings in the orchard again. It occurred to me that it might just be Harvey out on some desperate search for jade, so one night I came by, intending to lead the conversation in that direction. But all Harvey wanted to talk about were the new oriole nests. It wasn't just plaid this year, he insisted, it was definitely argyle. But while he went on about it, his eyes were too bright and he couldn't sit in one place for longer than a moment or two. If he wasn't jumping up to see how Nora was, he was straightening a picture or going over to the window facing on the orchard. Yes, he said when I finally insisted—yes, he'd seen the lantern. Several times, and always late at night. Somebody was sneaking around over there all right.

He said okay when I asked if we could turn off the lights and keep an eye out ourselves. (At least if we saw a lantern, I'd know it hadn't been Harvey.) So we sat in the dark with only the light from the kitchen door and the lamp in the stairwell. But he couldn't stay off the subject of the oriole nests long. He seemed to be putting a great deal of store in them.

"All right," I said at last, "I'll take your word for it. So they're argyle. So what?"

Well, he hummed and hawed for a bit, trying to put his thoughts into words. Then he said, "It's like a rainbow."

"You mean some kind of a covenant?" I asked.

He wouldn't go that far. "I mean like hope," he said.

"Well," I said, regretting the words as soon as they were out of my mouth, "it all sounds a lot like Breeze and Baddish's found art to me."

That shut him up for a real long time. Then he nodded and got up. He went into the kitchen and came back carrying a gin bottle and two glasses.

Now Harvey wasn't much of a drinking man. Nor am I when it comes down to straight gin. But I could see he needed to talk. And I'll give him this, he spoke without the self-pity that usually comes with the territory when you uncork a bottle. He said he held himself responsible for the way things had turned out—not his wife's condition, of course, but losing his job and now not being able to provide for her as he should. He should have finished his thesis, published in his field, and been more ruthless about class work, even if it meant spending less time with his wife and Portia. "And do you know what else I did?" he concluded in a voice breathless with amazement. "I made myself a brother to the muskrat and a companion to the kingfisher!" We looked at each other like he'd almost quoted Scripture.

Nodding decisively as if to reaffirm everything he'd said, Harvey fell silent and remained that way for a long time. Bad as the light was, I could tell from his face that he found it hard to accept that all those happy times he remembered had been wrong. Finally, as if out of nowhere, he said, "All that's left is the insurance policy. I'm worth more dead than alive." Just then a beam of light swept across the living room and we jumped to the window.

With all the lantern business, Baddish had started driving out from town regularly to work a spotlight through the trees. That night he must have thought he saw something. As we watched, he killed the lights, unlocked the gate, and drifted the truck down into the orchard. After a bit, we heard a shout and a shot. Later Baddish claimed he'd seen an Oriental in a shiny black suit running away, and fired when the man refused to stop. He swore the bullet hit the blade of the man's shovel. If you ask me, he hit one of his own No Trespassing signs. Anyway, some said

Deer Xing had come back to claim his jade. Others said it was a Red Chinese agent whose people had tortured Deer Xing into revealing where he'd buried the trove.

The next time I saw Harvey was in the checkout line at the Eat/Gas convenience store on the edge of town. I was on my way back from dinner at the Central Hotel. His spirits were pretty low. The doctors had told him the time had come for Nora to go into a nursing home. While he was describing the grim results of his day making the rounds of the local social agencies to see what financial help he could get, I saw Baddish drive by, heading out to the orchard. So did the town cop standing in line ahead of us—he remarked to the girl at the register that Baddish had better not try anything like a mantrap or he'd find himself in real trouble. I hadn't thought Harvey heard, but a few minutes later he turned to watch the cop leave the store and, half to me and half to himself, said thoughtfully, "With Carl's luck, he'd probably come out of it smelling like a rose."

"Come out of what?" I asked. But Harvey didn't answer. He just gave a small smile.

Three days later, when I heard Harvey had been killed, my first thought was that he'd committed suicide, maybe not knowing some insurance companies don't pay off on something like that. But it couldn't have been suicide. They found his body inside the orchard, on a path about fifteen feet away from a hole snipped in the fence. He'd been shot through the heart. The pistol that killed him lay a few feet away. There were no fingerprints on it, which there would have to have been if Harvey had done it to himself, since he wasn't wearing gloves.

Some envious types wanted to pin it on Baddish, even though he'd been out of town getting inducted into the American Academy of Arts and Letters. Others said Harvey might've surprised Deer Xing digging up his jade and paid for it with his life. Or was he, as others suggested, just another victim in a struggle between the East and the West over a jade scepter that made any man who possessed it the rightful Emperor of China?

Harvey Goodling's murder remained a mystery, preying on my mind long after the powers-that-be declared it death by party or parties unknown. The insurance company paid off. But Nora Goodling passed away in a matter of weeks and the bulk of the money went to Portia, who used it to put Kyle through architectural school.

There was a bad windstorm late that autumn. A day or so later, I happened to be driving by when I noticed something different about the Goodling place. As it still stood unrented, I turned in at the driveway to investigate. The apple tree in the back yard had heaved over during the storm and come down hard on the tool shed. I went over and stood at the fence for a bit, looking at the place where Harvey's body had been found, wondering what had really happened to him.

As I started back to the car, I saw something on the ground that made Harvey's last few minutes as plain as day. I could see him wiping the fingerprints from the pawn-shop revolver and tying it into a heart-high crotch of a tree with a length of fishing line. Then he threads the line through the trigger-guard and leads it down the tree until it's about five inches off the ground. Wrapping the line once around the tree, he leads it across the path and ties it off at the base of a tree on the other side. He probably tries a couple of dry runs with his foot to make the trigger click, imagining the trajectory of the bullet with his eye. Then he loads the chamber.

So Harvey Goodling found his way to make sure Nora got the money from the insurance policy and the care she needed. Like I said, I liked Harvey. He was under a great deal of pressure. Did he mean to implicate Baddish? Or did he really believe that with Baddish's luck, the man would come out of it smelling like a rose? I don't know. Maybe he'd have handled things better without Baddish's successes to measure his misfortunes against.

An oriole nest lay on the ground beside the fallen apple tree. The argyle design was almost perfect, the diamonds of yellow and blue wool and brown grass all neat and regular. Yet, like an engraver who decides at the last minute that the plate is not up to standard and crosshatches the whole thing with his stylus, the orioles had woven a long length of fishing line back and forth randomly through their design.

Well, that's the end of the story. You've been a real good listener. Time I was heading back home to Rumble Strips.

What's that? Yes, you're right. I've always thought that's a damn funny name for a town, too. When Sadie Rumble moved from the big city in the early forties to open her roadhouse, you can bet she thought she'd left exotic dancing behind forever. But when the Army base closed down and business started falling off real bad, well, she needed something to draw in the customers.

# Something's Happening at the Halliwells'

JEFFREY BUSH

**P**ete was biking down Division Road.

Or that, he told himself, was what he appeared to be doing—a thirteen-year-old boy pedaling down a country road on a bright June day, avoiding the puddles from last night's rain, on his way to mow the Halliwells' lawn.

Actually, he was deep within enemy lines, bringing out news of their secret plans.

He passed Mr. Cook driving a tractor slowly up the road in the other direction. Mr. Cook, unable to penetrate Pete's disguise, gave him a casual wave.

He passed old Mrs. Venable's fruit stand—or what seemed to be old Mrs. Venable's fruit stand. It was, in fact, a radar station, designed especially to spot a person like him. Mrs. Venable smiled vaguely—unaware of his desperate mission.

He approached the orange trucks from the gas company. Each week they were a little farther down the road, installing a natural gas line from Centerville to East Centerville. A number of men were to be seen around them, wearing orange helmets. Today, sitting by the side of the road eating their lunch, two or three of them looked at him without interest as he passed.

He had got by them!

Now it was up to him, and him alone, to carry word of the massive attack they were about to launch.

He pedaled furiously.

He had a vivid imagination.

Around the next bend, down a gentle dip, up again, and he was at the Halliwells', braking, turning into their driveway—blacktop, like the road—and taking a look at their grass. Yes, it needed cutting, all right.

Back to reality.

He leaned his bike against the wooden fence that separated their property from the field next door. He started around the house.

Surprise. By the back door there was another orange truck.

A man was sitting inside it, behind the wheel. He stuck his head out the window. It was a narrow head, with a big jaw, as if someone had stuck a saucer inside his mouth.

"You live here, kid?"

"No, I don't," Pete said politely.

"Whaddya doing here?"

The man wasn't wearing an orange helmet. And there was no lettering on the side of the truck.

"I'm here to cut the grass. What's the trouble?"

The man stared at him. "Gas leak," he said finally. He jerked his head at the Halliwells' back door. It was open. "Don't go in the house."

Gas leak?

"Okay," Pete said.

In as normal a manner as he could manage, he walked to the garage.

That truck wasn't from the gas company. It couldn't be. He knew it couldn't be.

What should he do?

Bike to the next house and call the police. Yes, but by the time he'd done that—and the police had got here—the truck might be gone.

He shivered.

In his imagination, he'd thwarted hundreds of evil plots. He'd always wondered what he'd do if he really had to confront one.

Thinking hard, he pushed the power mower out of the garage, past the man's watchful gaze, around the corner of the house, and out of sight.

Could he delay the truck somehow?

The other side of the house was blocked by the apple orchard. This side was where the truck would have to come—on the driveway, or on the six feet of grass between the driveway and the fence. He looked around. There was nothing to put in the truck's path—no lawn furniture, no stones from a stone wall. Even if there had been, the men—for there must be more than one—could easily move them away.

Maybe he could find something in the garage. Out of the corner of his eye he saw the man watching him as he walked back. In the garage were the things that were in everybody's garage—tools, a garden hose, some bags of fertilizer, half a dozen cans of motor oil, and a lawn roller.

The lawn roller! It weighed a ton. He pulled. He pulled harder. He got it going—out of the garage, onto the driveway, towards the truck.

Did the man know that you only used a roller at seeding time? And that Pete wasn't doing any seeding?

He didn't dare look up to find out.

He was used to pretending that he was in the midst of fantastic adventures. Now he had to pretend that he was doing something perfectly ordinary.

He felt the man's eyes on his back until he was around the corner of the house. He rested, panting. The roller blocked the driveway. But a couple of men wouldn't have any trouble pulling it away.

He thought of the cans of motor oil.

He walked back to the garage. The man was still watching him. It would look okay to take one can of oil—how could Pete take all six?

The man couldn't see him in this part of the garage. He ripped open a bag of fertilizer, dumped most of it out, put in five cans of oil, and loaded fertilizer back in on top of them. Dragging the bag with one hand, and holding the sixth can of oil in his other hand, he started past the truck, head down.

"Hard worker, ain't you?"

Pete jumped. He raised his head. The man was staring down at him with amusement.

He grinned. He couldn't remember a grin that had ever been so hard to produce.

"Sure am."

Before the man could say anything more, Pete dragged the bag around the side of the house. He glanced up to make sure the coast was clear, pulled out the cans, and punched them open with his knife. One by one he poured them on the blacktop. When he was done, the roller was surrounded by a pool of oil.

So much for the driveway. It was all he could think of, anyway. But there was still the six feet of grass between the driveway and the fence.

Did he have the nerve to go to the garage one more time?

He took a deep breath. As he rounded the corner of the house, he saw a second man. He had a round face and a mustache, and he was loading a cardboard carton onto the back of the truck. He saw Pete and stopped.

There was nothing for it but to keep walking.

"Back again?" the man with the big jaw said.

"Getting the hose."

Would they wonder why a garden hose was needed after last night's rain? Followed by two pairs of eyes, Pete walked to the garage, picked up the hose, and carried it around the side of the house. Scarcely conscious of what he was doing, he unscrewed the nozzle, attached the hose to its outdoor faucet, turned the water on, and pulled the hose across the driveway to the six feet of grass.

He stood up.

Was there anything else?

Of course. The power mower. He started it. Maybe the two men would think he was mowing the lawn.

It was time to call the police. He was cold with sweat, his shirt was sticking to his back, somehow he'd got oil into his eyes, and now, at last, he could admit something to himself—he'd never been so scared in his life.

"Telephone!" he cried, as he ran past a startled Mrs. Simpson. He dialed.

"Centerville Police, Sergeant Smith speaking."

"Something's happening at the Halliwells'!"

"Who's this?"

He hung up. When grownups found out who you were, they paid less attention.

Back at the house, crouching behind the hedge in front, he saw that everything was as he'd left it. The roller sat in its pool of oil. The water was running onto the six feet of grass. The engine of the mower was going in neutral.

A minute passed. It seemed like an hour. Where were the police?

His heart was thumping. And then, above the roar of the mower, he thought he heard the truck starting.

Yes! There it was, coming around the corner of the house, faster than it should. It stopped abruptly, a foot or two from the roller. The passenger door opened, and the man with the round face jumped out.

He rushed towards the roller. His foot went out from under him. He picked himself up, hands shining with oil, mouthing something to himself that Pete couldn't hear. He grabbed the handle of the roller and pulled. Both feet went out from under him, and he fell on top of the roller. The man with the big jaw jumped out of the driver's side. The two men seized the handle, pulled, and fell together.

They got up, waving their arms and yelling soundlessly at each other. Big Jaw had a bloody nose. Round Face was pointing at the six feet of grass beside the driveway. They got back in the truck. Big Jaw backed it up, aimed for the grass, and stepped on the gas.

The water from the hose had turned the patch of grass into a mud hole. The truck slowed, its wheels spinning. It reversed. Its wheels sank in deeper. It lurched forward. It stopped.

In the cab, Big Jaw was shaking Round Face. Round Face lolled in his seat, as if he'd hit his head on the windshield. Big Jaw jumped out, stumbled to the back of the truck, and tried to push. From a distance it looked as if tears of anger were mixing with the blood from his nose.

Which was when a police car turned into the driveway.

An hour later, after Big Jaw and Round Face had been handcuffed and driven away in another police car, and Mr. Halliwell had assured Pete that he'd rather have a bit of his lawn chewed up than lose his collection of antique silver, which had been in five cardboard cartons in the back of the truck, and Pete had agreed that yes, maybe it would be better if he came back tomorrow to cut the grass, Sergeant Smith said, "There's one thing I'm curious about. There are lots of gas trucks working on this road. How come you were so sure those two birds weren't fixing a gas leak?"

There was no mystery about that. "They couldn't have been," Pete said. "The gas line hasn't got this far."

Sergeant Smith was silent: "No, it hasn't, has it?" He put a hand on Pete's shoulder. "Well," he said, "thanks."

Pete grinned. It was a real grin, this time. But an exhausted one. And as he got on his bike, he didn't think he was going to do any more pretending, at least not for a while.

He had all he could handle being what he was—a thirteen-year-old boy pedaling down a country road, on a bright June day, on his way home after outwitting two burglars.

# The Dettweiler Solution

### LAWRENCE BLOCK

Sometimes you just can't win for losing. Business was so bad over at Dettweiler Bros. Fine Fashions for Men that Seth Dettweiler went on back to the store one Thursday night and poured out a five-gallon can of lead-free gasoline where he figured as it would do the most good. He lit a fresh Philip Morris King Size and balanced it on the edge of the counter so as it would burn for a couple of minutes and then get unbalanced enough to drop into the pool of gasoline. Then he got into an Oldsmobile that was about five days' clear of a repossession notice and drove on home.

You couldn't have had a better fire dropping napalm on a paper mill. Time it was done you could sift those ashes and not find so much as a collar button. It was far and away the most spectacularly total fire Schuyler County had ever seen, so much so that Maybrook Fidelity Insurance would have been a little tentative about settling a claim under ordinary circumstances. But the way things stood there wasn't the slightest suspicion of arson, because what kind of a dimwitted hulk goes and burns down his business establishment a full week after his fire insurance has lapsed?

No fooling.

See, it was Seth's brother Porter who took care of paying bills and such, and a little over a month ago the fire-insurance payment had been due, and Porter looked at the bill and at the bank balance and back and forth for awhile and then he put the bill in a drawer. Two weeks later there was a reminder notice, and two weeks after that there was a notice that the grace period had expired and the insurance was no longer in force, and then a week after that there was one pluperfect hell of a bonfire.

Seth and Porter had always got on pretty good. (They took after each other quite a bit, folks said. Especially Porter.) Seth was forty-two years of age, and he had that long Dettweiler face topping a jutting Van Dine jaw.

(Their mother was a Van Dine hailing from just the other side of Oak Falls.) Porter was thirty-nine, equipped with the same style face and jaw. They both had black hair that lay flat on their heads like shoe polish put on in slapdash fashion. Seth had more hair left than Porter, in spite of being the older brother by three years. I could describe them in greater detail, right down to scars and warts and sundry distinguishing marks, but it's my guess that you'd enjoy reading all that about as much as I'd enjoy writing it, which is to say less than somewhat. So let's get on with it.

I was saying they got on pretty good, rarely raising their voices one to the other, rarely disagreeing seriously about anything much. Now the fire didn't entirely change the habits of a lifetime but you couldn't honestly say that it did anything to improve their relationship. You'd have to allow that it caused a definite strain.

"What I can't understand," Seth said, "is how anybody who is fool enough to let fire insurance lapse can be an even greater fool by not telling his brother about it. That in a nutshell is what I can't understand."

"What beats *me*," Porter said, "is how the same person who has the nerve to fire a place of business for the insurance also does so without consulting his partner, especially when his partner just happens to be his brother."

"Allus I was trying to do," said Seth, "was save you from the criminal culpability of being an accessory before, to, and after the fact, plus figuring you might be too chickenhearted to go along with it."

"Allus *I* was trying to do," said Porter, "was save you from worrying about financial matters you would be powerless to contend with, plus figuring it would just be an occasion for me to hear further from you on the subject of those bow ties."

"Well, you did buy one powerful lot of bow ties."

"I knew it."

"Something like a Pullman car full of bow ties, and it's not like every man and boy in Schuyler County's been getting this mad passion for bow ties of late."

"I just knew it."

"I wasn't the one brought up the subject, but since you went and mentioned those bow ties—"

"Maybe I should of mentioned the spats," Porter said.

"Oh, I don't want to hear about spats."

"No more than I wanted to hear about bow ties. Did we sell one single damn pair of spats?"

"We did."

"We did?"

"Feller bought one about fifteen months back. Had Maryland plates on his car, as I recall. Said he always wanted spats and didn't know they still made 'em."

"Well, selling one pair out of a gross isn't too bad."

"Now you leave off," Seth said.

"And you leave off of bow ties?"

"I guess."

"Anyway, the bow ties and the spats all burned up in the same damn fire," Porter said.

"You know what they say about ill winds," Seth said. "I guess there's a particle of truth in it, what they say."

While it didn't do the Dettweiler brothers much good to discuss spats and bow ties, it didn't solve their problems to leave off mentioning spats and bow ties. By the time they finished their conversation all they were back to was square one, and the view from that spot wasn't the world's best.

The only solution was bankruptcy, and it didn't look to be all that much of a solution.

"I don't mind going bankrupt," one of the brothers said. (I think it was Seth. Makes no nevermind, actually. Seth, Porter, it's all the same who said it.) "I don't mind going bankrupt, but I sure do hate the thought of being broke."

"Me too," said the other brother. (Porter, probably.)

"I've thought about bankruptcy from time to time."

"Me too."

"But there's a time and a place for bankruptcy."

"Well, the place is all right. No better place for bankruptcy than Schuyler County."

"That's true enough," said Seth. (Unless it was Porter.) "But this is surely not the time. Time to go bankrupt is in good times when you got a lot of money on hand. Only the damnedest kind of fool goes bankrupt when he's stony broke busted and there's a Depression going on."

What they were both thinking on during this conversation was a fellow name of Joe Bob Rathburton who was in the construction business over to the other end of Schuyler County. I myself don't know of a man in this part of the state with enough intelligence to bail out a leaky rowboat who doesn't respect Joe Bob Rathburton to hell and back as a man with good business sense. It was about two years ago that Joe Bob went bankrupt, and he did it the right way. First of all he did it coming off the best year's worth of business he'd ever done in his life. Then what he did was he paid off the car and the house and the boat and put them all in his wife's name. (His wife was Mabel Washburn, but no relation to the Washburns who have the Schuyler County First National Bank. That's another family entirely.)

Once that was done, Joe Bob took out every loan and raised every dollar he possibly could, and he turned all that capital into green folding cash and sealed it in quart Mason jars which he buried out back of an old Kieffer pear tree that's sixty-plus years old and still bears fruit like crazy. And then he declared bankruptcy and sat back in his Mission rocker with a beer and a cigar and a real big-tooth smile.

"If I could think of anything worth doing," Porter Dettweiler said one night, "why, I guess I'd just go ahead and do it."

"Can't argue with that," Seth said.

"But I can't," Porter said.

"Nor I either."

"You might pass that old jug over here for a moment."

"Soon as I pour a tad for myself, if you've no objection."

"None whatsoever," said Porter.

They were over at Porter's place on the evening when this particular conversation occurred. They had taken to spending most of their evenings at Porter's on account of Seth had a wife at home, plus a daughter named Rachel who'd been working at the Ben Franklin store ever since dropping out of the junior college over at Monroe Center. Seth didn't have but the one daughter. Porter had two sons and a daughter, but they were all living with Porter's ex-wife, who had divorced him two years back and moved clear to Georgia. They were living in Valdosta now, as far as Porter knew. Least that was where he sent the check every month.

"Alimony jail," said Porter.

"How's that?"

"What I said was alimony jail. Where you go when you quit paying on your alimony."

"They got a special jug set aside for men don't pay their alimony?"

"Just an expression. I guess they put you into whatever jug's the handiest. All I got to do is quit sendin' Gert her checks and let her have them cart me away. Get my three meals a day and a roof over my head and the whole world could quit nagging me night and day for money I haven't got."

"You could never stand it. Bein' in a jail day in and day out, night in and night out."

"I know it," Porter said unhappily. "There anything left in that there jug, on the subject of jugs?"

"Some. Anyway, you haven't paid Gert a penny in how long? Three months?"

"Call it five."

"And she ain't throwed you in jail yet. Least you haven't got her close to hand so's she can talk money to you."

"Linda Mae givin' you trouble?"

"She did. Keeps a civil tongue since I beat up on her the last time."

"Lord knew what he was doin'," Porter said, "makin' men stronger than women. You ever give any thought to what life would be like if wives could beat up on their husbands instead of the other way around?"

"Now I don't even want to think about that," Seth said.

You'll notice nobody was mentioning spats or bow ties. Even with the jug of corn getting discernibly lighter every time it passed from one set of hands to the other, these two subjects did not come up. Neither did anyone speak of the shortsightedness of failing to keep up fire insurance or the myopia of incinerating a building without ascertaining that such insurance was in force. Tempers had cooled with the ashes of Dettweiler Bros. Fine Fashions for Men, and once again Seth and Porter were on the best of terms.

Which just makes what happened thereafter all the more tragic.

"What I think I got," Porter said, "is no way to turn."

(This wasn't the same evening, but if you put the two evenings side by side under a microscope you'd be hard pressed to tell them apart each from the other. They were at Porter's little house over alongside the tracks of the old spur off the Wyandotte & Southern, which I couldn't tell you the last time there was a train on that spur, and they had their feet up and their shoes off, and there was a jug of corn in the picture. Most of their evenings had come to take on this particular shade.)

"Couldn't get work if I wanted to," Porter said, "which I don't, and if I did I couldn't make enough to matter, and my debts is up to my ears and rising steady."

"It doesn't look to be gettin' better," Seth said. "On the other hand, how can it get worse?"

"I keep thinking the same."

"And?"

"And it keeps getting worse."

"I guess you know what you're talkin' about," Seth said. He scratched his bulldog chin, which hadn't been in the same room with a razor in more than a day or two. "What I been thinkin' about," he said, "is killin' myself."

"You been thinking of that?"

"Sure have."

"I think on it from time to time myself," Porter admitted. "Mostly nights when I can't sleep. It can be a powerful comfort around about three in the morning. You think of all the different ways and the next thing you know you're asleep. Beats the stuffing out of counting sheep jumping fences. You seen one sheep you seen 'em all is always been my thoughts on the subject, whereas there's any number of ways of doing away with yourself."

"I'd take a certain satisfaction in it," Seth said, more or less warming to the subject. "What I'd leave is this note tellin' Linda Mae how her and Rachel'll be taken care of with the insurance, just to get the bitch's hopes up, and then she can find out for her own self that I cashed in that insurance back in January to make the payment on the Oldsmobile. You know it's pure uncut hell gettin' along without an automobile now."

"You don't have to tell me."

"Just put a rope around my neck," said Seth, smothering a hiccup, "and my damn troubles'll be over."

"And mine in the bargain," Porter said.

"By you doin' your own self in?"

"Be no need," Porter said, "if you did *your*self in."

"How you figure that?"

"What I figure is a hundred thousand dollars," Porter said. "Lord love a duck, if I had a hundred thousand dollars I could declare bankruptcy and live like a king!"

Seth looked at him, got up, walked over to him, and took the jug away from him. He took a swig and socked the cork in place, but kept hold of the jug.

"Brother," he said, "I just guess you've had enough of this here."

"What makes you say that, brother?"

"Me killin' myself and you gettin' rich, you don't make sense. What you think you're talkin' about, anyhow?"

"Insurance," Porter said. "Insurance, that's what I think I'm talking about. Insurance."

Porter explained the whole thing. It seems there was this life insurance policy their father had taken out on them when they weren't but boys. Face amount of a hundred thousand dollars, double indemnity for accidental death. It was payable to him while they were alive, but upon his death the beneficiary changed. If Porter was to die the money went to Seth. And vice-versa.

"And you knew about this all along?"

"Sure did," Porter said.

"And never cashed it in? Not the policy on me and not the policy on you?"

"Couldn't cash 'em in," Porter said. "I guess I woulda if I coulda, but I couldn't so I didn't."

"And you didn't let these here policies lapse?" Seth said. "On account of occasionally a person can be just the least bit absent-minded and forget about keeping a policy in force. That's been known to happen," Seth said, looking off to one side, "in matters relating to fire insurance, for example, and I just thought to mention it."

(I have the feeling he wasn't the only one to worry on that score. You may have had similar thoughts yourself, figuring you know how the story's going to end, what with the insurance not valid and all. Set your mind at rest. If that was the way it had happened I'd never be taking the trouble to write it up for you. I got to select stories with some satisfaction in them if I'm going to stand a chance of selling them to the magazine, and I hope you don't figure I'm sitting here poking away at this typewriter for the sheer physical pleasure of it. If I just want to exercise my fingers I'll send them walking through the Yellow Pages if it's all the same to you.)

"Couldn't let 'em lapse," Porter said. "They're all paid up. What you call twenty-payment life, meaning you pay in it for twenty years and then you got it free and clear. And the way Pa did it, you can't borrow on it or nothing. All you can do is wait and see who dies."

"Well, I'll be."

"Except we don't have to wait to see who dies."

"Why, I guess not. I just guess a man can take matters into his own hands if he's of a mind to."

"He surely can," Porter said.

"Man wants to kill himself, that's what he can go and do."

"No law against it," Porter said.

Now you know and I know that that last is not strictly true. There's a definite no-question law against suicide in our state, and most likely in yours as well. It's harder to make it stand up than a calf with four broken legs, however, and I don't recall that anyone hereabouts was ever prosecuted for it, or likely will be. It does make you wonder some what they had in mind writing that particular law into the books.

"I'll just have another taste of that there corn," Porter said, "and why don't you have a pull on the jug your own self? You have any idea just when you might go and do it?"

"I'm studying on it," Seth said.

"There's a lot to be said for doing something soon as a man's mind's made up on the subject. Not to be hurrying you or anything of the sort, but they say that he who hesitates is last." Porter scratched his chin. "Or some such," he said.

"I just might do it tonight."

"By God," Porter said.

"Get the damn thing over with. Glory Hallelujah and my troubles is over."

"And so is mine," said Porter.

"You'll be in the money then," said Seth, "and I'll be in the boneyard, and both of us is free and clear. You can just buy me a decent funeral and then go bankrupt in style."

"Give you Johnny Millbourne's Number One funeral," Porter promised. "Brassbound casket and all. I mean, price is no object if I'm going bankrupt anyway. Let old Johnny swing for the money."

"You a damn good man, brother."

"You the best man in the world, brother."

The jug passed back and forth a couple more times. At one point Seth announced that he was ready, and he was halfway out the door before he recollected that his car had been repossessed, which interfered with his plans to drive it off a cliff. He came back in and sat down again and had another drink on the strength of it all, and then suddenly he sat forward and stared hard at Porter.

"This policy thing," he said.

"What about it?"

"It's on both of us, is what you said."

"If I said it then must be it's the truth."

"Well then," Seth said, and sat back, arms folded on his chest.

"Well then what?"

"Well then if *you* was to kill yourself, then *I'd* get the money and *you'd* get the funeral."

"I don't see what you're getting at," Porter said slowly.

"Seems to me either one of us can go and do it," Seth said. "And here's the two of us just takin' it for granted that I'm to be the one to go and do it, and I think we should think on that a little more thoroughly."

"Why, being as you're older, Seth."

"What's that to do with anything?"

"Why, you got less years to give up."

"Still be givin' up all that's left. Older or younger don't cut no ice."

Porter thought about it. "After all," he said, "it was your idea."

"That don't cut ice neither. I could mention I got a wife and child."

"I could mention I got a wife and three children."

"Ex-wife."

"All the same."

"Let's face it," Seth said. "Gert and your three don't add up to anything and neither do Linda Mae and Rachel."

"Got to agree," Porter said.

"So."

"One thing. You being the one who put us in this mess, what with firing the store, it just seems you might be the one to get us out of it."

"You bein' the one let the insurance lapse through your own stupidity, you could get us out of this mess through insurance, thus evenin' things up again."

"Now talkin' about stupidity—"

"Yes, talkin' about stupidity—"

"Spats!"

"Bow ties, damn you! *Bow ties!*"

You might have known it would come to that.

Now I've told you Seth and Porter generally got along pretty well, and here's further evidence of it. Confronted by such a stalemate, a good many people would have wrote off the whole affair and decided not to take the suicide route at all. But not even spats and bow ties could deflect Seth and Porter from the road they'd figured out as the most logical to pursue.

So what they did, one of them tossed a coin, and the other one called it while it was in the air, and they let it hit the floor and roll, and I don't recollect whether it was heads or tails, or who tossed and who called— what's significant is that Seth won.

"Well now," Seth said. "I feel I been reprieved. Just let me have that coin, I want to keep it for a luck charm."

"Two out of three."

"We already said once is as good as a million," Seth said, "so you just forget that two-out-of-three business. You got a week like we agreed but if I was you I'd get it over soon as I could."

"I got a week," Porter said.

"You'll get the brassbound casket and everything, and you can have Minnie Lucy Boxwood sing at your funeral if you want. Expense don't matter at all. What's your favorite song?"

"I suppose *"Your Cheatin' Heart."*"

"Minnie Lucy does that real pretty."

"I guess she does."

"Now you be sure and make it accidental," Seth said. "Two hundred thousand dollars goes just about twice as far as one hundred thousand dollars. Won't cost you a thing to make it accidental, just like we talked about it. What I would do is borrow Fritz Chenoweth's half-ton pickup and go up on the old Harburton Road where it takes that curve. Have yourself a belly full of corn and just keep goin' straight when the road doesn't. Lord knows I almost did that myself enough times without tryin'. Had two wheels over the edge less'n a month ago."

"That close?"

"That close."

"I'll be doggone," Porter said.

Thing is, Seth went on home after he failed to convince Porter to do it right away, and that was when things began to fall into the muck. Because Porter started thinking things over. I have a hunch it would have worked about the same way if Porter had won the flip, with Seth thinking things over. They were a whole lot alike, those two. Like two peas in a pot.

What occurred to Porter was would Seth have gone through with it if he lost, and what Porter decided was that he wouldn't. Not that there was any way for him to prove it one way or the other, but when you can't prove something you generally tend to decide on believing in what you want to believe, and Porter Dettweiler was no exception. Seth, he decided, would not have killed himself and didn't never have no intention of killing himself, which meant that for Porter to go through with killing his own self amounted to nothing more than damned foolishness.

Now it's hard to say just when he figured out what to do, but it was in the next two days, because on the third day he went over and borrowed that pickup truck off Fritz Chenoweth. "I got the back all loaded down with a couple sacks of concrete mix and a keg of nails and I don't know what all," Fritz said. "You want to unload it back of my smaller barn if you need the room."

"Oh, that's all right," Porter told him. "I guess I'll just leave it loaded and be grateful for the traction."

"Well, you keep it overnight if you have a mind," Fritz said.

"I just might do that," Porter said, and he went over to Seth's house. "Let's you and me go for a ride," he told Seth. "Something we was talking about the other night, and I went and got me a new slant on it which the two of us ought to discuss before things go wrong altogether."

"Be right with you," Seth said, "soon as I finish this sandwich."

"Oh, just bring it along."

"I guess," said Seth.

No sooner was the pickup truck backed down and out of the driveway than Porter said, "Now will you just have a look over there, brother."

"How's that?" said Seth, and turned his head obligingly to the right, whereupon Porter gave him a good lick upside the head with a monkey wrench he'd brought along expressly for that purpose. He got him right where you have a soft spot if you're a little baby. (You also have a soft spot there if someone gets you just right with a monkey wrench.) Seth made a little sound which amounted to no more than letting his breath out, and then he went out like an icebox light when you have closed the door on it.

Now as to whether or not Seth was dead at this point I could not honestly tell you, unless I were to make up an answer knowing how slim is the likelihood of anyone presuming to contradict me. But the plain fact is that he might have been dead and he might not and even Seth could not have told you, being at the very least stone-unconscious at the time.

What Porter did was drive up the old Harburton Road, I guess figuring that he might as well stick to as much of the original plan as possible. There's a particular place where the road does a reasonably convincing imitation of a fishhook, and that spot's been described as Schuyler County's best natural brake on the population explosion since they stamped out the typhoid. A whole lot of folks fail to make that curve every year, most of them young ones with plenty of breeding years left in them. Now and then there's a movement to put up a guard rail, but the ecology people are against it so it never gets anywheres.

If you miss that curve, the next land you touch is a good five hundred feet closer to sea level.

So Porter pulls over to the side of the road and then he gets out of the car and maneuvers Seth (or Seth's body, whichever the case may have been) so as he's behind the wheel. Then he stands alongside the car working the gas pedal with one hand and the steering wheel with the other and putting the fool truck in gear and doing this and that and the other thing so he can run the truck up to the edge and over, and thinking hard every minute about those two hundred thousand pretty green dollars that is destined to make his bankruptcy considerably easier to contend with.

Well, I told you right off that sometimes you can't win for losing, which was the case for Porter and Seth both, and another way of putting it is to say that when everything goes wrong there's nothing goes right. Here's what happened. Porter slipped on a piece of loose gravel while he was pushing, and the truck had to go on its own, and where it went was halfway and no further, with its back wheel hung up on a hunk of tree limb or some such and its two front wheels hanging out over nothing and its motor stalled out deader'n smoked fish.

Porter said himself a whole mess of bad words. Then he wasted considerable time shoving the back of that truck, forgetting it was in gear and not about to budge. Then he remembered and said a few more bad words and put the thing in neutral, which involved a long reach across Seth to get to the floor shift and a lot of coordination to manipulate it and the clutch pedal at the same time. Then Porter got out of the truck and gave the door a slam, and just about then a beat-up old Chevy with Indiana plates pulls up and this fellow leaps out screaming that he's got a tow rope and he'll pull the truck to safety.

You can't hardly blame Porter for the rest of it. He wasn't the type to be great at contingency planning anyhow, and who could allow for something like this? What he did, he gave this great sob and just plain hurled himself at the back of that truck, it being in neutral now; and the truck went sailing like a kite in a tornado, and Porter, well, what he did was follow right along after it. It wasn't part of his plan but he just had himself too much momentum to manage any last-minute change of direction.

According to the fellow from Indiana, who it turned out was a veterinarian from Bloomington, Porter fell far enough to get off a couple of genuinely rank words on the way down. Last words or not, you sure wouldn't go and engrave them on any tombstone.

Speaking of which, he has the last word in tombstones, Vermont granite and all, and his brother Seth has one just like it. They had a double-barreled funeral, the best Johnny Millbourne had to offer, and they each of them reposed in a brassbound casket, the top-of-the-line model. Minnie Lucy Boxwood sang, *"Your Cheatin' Heart,"* which was Porter's favorite song, plus she sang Seth's favorite, which was *"Old Buttermilk Sky,"* plus she also sang free gratis *"My Buddy"* as a testament to brotherly love.

And Linda Mae and Rachel got themselves two hundred thousand dollars from the insurance company, which is what Gert and her kids in Valdosta, Georgia, also got. And Seth and Porter have an end to their miseries, which was all they really wanted before they got their heads turned around at the idea of all that money.

The only thing funnier than how things don't work out is how they do.

# August is a Good Time for Killing

## JOYCE HARRINGTON

ugust is a good time for killing," the old woman said, peering solemnly over the honeysuckle. There must have been shock on my face, for she added quickly, "I mean weeds, of course."

"Of course," I agreed just as quickly. I knew she meant weeds. What else could she mean?

"There's not much else to do in the garden in August. Strawberries are finished. Peas are petering out. Tomatoes are still bearing but they're tired. Killing is the only thing."

"The peas were awfully good. Thank you again."

Was it true that she was a witch? Josh had refused to eat the peas; said they were poisoned and he didn't want to get turned into a frog or fall asleep for a zillion years. Fact of the matter was that Josh hated peas—canned, frozen, or fresh from Mrs. Abel's garden. Peter ate four and survived. I had eaten the rest, greedily enjoying every mouthful. I love fresh peas. Mrs. Abel couldn't have sent over a more welcome gift. And now I wished I could uneat them somehow. The ghost of those peas was rising in my throat and fuddling my brain, making it difficult to think or speak with any sense at all. Maybe they *were* bewitched.

"You should put those boys to work," she said. "And the honeysuckle is a good place to start. You have to cut it back quite severely. If you don't, it will take over."

"But it's so beautiful. I don't mind if it does take over. The boys thought you were offering them a job. To help you in *your* garden."

"Nonsense. I've gardened for years without a stitch of help, I'm certainly not going to start needing it now. But the honeysuckle is growing over onto *your* side. It's my honeysuckle, so I'm willing to take the responsibility for cutting it back. The least you could do is make your boys pull up the runners. They'll be all over the place if you don't. I assume you're too busy to do it yourself."

What could I tell her? Everything she said was a challenge. We seemed to be an affront to her sense of order—a young woman and her two sons living alone without benefit of a man around the house. Not unusual in New York City, but obviously not quite respectable in this quiet backwater town. Or was I being too sensitive? Was Mrs. Abel mean and spiteful to everybody? *Was* she, as Josh and Peter insisted, a witch?

"Well, I am pretty busy," I said. "I'm working on a book." And instantly felt queasy and self-conscious, as if I'd just mouthed some lame excuse for not having my homework done. I knew she had been a schoolteacher.

"So I heard." She dismissed my labors with those three words. "It's always been my experience with boys that if you keep them busy, they won't have time to get into mischief. I taught school for fifty years, you know."

"So I heard."

My sarcasm was wasted. She plowed on with her dreadful philosophy of how boys should be handled. It wasn't much different from her attitude toward honeysuckle. She must have warped a lot of young minds in her day.

"You must always keep the upper hand with boys. Now girls are much easier to control. Oh, once in a while you'll get a wild one—" she eyed me speculatively "—but for the most part you can handle girls with a system of rewards for good behavior."

Bribery, I thought. Just like the peas.

"I always made sure the boys in my classes had plenty of work to do. And I wasn't afraid to use the paddle."

"Were they afraid of you?" I asked.

"They respected me," she replied. "Lots of them come to visit me now that I've retired. They don't forget Mrs. Abel. They come to me for advice with their own children. And I tell them just what I told you—don't be afraid to enforce hard work and strong discipline."

I was dying to get away, but I didn't want to be rude. And a kind of horrid fascination glued me to my side of the honeysuckle hedge and kept me prompting her for more.

"Did you have any children of your own?" I asked.

"No. I've been a widow for a long time. I never thought once about remarrying after Mr. Abel died. He never came back from the Great War. They never even found his body. I have a flag. I raise it on Memorial Day." She sounded as if the flag gave her more pleasure and less trouble than the living man might have done.

"Now your husband," she went on. "He must have been a handsome man. The boys are quite good-looking. They don't resemble you at all."

I stared at the wart on Mrs. Abel's chin. Every witch worth her eye of newt has a wart on her chin; Mrs. Abel's had the requisite three long hairs growing out of it.

"He still is a handsome man. We're divorced."

"So much of that nowadays." She wagged her head and the corners of her mouth dripped sadness. "It's always the children who suffer."

"The boys aren't suffering. They're having the time of their lives." What a talent the woman had for raising hackles! She'd neatly put me on the defensive in the most vulnerable area of my already shaky emotional fortifications.

"It'll show up later," she assured me. "Mark my words, you'll have your hands full."

Mrs. Abel spoke in clichés, but she imbued them with such eager ill-will, such certainty of disaster, that I found myself glancing nervously over my shoulder to see if maybe Josh and Peter had emerged from the woods dripping blood or trailing broken limbs. The early afternoon continued blamelessly still and sun-filled. Bees and squirrels went about their business.

"Well," I said. "Back to work. It's been nice chatting with you." And what exactly did I mean by *that*? It was horrible chatting with her. Was I trying to be charming and disarming so she wouldn't cast an evil spell on me? I crossed the yard feeling her flat eyes boring malevolently into the small of my back. It made me walk funny, as if my legs had turned to stilts.

Our house is a dingy white clapboard affair, squatted at the edge of a little upstate town near a shallow creek and a pleasant wooded area. It is small, in need of paint, and its facilities are primitive, but the rent is cheap and as a sanctuary from the havoc of divorce and the hustle of the city it is perfect.

The screen door shrieked as I entered my sanctuary. The manuscript glared at me from a rickety card-table at one end of the screened porch. Blank yellow paper rolled onto the platen of my old Olivetti issued its challenge. The book, while not precisely the cause of the divorce, had played its part in the final breakup. It had been all right as long as I just diddled around writing an occasional clever little story for clever little magazines. Hal could afford to be proud and say, "This is my wife. She writes."

But as soon as the writing got serious, as soon as I got the grant from the Endowment and really started working on the book, as soon as the cooking fell off and the laundry got behind and dust accumulated on the hi-fi, Hal started obstructing me. In little ways at first—like calling me up from the office when he knew I was working and telling me his grey suit had to be taken to the cleaners immediately. Or inviting hordes of people over for dinner on the day *after* I'd done the weekly shopping so I'd have to dash out and do it all over again and spend the rest of the day cooking. And be hung over and worn out the next day, so there were two days lost from the book. It grew from an accumulation of petty annoyances to a monster bristling with lawyers, recriminations, hurt pride, and no return ticket.

I sighed and settled down in my swivel chair. I swiveled once, viewing my domain. Plants in pots helped hide the lack of paint. At one side of the porch, a lumpy daybed undulated beneath a bright Indian coverlet. I would make some pillows soon, turn the place into a regular den of Oriental luxury, maybe even put a priceless Persian rug on the splintery floor. I might even oil the hinges on the screen door. After I sold the book. I swiveled back to the Olivetti and groped for a thought.

"Ma! Ma! Josh found a dead body!" Peter came screeching across the yard.

"That's nice," I mumbled.

"Ma! Ma! No kidding!" Peter pounded up the stairs and through the screen door, letting it slam behind him. The whole porch shook and the Olivetti inched closer to the edge of the table. "There's an old dead guy in the woods! Josh is guarding him."

I shoved back from the typewriter and stared, disbelieving, at my younger son. Dead guys did not turn up in peaceful woods outside of lurid fiction. Or could this be some of Mrs. Abel's witchery in action?

"Oh, Ma! It's real weird. This old guy is in a cave and he has a long beard and he smells funny."

Peter was hopping up and down with fearful excitement. Stay calm, I told myself, and calmly said to him, "Maybe I'd better take a look."

I followed Peter across the yard and into the quiet aisles between the trees. How strange to be walking through August woods, trailing my capering child, played on by rays of tinkling sunlight, toward the possibility of a corpse. This couldn't be happening.

And it was not. When we reached the cave, a steepled indentation beneath two slabs of angled rock, the corpse was sitting up and talking to Josh.

"Sure we got bears. Ain't you heard 'em? They come in the night. Come for bacon, beans, and boys. Beans and bacon they like to eat. What d'you think they wants with boys?"

"Don't believe you," Josh challenged. "I ain't seen no bears."

"*Any* bears," I corrected automatically. "And don't say 'ain't.'"

Josh shrugged and kicked at a rock.

"Who are you?" I asked the revenant.

The bearded, funny-smelling, no longer dead old guy scrambled to his feet, knocking his head against the overhanging roof of his cave.

"Morning, ma'am. Afternoon. How dee do. Luther's who I am. You's livin' in my house."

"Your house?"

He was not old beneath his effluvium of cheap wine; I would guess around forty. His beard was patchy black and grey, his arms long, sinewy, and tanned. He wore a ribbed undershirt splotched with wine and sweat stains, grey pin-striped trousers that had come down in the world, and a pair of out-at-the-pinkie-toe sneakers.

"Yes, ma'am. I was livin' in that house. Miz Abel said I could. Then she said I had to leave, cuz you's was comin'."

"How long did you live there?"

The question seemed to puzzle him. He gazed off into the rustling top of the trees and scratched absently at the back of his head.

"Where do you live now?"

He shrugged and glanced over his shoulder at the tiny cave. In it there lay a grimy quilt, the batting poking through the ancient calico, an empty muscatel bottle, and a shabby zippered satchel.

"Can you paint a house, Luther?"

"I can paint," he said, nodding energetically. "I did paint for Miz Abel. She give me two dollars. Said I wa'n't worth no more'n that. I can wash windows. Set traps too."

"For bears?"

"Ain't no bears 'round here." His bloodshot eyes swiveled around at me, pityingly, as if I were loony. "Rabbits mostly. I gets twenny-five cents apiece." His tongue flicked out to lick dry lips, and he turned to gaze longingly at the empty bottle.

The boys had lingered until it was certain that Luther was neither corpse nor ghost, and then they'd scampered away toward the creek. I could hear them whooping and splashing. Luther hung before me, loose-limbed and expectant. What now? I thought of the small building at the back of the yard, no more than a shed really, designated by the rental agent as "the washhouse." I had done no more than poke my head into it and retained a hazy collection of a stone tub with a single faucet, a rusty gas ring, and a single light bulb hanging from a frayed black cord. Not much, but better surely than a cave in the woods. Was I about to hire a resident handyman? It would be nice to have the house painted. Painting was not included in the lease. It would be nice to get on with the book. I couldn't do both.

"Luther, would you like to paint my house?"

"Yes, ma'am."

"Would you like to live in the washhouse?"

"Yes, ma'am."

"I'll pay you." I hesitated over naming an amount. Best wait and see what kind of a painter Luther turned out to be, although anything would be an improvement.

As if he could read my mind, Luther stated proudly, "I paint real good."

"Fine," I said. "You can move into the washhouse this afternoon. It needs to be cleaned up and so do you. Then we'll go into town and buy some paint."

I walked away, leaving Luther to round up his belongings and say good-bye to his cave. It had always been a tenet of my city life that winos were harmless. Repugnant maybe, and a sad waste of good human material, but basically no threat at all. Luther had a quality of childlike simplicity. No. Not childlike. Children were far from simple.

I set a broom, a bucket, some soap, and a towel outside the washhouse, and for the third time that day confronted my typewriter. It must have been several hours later that I became aware of a tentative scratching at the screen door. The sun threw a long shadow across my yellow paper. Luther stood on the porch steps transformed. He wore white painter's overalls, clean but flecked with many-colored drips of paint. His face, bereft of beard, shone red above and white below, his chin oozing blood from tiny razor nicks. Good Lord! I hadn't asked him to shave!

"Time to get paint," he said.

"Right you are," I agreed. The book was alive again, running through the typewriter like a wild thing. I could be generous with my time. The boys trailed across the yard, obviously about to utter their eternal plaintive cry, "I'm hungry, Ma!"

"Hurry up!" I called to them. "We're going into town."

"Can we eat at McDonald's?"

"Why not!"

In the hardware store, the proprietor eyed me curiously as I shuffled through paint chips. The boys prowled, fascinated by nails in barrels and nuts and bolts in little wooden drawers with curved brass handles. It was an old-fashioned hardware store that carried the very latest in power tools and electrical appliances alongside stacks of Mason jars and rows of kerosene lamps. Luther clutched a bright red paint chip and stared at his sneakers as if already beyond hope that anything so beautiful could be his to work with.

"White," I said. "And some brushes and whatever else we need. A ladder, I guess."

"I can rent you an extension ladder, ma'am. No sense in buying one of those." The proprietor beamed at me with kindly fat-cheeked goodwill. "Luther doin' the job for you?"

"Yes." I looked around for the boys. They were hypnotized by a display of flashlights. What is it about boys and flashlights? I decided I would let them each choose one.

"Luther's a good enough painter." The proprietor's rich jolly voice called me back to the business at hand. "But he's slow." The man tapped the side of his head significantly. Luther continued to stare at his sneakers; the hand holding the red paint chip began to shake.

"And he has some funny ideas about color. Well, just look at him. I bet he's thinkin' it would be real nice to paint your whole house fire-engine red. Crazy!" The man spoke as if Luther were deaf or so deficient in understanding that he could say any cruel thing without penetrating to a nerve. "But if you want to get the job done, just make sure he stays off the bottle. Right, Luther?"

Luther's mouth twisted into a witless wet grin. He said, "Bub-bub-bub." His eyes filmed over into a semblance of idiocy.

"We'll paint the house white," I said, "but there's no reason why we can't have a red door. Let me have a can of this." I took the red paint chip from Luther's shaking hand and waved it at the hardware man's complacent smirk.

"Yes, ma'am," he said.

Later, with the painting gear stowed in the trunk and the ladder secured to the roof of the car, Luther's face returned to normal. Normal? The boys, in the back seat, shone their flashlights into each other's eyes and threatened mutual mayhem.

Luther said, "Time to eat?"

"McDonald's, here we come."

We carried our hamburgers and french fries home. I was not about to subject Luther to any more of the mindless bullying I had witnessed in the hardware store. It was for my own protection as much as for his. He had evolved his means of dealing with it; turning himself into a slack-jawed, drooling caricature of a mental defective. But I couldn't bear to watch that awful transformation again.

We ate in the twilit backyard, Luther and the boys munching in companionable silence while I pondered how I had managed to appoint myself protector of the downtrodden. It was totally out of character; I was far from overprotective with the boys and not notable for coddling my husband. My ex-husband. What was there about this alcoholic reject that evoked my righteous indignation? Was that all it was, or was I, God forbid, infected with missionary zeal? Did I have some inane notion that I could reform him, educate him, bless his life with meaning? Maybe he had all the meaning he could handle.

The boys crammed the last of the french fries into their mouths and swooped off shrieking across the darkening lawn, drawn by the wildly flailing beams of their flashlights. Luther gathered up the greasy papers, methodically wadding them into the smallest possible bundle.

"Time to paint now?"

"No. It's too dark. You can start in the morning."

"Don't pay no mind to that Miz Abel. Luther never did no wrong thing."

"Mrs. Abel has never mentioned you, Luther. Now I want to get some more work done. Good night."

As I entered the screen porch, I heard Luther's disjointed mumble fading across the yard to the washhouse.

"Paint in the morning. Get up early. Miz Abel is ugly. This one is pretty. Paint the door *red*. Nice. Miz Abel better not tell."

Tell what? I wondered, and then forgot as my fingers flew over the keys.

In the morning, I awoke to the sound of scraping. It was barely light and a fuzzy mist floated about two feet off the ground. It made the ladder seem to rise from incalculable depths up the side of the house and, for all I could tell, extend all the way to heaven. The scraping came from somewhere above. My little Ben windup alarm clock said 5:45 and my bed felt clammy from the tendrils of mist that had crept onto the porch and fingered my lumpy bedding. I scrambled into my robe and went outside.

Luther was on the ladder, a great white bird of pure light, elbows flapping as he scraped away old paint blisters from the flanks of the house.

"Time to paint now!" He beamed down at me.

"Time to paint, Luther." I went inside to plug in the coffeepot. Time for the book too, before the boys woke up. I left Cheerios and bananas on the kitchen table for them.

The scraping from above melted into a rhythmic slap-slap, which in turn blended into the tap-tap of words arranging themselves on paper. I vaguely heard the boys clanking spoons on bowls and then clump past me to offer their services to Luther. Good, I thought. Let him teach them how to paint a house. Just a few more lines and then on to the next chapter. Then I leaped at an imperative rapping on the screen door and whirled to see who was barging into my morning. It was Mrs. Abel.

"May I come in? I have to talk to you." Her wart pulsed with secrets to unfold. I opened the door and she creaked through.

"Can we talk in the kitchen? I don't want *him* to hear." She rolled her eyes upward and I wondered if she meant Luther or God.

We went into the kitchen. The boys had left behind a crunching of spilled sugar and some flaccid "O's" in milky puddles. Mrs. Abel tip-toed around a shriveled banana peel.

"I thought I ought to warn you," she mouthed, making up in exaggerated lip movements what she lacked in volume. Her teeth were long and yellow.

"About what?" I mouthed back at her.

"Luther. I see he's painting for you."

"Right. He seems to know what he's doing."

"Oh, he's a good enough painter. A bit . . ."

". . . slow? I know. But I'm in no hurry."

"That isn't what I came to tell you. Frankly, I hoped I wouldn't have to tell you this. Luther was supposed to go stay with his brother. I told him to go. He's never disobeyed me before."

"First time for everything."

"What?" Her flat eyes suspected irreverence, but she carried on. "As far as I knew, he went. His brother lives on the other side of town. Luther always has a home there, whenever he chooses to appear."

She stopped for breath and to marshal her thoughts.

"Coffee?" I asked.

"What? Oh. Yes, please. Two sugars, no milk. Luther killed a boy."

Coffee slopped into the saucer and from there over my thumb and onto the gritty linoleum.

"I didn't mean to startle you." She smiled. "But truth is truth and must be told, now that you've got yourself mixed up with him."

"I'm not mixed up. He's only painting the house."

"*And* living in the washhouse. I saw him hanging his quilt out to air. But of course you couldn't know anything about what happened here thirty years ago. You couldn't know the *danger* you're in—or your boys." She sipped coffee primly and smacked her thin lips. Either my coffee was to her liking, or her story was making her mouth water.

One thing was certain. Her evil was infectious. I wanted to rush out of the house and snatch Josh and Peter away from the contaminated person of the house painter. But a small voice said, "Wait a minute. Find out what *really* happened."

"What happened?" I asked. "Thirty years ago."

"What happened was that a boy who lived in this house, about eight years old—isn't your younger boy about that age?—was drowned in the creek. He used to go fishing and trapping with Luther, and then one night he didn't come home for supper. Luther was about ten years old then, living at home with his mother and father just down the road. They've passed on since. He was a child of their old age; a mistake if you ask me, and he never was very bright. Well, the parents of the missing child were very upset and a search was organized.

"They found Luther first, in a little cave in the woods. Oh, he was a mess, crying and blubbering and making less sense than usual. He never did have any backbone. I remember him carrying on the same way over an arithmetic problem. Anyway, all they could get out of him was that he didn't do it and he didn't know who did it. Well, *that* made them search even harder, and eventually they found the boy—Bobby Albright was his name—face down in the creek. They say you can drown in a teacup, but it's always been my opinion that you would need a little help. I've always believed that Luther held Bobby's face in the water."

"What did the police say?"

"Accident," she snapped. "Accident! There was a lump on poor Bobby's head, so they guessed he fell on a rock and drowned while unconscious. But I knew better. Why do you suppose Luther took it so hard? Guilt, pure and simple."

"But why would Luther do such a thing?"

"You and I need reasons, my dear. But Luther is different. He was a willful, disobedient child. One of those who stubbornly refused to learn anything, and no amount of paddling could make him a good student. Well, I just wanted to let you know what kind of person you have painting your house. If I were you, I'd keep my doors and windows locked at night."

"Wait a minute," I said. "If he's so dangerous, why did you give him permission to camp out in this house while it was vacant?"

"Oh, he's no danger to me. I know how to handle him. The owners asked me to keep an eye on the house, and what better way to prevent vandalism than to let it be known that crazy Luther might be lurking about the premises?"

"Has he ever done . . . anything else?"

"No. But who knows what he might do when he's full of wine. Well, I suppose you're busy." She glanced pointedly around my untidy kitchen. "And Lord knows I have plenty of work to do."

I stood at the screen door and watched her wade laboriously across the yard. What's worse than a witch? I thought. I hoped I wouldn't have too many more visitations from Mrs. Abel now that she'd sown her vile seeds of ancient gossip. With half an ear I listened to the slapping at the side of the house, and the low murmur of Peter's voice telling one of his favorite stories.

"So Dorothy had to get the broomstick but she got caught by the flying monkeys . . ."

"You gotta hold the brush like this," came Luther's voice. "And go this way, back and forth."

"And they all came to save her and they ran all over the castle and then Dorothy spilled a bucket of water on the witch and she melted and that was the end of her."

And Josh, ever the realist and puncturer of his little brother's balloons, said, "The Wizard was a fake and it was all only a dream. But Mrs. Abel is a real witch and she'll getcha!"

If you only knew, I thought, and went to take a shower, hoping to dispel the heavy sense of oppression that my visitor had left behind.

Later that evening, I paid Luther for his day's work. The front and one side of the house were finished except for the trim, and the boys had spent a glorious day covering themselves with paint. As I handed him a ten-dollar bill, his eyes shifted to the little house beyond the honeysuckle hedge.

"Miz Abel came here this morning," he stated.

"Yes, she did."

"She told you things about Luther."

I wouldn't lie to him, but I wondered how much I could safely tell him. I suspected that he was only crazy "north by northwest," but I wasn't ready to bank on it. "She told me about something that happened a long time ago. An accident."

He nodded gravely and sloped off across the yard to the washhouse. I wanted to call after him, let him know I was on his side, but if he didn't know that already nothing I said would make any difference.

That night I was very conscious of not locking my doors and windows. For a long moment, my hand hovered over the hook and eyebolt on the screen door, but then I reminded myself that this was not paranoid New York City. This was the safe, clean, all-American, true-blue small town of everyone's nostalgic dreams. Anyway, the flimsy hook wouldn't stop anyone determined to get in. I went to bed.

For a long time I lay listening to the sleepy murmurs of the boys in their nook under the eaves. After they quieted down, I listened to the hooting of owls and the rustling of trees in the mild night air. Once I got up and stared through the screen into the blackness of the backyard. I thought I'd seen a flash of light from the direction of the washhouse, but decided it must have been a firefly. At last I slept, but dreamed strange, struggling, blood-tinged dreams that kept me on the edge of consciousness, fading as soon as I opened my eyes. Toward dawn, I finally fell into exhausted and dreamless oblivion . . .

I was awakened by the slap-slap-slap on the side of the house. It was mid-morning of a hot humid day, and I'd lost precious hours from the book. I dressed quickly and went outside to see what progress the painters were making.

I rounded the side of the house and stopped in shock. Luther, on the ladder, twisted around and waved to me, grinning and pleased with himself. The front of his white overalls was streaked and splashed with red. My knees went weak and my empty stomach lurched. The boys were nowhere in sight.

"Where . . . ?" My nightmares were coming true. Mrs. Abel was right. My mind leaped to horrid discoveries in the woods or behind the washhouse. I stared up at Luther, wondering what to do next.

"Painted the door already," he announced proudly.

Josh pounded around from the front of the house and took my hand in his sticky one.

"Come and see, Ma. It looks terrific."

Peter followed, gripping a reddened paintbrush. Both boys were generously splattered with red paint.

"Can we paint the stairs red too?"

"No, not the stairs. That would be too much red." It was already too much red for one morning, but I let them lead me around to the front of the house.

The door had, indeed, been painted. Bright red and still tacky, it gleamed on the front of the house like the half-remembered blood-stains of my dreams.

"It looks very nice," I said. And tottered back into the house to plug in the coffeepot. While the coffee perked and I scrambled eggs, I chastised my hyperactive imagination. Was I going to let that vicious old woman distort my mind with her ugly suspicions? No, I was not. It occurred to me that her tale might be just that, a fabrication designed to frighten me into leaving. I didn't know what she had against me, but I wasn't going to be frightened out of my sanctuary. I called everybody in to breakfast. Luther ate with good appetite.

The rest of the morning I spent organizing my notes and my own feelings. I didn't know what to make of Mrs. Abel's story, but if anybody ever needed a friend, it was Luther. If he'd really killed that boy, why hadn't the police found out about it? Mrs. Abel had seemed so certain that he'd done it. Surely she would have told the police. They must have been satisfied that he was innocent, or at least not responsible. Why had she continued to believe him guilty for thirty years? And why try to frighten me off when all I was doing was giving him an honest day's work and a semblance of dignity? I was still puzzling over Mrs. Abel's purpose when I heard voices outside. I ran out and around the house to see who was there.

Josh and Peter were huddled together at the corner of the house, being uncharacteristically quiet. When I appeared, they bolted for the porch, but I sensed their noses pressed to the screen from the inside.

"Good morning," I said to the tall dry man in the quasi-military uniform with the small American flag sewn onto the sleeve. Luther stood dumb and downcast before him. There was no mistaking the family resemblance. Mrs. Abel had neglected to tell me that Luther's brother was a policeman.

"Morning, ma'am," he said, politely and deliberately removing his Smokey Bear hat. "I came to find Luther. I hope he hasn't been bothering you."

I said what was obvious. "Luther's been painting my house."

"Yes. Well, there's more to it than that. I called Mrs. Abel earlier this morning. She always knows what he's been up to."

My blood began to boil. "Luther hasn't been 'up to' anything. Mrs. Abel is a vicious old busybody."

I glanced at Luther. He was wearing his village idiot face, and his lips began to move in the slobbering "bub-bub-bub" I'd heard in the hardware store.

"That may be," said his brother. "But she didn't answer her phone. I called three times. So I came on over to see for myself."

"Luther's doing a job for me, and doing it well. Are you satisfied?"

"Not exactly." He turned to peer intently up the road toward the center of town. "The ambulance should be getting here soon. I called from over to her place."

"Ambulance? What for? Is she sick?"

"Not exactly. She's dead." His eyes, when they swung back to me, were a chilly grey. "May I use your phone?"

"Sure. But wait a minute. What did she die of? Heart?"

He paused with his hand on the screen door. I heard the boys scuffling away upstairs.

"You might say that. Somebody stopped it for her. With a pair of hedge-clippers."

Now that he'd opened up, I wanted him to stop. But he droned on in his official monotone.

"Somebody threw a bucket of water on her. Maybe trying to clean up the mess. Just made it worse. She put up a fight though. Somebody likely got a broomstick busted over his head. I got to make that phone call now." He went inside.

Luther stood beside the ladder, the red-stained front of his overall glowing obscenely in the noonday sun.

"She's a witch," he muttered. He took his painter's cap off and tenderly massaged the top of his head.

"Luther, don't." Everybody was telling me things I didn't want to hear.

"I thrown water on her but she don't melt. She hit Luther with that broom. Luther hit her with that . . . that . . ."

I sat down on the porch steps. Luther came closer, earnestly explaining.

"She hit Bobby with that shovel. Bobby taken two tomatoes."

"What tomatoes? Who's Bobby?"

"Bobby fallen down. She tell Luther help carry. Put Bobby in the water. She say Luther never tell nobody or else go to jail forever. Luther didn't do no wrong thing. Bobby was Luther's friend. She a witch. She kill Bobby."

It came together then and I wanted to cry. But my tears wouldn't help Luther. The only thing I could do was respect his confidence and hope for the best. But what would be best for Luther? To continue playing his role of village idiot, a role he was comfortable with? Or to spend the rest of his life in some institution for the criminally insane? Not if I could help it by keeping his confession to myself. Mrs. Abel had got what was coming to her.

Heavy footsteps shook the porch and the screen door screamed on its rusty hinges. I got up to face Luther's brother with what I hoped was a look of puzzled ignorance.

"Ma'am," he said with exaggerated respect. "I just talked with the station. It seems they think they have a suspect."

I looked at Luther. He had retreated behind his moronic facade.

"It seems they picked up this stranger for speeding through town. It seems they put two and two together and came up with five." Doubt clouded his steely grey eyes as he glanced at his brother. "It seems they're holding him on suspicion."

"Do you believe he did it?"

"I don't know what to believe, ma'am, I truly don't. All I know for sure is that one old woman is dead, and I can't say I regret her passing. But it's my duty to find out who killed her."

"And this stranger, this speeder, what about him?" My voice came strangely from my throat, taut and stifled. If I didn't speak, if I didn't betray Luther's confidence, would another man live wasted years in the wake of Mrs. Abel's malevolence? I couldn't speak. Only Luther could do that. I whirled on him, clutching his red-smeared sleeve. "Luther! Tell him! Tell your brother what you told me."

"Bub-bub-bub." Wet lips and vacant eyes. He was gone. This was no role-playing. Luther had crossed the line to the only safety he knew.

A gentle hand took my arm and held it firmly.

"Ma'am," said the expressionless voice. "I know. Luther told me. I've been waiting thirty years for him to tell me. Now it's too late."

I looked at the dry creased face under the silvery brush cut. The grey eyes had lost their chill, and I saw there a sadness deeper than any I had ever known. I felt tears in my own eyes then, for Luther struggling dimly in his silent prison and for this man with the sad grey eyes who must finally crucify his brother.

"Ma'am?" The man's questioning voice reached through my sobs. "Would it be all right with you if Luther finishes painting the house before I take him in? It would make him feel better, and I'll stay and keep an eye on him."

"Yes, oh, yes." I broke away and stumbled into the house. I had packing to do. All the clothes into all the duffel bags. All the toys, books, toothbrushes. The lid onto the typewriter. We would go back to the city. Back to a world I knew well and could cope with, where violence and evil were anonymous and did not reach into my life with red hands smearing me with indelible accountability.

Josh and Peter stood one above the other on the narrow stairway, watching, large-eyed and frightened, as I swept through the house indiscriminately tossing objects into boxes and bags, whatever was handy. "Get your things together, boys," I shouted at them. "We're leaving!"

"Aw, Ma," said Josh. "Can't we help Luther finish painting?"

I stopped in my tracks, one hand clutching a damp pair of swimming trunks. My children in their red-stained jeans, with streaks of red on their hands and arms and even in their hair, were telling me something. It was, after all, only paint. Luther had been their friend. He still was. There was nothing to run away from.

"I can't pack these. They're all wet. Sure, go and help Luther. We won't be leaving yet a while . . ."

On the outside of the house, the rhythmic slap of Luther's paintbrush is the most melancholy sound I have ever heard.

# Dead Standstill

## REX MILLER

On a sweater-chilly robin's-egg-blue-sky Tuesday morning in the second week of May, Nancy Hamilton was flat on her back, freezing where her sweater and shirt had worked up and exposed her skin to the cold plastic sheet, trying to make the family spa stop making those tortured, dying noises.

"I mean it," she whispered. "I'm going to *murder* you," she threatened the gargling thing. The innards of the fiberglass and wood four-person hot tub gurgled and burbled and moaned in response, sounding as if it was about to give up the ghost on its own.

Gentle efforts to reason with it had failed. Imprecations hadn't worked. She'd worked her way up to murderous threats.

What was it Mike used to say about how things wear down? Something about how you can't repeal the second law of thermodynamics. Alas, the great handyman was no more. Mike was history. Things had worn down. Their marriage, for instance.

Exasperated, she slammed the access door to the monster shut, and of course the hot tub motor immediately quit making the hideous noise and began purring contentedly. The old angry door slam—the oldest trick in the service manual.

"Un-be-liev-able." She laughed, pulling her shirt down and tucking it in, rearranging her sweater, and walking through the master bedroom and into the bathroom to wash the gook off her hands, proud of having single-handedly changed the spa filter.

When she turned on the faucet, the hot water heater made a moaning, gurgling noise.

If Mike was here, *he'd* be tending to all this stuff. Changing the filter, checking the frammis—whatever it was. This was man's work. She identified the sexist thought and rejected it.

In the kitchen there was a list of everything that was falling apart, going wrong, running down, breaking. She would go in and write *bathroom faucet* at the bottom of the list, and when she got hold of Mr. Emmert, their plumber, he could take care of everything at one time.

She missed having a man in the house. She missed the kids. And more than she cared to admit to herself at the moment, she missed Mike.

She couldn't face an attack of the guilts right now, and she decided some fresh air would do her a lot of good, so she got an old windbreaker and a scarf out of the closet and went out into the yard.

It was chilly, but the ten foot high cedar fence that closed off a large section of their yard, now Nancy's flower garden, managed to block off most of the cold wind.

As if it had tuned in on her mood, a bright yellow male goldfinch swooped down for a seed pit stop, landing virtually at arm's length from her. Amazingly unafraid as it availed itself of the feeder. She stood still for a minute or so enjoying the beautiful bird; then she walked over to one of the benches and sat down to relax and enjoy her yard.

It was a never-ending show at this time of the year. She sat, transfixed, as a dumb sparrow ran a hummingbird off the swinging feeder. Glossy grackles soared overhead registering their opinion. A male cardinal carefully cracked a seed and carried it away to his nesting mate. She always put seed out for her birds, and was inevitably rewarded by a serenade of song and a chorus of cheerful chirps.

She'd fed birds when they lived in the rental houses, too, but it hadn't been the same. These were *her* birds. *Her* yard. Once it had been their yard. But it hadn't worked out.

At thirty-eight, Nancy was petite, five feet two and a half inches tall, pretty, smart. A year ago she would have described herself as a housewife. The year before that a housewife and mother. But all that had changed.

In the two year interim, the accident had taken Davey, Nora had run away, and Mike had fallen in love.

It was a love affair with someone awesome in her wiles; a woman with whom Nancy Hamilton could not compete. Mike had fallen for the white lady. Cocaine. Or maybe cocaine and money in equal parts—what difference did it make now? He was gone from her.

It had all started when Dixie, Mike's aunt, had passed away and left Mike the money. Ninety-seven thousand and change. Such a godsend, they'd thought. And who would ever have imagined Dixie would have saved up all that money—all those hundreds and fifties hoarded away in a closet shoebox?

Until then the dream of building their own home had been out of reach. But when you added the ninety-seven thou to their certificates of deposit, it was just enough to do it. The first thing they did was send away for some blueprints. And even before the bank had transferred the funds, Mike was talking with a local contractor about the nineteen hundred square foot dream house they'd thought about for so many years.

Mike could never settle for anything ordinary. He had to be a big shot. They couldn't build on a lot in town. No. He was tired of living in those "boring tract houses in the city," so they bought a twenty acre country site beyond the city limits. That was just the beginning of their problems with the house: no city water.

The hard water had been a major problem at first. There was such an unusually high mineral content you couldn't drink the water, you couldn't wash your clothing in it—you could barely stand to bathe in it. But then there was the damn *pool*.

Mike had to have a pool. He insisted on it. It was all he really wanted, he said. You can have your courtyard and your garden, your sewing room, your spa, your plants, your built-ins, your kitchen. "But I get my pool." An outdoor, Olympic-size, below-ground, deluxe pool complete with all the gadgets and goodies the pool people said you couldn't live without.

Now Mike's pool was no more. It was a few feet away, long since filled with earth, covered in thick PVC, bordered in tubing and concrete, then topped with a layer of pea gravel.

She was just getting so she could look at the ring of gravel without feeling a stab of pain in her chest. Soon, she had been told, the heartache for Davey, their beauty of a six-year-old son, would fade and she'd find she wasn't missing him so awfully. "In time, whole days will pass and you won't think about the day your child drowned. A day, maybe even two, will go by without your blaming yourself for his death," someone had told her.

She'd just gone to answer the stupid telephone, she thought, glancing at the cordless hunk of hard plastic she carried with her everywhere now, her little Linus blanket. When Nancy had come back—not forty-five seconds later—their beautiful child was face down in the pool. The horror and numbing shock of it was still such that she had to close her eyes and breathe deeply to rid herself of the images.

Losing Davey had been the beginning of the marriage's disintegration.

Mike's social proclivity, as she called it, for drugs went into high gear. She supposed his dealing dated back to about that same time, and she knew he was moving a lot of narcotics so that he could keep up with his new country club buddies.

He quit his good job at Missouri Chemical, and he and his rich friends would suddenly disappear for long weekends "to Atlantic City on business," or "just down to the Mardi Gras to see this guy." And she didn't let herself think about all the women.

They fell like dominoes. Nora was next. Her beautiful, headstrong teenager. Small like Mama. Five feet tall and ninety-five pounds soaking wet, but with the hair and face and curves to make men of all ages stop dead in their tracks.

Nora had a good brain, she was sweet-tempered, athletic, interested in everything—her whole life was in front of her. But when they lost Davey, and then her dad left, too—that blew it. Within a few months she'd dropped out of school—an honor student in her senior year—and was dating this horrible sleazebag who had a small town garage and Hollywood dreams.

Nancy and Nora had never been the best at communication to begin with, and Nora blamed her for the breakup of the marriage. It was now Nancy's fault that her father, as well as her little brother, was gone. Pleas to stay in school fell on deaf ears. Gentle suggestions about Tony, her longhaired, sleazy beau, met blind eyes. A few months later Nora was gone. Nancy got a postcard, heartbreakingly without a salutation, that said, "I wanted to tell you don't worry about me. I'm fine. Tony and I are living in Colorado. We have a place in the mountains. Nora."

Not even "Love, Nora." No return address, naturally. Nancy forced the family woes from her mind and tried to concentrate on the flowers.

The ringed stone courtyard was visually pleasing, and it was bordered in landscape timbers that contained nearly three hundred feet of flowers and blooming shrubs—white and purple delphiniums, pale lavender hosta, yellow and white coreopsis, yellow shasta daisies, red and pink dahlias, Chinese holly, lavender and blue-spired veronica, purple hyacinth, white candytuft, blue geraniums and playcoden, royal robe violets—and everything was blooming now. If only it didn't turn too cold. She shivered a little, thinking about predictions for a May frost.

But the sound of the wind through the trees was an orchestral background to the birdsong. Maybe she could just sit out here smelling the honeysuckle and listening to the birds and everything bad would go away.

The interior court was a riot of pink and white weigela, Persian lilacs that were so overpoweringly fragrant they were all you could think about when you smelled them, hot pink crepe myrtle, tulips in every color of the rainbow, maroon columbines, lavender wisteria clustered among the Siberian squill, cinnamon and ostrich ferns, Spanish needle yuccas that survived *anything*.

Even the weeds were gorgeous. She loved the yellow sheepshire that grew around the reddish-orange climbing honeysuckle. Not as fragrant as its wilder, seductively-scented cousin, but the feathered friends loved it and the blooming cardinal shrubs and lilacs gave you all the aroma you could handle and then some.

Someday, she thought, I'll come out here and look at all the pretty flowers, and the ring of gravel will not look like Davey's grave.

"Hi, Mr. Clendennon, thank you for returning my call," she said into the phone.

"Well, I'm sorry it took so long, but I've been wiring a house for Elmer Carr over at Willow Point. So, you know, I been gettin' home late." It had taken nearly three weeks to get the electrician on the telephone.

"Oh, no problem," she said, lying. "I wonder if I could get you to fix my doorbell and my telephone?"

"Whatsa matter with 'em, Mrs. Hamilton?"

"The doorbell rings all the time and there's nobody there. It just goes off—day and night, you know? I thought it was kids playing pranks at first. And then the phone will ring and you pick it up and it's dead."

"Well, the phone and the doorbell don't have anything to do with each other, so—" He let it trail off.

"Couldn't the wires be crossed somehow?" she asked without thinking. Jim Clendennon gave her a five minute answer, but finally she got a commitment out of him to come over and look at the doorbell. He said he was "not empowered" to work on phones. Gave her another five minutes on AT&T and Ma Bell and Western Electric and General Electric and various other companies. Apparently getting the telephone to work right was now an affair of state.

She'd had Richie Lanning look at it. He had taken it apart after extracting her promise that she wouldn't "tell," and he'd even gone outside and shown her how you could tap her phone from the box on the side of the house, which was of very little interest to Nancy at the moment, thank you very kindly, but he was a friend of the family and she'd been polite.

The phone still rang at all hours with nobody on the other end, and the doorbell routinely went off at least a couple of times during every twenty-four-hour period, particularly unnerving in the middle of the night, as it was one of those that played a little chimey tune.

The consensus was that the culprit was either (a) a CB base station (CB base stations now got all the flak formerly reserved for ham radio operators in general—the public now knew the phrase "CB *base station!*"), (b) a garage door opener "on the same harmonic frequency" (as *what?*), (c) power tools down the road at a neighbor's house (in the middle of the night?) or none of the above.

Having obtained a guarantee from Mr. Clendennon, acknowledged master electrician of the entire tri-state area, and also the highest priced, she picked up the dreaded instrument and phoned her girlfriend Sondra Reynolds.

"It's me."

"You going?"

"I don't think so."

"Oh," Sondra whined, "you chicken."

"I know." She copped a plea of temporary fat thighs and told her she'd take her up on the invitation next time. A float trip. She'd surveyed herself in the cutout job in her bedroom mirror. The thighs were still okay. She just couldn't leave the house right now with all that was going on.

There was another call she was going to have to make soon, but she couldn't face that one today. With Nancy no longer putting in a four-day week at school, and the bi-monthly stipend from Mike now coming infrequently, the last of the checking account money was dwindling to nothing. Sondra told her she should get a lawyer and "sock it to him." But lawyers were anathema to Nancy after the endless problems they'd had with the house.

In fact, one of the reasons the float trip was out was that when she and Mike and Nora had gone away for two days, just a weekend at the lake, they'd returned to find their patio awash in water. It seemed the foundation had been built too low, and heavy weekend rains had seeped into the paneled, closed-in patio, the standing, blowing rain water soaking the carpeting and the baseboards.

The irony was that when they'd come into the money Mike insisted she quit her teaching job, arguing that she needed to "concentrate on the house." That she'd done. Since Davey's tragic drowning, it seemed that it had become her entire life. But she had to wrench her mind back to the work at hand. There was nothing to be gained stewing about her errant teenager in the Colorado mountains, or her doper of a husband.

That night Nancy Hamilton had a horrible dream of Davey's drowning, a nightmare in which she kept hearing a child screaming and choking, and when she sat up wide-eyed and fully awake at two ten A.M., the noise hadn't gone away. She heard a kind of "loud, gargling horror in the pipes," or so she described it to Red Emmert, after having literally shouted at Mrs. Emmert to put him on the phone or she'd be over to camp on their doorstep.

Mr. Emmert was there at seven, visibly irritated, but at least he'd come. Perhaps, to be fair, he was so snowed under he only worked on emergencies. Well, this was one of those. She told him about the many problems with the plumbing, the spa, the bathroom faucet, on and on. And of course nothing acted up while the plumber was there. He replaced a couple of washers and was gone inside fifteen minutes, leaving Nancy to consider the fact that she'd dreamed the whole thing.

Three days later she was taking a shower and suddenly all the cold water was off and the hot water was boiling out of the plumbing, scalding her, she was screaming, fighting to get out from under the shower. Again, Emmert came out, and again he could find nothing wrong.

"Miz Hamilton," he said, kindly, "I know you been through a lot and that with the little boy, you know, and I, uh, I think maybe, uh—" and she finished the sentence for him.

"I know what you're thinking. I guess maybe you're right." And she didn't protest. Let it go at that. Maybe the trouble was of her own making.

But the next morning she looked out the living room window and was chilled with fear at what she saw. Every other flower and small plant in the garden was either dead or dying. Her precious flowers! Even the large shrubs were suddenly beginning to look brown. She worked in the garden all day, watering, spading, mulching, but she couldn't kid herself about it. Something was wrong. She double-checked with the weather station, but there was no way the nights had been cool enough to cause this. Something had come up out of the ground and killed everything in the courtyard.

The following night she dreamt again, although she could not recall the specifics of the dream. Only that when she awoke shortly after one A.M. she heard not so much a gargling horror as a loud and unnerving bubbling noise in the plumbing.

This time she was taking no chances. She got the small tape recorder from the study, made sure it had two fresh batteries in it, and taped ten minutes of the noise coming out of the pipes.

"Hello," Mrs. Emmert said in her irascible snarl.

"Mrs. Emmert, this is Nancy Hamilton again."

"You gotta stop calling in the middle of the night like this. My husband gotta get his rest."

Nancy knew one of the Emmert kids from school. The girl was just like her mother: lazy, fat, petulant, mean-spirited, and hypochondriacal.

"Mrs. Emmert, just listen." She hit *Play* on the recorder, and a loud but undecipherable garble spit into the phone.

But when Red Emmert showed up she didn't need the recording—the noise was still bubbling away. It had grown louder, if anything.

"Well, I can tell you what *this* is," he said. "But this isn't the way you described the noise before."

"No," she explained, "I know. But it wasn't making this noise before. What the heck is it?"

"I'll tell you exactly what it is. It's a high water table. We got the same thing in some of the houses in town." He explained to her what a high water table was and how it could cause the bubbling phenomenon.

"But what can we do to stop it?"

"You cain't do nothing to stop it. Not till that water level drops back down."

"But won't this tear up the pipes and everything?"

"Nah. It won't hurt nothin'. Just don't run no more water than you have to."

That night the faucets began dripping. The pipes had stopped bubbling temporarily, but all the faucets in the house were leaking water—the newly washered hardware! Drip . . . drip . . . drip . . . *drip* . . . *drip* . . . DRIP . . . DRIP!

It was an irregular and maddening noise that woke her about four with a really loud and metallic ping . . . *ping* . . . PING; an increasingly loud noise coming from the direction of the kitchen. Almost as if someone was *making* the noise, like hammering on the kitchen pipes with a ball-peen hammer . . . *ping* . . . PING! BANG! Wait a minute. The noises were too loud for any dripping water. Suddenly Nancy was aware that these were man-made and she was frantic, fumbling first for the revolver she kept under the bed and then dialing the sheriff's office on the bedroom phone. A bored dispatcher telling her "we'll send somebody," trying to ask her a lot of questions and the pounding getting louder and louder.

She slammed the phone down on the idiot and, holding the weapon shakily in front of her, began to make her way down the darkened hallway between the master bedroom and the living room adjoining the kitchen.

Should she turn the lights on and scare away the intruder?

Just as she was going around the corner, the noise stopped and Nancy froze, and it was at that moment of insight she remembered that sometime after the problems with Mike had begun, she'd become afraid of the loaded firearm under their bed, and she'd removed the bullets. She could see the bullet box very clearly in her mind, a green and yellow box of Remington .38 Special "Plus P's." Very deadly, silver bullets just like the guy with the mask used. The one small problem—they didn't happen to be in the gun she was holding.

She was still standing there like a statue in marble, *Woman in Bathrobe Holding Empty Gun*, when the sheriff's vehicle crunched up in the driveway and she heard his loud banging on the front door. Nancy knew even as she answered the door, turning on the lights and breathing again, that there would be no one outside.

A week later and she was soaking in the tub and "rusty red-brown stuff began coming out of the plumbing." She shut off the faucets but not before something that smelled like excrement had seeped into the bath with her. She leaped out of the tub, then tried to wash it out and wash herself off with the shower, but more of the same. The smell was beyond anything imaginable.

She ran outside into the courtyard, nude, opened a garden hose, and miraculously it did not spew filth and she was able to rinse herself off.

By mid-afternoon she'd dried her body, dried her tears, and had two full-scale knock-down-drag-out screaming matches with Red Emmert's wife. So it was a combative woman who snatched the phone from the receiver on its first ring and, instead of her usual warm "hello," uttered a tight "Yes?"

She was floored to hear the once-familiar baritone say, "Nancy, it's me."

"Mike?"

"Sorry to bother you, but I need some tax stuff. You got a couple seconds?" He seemed curt and even colder than usual.

"All right," she replied, keeping her voice in an equally flat tone.

"I need to come over and borrow our last joint return. Do you still have all our returns in the metal file box?"

"Yeah. As far as I know. Mike, listen, we've got real problems. I need to see you about the house." With the word "house" the floodgates burst, and suddenly she was telling him about all the problems. About what a nightmare the house had become. About money worries. Letting it all flow into the telephone.

"I don't know what to do. The place is costing a fortune. I can't afford to keep paying plumbers. Mr. Clendennon is going to send me a big bill. The medical insurance is due. I've got Red Emmert's wife ready to kill me. I can't get him out here. I—"

"Emmert is about a hundred years old, number one. Call that guy Ducas—you know who I mean?"

"No."

"He does industrial work, mostly. I'll get hold of him and have him come out. You gonna be home in the morning?"

"Sure."

"Okay," he said. She extracted a promise from him to come out in the morning and try to help with the house. She would give him the tax records then. They could discuss her money problems.

True to his word, Mike was there bright and early, and the new plumber showed up soon after. The men agreed that the culprit was the septic tank.

"Red Emmert called that one right, Mrs. Hamilton," Ducas assured her. "You've got a real high water table out here. You can dig down about a foot and you hit bubbling water. That's what happened—that water is messing up the lines and that. It's got into the drain lines and I 'spect caused the crack in the septic tank, which leaked that sewage into your plumbing somehow—see?"

Mike knew of a guy who would help fix the tank and sink new drain lines. After Mr. Ducas was gone, she told him all about the noises, the false alarms, one thing after another, and he just stood there looking at her like she'd lost her mind. Listening to her run through her catalogue of household woes with undisguised irritation.

"You know, this is really great." He started to read her off but managed to bite his tongue and just shook his head. He seemed like a stranger with a familiar face. Once so tanned and handsome, he was pallid and unshaven. Her once fastidious husband appeared disheveled, his movements nervous and exaggerated. Nancy wondered if she had changed as much in his eyes.

"It's not my fault the house is coming down around my ears," she said in a soft and what she hoped was an unchallenging voice. "I can't afford to keep it up. And even when I go back to work, which I'm going to have to do immediately, Mike, I'm not going to be earning the kind of money this place is going to take. We've got to sell the house." He looked at her like she was crazy.

"This is a rotten time to sell." He talked about soft housing starts and a lot of things she didn't understand. But he said, "I guess I can ask around. See how difficult it would be to get a buyer for the place." Soon he was gone and Nancy was once again alone with the house.

The following two days were uneventful. Then, late at night, Nancy caught herself listening for a telltale squeak of floor in carpeted, reinforced flooring that she *knew* could yield no sound. Listening for the boiling, bubbling, mean essence of this ground that would spew up in the pipes as she lay in bed, unprotected and alone. She knew what she was doing to herself.

She knew so much about this house—she could stare at a pattern of flowers in her handpicked, hard-won wallpaper and see the sheetrocker's product, or the insulation that she and her man had helped to stuff carefully between the framework of the two-bys. See the house naked under its coat of many colors. She knew this baby, bad and good. And she knew there was a presence here besides herself.

Finally, when she fell asleep, deeply, she dreamed the worst nightmare yet. And in the dream she saw light catch on gold and saw it to be the hand of a man. A golden band on the hand of a man, she dreamed, musically.

Dreamed of a woman in a mirror. Soft, shoulder-length hair. Large and expressive eyes in a pretty, oval face. Good cheekbones. Nice nose. Small and well made. Wiry toughness under velvety smooth skin. Sturdiness of upper leg, slimness of ankle.

"Sometimes I forget how beautiful you are," a man whispers from so many months ago. Baby-talk nicknames. Giggled pillow secrets. A remembered foreplay to lovemaking. An aftermath of angry recriminations, talk of money and coke. "Have the goodness to lower your voice." They are not alone in the house.

She dreams of the little child. A boy so small, his tiny body wet and slickly smooth. Nancy will never forget the touch of his icy skin. She fights not to remember this so clearly in the vivid and painful dream, and as it segues to another incident, she still shivers from the screaming injustice of it, shakes from the extraordinary depth of abject grief.

She dreams she is awake and eyes like saucers stare into the luminous face of the bedroom clock. A noise.

This dream that knows no logic, no chronology, no mercy, has her wide awake and listening to the drip-drippppp—*ping*—PING! She is moving silently through the house, her footsteps deadened by seven thousand dollars' worth of wall-to-wall turquoise shag. Hammering from the kitchen.

Frozen, fighting not to breathe, she waits for the frighteningly-irregular pounding to resume. BBBAAAAMMMMM! A grenade-loud concussive explosion pounds against her senses and she springs for the nearest weapon.

Hand clutching gun. Where are the bullets? CALL THEM CARTRIDGES THE BULLETS ARE THE PART ON THE END, a man's voice growls from the past. Her shoulders shake as she sobs in her sleep, passing the leaded glass tiger who is so beautiful by day, but whose image in the vista of the nighttime garden is menacing beyond expression. A man's hulking shadow fills the hallway and she says, in a voice like a hard, clenched fist, *I have a gun* . . .

"Mike. I can't take it any more," she tells him. On the phone at the crack of dawn. She will not listen to soft housing starts, plumbing repairs, high water tables. "We've got to sell it," she screams into the phone, forcing back the tears that will soon come. "I can't take another night of sleeping pills, plugs in my ears, the house crying out to me, phones and doorbells ringing. Things leaking and dripping and breaking. I CAN'T TAKE IT ANY MORE!"

There are weeks Nancy never let herself think about again. Mike found a guy who would take the house off their hands—someone he'd met out at the club—she knew him vaguely and had never liked him. But it was the offer that was so ridiculous—fifty thousand dollars. It was a quarter of a million dollar house, conservatively, not counting the acreage.

Bad weeks. Savage time of illness and depression. They ended up closing the deal. When the smoke had cleared, she was left with less than eighteen thousand dollars, but at least she was out of the house.

Nancy and her friend Sondra had gone out to pick up her things at the house. She was in the courtyard looking at the place where Davey had drowned. The plastic around the gravel had worked itself up out of the ground and was circling the yard like ugly parts of big black serpents. Every shrub and tree had died—even the weeping mulberries in her once-romantic garden now stood barren and dry. The dead bushes resembled tumbleweeds on stalks. Weeping mulberry. Weeping peach. Weeping Nancy.

"Any problems?" Mike said to the guy from the bank.

"Nope. No problems." He hefted the attaché case in his right hand. Both of them laughed excitedly. "Does this look like problems?" He opened it.

"Jeezus!" There were stacks of beautiful portraits of Mr. Franklin. Federal Reserve note portraits. More than Mike had ever seen at one time. His buddy at the bank had a client, a big potato chip conglomerate, who decided they couldn't live without the Hamiltons' twenty acres. Mike and Nancy sold the land to a dummy corporation for fifty thousand. The corporation peddled it back through the bank for half a million. Mike and his pal split the difference. The dummy corporation dissolved. The principals vanished. The chip people had the land. Mike and the bank guy had the money tax free. The paper trail stopped dead inside the bank. You couldn't get cleaner at the laundry.

It was also nice not to have to go play games with his ex at odd hours. Nancy had been more work than he'd thought she would be. For a while there he had thought he was going to have to start salting the well water.

# Tall Boys

## ROB KANTNER

addy was dying. Not from the emphysema; that was three years from grabbing him. No: Daddy was dying because it looked like come November he'd have to vote for a Republican—or a Catholic.

"Even Truman don't want him in there!" Daddy ranted, waving his forkful of smother-broil chicken in the air. "He said Kinnedy ain't ready to be president yet, and I agree with him."

"Now there's a surprise," Ma said as she spooned a double helping of mashed potatoes onto my plate.

Daddy's lips whitened as he glared at her. "I always took a shine to President Truman," he said dangerously.

Ma stopped serving my brother Bill, straightened and stared at Daddy. "For heaven's sake, Lewis! Back when he was in, you said men under five eight shouldn't be dog catcher, let alone president!"

Daddy looked angrily perplexed. Across from me, Uncle Dan cleared his throat. I was hoping he'd point out that Daddy himself was only five seven. But Uncle Dan was just as gunshy of Daddy as the rest of us. Ironic, since he was the only person I ever knew for whom Daddy had grudging respect, bordering on awe. He observed dryly, "Well, Truman should know 'not ready to be president' when he sees it."

I snickered. "Let's eat!" Ma said, pointedly ending the political discourse as she sat down at the end of the table to my left. "Libby will just have to take supper cold. Say the blessing, please, Benjy?"

We linked hands around the table and I closed my eyes, trying to think of the words. Fortunately, I was saved by the scuffing of footsteps on our porch outside and the squeal of the screen door hinges. "Hi, everybody!" my sister Libby called from the door. "I want you to meet somebody."

She walked at a bounce toward the dining area, accompanied by a boy/man wearing a small respectful smile. Even to my unschooled eyes, he looked older than Libby. Than me, even.

Libby's black hair was parted in the middle and combed down smooth, cut at ear lobe level all the way around. Bangs curved down her forehead, arching over her dark eyes. She more than adequately filled her black sleeveless blouse and white striped shorts. A perky girl with a secret smile; my baby sister but suddenly no little girl any more.

Ma was looking at Libby. Uncle Dan, having sized things up, was examining his clasped hands. Daddy, leaning back in his chair with feigned casualness, studied Libby's friend with his smoky blue eyes, the kind of eyes that terrorized Union troops a hundred years before. "Where you been, Elizabeth?" he asked softly.

"A carnival out in Nankin Mills. Jill's brother took us. That's where I met Jimmy. He works in the carnival." She beamed at her friend. "Jimmy Herndon, meet my family. That's Daddy and Mama. This is my brother Bill, that's my brother Benjy, and over there's my uncle Dan Perkins."

Herndon was a big beefy razor-cut blond wearing a yellow sport shirt, dark slacks, and pointy-toed shoes. He stepped toward Daddy, big paw outstretched. "So nice to meet you, Mr. Perkins. Say, what a great house you have here! You know, I've seen a lot of the Midwest, but Detroit is—"

"How old are you, son?" Daddy asked. There was nothing but interest in his voice. He was relaxed there in his chair, head tipped back, the hard planes of his face benign. The hairs rose on the back of my neck.

"Twenty-four," Herndon said, dropping his untouched hand.

"Daddy—" Libby began.

"Did you know," Daddy said, "that Elizabeth just turned fifteen?"

Herndon grinned crookedly. "Well, we hadn't really—"

Libby threw an imploring look at Ma as Daddy said in a whiplike voice, "Fifteen years old! What kind of skunk did your folks raise you to be, courtin' a fifteen-year-old little girl?"

Herndon held up both hands. "Courting? I'm not—"

Daddy leaped to his feet, his chair crashing to the floor behind him. "Get out!" he shrieked, face purpling. His fury demanded more oxygen than his ruined lungs could possibly provide; he exhaled in hard puffs between phrases. "Get out! Get *out* of my house! You *son* of a bitch! Get out!"

Libby began to cry. Herndon, twice Daddy's size and well under half his age, took one step back, gave Libby an unreadable glance, then turned and strode out of the house.

My sister's round face was wet and white. "Thanks an awful lot!" she shouted to the room at large, then ran away into the living room.

My big brother Bill stared grimly into his lap. Uncle Dan looked levelly at me. My heart pounded as if I was the object of my daddy's wrath instead of a bystander. Ma had risen and now, as Libby's footsteps echoed up the stairs, she went to Daddy and put her strong arms around his thin shoulders. "Now sit down, Lewis," she said brusquely. "Sit down and rest and take some supper."

"Son of a bitch," Daddy muttered, the words punctuated by puffs. But he sat.

Ma looked all right, but in her own way she was as upset as Daddy, as indicated by the fact that she clean forgot about grace. "Come on, let's eat," she said, spearing her chicken. "Libby will just have to take hers cold."

"I surely do look forward to these Wednesday night suppers with your family, Ben," Uncle Dan said dryly.

"Daddy's been real poorly lately," I said. "And that dopey sister of mine must have a death wish or something, dropping that guy on Daddy like that. I mean, she ain't even officially allowed to single-date yet. You really think he's twenty-four, Uncle?"

"Was once, anyway. I have a feeling he's been a lot of things. In a lot of places."

The humid July evening was darkening the porch, which opened on three sides to our heavily treed front yard. I sat on the stone railing, facing Uncle Dan, who was half visible on the big oak glider. He was a thin, wiry man who looked younger than his sixty-two years, with a full head of neatly trimmed, graying auburn hair and a narrow unlined face highlighted by remote gray eyes. As usual he wore a light, neatly tailored suit with shiny black wing tips and a narrow black tie. His Panama hat sat on the glider next to him and a Camel cigarette smoldered between his fingers.

I was jumpy as hell, the Big Question sitting fat in my mouth. Uncle Dan knew that, and was enjoying the suspense. We both looked toward the driveway as Bill's '58 Fairlane Town Sedan backed along the side of the house and then took off up the street. "Where's he off to?" Uncle Dan asked idly. "His shift doesn't start till midnight."

"Probably gone to see Marybeth first," I mumbled.

"He's been at Ford's what, eight years now," Uncle Dan observed. "Think you'll be able to hang on that long, Ben?"

It took a moment for what he said to register. I stood, fists clenched, heart pounding. "Really, Uncle? When?"

"Monday week, afternoons, at the Rouge."

"Doing what?" Please, no sweeping floors.

"Hanging doors on Fairlanes and Galaxies."

I whooped. "Great! Beats sweeping floors."

My uncle inhaled on his cigarette. "Lot of good men sweep floors at the Rouge. I did it myself, for awhile."

"Hey, it don't matter! This is great! Now I can quit the freakin' grocery store and make some serious dough!"

"Sit down," he said softly. I complied. My uncle leaned forward. "You remember our deal. You're going to pass your courses next year and you're going to graduate high school. You're not a punk kid any more, you're a grown man, and you've got obligations."

"Yes sir, Uncle Dan," I said, toning down the excitement.

"I hear you're flunking anything, I'll get you fired out of Ford's. Hear?"

I wondered if he could really do that. Uncle Dan had seniority to burn, but was only a foreman. There was, on the other hand, a lot about him I did not know. That none of us, Daddy included, ever knew. "Yes, sir. And I'll pay you back for the car loan, right off the top."

"No hurry," he said, leaning back on the glider.

"Evening, Ben!" called a female voice from behind me.

I turned. "Oh, hi, Miz Wilder," I called back.

"Lovely evening," she said, smiling at us, strolling by alone in the gloom of the big trees.

"Sure is."

Uncle Dan was sitting up straight, peering past me. "Neighbor lady?" he asked softly.

"Lives up at the corner of Bentler."

"Mm. Nice. Miss or Missus?"

"Missus."

I caught him looking at me closely. After a moment he said, "Your mother was telling me about your new girlfriend. Debbie?"

I scowled. "Debbie Miller. She's not my girlfriend, just a sophomore chick who lives in the house back of us. Been hanging around here, and Mama's been egging her on, but there's nothing there. I'm playing the field," I ended bravely.

Uncle Dan's distant eyes were on me again, making me feel distinctly uncomfortable. I wished that I could smoke; it would have helped at moments like that. "Think I'll mosey along home," he said, as he stood and put on his Panama, "before Act Two starts."

That was fine with me. It was pushing eight o'clock; *Silent Service* was coming on. I walked with Uncle Dan down the brick steps and across the narrow lawn to the curb, where his brand-new Thunderbird convertible, the most expensive car Ford built, was parked behind my brand-new second-hand '51 Deluxe Tudor sedan. "What do you mean, Act Two?" I asked as we walked.

"Libby and her new, uh, beau," he said. He crushed out his cigarette, opened the door and got inside.

"Oh, I think Daddy done killed that thing dead," I grinned.

"I don't," my uncle answered, face bleak in the fading light. "I saw them together in there."

I had no idea what he meant. "Whatever happens, it won't affect me none," I said with bravado that was entirely felt.

"May you be so lucky, Ben." He started the T-Bird, waved, and pulled away up Bennett Street, motor purring, tires humming, taillights glowing red in the gathering darkness.

Three mornings later, I hoofed barefoot into the kitchen, tugging my blue National Foods uniform shirt down over my head. "Mama, I threw my newer work pants down the chute the other day. You washed 'em yet?"

She glanced at me over her shoulder as she rinsed off a breakfast bowl in the sink. "I finished the wash yesterday, Benjy. Those pants weren't in there."

"I *know* I put 'em down the chute."

"They'll turn up. Wear your old ones for today." She shut off the water. "Miz Wilder called a minute ago. Her husband's gone away on business, and she wanted to know if you could stop by there this morning and move some boxes for her. I said you could."

Move some boxes, I repeated silently. "Sure," I said, "I'll stop by there before I go to work."

"Bring me a pig's head from the grocery." She took down a dish towel and started drying her hands. "We're having Brunswick stew tomorrow."

"I'll bring you the dead pig," I grinned, "but I'll need some dough."

"Take a five out of Daddy's cash kitty."

"Daddy won't like that."

"You do like I tell you," she advised, "and let me worry about your daddy."

"Yes, ma'am." Easy for you to say, I thought. He doesn't ever hit *you*.

She finished drying and hung the towel back up. The house around us was Saturday silent. Bill was working overtime at Ford's; Daddy's schedule at Kerns Casket was four on and two off, causing his weekends to rotate around; Libby was out somewhere. My mother looked me over, and she seemed to decide. "Set down, Benjy. I got something important to talk to you about."

Nervous and uncomfortable, I sat. My mother took the chair across from me. Her squarish face was tired and her eyes lacked their usual fervor. Her blue housedress was already limp from early heat and humidity and work. She folded her hands, looked at them, then at me. "You probably ain't aware of it," she began quietly. "You got your own life these days. But there's trouble in this house."

I was afraid even to breathe. "What kind of trouble?"

"Your sister," Ma said, "is still seeing that boy. That Jimmy Herndon."

Inside I sighed, and thanked my lucky stars that it was Libby's ass in a sling this time, and not mine. "How do you know, Ma?"

"Just a feelin'," she said. "Your momma ain't a total dern fool, you know. I know a lot about what goes on in this house." I wasn't about to touch that one. After a pause, Ma went on. "For example, I had a feeling that William knew more than he was lettin' on. So I asked him last night, and I was right."

"William" was my big brother Bill on the wrong side of Ma. "Right about what?" I asked.

Her lips drew back from her teeth for a minute and her eyes were steely. "Up till Wednesday, William was picking Libby up from summer school classes and driving her to meetings with that boy."

I couldn't believe it. "So Bill was helping her?"

Ma nodded grimly. "Your brother is weak. Libby asked him to, and he didn't have the gumption to say no. Last night he spilled everything. He told me that Libby didn't meet that boy Wednesday, like she said. They met two weeks ago. She brought him here Wednesday night because she was going to ask us to let him stay in the extry bedroom till he could find a job. Supposably he was quitting the carnival so he could stay in Detroit."

"Wow. Daddy ain't heard all this, has he?"

Ma held up a work-worn hand. "Your daddy must never know. He is very poorly. He don't need aggravation."

And God knows we don't need him aggravated, I thought. "What are you gonna do, Ma?"

"I thought about forbidding her to see Herndon. But Jane Lee says if you forbid a teenager to date someone, she'll turn right around and do it anyhow."

Jane Lee was a local advice columnist whose counsel Ma ranked just below that of the Gospels. "Jane Lee knows best," I said, echoing what Ma herself had said down through the years.

She ignored the sarcasm. "Bill swears he stopped helping Libby as of Wednesday. That's all the help I can expect out of him. For the rest, I'm looking to you."

I gaped. "Me?"

"You," Ma said in a cold voice. "I want you to find out for sure if they're still seeing each other. If they are—" She stopped abruptly and took a deep breath before going on. "If they are, then you will find a way to break it up, and get him out of Libby's life for good."

I sat there in our kitchen, listened to the silence, felt the pressure, impaled on a dilemma. On the one hand, I'd been brought up to obey my parents instantly and without question. On the other hand, I wanted no part of Libby's messes. And I was not, as Uncle Dan said, a punk kid any more. I was practically a grown man now, tired of taking orders. Plus, I only had a week before I went to work afternoons at the Rouge. My free time was running short, and I didn't want to waste any of it making like some kind of half-assed Richard Diamond, Private Eye.

Forget it, old lady, I said silently. Find yourself another patsy.

My mother said, "I'm not asking you for your daddy's sake, or for my sake. It's for Libby's sake." She pressed her lips. "That boy is trouble. I just know it. Libby's too young. She's strong-headed. Rash. Reckless."

Here goes, I thought. "Ma, I'm—I wouldn't know where to start." Good going, big man, I thought, disgusted. Good thing Fast Eddie and the Bubbas weren't there to hear me.

She smiled at me. "You'll find a way. You'll do it because you're my boy, and because I'm asking you to, hear?"

"Yes, ma'am."

"You do as I say, now."

"Yes, ma'am."

"Take care of your baby sister."

"Yes, ma'am."

I locked up my Ford and joined Fast Eddie walking with a cluster of other customers up the long grassy meadow toward the carnival entrance. Thin-as-a-straw Eddie wore all black, as usual, and carried his Gibson acoustic slung by its black embroidered strap over his shoulder. He surveyed the sky with his dark eyes and held out his hands tentatively. "Think it might rain?"

"That's the chance you take, dummy, carrying that guitar around. What's it for, anyways?"

"Chicks," he said, his thin face wolflike.

"Well, you're on your own on that. I'm here to track down this Jimmy Herndon fella."

"I still don't get it, Benjy. What's talking to Herndon gonna get you?"

"I'm going to ask him if he's gonna hang around or leave town. If he's leaving town, our troubles are over. If he's hanging around, well—I'll have to figure out what to do then."

We got in line at the carnival admission booth. Fast Eddie studied me. "What's with you and the chicks department, Benjy? Having yourself a celibate summer?"

"I'm doing just fine, thanks," I growled, digging into my pocket for money.

Fast Eddie laughed. "You mean Debbie Miller? Your momma was telling me little Deb's got the hots for you. What a howl!"

"Forget it, man. She's ugly, she's stupid, and she's only fifteen."

"So, what's the problem?"

As such operations go, the carnival wasn't very big. Its dozen rides included a rickety roller coaster, dodge 'em cars, a merry-go-round, a couple of pivoting saucer rides, and the inevitable Ferris wheel. Organ music shrilled from worn-out speakers, and the humid air was drenched with the scent of sawdust, beer, and animal dung.

We hit the midway, which stretched out colorfully the length of a football field, flanked with booths manned by loud, practiced carnies. There weren't many customers. Some of the booths had none at all. It was perfect, but I didn't feel all that good. I was hung over, for one thing; as usual, Fast Eddie, the Bubbas, and I had put away a case of tall boys the night before. On top of that I was nervous. I'd never done this kind of thing. I didn't know where to begin. Oh well, I thought, just dive in and fake it.

"Over here, Fast," I said, gesturing us toward one of the carny booths. This was a sort of ring-toss game. You threw rubber rings at cases full of longnecked bottles. If you got a ring to stick over a bottle neck, you won a prize. The catch, of course, was that the rings were just barely big enough to fit over the necks, and the bottles were not seated solidly in the cases.

I ambled up to the counter. It was manned by a wizened, deeply tanned man in a baggy blue Truman shirt, ball cap, and loose pants. His face looked like it had collapsed on itself; it had no substance at all except for the wad of chew in his left cheek. As I approached, he sang, "Yes sir, yes sir, win a big prize today, win a big prize. Two chances for a thin dime, five for a quarter. What'll it be, young fella?"

"Hi," I said, grinning at him. "I'm looking for Herndon. Jimmy Herndon."

"This ain't the missing persons bureau. How many chances you want, now?"

"I don't want any. Look, I know Herndon works here at the carnival. Where is he?"

The carny stepped back and glared at me, tiny points of light burning in his remote eyes. "You're blocking paying customers. Pay up and play, or move on, kid."

I glanced around. No one else was there. Not even Fast Eddie. Bored already, he'd wandered across the fairway to the Rifle Range and was chatting with the overweight blonde who ran it. She beamed at him in a

way that women never beamed at me, and I felt the resentment that went
back to when Fast and I were six: *how in hell does he do it?*

I glared at the carny. "There's nobody else here, mister. Now I asked
you a question. Help me out and I'll be on my way."

The sawed-off ball bat came up with blinding speed, swung down and
smashed the counter top. I nearly jumped out of my shoes. The carny
raised the bat again and waggled the business end like Rocky Colavito,
staring hotly at me. "You heard me!" he screamed. "Get moving!"

I gulped. "Okay, okay. No offense." I backed away from the booth.
Several other customers were staring at me. The other carnies paid no
attention at all. Fast Eddie had vanished. So had the blonde lady.

I continued up the midway. Gradually my heartbeat got back under
control. Big deal, I told myself. You ran into a hard nose first time out.
Keep trying. Someone will come across.

Wrong. I worked the midway for better than an hour. I talked to carnies, concessions people, roughnecks and drivers. Leaving out the ball bat
part, they were as cooperative as the ringtoss man. Never heard of Jimmy
Herndon. Get moving, kid. Mind your own business.

They were lying. I was sure of it. But, I thought as I retraced my route
down the midway, there's no way to prove it. Dead end. I walked on,
bound for the exit, wondering where Fast Eddie was, wondering what to
do now—

"Hey, Benjy!"

I turned. Fast Eddie gave me the come-on wave. I trotted toward him.
"What's up, Fast?"

He looked excited. "Come here. Quick, before she changes her mind."
He led me between two of the carny booths. Behind the midway was a
sprawling grassy area parked full of trucks. One of them, a big panel job,
sat facing me with its tail doors swung open. Sitting on the bumper was
the blonde woman I'd seen Fast talking with earlier. She was smoking a
cigarette and looked nervous. "This is my friend Erma," Eddie said.
"Erma, this is Benjy. Now tell him what you told me."

Erma's close-cropped hair hadn't always been blonde. She stretched a
cowgirl outfit and big tall boots, and was ten years and fifty pounds ahead
of Eddie, not that it made any difference to him. She scanned me indiffer-
ently, glanced around, then said in a low voice, "Jimmy Herndon was a
roughneck here at the carnival."

I glanced at Fast. He was beaming. "I know that," I told her. "Where is
he?"

"I don't know."

"Tell him the story, Erma," Fast Eddie said.

She shut her eyes tightly for a minute. Then: "There was a big brawl last week in a bar up on U.S. 12 somewhere. A man got knifed. Throat cut, bled to death. Jimmy was there. Word is, he did it. He's hiding out. Cops are after him. He don't dare show his face around here."

"Nice guys your little sister hangs out with, Benjy," Fast noted.

"Shut up." I leaned close to Erma. She smelled of makeup and sweat. "You sure about this, Erma?"

"Swear to God." Her eyes flickered. "We're not supposda talk about him. Bad for business."

"I'll just bet." I stood. "Any idea where he went?"

She shook her head and inhaled on her cigarette jerkily. "I don't know, and I don't want to know. Jimmy Herndon is slick and tricky and pure trouble all the way through. You boys stay clear of him."

"We can't," I said, putting all the tough I could into my voice. "Him and me, we got business."

She smiled sadly. "Then be careful, boys. Be plenty damn careful."

After thinking it over, I decided to park in the lot of the Michigan Bank, across Grand River from Redford High. I couldn't park too close or Libby would spot me. I couldn't park too far away or I'd miss her. This was perfect. Hopefully.

As I waited, the radio whispered the three o'clock news: Tshombe, Katanga, the Democratic Convention, and today's All Star Game. It was a warm and muggy Monday, had rained earlier and would again. I smoked a Camel cigarette and thought about what I was doing. I'd bombed out with Herndon. Now to go at it from the other end. Follow Libby and see where she went.

Gaggles of kids left the building as summer school classes let out. When I spotted Libby, she was walking east along the sidewalk on Grand River, about to cross Westbrook. Headed away from home.

When she stopped in front of Sock's Texaco amid a mixed group of whites and Negroes, I realized she was waiting for a bus. I put out my cigarette and started the car. Libby didn't seem anxious or furtive. She wore a generously cut pleated shirtdress in light blue, with a big wide belt and sandals, and carried her textbooks as if they weren't important.

A DSR bus came along and roared to a stop. I wheeled my car into one of the eastbound lanes of Grand River as the bus gobbled up its passengers and continued toward the distant skyline of downtown Detroit.

The radio began to croon Percy Faith's "Theme from 'A Summer Place.' " I'd heard it to death already. I twirled the knob to the next station: Elvis doing "Stuck on You." Much better. I kept the left lane of Grand River, and followed the bus at the thirty-five mph speed limit. The back ad panel advertised Channel 7, WXYZing, Detroit's Big Station.

I wondered where the hell my sister was going.

The bus stopped at every major cross street. Each time I hugged the curb, watching fruitlessly for Libby as people got on and off. We passed near the National Food Store where I worked and I flipped it the finger as we went by, knowing I was out of there in less than a week. St. Mary's Catholic Ward's and Penney's, the Bow Wow Coney Island, the Belshaw plant. Traffic was light, but the speed limit was thirty now and we crawled. Winkelman's, Sears, Charlie's Cadillac and Dawson Edsel; downtown was rising before my eyes and still no Libby—

I damn near blew it. The bus stopped across from the Riviera Theatre; I watched the disembarking passengers idly and then scanned the marquee: A *Tall Story* starring Tony Perkins and Jane Fonda. When the bus moved on, I did too, and belatedly spotted Libby half-jogging across Grand River headed for the front of the theater.

Cursing myself, I U-turned in front of Kresge's and came back as several homebound commuters honked angrily. Libby was not in sight. One thing I knew for sure: she didn't need to come all the way down here for movies, not with the Redford Theatre right around the corner from our house.

I gingerly turned north on Riviera Street. Libby was half a block away, crossing the narrow street toward the front of a gaunt, gray, two story apartment building. As I rolled slowly that way, she went inside. I pulled into the Riviera Theatre's parking lot across from the apartment building, drove down to the end, and parked by a tree.

*Wesson Apartments* was engraved in stone above the door. The building filled the corner of Riviera and Yosemite streets, a modest looking neighborhood. I didn't know anybody down here. I wondered who in the hell Libby knew down here. I wondered what she was doing in there. Several times I opened my door, ready to go find out. Each time I shut the door and waited some more.

An endless, fidgety hour later, Jimmy Herndon came out of the Wesson Apartments with his arm around my sister. They kissed, he waved, and she walked away toward Grand River, stride bouncy, arms embracing her books.

I fired up the Ford and laid a hot streak of rubber as I swerved onto Riviera Street and rolled abreast of Libby. Her eyes widened when she saw me; then she looked resolutely ahead as she walked. "Go away, Benjy."

I kept my tone reasonable. "Need a ride, don't you?"

"I'm fine. Now go away."

I babied the Ford along, keeping even with Libby. "Come on, hop in," I said. "You really don't want to ride that sweaty old bus all the way home, do you?"

She looked at me suspiciously, then tossed her head in what passed for acceptance. I stopped the Ford, she crossed in front and got in. I managed to keep the lid on till we'd turned the corner and were part of the westbound rush up Grand River.

"You're not seeing that son of a bitch no more, Libby Perkins, or I'll break both your arms for ya, I swear to God!"

"I'll see him all I want!" she shouted back. "And you got no right to spy on me."

I calmed myself with difficulty: "Listen. Herndon's trouble. He done got into a knife-fight, and somebody died, and the cops are after him."

I did not get the expected shocked silence. "He didn't kill anybody," Libby came back readily. "It was all a big mixup. An accident. They're just picking on him."

"How come you know so much about it?" She didn't answer. "Don't tell me you were *with* him when it happened."

She shrugged and began to play with the window crank, mouth ugly. "What about you? You're not exactly Mister Simon Pure yourself. I've smelled beer on your breath, plenty times. And I know you're weedin' off every chance you get. And you prob'ly got some kind of trashy girlfriend stashed away somewhere."

"I'm seventeen," I said. "Makes all the difference."

"No," she shot back. "You're a boy and I'm a girl. *That's* the difference." She turned on the radio. It was playing "Itsy Bitsy Teeny Weeny Yellow Polka Dot Bikini." I shut it off on the third beat. Libby scowled and went on, "Mama put you up to this. She thinks just 'cause I'm a girl that I can't handle things. Well, I can. Every damn bit as well as you."

Silence prevailed till I made the turn onto Burgess, three blocks from home.

Libby said softly, "You just forget what you saw today. If you snitch to Mama and Daddy, I'll say you're a liar."

"Stay away from him, Libby."

"You can't stop me. Mama and Daddy can't stop me." She smiled. "Nobody can stop me. Nobody at all."

As we turned onto our street, I waved at Mrs. Wilder, and she waved back from her porch swing.

"So," Fast Eddie said from the shotgun seat, "we gonna thump some rump this afternoon or what, men?"

I slowed the '51 to a stop in front of Sun Ya's on Grand River as the radio played "Cathy's Clown." "We're just gonna *reason* with Mr. Herndon. That's all."

Fast grinned at me and jerked a thumb toward the back seat. "Is that why we're bringing along all this Bubba-beef? Because they're so articulate?"

I glanced in the rear view. The Bubbas filled the back seat with biceps, shoulders, football jerseys, and identical grins. "Reason with him," one of them said. "Damn straight," chimed in the other.

Their real names were Joe and Frank Szewczklieuski. But everybody had referred to them as Bubba, both singular and plural, almost as far back as I could remember. The handle was hung on them by my daddy. Being, like everyone else, unable to tell them apart, he was uncomfortable calling them Joe or Frank. And he never could learn how to pronounce their last name, no matter how patiently we tutored him. One day in frustration he called them Bubba, and it stuck.

It was a hot, sunny Tuesday noon. I'd worked the morning at the grocery and then collected the guys for our little visit to Jimmy Herndon. Libby was safely in summer school so I figured the coast was clear. My reasoning was, if I couldn't talk her out of him, maybe I could encourage him out of her.

The light changed to green, the song changed to "You're Gonna Miss Me," and the topic changed to the Detroit Tigers: sorry as hell, tied for fifth with the Washington Senators and going nowhere fast. I lighted a Camel and joined the badmouthing, which went from baseball to women, to beer to women, to Fast Eddie's new band to women, and from there, neatly, to beer.

"Hey, Ben," a Bubba said, "tall boys Saturday night."

"Your turn to buy," the other chimed in.

"Damn, that's right," I said. "Guess I'll be hitting the usual source. If I can catch Denny on duty. He still doesn't card, does he?"

"Nah," Fast Eddie said, "but I think he's on vacation."

"I'll figure it out," I vowed. "Don't worry, guys. It's only Tuesday. By Saturday, a case of tall boys will be ours."

We crossed Livernois; on the home stretch now. Fast Eddie rubbed his hands together. "I think we ought to take Herndon in an alley and lay waste to his face."

Eddie's zeal would have been disquieting if it were not so suspect. "Just let me do the talking, Fast," I said. "Y'all are along for moral support and that's all."

"You guys hold him," Fast said ominously, "and I'll hit him."

I rounded the corner and pulled into the half-full parking lot of the Riviera Theatre. We parked, got out, and crossed Riviera Street, making for the doorway of the Wesson Apartments. We'd just hit the sidewalk when Fast Eddie said blandly, "Hey, guys, I better stay out here and watch the car."

The Bubbas snickered. I glared at Eddie. "What do you mean, 'watch the car'? It ain't going nowhere."

He was already heading back. "I'll just sit on the hood and scare off the thieves. You guys have fun."

He waltzed away, whistling a cheerful tune. "Come on, guys," I muttered to the Bubbas.

The foyer of the Wesson was small, airless, and empty except for a row of metal mailboxes nailed to the cheap plaster wall. Each box had a name and not one of them was Herndon.

"What now?" I asked the Bubbas. Their only reply was a shared grin. I had a brainstorm. "Come on," I said, and led them to an apartment door. A brisk knock brought the face of a small busty woman with loose dentures, a small mustache, and a hairnet. "Yaaaassssss?" she asked, wobbling.

"Looking for Jimmy Herndon, ma'am," I said. "He lives in the building here. Big beefy guy? Blond? Works the carnival?"

"Upstairs," she said with a Smirnoff accent. "Try upstairs, the door with the Tigers decals." She slammed the door.

"Now we're cooking," I said. The Bubbas trailed me like a herd of steer, up a flight of narrow wood stairs to the second floor. I knocked on the door and it swung open obligingly.

I damn near swallowed my tongue.

It was a small one-room apartment with windows looking out over Yosemite Street. The Murphy bed was held down by the stark naked Jimmy Herndon, who gaped at us through the smoke of his cigarette, and a trim young dark-haired woman who, I realized as she gave a strangled "Eep!" and tried to cover herself, was not Libby.

"Excuse us," the Bubbas said in unison, having been raised to be polite.

"Want to talk to you, Herndon," I said sternly.

The big man's good-living face went sour for a second as he recognized me. "Oh, jeez. Okay. I'll see you in the hall there in a second, kid."

"Make it quick," I said threateningly, and pulled the door shut. "Hey, Bubba, trot on out there on Yosemite and make sure our little buddy doesn't slip out the window, okay?" One of them took off, clomping heavily down the stairs.

I lighted a Camel and smoked nervously. After a moment the apartment door opened and Jimmy Herndon came out, zipping up his pants. He grinned at me. "You're Benjy, right?"

"Ben. Ben Perkins. And you know why I'm here, so let's get on with it."

"Get on with what?" he asked pleasantly. His eyes clicked once to Bubba and then back to me, undisturbed.

"You and Libby. I want to hear you say that it's over."

"Well, okay. It's over. How's that, Benjy?"

His grin had not wavered. I dropped my cigarette to the floor and slowly crushed it out, feeling my heart pound and fists knot. "You smart-mouthin' me?"

He showed me palms. "No," he said deliberately. "Now don't get riled. I meant what I said. Libby and I are all through."

I loosened my hands marginally. "You give me your word on that?"

"Absolutely. Look, Ben—you don't mind if I call you Ben, do you?" He hooked a hand over my shoulder and led me slowly up the hall. "I like Libby. I really do. But she really is too young for me. I'm breaking it off. I'd already planned to, even before today."

"I see."

Herndon looked me straight in the eye. "As it happens, I'm leaving town for good. Tonight. So I'll be out of the picture. Fair enough?"

"Yeah. Okay." I gestured to Bubba. "Don't disappoint me, now," I warned Herndon.

"Don't worry, Benjy. I won't."


The rain was dumping in buckets the next afternoon as I sloshed the Ford up Lasher on my way home from work. I'd put in ten hours at the grocery and I was whipped, grimy, and grumpy. My boss, whom I'd un-wisely nicknamed Hitler, had been giving me the crappiest jobs in the place ever since I told him I was going to work at Ford's. Plus I was jumpy, wondering what kind of explosion waited for me at home. It had been twenty-four hours since my talk with Jimmy Herndon, more than enough time for Libby to find out that he was gone.

A familiar figure waved an umbrella to me from under the awning of Jim's Sweet Shop. I sloshed the Ford to the curb as my mother ran to the car, opened the door and piled in, dragging her umbrella behind her. "Lord have mercy, it's enough to strangle frogs! Thank you, Benjy."

"No problem, Ma." I wheeled the Ford away from the curb. "So, how's things around the house?"

"Things?" she asked absently as she glanced inside her prescription bag. Then she arched a brow. "Oh. Things. Well, son, I reckon *things* are just fine."

"In the baby sister department?" I asked carefully. "What's she been up to?"

"Nothing special. Came straight home from school, like yesterday. Studied awhile. Then went out with her girlfriends. There's a new movie at the Redford over there, something with Dick Clark." She must have taken my silence for skepticism, because she added, "I know that's where Libby went. I walked up here with her and her friends, since it was right on the way to Kinsel's for your daddy's prescription."

"Well, good," I said uneasily, swinging right onto Bennett.

"I don't know what you did, son, but whatever it was, it seems to've worked. I'm much obliged." She looked at me and wrinkled her nose. "Heavens mercy, what is that stench on you, Benjamin?"

"Hot sauce. Had to clean up a busted case of it."

She had her eagle eye on. "And those shoes! Why in the world did you wear those sorry old shoes to work?"

"Couldn't find my other ones. Looked everywhere."

She snorted. "You're too young to be going senile. First your pants, now your shoes."

"Sorry, Ma." I slowed down for our driveway. "I've had a lot on my mind."

She smiled at me. "I know. It was unfair of me, imposing on you the way I did. But I'm not sorry. You fixed it and it's over and I'm grateful, Benjy. Right grateful."

I wished I could be as positive as she.

But everything stayed calm. At least as calm as it ever was around our house. Daddy came home mean as a snake from a run-in with his boss at the casket company, and had another tantrum when the news came over that Kennedy had, as expected, been nominated. Libby returned from her movie and ate dinner with the family. Then she spent the evening curled up on the living room couch, industriously studying her English. She was in a fine mood. I began to think that maybe Ma was right. Maybe the Herndon episode was over. Maybe Libby would pass her remedial courses and go on to tenth grade in the fall and life would return to whatever passed for normal around our place.

I wanted to believe it. I had my own life to live, and only a few days left before hitting the line at Ford's. I wanted to cruise in my Deluxe Tudor, maybe turtle-race down Woodward Avenue, four cars abreast doing ten miles per hour; gobble Big Chief burgers at the Totem Pole, catch the Tigers playing the Yankees at Briggs Stadium this weekend, and, of course, have at least one more session guzzling Stroh's tall boys with Eddie and the Bubbas, assuming I could find a supplier.

But in the end I had to make sure.

I stood before the apartment door and took a deep breath as the Wesson Apartments breathed silently around me.

For the dozenth time since getting up that Thursday morning I wondered if I was being extra dumb, coming down here alone. But, I reminded myself, Herndon didn't seem all that tough. Big guy, for sure, with some experience on him, but mostly mouth. All lard and no hard, as my daddy would have said. I wouldn't need the Bubbas to handle him. If in fact he was still here.

I knocked on the door. After a moment it eased back, held cautiously by the dark-haired woman I'd seen Herndon with the last time. She wore a mint Grecian-sleeve dress with a polka dot sash around her slender waist. Her hair was pixie short and so was she: shapely but slight with the wiry build of a dancer. "You," she greeted me.

I wanted to tell her she looked better with clothes on, but caught myself in time. Not very nice, and untrue, besides. "Me," I answered, grinning. "Where's Herndon at?"

"Not here. Who cares where?" She smiled crookedly. "I sure as the dickens don't. I threw him out." She stepped into the hallway and pulled the door to. At my expression her face hardened and she pushed the door back open. "You want to search the place? Go ahead!"

"If I wanted to, babygal, I would." The line sounded better in my head than it did out loud. "What'd Herndon do, find somewhere else to live?"

"Somewhere else?" she mimicked sourly. "He never lived here. Hung around some, you know? But he never spent the night. We had some laughs, okay? But nothing big-time."

"Seen him lately?"

"You deaf or something? I threw him out, I toldja." As she looked at me, I saw that her eyes, outlined in black, were the exact color of her dress. "The other day when you were here, I listened through the door. That's how I found out about him and your sister. That tore it. I never planned to marry the bum, but I wasn't going to be part of any harem, either."

"Any idea where he went?"

"If he was smart, he got out of Detroit. Cops are looking for him. You knew that, huh? I called 'em myself to let them know he'd been seen in the neighborhood here. Maybe they caught him, ever think of that?"

Nope. Not hardly. "Sure I did," I said importantly. "I'm stopping by the precinct right after this."

"Uh-huh." Her hips swayed slightly as she gave me the cool green once-over. "When you're done with all that, whyn't you come back and buy me a drink or something?"

"Wish I could," I said, taken by surprise. "But I'm, uh, more or less seeing somebody, you know?"

"At least you're honest," she said, which made me feel guilty. She walked with exaggerated grace back into her apartment and smiled and winked at me over her shoulder. "I hope she knows how lucky she is," she said before closing the door between us.

I idled the Ford at the Schoolcraft traffic light. On the opposite corner sat the C & H Party Store. I wondered if they'd card me if I strolled in and bought a case. I had no idea, and I had no time now. But I'd have to figure the beer thing out pretty soon. Saturday was only two days off.

But I had something bigger on my mind than the need for a case of tall boys. It was a feeling I'd never had before, not quite this way. The feeling that something was going on behind the scenes. That a great big fast one was being pulled.

That I was being had.

"He never spent the night here," his ex-girlfriend had told me. Then where the hell was he living, between the knife fight and now? Had I even thought to ask her? Nooooo.

"She was going to ask us to let him stay in the extry bedroom," Ma had told me. Of course, the negotiation had never gotten that far, thanks to my calm, cool, collected daddy.

And Libby had been acting awfully happy last night for a hotheaded girl whose first great love had ankled her.

The light greened and I geared the Ford up to high, half watching my driving. "There's trouble in this house," Ma had said. Yeah. Things hadn't been right. I'd been waking up a lot lately in the dead of night. I'd attributed that to the jitters—starting work at Ford's would be no picnic, I knew —but what if . . .

That morning I'd been unable to find my prized Redford High baseball jersey. And Bill had complained about missing a jacket. Either the laundry chute was eating our clothes, or Ma was going senile, or—

"Jesus Christ," I murmured. I sailed through the red light at Greenfield without even thinking about it. Could anybody be that brazen?

By the time I reached our neighborhood, I'd decided what to do. It was wild-assed crazy, but it just might work—if I could only talk Debbie Miller, my local admirer, into going along.

She appeared, a ghostly, whitish-gray, faceless figure, behind the rippled glass of the porch door, and clicked the latch open. As I pulled the door, she put a finger to her lips and shook her head. I nodded. She turned and led me through the inner door into the house, through the kitchen, and up the carpeted back stairway.

The house had the sweet, foreign smell of strangers and was pitch black and thickly silent except for the faint tread of our feet echoing mutely on the old floorboards. My heart was racing, and I was pumped and primed and as ready to go as if it were nine in the morning instead of just past midnight. God alone knew what the next hour or so would bring.

Debbie closed her bedroom door behind us and faced me. In the faint light of her bedside lamp, I saw that she wore white full-length cotton pajamas over pink bunny slippers. Atop that she wore a white satiny quilted robe that reached from her ankles all the way up to a big button at her throat. She was about as physically inviting as a Barcolounger, which, I discerned in her opening comments, was no accident.

"Don't you lay a hand on me, Benjy Perkins!" she whispered sharply, gray eyes hard.

I sighed. So much for the big crush she supposedly had on me. Just as well. "That's not why I'm here," I whispered patiently. "I explained all that."

"Better not be. I'm not like that Beth Heinzeroth, sneaking boys into her house to do God knows what. I must be nuts to be doing this. I'm a good girl."

"I know. So listen, whyn't you keep yourself busy or something, while I do what I got to do? Go to sleep if you want. I don't know how long this'll take."

She rolled her eyes. "No, thank you. I'll just stay awake till you're done with whatever strange business you're mixed up in. There's the window. Help yourself. And keep it quiet or you'll wake my folks—and you know what that means."

I went to the window, pulled back the drapes, and notched the blinds. Across the narrow adjoining back yards, beyond a copse of trees, I could see the back side of our house, half black and half silvery in the moonlight. Behind me, I heard bedsprings creak as Debbie arranged herself Indian-style against her headboard. I glanced back at her and she raised her chin and stared at me defiantly. I made what I hoped was an innocent, reassuring smile, turned back to the window, knelt and looked out and watched, waiting for something to happen.

An hour went by like that. Nothing happened outside. Inside was another story. Debbie just couldn't sit still. She flipped through magazines and paced, cleared her throat and smothered yawns, and gave me a clench-jawed steely-eyed stare whenever I dared to look at her.

I was silently composing a speech in which I foreswore, for all time, any and all interest in her body, when I caught a motion outside at the northeast corner of our house.

It was Libby. She wore jeans and a sweater and nothing on her bare feet showing white against the grass. It was in the low fifties that night, cool for July, and she hugged herself as she walked purposefully in the moonlight to the double doors that covered the cement stairs leading down into our cellar.

As I stared, I felt disbelief. I also felt something else, something new: pure cold joy. Got you, you bastard. I got you, got you, got you.

Libby bent and gave the cellar door three taps. After a moment it rose a couple of inches. She opened it the rest of the way, stepped over the threshold and followed the steps down, swallowed up in the deeper blackness as the cellar door dropped shut behind her.

Now! I thought fiercely. Now to settle some hash! I stood abruptly. Debbie jumped. "What is it?" she whispered.

"Christmas time. Got to go, sweetheart." I headed for the door. "You stay here. I know the way out. And thanks, kid. You done good."

She stood, nervously tugging the robe tightly around her. "I thought you'd be here longer."

"Long enough. Go on, get some sleep." I opened the bedroom door.

She licked her lips. "I enjoyed it," she ventured.

I waved and stepped out. As I pulled her door shut, I distinctly heard one whispered word: "Bastard."

I closed the porch door silently behind me and moved at a fast trot across the Millers' back yard. In the weeds behind their trash barrel I found the Louisville Slugger I'd hidden there earlier. I hefted it and held it at my side as I crept around the copse of trees as quietly as I could. Too late. I heard the cellar doors creak shut and caught a glimpse of Libby rushing back the way she'd come. She'd been down there five minutes, tops.

Well, well. Now this would work even better. I crouched in the cool, damp grass, leaning on the bat, and counted to six hundred, plenty long enough for Libby to get inside, up the stairs, and into her room, out of harm's way. Then I stood and walked across our lawn, ducking under the clotheslines as I made for the cellar doors.

There I froze a moment. Not a sound from anywhere. I had to do this smart and quiet. I thought it through, then bent and tapped on the cellar door three times, just as Libby had.

After a moment the door rose an inch or so. I stood facing out, with my back against the house, waiting and watching, as it closed. I bent and tapped on it again. Stepped back and hoisted the bat this time, cocked and ready.

The cellar door rose, opening wider and wider, revealing a male arm and then a blond head as Jimmy Herndon ventured up the stairs, back to me. He'd just uttered the first syllable of Libby's name when the fat of my Louisville ball bat thonked him squarely above his right ear.

He collapsed as if switched off, splattering down onto the stairs. I dropped the bat, bent and took him under the damp armpits of his T-shirt and began to drag him out. He weighed a ton, but I didn't have far to haul him, and I was feeling too proud of myself to care. I'd done it. I'd taken

out the villain, like Richard Diamond, Sundance, Roger and Smith, Peter
Gunn—guys like that.

Finally the gagging and retching stopped. I had both big windows of my
'51 Ford open to the cool night air pouring in as I drove down the silent
desertion of Grand River, but even that wasn't enough to dull the stench
from the back seat.

"You had to do that, huh," I growled. "Ya had to puke in my brand-new
second-hand car. Thanks a whole lot."

"You were the one who hit me, kid," Herndon said hoarsely. "You get
slugged in the head, you puke."

All I knew was, it certainly wasn't something that happened to Richard
Diamond, Sundance, Roger and Smith, Peter Gunn—guys like that.
"Should of told me," I said. "I'd have stopped so you could do it on the
street like everybody else."

"Sorry," he said, tone wholly sincere. "Mind if I come up there?"

"I don't care."

"You're not going to hit me any more?"

"As long as you're peaceable I won't."

Jimmy Herndon stuffed himself over the seat into the front and arranged himself as far from me as he could get. I followed the night-
blanketed street as it lanced toward the heart of Detroit, doing about
sixty, catching the synchronized lights perfectly. After a moment Herndon
asked, "Where you taking me?"

"The train station. You promised to leave town," I said sourly. "I'm
holding you to it."

"That's just fine, Ben. I really appreciate it—"

"Just shut the hell up!" I shouted. "Quit acting like you're anything but
a crooked, devious, sleazy son of a bitch, okay?"

"I'm not all that bad."

"Aren't, huh? You been sneaking around with my sister. You been sleeping in the basement of my house every night. You had a whole bag of our
clothes ready to take with you. And you're wanted for knifing a guy. If that
ain't bad, what is it?"

"Survival." His smile was not kind. "Maybe when you're older, you'll
understand what I mean."

I swung right on 14th Street. It was foggier down here, the street lights
misty on the fronts of darkened houses and stores. "Well," I said, "this-
here punk kid done took you out, pal. And I could make things even
worse, as in turning you over to the cops. But I don't need the cops to fix
you. It'd be too easy, somehow. There's a lot more satisfaction in running
your ass out of town personally."

He absently rubbed his head where I'd hit him. "You're giving me a real break, kid. Thanks."

"No thanks needed. It ain't Christian charity. I just don't want my sister drug through the mud with you, hear?"

He was smiling at me. "You really are a pretty four-square guy, Ben. If there's something I can do for you before I leave, to make amends, just name it."

"Yeah. Right," I snorted. "At one thirty on a Friday morning." We were driving through a neighborhood of streets all named after trees. Nothing was open but the occasional bar. That gave me an idea. Yeah, right. Perfect!

As we reached Temple Street, I swerved the Ford over to the curb by a small building at the corner that said Temple Tavern. I put the brake on and dug in my pants pocket. "You want to make some kind of amends, go on inside there and buy me a case of Stroh's tall boys. Got it?"

I reached a five at him. He shook his head and came out of his pocket with a large wad of soft, often-folded currency. "Nope," he said firmly, "I'm covering it. Least I can do." He hopped out and strode into the tavern. Presently he appeared on the sidewalk again, embracing the case. I got out and opened the trunk; he put the clinking beer bottles inside.

Ten minutes later I delivered Jimmy Herndon to the Michigan Central Train Station, walked him inside, and watched him purchase a ticket to Chicago with several bills from his fat wad of soft currency.

When he completed the transaction, he turned to me, grinning. "Train leaves at six," he said. "Gonna wait around and wave a hankie as I depart?"

"Maybe I should. To make sure you go."

"Oh, I'll go. I promise." He looked around the cavernous train station lobby. "This town's too hot for me. I'm gone and I'll stay gone. You whipped me, Ben. I'm out of here."

I was exhausted. I was scheduled to do a twelve hour shift at the grocery, starting at six A.M. I had to get home and rescue what sleep I could. "Okay. Just don't let me see your face in these parts ever again."

Back behind the wheel of my '51, beating gears headed northwest for home through the misty night, I felt pretty damned good. I'd won. Libby had been smack in the middle of big trouble, and I'd sorted it out. It hadn't been pretty. I'd made mistakes. But I'd overcome every obstacle that appeared, and in the end I prevailed.

All for no reward—aside from the satisfaction of feeling like maybe I wasn't just a punk kid any more. . . .

The siren made me swerve and I nearly took out a lamppost at the Outer Drive intersection. A cop car hung to my bumper, red bubblelight and headlights flashing angrily, punctuated by the whooping siren. Heart hammering, I hauled the Ford to a stop in front of the Christian Science church. Damn it to *hell!* I thought. Nailed. Speeding. My first ticket.

The officer sauntered up to my door and peered down. "Benjy Perkins?" he asked, in what had to be one of the last Irish accents left on the force.

"Yessir." How the hell did he know my name?

"Would you mind stepping out of the vehicle, young feller?"

I did so, shaking. The cop took my upper arm and led me to the rear of the car. "Got anything special in the trunk, son?"

My homecoming was not pretty.

Daddy, who didn't bother to bail me out of the 16th Precinct till eight thirty the next morning, nearly ripped my head off. Mama met me at the door to inform me that I was the first member of the Perkins family ever to go to jail. My brother Bill, just leaving for work, shook his head ominously when he saw me. And Libby, my sweet little sister Libby, all angelic in her summer school clothes, tossed her head at my appearance and greeted me with "Morning, jailbird!"

I could handle Daddy and Mama and Bill. Time would take care of my problems with them. But I had to settle accounts with Libby. When she got home, late that evening, I barged into her bedroom and slammed the door. "We got to talk, Libby," I growled.

She was sitting at her dressing table, brushing her short brown hair. "What do you want, jailbird?"

"First off, cut out the name-calling. This jam I'm in is all on account of you."

Brush, brush. "Really? Did I put the beer in your car?"

"No." I stepped closer, about to lower the boom and grimly enjoying it. "I caught Herndon last night. Dragged him to the train station and ran him out of town. He knew about the beer and he called the cops on me, to pay me back."

The smile went. The brush stopped. Libby looked at it, turning it over and over. Then tears sprang into her eyes and she tossed the thing hard onto the dressing table. "You hoodlum!" she shouted, eyes hurt and angry. "How could you do that to him?"

"*I'm* the hood? What about him? He's the one who knifed somebody. He's—"

She buried her face in her arms, knocking stuff off the dressing table as she writhed. "I loved him and he loved me," she wailed. "He would have taken me with him. But you butted in before he could make the arrangements. You ruined everything."

"He didn't love you. Look at me, Libby. He had another girlfriend at those apartments the whole time. Look at me, damn it! He wasn't going to take you with him. What would he do that for? He's ten years older than you. He was just using you, Libby! You were had, and I do mean had."

She kept crying. I went to her and put my hands on her shoulders. She whirled around with the hairbrush and nearly raked my eyes out with it. "Stay away from me," she hissed.

"All I ever wanted was to help," I shot back.

"I'm quits with you. You ruined my life. I will hate you as long as you live."

"You're breaking my heart!" I sneered.

She turned to the mirror. "We'll see how tough you are when Daddy finds out about the cash kitty."

"What the hell are you talking about?"

"I lent it to Jimmy," she said, resuming her brushing. "Two hundred and ten dollars. He was going to pay it back before he left town. But you fixed that, all right. He'll never pay it back now, and I wouldn't blame him."

I remembered the wad of soft currency from which Herndon had bought my tall boys. He must have laughed his ass off. "You expect me to take the rap for that? Get real. I'll tell Daddy what you did."

"Go ahead. Try. Who's Daddy going to believe? You're nothing but a jailbird. You can't compete against his baby girl Elizabeth, so don't even bother to try."

She stood, gave herself one final inspection in the mirror, and walked out of the room.

And, for all practical purposes, out of my life. Down through the years, we've mostly met up at funerals. Daddy in '63. Mama in '67. The Bubbas in '70. Uncle Dan in '84. All gone.

So is the Riviera and the train station, both boarded up. National Foods is now a hardware store. The Totem Pole is a Burger King. Fourteenth Street is a war zone, and the Washington Senators became the Texas Rangers—prime competitors of the Detroit Tigers, who in the interim have been better and worse, then better, and are now worse.

The Wesson is still there. So is Redford High. Annie Wilder got divorced and moved away, I never did learn where. Debbie Miller became an English professor at the University of Michigan. My brother Bill married Marybeth and still works at Ford's. You know all about Fast Eddie Anger if you're into pop music at all.

By a very circuitous route, I ended up a private detective. Like Richard

Diamond, Sundance, Roger and Smith, Peter Gunn—guys like that, sort of. Fast Eddie was my client once. So, even, was Libby.

But it wasn't till tonight that I realized my very first client was my mother. Tonight, as I stood in the fairway of the Wayne County Fair, overrun with the memories triggered by the sight of the man running a ball-toss booth.

He stood behind the counter, twenty feet from me. He was too busy to notice as I stared at him, superimposing his image, etched clear in the bright lights of the County Fair midway, against the faded memories of three decades ago. Thirty pounds heavier. Hair grayish and wispy thin. Heavy lines had taken the face, and his bouncy swagger was gone. But it was definitely him.

I pictured myself going up to him. I had a lot of questions. Did he really knife someone? Did he ever get caught? How much jail time had he done in the intervening years? What was it like to be well past fifty and still roaming the country, working the shrinking carnival circuit for nickels and dimes? How many women had there been? How much money? How many promises? Did he ever think about the broken hearts and hurt feelings he left in his wake?

The ball-toss went momentarily vacant and Herndon, as if signaled by radio, turned, looked at me, away, then back: locking his stare with mine. I grinned, remembering the sound of the bat as it hit his head. Now, all these years later, I wished I'd hit him harder—

"Ben! Hey, Ben?"

I turned. Will Somers, a muscular blond eight-year-old, galloped up to me, followed at a distance by my friend Carole Somers, great with child and looking tired. "Found the johns okay?" I asked.

"Finally," Carole said. "Who's that man over there?"

"Who?" I parried.

"That barker in the ball-toss booth. You were staring at him. Do you know him from somewhere?"

I glanced over at Herndon, whose eyes were still fixed on me. "Nobody important," I answered. I took Carole in one arm, Will in the other. "Come on, I'll buy you something to eat."

# The Spring that Ellie Died

STEPHEN WASYLYK

The spring that Ellie died, the crocuses were up early and brighter than ever and the dogwood flowered with an exuberant abundance and Ellie loved it because, as her father said, she was an elf, a woodsprite, a child of nature. But two days had passed and we still had no firm idea of why Ellie had been found dead under the small stone bridge over the rocky creek.

It wasn't much of a bridge. Eight feet high at most, an archway of carefully fitted stones, with a waist-high abutment on either side of the road that curved in the shape of a funnel to direct traffic onto the overpass.

It wasn't much of a creek, either. Shallow enough to be waded easily, yet deep enough for trout to grow to a fair size. Studded with rocks below the bridge, it splashed and murmured and gurgled happily like creeks everywhere.

Ellie's battered bicycle was alongside the parapet, her body below the arch, her head resting on the large rock that had killed her, the water soaking the tattered jeans and the pullover shirt and swirling the long, dark hair and washing away the seeping blood and, seeing that slight body in the glare of my flashlight, I had almost cried, which wasn't what a hardened sheriff's deputy was supposed to do.

But my tears would have been only a prelude to those of the town because almost everyone knew and loved Ellie, and those tears in turn were only a prelude to the anger that the town directed at Sheriff Beeslip and me when we didn't come up with an immediate arrest.

I suppose that Beeslip and I went over it a hundred times.

Ellie had left the small shopping center at the edge of town at just about eight forty-five, pedalling her bicycle into the darkness toward her home a mile away.

Only a mile.

Even pedalling slowly, she would have been home in ten minutes, if Ellie ever pedalled slowly, which she didn't. So she must have reached the bridge in less than five.

Beeslip's theory was that a motorist had hit her as she passed over the bridge or had forced her into the abutment, smashing into the bicycle and catapulting Ellie to the creek bed.

It could have been. She had a large bruise on her forehead and several others on her body where she had landed on the rocks, but the doctor said the cause of death was a skull fracture from the large rock her head had struck. The bicycle was scratched, mortar from the bridge embedded in the tire, the light broken, and the abutment showed scratches and traces of red paint from the bike, but I couldn't understand why a car couldn't have passed with plenty of room, why the flashlight Ellie carried in a clip on the bike was next to the body, or how a thirteen-year-old who had practically lived on a bike since she was seven had been trapped against the abutment. She probably wouldn't have even started across the bridge if she'd seen a car coming.

"What's bothering you, Harvey?" My wife's hand reached across the space between the chairs on our small patio and squeezed mine. "It looks like nothing more than an accident. She could have been pitched over the abutment when a car squeezed her against the side of the bridge."

"Why didn't the person stop? Why wasn't it reported?"

"Panic. They'll come forward after they have a chance to think or realize you're sure to find out who they are. After all, it isn't as though someone would want to hurt Ellie."

I sat and meditated and let the warm spring night speak for me until I could get my thoughts together.

"I suppose what bothers me is that Beeslip and I haven't come up with anything, but I swear I don't know what more we could have done. We've talked to the people who live along that road a half dozen times. None of them saw or heard a thing, and all of them say they were not on the road at any time. We've alerted every auto body shop in a fifty mile radius to report anyone wanting small scratches or dents repaired. We've examined every car in the parking lots and on the road that caught our eye. Nothing. It's as if she pedalled into a vacuum and turned up dead."

"It could have been a complete stranger, just passing through."

"Not on that road. It goes nowhere and leads to nothing. Only the local people use it. Now, today, Beeslip told me some people driving over that bridge have seen something. What, they don't know. A light, a shape that appears for an instant and is gone. They're beginning to say that it's Ellie's ghost."

"People and their imaginations," she said. "I never heard anything more ridiculous in my life."

"Still, Beeslip wants me to go out there and take a look tonight. It's about time for me to leave."

"I'll come along."

"I don't know if Beeslip would approve."

"Never mind Beeslip. After all, I liked Ellie, too."

Fifteen minutes later I pulled off the road and turned off the lights. The only sounds were the subdued watery murmur of the creek swirling around the rocks, the cacophony of insects rushing the season, and the dull croaking of a frog somewhere upstream.

"Let's walk," she said.

I pulled the powerful flashlight from its clamp beneath the dash and we left the car. There was no moon, but the air was clear and the starlight bright so there was enough light to keep us on the road. We crossed the bridge and stood for a few moments on the other side.

"I don't see a thing," she said. "Where's your ghost?"

"I didn't say there was one. It's just that some people reported seeing something. Exactly what it was, if it was anything at all, remains to be seen."

Her hand suddenly tightened on my arm. "Shhh."

We stood motionless.

"What is it?" I whispered.

"I thought I saw something."

"In the dark? I didn't know you had the eyes of a cat."

"A darker shadow that seemed to move."

I pressed the flashlight into her hand. "Use this."

She held it out before her with both hands. The bright light suddenly stabbed through the darkness and focused on the far side of the creek.

A small shape darted beneath the bridge.

I grabbed the light, crossed the road and waited until I heard the faint splashing. I flicked on the light.

A young boy scrambled up the bank.

I sprinted across the bridge and cut him off.

He looked up into the light, his face white, eyes frightened behind the glasses.

"It's Deputy Caswell, Kevin," I said. "Come on up."

He scrambled the rest of the way, a small boy about twelve, with a thin face and slightly protuberant teeth, his shirt hanging loosely, his sneakers and jeans soaked. He was carrying a small battery lantern and I had a hunch I had discovered what the passing people had seen.

My wife came up. "Kevin MacDonald," she said, using the tone women always reserve for young boys caught doing something they shouldn't, "just what on earth are you doing here?"

"Investigating," he said.

"Investigating what?" I asked.

"Maybe Ellie's murder." His voice was angry and tearful.

"No one has really called it that," I said.

"I have. I know."

"You know what?"

"Who killed her." His voice was angrier now.

I took his shoulder. "You'd better come with me."

I put him in the back seat.

"Where are you taking me?"

"To my home," I said.

"Are you going to question me?"

"I certainly am."

"I don't want to talk about it."

"Okay," I said, as I spun the wheel. "Then I'm taking you to your parents."

"I'd rather you didn't. I told my mother I was going to the movies."

"With that lantern?"

"She doesn't know about that."

"I suppose there are other things she doesn't know about. Want to make a deal?"

"What kind of deal?"

"We go to my house for some ice cream, you tell me what you're up to, and I let you off on your corner."

"It's a deal," he said.

The general consensus was that Kevin MacDonald would grow up to teach one of the sciences at a university somewhere. Certainly, he was interested in nothing else. At the age of ten, he had backed one of the family cars out of the garage into a bed of petunias, lowered the garage door, and announced that henceforth the garage was his laboratory. Not quite the completely tolerant parent, his father had warmed his bottom for him for attempting to drive the car but had also compromised to the extent that half of the two-car garage was now indeed Kevin's laboratory, a decision his father had come to regret because one of Kevin's latest projects had been the concoction of a foul smelling mixture that allowed no one to enter the garage for a week and still permeated the entire neighborhood on a windy day.

At any rate, the kid was bright beyond his years, and if he had something to say, I was more than willing to listen.

I sat him at the kitchen table and watched him fiddle with the ice cream.

"All right," I said. "What were you doing out at the bridge?"

"Investigating."

"If you have some information, why didn't you bring it to the sheriff? You know we've been working on Ellie's death for two days."

"Well—" He dug at the ice cream as though he really wasn't interested. "I don't know anything definite."

"Definite or not, you should have told us what you had on your mind. After all, if there is any investigating to be done, we're in a much better position to do it than you are."

"I wanted to go to the sheriff with something he could work on. Who listens to a kid?"

"I do. Let's start at the beginning. You said Ellie was murdered."

"She might have been."

"And you say you know who."

He pushed the ice cream from him slowly. "There was a man who used to hang around the bridge, waiting for the girl."

"What girl?"

"The one he used to meet."

"All right, a man used to meet a girl out at the bridge. How did you know?"

"I like to go down to the creek at night and the bridge is one of my favorite places. It's interesting during the day, but you can see a lot of things at night, too. I sit quietly and wait. Then when I hear something, I turn on my light. There are some 'possums that live near the bridge. I've seen them more than once."

"What about the man?"

"When I turned on my light one night, I guess it was the first he knew someone else was there so he yelled at me to get out. I ran. Once he even threw stones at me. When you shone that light at me tonight, I thought you were him."

"Do you know who he was?"

"No. He would just yell, 'Hey kid, get out of there or I'll beat your head in,' or something like that and I'd run. He sounded as though he meant it."

"Suppose he was there tonight instead of me," I said. "What did you intend to do?"

"Get a look at him so I could tell the sheriff."

My wife rolled her eyes.

"You said he was waiting for a girl. How did you know?"

"Once you go over the bridge, there's a little road there that the fishermen sometimes use. The second time, I saw her go by and turn in there right after he chased me. I guessed he was waiting for her."

"How could you see her in the dark?"

"It's never really *that* dark, once your eyes get used to it, but the car had no top and when she passed, I could see her long hair against the glare from the headlights."

"Did you recognize her?"

"All I know is that it was a girl driving a car."

"What kind of car?"

"I don't know. I'm not interested in cars."

"How many times did you see the man?"

"Three or four."

"Two nights in a row, a week apart, exactly when?"

"Every time on a Monday."

I glanced at my wife. Ellie had been killed Monday night.

"Were you out there the night Ellie was killed?"

He had been answering quickly, without hesitation. This time he waited for a few long seconds and when he spoke, his voice was low.

"No, but I had told her about the 'possums. She said the next time she went by there at night she'd stop and look for them. I guess she forgot."

"Forgot what?"

"What I said. I told her about the man and not to go on Monday. Maybe I shouldn't have said anything about the 'possums at all. If I hadn't, she wouldn't have stopped and he wouldn't have—"

I broke through the pain and the tears in his voice harshly. "Hold it! You don't know that anything like that happened."

"You listen to me, Kevin," said my wife gently. "You had nothing to do with what happened there and I don't want you thinking that way. Do you understand?"

"Yes, ma'am," he said unconvincingly.

Oh hell, I thought. The kid didn't deserve this. He'd told Ellie about the 'possums and maybe she'd stopped to look for them and now she was dead and he was blaming himself. We could say what we wanted to, but he'd think his own thoughts and carry his own burdens, as unfair as they might be, and all we could do was hope we were smart enough to talk him out of it.

"I wish you'd come to us immediately," I said.

"I told you. I didn't think anybody would listen to a kid."

"There is one thing you must promise. Keep away from that bridge until I tell you it is all right to go back, 'possums or no 'possums. Any investigating of this unknown man waiting for the unknown girl will be handled by me and me alone. Is that clear?"

He glanced at me nervously. "Do you think that maybe Ellie didn't stop to look for the 'possums?"

"She probably forgot all about them right after you told her," I reassured him.

I was lying and he probably knew it. Looking for those 'possums was exactly the kind of thing Ellie would do.

My wife put her arm around him. "Always remember, Kevin, that you can't hold yourself responsible for what other people do or don't do."

He smiled suddenly. "Hey, you know what? I'm glad I told you. Are you really going to try to find out who the man is?"

"I really am. If he was there, he might be able to tell us what happened."

"Then why didn't he come and tell you himself?"

I shrugged. "You never know about these things, Kevin. He might think he has a good reason."

I had a pretty good idea of why the man hadn't come forward. The girl. It sounded like a lovers' meeting to me—one that had to be kept secret, which was why he'd chased Kevin in the first place.

But now Kevin was the only one who knew, the only one who could put the man at the bridge on Monday nights.

"Do you think the man would recognize you if he saw you during daylight?" I asked casually.

The thin shoulders almost touched his ears. "He had a flashlight but a kid is a kid to grownups."

He was probably right, but I couldn't gamble.

"Come on," I said. "I'm taking you home."

"A block from home," he said.

"Right to the door. Call it a bonus for your cooperation."

I explained things to his parents and asked them to keep him close to the house for a few days.

"One thing more," I told his father. "He has an idea that if he hadn't told Ellie about the 'possums, she wouldn't have died. He's blaming himself. You'll have to handle him very carefully."

He passed a hand over his face. "The poor kid. I appreciate your telling me and you can bet I'll be doing a lot of talking. Let's hope I'm as good a salesman as I think I am."

"Look at it this way," I said. "It's one sale you have to make."

The next morning Beeslip and I went out to the bridge. The lane Kevin had seen the girl turn into was about twenty or thirty feet beyond the creek and was used by fishermen who drove in to get off the road. It wasn't noted as a lovers' lane. Those were scattered elsewhere.

While Beeslip and I had checked it out when we first investigated, it didn't seem to have any bearing on the problem in front of us because we had construed the accident as having occurred on the bridge itself.

Now we went over it again.

Beeslip was a small, thin man in his late fifties who had trouble finding shirts that fitted properly, so he always looked as if he was wearing someone's hand-me-downs.

We walked down the little lane, which was only about three car lengths long before it ran into a big oak.

"You can see why they picked this as a meeting place," said Beeslip. "Once in here, no one can see you."

"Except a kid down at the creek studying 'possums."

"If the man had just kept quiet, even Kevin wouldn't have noticed."

"I don't think that concerned him. He didn't want Kevin to see the car turn in, which Kevin did."

"Kevin saw one car. How did the man get here?"

"Probably drove, too. There's enough room for two to park."

Beeslip tugged his too-long sleeves above his wrists in an automatic gesture. "You think they were here the night the girl died?"

"The odds say they were."

"I guess you'll want to stake out the place next Monday."

"If nothing turns up before then. They might think it's safe and that we're all through here."

We were walking back to the road when I stopped and squatted beside a bare patch of soft ground that showed the imprint of a tire.

"Forget it," said Beeslip. "If we had found that the morning after, I might think we had something. Two days later, it doesn't mean much."

"Only one way to be sure."

"Has to belong to a fisherman. We couldn't be that lucky."

I shrugged. "No harm in trying, is there? I'll make a cast and run it down to the state police lab. They can give us the make of the tire from the tread design."

"Go ahead. Dumber cops than us have lucked out."

I was back that afternoon. The lab said the tread design was that of a foreign made radial, which to me spelled import because while there might be one or two domestic ragtops around, most of them would be those little sports cars.

The lab man could tell me the kind of tire, but as he explained, there was no distinguishing mark like a cut or a nick, so there was no way to tie the cast into a specific tire on a specific car, which was all right with me for the moment. At least I had something to work on.

Beeslip listened, then called the Motor Vehicle Bureau in the state capital for the registrations of imported convertibles in the county. Their computer spit it out so fast, we had a list in the morning mail.

We went over it name by name, striking out those we considered too far away, since we felt the couple had to live in the immediate vicinity or they wouldn't be so secretive. We narrowed it down to an even dozen and I hit the road.

The first four were owned by young men, and the tire treads differed greatly from the one in the photo the state police lab had made for me.

The fifth was registered to a Debra Vanamen, the address a house just a little outside of town in a new development. I found the street, pulled up behind a green Mercedes and walked around it. There were no scratches or dents, the surface was mirror-like, but I had the feeling even before I looked that the tires would match. There was a trace of mud on the right rear wheel that looked a great deal like the loam alongside the creek, and I scraped a portion into a utility bill envelope I had in my pocket, folded it, and put it away carefully.

The woman who answered the door was an attractive, fortyish type with long, wavy brown hair with beauty parlor frosting.

"I'm looking for Debra Vanamen," I said.

"You've found her. Why are you looking?"

"Is that your car at the curb?"

She frowned. "Have I done something wrong? I don't remember breaking any traffic laws."

"Does anyone other than you ever drive it?"

"My daughter. And my husband on occasion."

"If your daughter is at home, I'd like to see her."

Her eyes were puzzled. "Come in."

I waited in the hallway while she went upstairs. I heard the murmur of voices and then she came down, followed by a girl who couldn't have been more than seventeen. The girl wore a white tennis outfit; her sun-yellow hair was parted in the center, falling to her shoulders, her face round and with a doll-like prettiness.

"This is my daughter, Leslie. Now what is this all about?"

"Last Monday night, a young girl was found dead at the bridge on the other side of town," I said. "You may remember reading about it."

She nodded. "Tragic. Hit and run, I believe."

"Possibly. A car like yours driven by a long-haired girl was seen in the vicinity."

"Good Lord," said the mother.

"I wasn't there," said Leslie quickly.

"You drove the car last Monday?"

She hesitated before nodding. "I still wasn't there."

"Perhaps you weren't," I said. "But the car was."

"You can't prove that."

"I think I can. The car was parked in the lane along the creek at the far side of the bridge. Now, if you weren't driving it, who was?"

"Why on earth should I go there?"

"To meet a man."

"Oh, God," said the mother.

"I met no one," said Leslie. "You can't prove that I did."

"You met the man several times. On Monday nights at about nine. We have a witness."

The mother made a sound deep in her throat and covered her mouth with one hand.

"Forget it," said the girl. "I wasn't there."

"I'd like to remind you," I said slowly, "that a young girl died. If you were not involved, you have an obligation to help us determine who was."

"I'm not saying anything."

"Leslie," said her mother. "There is no reason why—"

"Oh, Mother," said the girl wearily. "Please shut up."

I took them both to the sheriff's office. Beeslip could get no more from her than I did, and when her father and his attorney showed up, we had no choice but to let her go.

Beeslip and I drove to my house for lunch.

Halfway through his sandwich, Beeslip said, "I don't think there is any question the couple was involved somehow. If they merely witnessed what happened, she could have found something to say without giving the man's name. What I'd like to do is find the man."

My wife filled the coffee cups and replaced the percolator firmly. "You two are not too bright," she said.

"I don't deny that," I said, "but we're smart enough to always welcome assistance."

"If you'll think back a few years to when we were young, we did our share of parking in secluded spots but we never *met* there. The only reason a couple would have for meeting like that would be because they couldn't afford to be seen together. Now what is the obvious, overriding reason for that?"

Beeslip popped the last of his sandwich into his mouth and chewed thoughtfully. "The man is married."

"Exactly," said my wife.

"Hold it," I said. "If it was one of those things, she had a car and there are plenty of motels within easy driving distance."

"I thought we agreed they couldn't afford to be seen together."

"He could have met her there."

"You're assuming he also had a car," she said.

"What man doesn't?"

"Try a young married one, who can't afford two cars yet, or even the price of a motel room for his rendezvous, and whose wife uses the car on Monday evening, which leaves him free to meet the girl but he has to walk there. Now who, along that road, would fit that description?"

Beeslip and I were both halfway out the door before she finished talking.

His name was Ebert and he lived in the third house from the bridge. Ellie had lived several houses farther down the road.

He was tall, with loose black hair, a bony face, and a smoldering resentment against the world that showed in the dark eyes. We had no record on him, but we did find out he'd managed to get himself fired from every job he'd ever had because he had a hard, quick temper. At present, he was pumping gas in the service station on the main highway and his wife worked evenings in one of the stores in the small shopping center.

We brought him in and questioned him. He didn't even blink when I mentioned the name Vanamen, but I was sure he was the right man. The trouble was, he was no more inclined to answer than the girl, and we still didn't know how the two of them fitted into Ellie's death.

We were in Beeslip's office, Beeslip behind his desk and Ebert in a chair alongside, while I leaned on a filing cabinet and felt a flickering anger at the unconcerned expression on Ebert's face.

"I think I'll run a check on the Vanamen car," I said. "You probably left prints in it."

That jolted the unconcern from his face.

"The mud on the tire proves the car was there and your prints prove you were in the car. Even a good lawyer won't be able to explain that away. We already know you like to throw stones. Who's to say you didn't go a step further this time?"

He jerked his head around, his eyes angry. "You guys will railroad anybody, won't you? Well, I had nothing to do with it. I admit I used to meet that Vanamen broad there. But not last Monday. I told her I was no longer interested, that it was all over. I didn't need that kid sneaking around. The next thing would be for the story to get out and my wife to know. I love my wife. Vanamen was just a little fling but she was getting possessive. So I called it off. She was there Monday night, all right, but she was there alone. She called me the next day and gave me hell for not meeting her."

I stared at him. "She told you she was there?" I took a step, my expression causing Beeslip to come to his feet nervously. *"Didn't it occur to you she might know what happened to Ellie?"*

His eyes dropped. "Sure. Sure it did. But how could I tell anyone without saying what had been going on?"

"So you decided to protect your own hide. The kid was dead, but all you thought of was yourself."

"My wife," he said. "I told you—"

"What's she going to think of you now?"

He stared at the floor.

"If it's any consolation, her opinion of you can't possibly be any lower than mine."

We put him in a cell until we decided what to do with him, which was probably nothing.

So the girl had been there. I sat and thought about that beat-up bike and that nice, shiny Mercedes without a scratch on it. An idea came so I brought Ellie's bike in and dusted it for fingerprints.

I found two different sets, both feminine.

I showed them to Beeslip and he looked up, his eyes cold, and said, "Go get her."

When they were all there—the Vanamen girl, the parents, and the attorney—I took Ellie's bike and slammed it down before her and waited, but her eyes were fixed on nothing in particular.

"Would you like to tell us how your prints managed to get on this bike?"

She didn't say a word.

Beeslip sighed. "I suppose we might as well get the county attorney over here and have her charged."

The mother rose to her feet slowly as though she was bearing a great weight on her shoulders, a weight that diminished her and made her seem smaller.

"It wasn't her," she whispered. "It was me."

"You can't protect her," I said. "The fingerprints will say she was there."

She held out her hands. "See for yourself."

The muscles in Vanamen's face seemed to have lost all life. The flesh sagged, his mouth hung open, and his color had disappeared.

"Leslie was protecting me," she whispered. "She didn't want her father to know."

I looked at Beeslip. We'd assumed all along it had been the girl, because that's what Kevin had said—a girl with long hair—but now I remembered that Ebert had called her the Vanamen broad and hadn't given her a name.

"Don't say anything more," snapped the attorney.

He might as well have saved his breath because she'd been walking around with it for four days and there was no stopping the torrent of words now.

She'd gone there to meet Ebert and had become angrier and more frustrated as the minutes passed. Ellie had stopped to look for the 'possums and Mrs. Vanamen had seen the light on the bridge. She assumed it was Kevin, the reason Ebert had given her for breaking off the affair, and a burning resentment had made her pick up a stone and throw it as hard as she could.

In the dark, without a clear target, that stone should have missed Ellie by a mile. Nine hundred and ninety-nine times out of a thousand it would have.

This was the exception.

The stone hit Ellie and knocked her over the parapet. Mrs. Vanamen had seen the dark shape plunge and the flashlight fall and realized what she had done. She ran to the spot but could see nothing, so she went down and found Ellie dead. The anger and frustration were now fear and panic. All she knew was that she had killed someone with no way to explain how or why or what she was doing there, so she'd taken Ellie's bike and smashed it against the abutment several times to make it look like a hit and run, and had taken off.

"I didn't mean to do it," she said dully.

I suppose she meant that, but you don't hurl a stone at someone without malice in your heart, and trying to cover up the results will win you no points in any hall of justice.

Late that night I went outside for a breath of air before I turned in. I looked at the starlit sky and savored the balmy air that would soon turn hot and still. More flowers would bloom and the countryside would become lush and green as it had for countless years and would for countless more.

Even new generations of 'possums would find their way to the water beneath the bridge, perhaps watched by twelve-year-old boys armed with flashlights and curiosity, and there would be nothing to distinguish this spring from all the others that were inexorably the same.

Except the tragic, unnecessary death of an elfin wood-sprite with an insatiable thirst for nature, and a dark cloud in the happy memories of a small boy, who wanted only to share the thrill of discovery with a friend.

# So Long, Lana Turner

WILLIAM T. LOWE

This is not a simple car theft," I declared. "I think you may have a major crime on your hands here, officer."

"Let's hope not, sir," the young trooper said politely.

"Well, you just wait and see if you don't." I knew I sounded peevish, but I couldn't help it. First I'd had to walk almost two miles out of my way to call the troopers, and then wait almost an hour, and then when one shows up he looks like just a rookie.

I pointed at my evidence. "It's not just the New Jersey license plates up here in northern New York. It's the man's empty wallet. It's the safe deposit box key that was hidden. And the facial tissue with lipstick on it. Or maybe that's blood. All that looks mighty suspicious to me!"

"Yes, sir," he said, still very polite. "And you found these things over there in the high grass?" He made it sound like only a senile old man would go poking around in tall grass and weeds.

"I told you. I pick up empty cans." I shook my plastic bag of empties. "And bottles, too."

"Yes, sir. What makes you think these items are connected with each other, sir?"

"Because they weren't here yesterday afternoon," I said triumphantly.

We were standing on the side of a road about two miles north of where I live in Clinton County, New York. It's a simple two-lane road that runs between the village of Fountain and the larger town of Keeseville. There's a little turnout there, just a place to pull off the highway to stretch your legs or switch drivers or change a baby's diaper. It's small, only big enough for three cars at a time, surfaced with gravel and outlined with big stones. No picnic tables, and only one trash bin that hasn't been emptied for a year.

The turnout doesn't offer much in the way of scenery, but you can see the Adirondack Mountains to the south, and if you climbed a tree, you could see Vermont across the lake to the east. It was June but a nice breeze kept the black flies away.

"The sun was shining on an empty beer can," I explained again, "and that led me to find these things. I thought it was peculiar that they should all be here at the same time, so I walked down to Tim's Esso and called your dispatcher. That's a mile more than I usually walk." I didn't mean to sound so surly; it was just that I was excited. I'm a widower; I live with a married daughter and I build bird houses. Life is pretty dull, but now out of pure luck I was about to be involved in a police investigation.

"I'm sorry about that, sir," the young trooper said. "You could have waited for me at the service station."

"Oh, that's all right." I could tell he was sincere. "I'll cut back some tomorrow."

After I made the call, I'd walked back to the turnout to wait. I was sitting on a big rock when the New York State Police car pulled up, a dark blue sedan with a broad gold band on the sides and the state seal on the doors. The officer who got out was very young. I don't know why I had expected someone more my own age.

His name tag read MARION, S. He was tall and lanky, and I had to admit he seemed competent enough. He was wearing the new state police side-arm, the Glock 9mm semi-automatic pistol; I had read about it in the paper.

Right away I had to be entered in his notebook.

"Your name, sir?"

"Hank Foster."

"Is that H-e-n-r-y?"

"I prefer H-a-n-k."

"You happened to be walking by when you found some items you thought were suspicious?"

"No, I did it on purpose. I mean, I walk for my health."

"And you're retired, sir?"

I wanted to rattle my bag of empties at him and say I was in the salvage business, but I didn't. I admitted I was retired.

I put the things I had found on the hood of the trooper car. The wallet was the conventional type that goes in a hip pocket with pockets for credit cards and so on. This one was good leather, not plastic, and it was curved and flattened to indicate that it had been carried in a pocket for quite a while. Still, it was not worn or scuffed, not ready to be discarded. No initials on the outside, no identification on the inside.

Officer Marion S picked it up. "Maybe some tourist just bought himself a new wallet and stopped here for a break and decided to transfer his stuff from his old one to the new one." He didn't sound like he really thought that was what had happened, and I didn't either.

"No, I don't think so," I said. "He wouldn't forget his key." I held it up to make my point.

Someone had cleaned out the wallet before he threw it away, but he missed one thing. I almost missed it myself. Jammed down in one end, behind the flap where large bills go, was a flat safe deposit box key. You couldn't see it and you would never know it was there unless you happened to feel it with your fingers. No bank name; just three stamped numerals that must be the number of the box.

Marion S put the key in a small envelope and picked up one of the license plates. They were this year's issue, in perfect condition, not defaced in any way.

"You'll want to contact the New Jersey Department of Motor Vehicles," I began, "to find out who these plates were registered to . . ." Marion S gave me the same look I used to give a student who had said something quite obvious. I shut up, and we looked at the plates in silence.

I guessed he had the same questions in mind as I had. Why stop out here on the highway and take the plates off a car and throw them away? Answer: because someone is looking for that particular car. But why then attract attention by driving around in a car with no license plates on it? Answer: you wouldn't. You would have another set of plates ready to put on the car. Did the same person who owned the car also own the now-empty wallet? I didn't have an answer for that.

The young trooper was walking around the turnout, looking at a few old tracks in the gravel and the white painted stones that needed painting again. I stood by the trooper car and kept quiet.

He came back and picked up the New Jersey plates again. "You know, Mr. Foster," he said carefully, "there's a lot of cars that cross the border up at Champlain. Both ways. And not all tourists, if you know what I mean."

"I know," I said, but I hadn't thought of it before. Of course he meant all the smuggling that goes on in and out of Canada. Champlain isn't two hours away from this spot. There are ten border crossings in New York and Vermont, and Champlain probably is by far the busiest. Customs and the Border Patrol have their hands full. Smugglers use pleasure boats on the lake and the Amtrak train, but the favorite means is the private car. The biggest volume is in cocaine.

"I'll put the word about these plates on the computer, but chances are the car these belonged to is long gone. Up in Quebec or down in West Palm."

He glanced around the turnout again. "As for the rest of it, Mr. Foster, I think it's just coincidence."

I couldn't say anything to that. If there had been a crime, a murder perhaps, and if it was connected to cocaine smuggling, Officer Marion S couldn't discuss it with me. I was a civilian, and to him a pushy one at that. But I was sure of one thing: whatever was going on, I wanted to be in on it.

I tried to sound sheepish, which is not easy for me to do. "I guess you're right, officer." I paused for a moment to change the subject. "Can I ask you something?"

"Shoot."

"What's the 'S' for? Steve or Sam?"

"Steve."

"When you find out about those plates, will you let me know, Steve, please? I'll be here tomorrow."

He grinned at me. "Sure thing, Hank."

He picked up my trophies and drove away. I picked up my bag of empties and started home. I was jubilant. This had been a big event for me and it wasn't over yet; I still had my foot in the door.

A car passed me on the way to Keeseville. The driver was Lana Turner. I caught a glimpse of her bright blonde hair and her cheerful smile. I waved and she waved back.

Lana Turner isn't her real name. She's a young woman who reminds me of the sweater girl queen of my undergraduate days. About six weeks ago a car stopped alongside me on the highway and the driver leaned out to ask me a question. She was a young woman with great natural beauty—blue eyes, cute chin, a generous mouth. Her hair was brass blonde, and she wore a tight yellow sweater. I gave her the name Lana Turner.

She asked me where the Page place was, and I told her. She thanked me and smiled before she drove away. It was the special smile pretty young women can give to older men. It's warm and open and unguarded because they don't have to be wary of being misunderstood or thought flirtatious. It's a very rare smile, and one that a lonely old man will treasure.

I was dog-tired when I got home; those extra two miles hadn't been in the energy budget.

That night I went to sleep thinking about that empty wallet. What became of the credit cards and the baby pictures and the other trivia that must have been in it? Why would anybody stand on a highway in plain sight and clean out another man's wallet? Answer: he was looking for something and he was in a hurry to find it. What was so important? Answer: not cash; he would have found that right away and heaved the wallet with everything else inside it. It had to be something small, like a claim check, or a receipt. Or the hidden key he didn't find.

So what did happen to the contents, the bits and pieces of someone's identity? Answer: they were still there, somewhere around the turnout. Why was I so sure? Whoever had taken the wallet in the first place had been careless. First, he didn't find the key. Then he didn't dispose of the wallet very well; anybody could have found it. So he would have been careless about the little, unimportant things. And I would find them.

If I was lucky, I would have something else to show Trooper Steve Marion this afternoon. He would be glad to have me helping him on this case. I picked up my plastic bag and started down the road.

I am doing all this walking to avoid an operation I don't want to have, by the way. Last fall my seventy-year-old heart staged a mutiny. An angiogram showed that the left side was not working right; an artery was silted up or something. A cardiac specialist young enough to be my grandson told my daughter and me there was nothing to be too alarmed about; he did bypass surgery all the time and almost always successfully.

The bypass job didn't sound good. First they saw through the middle of your rib cage and make an opening large enough to hide a football. Then they root around and find the diseased artery and chop it out. Then they splice in a vein they have pirated from one of your legs. I said no. We negotiated; my daughter and the doctor on one side; me on the other. I won a six-month postponement during which I promised to eat sensibly, go to Sunday school, and exercise moderately.

That's what I'm doing. I walk about three miles every day. Of course I can't repair the damage to that one artery, but I can make the others work harder. The doctor says I'm still a prime candidate for a heart attack, but I do feel better.

That's how this stretch of road became an extension of my front yard. I know every crack and bump, every weed and tree. The empty cans and bottles began to bother me. At first I picked them up and threw them farther back in the bush. Then I began to save them. If I am going to spend so much time on this road, by thunder it is going to be clean.

Now I carry a bag for the empties. A local charity redeems them, and the money from the deposits goes to a children's hospital. There is a tiny sense of accomplishment, and I don't care what the natives think. They're as bad about littering as the tourists. Worse, because they live here.

On my exercise route I pass the Page place. This is a large garage set back from the road. A sign over the door reads PAGE AUTO REPAIR. Several cars are always parked in front and by the side of the building. A large field in the rear is crowded with other cars, new and old, kept, I assumed, to provide repair parts.

Farther back is the Page residence, a one story frame house. A small house trailer is parked on one side. There is a scraggly flower bed with a concrete bird bath. The house needs paint, the yard needs raking.

There always seemed to be activity around the garage. I knew Walter Page by sight, and if I saw him as I walked by, I would wave and he would wave or nod in return. He was a heavyset man with a ragged black beard. His son, Walt Junior, was one of those unfortunate kids whose life was already over.

He had been a football star in high school and had his picture in the paper twice. After graduation he could at least have gone into one of the armed services, but he didn't. Now he worked in the family garage and would never see the outside of Clinton County. The boy who had been so fast on his feet now walked with a flatfooted step and was getting heavy like his father.

Where Lana Turner fit into this family I didn't know. She must have been kin from somewhere, come for a long stay or maybe permanently. After she arrived a few weeks ago, the Pages brought in the second-hand house trailer that was parked beside the house; I assumed that was her living space.

Lana must have done the shopping for the household; I saw her every day or so driving back and forth into town. I felt sorry for her. She was too pretty to be stuck up here in the mountains. If she stayed, she would wind up like so many other young girls: too short a youth, too few choices, fated to marry a man who worked with his hands instead of his head.

"Pretty young woman," I wanted to say to her, "don't waste your life here. Don't let the world leave you; catch up while there's still time." I never spoke to her, of course. It was just an old man's thought as he trudged his endless miles. But I would wave, and she would wave back, and smile at me.

At the turnout I was lucky. The trash bin was the obvious place to start searching and in twenty minutes I had found three credit cards and a driver's license, all issued in the same name. They were in the bottom of the bin, the credit cards bent double and the license ripped in two. Digging for them was a filthy job, but I didn't mind. I was paying my dues in the detective business.

These things had to be from the wallet I found yesterday. Someone had stood right here and gutted the wallet, probably dropping them on the ground. Then he picked them up and rammed them down the side of the trash bin as far as he could reach. That might have seemed safe enough, but it was a careless way to try to hide a person's identification.

I sat down on the big rock to examine my discoveries. The credit cards didn't tell me much; the license was the jackpot. It was a buff-colored

New York license issued to a Thomas Swinney with a post office box address in Syracuse, New York. His height was five ten, his eyes brown, his age thirty-eight. The photo was too tiny to show much except a jowly face with a thin black mustache and hair. He could have been anything from a bartender to a truck driver.

I was delighted. I couldn't wait to introduce Mr. Thomas Swinney to my friend Steve Marion, the trooper. Even if this wide spot in a back road had been the end of the line for him.

When Steve arrived, I stood up. "Howdy, Mr. Foster," he said. I had hoped he might say something like "Howdy, partner."

"Those license plates were from a stolen car, all right."

"Yes," I said, trying to keep the excitement out of my voice, "and this may just be the man who stole it."

Steve was impressed with my finds. He didn't waste any time; he got on the radio in his car and asked for any available information. He wasn't being polite now; he was all business.

I sat on my rock and waited. I was sure we were on the track of some criminal activity. This area has a history riddled with crime. The road I walked on every day had seen its share of criminals. During Prohibition it was one of the roads bootleggers used to transport whisky from Canada down to Albany and on south to New York City. Big touring cars, loaded so heavily their springs were flat, crept down it at night to hide in barns during the day while the cargoes were split up into other cars and driven south.

Illegal liquor was big business then, but it couldn't hold a candle to the smuggling today. Illegal aliens get the most newspaper coverage. "Sixteen foreign nationals discovered in false floor of truck." They come from half the countries of the world to try their luck with the Border Patrol. Cigarette smuggling goes on constantly, but the customs agents can usually spot the contraband from fifty paces away.

The biggest game of all these days is narcotics smuggling. The wave of cocaine has swept north from Florida and reached into Canada. It travels north across the border by courier, and payment in the form of cash comes down, again by courier. Like cash, cocaine is small in bulk, easily concealed, worth more than its weight in gold.

Interstate 87 is our main north-south artery, since it runs from Albany to Montreal, four lanes all the way. But, as in Prohibition days, it is more discreet to use side roads for moving a load of coke or cash. And, as in the old days, the one place strange cars can go in and out unnoticed is the friendly neighborhood auto repair shop. Quite suddenly I thought of the Page place, just a mile away.

"Thomas Swinney's got a record. Grand theft auto." I jumped at

Steve's voice behind me. "Sorry, Hank," he said. "I didn't mean to startle you."

"That's all right," I said quickly. "So he's got a record? And I suppose you found out he's missing?"

Steve was puzzled. "How'd you know that? Yes, his P.O. says he doesn't know where Swinney is."

"His P.O.?"

"His parole officer. Says Swinney hasn't reported in the last month or so."

"Well, he's not missing. He's up here. We've just got to find his body."

Steve gave me a long look. I was afraid of what he might be thinking. Busybody old man . . . lives on TV shows . . . got lucky with a wild guess . . . Suddenly I thought Steve was going to tell me to forget the whole thing and go home.

Instead he asked me, quite seriously, "Why do you think this subject is dead?"

"Because," I said as carefully as I could, "somebody has tried very hard to hide the fact that Swinney was here. And somebody knows that other people will want to know where Swinney is."

Steve listened, but he shook his head. "You're reaching, Hank."

"Maybe, but I don't think so. Swinney didn't just happen to lose his wallet. Some kid didn't just happen to find it and empty it." I shook my head. "Swinney was important for something he had or something he knew. Remember the key, Steve."

By now we were sitting side by side on the rocks, Steve with his cap pushed back, me rubbing my bald spot where the sun had gotten to it. Steve looked at me thoughtfully.

"Where do you think this alleged body might be found?"

I had given this some thought; I was ready for him. "Remember now, this person, the killer, is careless, an amateur. He's got a body on his hands, or rather, in his car. Maybe he's panicky because he didn't pick a better time and place, or because pretty soon he will be missed from wherever it is he's supposed to be.

"Maybe he thinks of Lake Champlain. Certainly not far away and certainly deep enough. But this time of year the boat launches are crowded and he's sure to be seen.

"The Civil War iron mines around Palmer Hill are less than an hour from here, but you can't drive right up to the old shafts. You would have to carry or drag the body a long way. That would take time, and there's always the chance of being seen.

"Then he thinks of the old granite quarry on Route 9 below Fountain. Once you move a couple of sawhorses out of your way, you can drive up pretty close, and one pit is full of water. A few rocks in the pockets and that's the last anyone would ever see of Mr. Thomas Swinney."

Steve tugged on his cap. "We've got no real solid reason to think Swinney was killed around here." I was glad he said "we." "I don't have much to take to the lieutenant or the BCI."

I knew that meant the Bureau of Criminal Investigation. "Look, Steve," I said earnestly, "you've got a known felon, disappeared under suspicious circumstances, probably connected to the narcotics trade . . ."

"What makes you think that?"

"It figures. Boosting cars and running dope go hand in hand. I read the papers."

"It's not very much," Steve said, "but I'll lay it out for the lieutenant." He stood up and started toward his trooper car. "Is there anything else, Hank?"

The sun was hot and I was tired. "Yes. Drive me home, will you? It's time for my nap."

The next morning I got an early start. I climbed a fence and went cross-country, carrying an old pair of binoculars. I wanted to check on something at the Page place. In half an hour I was strolling along the highway as usual. I heard a car behind me and hoped it might be Lana Turner. I had missed seeing her yesterday.

It was Steve. He motioned for me to get in the front seat with him. "The Wilmington patrol picked up a body early this morning," he told me.

"Was it Swinney?"

"It was him." Steve tapped the radio. "They just got confirmation on his fingerprints."

I tried hard to appear casual. "So he went for a swim in the quarry."

"Nope," Steve said. "He was high and dry." I twisted around to face him and saw him grinning at me.

"Relax, Hank. You were close enough. A couple of geology students found the body on the road into the quarry late yesterday, and they phoned it in." Steve told me the students had been prospecting around when they saw a car dump something and drive off. Apparently the driver saw them and got panicky. The students couldn't identify the car or the driver.

"How was Swinney killed?"

"Blow on the head. Something like a jack handle or a poker. Dead about two days, like you figured."

"Anything in his pockets that might indicate what he was doing here?"

Steve shook his head. "A pair of needle-nose pliers and some short pieces of electrical wire. Stuff you might use to hotwire a car. He must have been good at that."

From the way he was looking at me I realized Steve was holding something back. "Come on, Steve. What else have you got?"

"You remember that safe deposit box key? It was Swinney's, all right, in a Syracuse bank. They got a court order to open it, and guess what they found. Ninety-three thousand dollars in cash."

My mouth dropped open. "Wow! That takes Mr. Swinney out of the bush leagues." I thought about it. "He couldn't make that kind of money stealing cars, could he?" Steve shook his head. "Then there's your narcotics connection, Steve."

"Yep. We thought of that."

We drove along slowly. The sun was already hot, and the top of Whiteface Mountain gleamed in the distance. I was afraid that at any minute the radio would send Steve off on other business, and I had something else to throw at him.

"Steve, you remember you said those New Jersey plates belonged to a blue two-door Dodge Diplomat? Well, I know where that car is. It's in the field behind the Page place."

He frowned at me. "You couldn't possibly know where that individual car is, Hank."

"Hear me out now. This morning I sneaked around there with this pair of glasses. That Dodge is sitting there right now."

Steve shook his head. "They probably built fifty thousand of that model and in that color scheme."

"So what?"

"It would be stupid to keep a hot car right there on the place."

"What better place to keep a stolen car than in a field of other cars? And especially if you plan to use it again."

Steve was deliberately dragging his feet. "You'd have to check the vehicle serial number to know it was the same car."

"Then you'll need a search warrant, won't you?"

He looked at me without speaking and I was afraid I had pushed too hard, but I kept on. This police business was exhilarating; I couldn't stop.

"You're not just looking for a stolen Dodge, Steve. Tell your lieutenant you're looking for a car that's been used to carry cocaine across the border. Maybe bring cash back into the States.

"During Prohibition they used to take the seats out of those big old Packards and Studebakers to bring down cases of scotch from Canada. Now they're running cocaine up and hiding it in spare tires and seat cushions and under the hood . . ."

"I know all that," Steve interrupted.

"That pair of pliers and electrical wire they found on Swinney. What does that suggest? Maybe he had figured out a new hiding place in a car. Not the radio, that's too small, but maybe the stereo speakers. Pull them out, stash the dope in the space, put the covers back on . . ."

Steve looked at me appraisingly. "You're guessing again, Hank. I admit you've been guessing pretty good, but you're guessing."

I was feeling so good I was absolutely reckless. "It's called deduction, Officer Marion. Basic deduction."

"Speculation," he said. "Pure and simple speculation." He put his hands on the wheel. "I've got to go. Drive you home?"

"No, thanks. I need the exercise. Tell me, Steve, are you going to try for a warrant?"

"I'll see what the drug enforcement boys say. Chances are they'll go for it. And to tell you the truth, Hank, that Page outfit has been known to dabble in stolen cars. They chop them up for parts." He reached for the ignition key. "I'll be in touch."

"Hang on a minute." There was something on my mind, and I had to speak up now.

"Steve, there's a young lady who lives on the Page place. Some kind of distant cousin, I think. She seems like a nice girl, and I don't think she could possibly have anything to do with whatever might be going on over there." I paused and glanced at Steve. He sat quietly, waiting for me to finish. "Anyway, I feel sorry for her. Old Mrs. Page can't be much company for her, and there she is, a single, attractive young girl there with a hardshell uncle and that young stud Walt Junior . . ."

Steve held up his hand to stop me. "Who are you, Tennessee Williams? I get the picture." He grinned, but it was an understanding grin. "All right, if we go in for a look around, I'll keep her out of it."

"Thanks, Steve."

I got out and he drove away. Now I felt better. I couldn't protect Lana Turner myself, but Steve had said he would look out for her. This detective work might be fun, but I wouldn't want to create any problems for the pretty young woman with a kind smile for an old man.

I felt so good I walked an extra mile on the way home.

Things moved fast after that. The next morning Steve said, "We got the warrant to search the Page place. The lieutenant says he'll have my hide if we come up empty."

"Don't worry. Tell him I'll help write up your commendation."

"Some drug enforcement boys will be here at noon. We'll go in then."

Steve was perfectly relaxed; I hadn't been so excited in years. A real police raid, just like in the movies.

"About the raid, Steve," I said, trying to sound as calm as he did, "will I be issued a sidearm, or am I going in strictly as an observer? Could I bring a camera along?"

Steve just stared straight ahead through the windshield. I wondered why he didn't answer my question, and I was about to repeat it.

"You've been a big help on this thing, Hank," he said finally. I noticed his face was getting red. "But you can't go with us."

I couldn't go? I was stunned. It was like a kick in the stomach. Of course they didn't want an old man along. Get out of the way; let the professionals take over. This is the real world; who needs a has-been schoolteacher. My own face got red. I opened the door and stepped out.

"Wait a minute, Hank."

"Save it, Steve," I snapped. I was furious but I was more hurt than mad. I had trouble breathing. I started down the side of the road and Steve followed me.

"Hold it, Hank. Please." I stopped and turned around. There was a strained look on Steve's young face. "Hank, take away thirty years and you'd be a great partner."

All right, it wasn't his fault. This was police work, and I was a civilian. "Thanks, Steve." I started down the road. "See you around, son."

Then a giant belt cinched itself around my chest and choked the breath out of me and a thousand needles stabbed into my left arm. The sky tilted violently and I blacked out. I think Steve caught me before I hit the pavement.

I didn't know anything else for three days. Steve got me to a hospital in time, and the repair work on my heart was successful. I won't be walking so much any more, but Steve and I are planning to do some fishing real soon. He told me the details of what I missed.

The troopers and the federal agents had their raid on the Page property and found things pretty much as Steve and I predicted. The DEA knew the crime families were delivering cocaine into Canada by concealing it in automobiles. They brought the cash payments down the same way. The families didn't trust each other completely, so they switched cars and cargoes frequently on the run from Florida to Canada and back again.

The Page place was just one of many transfer spots. Drivers were changed frequently, too, and that's where Thomas Swinney came on board. He made a number of trips between the Page place and other points in New Jersey and Pennsylvania. The spare license plates were just tools of the trade.

Swinney had made a lot of money and bragged about it, and that got him killed. By Walt Junior, who was jealous of Swinney's attentions to Lana Turner.

I guess I was wrong about her. Her real name was Judy something. She had a husband doing eight to twelve years in Dannamora. She was the real boss of the Page operation; the mob had planted her there to protect its interests, and she made a lot of the runs into Canada.

It seems she hated the mountains and she elected Thomas Swinney and his bankroll to be her ticket out of the boondocks. But one night up at the turnout, Walt Junior dissolved the partnership with a piece of angle iron. He searched for a clue to Swinney's money, but he was careless and didn't find the key. He and his father and an uncle are out on bail, awaiting trial.

So is the pretty young woman who reminded me so much of my college dreamgirl, Lana Turner. I can still see that bright blonde hair and that warm open smile. I can't believe I was entirely wrong about her. Anyone that pretty can't be all bad.

So long, Lana Turner. It was nice knowing you.

# To Kill a Cavanaugh

## BRENDA MELTON BURNHAM

S tate Senator William Cavanaugh departed this world from the back parking lot of his own grocery store. The three bullet holes in his upper torso added a certain notoriety to the whole affair. The Golden City *Courier* ran bold headlines for days.

All of which distressed me. No, that's not quite true. I began with sorrow and moved on to distress. Then I became angry.

First off, Willie was my cousin. At one time he and I had been boon companions, before he grew up and became just another typical Cavanaugh male—pompous, silly, and rich.

But that's beside the point. He was a Cavanaugh. As my mother used to say, "Always remember, Jane. Family is what counts."

Who would dare to kill a Cavanaugh?

"The police are handling it," my brother Harry assured me. "Chief Porter will find the killer." He'd been saying that the last four days, ever since Willie was shot.

"Had to have been a drug-crazed hippie," my youngest brother Arthur added. "After the money from the store." He'd been saying that all along as well.

"Maybe it was a drug deal," Harry's son Teddy joked, which made me so mad I sputtered.

"The only thing Chief Porter can find is his mouth when there's food around. A drug-crazed hippie? In Golden City? Everyone in town, including any drugtakers, knows Archie Babcock manages the grocery stores, and their income, for Willie." I didn't bother to acknowledge Teddy's contribution to the conversation.

Harry didn't try to argue with me. "Maybe if we offered a reward?"

"That's good," Arthur agreed quickly. "For information leading to an arrest or something like that."

"We could get it on the *Most Wanted* program on TV," Teddy chimed

in, his eyes wide with anticipation. "When they interview me, I could
say . . ."

"What we *could* do," I said, "is figure out who might've wanted to kill
him."

But none of them could imagine anyone wanting to kill Willie.

I sat in the parlor of my house—which had been my parents' house
before me, and my grandparents' house before them—and thought about
Willie. The Cavanaughs are a prolific family (one reason why they domi-
nated Kern County perhaps. Another was that they married money.), so
there were always lots of cousins around. We had taken lessons on the
piano in the corner, played hide and seek in the dark crannies, dressed up
in clothes from trunks in the attic. Outside there was the vast expanse of
lawn for games like Red Rover and Cops and Robbers and the orchard
beyond for picnics.

Willie had been a scrawny kid with thick glasses and a bad stutter. I
had been a plain little thing (My mother, a beautiful woman herself, was
always careful that no one should ever call me "Plain Jane." And no one
ever did, in my hearing.) with a badly scarred leg from the fire that had
killed my sister. In a family where physical attractiveness was the norm,
Willie and I did not fit the pattern.

So we were drawn together by a common age (having both been born in
that most momentous month: October of 1929) and a common bond.
And we had shared a secret, a secret I have never told to anyone. I
doubted Willie had, either.

During the summer of our eighth year, when the moon was full, we
would sneak out of our beds and find the spot of grass where the light
shone brightest. There we performed our "Moon Magic" dance. This consisted of jumping about a great deal and "rubbing" the moonlight onto
our bodies, all the while muttering incomprehensible gibberish that we
thought added to the spell.

What was the purpose of all this? For me it was to heal the scarred and
crooked leg—and even perhaps to make me pretty, I suppose. For Willie it
was to make him grow tall and strong and speak clearly. Not that we ever
actually told each other these things. There was no need.

Did the magic work? Well, although puberty came to him late, Willie
did grow as tall and handsome as any Cavanaugh male. Speech therapy,
and increasing confidence, cured his stuttering.

For me the success was less visible. My leg never lost its slight limp.
The scars never disappeared. On my best days I was never described as
"pretty." But my spine grew straight and my resolve stiff and strong. I
consider these traits far more desirable.

But I did not spend all my time woolgathering and reminiscing. I thought about the people who knew Willie. I did not agree with Arthur's theory of some drug-crazed individual. Nor did I believe it was an attempted robbery.

First, of course, there was his wife Imogene. One's spouse should always be considered suspect whenever there's a sudden death, I think. In any marriage of long standing there must be a number of reasons to wish yourself rid of your mate. (I myself have never been tempted to marry, and from the evidence I've seen, it has been one of my wisest decisions.)

Imogene was a large, lumpy woman with the temperament of rising bread dough. While in personal terms theirs might not have been the happiest of unions, it had been a successful one. Her father had owned a small grocery which he built into a chain that spanned several counties. Her money had helped launch Willie's political career; the Cavanaugh name had helped her overcome the drawbacks of looks and personality.

The next morning I baked a chicken casserole from one of my grandmother's favorite recipes and dropped by to visit the widow.

"Jane, how thoughtful of you," Imogene acknowledged. "Come in." She wisely was not wearing black; it wasn't kind to her.

Her son Leroy and his wife Ruthann rose to greet me as we entered the large living room, painted dark green and filled with heavy furniture upholstered in pink cabbage roses. I'd seen the very same layout in a 1953 *Better Homes and Gardens*.

"How nice of you to come by," Ruthann murmured. She was one of those wispy women who considered murmuring the height of gentility. "So few people bother after the services are over."

"We were just advising Mother that she ought to get shut of this big house now that Dad's gone," Leroy boomed, apparently expecting me to join in his plan. "Too much work. She'd be much happier living with Edith."

His sister walked into the room in time to hear his last words. "Why shouldn't she live with you and Ruthann?" she remarked in a tone that implied the discussion was not a new one. Edith had the Cavanaugh good looks; where she had gotten her sullen disposition was beyond me. "Billy's gone off to college now. She could have his old room."

Imogene smiled and said nothing.

"We were only thinking of you, dear." Ruthann's hands made vague little arabesques. "Since the divorce and all . . ."

The divorce had been a messy one. At one point Willie had actually gotten into a physical battle with his son-in-law, Chip, or so the stories went. In my opinion any man well into his forties who chased twenty-year-old dollies, continued to brag about his former prowess as a high school quarterback, and was still called Chip hardly lent luster to the Cavanaugh family anyway. That he and Willie had always been at loggerheads was of interest to me, however.

"Where is Chip now?"

"He's moved north to Topeka," Edith answered reluctantly.

Topeka just happened to be the state capital, where Willie kept an apartment while the Senate was in session. I noted the fact before returning to the earlier topic of conversation.

"Do you want to sell the house, Imogene?"

Before she could answer Leroy said, "No reason she should. Ruthann and I could move in here . . ."

"Oh, I see," Edith snapped. "You want the house, but you don't want Mother."

"You know she and Ruthann don't see eye to eye . . ."

"Imogene," I said, above the din, "could I have a glass of water? I forgot to take my pill."

"Of course."

She rose and led me out to the kitchen. I fished around in my purse for a bottle of aspirin to support my excuse to cut her out of the herd.

I dutifully washed it down with the water she provided, then repeated, "Do you want to move?"

She fiddled with her heavy gold wedding set and didn't look at me. "I don't know what to do, Jane. Willie always made the decisions, you know that." She sniffled into a handkerchief she pulled from her pocket. "What am I going to do without him?"

"Oh, for heaven's sake." I rinsed the glass and put it back on the shelf. "He's been off in Topeka these past twenty-five years messing up the state with the rest of those idiots and left you behind most of that time. He bullied you unmercifully when he was here. He went off with that silly little fluff, Tammy Nichols, from the grocery store not long ago and was gone for three days." Shock tactics and hard truths were always the best way to deal with Imogene. Otherwise she puddled around in meaningless pieties forever. "Didn't that bother you?"

"Yes." She continued to twist her rings. In the background I could hear the argument escalating in the living room. "It bothered me a lot. I was so . . . embarrassed. Hurt."

"You should've shot him then and not waited two whole months."

"Jane!" Her head jerked up, and she actually looked me in the eye. "I never would've shot Will. Never."

I believed her.

*    *    *

"Has Chip Woodruff been in town lately?" I asked my brother Harry later that day. He and Flora had invited me for dinner before the shocking events of the past week had occurred.

"He was here last week. Something to do with the divorce, I believe. You don't think he . . ."

"Why not? They never did get along. And if he thought Willie had anything to do with Edith's decision . . ."

"But he didn't," Flora interrupted. "Will didn't approve of the divorce."

This was news to me. But then I am not one to encourage gossip without good cause. Which there was now. "Really?" I remarked to my sister-in-law.

She nodded. "He didn't think it was good for the family name. Especially with him up for reelection this year."

"I thought he was retiring."

"Changed his mind," Harry answered. "Decided to 'have one more shot at it' is what he said to me."

"And the scuffle he and Chip had?"

"Dreadful thing really." Flora leaned forward in her eagerness to impart the information. "Edith and Chip were going at it pretty strong when Will and Imogene showed up. He yelled at Chip to leave his daughter alone and get out of the house. Well, Chip took offense at that, naturally, and said he wasn't about to leave his own place. Will said, 'I'll see you do,' and grabbed Chip." She paused for breath.

"And that's when Edith jumped in. On her husband's behalf. Can you imagine? Imogene said it was awful. It took her and Chip both to pull Edith away from her own father. Then Chip yelled, 'That's it. I want a divorce. This whole family is nuts,' and walked out." Flora leaned back in her chair, exhausted from her tale.

Before I could comment the front door slammed.

"They're here," Harry said, getting up from his chair.

I turned to Flora. "I didn't realize someone else was coming?"

"That's why we invited you, dear Jane. We wanted you to meet someone special."

Teddy came into the room with a dark-haired woman beside him. She was rather plain of face and wore a severely-cut navy blue suit over a trim figure.

Teddy took her arm and brought her to me.

"Jane, I'd like you to meet Susan. Susan, this is my aunt Jane."

"I'm so pleased to meet you," the young woman said. "I've heard so much about you."

Behind her Teddy beamed and Harry loomed anxiously. I had not at all cared for Teddy's first wife, who had died the year before in my back yard in a dreadful freakish accident.

I waited until three the next afternoon before going to the grocery store, figuring it might not be so busy then. I walked up and down the aisles. Tammy Nichols was nowhere to be seen.

"Excuse me," I said to Delores, the produce clerk, "is Archie around?"

"I think he's in his office, Miss Cavanaugh. Would you like me to call him for you?"

"No. I'll go back and talk to him there." Delores was the sort of person who would never dream of telling me I couldn't. Not that I would've paid much mind if she had.

Archie Babcock wore thick, wire-rimmed glasses and bow ties, and had a cowlick that made his hair stick up in the back no matter how much fancy stuff he sprayed on it. The latter gave him a tendency to swipe one hand across the top of his head a great deal.

"Miss Cavanaugh." He jumped up from his chair when I entered the small, crowded office. "Come in. Let me clear a place for you."

He set a box of canned corn on the floor and dusted the seat of the metal chair so I could sit down.

"What can I do for you?"

I figured that as long as I was here I might as well ask him a few questions, too. "What do you suppose Willie was doing in the parking lot at midnight?"

He jerked like a puppet in inexperienced hands, and I remembered, too late, that he was the exact opposite of Imogene. Archie panicked and grew defensive over nothing. His parents were strict Baptists who had raised their son with a heightened sense of guilt that was totally wasted on him. The man was as inoffensive as a tadpole.

"I, I don't know, Miss Cavanaugh. It was his store. He had the right . . ." the poor man gobbled like a turkey.

"I'm sorry," I said, through tightened lips. "I've been so concerned over this terrible incident, I'm not myself." I took a handkerchief from my purse and held it to my face.

Archie leaped to his feet again and was at my side immediately.

"Oh dear," he said. "Can I get you a glass of water? Anything at all? I am so sorry. This must have been terrible for you."

"I'm just so distraught over Willie's death. I've tried and tried to imagine why he would come down here in the middle of the night." I dabbed the cloth against my eyes.

"I know what you mean. Of course, there was the money . . ."

"The money?"

Archie twitched and rubbed his hand over his hair. "Well, yes. Chief Porter said I was to keep it a secret, but I'm sure he didn't mean from you, Miss Cavanaugh. After all, you're family. There was twenty-five hundred dollars missing."

"A burglary?"

"No, ma'am. I mean, not literally. We—Chief Porter and me, that is—figure Will came in and took it out of the safe himself because there was no sign of forced entry or anything."

That certainly put a different spin on things. It would be galling to think that Arthur's theory might be right after all. "It was very clever of you and Chief Porter to keep it quiet."

Archie beamed. The smallest glimmer of praise was like sunshine to his soul.

"I feel much better just knowing the situation is in capable hands." I rose from the uncomfortable little chair. "Oh, by the way, is Tammy Nichols here?"

"No. She had vacation time coming, so she's off this week. Is there anything else I can do?"

"You've been a great help, Archie. Thank you so much."

He reached to assist me to the door, but managed to stop himself in mid-motion. I pretended not to notice to save face for both of us. People like Archie are so tiring to be around.

Tammy Nichols lived in the Oak Terrace Apartments, a fancy name for a very ordinary structure. I knocked at her door a short time after leaving the store.

Several minutes passed before the door opened a crack.

"Yes?"

"Miss Nichols?"

"Yes."

"I would like to speak to you for a few moments if I may."

The door opened marginally wider. "I don't know what . . ."

"It won't take long."

She paused. I waited. Finally, she moved back, pulling the door with her, and I stepped inside. I suppose some people might regard her as attractive, but she was definitely not at her best that afternoon. The long auburn hair, which was her best feature, was uncombed, and the cotton duster she wore was wrinkled and stained. Her face tended to be sharp anyway; without its usual layer of makeup, she had a rabbity appearance that was most unattractive.

She waved me inside. I looked around and chose an old rocker with one arm missing. She seated herself on the couch opposite, tucking one bare foot under her as a small child does.

"Are you ill?" I asked, amazed even as I did so that I should be concerned about such a slovenly, unappealing creature.

"A touch of flu, I think. I'll be fine." She didn't sound as if she would ever be fine.

"Have you seen a doctor?"

She turned her head and said nothing.

"You're sick about Willie. Is that it?"

I could see her jaw clench. "He was a very nice man."

"Yes. He could be."

She looked back at me.

"And he was very nice to you?"

She lifted her chin very high. "Yes. He was."

"I should think not many people have been, have they?"

To my distress she began to cry. Loud, thumping, messy sobs that got her nose involved with the process as well. "We weren't doing nothing . . ."

"Anything."

"Anything. I know you don't believe that. Nobody would. It's just . . . he liked to brush my hair. For hours and hours, it seemed like sometimes. He even bought a fancy brush, all silver and shiny with some kind of special bristles."

My mother had had a brush like that. So many women did, years ago. I had an instant vision of the aging man using one on that reddish mass. Smoothing it . . . caressing it . . .

"Why, last time he was here I said something silly to him, and he even threatened to . . ." she giggled, "paddle me with it."

I tried not to show my repulsion. Why couldn't the man have just taken her to bed and been done with it, for goodness' sake? What did this tell me about Willie, other than something I didn't want to know? I recalled his mother, Helene, a woman I hadn't thought about in years, with a jolt. She had been a silent, almost invisible person—with beautiful red hair.

The spasm of laughter gone as swiftly as it had come, Tammy went on, almost unaware of my presence. "He needed somebody to talk to, and I listened to him, he said. He was so smart, you know what I mean? And he was lonely. He said that, too. Can you believe it? Somebody like him lonely? I mean, with all that money, and all those important people he knew?"

I handed her my hankie, since she was obviously in need of it, and said, "Was he here that evening?"

She nodded. "But he left about eleven. Honest."

"What did you talk about?"

"The election. He kept asking me—me!—what I thought. Should he do it or not? I said sure he should, we needed more like him. And he said, well, maybe it would be better if he didn't, after all he was getting older, and I said, no way, he wasn't old. And pretty soon he started getting real excited about it and saying yeah. Yeah, he should do it. You know. Like that."

"Did he give you money?"

Her face took on the sly, rabbity look again, and she didn't meet my eyes.

"Did he give you money that night?"

The chin popped up once more. "No, ma'am. He did not."

I was suddenly very tired. Tired of Willie, tired of this child and her emotions, tired of family secrets. I stood and headed for the door. Tammy got there ahead of me and opened it.

"Do you need money?" I asked as I stepped outside.

"No," she said. Then, "But thank you for asking."

I kept walking.

I lay down for an hour, something I rarely do, before fixing dinner. When I got up, I made a small salad and broiled a chicken breast. They were both quite tasteless, but I ate them and washed the dishes afterward.

Then I sat in the parlor, with a lamp turned low. The older one gets, the clearer the memories of childhood become. Soon, I thought foolishly, I shall be so addled that all I can think of will be events that happened years ago.

Damn Willie anyway. Why should I care what caused this man's death in a parking lot on a dark night? Because we had shared common experiences? Because, years ago, we had been allies for a brief while?

I looked across the room at my mother's picture. "No, my dear," she seemed to say. "Because he is family."

I switched the lamp up another notch and went to the phone. Harry answered on the third ring. After thanking him again for dinner the night before and after a few words about Susan ("Yes, Harry, I agree. She does seem a lovely girl."), I asked, "Do you remember exactly when it was Chip was in town?"

Harry seldom questioned things. He was quiet for awhile, then said, "I think it was on Tuesday. I saw him at lunch as I recall. He said something about picking up some papers from his lawyer."

"Do you know if he was going straight back to Topeka?"

"I'm sure he was. He said he had a fish about to bite on a Seville and had to get back." Chip was a car salesman; "Not just any car, either," as he liked to brag.

"When did Willie decide to run for reelection?"

"Just recently, I think. He made some remark to me a couple of weeks ago about 'wanting to get out of the rat race.' Then, only days before he died, he was saying things like 'having a new lease on life' and 'getting the perspective of young people' or some such. They were all such mundane cliches. To tell you the truth, I didn't pay much attention to any of them. Do they make any sense to you?"

"They might, Harry. Thank you." I hung up and dialed Tammy Nichols' phone number. When she answered I said, "This is Jane Cavanaugh. I'd like you to answer one question for me. Was Willie talking about your moving to Topeka?"

"I wasn't sure I could find work up there, but he said that wouldn't be no problem."

"Any problem."

"Any problem. I hadn't decided for sure, mind you."

"No, of course not. Thank you, Miss Nichols."

So Tammy was the "new lease on life." And if what Chip had told Harry was true, he was long gone when Willie was shot on Thursday night.

What about the twenty-five hundred dollars? Why would Willie need cash in the middle of the night? That made no sense at all. Unless . . .

I needed to talk to Archie one more time. I debated about calling and decided, with his temperament, it was best done in person.

Archie lived in a small bungalow on a quiet street in the older section of town. He answered the door immediately.

"Miss Cavanaugh. What a surprise. Won't you come in? I was just waiting for the ten o'clock news before I retired."

His house had a fussy bachelor look. He had dated Muriel Simpson for seven years as I recall, but when she turned thirty-three and had received no proposal, she married someone else and moved away. Archie had remained happily single.

"Thank you, Archie. I was sitting home alone, and as old women will . . ."

"I could never think of you as old, ma'am."

I waved away his compliment and took a chair. "I got to fretting about something."

He sat down across from me and waited.

"The money. Why would Willie go down to the store for cash in the middle of the night? Unless . . ." I paused, "he was being blackmailed."

Archie seemed startled by the idea. "But what would anyone blackmail Will about?"

"I don't know. Was there any problem with the stores that you know of?"

He shook his head emphatically. "I see all the books. I check all the figures."

"That's what I thought, too. You're much too good a businessman to let something like that slip by you. So it had to be in his personal life."

"I wouldn't know anything about that, Miss Cavanaugh."

"Didn't I hear once that you had political aspirations, Archie?"

He laughed and fiddled with his cowlick. "Not me. I'm just a grocer."

"So was Willie."

"Yes. But he was a Cavanaugh." A note of self-pity crept into his voice.

"He could have named you as his choice to succeed him. Put the word out, so to speak. Spoken for you to important people, that sort of thing. Isn't that the way it's normally done?"

"He was never going to give up that position. Never."

"Not even if the story got out that he was 'fooling around' with a younger woman?"

Archie smoothed down his standing hairs. "Who would say a thing like that?"

"Someone who wanted money, perhaps? Someone who intended to bleed him dry . . ."

"That's not true! I didn't want his money. I . . ." Archie's hair popped up again.

"No," I agreed. "You didn't want money. You only wanted to run for state senator. That seems eminently fair to me."

"He'd promised me. He said, 'Next time, Archie. Next time I'll step down and help you get my seat.' He promised."

"What happened?" I asked, very gently.

"He called me that night. Late. Told me to come down to the store. I didn't know what was happening. I rushed down and there he was, standing in the moonlight in the middle of the parking lot, grinning like a fool. 'Archie, I've changed my mind,' he says. Just like that. 'I'm going to run again.'"

Archie looked past me, maybe seeing Willie as he was that night. "I told him he couldn't do that to me. I had plans. I'm not a young man any longer. I can't wait forever. But he just gave me that silly grin.

"So I said, 'What about you and that Nichols girl? Huh? What about that? Folks wouldn't like it much if they knew about that.' Then he did the strangest thing. He looked up at the sky and that full moon, laughed out loud, and started dancing around like some wild Indian, rubbing his hands all over himself and making these weird noises. I thought he'd gone crazy."

Poor Willie. Dancing the Moon Magic one last time. "Where did the gun come from?"

"I always keep one in the car. In case of robbery, you know. I carry the money to the bank each day. Will bought it for me years ago. I'd taken it out of the glove compartment on the way over there. I didn't know but what he'd found the store broken into or something, the way he called so suddenlike and told me to meet him there." Archie removed his glasses and rubbed the bridge of his nose. "I was all tense anyway, and then, when he said what he did and started laughing and doing that stupid dance, I guess I saw red. So I shot him. Several times. I, I didn't mean to. Not really. It just happened."

We sat in his tidy living room and said nothing. I don't know what Archie was thinking about. I was thinking about Willie. He was such an unappealing little boy, and he became such a foolish man.

"What about the money?" I asked finally.

"I took it. I thought perhaps the police would think there'd been a robbery, and Will had caught them at it. They do think that, you know." He put his glasses back on. "I have it in the bedroom, the whole twenty-five hundred. I'll go get it for you right now."

"Not yet, Archie. Just let me think a minute." What was I to do? This ridiculous little man had shot and killed a Cavanaugh. I could ask for a cup of coffee and then slip the arsenic into Archie's cup while he was getting the money. I'd brought the poison with me just in case; the packet had been in the potting shed for years.

But it seemed such a waste of effort and energy.

I could call the police. Tell them what had happened and have them come out and deal with the offender.

And have the whole ugly story in the Golden City *Courier* for everyone to read? Tammy Nichols? Willie brushing that long red hair? The near-paddling? The Moon Magic dance?

"Archie, about the twenty-five hundred dollars . . ."

The police never did find the party who robbed the grocery store and shot Willie. Archie Babcock ran for Willie's vacant senate seat and won. I follow his activities very closely. Tammy Nichols moved to Kansas City, with a small donation from me to help her get started there. Imogene decided to keep her house. Edith continues to visit Topeka periodically, in some silly effort to get Chip back. Oh, and Teddy is engaged to Susan.

# The Maggody Files: D.W.I.

## JOAN HESS

Thursdays aren't the busiest days for outbursts of criminal activity in Maggody, Arkansas (pop. 755). Neither are Sundays, Mondays, Tuesdays, and Wednesdays. Long about Friday, things pick up in anticipation of the weekend, although when we're talking grand theft auto, it means some teenager took off in his pa's pickup. A hit-and-run has to do with a baseball and a broken window at the Pot o' Gold trailer park. The perpetrator of larceny tends to be a harried mother who forgot to pay for gas at the convenience store, most likely because one of the toddlers in the back seat of the station wagon chose that moment to vomit copiously into the front seat.

I say all this with authority, because I, Ariel Hanks, am the chief of police, and it's my sworn duty to drag the errant driver home by his ear, and send the batter over to mumble a confession and offer to make reparation. Why, I've been known to go all the way out to Joyce Lambertino's house to have a diet soda and a slice of pound cake, admire her counted cross-stitch, and take her money to the Kwik-Stoppe-Shoppe. And bring her back the change.

Other than that, I occasionally run a speed trap out by the skeletal remains of Purtle's Esso Station, where there's a nice patch of shade and some incurious cows. I swap dirty jokes with the sheriff's deputies when they drop by for coffee. Every now and then I wander around Cotter's Ridge, on the very obscure chance I might stumble across Raz Buchanon's moonshine still. It's up there somewhere, along with ticks, chiggers, mosquitoes, brambles, and nasty-tempered copperheads.

The rest of the time I devote to napping, reading, wondering why I'm back in Maggody, and doing whatever's necessary to eat three meals a day at Ruby Bee's Bar & Grill. The proprietor (a.k.a. my mother) is a worthy opponent, despite her chubby body and twinkly eyes. She's adjusted to having her daughter do what she considers a man's job, and she's resigned to my divorce and my avowed devotion to the single life. This is not to say I don't hear about my failings on a regular basis, both from her and her spindly, redhaired cohort, Estelle Oppers, who runs a beauty shop in her living room—and is as eager as Ruby Bee is to run my life. But I don't believe in running; there's nothing wrong with a nice, easy walk (except on Cotter's Ridge, and that's already been mentioned).

But the particular Thursday under discussion turned ugly. I was at the PD, yanking open desk drawers to watch the roaches scurry for cover. When the telephone rang, I reluctantly shut the drawer and picked up the receiver.

"Sheriff Dorfer says to meet him by the creek out on County 103," the dispatcher said with her customary charm. "Right now."

"Shall I bring a bucket of bait and a six-pack?"

"Just git yourself over there, Arly. Sheriff Dorfer's at the scene, and he ain't gonna be all that tickled if you show up acting like you thought it was a picnic."

It was not a picnic. I parked behind several official vehicles, settled my sunglasses, and slithered and slipped down a fresh path of destruction to the edge of Boone Creek. Harve Dorfer was talking to a man in a torn army jacket who was wiping blood from his face with a wadded handkerchief. A pair of grim deputies watched. Beyond them lay a lumpish form covered by a blanket. The rear half of a truck stuck out of the water as if poised in a dive.

"You're a real work of art," Harve growled, then stalked over to me, an unlit cigar butt wedged in the corner of his mouth. He aimed a finger at me, but turned and looked at his deputies. "Les, you and John Earl take this stinkin' drunk up to the road and have the medics check him. If nothing's broke, take him to the office and book him. If something is, go along with him and wait at the emergency room until he's patched up. Then take him to the office and throw the whole dadgum book at him."

I studied the object of Harve's displeasure. Red Gromwell was local, a young guy, maybe thirty, with a sly face already turning soft and greasy hair the color of a rotting orange. At the moment, he had a swollen lip, the beginnings of a black eye, and a ragged streak of blood down the side of his face. His knuckles were raw. His jacket was stained with blood, as were the baggy jeans that rode low on his hips out of deference to his beer gut. He gave me a foolish grin, dropped the handkerchief, and crumpled to the ground. The deputies hauled him to his feet, and the three began to climb toward the road.

"Drunker than a boiled owl," Harve said, firing up the cigar butt. "Says he and a guy named Buell Fumitory was out riding around, sharing a bottle and yucking it up. All of a sudden the truck's bouncing down the hill like one of those bumper cars at the county fair. Says he was thrown out the window and landed way yonder in that clump of brush. Buell over there wasn't as lucky."

I folded my arms and tried to be a cool, detached cop. My eyes kept sneaking to the shrouded body on the ground, however, and I doubt Harve was fooled one whit. I tried to swallow, but my mouth was as dry as the dusty road behind us. "Did Buell drown?" I asked.

"I can't say right offhand. He was banged up pretty bad from hitting his face against the steering wheel who knows how many times. It doesn't much matter—in particular to him. Red said by the time he could git himself up and stagger to the edge of the water, it was clear there wasn't anything to do for Buell. He did manage to climb back to the road and flag down a truck driver who called us."

"Red's not the heroic sort," I said, shaking my head. "He'd just as soon run down a dog as bother to brake."

"You know him?"

"Yes indeed. He works at the body shop and brawls at the pool hall. I had some unpleasant encounters with him after his wife finally got fed up with him and filed for divorce. Twice I drove her to the women's shelter in Farberville and urged her to stay for a few days, but she scooted right back and refused to file charges, so there wasn't much I could do."

"One of those, huh?" Harve said through a cloud of noxious cigar smoke.

"One of those." I again found myself staring at the blanket. "Buell Fumitory kept to himself, so I don't know much about him. He moved here . . . oh, a year ago, and worked at the supermarket. He came into Ruby Bee's every now and then for a beer. He seemed okay to me."

"According to this Red fellow, Buell was driving at the time of the accident. I reckon it's too late to give him a ticket." Harve snuffed out the cigar butt and looked over my shoulder. "Here come the boys with the body bag. Tell ya what, Arly," he said, putting his arm around me and escorting me up the hill, "I'm gonna let you have this one for your very own. I need Les and John Earl to finish up the paperwork on those burglaries over in Hasty, and I myself am gonna be busier than a stump-tailed cow in fly time with office chores."

I shrugged off his arm. "Like posing for the media with the latest haul of marijuana? This sudden activity doesn't have anything to do with the upcoming election, does it?"

"You just hunt up the next of kin and write me a couple of pages of official blather," he said. Trying not to smirk, he left me at the road and went down to supervise the medics.

As I stood there berating myself for getting stuck so easily with nothing but tedious paperwork, a tow truck came down the road. Once the body and the truck were removed, the squirrels would venture back, as would the birds, the bugs, and the fish that lurked in the muddy creek. The splintered saplings would be replaced by a new crop. Three months from then, I told myself with a grimace, there would be nothing left to remind folks about the dangers of D.W.I. In some states, it's called other things. In Arkansas, we opt for the simple and descriptive Driving While Intoxicated. Might as well call it Dying While Intoxicated.

"It doesn't make a plugged nickel's worth of sense," Ruby Bee proclaimed from behind the bar. She rinsed off the glasses in the sink, wiped her hands on her apron, and gazed beadily at Estelle, who was drinking a beer and gobbling up pretzels like she was a paying customer.

"That sort of thing happens all the time," Estelle countered. "They were drunk, and anybody with a smidgen of the sense God gave a goose knows it's asking for trouble to go drinking and driving, particularly out on those twisty back roads. Remember that time I was coming back from a baby shower in Emmet, and this big ol' deer came scampering into the road, and I nearly—"

"Nobody said there was a deer involved. Lottie said that Elsie happened to hear Red talking to some fellow at the launderette earlier this morning, and he said Buell was singing and howling like a tomcat and was a sight too far gone to keep his eyes or anything else on the road." She began to dry the glasses on a dishrag, all the while frowning and trying to figure out what was nagging at her. "The thing is," she added slowly, "I didn't think Buell was like that. He was always real nice when he worked in produce. One time I bought a watermelon, and when I cut—"

"I don't see why he couldn't have been real nice and also been willing to drink cheap whisky and take a drive."

"I ain't saying he wasn't," Ruby Bee said, still speaking slowly and getting more bumfuzzled by the minute. "But I'll tell you one thing, Estelle—he never came in here and guzzled down a couple of pitchers like Red did. Like Red did before I threw him out on his skinny behind, that is. It like to cost me three hundred dollars to get the jukebox fixed. And to think he busted it just because his ex-wife was drinking a glass of beer with that tire salesman!"

"He was hotter than a fire in a pepper mill, wasn't he?" Estelle said as she picked up a pretzel. "I wish somebody'd find the gumption to mention to him that what his ex-wife does is none of his business. It ain't like he bought a wife; he was only renting one. It's a crying shame he wasn't the one to end up in the creek so Gayle can get on with her life and stop having to peek over her shoulder every time she steps out of the house."

"How'd she take the news?"

Estelle lowered her voice, although anybody could see there wasn't another soul in the barroom, much less hanging over her shoulder like a lapel. "Well, Lottie said Mrs. Jim Bob happened to run by Gayle's with some ironing, and Gayle wouldn't even come to the door. Mrs. Jim Bob saw the curtain twitch, so she knew perfectly well that Gayle was home at the time."

"I don't see that she has any reason to . . ."

Estelle gave her a pitying look. "To avoid Mrs. Jim Bob? I'd say we all had darn good reasons to do that. I could make you a list as long as your arm."

"Unless, of course . . ."

"Unless what?"

"Well, if Gayle was . . ."

"I do believe you could finish a sentence, Mrs. Dribble Mouth, and do it before the sun sets in Bogart County."

Not bothering to respond, Ruby Bee stared at the jukebox with a deepening frown. "You know," she said about the time Estelle was preparing to make another remark, "the last time I saw Gayle at the Emporium, she was looking right frumpy. What she needs is a perm, Estelle, and you're the one to give it to her. I suspect it'll have to be for free; she barely makes minimum wage at the poultry plant in Starley City. Why doncha call her right now and make an appointment?"

"For free?" Estelle gasped. "Why in tarnation would I do a thing like that?"

Ruby Bee curled her finger, and this time she was the one to speak in a low, conspiratorial voice. Estelle managed not to butt in, and ten minutes later she was dialing Gayle Gromwell's telephone number.

The next morning I got the address of Buell Fumitory's rent house from the manager at the supermarket. He told me that Buell had worked there for most of a year, caused no trouble, took no unauthorized days off, and got along with the other employees.

Armed with the above piercing insights, I drove out past Raz Buchanon's shack to an ordinary frame house in a scruffy yard. A rusty subcompact was parked beside the house, but no one answered my repeated knocks. I considered doing something clever with a skeleton key or a credit card to gain entry. However, having neither, I opened the front door and went inside.

The interior was as ordinary as the exterior. It was clearly a bachelor's domain. There were a few dirty ashtrays and a beer can on the coffee table, odds and ends of food in the refrigerator, chipped dishes and a cracked cup in the cabinets. The only anomaly was a vase with a handful of wilted daisies, but even tomato stackers can have a romantic streak.

I continued on my merry way. The bedroom was small and cluttered, but no more so than my apartment usually was. The closet contained basic clothing and fishing equipment. The drawer in the bedside table had gum wrappers, nail clippers, a long overdue electric bill, and an impressive selection of condom packets. Perhaps somebody in the morgue would encourage Buell to continue practicing safe sex in the netherworld.

In the distance, most likely at Raz's place, a dog began to bark dispiritedly. As if in response, the house creaked and sighed. It wasn't a mausoleum, and I wasn't about to lapse into a gothic thing involving involuntary shivers and a compulsion to clutch my bosom and flutter my eyelashes. On the other hand, I recalled the blanketed body alongside the creek, and I wasted no time, pawing through dresser drawers until I found a stack of letters and an address book.

I sat down on the bed and flipped through the latter until I found the listing for Aunt Pearl in Boise. If she was not the official next of kin, she would know who was. The letters turned out to be commercial greeting cards, all signed with a smiley face. I made a frowny face, stuffed them back in the drawer, and returned to the PD to see if Aunt Pearl might be sitting by her telephone in Boise.

She was, but she was also hard of hearing and very old. Once I'd conveyed the news, she admitted she was the only living relative. Her financial situation precluded funeral arrangements. I assured her that we would deal with it, hung up, and leaned back in my chair to ponder how best to share this with Harve. There was very little of value at Buell's house. A small television, furniture that would go to the Salvation Army (if they'd take it), and a couple of boxes of personal effects. The pitiful car would bring no more than a hundred dollars.

The pitiful car. I propped my feet on the corner of the desk and tried to figure out why there was a car, pitiful or not, parked at Buell's house. He did not seem like a two-car family. Glumly noting that the water stain on the ceiling had expanded since last I'd studied it, I called the manager at the supermarket and asked him what Buell had driven. He grumbled but agreed to ask the employees, and came back with a description of the subcompact.

Red Gromwell drove an ancient Mustang; I'd pulled him over so many times that I knew the license plate by heart. The pickup truck in the creek had been gray, or white and dirty. I thought this over for a while (bear in mind it was Friday morning, so I wasn't preparing to foil bank robberies or negotiate with kidnappers).

I called the sheriff's department and got Harve on the line.

"You're not backing out on that D.W.I. report, are you?" he asked before I could get out a word. "I hate to stick you with it, Arly, but I'm up to my neck in some tricky figures for the upcoming quorum meeting, and one of the county judges says—"

"What'd you do with Red Gromwell?"

There was a lengthy silence. At last Harve exhaled and said, "Nothing much, damn it. We kept him in the drunk tank for twelve hours. This morning he called his cousin for bail money and strolled out like a preacher on his way to count the offering. I checked with the county prosecutor, but it ain't worth bothering with. If he'd been driving, we could cause him some grief. Not that much, though. Get his driver's license suspended, slap him with a fat fine. The judge'd lecture him for twenty minutes, and maybe give him some probation. The prisons are stuffed to the gills right now, and I sure don't need to offer the likes of Red Gromwell room and board, courtesy of Stump County."

I waited until he stopped sighing, then asked him to ascertain the ownership of the truck that had been pulled out of Boone Creek. He huffed and puffed some more while I wondered how badly the PD roof was leaking and finally agreed to have Les call the tow shop (sigh), get the truck's plate number (siigh), and call the state office (siiigh) to see who all was named on the registration.

On that breezy note, we parted. I did some noisy exhaling of my own, but all it accomplished was to make me woozy. It occurred to me that I was in need of both local gossip and a blue plate special, so I abandoned any pretense of diligent detection and walked down the road to Ruby Bee's Bar & Grill, the hot spot for food and fiction.

It was closed. Irritated, I went back to my car, drove to the Dairee Dee-Lishus where the food was less palatable but decidedly better than nothing, and promised myself a quiet picnic out by the rubble of the gas station. Twenty minutes later, I was turning down County 103.

"It'd be cute all curly around your face," Ruby Bee said brightly. "Brush those bangs out of your eyes and wear a little makeup, and you'd look just like a homecoming queen."

"I don't know," Gayle Gromwell said. She didn't sound like she did, either. She sounded more like she was real sorry about coming to Estelle's Hair Fantasies, even if the perm was free. Nobody'd said the event was open to the public.

Estelle nudged Ruby Bee out of the way. "I happen to be professionally trained in these matters," she said with a pinched frown. "Now, Gayle honey, I have to agree that those bangs make you look like a dog that came out of the rain a day late. I'm just going to snip a bit here and there, give you some nice, soft curls, and then we'll see if maybe you don't want an auburn rinse."

Gayle looked a little pouty, but this wasn't surprising, since she wasn't much older than twenty and still had a few blemishes and the faint vestiges of baby fat. She slouched in the chair and gazed blackly at her image in the mirror, refusing to meet Estelle's inquisitive eyes or even Ruby Bee's penetrating stare. "Oh, go ahead and do whatever you want. I know my hair looks awful, but I don't care. Why don't you shave it off?"

"It's going be real pretty," Estelle said nervously. This wasn't what she and Ruby Bee had hoped for, although Gayle had come and that was the first hurdle. She wiggled her eyebrows at Ruby Bee. "Don't you think Gayle here will have every boy in town chasing after her?"

Ruby Bee knew a cue when she heard one. "I just hope Red's simmered down. Remember when he put his fist through the jukebox because of that tire salesman? They charged me three hundred dollars."

They both looked at Gayle, wondering what she'd say. Her eyes were closed, but as they watched, a tear squeezed out and slunk down her cheek alongside her nose. Within the hour, they had the whole teary, hiccuppy, disjointed story.

"Two weeks ago?" I echoed, admittedly less than brilliantly. "The truck was purchased two weeks ago?"

"A private sale," Les continued. "I tracked down the previous owner, who said he'd advertised the damn thing for three weeks running and was about to sell it for scrap when some guy showed up with a hundred bucks."

"Some guy? What did he look like?"

"Nothing special. Dark hair, wearing jeans and a work shirt, sunglasses, cap. Average height and weight, no initials carved in his forehead or neon antlers or anything."

"And he didn't catch the guy's name, I suppose?"

"You suppose right. This was strictly cash-and-carry."

I tried once more. "What about the registration papers?"

"Never transferred."

I hung up and went to the back room of the PD to glower at my evidence. It didn't take long. The bloodstained handkerchief was in one plastic bag and an empty liter whisky bottle in another. I hadn't been in the mood to take scrapings of mud from the bank or water from the creek. Harve, the deputies, the medics, and the tow truck operator had all tromped around; if there had been a telltale footprint, it had been obliterated (and I couldn't imagine a footprint telling much of a tale, anyway).

There was no point in dusting the bottle for fingerprints. If I bothered, and then found Red and took his to compare, I'd have a lovely match. It was a policeish activity, but also a futile one. As for the handkerchief, I knew where the blood came from and I didn't care where the handkerchief did.

And I knew where the truck came from, but I didn't know who had bought it or why. I realized I again was making a frowny face. This was of no significance, but it led my thoughts back to the smiley faces on the cards, and that led me to the contents of the bedside drawer, the daisies, the white pickup truck, and before too long I was staring at the whisky bottle and wondering how I could prove Red Gromwell had murdered Buell Fumitory—soberly and in cold blood.

Then I realized I had the evidence in front of me. I went back to the telephone, called Les, and said, "Do you have a date tonight?"

"I don't think my wife will approve, but what do you have in mind?"

"What happened to Gayle's hair?" I said to Ruby Bee as I watched Gayle and Les settle in a back booth. "Didn't her mother warn her about sticking a fork in a socket?"

Ruby Bee leaned across the bar and whispered, "This ain't the time for smart remarks. I don't seem to recollect anyone complimenting you on that schoolmarm hair of yours. I happen to have something that you might find interestin', if you can shut your mouth long enough to hear it."

I meekly shut my mouth, mostly because I might have time to eat a piece of pie before the fireworks started. Before I could hear the big news, Estelle perched on the bar stool next to me, craned her head around until she spotted Gayle, and then turned back with a self-righteous smile. "I just knew that auburn rinse would be perfect. If Arly here would let me restyle her hair, she'd look just as nice as Gayle."

"So that's why I had to eat at the Dee-Lishus today," I said accusingly. I resisted the urge to run my fingers through my hair, which would have undone my bun and left me vulnerable to further cosmetological attacks. "Just once I wish you two would stay off the case. Believe it or not, I am more than capable of—"

"Gayle was having an affair with Buell," Ruby Bee said.

I did not relent. "I figured as much, and I did it all by myself. I did not require the assistance of two overgrown Nancy Drews to—"

"And Red found out," Estelle said. "Last week he busted in on 'em and made all kinds of nasty threats. I find that a mite suspicious, considering what happened last evening." She blinked at Ruby Bee, not blankly but frostily. "If Arly already knew about Gayle and Buell, why did I end up doing her perm for free?"

Ruby Bee retreated until she bumped into the beer tap. "Arly doesn't know everything. Just ask her if she knows that Buell didn't like to go carousing like some, and hardly ever got drunk on account of the medication he took for a recurring bladder problem. And wouldn't have gone riding around with Red if his life depended on it."

"Don't ask me anything," I rumbled. I was about to elaborate on my irritation when I spotted Red coming across the dance floor. He still looked a bit battered, the black eye having blossomed and the swollen lip giving him a petulant sneer. He was not wearing bloodstained clothing, however, and he moved easily for someone reputedly thrown fifty feet from a careening vehicle.

He froze in the middle of the floor, ignoring the couples cruising around him. His fingers curled into fists, and a muscle in his neck bulged like a piece of rope. Clearly, the first of the bottle rockets was lit. I slid off the stool and caught up with him as he reached the booth where Gayle and Les were sitting.

"What the hell did you do to your hair?" he asked Gayle. When she shrugged, he jabbed his thumb at Les.

"Who's this?"

She looked up defiantly. "None of your business, Red. We've been divorced for two years now, and you ain't got any right to act like a crybaby if I go out with someone."

"I didn't act like a crybaby when I caught you in bed with that wimp from the supermarket, did I?" he said, looming over her. "Guess you won't be romping with him any more, unless you aim to crawl in the casket with him."

Les put down his beer. "Now, wait just a minute, buddy. This woman doesn't have to take that kind of talk from—"

"Shut up or I'll shove that glass down your throat," Red snarled. "Now, listen up, Gayle Gromwell. You git yourself out of that booth and on your way home afore I drag this mama's boy outside to rearrange his pretty little face."

"You can't tell me what to do," she said sulkily.

Red pulled back his hand to slap her, but I grabbed his arm and hung on until he relaxed. "Gayle's right, Red—you can't tell her what to do," I said. "She's a single woman, and she's allowed to date whomever she chooses. In this case, she's chosen to date a deputy sheriff, which means you're threatening an officer of the law. In front of an entire roomful of witnesses, too."

He realized all the customers were watching and, from their expressions, enjoying the scene. Ruby Bee thoughtfully had unplugged the jukebox so nobody would miss a word.

"Okay," he muttered to me, then stared at Gayle. "You keep in mind what I said to you the other night, you hear?"

I tapped him on the shoulder. "Was this when you invited your old pal Buell to share a bottle of whisky and enjoy the moonlight?"

"Naw, that was yesterday after work. I went by his house to tell him I was wrong to bust down the door like I did. I told him that sometimes I go kind of crazy when I think about Gayle with another man. He was right understanding, and pretty soon we decided to run into Farberville and get ourselves a bottle. We was talking about deer season when he lost control of the truck. You know what happened then."

"Yes, I do," I said, nodding. "Why was Buell driving the truck you bought in Little Rock two weeks ago? You paid good money for it, and I'm surprised you weren't driving."

The bruises under his eye stayed dark, but the rest of his face paled. "I dunno. I thought he was soberer than me."

"It's a good thing you weren't in the Mustang, isn't it?" I continued, still pretending we were having a polite conversation. "I know you're awfully fond of it."

"Helluva car," he said.

"Which is why you bought the truck. You weren't about to total your Mustang that way. I checked around town today, and nobody saw you and Buell driving down the road in the white pickup." I crossed my fingers. "But Raz saw you drive by his place in the Mustang late afternoon, and come back by. He didn't see Buell then, but I guess he'd need X-ray vision to see a body in the trunk, wouldn't he?"

"What are you saying?" Gayle said, gulping. "Did he kill Buell?"

"I already told the sheriff all about it," Red muttered.

I shook my head. "You told the sheriff a stale old fairy tale, Red. You went to Buell's and beat him up, put him in the trunk, and drove to your place to switch vehicles. Then you collected the whisky, went out to the hill on County 103, and sent Buell down the hill and into the creek. He was unconscious, so he didn't have much of a chance to get out of the truck."

He gave me a frightened look. "You got any proof, cop lady?"

"You drained the bottle after the wreck, so we'd figure you were drunk. I found it in the woods. If you had it with you in the truck, then you and it went flying out the window together. Why didn't it break?"

"That doesn't prove anything."

"You'd better hope Buell's fingerprints are on it," I said, "and that the alcohol level in his blood indicates he was drunk." I waited politely, but he didn't seem to have much to say. "Oh, yes, and there's one more thing,

Red. You'd better start praying the blood on that handkerchief matches your type and doesn't have any traces of the medication Buell was taking."

"Medication?" Red said, sounding as if he were in need of some at the moment. He didn't improve when Les stood up, recited the Miranda warning, and cuffed him.

Once they were gone, I glowered at Ruby Bee until she headed for the jukebox, then sat down across from Gayle. "Red'll be out on bail by Monday. I suggest you spend the weekend thinking about why you're willing to play the role of victim. Get some counseling at the women's shelter if it'll help, and change the lock on your front door."

Her smile was dreamy. "Who'd have thought Red would actually kill somebody over me?"

"One of these days he'll kill you," I said, then left her to her pathetic fantasies and went back to the PD to brood.

During the course of the weekend, I'd be obliged to run in some drunks, bust a couple of minors in possession, and intervene in domestic disputes. With luck, we'd all survive, and on Monday morning, bright and early, I'd grab my radar gun and a good book, and head for that patch of shade . . . unless I decided to take a hike on Cotter's Ridge. You just never know where crime will erupt in Maggody, Arkansas (pop. 755).

# Early Summer

## JAS R. PETRIN

He weighed the ball thoughtfully in his hand, digging his fingertips hard into the stitching. A gust of wind whipped suddenly at his cap, blew his arm hairs warm, and rattled his trousers. He didn't like to pitch on windy days.

But the wind had brought summer early to Maple Siding, driving steadily out of the southwest for days, lashing old newspapers along the streets and bundling trashcans hollow down dust-stormed lanes. It sucked at the roofs all night like a hot dry breath, like a thing with intentions wanting in; and Joey's grandmother said it would bring trouble.

The devil's breath, she called it: "The last time it blew like this, young Mr. Kelly, the music teacher, climbed into his bathtub, unzipped his wrists with a razor and died—oh, he was *such* a tidy man."

To Joey and his friends the unexpected summer warmth meant an early ball season, mopping up the hidden, shadowed ices, edging the damp out of the grass; a wind to blow winter cobwebs out of the players and gust them into the streets, bristling with bats and catcher's mitts, puffing them all down to Kryger's empty lot like last fall's tumbleweeds melted free of the snow.

Now Joey fought his desire to crouch and gravel his fingers in Kryger's dust, afraid to switch the ball to his glove hand. On his left, through the edge of a narrowed eye he could see Herm Brown inching out from first towards second, teasing Joey, daring him; and straight behind and out of sight, Herm's brother Terry would be five feet out from second in a crouch; and all the time on third base, Bill the Thrill Moody waiting, hands on hips, feet splayed wide, impatient for his certain dash to home plate.

Tilston Whitley was up to bat.

Home Run Whitley had not struck out within living memory.

Joey usually tried to walk Whitley with an outside ball. But not this

time. This time he was going to knuckle-ball it right into Whitley's
puffed-up ribs. He'd get away with it, too. The others would be with him
—even half of Whitley's own team. Everybody hated Tilston Whitley.

Joey coiled up slow, tight, mean, then snapped himself open like a
spring, slinging the ball bullet-fast straight for Whitley's midsection.

Quick as a cat and grinning, Whitley stepped back and cracked the ball
high and hard into left field.

A howl of screams went up. The runners ran. Joey stood in fury and
despair, dazed. "Run, run!"

The runners pounded the hot spring earth into dust.

"Run!"

Then something changed. Now the cries held a note of panic. The
speeding players seemed to hesitate, shift direction, then flash away in one
lunging body like a startled school of fish.

"Run!"

And they ran.

Joey watched stupidly. Bill the Thrill, who was nearly sixteen and scared
of nothing, veered in his dash to home plate and pelted off after the other
streaming kids at full homerun speed. Joey turned slowly to face right
field. He jumped. Not twenty feet away and booming in fast came old
Kryger, red as rhubarb, sweating, breathing, reaching . . . Joey dodged
sideways.

Kryger had to correct his own headlong rush. One hairy hand closed on
Joey's dust. Joey flew for the safety of Mason's store twenty yards off—
Mason's wall, Mason's downspout, Mason's beckoning rooftop sanctuary.
It was three strides, toss up the glove, catch and hold, right hand on the
gaspipe, hang, swing, leap, and up. Kryger thundered in below, heaving
like a steamer and fog-horning:

". . . yard apes on my property . . . blah . . . baseball down your
throats . . . blah, blah . . . whale the damn out of you . . . blah!" He
shook the trough. "I know you, smart-ass boy!"

It was the usual Kryger tirade. He had two or three ranting versions of it
and Joey had heard them all.

Joey clung to Mason's chimney, panting up breath and the wind and
the red chimney-brick dust. Kryger prowled below like a bear, grumbling
and rattling the trough.

Then, from below, a cry of sudden pain.

A new explosion of curses. Hasty gravel-munching footsteps: Kryger
legging it away in retreat to his wrecking yard den.

Joey kneed and elbowed his way to the eaves and looked down. Kryger
was gone, all right. He had discouraged himself on a naked seam of down-

spout tin. There was wet blood black on the pipe, and round ink-blot stains of it spattering away over the gravel.

Joey grabbed his glove, skinned down the pipe and aimed himself home. Then he stopped. Where was his ball? It had been here—just here —on the ground. But now he saw only the grinning toothmarks of his own sneaker treads.

Kryger had stolen his ball.

He headed for home, his stomach sour and clenching. He found a rock to kick and sent it rattling over the pavement. Jim Slater, left field, melted out of a doorway and fell in beside him.

"First game of the season and Kryger busts it up."

"Yeah, and he stole my ball, too."

"I saw him. He grabbed it up and winged it over his fence into junk city."

"The jerk." Joey spat bitterly, neatly, and bull's-eyed a fire plug. "He couldn't bother us if we had a proper playing field like every other town around here."

"Let's get even. Let's phone the cops on him—tell them his junk yard's full of stolen cars."

"You kidding? They wouldn't listen to us. They'd hear a kid on the line and they'd hang up—they'd go back to torturing prisoners or something."

"You think they torture prisoners?"

"You think they don't?"

"It's lousy being a kid in this town."

"Sure is—they hate us."

Jim peeled off at his own street, glancing back. "Practice tomorrow? Just you and me?"

"Sure. After I do papers."

Joey rapped his stone away, just missing a wind-billowed puffball of a cat.

He thought how he'd set things right one day here in Maple Siding. He'd be mayor. He'd be the benefactor of amateur ball. He'd evict Kryger from that vacant lot, kick him heels over rump-roast out of that wrecking yard, too. There'd be room then for a ball park with a stadium that'd hold a thousand, ten thousand, fifty thousand cheering kids. He'd be the architect, the foreman, the crane operator, the mayor all at once. Yes. He could see it. They'd raise up a statue to Joey Parker when he died, right at the ball park entrance, a statue a hundred feet high with no pigeons . . .

But first he was going to become the greatest major league pitcher the world had ever seen.

*    *    *

Allison Davies ran down the wide damp-wood-smelling verandah of her house on Rougemont Drive and waved to young Joey Parker plodding dreamily home on the far side of the street and kicking a stone into the wind. She willed him to hurry. She had been Joey's babysitter once and she remembered Mr. Parker as a man full of discipline.

She set off down Rougemont, heading for the bridge—and Tom Barrett. She was determined to time her arrival there so he'd wait a bit: not so long that he'd be cross with her; just long enough to coax that appreciative glow out of his eye when he spotted her. She glanced at her watch: twenty past eight. She'd walk three more blocks straight along towards downtown, cross at the library, then cut down to the bridge along the tracks.

The wind seemed as anxious as she was; it pressed her forward like a friend.

She walked happily, conscious of her youth, her attractiveness, her new white and yellow spring jacket and matching sneakers, conscious too of the way men watched her pass, strangers boldly staring, those she knew shyly happening their eyes on her. There was a heavy, early-summer scent to the air, the pollen of a thousand flowering fields brought to her like a bouquet by the wind, and it was good, very good, she decided, to be seventeen and on your way to meet a young man at the edge of town.

She passed the convenience store and Mr. Johnston huddling bored as a sack in his car, waiting for his wife to fetch supper out in a plastic bag. Two thin ladies ballooned by on the wind, hooting, clutching at their hats and their parachute dresses; but Mr. Johnston's eyes followed Allison like thieves. She moved her hips for him and walked her shadow on up the street, and the wind took her away with the dust and the candy wrappers.

She passed Sturgis Road, Elm Street, Ash Street, crossed at the library, empty with all its lonely books. Here the tracks began their long, curving swoop into the Maple Siding station. She went between the rails, staggering her pace to find every second tie.

She dodged a splash of tar that might have spoiled her new sneakers.

It was getting darker now, but the wind was no cooler. The shadows stretched themselves out purple on the ground like paint, and the fading sky glowed yellow around the black-green tossing trees. Her thin jacket snapped in the gusts like a shroud. There was a hot-sand, train-oil smell, and a scuffed stone clinked against rusting steel.

A whole new atmosphere was enveloping her, the sound of creaking frogs and insects, the heavy swamp scent of tadpoles, water beetles, damp and decay. The wind snatched her breath from her throat and raced it away over the tall abandoned grass in hissing waves of black cattails.

"Damn."

She had misjudged her footing. Now one bright new sneaker came up spotted with mud.

"Allison, you're a fool," she told herself. "Couldn't even stick to the sidewalks like a normal person." But there was nothing to do, no turning back now, not time enough to retrace her steps. She did not want Tom to be angry with her.

She hurried forward only to halt a moment later in dismay. Ahead, a slew of oily mud and cinders stretched for fifty yards between the rails.

"Oh, damn and damn again!"

Now she would have to go back for certain, return all the way to the Rougemont crossing. She saw Tom in her mind's eye, walking away from the bridge, thinking he'd been stood up.

But . . .

Dipping away into the ditch in a quick plunge of tire tracks was a trail, the spoor of last season's bicycles. She knew it. She had cycled it herself not many years ago. It rose and fell through the scrub to the back of Kryger's wrecking yard, wound along his fence for a distance, then opened out into the vacant lot by Mason's store.

But the light was failing, the path was overgrown with scrub and likely to be muddy so early in the year . . .

The winds made up her mind for her, tilting her into the path like an encouraging hand.

There *was* mud at the bottom of the path, but only for a yard or so. She pressed her lips together and trudged on through it. Her shoes were a complete mess now; she couldn't make them any worse. "What will Tom say," she asked herself, "me twenty minutes late and plastered with mud —he'll be ashamed to be seen with me."

With a quick tiny thrill of alarm she saw how the dark was settling on her. She hurried, and the wind sighed the trees over and last year's dead leaves rattled around the path. Far off and faint, the steady croak of the auger on the vegetable oil plant came and went, came and went, like the pleading voice of a lost ship.

The tire tracks led her, and the treetops leaped above her.

And somewhere a breaking branch cracked sharp as a snapping bone.

She stopped.

That shadow . . . there on the path . . . A chill slipped down her back like a sprinkle of snow. Surely somebody was standing there, waiting, waiting, somebody silent, somebody still . . .

"Don't be an idiot."

She forced herself on. The slope of the path rose under her and she knew she would be up and out of the scrub in another minute.

Then behind her a shout:

"Hey!"

She nearly fainted.

She trembled herself around. Terror pounced. A man *was* standing on the path watching her. Then, just as suddenly, relief flooded through her like a warm tide and she pressed her hand to her breast.

"It's only you," she laughed in a voice that was still strained tight, tight, tight. "For a moment I thought—I don't know what I thought." She laughed again. "You almost scared the life out of me."

He approached grinning foolishly. He seemed a little frightened himself. There was something about his hand . . . He said, "Miss Davies—," then stopped. Perhaps the wind had carried his words away. He took her arm, lightly at first, as though to help her along; then he dug his fingers in hard with sudden vicious strength.

He began to draw her into the undergrowth.

Allison Davies was so shocked and astonished she couldn't even scream.

A mile away Joey Parker slammed up to his room. "Late!" they had pronounced; "No supper!"

He had gathered his breath to explain, but his father interrupted: "You got no business on private property. Told you and told you. The town'll get you kids a field, but you got to be patient. It's like a game. There's lots of players. You got to play ball."

Joey plumped down on his water bed, sending up a wave; and reaching into the desk drawer, he pulled out a candy bar that he had cached there himself against such emergencies. He chewed deliberately, gathering in his temper, fastening it down a bit at a time. Self-control, he told himself, was an asset to a ball player.

His room helped to settle him.

On the desk his pitching trophy, won last year on the school team. Other trophies large and small littering the top of his dresser. Bats, balls, gloves spilling out of a corner. And on every side, spreading up the walls and wrapping him warmly in, a mosaic of baseball cards, cutouts, posters.

There was Mantle, the slugger himself, staring back startled over one shoulder as though the photographer had surprised him; here Babe Ruth, Sultan of Swat, chin up, looking perplexed; and Willy Mays smiling broadly from a curled-yellow sheet of newsprint. Around these legends a throng of younger players shouldered up in high gloss colors, exerting dynamic poses and fluoride smiles.

Joey tossed his wrapper aside and switched out his light. The wind shuddered his window, drawing him to the glass, and he looked out. He could see right down the main rail line, follow it with his eyes all the way to Kryger's, where a single light burned like a mortuary candle against the moving dark.

Kryger would be there in that light, counting stolen baseballs . . .

Joey didn't think any more about it.

He went out the window and down the porch roof like the shadow of a hunting owl. He ran, and the black earth flowed under him.

The wind tossed his hair. The wind roared. The wind sighed a grey cloud streak over a watchful moon and swept overhead like the current of a great river, bending trees like lilies, sweeping him along between the shimmering steel rails.

At the bicycle path he didn't even hesitate, but plunged into the greater darkness of it without missing a step, his mind leading him along the invisible turns among the dodging bushes, under the choir voices of the hydro lines and the singing trees.

Once he might have heard something above the wind, a voice or the groan of a tree; but he passed on with his mind fixed. He stumbled over some small object, something loose, and he picked it up. A sneaker. He tossed it away.

Kryger's gate stood open.

He hadn't expected that.

It stirred on its hinges, beckoning, blustered by the wind.

Joey waited, hidden, watching, sorting the night for danger with a boy's natural instinct. There was nothing. Only the constant enormous breath of the wind.

He slipped inside.

It was a bizarre place to be on a gusting, clouded night. Alien, wonderful, a confusion of tumbled iron in wild provocative shapes. Some mad midnight sculptor might have strayed here out of a nightmare, casting a surreal trail as he wandered off into insanity. In the darkness there were few identifiable shapes.

But the ball he found easily. It lay in the open, catching the moonlight in an avenue of twisted black beams and arching hulks; perhaps a collapsed roller coaster had been dragged here with hooks. Joey tossed the ball out towards Mason's store. Now, he told himself, if the worst happened he would be able to get the ball in the morning.

And the worst did happen.

The gate crashed shut.

He couldn't see the gate from where he was, but there was no mistaking that galvanized hollow clank, that rattle of fumbled chain.

Instinct drove him to hide, powered his reluctant feet, clutched his hands for him, hauled him up the back of an old truck to the roof of a dead bus.

He lay there flat, waiting to be killed.

Kryger's heavy hands trembled, raked with a fiery pain from his scratches, and he toweled the sweat from his face with the hair of his arm.

Twice he had made the long walk along the tracks to the bridge and had found nothing. Yet the shoe was missing. That was a fact. He had seen that it was missing when he floated the body into the creek near the bridge. Quietly, quietly he had done it, not wanting to alert the lone boy, the sentinel boy who leaned on the bridge guardrail above, brooding out over the flat sighing night fields.

The body had slipped into the water easily. It was the missing shoe that was worrying him now. He had searched frantically back to the wrecking yard, searched from the gate to the old truck cab, fingered and palmed the cab's hidden places a dozen times; but he had not found it.

He had not found it.

Kryger sank down on a rusted rib of the butchered truck and knuckled his muddied knees. The wind calmed suddenly and a mosquito materialized, whining at his ear, wanting blood. He swung at it savagely. He needed to think.

What was the worst that could happen?

That the missing runner be found somewhere here on his lot.

He shook his head slowly over his knees. Why had he attacked a local girl? He had always told himself he would never do that. And so skinny, too. He could have easily driven to the city and had his pick of a thousand fatter girls, taken her on one of his little country drives. Then he could have hidden the body here. Like the others. He could have added it to his collection.

They were all here with him, Kryger's girls.

Kay, the chubby blonde, who had sung with one plump arm trailing from the window of his truck; he had put her in the trunk of the bustle-backed Dodge. And Liz—she had wanted to be called Elizabeth, she had an eye for style; he had nestled her in the Cadillac among the tire irons. And of course his favorite, little Rosa, who tinkled silver bangles against her olive skin; she deserved a Ferrari, but he'd had to settle her in a smashed Fiat.

But there was no point in this sort of thinking.

What he must do, first thing tomorrow, was dispose of the key to the back gate. What went on at night out beyond his back fence, out in the frog and insect ruckus, was no concern of his. With no key to the lock he could say that he never came and went by that way. He could say that he hadn't seen the key in months, couldn't recall it at all.

He felt better now that he had a story, even a not-so-very-convincing one. At sunup he would scour his property inch by inch. If the shoe was here he would find it and dispose of it. He hoped he would find it. The shoe might in some way lead to him. He looked at his scratches. He had bled. Maybe he should stay in the city until things quieted down. Maybe he should *retire* to the city. Then he could come out *here* for his girls and take them for *city* drives. Sheriff Coats's young wife now . . . Or the plump Mrs. Parker . . .

God, but that little thing had struggled. He would never have believed that a hundred pound girl could fight like that.

The wind was back, but he paid it no mind. He sat there in the night reliving his evening, sobbing into his hands with the pleasure and the terror of it.

"We don't want police," he said to the night, "not here, not here. . . ."

Joey lay trembling and flat on the rust while the stars stabbed at him through the scudding, billowing sky. He heard the snuffle of tears below and didn't understand. The world was too large for him, and he fell through space with it, spread-eagled under the timeless sky, crying to himself in his mind for his room and bed.

Eventually the rat-like sniffing faded below, and footsteps dragged themselves away.

Joey was able to creep his fear-sick body back down to the earth, worm it under the fence, pick up his ball, and sob his way home against the angry wind.

He slept late next day.

He was almost late for papers.

Most of the other carriers had already picked up their ink-printed loads and left the distribution point by the drugstore. Only Myrna Greene was still there, grunting her three large bundles into a wagon. There was something different in her expression: a frightened pleasure, an anticipation, as though she were at a favorite horror movie with the best scene about to begin.

Joey's Uncle Wilson had looked like that the night he'd come home with religion.

"Murder," she gasped with satisfaction, slapping the last bundle into place.

"So?"

You couldn't give credit to Myrna Greene for knowing anything.

"Not interested, huh?" Myrna Greene picked up the handle of her wagon, smiling her nervous, pained, hopeful grin.

"There's always murders in the city," Joey said.

But Myrna Greene was rumbling her wagon away. She shouted back, "It wasn't in the city, smart-ass, it was right here in Maple Siding. —Don't you read the papers?"

She grinned away with her load.

Joey tore the cover sheet off his top bundle and sucked in his breath. The headline was three inches high: LOCAL GIRL BRUTALLY STRANGLED! He swallowed and sat down in wonder to read, gasping. Allison Davies—his old babysitter! He shook his head over the ink. There had never been such a thing happen in Maple Siding during his short life, in spite of Grandma's tales.

And the paper said the body had been missing one shoe.

He delivered his papers quickly, the wind wrestling him for them. He was busting now to meet Jim Slater.

Jim was tall for his age, and lanky. He had a long, loose-jointed gait that he cultivated—he had admitted as much to Joey. He said it was the way a ball player ought to walk out on the field: quiet, laid back, with a lurking arm that could lash out and strike like a snake. "We'll go to Kryger's field," he said as the two of them came together.

"You nuts?" Joey related his night's adventure. "That guy's crazy, crying in the dark. And besides, he's sure to be watching out for me after yesterday."

"Nope." Jim spoke with authority. "He's not even in town. I saw him hit the highway this morning in his pickup, going like hell-knows-what."

"Which way did he turn?"

"North."

They both grinned. Any vehicle that left Maple Siding and turned north at the junction had to be going to the city. They'd have the run of Kryger's lot the rest of the day.

"But first," said Joey, "I got to make a stop."

They found the shoe after some casting about.

They found woodticks, too. Jim was annoyed. "What do you want that thing for, anyways?"

"It's valuable," Joey said, "as evidence."

They slung pitches across Kryger's lot at one another for an hour, fighting the wind, then went for ice cream. That was another good thing about Kryger's lot. Mason's store was handy with an inexhaustible supply of soft drinks and ice cream.

                              *    *    *

"The police are holding the Barrett boy." Joey's father rattled his newspaper over his soup. He liked to read the best articles aloud over the dinner table whether anyone else had read them or not.

"His poor mother," said Mrs. Parker, passing a lettuce leaf and a bit of carrot to Grandma. They were both always dieting, and always getting heavier.

"His mother says he got home that evening after about midnight. His excuse for being so late was that he waited for the Davies girl over two hours at the bridge." Mr. Parker glanced up. "Seems unlikely, doesn't it? When we were dating I doubt if I'd have waited two hours for you—it's just not reasonable for a person to do that." He shook the paper. "Says here the body was badly bruised . . . arms, throat, legs—she must have put up a struggle."

"Poor thing," said Mrs. Parker.

Grandma smiled over her lettuce as though it were a feast. "The wind brought her there, brought him, crashed them together. Murder," she said.

Joey jumped up from the table without excusing himself, snatched his ball and glove, and ran out into the sun and wind and baseball world.

"Look," he told Jim, "it's the same shoe. It's got to be. It's the shoe they're looking for."

"All right. It is the same shoe. So what?"

"Well, I don't know. I've got it. Maybe I should tell the police. They're looking for it."

"Help the cops? Are you nuts?" Jim slammed the ball so hard into his own glove Joey saw him wince. "What do you want to help the dumb cops for? They're part of—of *them*."

He made an insulting motion with his throwing hand that took in the adults of the whole town.

They were sitting knees up against the schoolyard fence, shirts off, chain link pressing checkerboards into their naked shoulders. The elms roared and thrashed above them like a wild green surf.

"What have any of them ever done for us?" Jim said. "Every town in fifty miles of here has a baseball field for its kids, some with bleachers, clubhouses, dugouts, everything. And we got nothing, nothing, nothing. We can't even play ball here in the schoolyard 'cause they're too cheap to buy the extra insurance. Help them?"

He spat long and slick into the grass.

It was all true, of course; but Joey still felt uneasy. "Allison Davies was my babysitter once."

"Sure. But she's dead now, isn't she? You going to bring her back?"

"It might help them nail the murderer."

"Crap! Anyone at all could have dropped that runner there. Picked it up somewhere else. Anyone. It wouldn't prove a thing. And anyways, they got Tom Barrett. You'd only complicate things. They wouldn't thank you."

"I guess you're right."

Joey pulled slowly and steadily on a long blade of crabgrass, seeking the inch of sweet white stalk. It squeaked out neatly and he slipped it into his mouth.

On the way home he loitered by the town hall and the court house. A force which he didn't understand held him there. He ought to go in, he told himself, and tell them about the shoe. He ought to tell them about Kryger's strange behavior, his crying in the junkyard night, his fear of police . . .

A car honked him out of the way. The back door let Sheriff Coats out, dragging Tom Barrett by the chain of his manacles. Tom Barrett's face didn't look murderous. It was as blank as a pie.

"Get along, you!" said Sheriff Coats.

Joe got.

He kept his lamp on, reading, until his father growled his whiskers in at the door and slapped the light switch. Joey closed his eyes, letting the footsteps creak his father away; then he reached his flashlight up from under the bed, made a tent of his sheet over his head, and went back to his baseball magazine.

The voices of his parents came and went below like water, and there was the clatter of tea things.

His father's voice rose like a wave.

"Another murder last night."

"But not here . . . ?"

"The city . . ."

". . . good. I mean, that's different, isn't it? You get to expect that sort of thing from city people."

"The folks at the office say there must be a connection with *our* murder. But I set them straight. 'Don't be fools,' I says, 'Tom Barrett was locked up tight as a screw the whole time right here in Maple Siding. What happened is some city cool-hander read about *our* murder in the newspapers and took the idea for himself.' "

There was resentment in Mr. Parker's voice. He might have been defending a copywriter.

"He's not locked up tight as a screw now," said Mrs. Parker; "the Barrett boy, I mean."

"I heard. The whole office was talking about it. Imagine letting a character like that out on the streets again. Insufficient evidence, they said at the hearing. Those fools aren't happy unless they got a confession signed in blood. And that damned defense counsel, Hugh Evans, arguing that the boy had no sign of a struggle on him, as if he wouldn't have cleaned himself up when he got home."

"Allison was just a slip of a thing. She couldn't have made a mark on a big strong man."

"That's right. And now Hugh Evans says the police got to find that missing shoe. 'Find that shoe,' he says, 'and you'll find yourself a murderer.' Silly old fool. I never heard such nonsense. That shoe could turn up anywhere. Somebody could find it and toss it in our garden. Would that make us murders? Ridiculous!"

"Somebody could just throw it over our fence."

"Sure they could. And we'd have a hell of a lot of explaining to do then, if Hugh Evans got his way. He'd make our lives miserable—damned miserable—just to protect his client."

"Maybe we'd wind up being his clients then . . ."

"If I had that shoe," said Mr. Parker, "I'd take and stuff it into Hugh Evans's mailbox."

Joey switched off his flashlight and came up out of his tented sheets breathing into the dark. Cars under his window wiped their headlights along the wall.

It was a great idea.

It was a dangerous idea.

He couldn't wait to tell Jim Slater.

And as he slept the night was calm with no disturbances: except that, for a time, Kryger hung upside down outside Joey's window like a bat, blinking vengeful eyes at him and working his teeth.

"You're crazy. You know that? Crazy."

They paid for their soft drinks and came out of Mason's air conditioning into a smother of hurricane heat. They let the wind kite them to shelter under a tree.

"Kryger really would be a killer if you tried that on him. He'd start with you. He's got something wrong with him, you know—a few shingles blown off. No telling what he might do if he got his hands on you. He doesn't have a full sack of beans, that guy."

Joey took a pull at his orange pop.

"I got that angle covered—he wouldn't get near me. It's a good idea, Jim. It could work. I think old Kryger's scared of the police already. Have you noticed that he never calls the police on us for trespassing?"

"That don't mean nothing."

"It must. He probably does have stolen cars in there."

"And what if he really is the killer? Have you thought about that?"

Joey snorted. "Kryger? That's a laugh. He's too old to chase girls. I bet he's over forty—fifty even. Nah, somebody else threw that sneaker in the scrub to get rid of it—Tom Barrett, most likely."

They were both quiet for a moment, thinking. Finally Jim said, "For all you know, it might not even be her shoe."

"It *must* be."

"Sure, but you don't *know*."

Joey thought about that. Then he said, "It doesn't make any difference if it is or isn't. Kryger won't know either, will he? I'm just banking that he doesn't want the police snooping around his place." He rolled himself out flat on the grass and watched a low cloud drag its white belly over the top of the tree.

The sound prodded Kryger like a stick.

*Clank*, pause . . . *clank*, pause . . .

He hunched himself to peer out into the yard. Through the fly-specked glass of his office window, he saw the smart-ass boy, the one that always ran up onto Mason's roof.

The kid stood on Kryger's own vacant lot, bold as a landlord, facing into the wrecking yard, rapping his ball off Kryger's fence. Kryger's reaction was rage. He had fierce thoughts of slipping out the back gate, circling around and coming up behind the kid—but he had already thrown away the back gate key.

Well, one shout, one scowl, one shake of the fist would send the kid galloping.

He bullied himself up into a good heat and crashed out loud through the door.

"Here! Get out of it—move!"

But the kid *didn't* move.

He flinched a bit, he nearly fumbled his ball; but he didn't break and run the way Kryger had expected. He just gathered up his arm and started in with the ball again.

*Clank* . . . *clank* . . .

Kryger felt something twisting and letting go deep in the workings of his gut; the same sort of feeling he'd got with the Davies girl, and with all those girls in the city.

He pounded up to the fence, swelling himself like a toad.

The kid stood firm. The ball came up—*clank*—flew back . . . came up—*clank*—flew back. Kryger rolled in like an engine, steam-valving and firebox-belching, ready to burst. He halted five feet from the kid, his nose just inches from the steel mesh.

The ball came up at his face—*clank*—flew back . . .

Kryger stood sweating, thick fingers winding, unwinding like rope in the steel links, fingers wanting to crush something. But he saw it was hopeless. The kid had him. There wasn't a thing he could do. He was penned up like a prisoner behind his own damn fence.

The kid was watching him closely, as though trying to find his moment; then he said in a thin voice, "Make you a deal."

"Deal? You want to make deals, trespassing on my land?" Kryger tried to go through the fence again.

"Deal. You let us play ball on this lot here with no more hassles, and we won't tell anybody about the shoe."

The shoe.

The whole sky, the sun, the wind seemed to gather and pound Kryger once like a hammer. It was as though he had just walked blindly into a wall, the breath was knocked clean out of him. If he hadn't been gripping the fence with both hands he would have sat flat down with the shock.

"What shoe?" he managed to whisper.

"That one." The kid turned and pointed.

A second boy, a long slow movement in jeans, stepped around the corner of Mason's store. He held up and dangled a shoe, spindled it, swung it into the air. It turned and turned.

White and yellow . . . yellow and white . . .

"I found it in your wrecking yard. There, on top of that bus." The kid pointed again.

Kryger remembered the long, slim, flailing denim legs. He looked at the bus. Yes, it was quite possible. He ought to have thought of looking higher up instead of bloodhounding about on the ground. Still, he reminded himself, nobody could prove the shoe had anything to do with him.

"It's got blood on it," the kid said; "yours."

Kryger realized he was still hanging on to the fence, hands high up, his welted and scratched arms bare to the boy's gaze. How that little bit of a thing had fought: country spirit; none of the city girls had matched it . . .

"How do you know it's my blood?" he asked weakly, trying to seem amused. He felt like giving the whole game up, walking straight on down to the sheriff's office, picking up the keys and locking himself in the cage. He'd say, "Here I am—Ollie Kryger. It was me strangled the Davies girl— and lots more, too, in the city." He imagined the sheriff savagely beating him in the hidden dark of the cells.

The boy was talking.

"Remember when you chased me up onto Mason's roof? You cut your hand on the downspout. Well, I took that shoe just now over to the downspout and rubbed the dried blood all over it. So it's got your blood on it, no doubt about that."

Here was hope!

It flickered a long way off in the forest of his thoughts like a candle in a distant window. These boys didn't really believe he had killed the Davies girl. Tight, straining cables began to loosen inside him.

"What is it you want from me, boy?"

"All we want—all *I* want—is for you to stop chasing us off this lot and breaking up our games. We don't hurt nothing of yours—you got no windows here for us to break. We don't cost you nothing. You leave us be, and we leave you be. Okay?"

Now Kryger stopped trying to heft the fence out of the ground and relaxed against it, the hard steel pressing his cheek. The world, which only a moment ago had leaped up under him, was leveling out rock solid again. These kids had nothing on him, nothing at all. They were attempting a clumsy frame.

Still, he must not force their hand. There *could* be some original stains of his blood on that shoe.

"Look, kid," he began, "—what's your name?"

"Joey."

"Look, Joey, I see what you're trying to do here. But you can't make a story like that stick. Don't you know these detectives got modern scientific equipment? They'll see right away what your game is—they'll match rust stains to the spout, or something."

"I won't tell them about the spout."

"Oh, but I will, won't I, Joey? I got to defend myself against a lie, don't I?"

The boy wavered. But he said with defiance, "We can rip the spout off right now, my buddy and me, and run with it. We can hide it someplace—"

Kryger forced a laugh. It took muscles he didn't know he had.

"Joey, Joey, that's no good. They'd see it was missing, they'd see it was freshly torn off, wouldn't they? I'd have to tell them how you tried to blackmail me. And blackmail is a crime. They'd make you talk, Joey. They'd get you down the basement of the sheriff's office and they'd make you talk, you know they would. They can get pretty mean, those cops, Joey . . ."

The boy appeared totally deflated now. His catcher's mitt drooped at his side, his large doe-eyes were desperate.

Timing, Kryger thought, is everything. He waited three seconds, four, then said:

"Anyways, Joey, you got me all wrong. All wrong. If one of you kids had only just come and asked me outright about using the lot, I'd have let you. I would have, Joey. You kids must think I'm a pretty mean old guy, but I'm not really. A man just likes to be asked, that's all."

Kryger paused for a moment to let that take effect, then added, "Try me now, Joey. Ask me straight out if you can play ball on my lot, straight out like a man, and hear what I've got to say."

The boy glanced back at the corner of Mason's store, at his pal, who looked bored with the whole business and wasn't dangling up the runner in a tease any more, but draping it carelessly in one hand at his side.

"All right," the boy said finally, "I'll go for it—can we play ball on your lot or not?"

Don't make it too easy, Kryger thought, don't get him suspicious. Aloud he said, "Can't you say please?—it's just good manners."

The boy heaved a sigh like all the sighs of all the bothered boys on earth. He turned so that his pal would not see his lips move, and lowered his voice.

"All right—*please.*"

Kryger screwed up his brow to affect deep thought. Then he said, "Why not?"

The smart-ass boy whooped and slung his glove into the air.

"But," warned Kryger, "don't you kids damage anything." It was a meaningless caution: there was nothing to damage.

The boy wheeled and fled over the gravel to his friend. He spoke excitedly, then the two shrilled with glee. The boy with the shoe flung it high in the air, and the two of them darted away.

The shoe rose swiftly, climbing against the blue early-summer air, arcing, tumbling slowly, slowly, yellow and white, yellow and white . . .

Kryger brought the shoe back into the wrecking yard, doused it generously with kerosene and put a match to it. The gay spring colors flared briefly into summer and turned black.

The smoke rose straight up.

There wasn't a breath of wind.

It was a glorious songbird morning, and like birds after a storm the Maple Siding ladies were emerging from their nests in new spring colors, chitchatting and tittering in the street.

Kryger watched them in their full-breasted plumpness. He breathed a little faster, anticipating.

He walked his big front gate shut in the gentle air. He overheard one of the kids whisper, "He's not so bad."

His lot surged like a sea with tumbling, laughing kids. They were squalling like gulls. The smart-ass boy was there on the pitcher's mound, and he waved to Kryger and Kryger waved back.

"Play ball!" Kryger bellowed, grinning.

Smart-ass boy, he thought, play your silly game.

Kryger was retiring.

To the city.

# Accidentally Yours

### ELLANE CAVENEY

As a lawyer in the rural community of Cram Corners, my caseload is rather sparse. Not that I'm complaining, since that leaves me lots of time for what I like best—hobby farming. I own forty acres just seven miles outside of town. We raise chickens, even though my wife claims they're dirty. (She's a city girl. I met Claire in college and brought her back to my hometown. After eleven years, she claims she's still adjusting.) We had goats for a while until I discovered that they ate expensive shrubbery, not grass, and that the milk tasted strange even when it was made into custard. I bought our three kids a Welsh pony and have since acquired an antique cart to ride in. I'm looking for a sleigh in good condition at a reasonable price. (Yes, I realize those terms are contradictory.) We have two feeder pigs appropriately named Breakfast and Lunch. But the huge hogs are going on six years of age because we bought them when they were adorable little piglets and proceeded to treat them as family pets. To this day, they follow our youngest son around like devoted puppies. Let me forewarn those who dream of a rural life: tender-hearted people shouldn't try raising their own meat, it's too expensive. I'm sure these Cheshire Whites are going to die of old age before we ever taste home-cured bacon. But then I have digressed from my subject, the most exciting, if regrettable, case I have defended to date.

First, let me introduce Janie Shannon. She grew up in Cram Corners. She was a few years behind me in school, but I knew her sister Anna. Janie was the quiet type, so quiet that I never really took note of her appearance until she became my client. I suppose she must be about twenty-five. She has short, curly brown hair and a flawless complexion. I can't tell you the color of her eyes for certain because she never looks anybody right in the face. After high school, she took a job behind the counter at Clarence's Drug. Most people say that Clarence hired her out of kindness. In other words, when the good Lord dealt, He gave Janie the cards missing

from a pinochle deck. Since I'd only met her over the lunch counter at
Clarence's, where she kept her eyes on the order pad and mumbled, I'd
come to the conclusion that she didn't have anything higher than a seven
or eight in the smarts department. Anyway, everybody felt sorry for Janie
when she was arrested for manslaughter, and I was asked to take the case
with local donations for my fee. It wasn't like my docket was overloaded at
the time (my only case being the McCallisters' divorce) so I accepted.

I'll never forget how dejected Janie looked at our first conference. She
had been arrested for killing Peter Krushyn but was out on bail (also raised
by the good citizens of Cram Corners). It seems that Janie struck Peter
with her '76 Chevy sedan when he was on his way back to the grocery
store he and his brother Paul owned. He'd just bought two hamburgers,
one order of fries and one of onion rings, plus two coffees. Their lunches
were much messier than Peter, who had a bruise on one thigh and a bump
on his head. Nonetheless, he was very dead. But let me get back to Janie
and her version of the accident.

"I rarely leave work before closing time," she whispered, so low that I
had to ask her to speak up. "I'd promised Mother that I would take her
books back to the library during my lunch hour. A simple little errand,
that's all." She heaved her thin shoulders. "I was driving slowly. I've never
had a speeding ticket. At least, I think I was driving slowly. I . . . I guess
I was daydreaming when Mr. Krushyn walked right in front of me." She
was shredding her hanky. Not a tissue, but a regular hanky, the kind my
grandmother used to tuck into her bodice. Rip. Rip. Rip. Most unnerving.
"I got so flustered. I tried to slam on the brake, but must have hit the gas
pedal instead. I really don't know. I don't remember. All I do remember
was this terrible thud."

"Just relax, dear." I patted her hand and felt her tense even more. "We
all make mistakes."

"But I make more than most," she murmured. "Even though I tally
everything twice, my customers are always having to correct me."

"I'm sure you make the errors in the customers' favor," I tried to con-
sole her.

"Oh, no! Please don't say such a thing in front of Clarence. I do try to
be so careful."

"I'm sure you do, dear."

"Are they going to give me the electric chair?" Her hanky now lay in
shreds on her lap and she began wrapping the strips around her fingers.

"Mercy, no, Janie! I'm sure Judge Croft will be most understanding."

"Sweet Judge Croft. Did you know he and my daddy graduated together? From high school, I mean. Of course the judge went on and
became important, and my daddy just went to work for the road commis-

sion. Oh, I have humiliated my family. Disgraced them! I killed a man. I really did. I can't believe it. I just can't believe it!"

"Don't take on so, Janie. I promise you everything will turn out all right."

"I don't see how." And she wept into the wadded fragments of her hanky. I handed her my monogrammed handkerchief, which she twisted and cried into and gave back in threads half an hour later.

I had no choice but to have Jane Shannon plead guilty to involuntary manslaughter, requesting leniency. The whole town showed up at the courthouse the morning of the hearing. Everyone's sympathy, quite naturally, was with poor, obscure Janie.

On the witness stand the girl told, tearfully, how she hadn't meant to step on the accelerator. Matt Corkran, our dayshift policeman, testified to the presence of skidmarks for the last six feet before impact. Character witnesses described how polite Janie was, how she always tried to give the correct change, and how she apologized profusely when she got the orders mixed up. Then Paul Krushyn took the stand.

"My brother crossed at that intersection 'most every day at noon," the fiftyish grocer stated. "We'd been ordering our lunch from the Dairy Barn since Pa ran the store. It was such a habit, and there was so little traffic on Route 17, that I reckon Peter wasn't watchin' when he stepped onta the pavement. 'Tweren't nobody's fault. Coulda been me in the road jest as easy, since we trade off who goes. Depends on who's busiest when lunchtime comes 'round. That day I'd been stacking soup so Peter went. Just his dumb luck. Miss Janie isn't to blame."

The packed courtroom nodded agreement.

The judge gave Janie a suspended sentence. I'm sure his conscience would not have permitted anything else. The whole town cheered, and the local weekly newspaper carried an editorial on the victory of justice in our great land.

Needless to say, I was a little surprised to see Janie in my office late one afternoon about a month after the hearing. Janie simply didn't visit people. Not even to thank them. She was too shy.

"Mr. Hodge," she began, taking a ladder-backed chair opposite my desk. "I just had to come and see you." I handed her a box of Kleenex and watched as she demolished them one by one in her nervousness. "I'm carrying a terrible burden and I must confess."

"To killing Mr. Krushyn on purpose?" I teased.

The girl raised her eyes, but the November shadows were long in my office and I still couldn't determine their color. A vague fear crawled up my back and sat on my shoulder.

"I can't live with myself," she whispered, "having lied to you. I mean, while I wouldn't want anyone else to know . . ."

"Have you spoken to your minister?" I asked, not wanting any share of the guilt I could feel emanating from Janie. This girl guilty? Impossible!

"I can't bring myself to tell Reverend Tolliver. You see, he's a second cousin on my mother's side."

"Janie, I really don't think I want to hear this."

"Yes, you do." She chewed her bottom lip for several seconds. "If I get up and leave right now, you would always wonder what really happened, wouldn't you?"

I shifted uncomfortably in my swivel chair.

"You can't be tried twice for the same crime," I advised her, "so you don't have to confess to *me*." Boy, did I emphasize that last word!

"I know." She made confetti of yet another Kleenex. "And I knew that I would never be convicted of manslaughter in this town. Mr. Krushyn knew it, too. I guess that's why he gave me five thousand dollars to run over his brother with my car."

"Oh, Lord!" I broke out in a sweat where I didn't even have pores.

"The brothers were having a difference of opinion about running their store." Janie took the last Kleenex out of the box. "One wanted to sell and move out of Cram Corners. The other didn't."

"I heard Paul had put the store on the market," I admitted, already savoring a warrant for his arrest. "Pray tell me," I had to ask, "why you would even consider . . ." but the word "murder" got stuck in my throat.

"Five thousand dollars is a lot of money. I wanted to take a cruise. You know, like on the Love Boat."

"Love Boat?" I repeated dazedly.

"Um-hmmm. I don't make much money at the drugstore. I've been saving for years and still have only three hundred and thirteen dollars in my account."

"I can't believe it. Janie Shannon capable of premeditated murder. I would never have imagined it possible. . . . Good grief, girl, you can't even get two orders straight."

"Well," Janie swallowed, hard. "I didn't exactly get it straight. That's why I put on my brakes in the end. But it was too late." Janie shook her head sadly. "Peter's the one who offered me the five thousand dollars. Fortunately, he paid in advance. And now, you and I are the only two who know the truth." She smiled. "I do feel so much better for having told you."

How nice, I thought, though I wasn't feeling very well myself. Sure, I was glad Janie had been handed a couple of aces from the Almighty's deck and that conniving Peter Krushyn had been left with a joker. But the

McCallisters had reconciled and I was living off my farming income. Oh, I was asked to represent a drifter who had been caught with some gems from the late Maggie Hofster's estate. But the way things had been going for me lately, the drifter would turn out to be Maggie's long-lost son who was only claiming his rightful inheritance.

Nope, I simply don't have faith in people any more. Not that I should trust animals, either. My left arm is in a cast following a spill from the pony cart and the chicken eggs we hatched so carefully in a hundred-and-fifty-dollar brooder all grew up to be roosters. Guess the Lord knew they'd be safe in our now-vegetarian household.

# A Soul to Tell

### JEREMIAH HEALY

"Mayay I have your attention. The Delta Connection, Business Express Flight 3557, with direct service to Nantucket and continuing service to Martha's Vineyard, is now ready for passengers through Gate 15. All rows may now board the aircraft."

I hefted my duffel bag and joined the line of folks handing little passes to the uniformed smile. An hour before, I'd locked "John Francis Cuddy, Confidential Investigations," and hailed a Boston cab to Logan Airport. It's cheaper to drive to Cape Cod and take the ferry to Nantucket, but I was on expenses, and the client on the phone had said the sooner the better. She also said I wouldn't be needing a firearm or dress clothes, just a camera and lots of film.

We made our way down a flight of stairs and onto a jitney bus with deep leatherette seats. Gas tankers, Marriott food service trucks, and baggage shuttles made for heavy traffic on the macadam. The bus driver pulled up to our plane, a twin prop Shorts 360 that looked a lot like our jitney with wings. I heaved my duffel into the open baggage hold near the tail. The maybe thirty of us filled most of the seats in the cabin, the takeoff reminding me of walking through a machine shop going full blast. When the pilot reached cruising altitude, the stewardess began pouring soft drinks.

The plastic cups were barely on the trays before we began our descent into Nantucket, the "Faraway Isle" of whalers. Gentle hills and moors, sporting a dozen shades of yellow, brown, and orange in the clear October air. My wife Beth and I used to talk about taking a getaway weekend to the island. Before the cancer took her.

On the ground, a guy wearing sonic earmuffs unloaded the baggage hold onto a cart and wheeled the cart to a glassless service window, through which he passed our luggage. Following the client's suggestion, I signed for a Jeep Cherokee at one of the rental counters and got a map and finger-traced directions to 76 Main Street, the bed and breakfast the client named.

There was only one architectural style on the drive from the airport, even the gas stations done in silver cedar-shake siding. The predominant trim color was white, a few nonconformists daring powder blue and even dull red. Once in town, however, there was a Federalist flavor to things, including a number of brick or clapboard mansions and cottages.

The inn turned out to be one of the white clapboard places, a friendly woman named Shirley registering me and asking what I wanted from my time on the island. When I said I wasn't sure, she rattled off ten or twelve spots I could visit, with brochures on what to look for when I arrived at each. After I was shown to my room and oriented on breakfast and next morning, Shirley wished me a good dinner and a good night.

Unpacking took only until four o'clock. Since the weather was clear and I didn't know what the client had in mind for my time, I decided to walk the town and harbor. Main Street angled downhill past quaint shops, spreading and petering out at wharves that held tiny shacks dolled up as art and crafts galleries. Not too many pleasure craft so late in the season, but still a lot of scallopers and charter boats.

At the sound of a hooting horn, people who had been lounging on benches or curbs suddenly gathered themselves and rushed toward a docking ferry. One couple doggy-walked a sea-kayak on its two-wheeled trailer, him at the bow, her at the stern, smiling tolerantly at the odd looks and snapshots being taken of them.

Leaving the harbor, I criss-crossed the streets, noticing the police station on South Water only by the one black and white Ford patrol car parked in front of it. As the sun set, I joined the rest of the tourists in what seemed to be the major preoccupation: reading menus posted outside restaurants and shaking heads at the high prices listed. I eventually settled on a reasonable place called Obadiah's, an old fashioned basement dining room on India Street. The wide-board pine benches were lacquered, the clam chowder and swordfish magnificent. I added a bottle of sauvignon blanc to the bill.

Upstairs, the sidewalks were rolling up. I walked off dinner for twenty minutes or so, appreciating the charm of the town in the afterglow of the wine. Climbing back up Main, I nearly broke my ankle twice on the cobblestone street, the stones themselves rounded but hummocky above the old cement.

At the inn, an equally friendly man named Mitch welcomed me all over again. After a few minutes of small talk, I went up to my room. In the spirit of the island, I went to sleep with the windows open and the door to the corridor unlocked.

\* \* \*

"I'd rather hoped to go deaf first, you see."

Eleanor Ware sat across from me, sipping herb tea from a delicate china cup. The cup was the only delicate thing about her. High forehead, broad nose, strong jaw. A whisper of makeup around the eyes, and black hair generously streaked with gray. The hair was pulled back and caught in a ponytail, as though she did that just once each day and undid it just once at night. The kind of clothes you see in a Talbot's window, all earth colors. Fifty-plus, and not the least bit afraid to show it.

Ware received me on a wicker settee in the solarium of a traditional Cape Cod, a railed wood deck visible through the sliding glass doors behind her. She already had asked me if I'd enjoyed the inn, and I already had told her that breakfast on the patio there had been great except for the yellow jackets. Apparently, the beautiful weather brought them out, wasps being "a small price to pay for sunshine in October." I'd just managed to get us onto why she wanted to hire me, but I was having trouble understanding her.

"Let me get this straight, Mrs. Ware. You want me to follow your husband around?"

"Yes, yes, but not for some—what do you detectives call it, 'ulterior motive'?"

"Investigator."

"Excuse me?"

"I'm an investigator. Detectives are on police forces."

"Yes, yes. Tell me, Mr. Cuddy. Are you married?"

"Widower."

"Oh. Oh, I am sorry." Her eyes blurred as she set the cup in a matching saucer. "Forgive me, Mr. Cuddy. And please forgive me too my joke about going deaf. You see, my husband Mycah has been in real estate ever since he came to the island—his office is just off Main Street. He turns fifty-five next February, and he's always promised to retire then. Mycah certainly deserves it, the man has worked day and night for decades and has always been a fine provider. But, with the boom in housing the last few years, he's scarcely had any time to spend with me. And I'm afraid, frankly, that in maintaining and expanding my own circle of friends . . . I'm just afraid that Mycah and I have rather lost touch with one another, that we won't have much in common once he retires."

"So you want me to follow him around?"

"Yes. To see what he does, how he spends his day. Then report back to me so that I can learn more about his interests and at least have topics of conversation when we begin spending more time together in a few months."

I shifted in my wicker chair. "Couldn't you just sort of ask him about that?"

Ware blushed. "Ask Mycah about what he does, you mean?"

"Yes."

"Oh, no. No, that would be . . . inappropriate. He'd feel that I didn't love him enough to have kept up with him."

I thought about Beth, all the time I spent away from her before knowing she was sick. Eleanor Ware's sentiment was a little corny, but I could understand it.

I said, "You want pictures of him?"

"Pictures?"

"Photographs. All the camera equipment I brought."

"Oh. Oh, I see. No, the island attracts a lot of naturalists, you see. When I suggested camera gear on the phone I meant for it to give you— do detec—sorry, investigators, call it 'cover'?"

"Close enough. I follow him around pretending to take pictures of the birds and the bushes."

"Precisely."

"You don't think he'll notice that."

"Mycah? No. No, everyone who visits Nantucket and rents a Jeep is sightseeing, and this is a small island with only so many roads. Even if he saw you more than once, he wouldn't give it a second thought."

"Do you want pictures of any of the people he meets?"

"No. Thank you, but no. Mycah must spend a good deal of his time showing properties to prospective buyers from away. From off-island, that is. I wouldn't be needing to meet or talk to any of them. I just want you to trail after him for, oh, say, three days? Then report back to me. Would that be satisfactory?"

"Three days at four hundred a day added onto my time to get here and get back, plus expenses."

"I assure you that I can afford it."

I looked around at the elaborate furniture, adjoining a living room with a baby grand piano but without a television. People who don't have a TV in their living room usually can afford it.

"What I meant, Mrs. Ware, is that you might not be getting much value for your money."

"I'm a fair judge of value, Mr. Cuddy. And besides, even if this is just a whim, I'd like to know. It will help me be a better helpmate to Mycah during his transitions from active professional to retired husband."

"You have a recent picture of him?"

She frowned. "Can't you just—what, 'pick him up' outside the house here?"

I gestured toward the front door. "Your house sits on this little knoll with a meadow in front of it. There's no place for me to conceal the Jeep, and even your husband would wonder about a car that picked him up right outside his driveway."

"Yes. Yes, I see your point."

"It would be a lot easier for me to latch onto him at his real estate office, and that way I could start this afternoon."

"Just a moment."

Ware rose and strode purposefully to the piano. She came back carrying a large photo, holding the frame at northwest and southeast corners like an auctioneer's assistant. "This is a portrait we had done at Bachrach's in Boston." The woman couldn't quite keep the pride from her voice. "I'm told they even had it displayed in their glass case on Boylston Street."

The photo showed Mrs. Ware sitting and a bold, assured man with auburn hair standing halfway behind her. His right hand rested on her shoulder, her left hand bent upward to touch his.

"You make a striking couple."

She blushed again and replaced the frame on the piano. Her sentimentality and strength made an attractive combination, and I found myself envying husband Mycah just a bit.

Resuming her seat, Eleanor Ware asked if there was anything else.

"What kind of car does your husband drive?"

"Cadillac."

"Model and color."

"Coupe de Ville, rather a burgundy. With all the dirt roads on the island, a Jeep would be more practical, but Mycah has always loved his Cadillacs."

"You know anyone on the local police force?"

My questions seemed to throw her. "The police?"

"Yes."

"What do they have to do with our arrangement?"

"Hopefully nothing. It's just standard procedure to check in with them when I start working in a new town."

"Is it . . . some kind of law or regulation?"

"No. Just good business practice."

"I see. Well, I have a problem with that."

"What is it?"

"On the telephone, when I called, you said that your licensing statute would keep everything between us confidential."

"That's right."

"Confidential even from the police?"

"I don't read the statute every week, but it just says I might have to reveal to a court, not the cops. Why?"

"Well, you see, I'm an islander. I was raised here, with the chief of police, among others. I would . . . It would be embarrassing to me for them to know that I'd hired you to follow Mycah."

"That's understandable. Tell you what. I'll just let the police know I'm down here on business, not what the business is or who it's for. Would that be all right?"

Ware seemed to think about it. "Yes. Yes, that would be fine." She reached down next to her chair and brought up a handbag from which she coaxed a fat envelope. "I'd like to pay you a retainer in advance."

As she counted fifties from the envelope, I said, "A check would be fine."

Ware stopped counting for a minute, weighing the bills in her palm as though that would somehow be a quality control on her tally. "No. No, I got the cash for this, and frankly, it makes it better."

"Better?"

"This is a small island, Mr. Cuddy. It's hard to have secrets, even harder to share them. That's why I wanted someone from away—someone like you—to help me. Paying you in cash means no snoopy bank teller will know my personal business."

Eleanor Ware finished counting and handed me the bills, being careful, I thought, not to let our fingers touch.

"Kate Hearn."

"John Cuddy, sergeant."

"Kate, please."

I released her hand. She sat back down behind a cluttered desk, me taking one of the metal chairs in front of it. The biggish patrol officer who had brought me into her office closed the door as he left.

Hearn said, "Chief's on vacation, off-island."

Mrs. Ware would be pleased.

Hearn inclined her head toward the door. "Ben said you're a private investigator."

"Yes."

"From Boston?"

"My accent give me away?"

Hearn laughed, one sharp bray. "No, it's just there aren't so many from the Cape, and I thought I knew most of the operatives from New Bedford and Fall River."

Her hair on the sides and back touched the collar of her shirt. The bangs in front were just past her brow. Any longer and she'd have to blow out a breath to keep them off her eyes, which were blue and steady. "So, what brings you to Nantucket?"

"I'm going to be driving around a lot with a camera, and I thought I ought to check in with you first."

"Uh-huh." The steady eyes never left me. "You're going to be driving around a lot."

"Right."

"Make, model, and plate?"

I told her. She wrote them down.

"Where are you staying?"

"Seventy-six Main Street."

"Good choice."

"I'm comfortable."

Hearn waited me out, then said, "Am I going to get a real answer to my question about what brought you here?"

"Confidential."

"Confidential."

"Sorry."

Hearn puffed out a breath, flipping the bangs. "Okay. Consider yourself checked in, then. But don't expect any favors without doing some yourself."

When I got up, we shook hands anyway.

High noon, but not much happening in downtown Nantucket. Three elderly women were window shopping, pointing politely and nodding at everything each one said. A hard-faced guy in a blue jogging suit was loafing on the hood of his car, arms and ankles crossed. He looked like he'd made his money young. Some kids of college age were camped on a curb, knapsacks as backrests, eating ice cream.

I could see the doorway to Ware Realty through the driver's side mirror. I studied a map of the island and fiddled with my camera like a tourist about to strike off for the afternoon. A burgundy Coupe de Ville occupied a parking space three down from mine. A tweedy middle-aged couple had gone into the realty office about fifteen minutes before, he seeming less enthusiastic than she did.

I was down to counting the number of ponds on my map when Mycah Ware came out holding a clipboard in his right hand. In tow were the middle-aged couple and a stunning redhead in a bottle-green dress that I would bet complemented her eyes. The quartet crossed to the Cadillac, the men taking the front seats, the women the rear, the redhead showing some leg as she climbed in. Even the guy in the jogging suit seemed to sit up straighter. Waiting until Ware passed me, I started up and after them.

I should have had ice cream with the knapsackers.

Ware took his customers to three houses, all indistinguishable to me under weathered shingles and white picket widow's walks. At each stop, Ware sashayed the woman in the couple all over the grounds, tapping and then holding a pen to the clipboard in his hands. The redhead tagged behind with the man in the couple, seemingly doing the same things with her pen and clipboard. Then everybody went into the house for half an hour or so.

The only change in the routine was the part of the island we visited. First west to the Dionis Beach area, then south to Cisco Beach, then east past the airport toward Low Beach.

While Ware and the redhead hucked, and the couple absorbed, I took photos. Of everything. Kids windsurfing in striped wetsuits, a woman in a straw hat painting a seascape on an easel, tufted grasses at the base of dunes. Double-rung fences of gray split rails, country mailboxes with little red flags, kaleidoscopic fields of wildflowers. Estuaries with small sailboats, moors of pumpkin-hued heather. Small trees bent over from the prevailing wind, briar patches even Br'er Rabbit wouldn't call home. You name it, I shot it, my eyes blearing and my back creaking.

At house number three, a blue Thunderbird with classical music wafting from the radio pulled even with me. Bent over my umpteenth wildflower, I looked up at the driver. Preppy face, short blond hair, the kind of guy who wouldn't look quite thirty until he was well past forty.

He said, "You okay?"

"Fine, thanks."

"Saw your car on my way into town, then saw you still here. Thought you might be broken down."

"No. Just taking pictures. Thanks, though."

"Any time." He waved and accelerated slowly away.

I wondered if I had just met one of Kate Hearn's officers out of uniform.

The Thunderbird was barely out of sight when Ware and the others left the house and piled into the Caddy. We drove back toward town, stopping at a classy private clubhouse set a hundred feet from its driveway. I stole the spirits from some more flora, trying not to notice the rabbit squashed flat near the entrance or the ravens licking their chops on the power lines. An hour later, the Coupe de Ville pulled back onto the road and went the rest of the way into Nantucket. The fabulous foursome disappeared into the realty office for half an hour more, then reappeared with vigorous handshakes and polite kisses all around. The wife in the couple was clutching a big manila envelope and beaming ecstatically; the husband was missing a shirt pocket with his pen and wearing an expression like he'd just been in a train crash.

Once the couple was out of sight, Ware and the redhead smiled at each other and went to the Cadillac. Off we went, this time toward the east along Milestone Road. I checked a couple of times for the Thunderbird but didn't see it.

When we got to the village of Siasconset, Ware and the redhead started house-hopping again. They'd circle around a place, clipboards in hand, Ware apparently giving her some tips as he pointed at exterior features, then to a form on her clipboard. At each house they'd go inside for half an hour or so, then come back out. These times I shot a towering, red-banded lighthouse; gray, dumpy hens that looked wild; and larger silver-shake mansions with English hedges and gardens.

After the third house, we again returned to town, dusk and a little fog heavy on the moors along the road. A block from the realty office, Ware came to a stop. The redhead and he shook hands theatrically, a pronounced "We-did-it" pantomime, then laughed. She got out of the Caddy and into a Mercedes convertible, the only one I'd seen on the island so far. Ware waited until she started up before he put his car in gear.

I followed Ware back to his own house, continuing on as he slewed into his driveway and put the Caddy in the garage via some kind of electronic door-opener. Figuring he was through for the night, I drove back to the inn, thinking over dinner that old Mycah had probably turned a tad more than four hundred for his day's work with the middle-aged couple.

I was getting better at keeping the yellow jackets out of my Wheat Chex.

On the patio in the backyard of 76 Main Street, I read the local newspaper and tossed sugar cubes to the sparrows. Past the overhanging branches, there wasn't a cloud in the sky, temperature at eight A.M. in the low sixties. Sweater weather. Mycah Ware might lead a boring life, but I could see why people would want to live their only one on Nantucket.

Reluctantly, I folded the paper and went around front to the Cherokee.

There were two sets of different elderly ladies window-shopping, three male knapsackers who spoke in German or Dutch to each other while they ate croissants and slurped coffee, and the same rough-faced guy in a different jogging outfit. The redhead's Mercedes was already on the street. I didn't see Ware's Cadillac, but I wasn't worried.

Just after nine, the redhead came out of the realty office. She was dressed in a conservative gray suit today, talking and nodding a lot to a short, squat, older woman who appeared to be calling the shots for a taller, younger woman from the same gene pool.

The threesome moved on foot toward my car, the jogging suit guy swiveling around, following the redhead with his eyes and sighing. I realized it might be a daily ritual for him, watching the best-looking woman on the island. As the redhead drew even with my car, she squeezed a smile at me into her nodding at everything the squat woman said. Up close, the redhead's face looked carefully maintained, and I bumped her age up toward forty. The squat woman's voice was raspy and commanding, and I decided I didn't envy the redhead her next few hours.

Hearing a car door slam, I looked back up the street. Mycah Ware, in rose slacks and a teal sweater, was crossing to his office. He went inside, staying maybe fifteen minutes before emerging, going to his Caddy, and taking off. I started up and followed him eastward to the Sankatay Head Golf Club, near the lighthouse from the day before. He pulled into the driveway. I stayed at the edge of the road and got out. I walked until I could see Ware at the trunk of his car, yanking out a bag of golf clubs and waving to a kid who hustled over to help him with it.

For the next six and a half hours, I counted four-wheel-drive vehicles (fifty-one, but some of them were doubles), species of birds (seven, with only the sparrows, seagulls, and starlings sure I.D.'s), and finally kinds of flowers (I quit at thirty). I even got cruel, snapping candids of overweight tourists on mopeds. They wore helmets at all the wrong angles and silently screamed through open mouths as they careened down the hill.

The Cadillac finally reappeared at the mouth of the driveway. On the way to town, Ware stopped for a couple of belts at the same private club, then continued home, putting his car to sleep again in the garage.

As I drove back to town, I thought it looked like a long thirty years in front of wife Eleanor.

It was just dark when I parked half a block from 76 Main Street. Before I could get out, a tall guy in a Mets baseball cap and sunglasses limped over to my driver's side with a map in his hands.

"I wonder if you can help me?"

My hand on the door handle, I said, "Sorry. I don't know the island too well."

The passenger's side door rocked open and the guy in the jogging suit got in, a Smith & Wesson Bodyguard revolver almost lost in his fist. "That's okay. We do."

The guy with the Mets cap lowered his shades. The preppy blond from the Thunderbird. I didn't like his smile much.

\* \* \*

"Okay, now pull over against that log there."

We were in the parking area for Dionis Beach. There was a big house with two peaked gables and a couple of smaller ones on the bluff, but all looked closed up for the season.

Jogging Suit said, "Turn off the engine."

I did.

"Put the keys on the dashboard."

Same.

"Now play statue for a minute."

Jogging Suit stayed where he was while Preppy got out from behind me. Preppy pointed a little automatic at my face while Jogging Suit opened the passenger's side and came around. Both leveled on me from ten feet away and at different angles as I got out of the car. Very professional and not a good sign.

"Assume the position on the hood."

I complied. They didn't bother with my wallet. Another bad sign.

Preppy said, "We're going to take a walk on the beach. You go first. Turn when we say. Don't do anything stupid."

I led them up the sandpath and over the cliff, sidewinding to the beach below.

Nobody around.

"Turn right and walk east, up the beach."

I started east, them clumping and squeaking in the sand behind me. It was a lot colder right along the water, the moonlight dancing off the waves. The beach stretched into the distance, but was only twenty yards wide before it abutted the cliff. Nowhere to run.

We'd scuffed about a quarter-mile along the bowed lines of flotsam when I asked, "Much farther?"

Jogging Suit's voice said, "Keep walking."

Before long, I heard the clattering of wheels on what must have been a boardwalked path. There was also a high-pitched but muted whine that took me a minute to place.

A man in a motorized wheelchair came onto the beach, the tires doing surprisingly well in the sand. He wore a Kangol cap low over his eyes and a muffler over his throat and under a heavy corduroy Norfolk jacket. The muffler was the same dark color as his sweater. He had what looked like calfskin driving gloves on both hands, one cradling a liquor bottle.

The Kangol Cap didn't speak for a good minute after we were close to him, probably to give me a chance to talk my way out of whatever I'd gotten into. I kept my own counsel.

Finally he said, "You know me?"

"I can't even see you."

Somebody kicked me behind the right knee. Cramping, I went down.
"View any better from there, Cuddy?"

I looked up and under the cap. Handsome face, youngish but strained
from the chair. Something familiar.

"I've seen your picture."

"The name's Branca. Victor Branca."

Branca. A rising wiseguy in the Boston-to-Providence axis. Then a ski-
ing accident, a total accident, if you could believe the papers, and he'd left
the slope paralyzed from the waist down. Six, seven years ago.

"Now you know my name, you know you answer my questions straight
when I ask them."

I said, "How come you know my name?"

A kick to the right kidney. I sagged onto that side and choked back
what was rising in my throat.

Branca said, "I ask, you answer. Got it?"

I tried nodding this time.

Seeming satisfied, Branca said, "You camp outside the real estate office
there. We figure, maybe you're tailing my wife. So we check with the car
rental at the airport and run you with some people we know up to Boston.
Turns out you're a P.I. Also turns out you look to be on Mycah Ware, not
my wife. How come?"

There wasn't any good way to say it. "Sorry. Confidential."

A shot to the other kidney. Felt like a different kind of shoe.

"These guys, they can do this kind of thing till you're just jelly inside.
How come you're tailing Ware?"

I shook my head and took a pointed toe just under the left shoulder
blade that had me twisting in the sand next to a pink tampon applicator.

Branca said, "This Ware, he's clean. We checked him out quiet but
good before I let my wife go to work for him. He don't juggle the books
there, he don't even have a partner he could be shorting on the take. So,
how come you're on him?"

I didn't bother to shake my head this time. One of the boys grabbed
me by the hair and pulled me up to my knees.

Branca motioned toward the sea. "You know, even when it's this cold,
them crabs out there like to eat." He waggled a finger at me. "Why're you
tailing Ware?"

"No."

Somebody remembered they hadn't whacked me behind the left knee
and let fly there.

Branca said, "Only one possibility. His own wife put a tail on him. Only
one reason for that, too. She thinks he's stepping out on her."

Through clenched teeth, I said, "No."

"Stepping out with my wife."

I got past the cramp. "That's not it."

"It's not?"

"No. His wife just wanted me to find out what he does."

"Why?"

I tried Mrs. Ware's retirement theory on him. It sounded lame even to me, and Branca didn't buy it. Then nobody said anything for a while.

Branca's voice came back, but different in tone. "When I had my accident, that was one thing that didn't get broken, you know? I thought Cynthia was still happy with me. I wanted to live as far away from a mountain as I could get, and this place suited me just fine. But without her, it wouldn't be so good."

If Branca were trying to sound wistful, he needed a little more practice.

"The people up to Boston there told me you were a stand-up guy, Cuddy. I ain't seen nothing different." Branca tapped the liquor bottle. "Boys?"

I got a whiff of the chloroform before one of them clamped the rag over my mouth and nose, but there wasn't much I could have done about it.

"Hey, Cuddy? Wake up. Come on. Up, up."

A strong arm was tugging on my left side. If I could have gotten to my feet, the smell of scotch would have knocked me back down. I wanted to crawl away from the man's voice with the scotch. I cracked my eyes open. The sunlight hurt, but I realized that the man was in uniform, the officer named Ben from the town police. And I was the one who stank of scotch.

Ben helped me up, snatching the empty Johnny Walker Black bottle from next to where I'd been in the sand. Ben waved to someone on the cliff who waved back. The lady in the straw hat at her easel.

I said, "What time is it?"

"Eleven fifteen."

My head was pounding as Ben made me start to shuffle up the beach.

Kate Hearn blew at her bangs and said, "So you drive out to Dionis Beach last night, tie one on, and sleep it off at the tideline."

"Like I said. I don't remember much."

"You look like you hit the ground without a parachute."

"I haven't slept on the beach for a while. Cold sand takes it out of you."

"So does a liter of scotch. You want more water?"

"Please."

I was handed another paper cup.

"This has been an exciting morning for us, John Cuddy."

"Wish I could say the same."

"Lost one of our stellar citizens to a terrible accident."

Finishing the water just kept me from gagging. "Sorry to hear it."

"Yeah. Mycah Ware, real estate broker. Know him?"

"We never met."

"His office is just a little ways from where you're staying. Or where you had been staying before you decided to bed down on the beach instead. Ben here couldn't find you at 76 Main. Shirley and Mitch were some worried about you. One of the patrol cars spotted your Jeep at Dionis and routined it in to us. That was when we went out looking for you."

"I appreciate it."

"Back to this Ware? Terrible situation. Fell down a flight of stairs this morning at a house he was sizing. Witness, one Cynthia Branca, saw him take the tumble. Frightened her near to death. Broke his neck, he did."

"Tragedy."

"Yeah, sure is. But since the witness is wife to somebody who's no stranger to violence, and since you checked in with me just two days before the accident, I thought you might have something to tell us."

I crumpled the cup. "I don't."

"Nothing at all?"

"Sorry."

"I'm sorry, too. I really am."

Hearn turned away and said, "You're free to go, Cuddy. But not to come back."

At the inn, I thanked Shirley for her concern. Cleaned up and changed, I packed my duffel bag, got into the Cherokee, and started out.

There were two other cars in the driveway of the Ware house, so I edged the Jeep into the bushes on the shoulder of the road and walked up to the front door. A solemn woman of about fifty ushered me inside. There were three other similar women looking sympathetic in the living room and two older men looking useless and restless. Eleanor Ware was sitting on the couch, the centerpiece of the tableau.

She rose when she saw me, a handkerchief to her nose and mouth. "Thank you for coming."

"I know this is a difficult time for you, Mrs. Ware, but could I see you for just a few minutes?"

"Certainly." Turning to the others, she engaged each in eye contact. "We'll be on the deck. Please help yourselves to the refrigerator, and thank you again for coming."

Once outside, she slid the glass door shut in its track and joined me at the railing overlooking the moor below the knoll.

I said, "I have something you need to know about your husband's death."

"Go on."

I told her about Branca and the boys, that I thought they killed her husband in front of Cynthia to whipsaw her back into line.

Eleanor Ware let me finish before arching an eyebrow and allowing a twinkle into her eye. "Clever, killing two birds with one stone like that."

I was afraid she was losing her grip.

"Mrs. Ware, I don't think you understand. Branca thought—"

"That I believed my husband was having it on with his wife when they 'inspected' those houses. I may have been—is the word 'adultered,' Mr. Cuddy?—but I'm not stupid. That's exactly what Mycah was doing."

I had to hold onto the railing. "He was seeing Cynthia Branca, and you knew it?"

"Of course. Oh, Mycah was *ever* so discreet. No lipstick on the collar. I assume he stripped before he even touched her each time. But he'd grown so . . . inattentive. A wife really can sense these things."

"Then why did you have me follow him?"

"Now why do you think?"

"Jesus Christ."

A wry smile. "You see, Mr. Cuddy, Mycah wasn't just unfaithful. He wasn't even just inattentive. He was boring. God, I can't begin to tell you how unbearable it is to be on an island you love with a man who bores you to tears. I dreaded his retirement. A few hours a day with Mycah was one thing. But the rest of my waking hours for the rest of my life? Inconceivable."

"You set him up."

"I did not. And neither did you. In any way. I'm sure Mr. Branca's reputation is known to you. I know it wasn't to Mycah, or frankly even to me until I did some rather thorough research. But that research convinced me that Mr. Branca would deal with Mycah because of what Mycah had done to him, not because of what Mycah had done to me. And you and I had virtually no role in that."

"Wait a minute. You flew me down here just to get Branca's attention?"

Ware looked at me. "I researched you, too, Mr. Cuddy. You'd lost your wife young. I thought you'd find my desire to be closer to Mycah in his retirement . . . admirable. I felt it would work. And it did."

"Why not just tell him yourself?"

"Tell Branca? Speak to a mobster and inform on Mycah? Just what sort of woman do you think I am, Mr. Cuddy?"

"The sort who'd pull the switch on her own husband rather than just divorce him."

"Divorce would have been too . . . public. Besides, Mycah made his own bier and shortly will lie on it. I am sorry that you were—is it 'roughed up'?"

"Yeah. I still don't see why you needed me, though. You didn't want to talk to Branca, fine. Send him a note, an anonymous tip."

She looked out over the moor, the breeze ruffling the heather in a wave pattern like an ocean of iced tea. "No. No, you don't see it at all. It's as I said to you when we first met. This is a small island, and therefore secrets are very dear. If I'd done everything myself, I wouldn't dare share it with anyone here." She gestured back at the living room. "With anyone in there."

Mrs. Ware turned to me. "I needed someone bound by confidentiality, but I could hardly hire a lawyer to follow Mycah about. You see, Mr. Cuddy, I needed *you*. Otherwise, I wouldn't have had a soul to tell."

# Just an Unofficial Investigation

### E. N. WELCH

The body might not have been found for hours if Hattie Scheffel's scruffy orange tom had come in for breakfast, but he hadn't, even though she had hoped his prowling urges were only dim memories by now, and thus she had ventured the faint, steep trail behind her house into the ravine. She picked her way across the treacherous rock bed, late fall drifts of red and brown and yellow leaves concealing slippery pockets of decaying vegetation. It made good mulch for her chrysanthemums, but Mort had always scolded that she'd break her neck down here, ought to stick to sidewalks at her age, but Mort had been gone for three years and she couldn't bear it if anything had happened to old Rufus, too. As she passed under the narrow wooden footbridge spanning the ravine, she saw the red stripe on the sleeve of the tan jogging suit, then another down the side, and forgot caution.

He lay on his stomach, legs and arms casually outstretched, at least as far as fat, stubby limbs that filled the sleeves and pants could extend. She brushed aside the twigs and leaves that had settled on him, threw a larger broken branch out of the way, and pulled at his fleshy left shoulder until she had rolled the top half of him over. His head flopped back, and she recoiled at the open, sightless eyes and slack mouth. The faint yapping of a dog came to her then, and up ahead, through the trees that climbed the left bank, she caught a glimpse of a chain link fence at the brow of the slope. Evelyn. Evelyn would be up, getting ready for school. Evelyn would know what to do—besides, he was *her* superintendent.

"Miss Ellerby? May I come in?"

Evelyn Ellerby looked over her shoulder at the stocky figure standing inside the door. "Of course. I'm just trying to roll this map up. Like window shades—always unsprung or broken."

"Let me." He moved to her side, and realized that he had to stretch, while she easily reached the bracket high overhead. He grinned up at her as he wound the spring. "Raymond Garza." He tested the tension, and the map rattled back into place.

"Yes, I saw you with Avery Henning before the last class. You're the— what *do* I call you?"

"Ray." He liked her directness. "No titles necessary—this is just an informal—"

"Investigation?" For a moment he was a student again, defensive against the teacher's authority. He tensed under her scrutiny, certain that her appraisal took in every detail, from broad, round face to barrel chest to shiny black shoes and by the time she got back to the little dark eyes in the squint wrinkles, she had him nailed, probably knew whether he wore briefs or jockey shorts, which side of the bed he slept on. He'd hate to be a kid in her class with something to hide.

"Well, sort of. Not really." He didn't know how to explain it—that Chet Williford, who some said wielded the real clout in the capital, knew all the right buttons to push, was a cousin of the late Superintendent James Tilbury, hadn't been satisfied that Cousin James had lost his footing while jogging early one crisp morning and plummeted to his untimely demise. The buttons he pushed were connected to circuits that wound through the state education office into the attorney general's bailiwick. "Just look around, talk to some people, make him happy," Ray had been instructed.

The town was a quiet, pretty little place, off the tourist itinerary, where the biggest event of the year was the two-day Pecan Festival. Ray couldn't remember ever having heard of a newsworthy item from here, hadn't even known the school superintendent had died until he was told.

"But Mr. Tilbury was an important man—"

She raised an eyebrow.

"—and being superintendent, he had connections at the state level, and his friends—"

Both eyebrows lifted.

"—just want to make sure the findings are correct as reported." He let his breath out. "And since Mrs. Scheffel came to you after finding him, and you were the second one to see him, Mr. Henning suggested that I talk to you."

"There's not much to tell—the police took my statement, and Clay— Chief Dyer—should have it and Judge Blankenship's ruling."

"He does, ma'am, and I've seen all that and talked with Mrs. Scheffel, and yesterday I spoke with Mrs. Tilbury at her daughter's. But since you teach here as well as live in the neighborhood, I thought you could—"

She cut him off with a laugh. "Ray, everyone in this town lives 'in the neighborhood.' There are only about six thousand people, not counting those out in the county, and you can walk to everything there is here. And speaking of that, if you like, you may walk along with me to my house—I have an aerobics class at four, and Henry the Eighth will be expecting his dinner."

"Henry the Eighth?"

She took her jacket from the closet near the door and shrugged into it. Ray mentally kicked himself for not being quick enough to help, but if she noticed his lapse, nothing in her manner indicated it. Then he remembered—*Miss* Ellerby, longest tenure on the faculty, chairman of the History Department, high school fixture, town landmark, single and independent.

"Ah, yes, Henry. Victim of bad press, I'm afraid, just like my Henry. He was a stray when I took him, and the alleged sire of every litter of pups born that year. I let him enjoy the reputation—didn't tell anyone the vet discovered he'd already had his credentials removed. But I keep him fenced, and he's good company. Good watchdog, too—barks at everything, even things that aren't there."

He watched her, keeping a bit back, as she locked the classroom door and strode down the hall. She cut a regal figure: stylishly short silver hair; straight, trim back in a well-cut suit softened by the ruffles at blouse collar and cuffs. Her legs embarrassed him; she had to be at least twenty years older than he, and here he was ogling an old lady's legs like some kind of pervert. Altogether a formidable woman. He was chagrined to see that her pumps were nearly flat-heeled, and hurried to catch up with her.

Outside the sun was bright, but the air was decidedly chill, with the cutting edge that characterized fall in this part of the state. Ray was glad he had zipped the lining into his coat.

The wide street leading from the high school was lined on both sides with houses whose architectural styles capsulized the previous hundred years, from porticoed Greek Revival and turreted Victorian Gothic to 1930's front-porch bungalow and ranch-style modern.

"Over there," Evelyn Ellerby gestured toward the right, "beyond the houses you can see the trees along the edge of the ravine. My yard backs up to it—a block over, four blocks down. The Tilburys lived two blocks in the other direction where the new houses are being built. She left last Saturday, right after the funeral, and I think it's already for sale. That's *her* daughter, you know, not his. She kept to herself, didn't socialize much. Mousy sort."

Ray couldn't decide if she was factual or critical. "Right," he said, and followed her around the corner.

"He jogged nearly every morning, same route most days—although you couldn't tell by looking at him." Now he knew; it was criticism. "Up Elm to Pine, then across the footbridge to the other side of town, down Main to Highway 14 and back around to Elm—about four miles, I'd say. Go left."

"Miss Ellerby, Mr. Henning suggested that—well, that you would—could—help me with the school people. Oh, he was very polite, answered all my questions, but frankly, he seemed—reluctant."

"Of course, Mr. Garza—Ray. School people don't talk. Didn't you know that?" Her eyes were smiling behind the lenses in the soft pink frames. "We've been taught to present a united front, to be wary of outsiders, and to speak only through official channels. And this is upsetting. Mr. Tilbury had been here only since Mort Scheffel died—not even three years, and there have been a number of—changes—we've had to adjust to. Now Mr. Tilbury has had an unfortunate accident—fell from the bridge and broke his neck, but here you are, a week later, digging around—for what?"

"I don't know yet. Maybe nothing. First, I'm going to go over the police report and the judge's, and then I want to ask around, find out if anyone was out last Wednesday morning early."

She laughed at that. "How long do you plan to stay? This is an early-rising town."

"Well, at least find out if anyone wanted Mr. Tilbury—gone."

"Look down there." She halted at the curb and pointed right. Less than a street, more than an alley, the pavement ended behind the houses on either side at a well-worn dirt path that sloped through the trees toward a narrow bridge with low railings. On the other side, the trees and undergrowth were denser, obscuring the town on that side. "This was never meant to be a road through here, just a convenience for people. I recall when my father and Hattie Scheffel's brother and some of the other neighbors built the first walkway there, so the kids wouldn't have to walk so far to school. The Scheffel place is on the other side of the trees, fifth house on the right, and Main Street is straight ahead, about three blocks."

She pushed her cuff back to check the time. "I really have to hurry now for my class. Tell you what—if you're still in town tomorrow evening, why don't you come by about five for a drink and we'll talk then."

A drink? Miss Ellerby, the school teacher? Something of his astonishment must have shown in his face.

"Or tea," she amended, and smiled at his discomfiture.

"Either one, ma'am. And thank you, I'd like that."

He watched the graceful figure in the smart suit cross to the opposite curb. "Oh, Miss Ellerby. May I ask a very personal question?"

She turned toward him, waiting.

"Just how old—" He winced; there was no tactful way to put it.

She studied him for a moment. "Sixty-three." Then she smiled warmly and walked away.

Damn! Legs like that at sixty-three, and he bet all the rest was original equipment, too. He wondered if Sylvie's legs would hold up that well, and across his mind flashed the image of his mother-in-law; he shook his head sadly.

Thursday had been a day of surprises, puzzling and unexpected, for Ray Garza, and the bits and pieces he had gathered, together with names and faces, floated through his mind, colliding, drifting, rearranging, rejecting. He found himself looking forward to five o'clock, counting on Evelyn Ellerby to be his sounding board, instinctively depending on her logic.

The house somehow fit her. It was a modest late Victorian, superbly proportioned, delighting the eye with gingerbread whimsy and welcoming with wide porches and wicker and yellow flowers. He heard the dog bark from the back as he climbed the steps. The door opened, and there stood Miss Ellerby, looking as Miss Ellerby should, unschoolmarmish and casually chic in a silky shirt, faded jeans, and running shoes.

He was as unprepared for the interior as he had been for everything else that day. No cosy clutter here, but bare, bleached floors, muted pastels on low-slung couches and chairs, glass and chrome, warmed with greenery and good prints and charm. He had seen less taste in glossy magazines on coffee tables. She smiled at his astonishment.

"People who don't know better are surprised to find that teachers don't always live according to *their* expectations. That's one-dimensional thinking. And you look as if you've done a lot of thinking today. What can I get you?"

He debated. "Tea, if you have it," he said finally. Stereotypes die hard.

The chair was as comfortable as it looked, his hostess solicitous, the tea hot and fragrant. With another little jolt, Ray realized it had been the right choice.

"It's been a confusing day, Miss Ellerby. I'm not sure *what* I've found."

"Oh? How so?"

"In a town this size, I thought the death of the school superintendent would be a cause for concern; instead, it doesn't seem to matter—at least not in the usual way." He consulted a small notepad. "Jack Wilson at the real estate agency, for example, was more excited that he's already found a buyer for the house. At the school business office, everything of his— personal effects, pictures, certificates, papers—were packed away in grocery cartons before the funeral. His wife never picked them up, so I've taken them with me. His staff seemed anxious to be rid of the stuff. Mr.—

here it is—Mr. Lawrence Gough, his neighbor, said that he hoped Mrs. Tilbury would be happier now, and three members of the board told me they were too busy to see me today, if I made an appointment they would try to work me in soon. What's going on here?"

She took a sip of tea first. "People at the top often have to make—unpopular decisions."

"Surely they can't all be unpopular. Did *you* like him?"

She stirred her tea absently, as if considering. "No, I didn't like him." Then she looked up, seemed to have reached a decision. "No, he wasn't the sort of person one likes, but I don't think that mattered to him. He was a small man, you know. Power was more important to him."

"If he was so disliked, why was he hired? Why did they keep him on?"

"Ray, Mort Scheffel had been in the district thirty-eight years when he died, twenty-six of those as superintendent. We had a sound academic program, a good band, fine athletic teams—but nothing flashy. We just turned out nice, achieving youngsters who could hold their own anywhere. When Mort died, there was some in town who wanted to change that. Although we had well-qualified applicants from the district, like Avery Henning and Travis Mills, the business manager, the loudest prevailed, and James Tilbury was hired. He'd been around, 'left his mark,' they said, on other schools." Her mouth twisted wryly. "It didn't take long to find out what the mark was."

"What did he do?"

"Just—things. I don't think I should discuss it with you; some of it was rumor, unprovable, but it was school business and—"

"I know—teachers don't talk. But you could save me some time, and you've been more—helpful—than anyone else, Miss Ellerby."

"Because I'm immune. Oh, I know that sounds conceited, but it's so. I'm 'old family,' kin to half the town, been here almost forever—and besides, I'm retiring this year. But only a few people know it—some special friends—so please don't mention it. More tea?"

As he passed his cup into her extended left hand, he saw below the edge of her sleeve the yellow-green remains of fading bruises circling her forearm. "Nasty business."

She tugged the sleeve down. "Reaching under the fence to pull the grass. I do like a neat yard, and that's the one thing Honey won't do. At my age one bruises so easily."

"Honey?"

"Lee Wayne Hunnicut. Went to school here in the sixties, played football. No scholar, but he tried hard. Then he went off to the service—Vietnam—but they sent him home. Honey hasn't been the same since—can't tolerate pressure. But he has a disability pension, and he does lawns and odd jobs, painting, just about anything—but he won't pull the grass from under the fence!"

They drank in silence and Ray studied the framed drawings and the print over the fireplace. He wished he knew more about art, had the feeling these were artists he should recognize. He'd buy a book when he got home.

"Miss Ellerby, didn't James Tilbury do *anything* right?"

She retreated behind her glasses, thinking. "Well, yes, he did get the bond issue passed for the new elementary school. But the new state law about maximum class size forced the issue."

"So they kept him on—even though he was a disaster."

"Of course. They had to. For one thing, it was a matter of pride—it doesn't slide down easily, and some of the board members had fought so hard to get him, they just couldn't admit they'd been wrong. And the money—we're not a rich district. They would have had to buy up his contract, and it had nearly two years to run."

"Then they could have waited out the two years and not rehired him."

"Yes. And in the meantime—"

"He could have done a lot of damage." She jerked her head up, down, in quick agreement. "Such as?"

She sighed and set her cup down, settled her glasses on her nose, spoke hesitantly. "Ray, you must understand that a district gets its reputation largely from the high school—the band, football, basketball, all the athletic teams, the speech and drama and other competitions—and that would be where the new superintendent would begin to—make his presence felt. Mr. Tilbury found a great deal to criticize in many areas—from the top down."

"You mean—fire the principal? Mr. Henning?"

"I heard Mr. Tilbury had a friend he wanted in the job. Avery Henning is one of the finest, most dedicated educators I have ever known. His home is here—where could he start over at his age? And Chuck Ninneman—so his team doesn't go to the finals. He runs a splendid program, teaches those kids values and sportsmanship and decency. As for Asa DeWitt, why, the band hall is home for any kid with a problem. His band ranks very high, but that wasn't good enough for our Mr. T. And there were others."

Ray had caught the intensity in her voice, her distress. "Tilbury really 'left his mark' on you."

"These are my friends, people I know. They're dedicated, good—and their lives were being disrupted, destroyed—for one man's ego."

Ray stared at the picture over the fireplace, straining to read the signature.

"Miss Ellerby, if James Tilbury didn't just fall off that bridge—if some-one helped him over the side—you've just suggested a number of pos-sibilities to me."

"Yes, I know." Ray was surprised again, a little let down; he'd expected a shocked protest. "But you would hear this anyway, and I'd rather you hear it from me. You see, I'm absolutely convinced that James Tilbury's death was an accident."

He wished he had the police report here; he wanted to read it again.

"Maybe," he conceded. "But I'm still curious. An unpleasant, powerful man, plenty of motive, a timely misstep—isn't it all just a little too—"

"Coincidental? Perhaps, but don't forget—there *is* a reason the word exists."

The sun was low and the air no warmer late on Friday afternoon when Ray arrived at Miss Ellerby's, uninvited, but, he was sure, not unexpected. There was no response to his knock, either from within or from the back yard. He retraced his steps across the manicured lawn to the drive and around to the gate in the chain fence; there were no untidy grass fringes that he could see all along its length. Then he saw her emerging from the ravine—first just her head, then the rest of her as she climbed the sparsely wooded slope. At the back gate she called, and a dark, shaggy dog bounded through the opening, wheeled, and began to run in happily aim-less patterns, scouting his territory. He spotted Ray just as Miss Ellerby raised a hand in greeting, motioning him into the yard, and the creature shot toward him, all ferocity and noisy yapping.

Henry the Eighth was less impressive than his name—a medium-sized, longhaired black mongrel with watchful, intelligent eyes, golden-brown ears and legs, and a curled plume of a tail. He sniffed at Ray's shoes, wagged his acceptance, and ambled off to complete his interrupted in-spection.

Miss Ellerby led him into the house. "Henry's been digging out again. I thought I'd fixed it, but I'll just have to get Honey to patch on a row of wire. But I did double duty—as long as I had to go looking for him, I picked up some wood for a fire—not much, of course, the animals need it, but Honey hasn't brought my firewood yet. What do you say to the first fire of the season, and—tea, is it?"

He took the canvas carrier from her and hefted the load of arm-thick branches. "Not a very big fire, I'm afraid, but yes, I'd like that—and tea."

She refused his offer of help with either, and he sank gratefully into a chair before he remembered he had planned a closer look at the picture over the fireplace.

"You were quite busy today. I saw you several times at the school." She set the tea before him and busied herself with arranging the puny logs on the grate.

"Miss Ellerby, you held out on me," he accused. He took the notebook from his pocket and flipped the pages.

"Oh, really? I thought I was being discreet."

He referred to his notes. "James Tilbury left his house, as he usually did, between six thirty and six forty-five—that's according to Mrs. Annaruth Mims across the street."

"My mother's cousin."

"On Pine he jogged by several people—out getting the paper—didn't speak to any of them. After that no one saw him until Mrs. Scheffel—and you know what happened after that."

"Took you all day to find that out?"

He rolled his eyes at her. "Avery Henning, the man Tilbury wanted to replace, had a church breakfast meeting at seven, but he was cooking, so he left his house about six fifteen. Chuck Ninneman told his wife he had some things to do at the gym; he left her in bed, but she thinks it was around six thirty, six forty-five. Willard Roman in the Math Department walked down Pine, across the bridge, to meet Bill Weems and Hector Sorbino—they jogged—for breakfast at the Pancake Palace. They do that once or twice a week. Millicent Ayres walked her dog over to the high school about six thirty. Asa DeWitt said he was going to the band hall early—good grief! Doesn't anybody sleep in this town?"

Miss Ellerby put a last broken branch on the minuscule fire and straightened. "I said it was an early riser's town."

He ran a hand over his face and said tiredly, "Well, there *were* a couple of things that bothered me."

"Ray, Tilbury fell—an accident. You're stirring things up needlessly."

He ignored her remark. "Gloria Eberhardt—boy, I don't remember that we had teachers like that in my high school. Mr. Roman said he saw her driving through town. She got pretty upset with me, told me she had a—personal errand."

"Yes, I know. She came to my room at lunch."

"A girl like her—what is she doing here? Why is she teaching?"

It was her turn to ignore his implications, but he caught her narrowed glance. "Gloria likes teaching, likes it here. She's going to marry Dennis Heilmann—as soon as he gets his divorce." She sighed. "Dennis was rather—wild—as a boy, had a mean temper. And he married very young. His wife left him a number of years ago and he sort of drifted—until Gloria. He's started a business now, but things take time. Meanwhile, sometimes Gloria—well, you know."

"Spends the night at his place."

"Please don't make things harder for her. She needs her job." She affected a noncommital tone. "Tilbury found her—very attractive."

He digested that, filed it away. Miss Ellerby poked at the dying fire.

"Something else—Lee Wayne Hunnicut had a run-in with Tilbury last spring and Tilbury called the police. Had him charged with trespassing—something about your dog, Miss Ellerby."

"Yes." She nodded. "That's right. Henry got out and took off, and Honey went after him, caught up with him blocks from here in James Tilbury's yard. Tilbury claimed Henry had turned over some flower pots, kicked him, I don't know what all. I took care of it—it *was* my responsibility."

Ray slapped the little notebook shut, replaced it in his pocket, and slid down in the chair, lacing his fingers behind his head. He concentrated on the print, the separate daubs and splotches of color that somehow formed themselves into a garden vista. One side of his mouth pulled up in disgust.

"Well, that's just dandy! That seems to make it unanimous."

Miss Ellerby lifted her elegant sweatered shoulders in a gesture of helplessness and then leaned forward, tense and earnest. "Ray, remember learning about the witch hunts of the seventeenth century? Those pious, well-intentioned people chose the proof they wanted and found their witches—because they were convinced they existed! Isn't that rather what you're doing? Isn't it possible that James Tilbury wasn't liked *and* died in an accident?"

He didn't answer for a moment. Then his voice was conversational, offhand. "You saw the body before the police arrived. Did you notice an abrasion behind the right ear? There was very little blood, some bark and debris stuck there, according to the investigation report."

Her eyes opened wide. "Heavens, Ray! The man was *covered* with scrapes and cuts and litter. It's a long way down!"

"He *could* have been struck from behind."

"He *could*—and probably did—bounce off a tree limb!"

"He was found face down."

She snorted. "Who knows *how* he started out? He certainly couldn't drop like a rock—not through all those trees growing in the ravine."

He had a sudden image of Miss Ellerby squatting beside the fireplace, feeding the scavenged branches into the flames. "You're quite convinced, Miss Ellerby, that it was an accident. What makes you so sure?"

"I have no proof, if that's what you mean. It's just that—" He had shaken her certainty. "I don't know what happened exactly, but I *do* know these people here. They're my friends, people I've shared my life with, and I—"

His eyes traveled down the slim, jean-clad legs to the thick-soled jogging shoes, and he finished it for her: "—take a two-mile walk every morning—over that bridge."

Henry the Eighth's frenzied barking must have alerted Evelyn Ellerby to his presence because she showed no surprise to find Ray waiting in the cold half-light of early morning. His hands were jammed into the pockets of his parka, the hood snugged low over his forehead, up around his chin. Her grey fleece jogger intensified the silver of her hair; the open blue jacket echoed her unfaded blue eyes. She looked trim and fit, and far more alert than he felt.

"You'll have to speed it up. Doesn't do your heart any good if you stroll."

Ray obediently lengthened his stride and tried to synchronize his pace with hers; six steps later he was off-beat again, lagging, and double-stepped to bring himself even with her. He realized the absurdity of their progress and would have laughed if he'd had breath enough.

A block ahead a black-jacketed figure trotted across the intersection, throwing a wave in their direction, and disappeared behind a house. "Weems," Miss Ellerby said, as she acknowledged his greeting. Farther down the street, another figure, pumping arms and legs, receded. She motioned with her chin: "Chuck Ninneman."

Her merciless rhythm never faltered, not even as she rounded the corner toward the bridge; Ray, on the outside, fell into a lope. At the edge of the pavement, he dropped behind to let her lead the way and finally abandoned the effort. When she halted at the bridge and looked back, he grinned sheepishly and plodded toward her.

"It goes easier if you breathe through your nose. Gets more oxygen to the muscles."

He nodded, unwilling to risk a breathless answer, certain she could hear the knocking in his chest. He wasn't a bit warmer, either.

The weathered timbers of the bridge, napped and greenish, were less than six feet across. Low railings on either side, thirty-four inches high (Ray had measured), were affixed to uprights three feet apart. Fallen leaves formed a thick mat underfoot, a moist and spongy layer of rotting vegetation hidden beneath an ever-renewed covering—brittle, lobed oak leaves and papery, hand-sized sycamore, limp mini-fronds of elm, black scatter-shot kernels of tallow and acorn caps. In the middle the way was relatively clear, the drifts piled along the edges. Ray wondered who would design a bridge with railings so low he couldn't lean.

Miss Ellerby read his thoughts. "My father used scrap lumber; it was for the children, as I said. Since then somebody just patches it when it needs fixing, but it's never been completely redone."

He stepped closer to the edge, putting his feet down squarely, feeling the topmost leaves slide under his feet. He stared down through the nearly naked branches below, down to the rounded mounds of rock outcroppings in the ancient stream bed. The morning sun had not yet reached those depths, barely lit the tops of the trees on either side.

"Miss Ellerby, I didn't sleep much last night. I have to decide today whether to let this go or to request an official, full-scale investigation into Tilbury's death."

"I thought somehow you were bent on the latter."

"No, it didn't start out that way at all. I came here as a—favor; somebody pulled some strings. I thought it would be cut and dried, and everybody would be happy, and that would be the end of it. Now, I don't know." He rubbed his icy hands together; Miss Ellerby balanced easily beside him, oblivious of discomfort.

"I think you make too much of what you think you've found. You think you've found motives—plural—for murder, but murder is a desperate act. Have you measured the strength of those motives? There are usually alternate methods of handling even the worst of situations—and most people recognize that."

"That's just it! Too many people, too many motives—probably some I haven't even discovered."

"Ray, why can't you just accept that—"

There was only the swish of leaves and the hollow drumming of padded feet on the wooden bridge an instant before the black and golden shape hurtled between them, ears flying, plumed tail streaming, the autumn-hued leaves swirling in his wake. Ray half-turned, startled. Then he was falling, the thin, sere leaves slipping, his right foot digging for stability in the moldered ooze below, and he knew with frightening clarity that his momentum would carry him over the railing, into space, crashing through the trees—Desperately, he bent his left knee, pitched to the side, and clutched at the arm reaching out to him.

"—it was an accident," she finished.

Crouching there, shaken, he heard her voice, distorted by the blood pounding in his ears. Over his fingers gripping her forearm, he read in her eyes the confirmation of the astonished question in his, and he knew—he *knew*, could almost see—how James Tilbury had fallen to his death.

He snickered, wonderingly, and then he was laughing, deep-chested, uncontrollable laughter that mingled relief and disbelief with an overtone of hysteria. It was joined in unconscious duet by Miss Ellerby's clear soprano peals, amplified in the chill, still air, and the sound reverberated against the sides of the ravine, through the trees, and carried up and out and away.

Ahead of them, Henry the Eighth ranged through the fallen leaves and scrub, nosing his erratic way in a meandering loop down the slope to the rocks below. At the bottom he paused, head cocked, listening, and looked up through the branches at the two figures on the bridge, and his gaping jaws and lolling tongue mimicked a satisfied smile.

At the first school board meeting of the next fall term, the assembly room was packed, but Miss Evelyn Ellerby wasn't there, was, in fact, on a walking tour of the Yorkshire dales. The new superintendent of schools, Avery Henning, read a petition (initiated by the high school faculty but signed by over two thousand registered voters) requesting that the new elementary school be named for a long-time teacher, Evelyn Ellerby. So confident was everyone of its acceptance that the next item on the agenda was the unveiling and presentation of a portrait of Miss Ellerby to hang in the foyer of the school. The photographer had caught her strength and grace and wit as she gazed into nothingness over the head of the tawny-eared dog that leaned adoringly against her.

A small engraved brass plaque on the lower rim of the frame read simply: "In grateful recognition of your contribution to education." It was as close as they could come.

# The Sounds
# of Sunday Morning

## Augusta Hancock

Just before the hymn began, the Rev. Jesse Seeker heard Clint Royce's mower chugging up the hill. The Rev. Seeker envisioned Clint seated on the mower in the field that sloped down to the cove beyond and below the church. Clint was a bony-faced, hardworking man who never appeared in the little white church on Sunday mornings, although his mower was often heard outside, roaring near and fading away, returning and diminuendo again, up and down the long field—as if Clint were working his way toward God, then turning back again.

The Rev. Seeker was as concerned about people outside the church as he was about his congregation. When Clint's wife died a couple of years back, the Rev. Seeker had tried to offer Clint some consolation, had hoped Clint would come to church. Clint's wife had come to services, and once in a while Clint would come with her. But since she'd died Clint had never set his foot inside the church. He worked like a demon. He did not seem to have God on his mind.

The sound of the mower was drowned out by the voices of the congregation—vigorous, if not always on key—and the organ, whose pitch and tone, altered by the damp salt air, were still loud. The outside noises were conquered for the moment.

Clint Royce owned not only the mower but also a grader that sometimes chugged past with noisy insistence. Dave Easton, who lived next door to the church, had a pickup truck with an ailing muffler, in which he did errands during the Sunday service. A little plane out of Wellsworth took sightseers over the coast on Sunday morning, the pilot flying low to point out the coves and lobster pots, the churches and spires and the cars that showed the sizes of the congregations. Meanwhile, outside this church, the normal traffic on the road—including the motorbikes that the young Torreys had acquired this summer—added to the texture of sound.

The Rev. Seeker could do nothing to stop the various Sunday-morning

noises, so he used them as best he could. He thought of them symboli-
cally, sometimes wrapping his ideas around them. He dreamed of a service
or sermon in which he could get all the sounds to come in—or go out—on
cue.

"And an angel of the Lord appeared." A plane would sound overhead.

"Enter into the house of the Lord." Varooom.

He often gave sermons on the dangers and distractions of the modern
world. In the orchestrated sermon, perhaps all the motor sounds could
come in at once. Then he could say, "Put them behind you"—and all the
machinery would stop.

It wouldn't be reverent enough and dignified enough for some people,
but it would be attention-getting.

What usually happened was that, when he had expressed his most
inspiring thought in the most beautiful phrasing he could muster, he got
the raspberry of a passing motorcycle.

Nature also made sounds. Sometimes when the Rev. Seeker paused
dramatically after presenting a great moral question, he was answered by a
guffawing gull.

There were many possibilities, but no way of orchestrating the sounds,
except by happy—or unhappy—accident.

This Sunday, as the hymn ended, the sound of Clint's mower receded.
That meant only that he was going downhill, away from the church. He
would be back. Meanwhile, the Rev. Seeker could hear a faraway plane.

Now Dave Easton left his house next door in the pickup truck with the
roaring muffler. His wife yelled at him over the sound. Did Dave go out
on Sunday mornings because his wife yelled at him? She was pretty, but
her voice was not gentle. She seemed a decent woman; she did not seem
happy with Dave. He was always running around, not accomplishing
much. He would have gone out in the truck, yelling or no yelling.

Dave's dog began barking its resentment at being left behind. If only
the Rev. Seeker could say in his sermon "the hounds of hell" and have the
barking commence. But he didn't give sermons on the hounds of hell.
Perhaps he should. Perhaps there was a heavenly message in that yowling.
Everything fit into God's pattern somehow.

Now the truck noise had faded, but the plane was overhead. As he
began his sermon, a sound like a shot punctuated his phrase. It probably
was a shot. Hunting season began in a few weeks. Jeb Reed would be down
behind his barn doing some target practice.

"Do unto others . . ." The Rev. Seeker thought of the poor deer.
There were too many deer around. He had to make himself think of it that
way. Deer ate the vegetable gardens of his flock.

The dog was still barking. Dave's wife yelled at it. The mower was receding downhill.

In the middle of the sermon, a boat motor started up, probably down in the cove. Unfortunately, the Rev. Seeker was not preaching about the perils and metaphors of the sea, but of the difficulties of living on land. The mower coming back up the hill toward the end of the sermon came in too late to make a point. He wondered if the mower was developing engine trouble. It suddenly seemed louder.

The next round of ammunition started just in time to be drowned out by the last hymn.

As soon as the service ended, silence descended, the wonderful silence that had been a charm of this place when the Rev. Seeker had first come here, before its residents became habitually and insatiably seduced by the charms of the combustion engine. Now most of them liked nothing better —no matter how short the distance, how pointless the errand—than to rush around in their various vehicles. They felt good driving or working something powered by the noisy magic of a motor. Instead of phoning to see if someone was in a certain place, they jumped in a car or truck and went to see. It made some sense; a lot of their work was outdoors where they wouldn't hear a phone. Still, it seemed a little frenetic. The noise which passeth understanding.

As he walked down the aisle, he wished that his congregation could feel about God as they felt about the combustion engine. He could call a sermon "The Combustion Engine." That should draw good attendance.

When the church doors opened and he began to speak to his congregation as they filed out, Dave's dog started howling, counterpoint to the slamming of car doors and the starting of engines. Even those who lived a quarter of a mile away had come in cars.

Tom Lawson and his wife filed by and shook his hand.

"It sounds like the hunting season's about to start," said the Rev. Seeker. He associated Police Chief Lawson with guns, although Tom was unarmed and in his Sunday civilian suit, and didn't much like guns anyway—yet he was fairly good with one.

"As long as they stick to deer, it's no problem for me," Tom replied. "That was a good sermon, in spite of the sound effects."

In the afternoon, the world was absolutely silent. There was not even a breeze. The Rev. Seeker sat on his porch and looked at the apples that hung heavy on his old tree. The spruces were still. There was no noise on the road. Even the birds were silent. Behind him, the refrigerator hummed, but there was no other sound until a squirrel fussed, chirruping in the apple tree. The Rev. Seeker thought of the morning racket and was glad that he could enjoy irony.

\* \* \*

At three o'clock, Tom Lawson was painting the porch trim at the back of his house when the phone rang. It was Dave Easton's wife.

"I don't like to bother you on Sunday, Tom, but Dave went off in the truck this morning—"

Yes, thought Tom, I heard him during the church service.

"—and he hasn't come back. He's never done anything like this before. I've asked everybody I can think of, and nobody's seen him. It's downright queer."

"Where was he headed when he went out?"

"He was going over to Jeb Reed's to do a little shooting practice. But I drove over there, and Jeb says he never came."

"That's no distance at all. Could he have set out to do something else first?"

"Not as I know of. Even if he'd done something else, he'd of been home by now."

Tom had heard that Dave and his wife weren't getting on so well. But it didn't seem likely that Dave had just skipped out.

"You and he didn't have a fight or anything this morning, did you?" Tom thought of her yelling over the sound of the truck muffler during the service.

"We certainly did not."

"I'll see what I can find out."

Tom hung up, wiped his brush, put it in paint remover, and called to his wife to say that he was going out.

He stopped by Jeb Reed's, but Jeb didn't know anything. Tom saw no trace of Dave or the truck as he passed along the road. He looked out over the field where he'd heard Clint mowing, then he passed the church and came to Dave's house. Dave's wife's car was parked in front. The dog came around and barked and howled at him. Dave's wife was tearful and ignorant.

Tom went to see the Rev. Seeker. They had ironed out problems together in the past.

"Before I go all along the road looking in every bush and alder for Dave, let's you and me think about what we heard this morning," Tom said. "We heard Dave go off, and we heard some other things. As usual, there was a lot of noise. I sometimes think people save up all their noisy chores for Sunday morning just outside the church."

The Rev. Seeker smiled. He'd always liked Tom Lawson, always thought he was very perceptive.

"I'm wondering if what I heard this morning adds up to anything,"

Tom went on. "I know you were concentrating on the sermon and the service, but could you remember what you heard and when you heard it?"

"I think I could."

"Let's play a little game. You write down what you heard in the order you remember hearing it, and I'll do the same thing."

The Rev. Seeker went to what he called his "sermon desk" and got paper and pencils.

The two men settled down on the porch, looking out past the apple tree toward the sea and the cove. It was going to be a good sunset, thought the Rev. Seeker. After a time, in which they alternately reflected and scratched pencil to paper, they looked at each other and nodded.

The Rev. Seeker began. "There were some traffic noises. Nothing in particular I could sort out. Then there was Clint's mower close to the church. That began just before the sermon. He went up and down a few times. Then Dave went out in his truck. His wife yelled at him, and his dog barked. Then I guess I heard the mower again, but probably not as close as before. Then there was a plane. I'd heard it faraway, but now it was overhead. After the plane, there was shooting practice, first a single shot and then a group of shots. The mower—it seems to me that it went away. Then I heard a boat—it seemed to be starting up. Sounded like a lobster boat, probably in the cove. Then I guess I heard the mower coming back. It sounded even louder than before. You see, I try to work these sounds into the sermon—might's well do something with them—so I think I've got it just about right."

Tom smiled. "We have the same pattern of what we heard. But there's one more thing about the sound of the mower. It seems to me that there was a time when that mower was kind of idling. Its sound was a little different then."

"Yes. That was while I was talking about hanging in and holding on, and it seemed appropriate that the mower was in a holding position. It was as if Clint was having trouble with the engine because then it got going louder than ever."

"That was just after the plane. As the plane noise went away, I heard that mower holding. Then there was a shot, and the mower was still making that sound."

"Yes, I was talking about holding on despite all disasters and distractions, and the shot came while the mower motor was idling. The sounds worked in with the sermon better than usual this morning."

"The boat—any ideas about that?"

"Nothing I could be sure of. Clint's brother keeps his lobster boat down in the cove. His boat doesn't speak as distinctively as Dave's truck does. But I was thinking, when I heard that boat, that Clint makes noise on land

and his brother on the water. The pattern fit the phrasing of what I was saying."

"Thank you, reverend. You've helped."

"It seems to me Dave's dog was barking longer and more frantically than usual."

Tom looked reflective. "Thanks. I hadn't thought about that."

Tom called the pilot of the little sightseeing plane.

"I didn't see anything special. I saw the church and the cars outside. There was nobody around except two men in a field just over from the church."

"What were they doing?"

"One of them was sitting up on a mower. The other was standing in the field, making some gestures with his arms. I didn't pay too much attention. I had to pull up then and bring her about to go over toward Carman's Cove and point that out to the passengers, so I couldn't see that field any more."

"Was there a truck there?"

"Yeah, I guess there was. In the dirt road that goes into that field."

"Have you talked to Clint?" Tom's wife asked.

"I'll talk to him very shortly. I've got one more thing to do before I go to see Clint."

"You'd think somebody would have heard that truck. It sure has its own loud voice."

"But nobody says they heard it."

Tom went back to the field. The mowing job on the far side didn't go in long, straight sweeps the way the rest did. He walked from the field to a bordering wooded area, which led to an old quarry long since grown up in trees. Generations ago, the Royces had quarried granite. Tom stumbled through the brush-covered rocks till he came to the edge of the quarry. Some of the scrub branches were broken. The truck had mostly disappeared down in the tree growth, but part of its rear end was visible. Tom could even see through the leaves the license plate and the tailpipe of the ailing muffler.

Tom drove up to Clint's house on a dirt road near the church, across the road from the field. The mower and the grader were out back. Clint's station wagon was parked in front. The house was quiet.

Tom knocked. Footsteps. Clint opened the door and nodded at Tom. He never had been much of one for words.

"I'm wondering if you've got any idea where Dave Easton might be," Tom said as he stepped inside.

Clint shook his head. "Nope."

"I guess you and him were talking in the field while you were mowing. During church. I guess nobody else has seen him since."

Clint frowned. It was clear that he hadn't expected Tom to know that much.

Clint looked around uncertainly.

"That first shot wasn't Jeb practicing, was it? Jeb started shooting a little later. The sounds were different. The first shot came from a different gun, from the direction of the field where you were mowing. Dave's truck must have got run down into that old quarry while the mower was running. The mower masked the sound pretty well."

Clint moved quickly. Tom cursed himself for not having seen what Clint was going to do. Turning fast, Clint moved from the hall into the kitchen and slammed the kitchen door in Tom's face.

By the time Tom got the door open, Clint had disappeared out the back door. Tom thought Clint would try to get away in the station wagon —although Tom's car was blocking it—but Clint abandoned the combustion engine and reverted to nature. Tom glimpsed him running through the woods and took out after him.

Shots rang out. Jeb's practice range was straight ahead. Tom heard a cry. He ran around the long way yelling at Jeb to stop shooting.

But it was too late.

The following Sunday, the Rev. Seeker stepped into the pulpit. Outside the church the excited voices of children biking past splashed the air. He should have been talking about the youth of today. But his mind and those of the congregation were on other matters.

Last Sunday evening Clint's brother had come to the Rev. Seeker's house. He sat looking at the afterglow over the cove, twisting his cap in his hands.

"Clint was on the mower when Dave drove up yelling about how Clint should leave his wife alone. Clint hadn't done nothing with Dave's wife. She was a nice woman, felt sorry for Clint, wanted to ask Clint to dinner with her and Dave. That was all. Wanted to take Clint something extra she'd cooked. But Dave didn't like that. Dave never did have much sense. Never did much of anything. But he thought he owned that woman.

"Dave pulled a gun on Clint when Clint was up on the mower. Dave probably didn't mean anything except to scare Clint. But Clint couldn't know that. He jumped down off the mower and wrestled the gun away from Dave. Clint's stronger than Dave. Dave grabbed Clint's hand and the gun went off. I can't say how much Clint meant to shoot him, how

much was accident. Clint gets pretty mad. All I know's what Clint told
me.

"He saw Dave was dead, and he put him on the mower and brought
him down the hill and asked me to take him out in the boat. I shouldn't
have done that, I know, but there was my brother in trouble and there was
that corpse that looked like it wanted to be got rid of, and there was my
boat and that big sea, so I took the body and the gun out and dumped
them."

Just as he was finishing his confession to the pastor, Tom Lawson came
in and found him.

All these things were going on in Rev. Seeker's mind as he was delivering the sermon. The truck, the mower, the grader would no longer interrupt him. And the little sightseeing plane stopped running after the Labor
Day weekend. Right now there was no boat motor and no nearby guns.
Clint's brother had been arrested as an accessory, and Jeb Reed's gun
license had been suspended. Jeb hadn't meant to kill Clint, of course.
Clint just happened to be where he was shooting. All the noises of last
Sunday were quieted, except for Dave's dog, who was barking and howling
in the direction of the church because Dave's wife had come to church
this morning and was sitting in the front row, tragic and contrite. Jeb
Reed was sitting next to her.

If they'd all been in church, instead of making all that noise, none of
this would have happened—or maybe it would have happened some other
way. But the Sabbath is the day for doing all the noisy chores that you
haven't had time for all week—including murder.

As he was talking about the blessings of God found in nature, he heard
the drilling of a well. That shouldn't be a Sunday sound, but it was appropriate to his sermon. He began to think of its possible criminal implications. Perhaps he could build a sermon around the idea of detection.

The Lord works in mysterious ways. That was his theme now.

His last uplifting words of hope were drowned out by rock-blaring music from a passing, open-windowed car.

# The Young Shall See Visions, and the Old Dream Dreams

## KRISTINE KATHRYN RUSCH

Nell rubs a hand on her knickers and grips the bat tightly. Her topknot is coming loose. She can see strands of hair hanging in front of the wire frames of her glasses.

"What's the matter, four-eyes? You nervous?"

She concentrates on the ball Pete holds in his right hand instead of the boys scattered across the dusty back lot. Any minute now, he'll pitch, and if she thinks about the ball instead of the names, she'll hit it.

"You hold that bat like a girl," TJ says from first base.

Nell keeps staring at the ball. She can see the stitches running along its face, the dirty surface disappearing into Pete's fist. "That's because I am a girl," she says. It doesn't matter if TJ hears her. All that matters is that she spoke.

"Pitch already!" Chucky yells from the grassy sideline.

Pete spits and Nell grimaces. She hates it when he spits. With a sharp snap of the wrist, he releases the ball. It curves toward her. She jumps out of its way and swings at the same time. The ball hits the skinny part of the bat, close to her fingers, and bounces forward.

"Ruuun!" Chucky screams.

She drops the bat and takes off, the air caught in her throat. She's not good at running; someone always tags her before she gets to base. But the sweater-wrapped rock that is first base is getting closer and still she can't hear anyone running behind her. She leaps the last few inches and lands in the middle of the rock, leaving a large footprint in the wool. A few seconds later, the ball slams into TJ's palm.

"You didn't have to move," TJ says. "The ball was gonna hit you anyway."

"Pete always does that so that I can't swing." Nell tugs on her ripped, high-buttoned blouse. "He knows I hit better than any of you guys, so he cheats. And besides, the last time he did that I was bruised for a week. Papa wasn't gonna let me play any more."

TJ shrugs, his attention already on the next batter.

"Nell?"

She looks up. Edmund is standing behind third base. His three-piece suit is dusty and he looks tired. "Jeez," she says under her breath.

"What?" TJ asks.

"Nothing," she says. "I gotta go."

"Why? The game's not over."

"I know." She pushes a strand of hair out of her face. "But I gotta go anyway."

She walks across the field in front of the pitcher's mound. Pete spits and barely misses her shoe. She stops and slowly looks up at him in a conscious imitation of her father's most frightening look.

"Whatcha think you're doing?" he asks.

"Leaving." Her glasses have slid to the edge of her nose, but she doesn't push them back. Touching them would remind him that she can't see very well.

"Can't. You're on first."

"Chucky can take my place."

"Can't neither. He's gotta bat soon."

She glances at Chucky. He's too far away to hear anything. "I can't do anything about it, Pete. I gotta go."

Pete tugs his cap over his eyes and squints at her. "Then you can't play with us no more. It was dumb to let a girl play in the first place."

"It is not dumb! And you've gone home in the middle of a game before." She hates Pete. Someday she'll show him that a girl can be just as good as a boy, even at baseball.

"Nell." Edmund sounds weary. "Let's go."

"He's not your pa," Pete says. "How come you gotta go with him?"

"He's my sister's boyfriend." She pushes her glasses up with her knuckle and trudges the rest of the way across the yard. When she reaches Edmund, he takes her arm and they start walking.

"Why do you play with them?" he asks softly. "Baseball isn't a game for young ladies."

He always asks her that, and once he yelled at her for wearing the knickers that Karl had given her. "I don't like playing dollies with Louisa."

"I don't suppose I'd like that much either," he says. When they get far enough away from the field, he stops and turns her to him. There are deep shadows under his eyes and his face looks pinched. "I'm not going to take you all the way home. I just came because I promised I would."

"You're not gonna see Bess?"

He shakes his head, then reaches into his pocket and pulls out the slender ring that cost him three months' wages. The diamond glitters in the sunlight. "Karl's back," he says.

Nell traced the nameplate. Karl Krupp. She hadn't imagined it; the name didn't disappear under her touch like so many other things did. Her fingers, with their swollen knuckles and fragile bones, looked defenseless beside that name. Slowly she let her hand fall back onto the cold metal rim of her walker. He would be how old now? When she had been ten, he had been twenty-five—a fifteen-year difference that would now make him . . . ninety-five. She glanced at the door to his room. It hadn't been open since he arrived, and that frustrated her. She wanted to see how badly age had changed him.

She supposed it hadn't changed him much, since he was in Household 5. The other residents were reasonably intelligent and ambulatory—except for Sophronia. But the nurses had removed her as soon as her senility became evident. Nell's own memory lapses and growing tendency to daydream worried her. She wasn't sure how much provocation the nurses needed before they moved her to a more restrictive household.

Nell lifted her walker and moved away from the door. She didn't want Karl to catch her snooping. Her name was different and she certainly didn't look like the scrawny tomboy he had known, but she didn't want him to know that she was watching him until she knew exactly what she was going to do.

Karl slouches indolently in the settee. His long legs stretch out before him and cross at the ankles, his left arm is draped across the armrest, and his finely chiseled head rests against the upholstered back. He should not be comfortable, but he clearly is.

Bess sits in the armchair across from him, leaning forward. Wisps of hair frame her flushed face, her eyes sparkle, and her hands—looking naked without Edmund's ring—nervously toy with her best skirt.

Nell lets the door swing shut. Karl doesn't turn at the click, but instead says in his deep, rich baritone, "Is that my Nell?"

She freezes, not expecting the well of emotion that voice raises in her. She imagines herself running to him and burying her face in his neck, then pulling back and slapping him with all her strength.

"Nelly, it's Karl." Bess can't quite keep the happiness from her voice.

"I know," she says, flicking dried mud off her thumb. She is covered with sweat, her glasses are dirty, and her topknot is coming loose. She probably doesn't even look like a little girl.

"Nelly . . ."

She hates the nickname almost as much as she hates Bess's tone. "I'm gonna go wash up."

"Go around front so you don't get mud on the floor."

Nell suppresses a sigh and turns around to let herself out. Just then her father opens the door, bringing with him the scents of tobacco and hair tonic. He ignores his youngest daughter's appearance and starts to go into the parlor.

"Who owns the fancy Model-T? Is it yours, Edm—?"

He stops just inside the parlor and Nell takes a step forward so that she can see everything. Karl rises quickly and extends his hand. Bess is biting her lower lip, and Papa has flushed a deep scarlet.

"I told you," he says in his lowest, angriest voice, "never to cross my threshold again."

"Mr. Richter, things have changed."

"I don't care if you've become the richest man in the world. You are not welcome here." Papa's voice grows even softer. "Now get out."

"Sir, please—"

"Get. Out. Or must I escort you?"

With one swift, graceful movement, Karl sweeps his hat off the table and places it jauntily on his head. He nods at Bess, steps around Papa, and musses Nell's hair as he goes out the door.

Papa doesn't move until he hears the automobile crank up. Then he says tightly to Bess, "You know he's not allowed to be here."

"But he's different. He's got a new job in Milwaukee, and he's got *prospects*, Papa."

"Fine. Let him find another girl."

Nell leans back against the door. They have forgotten that she's there.

"Papa." Bess rises out of the armchair. In her high-buttoned shoes, she is almost as tall as her father. "Things are better. He promised."

"Oh? Did he promise he would never hit you again, or did he just talk about money?"

Bess whirls away and looks out the window. "Papa, that's not fair."

"No, it's not fair." Papa pulls his watch from his pocket, opens it, and then closes it without looking at the face. "But I don't want him back. After he hit you, I heard Nelly crying herself to sleep every single night."

Nell's face grows warm. She thought no one knew.

Papa stuffs his watch back into his pocket and adjusts his waistcoat. "Now, I would like some dinner."

Nell slips out the front door and heads around the house to the pump. Her body is shaking. She remembers Bess's swollen and bruised face, but she also remembers the fun they had laughing on the front porch with Karl. Her tears those nights hadn't been just for Bess. They had also been for those summer afternoons filled with laughter, lemonade, and Karl mussing her hair.

Even though it was difficult, Nell liked to walk. She felt that each slow step added a minute to her life. Without her walker, she would have to use a wheelchair—and the wheelchair was a sign of weakness. Lifting the walker and then taking a step gave her the same sure feel that she used to have after hitting a home run the way Karl had taught her to.

Sometimes she spent the entire day walking up and down the hallways. She got to go outside on those rare occasions when her family visited. They took her out so that they could avoid talking.

Each household was painted a different color. The walls in Household 5 were robin's egg blue and covered with artwork done by the residents. Shortly after Karl arrived, a painting of a multi-colored spiral had gone up beside his door.

Nell found her gaze drawn to the painting. She pushed her glasses up so that she could study it. The spiral had rungs, like a ladder. At the bottom, instead of a signature, was a notation that tugged at a memory she couldn't reach: deoxyribose nucleic acid. She read the phrase twice, then saw with a start that Karl's door was open. Strains of a Chopin étude slipped into the hallway. Intrigued, she leaned closer.

The residents were encouraged to fill their rooms with their personal effects. Most rooms had a television set, a stuffed armchair covered with a quilt, and a cross on prominent display. But Karl's room was lined with bookcases, and the bookcases were full. Karl stood near the door, holding a book in his hand.

"It's the pretty woman from across the hall." His voice hadn't changed. It was still rich and full, and it still sent shivers down her back. His black hair had become silver and his skin was covered with delicately etched lines. Age hadn't bent him. He extended his hand. His movements were as graceful as ever. "Would you care to come and visit for a moment?"

Nell found herself staring at his hand. The last time she had seen it, it had been covered with blood. "No, thank you," she said. "I'm taking my walk."

"Surely you have just a moment—?" He inclined his head toward her, waiting for her to give him her name.

"Eleanor," she said.

"Eleanor?" He took a step back so that she could pass him. She hesitated, then smiled a little bit at herself, realizing that this was the man who had given her a taste for charm.

"A moment." She turned her walker and started toward him, feeling awkward for the first time in years.

He watched her shuffling movements. "Arthritis?"

She shook her head. "I broke both hips pinch-hitting for some Little Leaguers in 1975. The doctors said I'd never walk again."

"Did you win?"

She looked up at him, startled to find herself only a foot away. "I'm walking, aren't I?"

He chuckled. "No, no. The game."

"Oh." She pushed the walker through the doorway. Bookcases made the entrance narrow. His room smelled like ink and old books. "We lost by three runs."

"It's a shame," he said quietly. "You should always win your last game."

She stopped near the window. He had a view of the back parking lot. "Who says it was my last game?"

She turned and looked at his room, then. It was filled with books. A desk covered with papers stood in the center of the floor and a stereo, like the one her granddaughter was so proud of, took up a shelf of one of the bookcases. The bed in the far corner was neatly made and covered with a manufactured spread.

"Would you like to sit?" He pulled a chair back for her. Nell shook her head.

"Tea then?" He reached behind him and plugged in a coffee machine. Cups, canisters, and vials filled with liquid rested beside the machine.

"What are you doing here?" Nell's question slipped out. He turned sharply to look at her. Nell felt herself blush. "I mean, you don't look as if you need to be here."

He smiled and the lines cascaded into wrinkles. "My grand-nephew runs this place. He figures I'm getting too old to live alone."

"But there are other places to stay if you're in good health. You don't seem to need medical care."

"I don't yet." He hooked his thumb in his front pockets and leaned against the door frame. Nell wondered if he'd stop her if she tried to leave. "I'm helping him with some research."

Nell glanced again at the desk. Some of the papers lying there were covered with the same spiral that was near the door.

"We're trying to find a way to slow down the aging process," he said. "You've heard of Leonard Hayflick?"

"No."

"Hayflick is a biologist who found that cells have a clearly defined life span. He figured that the life span was determined by the number of cell divisions instead of chronological age. But some cells deteriorate before they reach their maximum divisions. And that, some believe, causes aging. Follow me?"

Nell realized she had been staring at him blankly. "Sorry."

"Let me put it simply," he said. "Everyone can live to a certain maximum age, but not everyone reaches that age because of physical deterioration. What we're trying to do is prevent that physical deterioration so that people can live out their entire lives."

"What is this maximum age?" Nell asked.

Karl shrugged. "We don't know. But some people have claimed that they were well over a hundred. And I just read about a woman recently whose baptismal records prove she is a hundred and twenty."

"Why are you telling me?"

"You asked, Nelly."

Nell's entire body went cold. She gripped her walker tightly and tried to think of a way she could get out of the room.

He took a step toward her, and she cringed.

"I'm sorry," he said softly. "I should have let you know right away that I knew who you were. My family stayed in Wisconsin, Nell. They let me know what was going on in your life. I knew you were here well before I came."

"What are you going to do?" Her voice trembled.

He took another cautious step toward her. "Well, first, Nelly, I'd like to explain about Bess."

"No," she said and her fear was as real as it had been that sunlit July morning when he had clamped his bloody hand against her mouth. "If you don't let me out of here, I'm going to scream."

"Nelly—"

"I mean it, Karl, I'm going to scream."

He opened his hands wide. "You're free to go, Nell. If I wanted to hurt you, I could have done it a long time ago."

She pushed the walker before her like a shield. Her hands were slipping on the metal. As she passed Karl, she didn't look at him.

The walls seemed narrower and the distance to her room much too short. When she got inside, she closed the door, wishing that it would lock. But she knew that part of her fear was irrational. There wasn't much a ninety-five-year-old man could do to her here, not in this home filled with bright lights and young nurses. All she had to do was scream and someone would come to her. They didn't ignore screams in Household 5.

Nell tugs at her knickers. No matter how tightly she ties them, they always stay uncomfortably loose about the waist. She has been reluctant to slide into a base like Chucky tells her to because she's afraid that if she does her knickers will come off.

She takes the path that goes through Kirschman's apple orchard. Mr.

Kirschman hates it when the kids take the shortcut through his orchard, but they do anyway.

As she turns the corner to the center of the orchard, someone clamps a hand over her mouth and drags her back against the tree. The hand is tight and slippery. It smells like iron.

"Nelly, promise not to scream if I let you go?"

The voice is Karl's. She nods. Slowly he releases her.

"What were you trying to do?"

He raises a grimy finger to his lips. His dark hair stands out in sharp relief to his pale skin. "I don't want you to go any farther, okay? I want you to go back and get your father right away. Promise?"

Nell nods again. She's staring at his stained white shirt and she realizes that it is covered with blood. She wipes at her mouth and her hand comes away bloody.

"Nell—"

She turns and starts to run, not realizing until she's rounded the corner that she's disobeyed Karl. There, lying across the orchard path, is her sister. Bess's hair is strewn about her, and her blouse is covered with blood.

"Nell, it'll be okay, just—"

Nell screams. Karl is standing behind her. She pushes him out of her way and runs down the orchard path toward home. This time running seems easy although the air still catches in her throat. She can't hear Karl behind her, and as she nears the house, she knows she's safe. Karl won't hurt her, Karl would never hurt her. The only one Karl hurts is Bess, and that is Bess's fault because she doesn't listen to Papa and now it's too late, it's all too late because Nell has left her there, bleeding and helpless, with Karl, the man who hurts her, the man whose hands are covered with blood.

"Did I ever tell you that my sister was murdered?"

Anna smoothed her already neat skirt and sighed. "Yes, Mother." Her tone said, *A thousand times, Mother. Do I have to hear it again?*

Nell clutched her hands in her lap, trying to decide if she should continue. Anna would never believe her. Even though she was fifty-five, Anna rarely thought about anything more serious than clothing and makeup. And, of course, she had never known her Aunt Bess.

"I saw the man who killed her."

Anna suddenly became stiff, and her eyes focused on something beyond Nell's shoulder.

Nell's heart was pounding. Her oldest, Elizabeth, would have listened. But Bess had been dead for six years. "I think I told you this once," Nell said. "But the man who killed her—his name was Karl—also killed her fiancé, Edmund. And they never caught him. And it used to frighten me, thinking that someday he'd come back for me."

"That was a long time ago, Mother." Anna's voice had an edge to it.

"I know." Nell's fingers had grown cold. "But I wouldn't be telling you now if it weren't important."

Anna looked at her mother full in the face, a deep, piercing look. "Why is it important now?"

"Because he's here," Nell whispered. The words sounded too melodramatic, but she couldn't take them back. "He's across the hall."

Anna took a deep breath. "Mother, even if he were here, there's nothing he could do. He probably doesn't even remember you."

"He remembers," Nell said. "I talked to him."

"Even so." Anna reached out and took Nell's hand. Her palm was warm and moist. "He's an elderly man. He probably won't live long. If we called the police and they verified what you said, he probably wouldn't even make it to trial. I mean, who else knows about the murder, besides you?"

"My father knew and—"

"Anyone living?"

"No." Tears were building in Nell's eyes. She blinked rapidly.

"Then it would be your word against his, and frankly, Mother, I don't think it's worth it. I mean, what can you gain now? He'll die soon and then you won't have to worry."

"No." A tear traced its way down Nell's cheek and stopped on her lips. She licked it away quickly, hoping Anna didn't see. "He won't die soon."

Anna frowned. "Why not?"

"He's working on an experiment to prolong his life."

"Oh, for God's sake, Mother." Anna pulled her hand away. "How many other people have you told this piece of nonsense to?"

"I haven't—"

A nurse knocked on the door and walked in. She set a tray next to Nell's armchair. "I have your medication, Nell."

Nell reached over and took the Dixie cup. The liquid inside was brown. "This doesn't look like my medication."

She looked up in time to see Anna shaking her head at the nurse.

"Just drink it, Nell," the nurse said in her fakely sweet voice, "and it'll be all right."

Nell took a sniff of the cup. The contents smelled bitter. "I really don't want it."

"Mother," Anna snapped. Then in a confidential tone to the nurse, she said, "Mother is having a bad day."

"The past few days have been difficult," the nurse said. "She hasn't gone to meals and she won't leave her room at all."

"Is that true, Mother?"

Nell swirled the liquid in her cup. Sediment floated around the bottom. Suddenly she realized that it didn't matter. No one would care if Karl poisoned her. She put the cup to her lips and drank before she could change her mind.

The liquid bit at her tongue like homemade whisky. She coughed once and then set the cup down. "I don't see why you want to know," she said.

Anna pursed her lips. "Mother, really."

Nell rubbed her tongue against the roof of her mouth, but she couldn't make the taste go away. She grabbed the side of her chair and got to her feet. Her hips cracked slightly when she stood. The nurse handed her the walker.

"Where are you going, Nell?"

Nell didn't reply. She moved the walker toward the sink, and got herself a drink of water.

"I'm afraid my mother may not be well," Anna said softly. "She was just telling me that the man across the hall murdered her sister, and she's afraid that he's after her."

"Mr. Krupp? I wouldn't think so. He's been bedridden since he came here."

"Maybe you should say something." Anna stopped speaking as Nell turned around. Nell made her way back to the armchair. The nurse took her arm as she sat down.

"Nell, I understand the man across the hall frightens you."

Nell looked up at the nurse's round face, trying to remember her name without glancing at the name tag. "No. Whatever gave you that idea?"

"Your daughter was saying that he made you nervous."

The name tag said DANA, L.P.N. "I haven't even seen him and he's very quiet. Why would that make me nervous?"

The nurse smiled and picked up the tray. "I was just checking, Nell."

Anna waited until the nurse left before speaking. "Why did you lie to her, Mother?"

"I don't know why you come visit me," Nell said.

Anna slid her chair back and stood up. "I don't know either sometimes. But I'm sure I'll be back." She picked up her coat and slung it around her shoulder. "And, Mother, it's better for you to socialize, you know, than to stay locked up in your room. Talking to other people will give you something to think about, so that your mind won't wander."

She walked out. Nell waited until she could no longer hear the click of Anna's high heels on the tile floor. "My mind doesn't wander," she murmured. But the nurse had said that Karl was bedridden, and he had looked so healthy to her. Nell sighed and then frowned. What would he be doing in Household 5 if he couldn't get out of bed?

Nell picks up the bat and takes a practice swing. Her dress sways with her, but she won't wear the knickers Karl gave her. Bess has been dead for a week, and Nell is lonely.

"What are you doing here?" Chucky asks. They are alone. The other boys haven't arrived yet.

"Wanna play," she says.

He frowns. "In a dress? Where are your knickers?"

"Threw them out." She hits the bat against the dirt like she's seen Pete do.

"You can't run in a dress."

"I can try." Her anger is sharp and quick. She hasn't been able to control her moods since Bess died. "I'm sorry."

Chucky ducks his head and looks away. "It's okay."

"I'm sorry," she says again, and looks at the playing field. The grass has been ruined near the bases. Sometimes she thinks baseball is the only dream she has left. Now, with Bess dead and Karl gone, even that seems impossible. "I'll just go home."

"No," Chucky says. "I mean, you can play."

She smiles a little and shakes her head. "Not in a dress. You were right."

"Wait." He touches her arm and then runs to his house, letting the porch door slam behind him. She goes to home base and swings the bat again, pretending that she has hit a home run. It is a good feeling, to send the ball whistling across the creek. She loves nothing more. If only she were a little boy, she could play baseball forever. Karl once told her that she could turn into a boy when she kissed her elbow. She tried for weeks before she realized that kissing her own elbow was impossible. She will never be a boy, but she will be good at baseball.

Chucky comes back. He thrusts some cloth into her hand. "Here," he says.

She unfolds it. He's given her a pair of frayed and poorly mended knickers. "Chucky?"

"They don't fit me no more. Maybe they'll fit you."

"But isn't your brother supposed to get them?"

"Nah," he says, but doesn't meet her eyes.

"I don't want to take them if it'll get you in trouble."

"It won't." He studies her, sees that she's unconvinced. "Look, you're the best hitter on the team. I don't want to lose you."

She smiles, a real smile this time, one that she feels. "Thanks, Chucky."

Nell resumed her walks again, making sure that she took them around medication time.

Karl's door remained closed for days, but she finally caught him in the hallway, switching Dixie cups on the trays.

"You're switching my medication," she said. She stood straight, leaning on her walker, knowing that he couldn't touch her in the halls.

"Yes, I am," he replied.

She swallowed heavily. She hadn't expected him to admit it. "Why?"

"I guess I kinda feel like I owe you, Nell."

"For killing Bess?"

He set the cup down on the tray marked with her room number. His hand was trembling. "I didn't kill Bess," he said quietly. "I killed Edmund."

"You're lying."

He shook his head. "I was going to meet Bess that morning in the orchard. We were going to run away together. Edmund got there first, and he killed her. So I went and I killed him."

Nell could feel the power of that morning, the sunlight against her skin, his bloody fingers across her lips. "Why—didn't you tell somebody?"

"I still committed a murder, Nelly."

That's why he had told her to get her father. That's why he had never come back to kill her, too. "Why—" She shook her head in an attempt to clear it. "Why did you come back here?"

"Wisconsin is my home, Nell." He was leaning on the cart for support. "I wanted to die at home."

"But your experiment?"

He smiled. "I've outlived most of my siblings for a good twenty years. And the formula wasn't quite right for me at first. We've changed it, so yours is better from the start."

"Mine?"

"Nelly." He bowed his head slightly and ran his fingers through his thick, silver hair. The gesture made her think of the old Karl, the one who had taught her how to laugh and how to hit home runs. "What did you think? That I was poisoning you?"

She nodded.

"I'm not. I'm trying the drug on you. I know I should have asked, but you didn't trust me, and it was just easier to do it this way."

"Why me?" she asked.

"Lots of reasons." The cart slid forward slightly and he had to catch himself to keep from falling. "I don't know many people who still play baseball when they're seventy years old. Or learn to walk again when the doctors say they can't. You're strong, Nelly. The power of your mind is amazing."

"But what if I don't want to live any longer?"

"You do or you wouldn't be out here, trying to catch me."

"I have caught you." The hallway was empty. Usually it was full of people walking back and forth.

"I know," Karl said. "What are you going to do? Call a nurse, tell them to arrest me? There's no statute of limitations on murder, you know."

Nell studied him for a moment. He was thin and his skin was pale. He was ninety-five. How much longer could he live?

"I don't want any more of your medication," she said.

He stood motionlessly, waiting for her to say something else.

She moved her walker forward, on the other side of the cart. "And I don't want to talk any more."

She didn't let herself look back as she slowly made her way down the hall. Imagine if she could walk without a walker, without pain. Imagine if she could live longer than her father, who had died when he was ninety-eight. She wasn't ready to give up living yet. Some days she felt as if she had only just started.

When she reached her own door, she stopped and looked back at Karl's. Once she had believed in Karl and his miracles. She did no longer.

The world has reduced itself to the ball clutched in Pete's hand.

"Throw it straight," Chucky yells.

Pete spits. Nell barely notices. She watches that ball, knowing that when he throws it she will hit it with all her strength. Time seems to slow down as the ball whizzes toward her. She knows how the ball will fly, where it will end up, and she swings the bat down to meet it. There is a satisfying crack as they hit and time speeds up again.

"Holy cow!" Chucky cries, but Nell ignores him as she drops the bat. Out of the corner of her eye, she sees the ball sail over the creek. She runs as fast as she can. Her right foot hits first base, and she keeps going, flying, like the ball. It disappears into the weeds behind the creek as her left foot hits second. Her glasses bounce off her nose between second and third, and she is navigating according to color. Her lungs are burning as her left foot hits the rock that is third base.

"Go, Nelly! Go!"

She runs toward the blurred shapes behind home. There is a stitch in her side and her entire body aches, but she keeps moving. She leaps on home base and her team cheers, but she can't stop. She has run too hard to stop right away, and she crashes into Chucky, who hugs her.

"Great!" he says. "That was great!"

She stands there, savoring the moment. Karl would have been proud of her. But Karl would never know. She wipes the sweat off her forehead and says, "I lost my glasses."

As Chucky trudges out to retrieve them, she realizes she can get no higher than this; her tiny girl's body, for all its batting accuracy, will prevent her from going on. But she doesn't care. If she can't play on a real team, she will hit home runs until she is a hundred, long after these boys are dead.

"That was great, Nelly," Chucky says as he hands her her glasses. "Really great."

She checks the lenses, which haven't cracked, and then bends the frame back into shape. "Not bad for a girl," she says with a glance at TJ. Then she goes over to the grass and sits at the end of the line, hoping that she'll get another chance at bat.

The sound of running feet woke Nell up. She had heard that sound before. Someone had died or was dying and they wanted to get him out before the other residents knew.

She grabbed her glasses and got out of bed, carefully making her way to the door. They were gathered in front of Karl's room. Two men wheeled a stretcher out. The body was strapped in and the face was covered. Quickly they pushed him out of sight.

She crossed the empty hallway. The tile beneath her feet felt cold and gritty. They had left Karl's door open, and she stopped just outside it, catching the smell of death under the scent of ink and books.

"Nell?" One of the nurses started down the hall toward her.

"Is he dead?" she asked.

"Mr. Krupp? I'm afraid so. I'm sorry if it disturbed you."

"No, not really," Nell said. She drew her nightgown closely about her chest. She was getting cold.

"He probably shouldn't have been in this household," the nurse said. "He was much too sick, but his family wanted him to have a private room."

Nell wondered how the nurse expected her to believe that. One glance inside Karl's room made it obvious that he hadn't been bedridden. Nell surveyed the room once more. The desk top was bare and the vials were gone, but otherwise it looked the same.

The nurse finally reached her side. Nell recognized her as the round-faced one who usually gave her her medicine. Dana, L.P.N.

"How did you get out here?" Dana L.P.N. asked.

"Walked," Nell said.

Dana L.P.N. shot her a perplexed look. "Well, let's get you back to bed, shall we?"

She put her arm around Nell's waist and helped her back to the room. The support wasn't necessary until they reached the door. When Nell saw her walker in its usual place beside the bed, her knees buckled.

"Nell?"

Nell straightened herself and pushed out of the nurse's grasp. She made her way to the side of the bed and lightly touched her walker. "I'm fine," she said.

She climbed into the bed and lay there until she heard the nurse's footsteps echo down the hall. Then she got up and walked slowly around her room.

*You're strong, Nelly,* he had said. *The power of your mind is amazing.*

She walked to the door and stared at Karl's empty room across the hall. The drawing was still there, its spirals twisting like a malformed ladder. Beneath the stunned joy that she was feeling, frustration beat at her stomach. She would never know if it was her own determination or Karl's bitter medicine that made her legs work again, just as she would never know if he had actually killed her sister or if he had been lying. She wanted to believe that it was the power of her own mind, but her mind's healing took time. She had started to walk within days of receiving the medication.

Nell went back to the bed and sat down, wondering what Anna would say when she learned that her mother could walk again. Then Nell decided that it didn't matter. What mattered was that her feet which had run bases, chased two children, and carried her through decades of living worked again. Once she had vowed to hit home runs until she was a hundred. And maybe, just maybe, she would.

# Best of Luck!

## VICKIE DUBOIS

Flit. Flit. Flit. Thunk!

Adelia Quirk's blue-veined fingers sifted through the morning mail. It rapidly formed two stacks. One, in the center of Harry Fendley's walnut desk, contained bills, notices of upcoming auctions, and a few other odds and ends that might interest the owner of Fendley's Used Cars. The other stack, on the bottom of Fendley's round metal waste-basket, contained junk mail, flyers for some even-more-interesting auctions, and an invitation to a political supper honoring the local congressional representative—the same fellow who smiled down from a chrome frame on the wall with a brotherly arm draped around Harry Fendley himself.

Harry would be sorry to miss that, Mrs. Quirk thought with satisfaction, a smile twitching her thin lips.

Adelia Quirk was a slight woman. The translucent powder on her ivory skin and the muted lipstick that faithfully recreated her fading lip line were concessions to her age and station in life, not vanity. Her thin gray hair had been permed and stood fluffed up, something like a dandelion puff.

She pushed her reading glasses back up the bridge of her thin nose and considered the title to a '79 Buick. A flick of the wrist and it too went spiraling down into oblivion. She felt positively giddy with excitement. She ventured a quick glance over her shoulder and made certain Harry Fendley wasn't lurking about—he was very good at lurking.

Three more missives rapidly joined those on the desk. The last she frowned at thoughtfully. The address was neatly printed. There was no return address. It was somehow naggingly familiar.

Her thumb savaged the flap of the envelope. She realized why it looked familiar. She'd seen dozens like this during the thirty years she'd worked as secretary at Endicott High School, before she had retired last spring. With a disgusted sniff, she balled up the paper and tossed it.

"MRS. QUIRK!"

The shout, delivered from about three feet behind her, had the intended effect. Mrs. Quirk jumped as if brushed by a live wire. She reached down, groping for the edge of the desk for support. Her heart had given such a mighty leap it had to be still for a few seconds before it could continue beating. When it did, she turned a baleful eye on her tormentor.

Harry Fendley smiled. "Mrs. Quirk, you mustn't throw away letters from my constituents. That might be from some good citizen with a problem." Harry Fendley was president of the County Board of Supervisors and a fat cog in the local political machinery.

Harry dived into the wastebasket, puffing as he bent over his great cauldron of a stomach, and rummaged about. Mrs. Quirk watched in fascinated horror, then sighed with relief when he came out with the crumpled letter—nothing more.

Harry Fendley made little puffing sounds as he straightened. He was a short man, round with a shiny bald head. His baldness was acutely emphasized by great dark brows that crawled up and down his forehead above little chinquapin eyes. He smiled benignly. He couldn't help smiling—a boa constrictor couldn't help flicking out its tongue.

I need to increase my Valium, Mrs. Quirk thought, her knees still shaking in her support hose. Maybe Fendley should take nerve pills, too. I could share mine . . . a couple of dozen in his coffee would do wonders for *my* nerves.

"Now, Miss Adelia," he said as he sat behind the wide desk and began to uncrumple the letter, "you're a good secretary, but you don't understand politics. Never throw away a letter before I see it—no matter what kind of crackpot it's from." He shook his head as if chiding a slow child. A look of concern formed on his features, his eyebrows crawling together above his pug nose like two black fuzzy caterpillars kissing.

"Why, you look pale, Miss Adelia. You are feeling all right, aren't you? Working to pay off George's IOU's might be too much for you. After all, it wasn't your fault George took to gambling—and was so bad at it. Many a night I told him, 'George, quit this playing cards and go home to Miss Adelia before you get yourself into trouble.' But he just wouldn't listen. Too bad he didn't have more life insurance; a real lack of foresight.

"I really am concerned for you, Miss Adelia. Why don't you stop being so stubborn and let's settle this thing. Eight acres is really too much land for a widow lady like yourself to keep up and, well, I don't want to scare you but you really ought not be alone way out there at night. Now, why don't you sign your house and property over to me, and I'll give George's promissory notes to you . . ."

Because I'd rather torch it first, worm! she thought indignantly.

When she didn't reply, Fendley turned his attention to the letter trapped beneath his pudgy paws. His eyes followed a few lines and he looked up with a delighted smile.

"Mrs. Quirk, have you any idea what you were throwing away?" Not waiting for her answer, he tilted the page to the light and read:

"THIS LETTER IS NOT A JOKE. IT WILL BRING YOU EITHER GREAT LUCK OR TERRIBLE MISFORTUNE. DISTRIBUTE THIR-TEEN COPIES OF THIS LETTER WITHIN FIVE DAYS . . ."

"It's a chain letter, Fendley." Mrs. Quirk cut him off impatiently. "The kids at school were forever passing these good luck, bad luck . . ."

"Just make thirteen copies, Miss Adelia. Don't you know that we have to share this good fortune with our friends?" Fendley pushed the paper toward her, then sat back like some benevolent Buddha, steepling his fingers over his paunch. "Let's see . . . send a copy to Robert Barnes."

"The man who ran against you in the last election?" Mrs. Quirk asked in surprise.

"Yes, the very same. And send one to James Hollingshead, the mayor of our fair city . . . one to Leroy Jacobs . . . and one to his wife Evelyn, too . . ."

Mrs. Quirk eyed him with something nearing appreciation as she jotted down the names of a dozen of his political and personal enemies, as well as a former secretary. The man had a highly developed sense of pettiness.

"Close the door on your way out, Mrs. Quirk. I'm expecting a friend and I don't want to be disturbed."

As she entered the outer office with its large plate glass windows, Mrs. Quirk spotted a young couple outside circling a dinosaur of a station wagon that had been crouched on the lot for a disturbingly long time. They wore the look of fish determined to be hooked. Since the other salesman hadn't come in yet, Mrs. Quirk saw her duty. She marched out and informed them that Mr. Fendley didn't want to be disturbed.

As she made her way back across the graveled lot, she thought that the sun shone a little bit brighter . . . the wind had a little less chill in it . . . a good deed had been done.

"The trouble with Harry Fendley," Mrs. Quirk muttered as she sealed the thirteenth envelope, "is that he wasn't stillborn." And that had been rather shortsighted of his mother, considering how he'd turned out.

Mrs. Quirk sat a little straighter in her chair and made a mental note to be more kind. The truth was that she just didn't like most people, and she'd found most people were kind enough to return the sentiment.

There were exceptions. It was sad, but true, that she didn't enjoy such a relationship with her neighbors. They all seemed determined to like her although she'd always gone to pains to be herself around them.

The trouble with the Andersons, whose three acres of scrubpine flats wedged between her property and the Red Mound National Forest, was that she'd known them both since they'd been having accidents in their pants. They both tended to treat her with the same indulgent affection they might bestow on an eccentric but harmless old aunt.

On the other side of her property lay five acres of flats, denuded of pines, that belonged to the Effersons.

The Effersons were a special curse—back-to-the-earthers. Not the stick-to-themselves survivalist branch of the family but the hearty gee-look-what-we-did-today group—always running over with homemade jams of exotic origins, goat cheese, or cucumbers which had been subjected to strange rites and packed into jars labeled *Pickles*. For all that Mrs. Quirk had made a point of being herself with them, they were as difficult to put off as a pair of frisky puppies.

On the other side of the Effersons, dividing their property from more of the national forest, was the Chickasaw River. Beyond the Andersons was Wooten Creek and more of the forest. This stretched into a vast unpopulated tract on the other side of the interstate highway. Mrs. Quirk knew that she was in no danger of a neighborhood mushrooming up there, for what the Department of Interior owns, no man taketh away.

Behind Mrs. Quirk and her neighbors another vast tract of pine forest stretched for miles. This was owned by Acme Paper, Inc., a notorious landgrubber snatching up any unguarded morsel of land while refusing to sell an inch. This, though more pleasant than a subdivision, was not as nice as if it had been part of the national forest. For, every decade or so, the trees were clear-cut and replanted—in *rows*. Rows of pines were an offense to the human eye.

Of the three parcels of land, Mrs. Quirk's was the prime property. It was the high ground between two flood flats. The Chickasaw River on one side and Wooten Creek on the other periodically flooded their banks. Mrs. Quirk's house stood on a long, raised finger of ground, a ridge carved by the southernmost edge of a glacier millennia before and weathered round. Her place stayed high and dry.

Harry was up to something, and she wasn't so much of an old fool that she couldn't guess it involved her house and land. If only she could figure out why he especially wanted *her* land.

She knew Harry hadn't offered her this job just so she could pay off George's debt. He'd offered it to her, accompanied by his favorite campaign smile, to soften her up into signing over her deed. Harry had great faith in his powers of persuasion; after all, he was a used car dealer.

A Brooks Brothers suit, carrying blueprint cylinders, disappeared through the door of Harry's office. Mrs. Quirk wondered, were they blueprints, or land survey maps? She listened at the door. Nothing. No sound. Harry had probably had the walls insulated against long-range listening devices—and nosy secretaries, she decided with a snort.

Actually, Mrs. Quirk was a bit ashamed of all the fun she was having. She'd had little to occupy her since her retirement. Then George had died, and had surprised her for the first time in twenty years. She'd discovered, after the funeral, that the Wednesday night prayer meeting he'd faithfully attended the last few weeks of his life had actually been a high-stakes card game in the back room of the local bar. Fendley held promissory notes from George's losses, all duly signed and witnessed. Fendley hadn't, of course, been directly involved in the card game—gambling being illegal.

Strangely, she wasn't angry with George. The truth was that she'd been rather pleased to find out he'd had the gumption to sneak around and do something—not that she wouldn't have put a stop to it if she'd found out.

She knew that, by law, she was obliged to pay. She also knew that Harry couldn't legally take her house away.

Nope, he sure can't, thought Mrs. Quirk complacently as she began to tear stamps from the brass stamp dispenser. Judging from the way Harry had been more and more impatient with her refusal, time must be running out for whatever he was cooking up. Mrs. Quirk pulled the thirteenth stamp from the dispenser, and her natural frown deepened. She lifted the lid: empty. There was only the one stamp left, and one of the chain letters —and the corner of her utility bill stuck out of her purse.

She glanced from one to the other. Of course it was really no contest. She tossed the thirteenth letter beneath the tray in her desk drawer, passed the last stamp across the tip of her pink, pointed tongue, and affixed it to her electric payment. As much as sending a bad luck chain letter to one's enemies appealed to her, one had to maintain perspective. After all, it was one thing to appreciate Harry's well developed sense of pettiness, but quite another to buy one's own stamps.

Adelia Quirk cast an uneasy glance at the lowering clouds as she waited for the light to change. Since the weather had worsened a few days before, the crisp, sunny cool of fall drearying into the damp cold of winter, Fendley had developed a passion for the news—or rather, for sending her arthritic joints across the street to buy a newspaper. Even though she'd wrapped up in her heavy wool coat, the buffeting wind knifed through. It made her nose runny. Damn Harry Fendley. He probably hoped she'd step in front of a semi.

The light changed and she started across, after checking the speeding Peterbilts.

Harry had become even more short-tempered with her the last couple of days. He definitely wasn't the Friendly Fendley she'd come to know and loathe. She judged it wouldn't be long before he would deal on *her* terms. Of course she could more easily decide what those terms would be if she could find out what he was up to. But he'd also been more secretive the last few days, and she'd had little time to pry.

The business had taken an upswing lately. There had been more customers on the lot than Fendley and the other salesman could handle. Mrs. Quirk had barely been able to keep up with the paperwork.

As Mrs. Quirk pulled out the newspaper, the first large drop of rain splattered atop the rusting yellow vending machine. A moment later another drop sideswiped her nose. She uttered a rather imaginative rudery as she hurried back to the corner.

Later, as she thought over what had happened next, Adelia Quirk realized that she'd known—somehow—that the brown and tan pickup wasn't going to stop. It hadn't been moving that fast, but it had rolled right through the red light. James Hollingshead's Lincoln *had* been traveling fast. As mayor of Endicott, he had ignored the traffic laws with impunity for years.

He was not, however, immune to the laws of physics. Both he and Robert Barnes, driver of the pickup, were declared dead at the scene.

It was a scene Mrs. Quirk could still see vividly that evening as she sat soaking her feet in a tub of warm water. She hunched over with a bright granny-patch afghan she had crocheted from odds and ends of yarn wrapped around her shoulders. She held a tissue pressing her nostrils together against a persistent sniffle as the warm water seemed to soak the chill out of her bones. Whenever her lids closed, drowsily, the scene replayed until she became so irritated that she banished it from her thoughts.

She had known the two men well. She knew everyone in Endicott well. A useless waste of human life, she decided, the both of them. Neither of them was worth a damn. Still, it was an unfortunate accident.

Probably mechanical failure, the officer at the scene had hazarded. Barnes had obviously tried to avoid the crash. The pickup's brakes must have failed.

The telephone rang. Mrs. Quirk eyed it with some displeasure before answering. "Hello, Virginia," she said without enthusiasm, upon hearing her sister-in-law's voice. "I guess you want to talk about the accident."

"What accident?" was the reply. Mrs. Quirk could have bitten off her tongue. Now she would have to spend half an hour going through the details again. She was spared when her sister-in-law went on: "Oh, you mean the Jacobses. It was no accident. Leroy meant to shoot her!"

"Shoot her—who?"

"Evelyn. He shot Evelyn—and that insurance salesman she'd been slip-pin' around with. The whole thing was so tacky. Leroy would leave for work at seven thirty and the insurance man would be at the house by eight. Evelyn would never even get out of bed. Only, this mornin' Leroy came back."

"I don't want to hear about it. So please don't tell me what Leroy said when they arrested him—and how many minutes of coverage the TV people gave it on the six o'clock news . . ."

"Leroy didn't wait for the police," Virginia interrupted, then said, somewhat subdued, "He shot himself, too. Can you imagine? That, and the accident on Main Street—you did hear about the accident on Main Street?"

"Yes." Mrs. Quirk rolled resigned eyes heavenward.

"And Johnny Hovatter getting drunk and falling off one of his horses and breaking his neck?"

"What? When did that happen?" Mrs. Quirk asked.

"Really, Adelia, you should keep up with what's happening around you. It was in this morning's paper." Fendley's newspaper had ended up serving her as a rain hat. Her own morning *Clarion Herald*, which was delivered somewhere around one P.M., had been thrown, with her delivery boy's unerring eye, into the only mud puddle in her driveway.

Virginia's voice rattled on. "For a town of no more than twenty-five thousand a lot of things have happened. Now, if we were New York, or somewhere—but that's what I was calling you about before you started questioning me about those other things—when are the Effersons moving out? Do you think they'll go back to New York—that is where they're from, isn't it?"

"The Effersons? They wouldn't sell out. Just a few months ago a Clarksville man was trying to buy . . ." Even as she said it Mrs. Quirk was remembering that it had been some time since they had trotted over bringing huckleberry jam or goat's cream. Cucumbers were out of season.

"They didn't sell. Frieda Wilson's daughter, who works at the court-house, said at the beauty parlor that there was an error in their title going back sixty years. The rightful owners had them served notice. They did offer them a small cash settlement in exchange for their promise not to challenge the thing—which would have been useless anyway from what Frieda said . . ."

With a patience that amazed herself, Mrs. Quirk bore the remainder of "what Frieda said." When the subject matter rambled on to what Frieda's mother was paying to have her house painted, Mrs. Quirk reminded her-self firmly to be kind. Virginia couldn't help it if she was an idiot.

After she'd hung up, Mrs. Quirk called the Effersons, who confirmed the news. It seemed the old farmer had sold their five acres of river front- age on the Chickasaw to a logging company some sixty years before. The logging company, a fledgling business, had had a falling out over payment with the farmer, and he'd reclaimed the property. The trouble was, he hadn't bothered to straighten it all out at the courthouse. The logging company hadn't gone out of business. Today it was known as Acme Paper.

"When did you find out something was wrong?" Mrs. Quirk was drawn to ask.

"I had a bad feeling a few months ago when a survey crew was shooting the lines for the paper company and they didn't stop at my back fence," Gary Efferson explained. "The foreman showed me his plat when he was finished sketching, and it made my stomach curl.

"We found a home for Zelda, though," he went on. "That's some comfort. I think we might try building a soddy in Wyoming next . . ."

When Mrs. Quirk hung up the phone, she felt angry. However irritat- ing the Effersons could be, they were *her* Effersons. She didn't like this turn of events, not one little bit. Now there would be five more acres of pine trees planted in rows.

At least they'd found a home for Zelda, the goat who made the cheese. She only hoped that it wasn't with a family that liked barbecued goat.

The whole mess was still on her mind when she arrived at work the next morning—until she was greeted by a broadly smiling Fendley.

"I've sold that blue Buick, Mrs. Quirk. Here's the people's name and address, if you'd get the paperwork started . . . ?"

"You can't sell that Buick, Fendley. The state will revoke your license if you sell a car without proper title."

Fendley waved her away airily. "The cleaning woman found it stuck to the bottom of my wastebasket. God only knows how it got there."

God or someone, Mrs. Quirk grumbled to herself.

She really wasn't paying attention when Fendley went on to tell her about the new salesman he'd hired to keep up with the crush of custom- ers. She felt as though the world plane had taken a slight but definite shift to the left, and she was a little off-balance.

That sense of wrongness grew later, when the mailman told her about the town alderman who'd been electrocuted by high voltage wires while putting up a TV antenna early that morning. And how another man, passing in a car, had happened to see the accident and had rushed to help —only to die, too, when he'd tried to jerk the man free of the antenna pole.

As he said the name of the second victim, Mrs. Quirk realized just what had been niggling at her. Both were from Fendley's chain letter list—as were the people who had died yesterday.

Mrs. Quirk sat down heavily at her desk. It really was an ugly coincidence. Sending people chain letters didn't make them die, a very logical part of her mind argued. These people did, came the reply. Then, why not Fendley? Fendley had gotten the original—the ones she'd mailed were only copies.

She suddenly remembered the almost unbelievable upswing in car sales —and she remembered the wording of the letter: great luck or terrible misfortune . . .

Fendley, smiling viper that he was, hadn't broken the chain. What if the people he'd sent the letters to had?

Mrs. Quirk felt slightly ill—and completely culpable. My God! She had even enjoyed the idea.

"Fendley, we have a problem," said Mrs. Quirk as she entered his office without knocking. He glowered at her, then hung up the phone without even saying goodbye to the person on the other end.

"Yes?"

"Fendley . . . Harry . . . I don't know any other way to say it . . . Harry, people are dying."

He regarded her as if she had just declared that the world was round. "Miss Adelia, people die every day."

"I mean, Fendley, the people you had me send those chain letters to are dying!" She named them. "*Seven*, Fendley, *seven* people have died."

He blinked owlishly at her. "It's just some odd coincidence." But the look on his face glowed with possibility.

Mrs. Quirk didn't like the effect her revelation had on him. Gleeful was the word that sprang to mind as she watched the strange light dancing in his eyes. She felt slightly ill.

"Fendley, I don't know what you can do—but for God's sake, do *something!*" she said sharply.

Black fuzzy eyebrows crawled upward in response. "What?" he asked reasonably.

"*What?*" What indeed. Mrs. Quirk had no answer.

The strange light in his eyes suddenly encompassed her. "Miss Adelia, are you feeling all right? You seem a little disoriented this morning. I talked with your sister about you a while back, and she was a bit concerned." His new tack was obvious.

She pinned him with a bright blue eye that had nothing of senility in it. For an instant his smile faltered. "A competency hearing?" she asked, a sardonic brow quirked above the frames of her bifocals. "I'd love it. Then—" she smiled thinly "—I wouldn't be responsible . . ."

It seemed to Fendley that her last words hung on the air long after she'd left the room.

Minutes later Mrs. Quirk was leaving the office with her personal belongings in a box under her arm and a potted geranium in her hand. On her way out, a pert blonde, whose sweater fought mountain and valley to no avail, stopped her in the doorway.

"Do you know if there's an opening here for a secretary?" the blonde asked hopefully.

Mrs. Quirk thought she could be forgiven for dropping the geranium on the woman's foot.

For the next twenty-four hours Mrs. Quirk sat in her living room and drank enough hot black tea to put the high-pressure TV ads for denture cleaner to the test. All of her considerable will was focused on disbelieving. When she called the mortuary, she was rewarded to find that business had lulled. No one else in Endicott had died.

No sooner had she replaced the receiver than the phone rang, and she found that the local animal population had not been so fortunate. The call was from Coleen Anderson, her neighbor, who confided that she had been receiving rude phone calls for the past month that had grown increasingly threatening. There had also been prowlers at night. Then, last night, three dogs had been left on her lawn, their throats cut. Coleen had broken into sobs.

Mrs. Quirk decided that it was time to call a war council. An hour later, the Effersons and the Andersons were bending near as she unrolled her own survey plat on the kitchen table.

Greed, thought Mrs. Quirk later, was what made the world go round, and Harry Fendley's world spun very fast indeed these days.

It was the next morning that she heard about the fire at Emilio's. The restaurant, which occupied a building used as a warehouse in the forties, had been a favorite dining place in Endicott. A great many diners had been inside when the flames broke out. There were seven victims of the fire.

As the news announcer gave out the names of the dead, Mrs. Quirk got out the list of letter recipients she had reconstructed and grimly struck four more from it.

Eleven. Of the original thirteen, only two remained alive. As far as she knew, they were still alive. One, John McLean, was the half-owner of a rival car dealership. The other was Fendley's former secretary. With bile lapping at the back of her throat, Mrs. Quirk gathered her purse and coat and went out.

Hartley and McLean Auto Sales, situated temptingly just beside the interstate frontage road, was a much finer operation than Fendley's. They sold new cars as well as used. Gleaming new units sat row on row, while brightly colored plastic pennants snapped overhead in the crisp breeze. The used car section was a neat display of choice late models, sold with warranty. The only thing that Mrs. Quirk noted missing was customers. Inside the plate-glassed showroom, four salesmen were deep into a bridge game.

She found McLean in his office, throwing darts at an old campaign poster of Fendley. There were a great many holes on Fendley's nose. However, at the moment, his aim seemed to be off. He couldn't even land a facer.

He looked around as she plunked down in a chair. "Mrs. Quirk! I thought you were dead!" He didn't seem unduly pleased to discover his mistake.

"And I see you're still the same vicious little hellion who used to sit in the outer office at school waiting to be paddled by the principal about once a week," she snapped back. She was tired.

"You were a lot more frightening than the principal, Quirk." He laughed, then shot his final missile. It seemed destined for Fendley's ear but dropped suddenly just before impact.

"What can I do for you?" he asked as he sat down behind his desk.

"I'm not dead," Mrs. Quirk said with utter seriousness, "but *you* are, unless you can do something immediately." McLean sat silently as she told him what was happening, the expression in his eyes changing from shock to disbelief. Even before he spoke, Mrs. Quirk knew that she'd wasted her time.

"Yeah, I remember something like that in the mail. My secretary threw it away. So what am I supposed to do, make thirteen copies and send them out? And then what's supposed to happen to the thirteen people I send copies to?" he asked, rocking lightly back and forth in his low-backed swivel chair.

Mrs. Quirk felt as though a fist had connected with her diaphragm. Of course! Why hadn't she seen the danger before? If McLean sent out his copies, then what was the fate of the people he sent them to? And if those thirteen sent out their copies, then it would be thirteen times thirteen in danger. There *was* no escape, she thought as she rose on wobbly legs.

McLean burst out laughing. "Tell Fendley I don't know what the joke's about but he certainly got the right person to play the part. Quirk, you deserve an Oscar. You almost had me thinking you believed what you were telling me." His laughter filled the room.

"Did you call someone?" one of the salesmen asked, sticking his head around the door jamb. Mrs. Quirk made her way past him and through the door.

"No, no," McLean said behind her. "Quirk was just telling me a joke." Already in the hall, Mrs. Quirk heard him laugh again. She didn't see him rock back and lose his balance. She did hear the sickening thump as the base of his skull hit the corner of the filing cabinet, and the salesman's startled yell.

She clutched her purse a little tighter as she went on out of the building without looking back.

Fendley's eyes were overbright. He seemed to be suppressing a smile as Mrs. Quirk faced him in his office. "Twelve, Fendley. Twelve dead. McLean just cracked his skull open after I tried to tell him about your sick joke." Fendley giggled in delight and beat a tattoo with his heels on the floor. Mrs. Quirk watched his reactions with horror.

"Fendley! In that restaurant fire people died who weren't even on your list! What's wrong with you?" She itched to slap him.

"Wrong?" He moved to a closet and opened the door. Mrs. Quirk saw that he too had reconstructed the list. His was in large letters on poster paper. He took a red marker and drew a line through McLean's name, then eyed his handiwork with satisfaction. "Nothing at all wrong, Quirk. Oh, but I wish I'd known . . . then I'd really have used those letters effectively . . ." He smiled delightedly as his little brown eyes glazed over with power-lust and madness. Then they focused again—on her. "Very effectively, but no matter."

Mrs. Quirk looked at the last name: Becky Ward. "What about Becky? The girl has a husband and two kids."

He lifted his shoulders, palms up. "What?"

"You *could* wish her well! May God damn you, you're responsible for this."

His smile grew cruel, his small eyes narrowing beneath his heavy black brows. "Becky wasn't very nice to me when she worked here."

"Meaning that she wouldn't let you catch her when you chased her around your desk. Fendley, you're a two-hundred pound waste of human flesh."

He glowered malevolently at her as she stood up. Mrs. Quirk felt faint. She wasn't used to her circulation thundering in her ears. Fendley was probably wishing *her* dead, she thought without emotion.

She felt a little less dizzy as the light flashing on his phone distracted him. "Tell the congressman I'll call him back in a few minutes," he told the congressman's secretary tersely after he answered it.

"Go ahead and tell Haroldson what progress you've made in acquiring the rights-of-way." It was really a shot in the dark, but she was pleased to see that it had struck home.

"How did you know?" he demanded, putting down the phone.

Mrs. Quirk shrugged. "My friend Gary Efferson is an avid reader of the financial news—surprisingly. He noticed that the congressman's wife had acquired controlling interest in Acme Paper. Haroldson's wife also directs the development company he ran before he was elected. It's not hard to figure out that our properties—the Andersons', the Effersons', and my own—form a stopper in the Acme Paper bottleneck, cutting off direct access to the interstate. With a major city only forty-five minutes away, development of the Acme land should be worth millions.

"The congressman probably paid you a generous amount with which to purchase the land and then sell it directly to Acme. But you made a game out of getting the properties for little or nothing."

"Almost right," Fendley smiled. "Actually my good friend Haroldson offered me a piece of the action. George, poor fool, had already wandered into the Wednesday night card game and started losing money before my deal with Haroldson. Too bad he died before I got that deed.

"But you know the best part, Quirk? There's not a thing you or anyone can do." He giggled. "Now run along to Becky Ward. Tell her to send out thirteen letters! Tell her to send one to *me!* And I'll get your sister to stop those commitment proceedings I had her start against you." His giggle grew into a sideholding, gurgling laugh.

Adelia Quirk's blue eyes brightened with a knowing light. "Sorry, Fendley," she told him soberly, although he couldn't hear her above the sound of his own laughter, "but Becky wouldn't know what I was talking about." She closed the door on his hysteria.

In the outer office, the new secretary moved hurriedly out of the way as Mrs. Quirk opened the desk drawer. "Sorry, dear, just something I forgot to mail," she told the blonde as she slipped the thirteenth letter from beneath the drawer tray and into her purse.

Remembering a certain Buick title, she decided to wait until she got home to burn the letter. Although that might not be necessary—hadn't that been a shriek coming from Fendley's office? Then again, she had never been able to hear much from in there. . . .

# My First Murder

## STEVE BARANCIK

Come summer I'm the luckiest kid in Pierson County, because my dad's the sheriff. When I get out of school, rather than make me work the fields, he makes me an unofficial sheriff's deputy—even got me an official Unofficial Sheriff's Deputy badge—and I tag along in his squad car and help out around the office while he makes the world safe for the good folk who live here.

Mom doesn't exactly approve, but then again she doesn't wear the gun in the family. In fact, just last week she was saying to Dad that sheriff's work wasn't a healthy thing for me to get too exposed to, said that I'd grow up thinking folks just killed each other all the time. I set her straight on that one. I told her that the greatest number of murderings occurs late in the evenings, early in the mornings, and on weekends. Definitely not all the time. She still wasn't satisfied. She gave Dad her "I told you so" look.

Not that all that much of what a sheriff does involves dead folk and those that make them that way. Most of Dad's work is actually pretty tame stuff, like when somebody's feathered livestock becomes somebody else's feathered livestock, and the first somebody hadn't exactly approved the deal. Not that that's boring or that it isn't important; it takes a good brain to figure out any kind of crime.

And my dad'll tell you that I've helped figure out a few. He says I'm already a little smarter than some of his deputies, and heaps smarter than the others. Still, Dad says he can't put me on the payroll on account of something called "neppertizzum." I think it means that I'm only twelve years old.

But, like I said, I've helped out on a few cases, and even solved some all by myself. The one that's tacked to the front of my brain right now, on account of I'm proudest of it, is the Sampson murder, the first murder I ever solved. You yourself probably wouldn't have figured it out, even my dad didn't, but I'm betting you're plenty smart enough to follow along.

The time was last summer, a Sunday in July to be exact, when the call came in to Headquarters. Someone had been murdered, or was dead with a few holes in him, out at Chief Okeedokee's Wilderness Campground, down by the river. Dad told me to drop what I was doing so that we could race out to the campground and get started while the blood was still wet.

Joe Barton, the owner of the campground (you guessed it: there's no Chief Okeedokee), met us at the entrance. Dad waved him into the car, and we continued down the dirt road towards the campsites.

"It was Cory Sampson," said Joe. "He and his wife have been camping here since Friday. Nobody saw who did it." Joe paused and then continued, sounding a bit worried. "You don't think there's a maniac still running around in the woods looking to kill someone else, do you?"

"That would be unusual," said Dad, but I don't think Joe took big heaps of comfort from it, seeing as how things were already running a little bit towards the unusual for him that day. Dad's as straight as an arrow, which is why he goes unrun-against at every election. But talking, smiling, and comforting aren't his biggest strengths; his shyness gets in the way. Still, folks like him all the same.

"Any other fusses this weekend?" asked Dad.

"Matter of fact," said Joe, "a couple campers complained yesterday about the Sampsons' playing their rock and roll music too loud. Seems they had some speakers hooked up in the back of their truck to the radio inside. I asked Cory to turn it down, and he just turned it off altogether. No big deal. Hardly seemed like enough for somebody to kill him over."

"Hardly," said Dad.

We were the first unit to the Sampson campsite, but as you can imagine every other camping couple and their kids were already on the scene. Dad groaned. Still, somebody had had the good sense to take a nylon cord and make a ring some ten feet across around the body, and nobody was inside that ring. That was more good sense than you could usually expect from folks. Sometimes they seem about ready to start cutting off souvenirs. Why, once I even saw a guy taking pictures of the wife and kids next to a fresh dead body. Cursed to beat the band when I told him he had the lens cap on.

Before we even got out of the car everyone was at Dad's window trying to make their statement, offering important information like, "Somebody's been killed full of holes," and, "Nobody knows who done did it." Dad searched out Sylvie Sampson, wife of the newly dead man, and offered her the privacy of the squad car, now that we were out of it, which she accepted. Then Dad told everybody else to line up in alphabetic order by last name, and once he'd finished looking at the scene and talking to Sylvie he would take their statements. Everybody groaned, especially the

Wynfeldts, but they all did as told. It's hard to believe when you hear about city folk rushing away from a scene and not wanting to get involved. Small town folk'll take their action and story makings wherever they can get it.

Cory Sampson was dead all right. He was lying face up in a patch of thick weeds and grasses about two feet high. He'd been shot three times from the front. The killer was no dead-eye. One shot'd hit Cory in the thigh, one in the shoulder, one right in the old fuel pump.

Right next to Cory, as clear as if he's lain down in the snow and rolled from his front to his back, was a patch of greenery all matted and flattened by Cory's own personal blood and gore. From this I figured Cory must have rolled halfway over before breathing his last.

There'd been too much "witnessing" around the campsite to figure out where the killer might have done the killing from. Still, there were three exit wounds in Cory's back side, so a search of the area would probably provide some lead leads. We'd need to find at least one of the bullets to figure where the killer stood and what kind of gun he shot.

When another unit showed up, Dad started giving out chores. He told his deputies to keep their eyes pried for a gun, bullets, and anything else that might seem out of place. Like gloves, say. He also radioed for a couple of metal detectors or, if no can do, some rakes. Then he went to the car, offered Sylvie his sorrows and such, and led her away from the crowd for some questions. From the looks of her I'd say she was grieving a good four on a ten scale.

It wasn't my place to sit in on such a sorrowful interview, so I did some investigating around. I asked Joe to point out the folks that had complained about the Sampsons' music, but they didn't look much like the killing type.

I wandered over to the body and noticed something that hadn't been there for the seeing before. In the flattened patch *next* to the body, the patch that was Cory Sampson's face down and second to final resting place, most of the blood had already dried but there were two little pools still plenty wet. Why not three, I wondered, since all the wounds had been bleeders?

Strolling onwards, I came to the Sampson truck. The windows were open, and when I got close, I heard a soft clicking from inside. I poked my head through the window, careful not to touch anything. The tape deck had been left on. When the tape had done the machine hadn't stopped; it was still trying to click forward. The tape case on the seat was done in a human hand. The group was called "Demon Freshened Borax," and the album was titled *Songs of Death and Parties*. I guessed that the music fell something short of Loretta Lynn. Still, I had what I wanted: an excuse to check in on Dad.

"Dad? Sorry to interrupt. I just wanted to tell you that Mrs. Sampson's tape deck in her car is on. Can I turn it off so her battery doesn't croak?" Right then I realized croaking wasn't a real tasteful subject for the moment, and turned to Mrs. Sampson to apologize as soon as the word had left my mouth. Indeed she'd turned a fine shade of pale. "Sorry, Mrs. Sampson," I said.

Dad told me that his talk with Mrs. Sampson would be over in a couple of seconds and then, turning to her, said she could turn off the tape herself then. But, he added, saying sorry all the way, she'd have to leave the truck and camping gear behind. He promised it would all be given back to her as soon as possible, probably the next day. She nodded. He called a deputy over to drive her home.

Once she'd gone I dragged Dad over to the body to show off my discovery. But the blood had dried all up, and you couldn't see what I'd seen before. I tried to show Dad how the blood was thicker near the two spots I'd seen, but he wasn't much interested.

"The coroner'll be here in a few minutes," he said, humoring me some. "You can tell him what you think you saw. Meanwhile you can sit in while I interview some witnesses."

Dad called the Wynfeldts first, which no one else was too happy about save the Ventons, who figured they'd be next. The Wynfeldts' was the nearest campsite to the Sampsons', and Sylvie'd been there when the shots that killed Cory were heard.

Mrs. Wynfeldt did most of the talking, or at least she did it louder than Mr. Wynfeldt. At around three Sylvie'd come over to their campsite and asked to borrow some matches. Mrs. Wynfeldt sent Mr. Wynfeldt to scare up a spare book, while the two ladies made neighbor talk. When Mr. got back with the book Sylvie and Mrs. continued the conversation, "bringing it toward a decent conclusion" was how Mrs. Wynfeldt put it, when they all heard the three shots loud and near. Mrs. Wynfeldt let Mr. Wynfeldt demonstrate here. "Bangbangbang," he said. "Just like that." The bangs came all within a second or less they both agreed.

The shots sounded like they'd come from the Sampson campsite, and hardly a moment passed before a worried Sylvie Sampson was running, "like the wind," said Mrs. Wynfeldt, towards her poor husband. Mrs. Wynfeldt shook her head real sad.

"Didn't much matter how fast she run," summed up Mr. Wynfeldt.

The rest of the witnesses had nothing useful to add, but don't try and tell them that. They all agreed that the shots had come rapid and regular, "bangbangbang" as Mr. Wynfeldt put it. No one had seen nor heard anyone running from the scene. By the time we'd given all of them their say it was dark.

Dad checked with his deputies and the coroner to see what they'd found meantime. What they'd found was two bullets; they'd searched like crazy for the third but no go. No gun or gloves, neither. From the bullets they figured the gun was a cheapie, and though they'd work on it it didn't figure to be traceable. As crime scenes go this one wasn't going anywhere.

I wandered around some more while everybody was cleaning up. I looked inside the truck to see if Sylvie had turned the tape off. She had, but that wasn't all she'd done. She'd taken the tape, too. Sylvie must have felt pretty attached to that tape, though I hadn't figured it for mourning music. Still, since my first observation hadn't gotten much of a welcome from Dad, this one I kept to myself.

During the drive home I asked Dad what he thought. He said that since the physical evidence hadn't done a whole lot of pointing, he was going to do some personal prying: dig into Cory's and Sylvie's home life, see if they'd taken out any life insurance recently, see how their relations related, check Cory's business connections and whether he owed anybody. That kind of stuff. "Beating the motive bushes," he called it.

I asked whether he thought it funny at all that Cory seemed to have been killed at probably the only time him and Sylvie had been separated that weekend.

"You mean like maybe she had him killed while she was fully alibied?" I nodded.

"Yep, it's possible," said Dad. "But it's more likely that whoever killed him had been waiting in the leafy wings all day for just that moment."

Dad had a point.

The next day didn't shed much extra light on Cory Sampson's sudden decline. The gun wasn't traceable. Not the third bullet nor any other physical evidence was found. The shots were figured to have been shot from the woods, so the getaway'd probably been made by foot, not wheels. No big surprise, since the witnesses hadn't seen nor heard a car leaving the scene.

Friends, family, and neighbors told that the Sampsons had never been the most get-alongingest couple, not even close, but that lately they'd seemed as happy as bugs in rugs. I'm no expert on marriage, but it seemed to me this pointed one small finger towards Sylvie, because I figured if you were planning to kill your husband you'd start acting nice to him so that folks wouldn't think you'd done it. Still, it was just a hunch, not the sort of hard evidence you get to fry someone for.

There had been no new insurance taken out on Cory's life, but the policy he already had wouldn't leave Sylvie washing other people's under-things, if you know what I mean.

Coming home that night I asked Dad what he figured to do next. He stared out over the dark road shaking his head back and forth. "I just don't know," he mumbled. I decided to spend the next day working alone. I had an idea, which was one more than Dad had.

First thing in the morning I hopped on my bike and rode to town, forgetting that the record store doesn't open until ten. Oops. I leaned up against the store. The more I thought about it the more I had Demon Freshened Borax on my brain. Why did Sylvie take the tape? Sure, she might have done it for no reason at all, but it was worth checking out. I don't know what I expected to hear, but it was worth a try.

At ten Mr. Stone showed up and let me in the store, but he had no copies of *Songs of Death and Parties*. "Doesn't sound like little boys' music," said old Mr. Stone.

"It's for my mom," I lied.

Mr. Stone frowned some. "I suppose I could call around for you and see who might have it."

I gave him my best "respect your elders" smile and told him that would be much appreciated.

He finally found a copy for me at The Headbanger's Ballroom, a record store some ten miles away, in the county seat the next county over. Have bike will travel.

"Serious music, man," said the hairy creature behind the counter with the rings in his nose. He seemed to like my choice.

The sticker on the wrapper said, "This album contains lyrics that will offend anybody." "Highbrow music?" I suggested.

"That album'll kill brain cells, man."

I told him how much I was looking forward to that and gave him my money. Then I sped home.

Not ten seconds passed from when I'd put the album on Dad's stereo before Mom shut every door in the house between her and me. I lay back on the couch with the lyrics and tried to follow along. The way they sang it wasn't easy. The first song was titled "Things Me and Sis Do with Knives." The lyrics would turn your dog's face red. The song ends with a scream, sounds like Sis finally stuck the knife in him.

The second song was titled, "Let the Party Begin." Three sounds, real loud with no music behind them, is what they used to set the beat at the beginning. They went like this.

"Bangbangbang."

\*   \*   \*

I called Dad and begged him to pick me up right away. When he came I was waiting with a shovel, garden shears, and a gas-powered leaf blower I'd borrowed from the neighbors. In my pocket I carried a homemade tape I'd made of the three shots on the album, with three minutes of silence going before them. "What's going on?" asked Dad while I loaded everything into the trunk.

"I'm going to show you how Sylvie killed Cory," I answered. "Let's go to Okeedokee's."

Dad looked first at my equipment, then at me like I'd lost a few of the brain cells the record store creature talked about. "He wasn't killed with a leaf blower," said Dad, sarcasticizing.

"Remember the duck rustlers," I said, speaking of the first case I ever solved. "Remember Peeping George?" I gave him my hurt look, which almost always works. "Aren't I an official Unofficial Sheriff's Deputy?" I whined.

"Okay, okay," said Dad. "Let's get going."

I loaded the tape into his car deck and looked at the clock. Three minutes. I turned up the volume a tad. "I'm playing a tape," I said.

"I don't hear anything," said Dad.

Now you know why he's the sheriff. "You will," I said.

As soon as the shots came I knew I'd turned up the volume a little high. Dad hit the brakes, spun the car, stuffed me under the front seat, and dived out the door with his gun drawn. To say my ears were ringing wouldn't be but half the truth; it was more like someone was playing squeezebox on my brain.

"Uh, Dad," I said, painfully and fearfully. "That was my tape."

God bless him, he didn't even point the gun at me.

Over the rest of the drive I explained, real loud, how I thought Sylvie Sampson had used a tape just like this one to make it seem like Cory'd been shot while she was fussing over at the Wynfeldts. I told him how she'd palmed the tape before leaving the scene, and how the deck had been on when we got there. He thought it was all very interesting, but he said there weren't ways to prove it.

That, I told him, is why we're going to Okeedokee's. I explained I'd have to mess with the crime site some, but he said it was okay since his men were done with it.

Once we got there we took the gardening tools out of the trunk. Dad didn't look like he had a whole lot of faith in me, and, in fact, I wasn't all that sure myself that my hunches'd turn out right.

First thing I did was cut the bloody flat grass patch—the one that was next to where we'd found Cory's body—right down to the ground. While I did I told Dad how my thinking went.

"Do you agree," I asked, "that it looks like Cory rolled himself over, or somebody rolled him over, after he was shot?"

Dad nodded.

"Well," I went on, "I think we can figure he didn't roll himself over. Sure, someone who's just been shot is going to want to get away and get help, and he might not be fit for standing, but I don't think he'd choose crabwalking over crawling. This isn't the county fair. If he landed on his front side he'd want to stay that way and move as best he could."

Dad nodded his head, looking impressed for the first time. He hadn't thought of that. "So what do you think happened?"

"I think Sylvie turned him over."

"Why?"

I didn't answer the question because I'd done with the grass clipping. Yanking the cord I turned on the blower and blew everything away. What was usually orange soil beneath was, as I'd figured, deep blood red all under the body. I picked up the shovel and handed it to Dad.

"What do you want me to do?" he asked.

"Take an inch off the top," I said. "Just an inch, no more, all the way around."

Dad did as he was told. It must be fun having deputies.

"Why am I doing this?" he asked.

"You probably don't remember," I said, "because you didn't take it real serious, but right after we got to the scene I tried to tell you I thought Cory'd been shot only twice before he hit the ground."

"Impossible," said Dad. "Gravity doesn't work that fast. The shots came too quick for him to have got plugged standing up *and* on the ground."

"The tape," I reminded him. "Look, if I show the last plug came while he was on the ground, will you be convinced Sylvie faked the shots everybody heard?"

"Me and a jury," he said.

Dad finished digging, and when I looked down I felt pretty good. At that level the blood had only dripped down in two places, and they matched up just right with the thigh shot and the shoulder shot. Even though the heart wound bled the most. I looked at Dad. "Since Cory was face down here, the blood'd leak direct into the ground, going the deepest straight under the source. Right?"

"Right," Dad admitted.

"Shoulder," I said, pointing to the top spot. "Thigh," pointing to the lower one.

I grabbed the shears and started cutting like crazy in the patch where Cory'd actually been found, facing up. I pictured his chest and aimed for there. Once I'd cut a circle a foot around, I picked up the blower and yanked the starting cord with style. "You are about to see," I yelled, "a .38 caliber hole in the ground."

With a .38 caliber bullet six inches below it, the final proof that the three shots everybody heard weren't the three shots that killed Cory Sampson.

When faced with the evidence, Sylvie wasted no time till confessing. She'd been thinking of killing Cory for months but hadn't been able to figure out how to get away with it. Then one night Cory brought home the new Demon Freshened Borax album, which she hated, and the second song gave her the idea.

She recorded only the three shots, just like I'd done. Then she bought an unregistered .38 and a silencer, making sure to load it with only three bullets, no more or less. That weekend she waited for a noisy moment to shoot Cory, just to be sure that the silencer was plenty silent. When someone started cutting wood with a chainsaw she had her chance. Coming towards Cory from the woods, she called his name so he'd face her and shot him twice. She wasn't real pleased with her aim, but he went down just the same. Then she rolled him over and gave him the third shot, which she'd saved for insurance, aiming it right at his heart from three feet above. Pleasant dreaming, Cory.

She walked, calmly, down to the riverside to dump the gun, and the gloves she wore case the gun was found. Then she went back to the truck, turned the deck on with the volume on "high," and loaded the tape. She then walked to the Wynfeldts to put her five hundred feet from the scene and socializing when the shots rang out.

Sylvie's mistake was being too careful, trying to ditch the tape after someone, namely me, already had seen it. If not for that she probably would have gotten clean away with the whole thing.

Dad offered me a deal. He'd make sure I got credit for solving the Sampson killing, name in the paper and all that, if I promised not to run against him for sheriff next year. I tried to hold out for an expense account—no go—and eventually I agreed. I think I can wait till I'm fifteen.

# Death of an Otter

## JOSEPH HANSEN

The bunch of flowers in his hand caught her attention for a moment, no more than that. She turned her head away. He had got used to how short they kept her hair. It made her head look like a small boy's, and the absence of makeup added to that effect. Never mind. Her head was a beautiful shape, and her skin and features were good—she'd never needed makeup. This visit was the same as always. When the nurse opened the door to her room, and he saw her seated in sunlight from a window, and the nurse said cheerfully, "Look who's come to see you," and she turned that brief, blank look on him, his heart made as if to surge out of his chest.

He wanted to rush in and take her in his arms, and hold her close, as he had done a thousand times in their lost years together. But he couldn't do that. Once long ago, when the doctor had told him she seemed better, less withdrawn, more her old self, Hack had tried it. It was a mistake he'd never forget. She had watched him come to her without a sign of alarm, but when he'd put his hands on her shoulders, she'd started to scream. Her eyes filled with horror. She beat and scratched at him, kicked at him, writhed, struggled. Nurses, attendants, a doctor had come. She was sedated in a few short minutes. But to him, her screaming seemed to go on and on.

It wasn't him she was frightened of. He knew that. She was back again in those nightmare hours aboard a stinking tub of a fishing boat up from Mexico with a cargo of brown heroin. That night was long ago, but it looked as if she was going to live in it forever. The early hopes of the doctors had proved wishful thinking. Her times of drugged calm grew longer, but she never once spoke. And when the terror swept over her, it was as if no time at all had passed. He blamed himself for letting the metedors take her, though he didn't fairly see how he could have prevented it, even if he'd foreseen it. It had happened fast.

Hardest of all to live with was that somehow he ought to have foreseen it. He had been a peace officer for a dozen years when it happened. He had them, and they knew he had them—unless they crippled him. And they did that by snatching Linda. Then he'd lost his head, and called for backup. His fellow officers had dropped the metedors bloody and dead in the bottom of their boat. They'd given Hack Bohannon back his wife. But they'd been too long getting there, and she was lost to him. He sat now in a creaky white wicker chair opposite her, and talked quietly about his stables, his horses, the horses he boarded for others.

She looked at him sometimes, briefly. He wasn't sure what understanding, if any, was in those looks. But once, when he was telling her about this spring's foals, wobbling up from the straw on their spindly legs, he thought she smiled for a second. Maybe not. Maybe it was the shadow of leaves from the tree outside the window touching her mouth. But he wanted to believe it was a smile. When the nurse came with a vase for the flowers and by glancing at her watch indicated it was time for him to leave, and he rose with his sweat-stained Stetson in his hand—he wanted to bend and kiss the mouth where that possible smile had appeared. But he only said, "Be good. I'll be back next Monday." Out in the cool, dim hallway of the lumbering old house, he wondered why he'd said such a damned fool thing. She'd never been any way but good in her life.

Gloom always settled in him after these visits. He had never brought anyone along before. Today he had brought T. Hodges, a young deputy from the sheriff station where he used to work. She was the first woman friend he'd made since he and Linda had been wrenched apart. She was very different. Oh, slight like Linda, yes, but dark, with a way of smiling with her eyes because she was self-conscious about her teeth—the upper ones stuck out a little. He wasn't sure why she'd asked to come along with him today. Maybe because she sensed the visits were hard for him and made him feel more than commonly alone.

He judged her to be too young to have to face this kind of situation, even at second hand. He'd told her no before. Then, because it seemed to hurt her, this time he had said yes. But she'd been troubled on the ride over the mountains from the coast, and quiet. She'd got out of the old pickup and walked with him across lawns past flowerbeds in the morning sunshine. Quiet. She'd even climbed the steps to the great verandah of the house, but there she had lost her nerve. He'd crossed the porch to the door and rung the bell before he missed her and looked back. She stood at the top of the steps, tears glistening in her dark eyes and shaking her head. "I can't," she said. "I'll wait here."

He came out onto the porch now, put on his Stetson, looked for her.

She was far off across a downhill sweep of grass, sitting alone on a green bench under a willow. He went down the steps slowly, and stood at the foot of the steps and waited for her to come to him. She came, at a slow walk, head hanging. When she reached him, she looked up, ashamed. "I guess I'm a coward," she said. "I didn't know that. I'm sorry, Hack. I wasn't any help to you at all, was I?" He gave her a small hug, left the arm over her shoulder, started with her toward the truck. "How was she?" T. Hodges asked.

"She almost smiled today," he said. He twisted the rusty handle, pulled open the rusty-hinged cab door for her. She climbed up and sat on the cracked, tape-mended seat. He slammed the door, went around and got in at the driver's side, slammed that door, the tinny sound loud in the mountain stillness. The cab smelled of timothy hay and of the dried manure underfoot on the tattered rubber floor mat. He brought the engine noisily to life. "Ah, hell," he said. "I'm making it up. She was just the same today. She isn't getting any better." He let the handbrake go, and rolled the rattly truck off across crackling gravel.

Along Highway 1 north of Madrone, buildings had gone up lately—motels, and places to eat. Stucco and neon. He didn't like them. When there'd come a chance, he'd voted against them. He'd written a protest letter to the local weekly paper. He'd never run into anyone who wanted them. Yet up they went, didn't they? There, damn it, was a whole new shopping center—boutiques, boulangeries, cafes serving nothing but crepes. Then there were isolated hamburger joints and fried shrimp counters. A good many hadn't made it. Some stood boarded up, bleak in the cold spring sunlight off the ocean. Others kept changing hands.

Here was an ugly white place repainted, paper banners taped to it, GRAND OPENING, last Saturday's date. A woman in a green down jacket and blue-jeans was up on an aluminum ladder yanking the highest of these signs down. She turned her head so he saw her face just as he passed. He was startled, and put a foot on the brake pedal. He edged off onto the road shoulder. T. Hodges looked at him curiously. "Somebody I used to know," he said, and watched the dusty side mirror until the highway was clear, and swung onto it, and headed back for the place. She was tearing down the paper signs from the windows now. He got down from the truck and walked over to her. "Dorothy Hawes?" he said.

She turned, the wadded paper signs clutched in her arms. The sea wind blew her gray hair across her eyes. But she saw who he was. And showed alarm before she caught herself and smiled. "Why, Hack Bohannon. How are you?"

"When did you come back?" he said.

"A few weeks ago." She tossed her head to let wind blow the hair off her face. "I should have let you know, but I've been busy setting up shop here."

"How long has it been?" he said. "Twenty years?"

"Eighteen," she said, "but I never thought of it as anything but temporary. I hated Los Angeles." She gave a shudder that had nothing to do with the wind chill factor. "But work was easier to find there. I was on my own, wasn't I?" Her young husband had drowned, leaving her with two girls scarcely more than babies. "Mouths to feed, and all that. Sometimes we need cities, no way around it."

T. Hodges walked up, interested. Bohannon said, "Dorothy Hawes, Teresa Hodges. She's a deputy sheriff."

"And you? You must be a captain by now." Dorothy Hawes's blue eyes rested for a moment thoughtfully on him. "You were the best they had. The one who cared."

Bohannon shook his head. "I quit some time back. I keep horses now. Up Rodd Canyon."

The Hawes woman said, "I'm not surprised. There's no justice in this world." She turned away. "Come on. Have lunch. I'm in need of customers." She laughed, struggling, arms filled with the crumpled paper, to open the door. He opened it for her. They all went inside. The restaurant, white and cold as the innards of a refrigerator, smelled good. The smells came warm from the kitchen, onions and herbs, chilis, cheeses. "You've got your choice of tables." Hawes made for the kitchen swing door, calling out something in Spanish to whoever was beyond it. She vanished, but she was back in a minute, unburdened of the signs.

"We planned to picnic on the beach," T. Hodges said.

"All right. I think I can scare up a picnic basket. How does chicken sound? Rotisseried. Mustard and honey glaze? You'll love it. A slab of Monterey jack? Sourdough bread delivered by hand fresh from San Francisco this morning? My wine license isn't here yet, but I'll slip you a bottle of something wonderful, if you promise not to tell." She grinned at T. Hodges. "Or am I suborning you?"

"Not if you let me pay for it."

"It will only take two minutes." Dorothy Hawes bustled back to the kitchen. "And you'll be on your way."

The basket stood on rough rocks. The wind off the ocean was strong. A tablecloth had been folded into the basket, but they didn't try to lay it out, nor to set plates and glasses on it. They tore the chicken apart with their hands, ate with their fingers. Bohannon used his clasp knife to cut the bread and cheese. The wine was good, bright and clean-tasting. Everything was delicious. The sea air helped make it that way. But the wind was too cold to invite sitting still for long. They closed up the bones and crusts in the basket, climbed down to the sand, and walked.

It hadn't been a talky lunch, and they didn't talk as they walked, either. The only sound was the slap and slither of the surf on the sand, and the crunch of their soles in the sand. The water, moiling around shoreward rocks, was a dozen different shades of blue and green. Out farther, beds of brown kelp rose and fell heavily on the sparkling swells. Bohannon felt good that T. Hodges was with him. The gloom was lifting already.

Then they rounded a clump of rocks. She was a couple of steps ahead of him, she gasped, she stopped in her tracks. And he saw what she saw. Lying in the surf, thick fur matted, eyes half shut and glazed over, stiffened body rolling in the wash of the tide, was a sea otter, a big fellow, maybe sixty pounds. A dark hole was in the skull behind the left ear. Hack knew it for a bullet hole before he passed the basket to T. Hodges, crouched, and picked the dead animal up. Cradling it, heavy, cold, wet, against him, he started back along the beach to find the truck. T. Hodges had recognized the bullet hole, too. She hurried after him.

"I can't believe it," she panted. "He was drunk. Nobody thought he meant it."

"Looks like he did," Bohannon said.

Madrone had a white barn of a building for meetings. In the big pine plank hall dances were held, rummage sales when rain and cold wind sent folks indoors, community suppers, shows of paintings by local artists, political gatherings in election years. Last night, the folding chairs that often stood in stacks along the walls had been brought out into the middle of the room and set up in rows. Some were metal, some wood, but none was empty by the time the meeting got under way. The dirt parking area outside was jammed with cars. Cars stood along the road shoulders, too, north and south.

The meeting was about sea otters. The inshore waters off Madrone, and for about two hundred miles up and down the coast from Monterey to Morro Bay, were a sea otter refuge. Once nearly wiped out by fur hunters, the animals had come back under government protection. There were nearly two thousand now, breeding, feeding, playing in the massive kelp beds. Tourists parked alongside Highway 1 to watch them through binoculars. They were clownish eaters, lying on their backs, flat rocks on their chests, cracking abalone, sea urchins, spiny lobsters against the rocks, stuffing their mouths. Gulls circled for scraps. It made a show.

But it didn't amuse the men who once made a living here diving for abalone. An adult sea otter can eat twelve pounds of abalone in a day. It didn't amuse the operators of fishing boats who had been forbidden to use gill nets in the shallow waters to catch halibut. Too many otters got caught and drowned in gill nets. Now the federal government, worried about offshore oil rigs coming into the area, proposed moving some of the sea otters to an island off Southern California, in case there were oil spills. So there would be a seed colony, in case the Central Coast otters all died.

A good many speakers took the microphones at the meeting. An oil company spokesman, in a shirt and tie, said there was no risk to the otters. Sturdy old Sharon Webb, in jeans and hiking boots, who'd spent decades battling to save nature from the ravening greed of men, said the transloca-tion was well worth a million tax dollars. A commercial fisherman from down the coast who made his living off the abalone around the island protested. Everyone got his or her say. Bohannon found the slat seat of the wooden folding chair hard under his butt after a while, and kept looking at his watch. The meeting went on a long time, mostly in circles. But fire-works broke out at the end, and all who stayed got some excitement to cut the boredom and send them home with something to talk about before bedtime.

Brick Lightner had a seat down toward the front, where the federal and state wildlife people sat at a table facing the crowd, trying to field ques-tions and monitor speeches. Lightner, a balding, bony man in a torn, greasy leather jacket, had called out more than once, "Aw, sit down and shut up," during this talk and that. Afterwards, someone said he'd kept mumbling "goddamn commies" under his breath. And firing up his breath from a pint whisky bottle in his jacket pocket. But he'd made no effort to get a microphone and talk himself.

Until the chairman, a young naturalist for the wildlife service, a sun-burned kid who kept an eye on the otters through a telescope from Piedras Blancas lighthouse during business hours, said it was late, and made polite remarks about how important it had been to hear all sides of the question, and how other local meetings like this would be held up and down the coast before any decision was made, and thanked everybody for coming.

Then Lightner roared to his feet, shouting, waving his angular arms, his long, stringy, reddish hair flying. "We don't need no more meetings. Jesus Christ, isn't there one suffering soul in this room with a little common sense? Just what did a damn sea otter ever do for you? Any of you. Can you answer that? Did a sea otter ever give you a dollar for a loaf of bread or a gallon of gas? Did a sea otter ever pay your rent or the taxes to send your kids to school?"

People had already started scraping up out of their chairs to leave, but nobody left. Not now. Some stood in front of their chairs, many with arms half into coats they had begun to put on. Some sat down again. But nobody said anything. Everybody listened, a good many of them with mouths half opened—making themselves look to the viewer as stupid as Lightner seemed to think they were, though Bohannon knew they weren't. Lightner raved on.

"You know the answer to that. The answer is 'no.' But I'll tell you who does give you a dollar now and then, who does pay your rent and taxes. Me, and men like me. And where do we get those dollars? From abalone and halibut, that's where. My old man fished this coastline thirty years and me after him. Until the goddamn government let those useless animals here to eat up everything under the water and leave nothing for us. Nothing."

He had been facing the crowd. Now he turned and jabbed a knuckly finger at the government people at the table. "And now you come telling us you're going to take two hundred fifty of these devouring locusts and put them someplace else on the coast to take away the honest livelihood of other fishermen. Because the sea otter is an 'endangered species—' " he spoke the words with a mincing sneer "—and has to be protected." Spittle had collected on his mouth. He wiped at it angrily with the back of a hand.

"Well, let me tell you who's the endangered species. It's you and me. Hell, there's two hundred thousand sea otters up off Alaska. Maybe more. Too many to count. To listen to folks talk here tonight, you'd think if we don't watch out sea otters was going to disappear any minute now off the face of the deep. Well, they ain't. But I'll tell you where they are gonna disappear from. They're gonna disappear from this stretch of coast right out here." He made a wide gesture with a ragged arm. "And do you know how? It won't be the government that does it. For a million dollars. It'll be you and me, my friends, my fellow citizens." He managed a kind of crazy smile now, and a crazy-wise nod of his head. "We are gonna vote.

"And I'll tell you how we're gonna vote. Ain't a pickup truck around here hasn't got a rifle racked up over the back window. Now, you know that's so. I don't quite know why. Hasn't been a bear sighted around here in twenty years. Hasn't been a cougar. They don't let you shoot the deer. Those rifles are there because it's your God-given right as an American to have them there, and that's enough. It's in the Constitution."

"Go home, Brick," somebody shouted. "Sleep it off."

"Wait a minute. I said we was gonna vote. And I'll tell you how. We're gonna vote with bullets. Gonna put them rifles to some use. Every man jack here is going down to the beach tomorrow at sunup, take that rifle down, and shoot himself half a dozen sea otters."

People jeered, moaned, and began to leave.

"Hold on. You want to solve this problem or not? All these sons of—"

he waved drunkenly at the table "—bureaucrats are gonna do is talk, talk, talk. We have to eat, we have to feed our kids. Sea otters are nothing but vermin. Getting a few of them out of here won't change nothing. Still won't be no abalone. Still can't drop gill nets. They all gotta go. And I promise you, I'll kill my share. And if the rest of you got any guts, you'll be out there with me tomorrow, and do likewise. If we don't do it, nobody will. Use your common sense."

But by this time, no one was listening any more.

When they swung in at the sheriff's station and parked on the leached asphalt of the lot there, under the high hedge of big old ragged eucalyptus trees, it was time for T. Hodges to go to work. They got out of the truck. The truck bed was strewn with grit, straw, spilled oats. Bohannon lifted the stiff carcass of the otter out of it and followed T. Hodges into the station through the side door. He stopped at Gerard's office. She gave him a small smile and went on out to the reception and communications desk in the front room.

Bohannon worked the knob of Gerard's door awkwardly, pushed the door with his shoulder, stepped in, and laid the damp, dead body of the otter on the floor. Gerard was seated behind his desk, talking on the telephone. He watched Bohannon with raised brows, told the caller, "I'll get back to you," and set the receiver in place. He stood up and came around the desk, and stood staring down at what Bohannon had brought him. Sea water pooled around the dark form on the sleek vinyl tiles. "Son of a bitch," Gerard said. "He went and did it."

"I don't know if there are any more," Bohannon said. "I didn't look. I just came with this one."

"There better not be any more," Gerard said darkly. "What a crazy fool." He dropped disgusted into his chair again. "I knew the day his mother died, we were in for it. Nance was the only one who could control him."

Bohannon grunted. "Some of the time."

"Well, she broke his bottles," Gerard said. "That helped. I'm only saying, this is the worst."

"The fine is twenty thousand dollars, which I don't think he's got. He'll lose his boat. Maybe his house."

"He won't need them," Gerard said. "He'll be in jail for a year. Maybe the worst was that last time he beat up Lucille. Blood all over the kitchen. Little Nolan screaming in a corner. When I saw her face, I thought she was a goner. She didn't look human any more."

"I wasn't here for that," Bohannon said.

"No, I'm wrong again," Gerard said. "The worst was Bob Hawes drowning."

"The storm did that," Bohannon said. "Wonder was, everybody on board didn't drown. Yes, Brick was the skipper, and he shouldn't have been drunk. But Bob's death wasn't his fault. The jury was right."

"I guess so." Gerard looked at the open door of the office and shouted, "Vern!" An echoing "Hoy!" came from someplace in the building. Heels thumped in the hallway. A fairhaired young fellow in uniform appeared in the doorway. Gerard told him, "Take Tommy with you, and go pick up Brick Lightner. You know where he lives? Charge him with—"

"Aw, no." Vern saw the otter on the floor. He looked stricken. He stepped into the office and crouched over the dead animal. "Shot?" His voice wobbled. He stroked the brown fur. "Aw, hell." He looked up at Gerard, tears in his eyes. "This? You mean that crazy drunk did this?"

"He threatened it last night," Bohannon said. "Everybody at the meeting heard him."

Vern pushed grimly to his feet. "Okay, we'll pick him up." He started out of the room, swearing under his breath.

"Vern," Gerard cautioned. "Keep your temper."

"Yessir," Vern said. In the hallway, he called out, "Tommy, let's go." And two pairs of boots banged off toward the parking lot door. It slammed behind the young officers. Gerard lifted the telephone receiver and said to Bohannon:

"I'll notify Fish and Wildlife. You want to get us some coffee?" His finger hesitated over the push buttons. "Where did this happen?"

"Old Bull Cove. You know it? The kid in the lighthouse couldn't have seen it. There's a tall bluff."

"I know it." Gerard nodded and punched the buttons. Bohannon went for the coffee. It simmered in a glass urn on a hotplate near T. Hodge's desk. She was wearing her headphones and little mike on its curved wand, and her hands were busy on a keyboard, typing up records. He carried mugs of coffee back to Gerard's office. The lieutenant was on his knees, examining the otter. "Looks like a 30-30. That's what Lightner owns." He got to his feet and accepted the mug, steam curling on the surface of the coffee. "Sit down," he told Bohannon, and went around behind the desk again and sat down there.

Bohannon stepped over the otter and took a chair. "Wildlife going to patrol the beach, looking for more?"

"Right," Gerard said. "They'll pick this one up and give it a thorough going over. They sounded grim."

"I don't remember its ever happening before." Bohannon poked into the ragged breast pocket of his old Levi jacket for a cigarette, lit the cigarette, pawed in the papers on Gerard's desk for an ashtray, dropped the kitchen match into it. "There's a stiff fine for even taking firearms onto the beach. Signs posted all along the highway."

"Yeah, well—" The phone rang, and Gerard picked it up. He listened for a few seconds, grimaced, said, "Okay, forget him for now. Go talk to Lucille Dodson. See why she didn't report it." He banged the receiver down. "Lightner's not home. His boat's out. At the dock, they say he took it out at dawn."

"Carrying his gun?" Bohannon said.

"In plain sight." Gerard nodded. "But there's worse news than that. He had little Nolan with him."

The Dodson place stood among pines in Settlers Cove, a handsome place of redwood planks, decks, glass, strong angular beams. Eliot Dodson was some kind of electronics whiz, a trouble-shooter whose work took him off on jets a good many times a year. Sometimes as far away as India and Japan. After that last awful beating Brick had given Lucille, she'd been in the hospital a long time while they put her broken face back together. She had met Dodson there when he was recovering from intestinal surgery of some sort. They had married when Lucille's divorce from Lightner was final. Lucille had won custody of the one child, a freckle-faced, red-headed boy of seven, named Nolan after a famous baseball pitcher.

The tan and gold county car with the strip of lights along its top stood at the foot of zigzag wooden steps that led up to the Dodson house. The radio inside the car crackled on and off. Bohannon braked his pickup on the winding road to let Gerard run out. Gerard worked the door, opened it, jumped down, turned. "Can't you spare the time? I'd like you to hear what she says."

Bohannon looked at his watch, grimaced, reached across and closed the passenger door, then wheeled the truck to the road edge and left it angled in the ditch. Old George Stubbs and young Manuel Rivera would keep everything going at the stables till he turned up—though he didn't feel it was fair to leave them to it for so long. He followed Gerard up the stairs. The two young officers were standing in a big room with a fieldstone fireplace, talking to Lucille, who was also standing. She was fairhaired and slender. Married to Brick Lightner, she'd dragged around in jeans and sweaters, hands chapped, hair ragged, looking twice her age. Marriage to a decent man had changed that. She stood straight now, and though anybody with half an eye could see her face had been patched up, she looked prettier than she'd ever done at Brick's.

"Mrs. Dodson?" The glass sliding door to the front deck, which was strewn with long brown needles from the pines that crowded around, stood open and Gerard stepped through it. "Lieutenant Gerard." He nodded his head back to indicate Bohannon, and spoke Bohannon's name by way of introduction. Lucille gave them a mechanical smile.

Vern said to Gerard, "Brick walked in and took Nolan out of his bed. The boy was dressing when Mrs. Dodson heard them talking and went in to see."

"It was four thirty in the morning," she said. "He had no right to come here, you know. There's a court order. He can't come within two hundred yards of this place."

"She told him not to take the boy," Vern said.

"He'd lost the right even to see Nolan," she said. "For touching him, he could go straight to prison."

"But he had a gun," Bohannon said.

She nodded bitterly. "And I think he would have used it. He was terribly drunk. He could be that way and still walk around. A crazy look in his eyes. It was this sea otter business. He was going to kill them all. From his boat. And no one would be able to punish him for it—not if he had Nolan with him. If they tried to capture him—" her voice trembled, and she bit her lower lip hard so as not to start to cry "—he'd kill Nolan and himself."

"And you believed that?" Gerard said.

She eyed him coldly. "Would you take a chance, if it was your little boy?"

"No, ma'am," Gerard said. "I guess I wouldn't."

"He said not to set the law after him," Vern said.

Gerard looked at her. "And you didn't." He held up a hand. "No, wait. You didn't notify us. We came to you because someone at the dock saw Brick with the boy when he took his boat out this morning. You didn't do anything he told you not to. Remember that. Rest easy with that."

"Are you going to call the Coast Guard?" she said. "For the death of one animal, you're going to force him to murder his own son?"

"We won't let that happen," Gerard said. "But I wish you'd reported this as soon as he left here. We might have stopped him before he got to the boat."

"I was afraid for Nolan. No—" she shook her head angrily "—what I should have done was follow them in my car and make him take me along. My mind wasn't working."

"It happens to all of us." Bohannon remembered again the time with the smugglers. "Where's your husband?"

"Seattle," she said numbly. "He's flying to San Francisco. He'll drive down from there."

"That's good." Gerard turned for the door, turned back again. "Try not to worry. Brick's got a loud mouth, you know that. But it's one thing to beat up your wife, it's another to go up against a whole community."

"He killed that otter, lieutenant. He isn't thinking like a normal person. He says he has nothing more to lose."

"He won't kill his son," Bohannon said. "As for himself—we're all scared of dying, when it comes down to it. He'll turn up with his tail between his legs. You'll see."

She regarded him steadily for a moment, wondering, worrying. Then she drew breath, said "Thank you" to them all, and they trooped out, heavy-footed, boots noisy on the deck planks and the steps going down. Somewhere distant, a bluejay squawked in the afternoon silence of the pines.

Horses waken with the sun. And Hack had worked a couple of hours in the stables when he came into the pine plank kitchen at seven forty-five. The place was aromatic with breakfast smells. Stubbs, wrapped in a mighty apron, worked at the towering old cooking range. He didn't hear the flap of the screen door, nor the thump of Bohannon's old boots on the planks. The battered portable radio on the counter beside him was too loud. Mostly what radios brought up here in these canyons was static mixed with a few faint strains of music. Country and western? Bohannon walked over and switched the radio off.

Stubbs, turning over golden slabs of fried mush, gave him a startled look, white cottony eyebrows raised over round, china-blue eyes. He was in his seventies, a one-time rodeo rider, crippled up now from too many broken bones, and from arthritis in wet weather. But he did more around the stables than most men half his age could do, and cooked besides— though it sometimes pained Bohannon so much, watching him limp and wince, that Bohannon pretended he preferred his own cooking to the old man's. It was a wry, running joke between them.

"You shouldn't be so quick to switch off radios," Stubbs said. "You might learn stuff to your advantage."

"Is that right?" Bohannon stretched a long arm around Stubbs's stocky form to snag a tall blue and white specked country coffee pot off its burner. He tilted coffee into a thick mug, set the pot back, started off with the mug. "Such as?"

"Such as, the Coast Guard found the *Abalone Queen* just after sundown, adrift twenty miles out." Stubbs took eggs from a big old refrigerator, slammed the door. Bohannon drew out a chair at the round deal eating table in the middle of the kitchen and sat down. Stubbs laid the six eggs carefully on the counter. "Adrift, because Brick Lightner was passed out drunk. His boy was trying to get at the engine because the starter wouldn't work. But he wasn't strong enough to pry up the trap door. He's only ten, or something like that."

"Ten would be about right." Bohannon was wondering whether he shouldn't shower before breakfast. "So they rescued them both, and Brick is in jail again, right? For killing the otter?"

"You'd think so." Stubbs lifted a lid off a black iron skillet and turned over sausages that sizzled. He set the lid back on with a clack. "But they had to let him go." Stubbs turned from the stove and blinked at Bohannon with a little smile. "That surprises you, now, don't it? You know why they had to let him go?"

"I guess you're going to tell me," Bohannon said, and pretended indifference, lighting a cigarette, tasting the coffee. It was too hot. He burned his mouth. "I guess that radio is a cornucopia."

"It's a Sony," Stubbs said, "but it talks English. He had the wrong gun, that's why. It was a deer rifle killed that otter. Like you said last night. But the gun Brick Lightner had on board his boat—it was a shotgun."

"I'll be damned," Bohannon said mildly.

"And there's more," Stubbs said.

Bohannon gave his head a shake. "I don't know how much more I can stand. Didn't Lucille press charges for Brick snatching Nolan? She and her husband got court orders against him for that."

"Didn't say nothing on the radio about that part," Stubbs said again. "See? I told you it was no cornucopia."

"Just a simple Sony," Bohannon said. "What more?"

"Brick Lightner wasn't back at his place more than a few hours when somebody come in and shot him dead."

Bohannon stared. "Who? What for?"

"There now." Satisfied, Stubbs turned back to his cooking. "I got you good, didn't I? I said you ought to listen to the radio."

"Who was it?" Bohannon asked.

And a voice said, "They want it to be me."

Bohannon turned. The voice came in from the long, covered plank walk that fronted the house, came in through the open door and windows of the kitchen. It was a fine, fresh morning, nippy but sunny and blue-skied. Sage and eucalyptus perfumed the breeze. Bohannon thought he knew the voice. The silhouette at the screen door made him sure of it. It was Sharon Webb, chunky and hippy and stalwart. He went and opened the screen door.

"Come in," he said. "They bound you over?"

"I drove to the sheriff like a bat out of hell to report a murder," she said, "and next thing I know I'm being booked and fingerprinted. Said the gun in my pickup had been fired. Nobody's fingerprints on it but mine.

I'm out on bail because Ford Larrimore—" she meant the judge "—is a dear old friend. And I pay my taxes."

"Have some coffee?" Bohannon said.

"Breakfast, Miz Webb?" Stubbs said.

"I'm too angry to eat," she told him, "thank you." She said to Bohannon, "But, yes, I'll drink some coffee."

"How did you happen to find him?" Bohannon asked after they sat down at the table together. "Was he dead when you got there?"

"No way." She gave her cropped gray head a shake. "He was alive and ornery as ever, and I was giving him a large piece of my mind over shooting that otter."

"How did you know he'd come home?" Bohannon said.

"I guess you can't get TV up here, can you?" she said.

"Not even cable," he said. "Was it on the news?"

"At eleven. That they'd towed the *Abalone Queen* in, and weren't holding Brick in the killing of the otter."

"Because he had the wrong kind of gun," Bohannon said.

"Fiddle-faddle," Sharon Webb said. "Why hadn't he stashed his 30-30 aboard the boat earlier, days ago? Why didn't he throw it overboard after he shot the otter?" She gulped coffee and set the mug down loudly. "Of course Brick Lightner killed that otter. You heard him say he was going to. Who else would, anyway? For what reason?"

Bohannon shrugged. "So now it's your gun that's in question. Somebody used it to kill him while you were in the kitchen, talking to him? Is that how it was?"

"Bullet went spang into his back while we stood there talking." Bohannon's cigarette pack lay on the bleached white surface of the table. She reached for it with stubby, shaking fingers, pulled a cigarette from it, set the cigarette in her mouth. "I shouldn't do this. Poisoning myself, poisoning the atmosphere. But I keep seeing the look on his face when the bullet hit. Like the devil had grabbed him. He wasn't surprised—he was plain terrified." Bohannon used a thumbnail on a wooden match and held the flame for her. The cigarette smoked. She inhaled the smoke, and closed her eyes for a moment gratefully. She let the smoke out through her snub nose, opened her eyes, and looked into Bohannon's face. "I need your help. Everyone knows how I hated him. It's as natural for the sheriff, the county attorney, any jury to decide I killed him as it was for me to decide he killed that otter. Which he did, damn it."

"I'll see what I can do," Bohannon said.

The Lightner place was not yet an eyesore, but it was getting there. Yellowing white paint peeled from the clapboards, window screens were torn and curling, and trickles of rust had run down from the corners of the windowsills. The composition shingle roof showed seams of graying tar at leakage points. Weeds sprouted through the crushed abalone shell that paved the ground. Beside the house was a dory tilted on blocks, half scraped of its paint, a job begun and abandoned long ago. A strip of shiplap had sprung loose from the warp of rain and sun. Bohannon rolled his dusty pickup past, looking at the neighborhood. The houses were small, old, and, because of the humpiness of the foothill terrain, scattered. The nearest place on Lightner's side of the patchy roadway was downhill and cut off by a stand of brushy trees. The house in sight across the road was steeply downhill, too. They wouldn't have seen anything that happened at Lightner's from there. But by craning his neck, he caught a glimpse of blue paint up the slope. He took a wrong turning and got lost for five minutes. Then he found the road.

The blue paint was on window frames and the door of a place made out of native stone. Eccentric. A fairytale cottage. Rocks in terraces made a garden in front, with too many plaster elves and iron deer and flamingos. There was also an ugly precast cement fountain. Bohannon climbed in his worn boots among these frights and rapped at the door, which was arched at the top. He expected a gnome to open it. But it was an old man, barechested, grizzled, muscular, leathery. Of course. Carl Tunis. Crazy Carl. It had been years since Bohannon had called him to mind. His lunatic letters used to appear in the paper all the time. But if Bohannon had been asked, he'd have said Tunis was dead.

He wore grimy brown walking shorts and sweaty sandals. He had a handful of prunes, and kept popping these into his mouth and chewing them with false teeth that rattled like castanets. He held the hand out to Bohannon. "Have a prune, sheriff. I'm eighty-three years old, and I do a hundred push-ups a day. You're breathing hard. From those steps. I can run up those steps top speed and never notice. I'm healthy because I eat only dried fruits, raw vegetables, and nuts."

"No, thanks," Bohannon said. "Did you see or hear anything down at the Lightner place last night?"

"I go to bed with the chickens," Carl Tunis said. "It's the law of nature. Man's an animal, just like a horse or a cow. They go to bed when the sun goes down."

"Last night—the shot that killed Brick Lightner didn't wake you up?"

"Matter of fact, what woke me up was all the cars," Tunis said. "A person doesn't live in Madrone to sleep in the middle of roaring traffic. A person expects quiet up here at night. I got up and looked out. Good moon last night. Lightner's looked like a parking lot." Tunis blew a prune pit past Bohannon's ear, and clapped a hand to his mouth to keep his teeth from flying after it.

"You recognize any of the cars?" Bohannon said.

"Shiny big one, looked expensive, European, I think. Lightner's red pickup, of course. That Webb woman's ditsy little Jap pickup. And a pale colored van. Four."

"Did you see any of the drivers?"

"Shadowy," Tunis said. "The gun went off. I seen the fire from the barrel. Outside in the back. Heard glass break, too. Window glass it was, I guess, from the radio."

"Which car drove off first?" Bohannon said.

"Fancy new one. Tall man got in it. I don't know him. It's too far. Turn yourself around and look down there. You can see how far it is. And Brick Lightner, he doesn't trim the trees, does he? Hard to do that from inside a bottle." The old man cackled at his joke. Bohannon turned as ordered, and had to agree it was hard to see. Tunis said, "He wore spectacles, though. You know, a man wouldn't have to do that if he'd eat raw carrots every day. People go against nature. It's what kills them. I'm going to live forever." He pounded his barrel chest with his fists, stood straight, drew air in noisily, exhaled it. The loose false teeth glared white in the morning sun. "It's a wonderful thing, the gift of life. People shouldn't mistreat it."

"Did you see Sharon Webb leave?" Bohannon said.

"That woman is a meddler," Tunis said. "Can't leave things alone to take their natural course. If you're a meddler, you're going to meddle once too often. I've got nothing against a person playing a tune. It's when they expect everybody else to dance to it, the trouble begins. Yes, I saw her leave, slam out through the kitchen door in a panic. He wouldn't dance to her tune, now would he—Brick? And she got fed up with it, and killed him. People will drive you crazy if you let them." He wagged his head of dirty white locks. "Trick is to breathe deep, control your heartbeat, stay serene."

"Who did the van belong to?" Bohannon said.

"Beats me," Tunis said. "Nobody from around here."

Bohannon wanted Gerard with him now, but when he rang the sheriff station from the pay phone by the new 76 station on the highway, Gerard was out in a patrol car someplace up a canyon on business involving stolen cattle. Bohannon frowned at the glittery steel pushbuttons of the phone and chewed his lip. He could ask for uniforms to back him up. If he was sure. He wasn't sure. Not a hundred percent. At last he mumbled thanks and hung up.

Householders were out walking expensive dogs up and down the steep, crooked trails of Settlers Cove. New houses were being built all over, which meant the pines were thinning out. But there were still enough of them to keep the roads in chilly shadow this early in the day. He left the pickup at the foot of the zigzag wooden stairs, behind a dark red Mercedes on whose glossy finish pine needles pattered. Lucille Dodson owned a VW Rabbit. He scuffed with a boot at the little tire imprints in the packed roadside earth where she parked it. He read his watch. She must be taking Nolan to school.

The sliding glass door from the front deck was open again. He could see straight through the house to a rear deck built around the trunks of three big pines. Out there a tall man sat on a bench, sections of the morning paper open on his knees, sections at his feet on the rough redwood planks of the deck. He had a mug of coffee with him, but he wasn't drinking from it. He wasn't reading, either. He was looking away into the woods. Through horn-rimmed spectacles with big round lenses.

"Eliot Dodson?" Bohannon called.

The man's grayhaired head jerked around. He stood up, the papers sliding off his lap. He peered through the shadowy rooms of the house at Bohannon standing in pine-needle-splintered sunshine. "Who are you?"

"Bohannon, private investigator. May I come in?"

Dodson came into the house, rounded a dining table, stepped down into the living room. "Why should you?"

"Sharon Webb has been arrested for the murder of Brick Lightner last night, and she's asked me to make inquiries for her. Says she didn't do it." The man had come no nearer. Bohannon still had to raise his voice. It was quiet in these woods. It didn't seem right to him for everybody with ears to hear him. He stepped indoors. "A witness saw you at the Lightner house around midnight. I thought you could tell me what happened there."

"What witness?" Dodson said.

"A neighbor. He saw your car. He heard the shot, the breaking window, saw you run to your car and drive off."

"It was dark," Dodson said. "It wasn't me."

"There was a bright moon," Bohannon said. "He had your description right. He described the car."

"I'm calling my lawyer." Dodson took steps.

"What for? You're not being accused of anything. All I need is a witness. Witnesses don't need lawyers. Suspects need lawyers. Am I supposed to suspect you of a crime? You surprise me."

Dodson looked uncertain. "What do you want to know?"

"Sharon Webb claims she was in Lightner's kitchen, talking to him, when he was shot. My witness says he saw her come out the back door, but that doesn't prove she was inside when the shot was fired. Was she?"

Dodson's thin mouth worked. He sat down on a long couch, picked up a phone off an end table, but he didn't push any buttons. He set the phone back. He sighed. "All right. When I got home here from San Francisco, and learned what he'd done to Nolan, I drove over there, yes."

"Had he hurt him?" Bohannon said.

"Not hurt in the common meaning, no. But he'd roused him out of a sound sleep, dragged him off to sea in the dark, passed out drunk. The boat was drifting, the boy couldn't start the engine. He couldn't get to it under the planks. It was terrifying. The child was a wreck."

"And you were going to do what to Lightner?"

"I was—I was—" Dodson's long, pale face grew red. "Ah, hell. I was furious. I don't know what I was going to do. There's a court order forbidding Brick to touch the boy. I'm trying—I'm trying to be a decent father to him, a proper role model. And that grungy drunk—"

"I know how you feel," Bohannon said. "Did you hear them talking? Did you look through the kitchen window? You're tall enough."

Dodson eyed him sourly, reached for the telephone again, didn't pick it up. He drew a deep breath. "Yes," he said, "I did. She was in there. Yelling at him about killing that otter. He had a bottle in his hand, and kept swigging from it, and grinning at her, mocking her. You know what he thought of women. Then the gun went off. He pitched forward on his face. I'll never forget it."

"And you ran like hell," Bohannon said.

"So would you. Everyone knew I hated him. Twenty people can step forward and testify they've heard me say I'd like to kill him. I never meant it."

"Did you say it last night?" Bohannon asked. "Where anybody heard you?"

Dodson looked sick. "We called Dr. Hesseltine to give Nolan a shot so he could sleep. The poor kid was shattered." Dodson eyed Bohannon gloomily. "The doctor heard me, loud and clear. You know Belle. Tough old dame. She said I was the one who needed the shot. I roared out of here. I wanted my hands around that bastard's throat."

"Brick could take you out, drunk or sober."

"I wasn't thinking," Dodson said.

"The ride over there didn't cool you off? You didn't realize you couldn't brace him with your bare hands? You didn't see the rifle in Sharon Webb's pickup and—"

"No." Dodson stood up sharply. "Absolutely not. It wasn't me. There was someone else there. I heard them moving around back of the house, brush crackling."

"But you didn't see who it was?"

"There wasn't time. The gun went off, and I knew if I was caught there, I'd be blamed."

"There was a light colored van there," Bohannon said. "Maybe the shooter came in that."

"I saw it, but I don't know who owns it."

Bohannon made a face. "Nobody knows." He sighed. "Come on, Mr. Dodson. Let's go over to the sheriff's and get your story on record."

"And set your client free," Dodson said.

Bohannon blinked. "You have something against her?"

"Not a thing." Dodson sat, picked up the phone, punched a number. "But if she didn't do it, won't they put me in her place?" He broke off to speak a man's name into the phone. He listened, grimaced, grunted "Damn," and slammed down the receiver. For a moment, he slumped back on the couch, eyes shut, mouth a line of disgust. Then he sat up, blew air out noisily, ran fingers through his hair, and looked at Bohannon. "Lawyer's not available. My old buddy. Europe. Three weeks. I'm in for it now, right?"

"Only Sharon Webb's fingerprints are on that rifle."

Dodson grunted. "But I was wearing gloves, wasn't I? It's an ingrained habit since I bought the Mercedes. Body oils discolor the leather on the steering wheel."

Bohannon shrugged. "If it comes to that, the county will furnish you a lawyer. But it won't come to that."

Dodson stood up. "Just let me use the bathroom."

He didn't come back from the bathroom. When, after a long minute, Bohannon called out his name and went looking for him, the bathroom window stood open. Down below, the Mercedes' diesel engine rattled to life. Bohannon ran through the house to the deck in time to see the broad, shiny car roll off down the trail.

When he reached the foot of the zigzag stairs among the fern and poison oak and the chilly shadows of the pines, he heard a car coming. It rounded the bend above, and it was Lucille Dodson's white Rabbit with the black cloth top. She parked in those four little dents the wheels had made in the road edge and got out, looking puzzled to find him there. She brought a shoulder bag out of the car, let the door fall shut, and came up to him. Quizzical.

"Where's Eliot?"

"You tell me," Bohannon said, and outlined for her what had happened. "Where would he go to hide?"

"He has no reason to hide." She looked along the road as if she expected him to come driving back up it right now. As if maybe he'd gone out for a newspaper or cigarettes. "He didn't kill Brick Lightner. He couldn't. He's the gentlest man in the world." Gazing up at him, her face like some badly bruised flower, her eyes filled with tears. "He's not capable of violence, Mr. Bohannon."

"He admitted he was in a rage last night," Bohannon said. "Over what Brick had put Nolan through."

"Nolan's all right," she said. "He's just fine this morning. As if nothing had happened."

"But last night he was so shaken up you had to phone Belle Hesseltine to quiet him down. And Eliot says Belle heard him say he was going to kill Brick."

"Words," Lucille scoffed. "He was upset. Surely Belle understood that. She's a very wise old woman."

"He went there, just the same," Bohannon said. "And Brick Lightner was killed. So maybe it wasn't just words."

"Excuse me." She brushed past him and started up the stairs, quickly, angrily.

"You going to phone him?" Bohannon called.

She stopped, turned back. "I don't know where."

"He shouldn't have run," Bohannon said. "It makes him look guilty as hell. If he calls, tell him to go to the sheriff and tell him what he told me."

"To help you earn your pay?" Lucille turned, climbed a few steps, turned back again. "Do you know the real irony of all this? I mean—if the Webb woman did kill Brick?"

"Tell me the real irony," Bohannon said.

"Brick didn't shoot the otter," she said.

"Not with that shotgun," Bohannon said, "but—"

She shook her head. "Not with any gun. Nolan told me on the way to school just now. Brick heated a can of chili for Nolan's breakfast, then passed out on his bunk. All he did all day was sleep, drink, sleep. With Nolan at the helm. He steered strictly away from the kelp beds. And Brick never once picked up a gun."

"A dark red late model Mercedes complete with license number," Gerard said. "It won't be hard to spot. We'll have him soon." He smiled wryly at Bohannon across his paper-work-strewn desk. "You've done it again, Hack. There'll be formalities, Miz Webb. But as far as the sheriff's department is concerned, you're in the clear."

The stocky little woman gave him a grudging smile for a moment, then looked grieved. "That poor little boy—he never seems to end up in the right place. And as for Lucille, why is it some women are so wretchedly unlucky?"

"She doesn't have a gift for picking husbands," Gerard said. "That's for sure."

Bohannon made a face. "I don't know. She calls Dodson gentle. And she ought to know the difference. I wish I was as sure as you that he did it."

"Gloves smeared the prints on Miz Webb's rifle," Gerard said, "in just the places where prints would be when someone held it to fire it. And he admitted to you he wore gloves."

"He also said somebody else was there," Bohannon said. "Out behind the house in the dark."

"Maybe Brick had some woman there and sent her outside when Miz Webb here showed up. Or she went outside on her own, so as not to be seen with Brick. Who would want to?"

"The owner of the white van," Bohannon said. "Sharon here saw it, too." The little woman nodded her cropped gray head. "That makes three witnesses now. You know of any woman of the type that would go with Brick Lightner who drives a white van? Or why he'd let some pickup from a tavern drive herself to his place?"

Gerard snorted. "Makes it too easy to leave."

"And when she got a look at that house inside," Sharon Webb said, "she'd want to leave. It's filthy."

"If it was the killer," Gerard said, "we need a motive. We know both Miz Webb and Eliot Dodson had it in for Brick, and why." He raised eyebrows at Bohannon. "Who else, Hack?"

Bohannon stared at him for a minute, then stood up. "You want to drive Sharon home?" he asked Gerard. "I just remembered something." He left the office at a run.

He rapped the aluminum screen door, through which he could smell cooking. The sea breeze blew on his back. The sun glared off the fresh white paint on the stucco of the back of the building. A fat Mexican woman in an expanse of chili-smeared apron came and pushed open the door. He held out the picnic basket to her. "Thank Señora Hawes for this," he said. "The plates and tablecloth and glasses are inside." She smiled with marvelous teeth, and dimples showed in her terracotta cheeks. She nodded, and reached for the basket.

"I will tell her, señor," she said.

"And say I'm sorry I missed her," he said. "The meal was delicious. Did you cook it?"

The plump shoulders moved in girlish embarrassment and pleasure. "Sí, but the recipes, they are Meeses Hawes's."

"Where is she today?" Bohannon asked.

"You know her daughters? In Lompoc. The one who was just married a few months ago. And now she and her young husband, they have found a house. They wanted Meeses Hawes to come look at it and see whether it is right for them." The fat woman craned back to look at something. "She ought to be returning soon." The smile came back. "Thank you for the basket, señor."

"Thank you," he said, turned away, turned back. "Tell me. The other morning, the morning when Mrs. Hawes packed that basket for us—you remember?"

"Sí, señor." She nodded.

"A truck delivered bread to you from San Francisco," he said. "Is that right? Were you here to receive it?"

"Meeses Hawes," the woman said, "she live upstairs." She stepped out and pointed to a flight of steps that climbed to rooms over the restaurant. "They come with the bread very early. I am not yet here. She meets them and takes the bread inside here to put in warming ovens." A shadow of misgiving crossed the round face. The woman cocked her head at him. "But that morning, when I arrived, the bread was stacked outside here, on this step."

"Mrs. Hawes wasn't here to receive it?" Bohannon said.

"She came late that morning," the woman said. "I remember. How did you know, señor?"

"Not from upstairs," he said. "She came in her car, right? Where from, do you know?"

"Sí, it is as you say," the woman said. "But no, I do not know from where." A timer bell rang behind the woman in the kitchen. She gave a start and pulled the screen door shut. "You must excuse me now, señor. The cooking."

"Thank you," Bohannon said. He turned away, and the wind took his hat. He grabbed for it, missed, it hit the sandy earth and rolled along at the base of the wall. The wind was brisk, he lunged after the hat, it reached the corner of the building and disappeared. He rounded the building corner and grabbed the hat and sprawled. He was climbing to his feet, slapping the grit off his clothes with the hat, when a white van swung in to park beside the building. The driver was Dorothy Hawes. She saw him through the windshield, gave him a wave of her hand, and climbed down out of the van. Her smile was half wince against the brightness of the sun and the stiffness of the breeze.

"Why, Hack, how nice to see you again."

Bohannon went to her, and kicked the left front tire of the van. He said to her, "I guess not," and squatted, and from in front of the tire gathered up what his scuffed boot had knocked loose. He rose and held it out in his hand for her to look at. "You know what that is?"

"Kind of shiny." She was mystified. "Like seashell."

"Abalone shell," Bohannon said. "And there's only one place around here that's got a yard full of that, any more. Brick Lightner's." He walked around the truck now, stooping, digging with his clasp knife at the treads of the other tires. "This van was parked there the night Brick was shot. Three people saw it." He folded the blade into the knife and dropped the knife into the frayed pocket of his jeans. "Why did you do it, Dorothy? First kill the otter, and then—"

"Because they let him go," she cried. "That was all I meant to do. I never meant to take a human life. I'm not like him. I'm not, Hack. You must believe that. He killed my husband. He killed Bob, as sure as sure can be. You know that's true. And the court blamed the storm and let him off. Let him off scot free to drink and bully his life away."

"Easy, Dorothy." Bohannon put hands on her shoulders to try to calm her. She shook him off.

"I'm not like that. I thought if I killed the otter, he'd get his punishment at last. Then I saw on the TV news he had the wrong kind of gun and they had to let him go, and that's how it would always be, wouldn't it? The law would never get him. I told you the other morning, there is no justice. And you know that, Hack."

"No justice in murder," Bohannon said.

"I only went there to—" she wrung her hands, looked at the sky, turned with a jerk to look at the sea, tears streaming down her face "—I don't know, to tell him to his ugly face the awful thing he'd done to me, drowning my Bob, the lonely, drudging life he'd sentenced me to."

"And just by luck you saw the rifle in Sharon Webb's pickup? And there was a clear shot through the kitchen window, right between Brick's shoulder blades, and you decided there was justice, after all? And you were the instrument?" He stepped around the van, yanked open the door, climbed in, opened the glove box, found what he expected, got out of the truck. She was watching him. He held up a pair of driving gloves. "I guess not. You took your own rifle, didn't you? But if you used Sharon Webb's and left it there, it would point suspicion completely away from you, right?"

"I didn't mean to get her into trouble," Dorothy Hawes wailed. "I'd have come forward to take the blame, Hack. Truly, I would. You see, both my girls are grown and married and secure now. Now I could do what I'd waited all these years—" She put her hands to her mouth and gave her head a frightened shake, her eyes wide, watching him. "No. I didn't mean that."

"You came back to kill him," Bohannon said. He jerked his head at the restaurant. "This was only a cover. You came back to kill Brick Lightner, and that was all you came back for." She seemed to lose starch all of a sudden. The tears that ran were tears of exhaustion. She swayed, and he stepped over to hold her up. "Come on," he said gently. "It's all over now." He led her toward his battered truck, helped her up into it, slammed the door. When he climbed in on the driver's side, she was slumped over against the door, cheek pressed to the dusty glass, gazing at the sea, if she was gazing at anything at all. He started the engine, let the brake go, turned the wheel. "You shot the otter, so you do own a rifle. Where is it?"

"I felt so sickened." Her voice was toneless with misery. "I hated myself for killing a helpless creature."

He wheeled the truck out onto the highway.

"I never wanted to kill anything again," she said.

"Nothing helpless, anyway," Bohannon said.

"The rifle's in the restaurant. Behind the counter, under the cash register." She was silent for a while as the truck rattled towards town. Then she said coldly, "He deserved to die," and that was all she said.

He drove the crooked two-lane blacktop road over the mountains slowly, shifting down a lot. A horse trailer swung along behind the pickup this morning; its passenger was a gangly weanling who had never been trailered before. Rivera had rigged the trailer with a rail to hold him steady, but careful driving was needed all the same, no sharp turns, no abrupt stops and starts. It grew tiring. His muscles ached with tension and he sweated.

The tall, rambling old house with its white jigsaw-work verandahs stood quiet among the spring-green foothills. The windows reflected clear blue sky. When they got out of the truck into the stillness, a freshening breeze cooled him. He unbolted the trailer door and let it down to serve as a ramp. Talking softly, he stepped up into the trailer and stood a while, stroking the colt's copper-colored coat. He took a handful of grain from a pocket and let the soft mouth of the colt lip it from his hand.

He unhitched the youngster and by the halter turned him around and led him down the ramp. His coat glowed in the sunshine. T. Hodges smiled. "Isn't he lovely?" she said. But Bohannon heard the closing of a door and looked toward the mansion. He had phoned ahead for approval

of his plan. And there was Linda on the porch, a nurse with her. He took
the halter and began walking the colt up the long lawn past the flowerbeds.

Linda didn't move. Maybe she was daunted by the outdoors, all that
sunlit space in front of her. But as he neared the house, the colt nodding
obediently beside him, he thought she was watching. Not something dark
and horrible in the past, but what was happening here and now. Then he
was close enough to be sure her gaze was on the beautiful young animal
who, when Bohannon paused, did a little quickstepping on his knobby
legs.

"Linda?" Bohannon called. "Come see the colt."

She hesitated. She glanced at the nurse. The nurse smiled and nodded.
Linda moved, stepped out, not quickly, almost as if walking were a new
sensation. She reached the top of the long steps and halted. Worry flickered in her face for a moment, then passed, and she came down the steps.
Slowly at first, then more quickly. She knelt on the grass, circled the neck
of the little horse with her arms, and rubbed her cheek against the smooth
coat. Her eyes shone. Then she saw T. Hodges, and got to her feet. She
smiled.

"Hello," she said. "I'm Linda Bohannon."

# Dark Places

## JAMES McKIMMEY

Sheriff Orville Bundy stood beside a dusty courthouse window looking down over his town toward where it had happened. Ghost Bluff was built on the steep slant of a large Nevada cliff, with its crosstown streets forming natural descending tiers. The highway which ran through the community and beside which the courthouse was built created the top tier. And down there, to the north and east, was where the last paved avenue ended.

From his position, Bundy could not see a small portion of the community that lay below and beyond. But he knew that, starting from the north end of the last lower street, there was a graveled path that curved down to yet another short tier where but one house stood alone beside a slow-running narrow river. It was where Janis Cramer had lived with her infirm mother.

Janis, twenty-two, had gotten off work at Ed Hill's pharmacy just past five in the afternoon two days ago. As usual, she'd walked down sidewalks to the final paved street. Then she'd used the graveled path to continue on her way in the September sunshine.

Because of the way the path curved in its descent, a length of it was invisible to anyone not on it. Midway along that length was a cave. And in the cave's jet darkness they'd found Janis's body sprawled on the hard dirt floor.

She'd been struck on the head with something hard, probably with one of the rocks scattered about just inside the entrance, although none of them showed any evidence, such as a bloodstain, to establish the fact. The murderer had used so much force that her skull had been broken as though it had possessed no more resistance than a piece of delicate china. It was Bundy's conjecture that the killer had then left the cave with the rock in his hand and had thrown it away somewhere else.

That had been day before yesterday, Bundy thought. And by now he and his deputy, Harvey Plummer, had questioned everyone who could be of assistance, including Janis's mother, who'd phoned Bundy's office when her daughter hadn't gotten home as expected.

There was no longer any doubt about the identity of the others who had walked at that time of day down the curving, descending path that went past the cave's mouth. Two housewives, a newspaper boy, a TV repairman, and a telephone lineman had offered combined information indicating that only two other people had taken Janis's route at a time that would have allowed them to kill her.

They were George Ferris and Skipping Sam.

Bundy had arrested both. They were now in cells of the jail. One had to be guilty.

But the problem was, Bundy thought wearily as he turned from the window and settled down into a wooden swivel chair behind his desk, which?

Bundy was short with great girth. He wore a tan Western-styled uniform and was rarely seen not wearing the wide-brimmed white hat on his head right now. He owned a perpetually florid face made round by fat. His pale blue eyes could charm or intimidate depending upon his mood. He had been sheriff of this town and county for twenty-one years. Respect for law here was healthy.

"Harvey!" he called suddenly. His voice had the sound of an outsized bullfrog's croak.

The door of Bundy's office opened almost immediately, and Deputy Harvey Plummer stepped in. He looked at the sheriff expectantly. Harvey was twenty-eight and six inches over six feet, appearing to be skinny in his uniform. But Bundy knew from experience that he was in fact leanly muscled and strong. His face was narrow with heavy-lidded gray eyes. His ears were large and stuck out almost sideways from his temples. Although Harvey owned a zealous, self-righteous compulsion to correct others whenever he believed them to be in error, Bundy had decided some time ago that he was the best deputy he'd ever had or ever would have.

"Go get Sam, Harvey. I'm going to give him one more runthrough."

"He's awful peeved over being stuck in the cell that way, Orville," Plummer said in a high, reedy voice. "He might not want to come."

"Tell him if he doesn't do it in a hurry, I'll drag him in here myself!"

"That might do it."

While Plummer was getting Skipping Sam, Bundy reflected unhappily on the loss of Janis Cramer as he stared at the scarred surface of his ancient desk where everything was always kept in perfect order under the bright illumination of a large, shiny, solid-brass swing-arm lamp with matching metal shade that the Chamber of Commerce had presented to him a year ago for meritorious community service.

Ed Hill's pharmacy, with its offering of medications, paperbacks, magazines, toiletries, watches, greeting cards, cigarettes, cigars, candy, wine, beer, and innumerable other items, had become a comfortable meeting place for local citizens. Ed stood behind a counter on an upper level of the store and filled prescriptions. Janis, below, took care of all of the rest.

She'd been born, raised, and educated in Ghost Bluff; and if there had ever been anyone in town more generally loved, more popular than she, with Skipping Sam running a close second, there was no one still alive who could say who it might have been. She was sweetly pretty with a husky voice that could charm the most irascible of dispositions. Sheriff Bundy always looked forward to running out of his blood-pressure pills so that he could go in for a refill and talk with her while Ed counted them out.

Her soft azurine eyes would look at you merrily, sometimes mischievously, as she chatted away, showing her infectious smile. And there was never a hint of malice or cunning or dishonesty because she was simply incapable of any of them. She had somehow remained so innocently naive, devoted to old fashioned values taught her by her mother, that that in itself had protected her from exploitation. Town talk had told Bundy that the young men who took her out had developed a code of conduct among themselves until she decided which she would marry. Should one of them overstep the bounds, and should she allow it to be known, he would have to answer to the rest.

And it was also that same innocent naiveté that had finally invited that which had happened to her. Someone had finally, and drastically, overstepped, Bundy was certain.

The coroner's report had indicated that she had not been sexually molested. But there was no doubt in Bundy's mind that someone had misinterpreted as a personal invitation the warmth she gave to everyone. He had then, one way or another, lured her into the cave. When she'd finally resisted him, he'd reacted violently by picking up a heavy rock and killing her. It had been done so swiftly that she hadn't even had time to leave a scratch on him.

The killer was either the stranger, George Ferris, new in town, or it was the person everyone in Ghost Bluff had loved almost as much as they had Janis, Skipping Sam.

The door opened again as Deputy Plummer said, "Here he is, Orville." Bundy pointed to a wooden straight chair, and Sam, looking miffed, put himself on it. Deputy Plummer sat down beside him, placing a palm meaningfully on the butt of the revolver jutting up from the tooled leather holster strapped at his waist.

Wearing a faded red-checked shirt, bleached jeans, and ankle-high boots, Sam was white-haired with a deeply browned face lined by time and weather. Of medium height, he was wiry and trim and moved with a springy quickness owned by some men half his age. How old he actually was no one knew, including Sam. He'd come into town on a bus twenty years ago, not remembering where he'd come from or why he'd arrived at Ghost Bluff. His wallet had contained no ID. But it had held enough money to allow him to move into an attic room in Mrs. Gibbons' boarding house.

After that, he'd demonstrated that what he liked doing most was walking, which he did with speed, energy, and one-minded purpose, although often he had no purpose. When he was in full stride, his face reflecting pride and satisfaction, he sometimes skipped.

It quickly became apparent to everyone that somewhere in his history something had happened that had simplified his thinking mechanism to bare basics. And he was given sympathetic help by those who knew how to put on charity efforts to raise money for his use. In time, he became a fleet-footed delivery man for businesses in town, earning just enough to keep his place at Mrs. Gibbons'. In time, it seemed obvious that Skipping Sam was totally harmless.

But now Janis Cramer was dead. And Skipping Sam had been observed by several to have been able to have been where she was murdered at the time she was. The other suspect, George Ferris, insisted he'd seen Skipping Sam come out of that cave at that same time.

Now Skipping Sam looked at Sheriff Orville Bundy. In his silver eyes was the resentful expression of any child who feels he has been unjustly accused and unfairly used.

"Sam," Sheriff Bundy said gently, "I've got you here for your own good. I want you to understand that."

Sam's expressive face shifted to a look of accusation. "It ain't for my own good, keeping me from the outside!"

"Yes, it is," Bundy said, meaning it. Everyone in town knew that Sam had been arrested as one of the suspects. Some had already convinced themselves that it was Sam, not the stranger, Ferris, who had killed Janis. Bundy had overheard some of that opinion expressed at the Blood Bucket Bar and Casino the night before. But it was only human nature, he'd decided, considering that Sam wasn't playing with fifty-two cards.

"Ain't," Sam said, putting one ankle over another and staring at his walk-worn boots.

"You walked down past the cave two days ago, didn't you, Sam? A bit after five in the afternoon?"

"I ain't sure about any such thing like that."

Sam had already admitted to that much several times since Janis had been killed. But now he was beginning to forget, which Bundy had been expecting. And so what else had he forgotten? Picking up a rock, smashing Janis's head, running out frightened, throwing the rock away where it hadn't yet been found, then lying about what had happened until lying wasn't necessary because he couldn't remember any more?

Feeling frustration, Bundy said, "Do you remember where Janis Cramer lived, Sam?"

Sam became more alert and smiled for the first time, his face lighting up, eyes sparkling. "She's a nice girl! I go into the drugstore every day to see her! I'll go in tomorrow, too! And she'll say, 'Well, look who came skipping in! My goodness, if it isn't Sam!' "

He'd now forgotten that she was dead, but he could still remember that greeting because he'd been hearing it for so long. But how had he really been interpreting that daily welcome?

"Janis's house is down there on the river, Sam," Bundy said.

"Next to it," Deputy Harvey Plummer corrected. "Not on it."

"You know what I mean!"

"It's not right to say a house is *on* a river when it's *next* to it!"

"Harvey?" Bundy said threateningly, holding up his right thumb and jabbing it at him. Plummer closed his mouth and remained quiet with effort, looking almost as resentful as Skipping Sam had a few moments ago.

Bundy looked back at Skipping Sam and was suddenly aware that Sam now owned the stale, musty odor of the jail. Fastidiously clean, he'd always, until now, given off the fresh smell of the outdoors. That brief sparkle of his eyes had dimmed away, too. It was depressing.

"Do you know where the river is, Sam?" Bundy asked quietly.

"Why wouldn't I know where the river is!"

"And is that why you went down the gravel path past the cave day before yesterday? Just to walk beside the river?" Witnesses above had seen him going down the path. But Janis's mother, who each late weekday afternoon always sat beside a window watching for her daughter's return, had not seen Sam arrive down there—or anyone else, including the other suspect, George Ferris, who had freely stated that he'd turned around before going that far because he was out of shape and tired of walking. "Sam?"

"Maybe." But there was a lack of certainty.

"Then why didn't you go all the way down there? What held you up from doing that?"

Sam only looked confused. And Bundy knew that he might have changed his intentions for no good reason at all.

"Deputy Bundy?" Sam said, his eyes brightening again as he leaned forward eagerly toward the sheriff.

"*Sheriff* Bundy!" Harvey Plummer said righteously.

"Sheriff Bundy?" Sam said, correcting himself. "All I want is to be set free so I can go back outside and deliver what I got to deliver and then go home when I'm wore out and have some good supper with Mrs. Gibbons and go to my room and sleep tight and then get up and do that again the next day. I wouldn't cause anybody any trouble ever!"

Bundy looked deep into Sam's anxious eyes and made up his mind. Sam hadn't killed that girl, he told himself. It wasn't possible.

"Deputy?" Sam pleaded to Bundy.

"*Sheriff*," Plummer corrected.

Bundy said, "If there's any way in this world I can let you out to do that, Sam, I by God will!"

Plummer took Skipping Sam back to his cell and returned with George Ferris, who sat down where Sam had been, with Plummer himself beside him, palm again resting on his revolver.

Ferris smiled insincerely at Sheriff Bundy. He was a compactly built man of six feet in his forty-second year with a pale, angular face; his nose was small with oddly flared nostrils, and his dark eyes had the guarded look of someone unceasingly suspicious of everything.

His black hair was cut in a fashion reminiscent of the fifties, and Bundy guessed that he dyed it. He wore a shiny blue Western-styled acrylic shirt with imitation pearl buttons on the pocket flaps, at the cuffs, and running down the front. His bluejeans owned a permanent press. His Western boots were burnished gold with man-made shafts and composition soles and heels. Bundy had a keen eye when it came to cowboy boots. Ferris had purchased his counterfeit outfit in Los Angeles whence he'd come a month ago, Bundy had decided.

Because Ferris had also moved into Mrs. Gibbons' boarding house, Deputy Harvey Plummer had gone there and collected both his and Skipping Sam's extra clothing and toiletries to bring to the jail.

Remaining silent, letting Ferris hold on to his false smile, Sheriff Bundy slid open the middle drawer of his desk slightly and looked at a key there.

It was a short flat brass key made to fit a Yale lock, the kind of lock that was on Mrs. Gibbons' front door. When Skipping Sam had been searched, after being arrested, they'd found an identical key in his right front trouser pocket, the place where most men carry keys. A search of Ferris had not produced such a key.

Plummer had found the one in Bundy's drawer on the gravel path about twenty-five feet from the entrance to the cave. Although he'd picked it up carefully to preserve fingerprints, it had been smudged in such a way that there were none. Nevertheless, it was obvious that it was Ferris's. He'd somehow accidentally dropped it, probably in the process of pulling out his cigarette lighter, Bundy and Plummer had judged. He carried the lighter in his right front trouser pocket, and there had been a butt of his brand of cigarette on the path near the key.

But the key was doing them no good, Bundy thought angrily. It had been found outside the cave, not inside, and Ferris had freely admitted to being outside the cave.

Bundy had run a check immediately on the man. Everything he'd told them about himself appeared to be true. A bachelor with no criminal record, he'd owned and run a video game arcade in Hollywood. His explanation about why he'd sold it and come here was simply that he'd grown tired of city living, had always loved Western movies, and had chosen a Nevada town with a name that might have fitted into one of those movies. He'd fallen in love with Ghost Bluff and intended to start up a new arcade here after he'd rested a bit.

It was Bundy's instinctive feeling, however, that he'd run away from something. But whatever it was, it wasn't, as yet anyway, on police records.

"The old man won't admit killing that poor girl?" Ferris finally asked.

Bundy hadn't liked him on sight. Now he hated him. The man had killed Janis, Bundy was now certain, which left an invalided lady alone in a house by the river. He was attempting to place all that blame on the guileless Skipping Sam, who was incapable of defending himself. But Bundy knew that he was going to have to do better than simply hating if Sam were ever going to get out to skip freely again in the outdoors he loved so much.

"Tell me again, Ferris," Bundy said shortly.

Ferris shrugged and went through it again.

He'd spent most of the day in his room looking at his small TV set. He'd finally decided to get some exercise before dinner. Walking to the river seemed like a good idea.

And so he'd gone down that graveled path. When he'd reached the mouth of the cave, he'd heard a sound in there like something struck with a hammer and cracking as a result. Then he'd seen Skipping Sam come dancing out, eyes looking wild. There was a sizable rock in Sam's right hand. Sam had disappeared up the path with it, heading back into town.

"Sam says he never saw you."

"He wasn't seeing anything except his way out of that cave."

"Did you wonder what he might have hit with that rock?"

"It went through my mind he could have used it on the head of some-body's dog. You can't trust a crazy like that."

"But you didn't go into the cave to investigate."

"A sight like that would have been enough to make me faint! But if I'd known it was that lovely, lovely girl—"

"Lovely, lovely," Bundy said. "Were you attracted to her?"

"Who wouldn't have been, sheriff?"

"I'm told you've been going into the pharmacy a lot lately, just to buy cigarettes. You can buy cigarettes in a lot of places in this town."

Ferris nodded agreeably. "I could have bought cigarettes at the grocery from Ozzie Bates, that mean, ugly soul. Or—from the girl in the pharmacy, same price, like I did. Why do I have to account for that?"

Bundy rubbed a hand along his round chin, irritated by Ferris's facile but unassailable answers, thinking how right things had been for Skipping Sam only a week ago. Mrs. Gibbons had used some of her savings to give Sam the finest treat he'd ever had.

She and Sam had taken an early bus to Reno, then flown south to go to Disneyland. They'd spent most of the day there, with Sam taking one ride and then another, not afraid no matter what kind of ride it was, happier than any seven-year-old could be. They'd flown back that night. And Sam had absolutely glowed with the pleasure of it until he began forgetting where he'd been. . . .

Sheriff Bundy at last realized what he was going to do. He said abruptly:

"I'm tired of your lying, Ferris!"

The sudden change of approach made Deputy Harvey Plummer sit more erectly. Ferris's eyes narrowed.

"When Harvey and I questioned Mrs. Gibbons," Bundy said, "she told us something nobody else around here ever knew about Skipping Sam before. When she took him down to Disneyland, he wouldn't get on a single ride if it took him into the dark. She found out a long time ago that he won't sleep in his room in the attic without a light."

"Orville?" Plummer said.

"There's no way Sam would have gone into the cave where we found the girl. It's pitch black there. And Sam's deathly afraid of dark places!"

"Orville," Plummer said more loudly.

Bundy took the key out of the drawer and slapped it down on his desk with a crack, saying, "We searched that cave again today. We found what we should have found the first time. This key!"

"Orville!" Plummer said, half-rising.

But then, noticing Bundy's right hand, he snapped his mouth shut and sat down as Bundy said to a tensing Ferris:

"Sam was carrying his key when we arrested him. But you weren't. You knew you'd lost it, didn't you? But you didn't know where. All you could hope for was that it wasn't in that cave. But that's where we found it. And it had one of your fingerprints on it!"

Plummer's mouth opened, but he forced it closed again.

Ferris's face had now turned even more pale. He gripped and ungripped his hands over his knees, the knuckles white. Then his eyes assumed a distant, almost trance-like look, as he said: "I was waiting for her by the cave when she came down the path. She smiled at me like she'd been doing all along. I knew what she had in mind. So I told her I'd always been nervous about what might be in the cave. And she said there was no reason to be. All the kids, when they weren't in school, played in it. Then she stepped inside and said, see? It's safe, she said."

His mouth curled at a corner.

"But when I went in after her, she started struggling. I saw a rock and picked it up fast because she'd tricked me—like the others! I pulled her into the dark . . ."

Ferris's eyes suddenly refocused. He bent forward and yanked up the brass lamp by its swing arm. He swung the heavy base with a mighty, vicious sweep at Bundy, who managed to slam himself backward just in time, falling out of his chair as the metal shade flew off the lamp and into a wall with a reverberating clang. The bulb popped and shattered, shards of glass flying everywhere.

Ferris started to crawl over the desk after Bundy, lifting the lamp again. But Plummer dived on his back and wrapped long arms around him. Bundy scrambled to his feet and swung a fist in the direction of Ferris's jaw, finding it. Ferris was stunned just long enough to get handcuffs on him. Then they wrestled him down the hall and into his cell.

Late golden sunlight poured softly over the town so that there were long shadows. Sheriff Bundy, from his window, could see Sam hurrying along a sidewalk with high energy. Bundy smiled and turned around, saying to Deputy Plummer, "It's good to see Sam out there walking again, Harvey."

Plummer nodded. "It worked out all around, didn't it, Orville? But I'll always be sorry about Janis, of course."

"Yes," said Bundy. "So will I."

"And her mother."

"She'll get a lot of help from this town."

"It's the way it is, here. And at least Ferris isn't going to murder any more girls than the three he finally admitted to killing. Thanks to you."

"I only did what I could think to do."

"And I almost ruined it, didn't I?" Plummer said guiltily. "When you said Mrs. Gibbons told us Sam wouldn't get on a ride at Disneyland if it took him into the dark, and wouldn't sleep in his room without light, all because he was afraid of dark places, I just about blurted out that she'd never told us anything like that and that Sam wasn't afraid of a single thing in this world!"

"Well—"

"Then you said we'd found the key in the cave when I'd found it on the path. You said Ferris's fingerprint was on it when it wasn't. And I just about shouted out that none of that was true, either. I would have if I hadn't seen your thumb jabbing away at me!"

"It's not my style, lying away like that. I don't like doing it. But—"

"He never would have confessed if you hadn't! You did the right thing. And I near put the kibosh on it. Boy! I think *I'm* so right. And all along I'm wrong. I apologize, Orville."

"Don't apologize, Harvey."

"That's a bad habit, my correcting everybody the minute it seems like they're making a mistake. I'm going to quit it! Forever."

"That's fine. Now what do you say we close shop?" He walked to the door. "Cross the street and have a beer at the Blood Bucket."

"Street?" Plummer said as he followed the sheriff down the hallway. "That's the highway, Orville!"

Bundy went out the front door of the courthouse and down three concrete steps to the sidewalk.

He could again see Skipping Sam as the wiry old man headed toward a setting sun with bounding strides.

"Now this here we're crossing, Orville," Plummer said indignantly, "isn't any street. This here's Highway 3!"

Bundy saw Sam suddenly take a long, joyful skip.

"I'm telling you, Orville, you can't call this just a street! This here is U.S. Highway 3! And it has been ever since I was born!"

But Bundy simply continued on his way toward that beer, grinning, not responding. If he'd ever really wanted anything in his life, it was to see Sam skip again. And he just had. He wasn't even going to do so much as jab a thumb in his deputy's direction, he told himself, no matter if Harvey kept it up all night. This was one time when he felt too good to mind.

# Summer Notes

### KAREN PARKER

They were sitting on the screened porch in the late afternoon, the old man and the child. She was crosslegged on the day bed, eating graham crackers spread with honey, and she brushed crumbs from her shorts and T-shirt onto the sandy blanket. Her grandfather was moving gently in a large rocking chair. It drove well.

Somewhere along the row of cottages a screened door slammed, then slammed again. Must be the Metcalf twins, Emily thought. The door on this cottage had lost its coiled spring so it didn't close on its own. You had to bang it shut. She wished her dad had noticed this when he rented the cottage and asked that it be fixed.

Emily licked her fingers. Her granddad didn't mind if she ate before supper. She was glad her mother had gone to the beach for the afternoon. She hoped her granddad decided to stay with them when they went home at the end of the summer.

He didn't shave his whiskers every day like her dad did. His face was bristly, then clean for a day, then bristly. Emily looked at him admiringly. He felt her look, glanced at her, smiled. They got on well together.

A sigh of contentment over the snack came out of her as she drew her knees up under her chin. She put her cheek on her knees. Granddad continued to rock slowly.

A group of boys were throwing a ball over a cottage a street away. Their cry of "Eeeny-eeny-ei-nor, here the ball comes over" drifted lazily across the heat.

Emily rubbed her cheek across her knees. "What's a suicide?" she asked.

"Hmmm?" asked Granddad, drowsily.

"Suicide. What is it?"

"When you kill yourself."

"Oh, I thought so."

He squinted one eye at her. "Why did you want to know?"

Emily ran her fingers along a scratch on her leg. It was forming a ridge.

"I just wondered. I heard some people talking and they said there'd have to be a suicide."

Her grandfather rocked and thought for a moment.

"You must have misunderstood. You don't do a suicide. You do a murder. I mean—a suicide is self-directed. You must have heard wrong."

"No," said Emily. "That's what they said."

"Who?"

"The people."

One thing he had learned in life. Patience. "What people?" he asked and the lack of irritation in his voice encouraged her to explain.

"I was sitting under the dock—" she glanced at him but he didn't look alarmed "—and two people walked out to the water and the man said it would have to be a suicide and the lady said, 'I agree,' and then they walked back and didn't say anything until they were on land and she said, 'You'll have to arrange it,' and he said, 'I know.' And then they were gone."

Chet stopped rocking. He looked at his granddaughter and she looked back. He'd gotten to know her pretty well these past weeks—before that he'd only seen her once or twice a year. She was bright for eight years old. He took her seriously.

"Did they see you?" he asked.

"No. I was underneath. You have to crawl on the bank—don't tell Mom —and sort of squeeze through by some rocks. But it's nice. Like a cave."

"Could you see them?"

"No."

"Well, that settles that," Chet said. He went back to rocking. Emily checked between her toes for sand.

"I know who they are," she said.

He stopped rocking again. "How?"

"I seen them"—"saw," he corrected—"saw," she said, "them a few times in the store buying soda pops. I recognized her voice—she's real pretty—she hisses when she talks."

"Hisses?"

"She says—um—'Thisss is the way to drink from a sssstraw.' "

"Oh." He went back to rocking.

The late afternoon air was hot and stale. One of the locals, the man who delivered blocks for those still using ice boxes, said the daily doldrums happened because all the land breeze had blown out to sea and there was a lapse before it began to blow back.

"You feeling okay, Dad?" Alice asked at supper.

"Sure," he said. "Why?"

"You seem quiet."

"Just thinking, I guess. I like this newfangled meal—what did you call them, open-faced sandwiches?"

Alice grinned at Bert, who was eating a bit reluctantly. He liked his supper to be hot and hearty.

"I'm glad you like them. If I'm going to be a beach bunny all afternoon, I have to make a quick meal. No fussing."

"I offered to buy fish and chips on the way home," Bert grumbled goodnaturedly.

"Too greasy. All that oil I put on my body made me not want to eat anything cooked in it."

"Oh, Mom, that's awful," said Emily. She made a face.

After supper her grandfather suggested a walk. The cicadas were still shrilling. They walked along the narrow dusty road between the rows of cottages. There was a breeze now; it smelled damp and fishy but not unpleasant.

"I wish it was always light at night," she told him. "I like going to bed before it's dark."

"Are you afraid of the dark?" he wanted to know.

"Sort of."

"Well, one night we'll make friends with it. Then you'll never be frightened again," he told her.

"Really?" she asked.

"Uh-hum." He stopped in front of the store. "Want to share a popsicle?"

"Sure."

They had a bit of a discussion over what flavor. Emily did not want chocolate. Her gramps wasn't partial to orange. They settled on root beer.

"Are those people here?" he asked casually when they were standing at the cash register.

"Nope," she said, knowing who he meant. She was anxious in case the popsicle broke unevenly and they'd only have part on the stick and the rest in their fingers. It melted so fast and her hands got sticky. But the popsicle broke neatly and evenly. "You're a popsicle expert," she told the storekeeper when he had smacked it on the counter and divided it exactly in half. "Thank you," he said.

The next day they went to the store twice—once in the morning, once in the afternoon. The couple was not there.

Emily's mother did not go to the beach that day, so Emily did not have an afternoon snack. When the cottage got hot from supper preparations— "If I boil water this place heats up," her mother complained again and again—Emily and her gramps went outside and sat on the fallen tree at the end of the street. They could see the harbor from there. And two little boys were on a stoop nearby blowing bubbles.

"I wish you could poke bubbles and they wouldn't break," she commented and then in the same tone of voice, matter-of-factly, she said, "That's them," and slightly inclined her head toward a passing car with a couple inside.

Part of Chet's mind marveled that she was so discreet, even at eight years of age. She knew darned well he had gone by the store twice to see if they were there. She knew he was curious and interested. He would have expected her to shout and point. Alice, as a child, would have done so.

The rest of his mind was in amazed shock. The man in the car was the owner of the large inn at the center of this holiday town. The woman was his receptionist. He knew the wife of the innkeeper when he saw her. Pleasant. Middle-aged. Mother of two sons. A suitable companion for her middle-aged husband. The receptionist was a bit of a floozy, Chet thought. And likely half his age.

Chet didn't sleep very well that night. He kept thinking of the words "have to be a suicide." The remonstrances, "Don't be a fool," "It's none of your business," and "She likely heard wrong," helped. But not for long.

Somewhere near dawn he made a decision and then he slept soundly.

At breakfast it was his turn to work the ancient toaster with the flip-down sides.

"It's going to be another scorcher," Bert announced. He said this every morning and it always was.

"Don't forget I like my toast dark on one side and light on the other," Emily reminded her gramps.

"What are you going to do when we go home and you have to put up with the pop-up toaster again?"

Emily shrugged. It was silly trying to figure out things ahead of time. How could she know now how she would feel then?

"The perils of progress," murmured Chet.

"Well, let's do the groceries early," Alice said. "You coming, Dad?"

"Nope—I think I'll stay," he answered. "I intend to just relax and read," he added quickly as Emily looked over at him and he was afraid she would want to stay with him.

When they had gone he got Alice's rubber gloves from under the sink. They felt wet inside. He didn't know how she could stand to wear them. He liked the feel of soapy water on his hands.

Then he shut himself in his room with a newspaper, an old jar of mucilage he'd seen in a cupboard, the scissors. Already it was hot in the room, but he did not push the flowered chintz that acted as curtains back on the string that doubled as a curtain rod. He left them closed.

He leaned back against the wall and peered out the crack between the curtains and the window. He could only see a few feet of the cottage next door.

Then, when he'd put stuff out on the bed and sat down on the rickety chair beside it, Mrs. Ambrose next door called out something to one of her kids, and Chet jumped guiltily. "Just not cut out for this sort of thing," he told himself as he got to work.

An hour or so later he had two letters written in words cut from the newspaper and pasted onto plain white paper.

The first one said, "The only suicide to happen had better be yours."

In block letters he addressed an envelope to the innkeeper at the inn. It felt weird to write with rubber gloves on.

He'd debated a bit before making the second letter, but he went ahead. It said, "Someone is out to hurt you. Take care. A friend." He addressed it to the innkeeper's wife at their home address.

He used water to put the stamps on the envelopes, feeling over-cautious.

Then he put the glue and gloves and scissors back and ripped the cut pages of the newspaper into shreds which he flushed down the toilet.

With a quick glance up and down the street to make sure Alice and Bert weren't on their way home, he went around the cottage and across to the next road by the back route. Several streets away he located a mailbox and dropped the envelopes inside.

"Well, that's that," he said to himself.

A day later Chet and Emily were on their way to the beach. "Do you want to see if those people are in the store?" she asked him.

"No, I don't need to. I took care of it," he told her.

"Oh," she said and looked at him but did not ask anything more.

The next day Chet saw the receptionist in the laundromat. She looked tired. Chet wondered if something was bothering her sleep. He thought he should feel pleased, but he didn't. He felt empty. But somehow satisfied.

On the weekend Bert added to the lunchtime conversation by commenting, "Saw a police car in front of the innkeeper's house today."

"Wonder why?" Alice asked. "I hope the boys are okay." The eldest boy worked in the local drugstore and was friendly and helpful.

"Maybe a problem at the inn," Bert said.

"Likely that," Chet agreed.

The rest of the summer passed uneventfully. Emily crawled several times under the dock, but she didn't hear any more interesting conversations.

Chet decided he could put up with his daughter's family—and they with him—so he started to make plans to close down his apartment and move in with them when they went back to town.

The day before they left the cottage for the summer, Alice heard in the post office that the innkeeper's wife was getting a divorce.

Emily was sitting on the worn linoleum sorting through her summer collection of shells and stones, trying to select the ones that would fit into the single box her mother had agreed she could take home.

She stopped her activity, looked up at her granddad. "There won't have to be one now, will there?" she asked.

He knew what she meant. "No," he told her. "Not now."

# A Matter of Thin Air

### LAWRENCE TREAT

It was pure coincidence that a week or two previously Chief Willy Wharton of LePage County had happened to drive by just when a car had been stopped for a traffic violation. That was when he first noticed them —two chattery, protesting women falling all over themselves with explanations. The traffic blocked them from his view, but he could hear their protests.

A truck had gotten in their way, a dog had run out in front of them, the sun had been in their eyes, they'd merely followed another car coming out of the driveway. Excuses spilled out of the pair of them like a paddlewheel churning up river water.

There was no reason why they meant anything to Willy, and he soon forgot about them.

When Julian arrived, Willy was luxuriating in the orthopedic chair that Kate had given him for his last birthday, and the knock on the door startled him.

He said, "Come in," and an underfed little man with light blue eyes and a scrawny beard the color and texture of wet hay stumbled in, almost fell on his face, and had to grab the edge of the desk for a prop.

"Sorry," he said. "Lost my balance."

"That's okay," Willy said. And with the gesture of somebody handing out a free ticket for the Superbowl, he said, "Sit down. What can I do for you?"

"Name's Julian Arbell," the man said, and he stammered for a second or so before he managed to blurt out the reason for his visit. "Pa's missing. Disappeared. Into thin air. Like that." He waved his arms as if he were trying to semaphore.

"Arbell?" Willy asked. "The Amos Arbell who lives over in Ottoville— that your father?"

"Was," Julian said. "I came all the way from Richardville to run him a funeral he'd be proud of, and where is he? Gone. I got the coffin, but what's there to put into it? Nothing!"

"You're an undertaker?" Willy said.

"Me? Not on your life!"

"Then why the coffin?"

"Got a bargain. Water damaged and real cheap, so I bought two of them. One for my wife, one for Pa. Saves me two hundred dollars, cash."

Willy put that one in the back of his head, where he stuck off-beat ideas that made no sense. Man's got a coffin, and consequently he kills somebody so he can use the coffin.

"What makes you think your pa's dead?"

"Phoned and said so."

"Look," Willy said. "If he was dead, how could he phone?"

"Pa could do anything."

Willy scowled, took a deep breath, and humped himself up in his chair, more or less like a sleepy tiger stretching.

Julian got the signal.

"Well," he said, "he didn't exactly tell me he was dead. Said they were killing him, and what Pa says, is."

"Who's they?"

"Florry. Minnie."

"Who are they?"

"Wife. Her sister."

"Did you ask them about your pa?"

"Nope."

"Why not?"

"They're gone, too. Empty house."

"Maybe they all went away on a trip."

"Not together. Hated each other. They been trying to kill Pa for years, but botch it every time."

"You were fond of your father?"

"Nope."

"When was this, when he called to tell you they were killing him?"

"Week ago Tuesday."

"Why'd you wait so long?"

"Blues."

"I don't get it."

Julian tugged at the seventy-eight or so hairs of his beard and got no satisfaction out of it. "Blues," he said.

Willy humped himself up again and made as if he'd take a deep breath and blow Julian clean out of the window. "Blues," Julian said again. "That's our school team. Going into the finals. Got to support them."

As a good American dedicated to law and order and the sanctity of team spirit, Willy couldn't dispute the premise. "Have you been to the house?" he asked.

"Just come from there. Nobody around except Casper. Caretaker. Been there twenty years, but not very bright."

"I think I'd better go see the place," Willy said. "Come along, we'll take my car."

On the way, Julian gave him a rundown of the Arbell history. "Pa made a fortune," Julian said. "Lumber business, Oregon. Ma died there. Left Pa pretty lonesome, so he married her nurse. Florida. Comes from a family that name all their children after the states. Brother's Tex. Ken's another brother. Kentucky. Minnie, she's Minnesota. She moved in as soon as Florry got married."

"Any servants in the house?"

"Dunno."

"Does your father have any friends?"

"Nope."

Casper met them at the house. A product of junk food and packaged dinners, Casper had a forty-inch waist and size forty-eight pants, which he held up by a kind of waddle and an occasional hitch with his left hand. He unlocked the door as if he were selling his birthright, and half price at that.

As Willy told Kate that evening, the joint looked baronial, full of uncomfortable chairs and expensive stuff that belonged in a museum. There was an archway between the cathedral-ceilinged living room and the banquet room, which Amos probably called a dining room, and a full suit of armor stood there to guard it. Just to make sure that Amos wasn't inside, Willy flipped up the visor. Amos wasn't.

With that settled, Willy got down to business, which was mostly snooping around and noting things like the silverware in the dining room and the dog bed in Amos's room and the mail that had piled up inside the front door.

The absence of the dog bothered Willy. Questioned as to its whereabouts, Julian said, "What dog?" And Casper scratched his chin and said, after thinking it over, "Dunno."

In the evening Willy went over the case with Chief Dan Moorhead, his counterpart in Morgan County. Although the two counties were in separate states, they had a common border along which stood the Right Side Bar & Grill, so named because it was on the right side of the state line, where liquor taxes were lower. There, by custom, the first booth on the right as you came in was reserved for the two chiefs, who usually met around eight in the evening and talked business.

There were certain similarities between them, and certain differences. While they ran to about the same longitude, for instance, Willy was spread thinner and had less bulk. The main difference between them, though, was internal. Dan's knowledge was encyclopedic and he stayed up nights reading technical treatises on anything from viruses to the infinite extent of the universe. Willy, however, was happily married and devoted his spare time to enjoying the existence of Kate.

When he got to the bar that evening, Dan was already there. According to ritual, Willy waited until after the first beer before broaching anything except the basic amenities. At the proper time he stated his problem.

"Got a vanishing act," he said. "Man named Arbell has evanesced." Willy liked the word and lingered on it before repeating what Julian had told him. "That's all I knew until I started looking around the house," Willy said.

"And then what?" Dan asked, looking as if he'd been brought up on vitamins and buttermilk.

"Then I looked in Florry's desk. Sort of interesting, too."

"Hepplewhite?" Dan said.

"Hepplewhite?" Willy asked. "Where does he come in?"

"You were describing the desk," Dan said.

"Well, I was going to tell you what was in it, which wasn't much. Some unpaid bills and a cash statement of what she spent for running the house, and Amos didn't give her much. A real miser, if you ask me. So where was the dough?"

Dan was willing to play straight man once in a while. "Where was it?"

"In the same bank that Amos always used, only his account was closed out. Phil Jameson, he's the manager. Had a shot at the Chicago Cubs a few years ago, but couldn't make it."

"He told you where she was?"

"In California. And she has a brand new account, in her own name, and there's fifty grand in it."

"Makes sense," Dan said. "She got hold of his money and then killed him and ran away." Dan grinned. "With the bank manager."

"Phil Jameson," Willy said, "has a good job, a fine wife, four children, and he plays third base on the Ottoville softball team. Why would he run away with a pair of forty-year-old sisters?"

"We were talking about the dough," Dan said. "How did she get hold of fifty grand?"

"Power of attorney, and everything's strictly kosher. I checked. She has been selling Amos's stock and putting the proceeds in her own name. Half a million so far, and another half to go."

"Find the body and get hold of Florry," Dan said. "Willy, it looks like you got yourself a homicide."

"Maybe," Willy said. "Anyhow, I found out that Florry is staying at the Beverly Hills out in L.A., so I called her and she said she was okay where she was and she didn't know anything about Amos, but she and Minnie were having a great time and didn't expect to come home yet, and then she hung up on me. Dan, she seemed too damn sure of herself."

"Any idea when she's coming?"

"Tomorrow. I called her right back and told her this was a homicide investigation and—well, after I told her a couple of other things, she allowed as how she'd take the first flight she could get, which turns out to be tomorrow night."

Willy was there in plenty of time. He figured that, after a couple of changes of planes and with a police investigation to worry about, the sisters would be pretty tired when they finally got to the LePage airport. He was wrong, however. They looked chipper, and they practically skipped down the stairway from the plane.

He spotted them right off. Florry was all cushions, even her face was like a small, pink pincushion, but if she was pure cotton, Minnie was made of emery cloth. No soft spots in her, and Willy had the feeling that if he bumped into her, she'd rub the skin off.

He walked straight up to them and introduced himself. "I'm Chief Wharton, and I thought we might sit down for a while and talk about—"

Florry opened the barrage. "It's so nice of you to meet us. I didn't think policemen were so polite and—" Minnie finished the sentence: "Nobody's been nice to us. We almost lost our bags and one of the handles was broken." Whereupon Florry got into the act again. "We don't want to bother you with our troubles, but what about Amos?" And Minnie chimed in, "You got us so worried about him. Do you know where he is?"

They went at it like that, presto, staccato, never letting up, never answering a question and never stopping their avalanche of words. When Willy wanted to know when they'd last seen Amos, Florry said it was after the Bob Hope show last Wednesday, but Minnie said that wasn't Wednesday, it was Thursday, and Florry said it didn't matter, it was the time he'd said Shakespeare used Mobil oil, whereupon Minnie said that wasn't Shakespeare, it was Shelley, and Florry said Shelley who, and they argued about that for a while and finally agreed that Amos would probably show up when nobody expected him, all he was doing now was making everybody worry and spend the taxpayers' money looking for him when he'd gone off somewhere and forgotten to tell anybody where he was going.

Willy realized that, far from being tired, they were building up to a peak of energy. He also realized that they'd probably rehearsed their act and that they enjoyed baiting him.

They fielded the matter of the dog as if they'd been expecting the question. Florry said, "That awful dog!" Minnie said he bit people, and the two sisters began arguing about how many times he'd bit the postman, and then they disagreed as to whether he was an Alsatian or a shepherd or a police dog, and what was a police dog and how much did it cost to feed the dog and was he a good watchdog and what kind of dog they had when they were children.

Willy gave up and managed to mention Julian, whereupon the sisters went to work taking Julian apart. They were full of the injustice of how he'd inherit everything under his father's will and how Florry wouldn't get a cent. Willy knew all about that, he'd checked with the Arbell lawyer and knew that she'd signed a pre-marital agreement and had gotten ten thousand dollars. She kept saying she'd spent it long ago and didn't know what she'd do now.

Willy told himself he knew damn well what she'd do. In fact, she'd done it already. She'd grabbed all the money available, and she was interested in getting hold of the rest of it. Willy admitted freely that he'd been out-maneuvered, out-generaled and certainly out-talked, so he sent the sisters home in a taxi while he drove back to the peace and quiet of Kate.

"I made a mistake," he told her. "They ganged up on me, but wait till tomorrow when I get Florry alone."

Florry was on the phone, however, shortly after he got home. "Mr. Wharton? This is Mrs. Arbell and somebody got in the house and stole everything, so you'd better come here right away and do something."

"Nothing I can do now," he said. "Don't touch anything, and I'll be around in the morning."

"I'll touch anything I want to because this is my own house, and I want you to come here immediately."

"Tomorrow," Willy said, and hung up. And when the phone rang a few seconds later, he took the receiver off the hook.

Still, all things considered, he wished he had this kind of a larceny investigation a little more often. Although Florry heckled him and Minnie piled it on, Willy had the whole business solved right off. First, he noticed that neither the door nor any of the windows had been forced, which meant a key had been used. As for the key, Julian had his own, so Willy figured he'd either drive up to Julian's or get in touch with the police there. Chances were, there wouldn't be much trouble. Julian would have the loot and would probably admit it.

Just to make sure he was right, Willy found Casper, who told him Julian and his coffin had been there yesterday afternoon, and that he'd filled up the coffin with something or other. Casper didn't know what.

When Willy returned to the main house, Florry was trying to put the knight together. It looked as if Julian had taken it apart, but had decided that the pieces were too bulky to bother with. Florry was trying to fit the tasses together and getting them mixed up with a cuisse, so Willy told her to forget about it, he'd fix it up for her, he was an expert on armor and he'd get around to it after he'd recovered the rest of the stuff and restored whatever had been taken.

"But how do you know where it is?" she demanded, and her eyes got big with curiosity or wonder, or maybe she just made them big for Willy's individual benefit.

"I know," he said, "so stop making a nuisance of yourself." And that left her silent and she just gaped, maybe for the first time in her life. Even Minnie looked impressed. Still, shutting Florry up for a few minutes didn't help him get places with a homicide investigation, and the best he could do was tower over her and watch her wilt and then walk off and tend to other business.

The most important other business was getting hold of Julian and having a heart to heart talk with him, but Willy could just as well have stayed back in his office in Forsyth. Julian merely repeated his belief that Amos was dead. Under his will everything belonged to Julian, so Julian had loaded up a few of his own possessions and brought them home, and what was wrong with that?

The net result was that Willy was a little late in arriving at the Right Side Bar & Grill that evening. "Thought you weren't coming," Dan said. "What happened?"

"Been busy," Willy remarked, and signaled to the bartender. "I," he announced, "am stumped." He waited for Dan to object, and when Dan didn't, Willy heaved a sigh just deep enough to blow a couple of paper napkins off a nearby table. Then he stated his problem. "I've got a moron, an amateur undertaker, and a pair of nonstop talking females, so what do I do with them?"

"Wait them out," Dan said. "People who talk too much give themselves away."

"Not these two," Willy said glumly. "They been practicing up all their lives, and they don't make mistakes."

"Tail them for a day or so. They'll do something stupid. Always happens." Dan, however, spoke with less than complete conviction. He was saved from going into the matter when Tony, at the bar, yelled something over the noise of the crowd. Dan interpreted it for Willy.

"Tony wants you," Dan said.

Willy turned around. "Yeah?" he said. "What's the trouble?"

Tony motioned and got nowhere. Then he took a deep breath and let out the full power of his voice. It ripped through the crowd like a bull charging through a cornfield, and in simple admiration for his lung power, the room went silent. Tony then spoke in a normal voice. "Phone," he said.

Willy got up and marched over to the corner of the room, where Tony handed him the receiver. "Chief Wharton here," Willy said into the receiver.

A man's voice answered. "If you want to find Amos Arbell, try the R.W. Nursing Home." And the phone clicked.

Willy returned to his table and sat down. "Funny the way your mind works," he said to Dan. "As soon as the guy said nursing home, I remembered an incident that happened a couple of weeks ago. Maybe less. I was stuck in traffic and this car came barreling out of the place and almost rammed a police car. The cop started bawling them out, only the women in the car turned the blame around and made out it was his fault. His or somebody else's. Anyhow, they talked themselves right out of that ticket, and I can hear them right now. Those voices, I don't know how come I forgot them, because they belonged to Florry and her sister Minnie."

"Then whoever called you just now knew what he was talking about."

"Maybe," Willy said. "I'll find out in the morning because if Amos is really there, he'll keep, and I may as well give him a good night's sleep. And the same to me."

He got to the nursing home a little after nine and identified himself to a big, thick-lipped manager named Moriarty. Moriarty drummed one square-nailed finger on an unpaid bill and was probably thinking of all the violations Willy could dig up, but when Willy stated his business, Moriarty was all smiles and acted like a men's wear salesman telling a customer how well he looked in that jacket.

Arbell?, Moriarty kept saying. Amos Arbell? Sure, he'd been admitted there about ten days ago. Came with his wife and sister, and they'd paid for a full month in advance. Did Willy want to see Arbell's record? Everything was in order. Regular medical exams every day. Not that Arbell needed them. A little senile, sure, but otherwise he'd been in good health. No need to worry about him. He'd been okay when he left.

"Left?" Willy exclaimed. "He's not here?"

"Left yesterday. As a matter of fact he sneaked out, so I phoned his wife and she said not to worry, it was okay, don't bother and don't bring in the police, she knew where he was. Not that I had any obligation to notify the authorities, but we lean backwards to take care of our clients."

Willy digested the news and saw that the case was more mixed up than ever. In fact, there was no case at all. Amos was senile and Florry had put him in a nursing home and gone to California, after putting most of his money in her name. Which she had a perfect right to do. As for Julian, he'd bought a coffin and wanted to get some use out of it, and when his father wasn't home, Julian decided he was now an orphan and had inherited the estate. And the only thing wrong was why Florry hadn't told this to Willy in the first place. And since she hadn't—

Willy, thinking hard and checking off all the possibilities, did what any cop would do under the circumstances. He reached into his pocket and took out a picture of Amos Arbell. Just to make sure. Just in case.

"Him?" Willy said.

Moriarty shook his head. "Who's he? Because I never saw him before in my life."

"That's Amos," Willy said, "and your customer isn't." And Willy stood up, wondering if Florry had outsmarted him. But whether she had or not, Willy had a full day's work ahead of him.

He was jubilant when he walked into the Right Side Bar & Grill that evening and sat down opposite Dan.

"Well?" Dan said.

Willy, who liked to be cryptic, outdid himself. "The dog did it," Willy remarked. "Or at least he started things off." And that was all Willy said until after the ritual of the beer had been completed. Then Willy explained the dog.

"It was a male named Priscilla," Willy said, "and everybody hated it except Amos. What happened was that it took a bit out of Casper. Here." Willy rose up in his seat and tapped his behind gently. "And Casper got mad and slugged it with a crowbar. But a guy like Casper, it's easy to break him down and tell when he's lying."

"Was he?" Dan asked.

"No. He told me exactly what had happened, and he was glad to get it off his chest. After he killed the dog, which Amos liked a lot better than he liked his wife, his son, and his sister-in-law combined, Casper just stood there with the crowbar and he was still standing there when Amos came along. When Amos saw the dog, he flipped and lit into Casper and gave him a shove, which Casper found a little hard to take. Like he said to me, first he got bit and then he got bawled out for getting bit and then he got pushed around. It was all too much for him, and he made a pass at Amos with the crowbar."

Willy grimaced. Dan said, "So who's in the nursing home?"

"Florry's brother, Tex. She had it all figured out long ago. She'd thought of all the things that could happen and how she could take advantage of them and she'd been wondering how to get rid of Amos without his will going into effect. So when Casper killed him and asked her what to do, she said bury Amos and don't tell anybody. Just bury him far away, somewhere in the woods where nobody can find him.

"She was pretty sure of Casper. He was too dumb to realize what he'd done and he'd forget about it, so she put her plan into effect. First of all, she entered Tex in the nursing home, but under the name of Amos Arbell and with instructions to act senile and take a walk after a week or so. That way, Amos's existence would be fully documented, nobody would think of looking for his body, and Florry could forge her power of attorney and get to work helping herself to his assets. And it all would have worked—there would have been no reason in the world to investigate, and I would never even have heard of the Arbell problem—except that Julian bought a couple of coffins and persuaded himself that Amos was dead and that his death was a police matter. Which changed everything. Florry had to stall me off, keep me away from Casper, and make me think that Amos had been in a nursing home and disappeared from there. I wasn't supposed to go into anything previous to that disappearance."

"Did you get a confession?"

"Me?" Willy said. "When I accused them and tried to get a description of Tex so we could get hold of him, Florry said he had brown eyes and Minnie said they were green, and Florry admitted there was some green in them. When I questioned them separately, they gave me contradictory descriptions. I think they had it figured out ahead of time. Florry said he was six feet tall and was blond, Minnie said he was five six and had brown hair. Around that time, I had me an inspiration. I turned them loose on an assistant D.A."

"They can't hold out forever," Dan said. "If a guy keeps at them, he's bound to break them down. They're accessories after the fact. Or at least Florry is, so how's she going to get out of that?"

"Maybe she won't," Willy said, "except that there's still one little problem. No *corpus.* Casper took the body out somewhere and buried it, but he can't remember where."

# A Man Around the House

### VIRGINIA LONG

I went out to the mailbox to get my mail as soon as the carrier passed. I still didn't see Myra Ledbetter out getting theirs, and I decided on the spot I'd just stroll over there and see what was making her so scarce lately. I counted back and it was four days I hadn't seen hide nor hair of her.

We're not the closest of friends, but she and Judson are the nearest neighbors I've got out here on the edge of town, and I like to keep an eye on her. She can be a little sneaky—like buying that new kitchen stove last month without even telling me she was thinking about it. And then getting so huffy when I asked her how much it cost! It seems to me neighbors shouldn't have any secrets from each other. I certainly tell her everything I think about, even if she doesn't always seem to appreciate my frankness.

It was a pretty fair walk along the town road to the Ledbetters' mailbox and then on up their drive, and I was looking forward to a cup of tea and maybe some of that good coffee cake she makes. Of course it isn't as good as mine, but no matter how many times I've offered her my recipe, she keeps right on using her own.

I've never been one to stand on ceremony, so when I finally climbed their porch steps, I just opened the door, stuck my head in and yelled, "Myra?"

There wasn't any answer and I was about to walk in and see if she was back in the kitchen when I heard heavy steps on the back porch, then through the kitchen and hall, and Judson Ledbetter stood there frowning at me. He didn't look any smarter or cleaner than usual.

"Hello, Judson," I said. "Haven't seen Myra for four days and I thought she might be feeling poorly."

"She's gone." That's all he said. Not one word of explanation.

"Gone? What do you mean gone?" I never knew Myra to go anywhere by herself in all the years I've known her, and that's since before I lost poor Martin ten years ago.

"Just gone. Just hauled off and left." He stood there in that hulking way he has, and didn't even have the gumption to look me in the eye.

I sniffed and turned to leave, since it didn't seem like he was going to tell me any more about it. But then he sort of growled, "You mean you ain't heard anything from her?"

I turned around again. "Well, of course not or I'd know about her not being here, wouldn't I?"

He met my eyes this time and he looked downright puzzled.

I was a little tuckered out from the walk, so I decided to take the short cut through the back lot. I was almost to the place where our property meets, just short of a thicket of sweet gum trees, when I saw it.

It was a grave. It couldn't hardly have been anything else. It was just the right size and humped up just the right way. And the dirt on the hump was fresh-turned dirt. I'll tell you, I didn't waste a minute getting on home, backing my car out of the garage, and heading for town.

I was still huffing and puffing when I hurried into the town marshall's office and ran smack dab into the mayor coming out. His name's Claude Mitchell and even if he's a little too short and a little too round, he's still a fine figure of a man. Being a bachelor all his life, he's probably a little too set in his ways, but a smart woman could get around that. I wasn't in too much of a hurry to hold in my stomach, pat my hair down, and pass the time of day for a couple of minutes. He didn't remind me one bit of poor Martin, but just seeing such an eligible fellow reminded me how nice it would be to have a man around the house again.

He seemed to be in kind of a hurry, too, so it wasn't long before he touched the brim of his hat and went on his way. I rushed on in to see the marshall.

"Good morning, Buddy. How's your mother doing today?" In a small town where you know everybody, you've got to observe certain manners even if there's something important on your mind.

"Doing a little better, thanks. I'll tell her you asked." He's a nice boy, Buddy is—thirty or so now but I still think of him as a boy. Real good to his mother, too.

I took a deep breath. "Buddy, there's something awful I have to tell you. Myra Ledbetter has disappeared and I swear to you there's a new grave out there in their back lot."

He stood up and looked at me like I'd taken leave of my senses, but after I told him the whole story he sat back down and studied about it for a spell, tapping a pencil against the side of his boot and frowning. Finally he said, "Well, seeing as how I'm the only law in Kester Corners, I guess

I'll have to look into it. I'll just sort of pay old Judson a visit and see what he's got to say about it."

It was out of my hands now, and I breathed a sigh of relief. Buddy said he'd call me if Myra did turn out to be buried there. They'd probably need my testimony or something. He didn't seem too sure about it, but then he's hardly ever had to worry about much more than settling a fight at the pool hall or making people keep their dogs quiet at night.

Well, the upshot of the whole thing was so embarrassing I was glad there wasn't anyone else around when Buddy came by my place later that afternoon. Seems Judson told him his deep freeze had gone on the blink and he had a whole bunch of meat go bad on him before he discovered it. So he'd just bundled it all up and buried it out there in the back lot.

Buddy said he felt pretty silly about it, but he went out and dug it up. Sure enough, there was eighty or a hundred pounds of hamburger, chicken, and fish that he could see through the plastic bags, already beginning to turn sort of brown and green and smelling to high heaven.

Luckily Buddy's mother and I have been good friends for a long time, so he didn't tell me off like he might have if I'd been anybody else. But, like I said, it was embarrassing. All I could do was say I was sorry.

I didn't sleep very well that night, and I kept thinking Judson must be pretty upset about the whole thing. And even if Buddy hadn't told him it was me that started it, he could have figured that out even with what little brains he had.

So early the next morning I decided I'd go over and apologize. I made up a batch of doughnuts for an excuse—Myra never could make a decent doughnut—and I went cutting through the back way again even if it did mean I had to pass that pile of dirt.

I got to the edge of the sweet gum trees before I saw him. He was just finishing up, it looked like, taking the shovel and patting down the loose soil tight and hard to make it look like it wasn't piled any higher than it was yesterday. But it was!

I know Buddy told me he put everything back just the way it was, and there wasn't any good reason for Judson to be filling it in again—unless he'd added something else to what was already down there in that hole.

I hung back in the cover of the trees and watched Judson. He got all through and then stood there looking around, and I'll be switched if he didn't have that same sneaky look on his face that Myra always had when she was bound and determined I wasn't going to find out something.

Well, I had found out something and I wasn't going to let Judson Ledbetter put anything over on me or Buddy Wilkes or anybody else. I got the car out and went hightailing it in to town again. But by the time I got there, I was beginning to have some second thoughts about how Buddy was going to take it. So I stopped at the drugstore and wandered around for a spell, pretending like I was looking for something special but really just thinking it all over real good.

I saw John Bascomb watching me from behind the pharmacy counter and gave him a big smile. Wouldn't hurt to do a little advance preparation —in just a couple of months his year's mourning for Edna would be up, and then I could really turn on the charm. He looked thin—needed a lot of good home cooking to put some meat on his bones, and if I do say so, there's not a better cook in Kester Corners than me. Maybe I could start out by inviting him to dinner after Sunday church. It sure would be nice to have a man around the house again.

Finally I decided it was nothing more or less than my duty to tell Buddy Wilkes what I'd seen. Then I'd leave it up to him what to do about it.

Well, Buddy wasn't very sure what to do, but he takes his job real serious and when he understood that Judson really had dug that hole out and filled it up again, he thought maybe he'd better go out and at least talk to him. But he said I had to go along this time since I was the one making the complaint.

We went out there in Buddy's car and Judson was sitting on the porch when we drove up. He looked at us with that dumb suspicious look of his, and we sat down on the steps like we'd just come to pass the time of day. After a while Buddy asked him if he'd heard anything from Myra yet, and Judson shook his head, looking straight at me like he thought I might have something to say. I just stared back at him with my lips shut tight. How would I hear anything from a woman buried five feet deep out in his back lot?

"Well, Mr. Ledbetter," Buddy said in a kind of tired voice. "I hear you dug up that hole again so I guess I got to look at it again, since there don't seem to be any real proof that Mrs. Ledbetter just went away."

Judson gave him a funny smile and stood up, and we all walked on back to where the pile of dirt was. Buddy was sweating a little already, just thinking of all that work to do all over again. He burst out, "Why don't you just tell me what you was doing fooling around with it this morning?"

"Coyotes was trying to get to that durned meat. I shot two of 'em and dumped 'em in there with the other stuff."

"Mr. Ledbetter, I ain't seen a coyote this close to town since I was a little bitty kid." Buddy looked plain exasperated, and he took up the shovel and started digging.

Nobody said anything for about ten minutes, and when Buddy got down to where we could see what was in the hole on top of the spoiled meat, there wasn't anything for any of us to say. They looked like mangy, yellowish-grey dogs and their fur was all matted with dirt and blood, but they were coyotes, all right.

Buddy's face was red and sweaty and he looked even madder when he started tossing the dirt back in. But this time it was me he was mad at. I apologized, excused myself politely, and went walking back home, not even remembering I'd left my car sitting downtown in front of the drugstore.

It had been such a busy day, I'd forgotten all about my mail. I went out to get it, mostly hoping it would give me something else to think about. You could have knocked me over with a feather when I saw a letter from Myra Ledbetter. There wasn't any return address on it and I couldn't make out the postmark, but I knew her handwriting when I saw it. I didn't even wait till I got back to the house. I tore it open and read it while I was walking up the drive. It said:

> Emily:
>
> I'm leaving this place for good, but I don't want to go off without telling you exactly what I think of you. You've stuck your prying nose into my affairs for the last time and if you can spare any time from flirting with every ragtag leftover man in town, I give you leave to latch on to Judson. He's a poor excuse for a man, but from what I've seen you don't care what size or shape they are long as they wear pants. No use anybody trying to find me. They couldn't drag me back with a team of horses.
>
> Myra Ledbetter

Well, that settled that. It was no more than my duty to tell Buddy there wasn't any sense in going digging around the Ledbetter place again. Myra really had gone off somewhere and I had the proof of it. I hoped he'd take my word for it. I didn't look forward to showing him that letter. Just goes to show you how ungrateful a woman can be, after I'd befriended her and given her so much advice.

I decided the first thing I ought to do was go over and apologize to Judson and tell him I'd finally heard from Myra like he seemed to expect I would. When I thought about how much he seemed to expect it, I looked at the envelope and saw it was stamped "Missent to Kenton, OH." That accounted for its being five days coming. It seemed to me it would have saved us all a lot of trouble if the post office had done its job right in the first place.

I cut through the back way again, since there wasn't anything to worry about now. But when I got to the sweet gum grove I slowed up just from habit, and there he was again!

Judson was all by himself—I guess Buddy didn't waste any time getting away from there—and he had the whole darned thing all dug up again. The plastic bags full of rotten meat and fish were propped up on the side of the pile of dirt, and I watched him lower a big, blanket-wrapped bundle and a suitcase into the deep hole. Then he took a black purse and dropped it in. I could hear it thud when it hit. Next he picked up the plastic bags by the corners, lowered them into the hole, and placed the coyote carcasses, holding them by the legs that were stiff by this time, in exactly the right position. Then he started shoveling all the dirt back in.

I had the picture now. I'd seen the frost on the blanket and the suitcase, and it wasn't hard to see why all that meat spoiled. There was something more important that needed the space in the deep freeze. The letter puzzled me for a minute till I figured out that Myra had it in her purse ready to mail at the first town she went through after she got away from Kester Corners. My guess was that he got mad when she told him she was leaving him, probably didn't even really mean to kill her but it just turned out that way. And when he found the letter in her purse, he figured that was the perfect proof that she really had left, so he drove to some nearby town and mailed it.

Clever, clever! I'd always thought Judson was a stupid clod, but now I realized that Myra had probably fostered that idea as a protective measure so I wouldn't set my sights on him. Actually he was smart enough to fool me and Buddy Wilkes and almost anybody. And strong, my goodness! I watched him swinging the shovel with hardly any strain at all, putting all that dirt back again. He was such a big, solid-looking man, and it reminded me that poor Martin had been a big solid man, too, rest his soul.

I leaned against one of the sweet gum trees and thought about how nice it would be to have a big, strong man around the house to—oh, lordy, lordy! What was I thinking of?

I heard a car on the road and went tearing back to my house just in time to see Buddy pulling into the driveway with my car. Like I said, he's a good boy and he even agreed to walk over to that back lot with me one more time.

And this time I didn't have to apologize to anybody.

# A Day
# at the Lake

## ED POOLE

illy Joe was walking down Cedar Lake Road carrying his fishing rod over his shoulder and his tackle and bait in a burlap sack. The spring sun warmed his back through his T-shirt and his brogans made dusty little clouds as he walked down the dirt road. Woods bordered the narrow road so closely that two cars could pass each other only if both drove with their right wheels in the shallow ditches.

Billy Joe was daydreaming about what he would like to do tomorrow to celebrate his eighteenth birthday when he heard a siren in the distance. Daydream was about all he could do because Pa sure wasn't about to turn loose of any of his money. Ever since Ma died, Pa had been spending his money on hard liquor and the fancy ladies at Lonzo's Bar and Girl. Actually, it was Lonzo's Bar and Grill, but everyone called it Lonzo's Bar and Girl. Mostly just to aggravate Lonzo.

The siren was getting louder. Billy wondered why the sheriff would be coming down Cedar Lake Road with his siren on. The road dead-ended into Cedar Lake. Maybe someone drowned. Yeah, that was probably it. Billy stepped down in the ditch to get out of the way just in the nick of time.

A black BMW came hurtling over a small hill in the road, becoming airborne for an instant before slamming back to earth. As it shot past Billy Joe, someone threw a large brown paper sack out of the passenger side window. The sack ricocheted off a pine tree and fell into a big briar patch.

Before Billy Joe could move, the sheriff came roaring past with his blue lights and siren going. Billy Joe watched until the two cars disappeared over the hill overlooking the lake.

Billy Joe used a long stick to retrieve the sack from the briar patch. It felt pretty heavy. He unrolled the top and opened it. Inside was a large plastic storage bag of white powder. It must've weighed close to four pounds. Now Billy Joe knew where the money to celebrate his birthday would come from. In fact, he would probably be able to celebrate quite a few birthdays to come.

Billy Joe took the bag about three hundred yards farther into the woods and shoved it up inside a hollow at the base of a big oak tree. Once one of Billy Joe's hounds had chased a coon into that hollow. That didn't sit too well with Billy Joe because the dog was supposed to be trailing a deer Billy Joe had wounded. Billy Joe wedged the bag up in the hollow with pieces of dead limbs that were lying around under the big oak. It was a shame to see such a magnificent tree dying, but whatever was causing the insides of the oak to rot would eventually kill the rest of it.

With visions of visiting one of the fancy ladies at Lonzo's spinning in his head, Billy Joe took a shortcut through the woods to the lake. When he got there Sheriff Hamilton had his pistol trained on two men who were leaning against the side of the BMW while his deputy, Arthur Monroe, frisked them. One of them was tall and thin with long greasy hair and a pockmarked face. The other one had reddish-blond hair and the build of a fireplug.

"They're clean, sheriff," the deputy said as he stepped back from the men.

Sheriff Hamilton swore, and then he noticed Billy Joe. "Come on over here, Billy Joe. I want to talk to you."

Billy Joe sauntered over while taking another look at the two men. One of them turned his head to look at Billy Joe.

"Boy! You keep that head down like I told you or I'll tear it off," screamed Sheriff Hamilton. The man looked down quickly.

"Billy Joe, did you see these guys throw anything out of that car when they came past you?"

"No sir, sheriff. I didn't see nothing."

"Hmmm. I was thinking they might have popped over that little hill and thrown something out before they realized you were there. That was the only time they were out of my sight long enough to get rid of anything. Are you sure you didn't see them throw anything out of that car? Anything at all?" Sheriff Hamilton asked, squinting his eyes and looking down his nose at Billy Joe.

"I'm sure, sheriff. What did they throw out?"

"Never you mind. Get along with your fishing. And I better not find out you lied to me."

It was a fact that Sheriff Hamilton didn't feel the need to be nice to you if you couldn't vote. He'd have probably been a little nicer to Billy Joe if he had known Billy Joe turned eighteen tomorrow.

Billy Joe went down to the edge of the lake and started casting for large-mouth bass. While he fished, he kept looking back up the hill to see what

Sheriff Hamilton was going to do with the two men. Billy Joe's plan depended on their paying him a finder's fee for returning their property, and they couldn't do that if they were locked up.

Billy Joe could see but not hear Sheriff Hamilton raising hell with the men. He figured the sheriff didn't have anything to hold them on or they would already be on their way to jail. Deputy Monroe started walking back up to Cedar Lake Road, looking along both ditches as he walked.

Two large-mouth bass and an hour later the deputy returned empty-handed. The sheriff spat a glob of tobacco and stomped around screaming at the men. He finally stopped ranting and wrote the tall one a ticket. The man signed the ticket; then they got in their car and drove away with the deputy following closely.

Billy Joe settled down to do some serious fishing. If his plan worked, it would be a couple of hours before the men would be able to shake the sheriff and return.

It was closer to three hours before Billy Joe saw the BMW come over the hill. By then he had enough bass to last a month. He reeled his line in, put the fish and his tackle in the burlap bag, and waited in the shade of a pine tree for the men to walk down to him.

The tall one wasted no time. "Where's our stuff, hayseed?" he asked. The short one just scowled and opened and closed his hands. Trying to look menacing, Billy Joe supposed.

Billy Joe shrugged his shoulders and played the country bumpkin. "I don't believe I know what you're talking about. If you lost something, I'll be happy to help you look for it. Is there a finder's fee for the person who finds it for you?"

"Don't be stupid, kid," the short one said, rolling his shoulders and moving forward zigzag like a boxer. "I'll knock your ass out, and you'll wake up on the bottom of that lake."

Billy Joe held up his right hand to stop him. "Before you do anything rash, I think you ought to take a look behind you."

The short one kept his eyes on Billy Joe while the tall one looked. Sheriff Hamilton's car was sitting at the top of the hill.

"Okay, kid. We play it your way," the tall one said. "How much of a finder's fee do you want? Five thousand enough?"

Billy Joe thought for a minute. If he was willing to offer five thousand, he'd probably be willing to go higher. "No, I want ten thousand dollars to help you find what you're looking for."

The two men looked at each other. Then the tall one said, "All right, but it'll take us a couple of hours to get the money together. How about we meet back here at midnight?"

"Fine," Billy Joe said. "You have the money; I'll have your stuff."

They went back to their car and drove slowly back up the hill past Sheriff Hamilton. While the sheriff was watching them, Billy Joe slipped into the woods that bordered the lake and started making his way back to where he'd left the bag. He didn't want to run into the sheriff again.

The sun hid behind a cloud, and a spring shower soaked Billy Joe as he ran through the woods. He rushed up to the hollow tree only to have his dreams come crashing down around him. The plastic bag and the paper sack it had been in were lying on the ground at the base of the tree, ripped to shreds. The rain had already washed away most of the powder, and what was left wasn't worth trying to save.

"Damn!" Billy Joe said. He must've trapped the coon in the tree, and the coon tore the bag to pieces getting out.

Billy Joe was not one to cry over spilt milk, but he knew those two guys were going to be mighty upset when he told them what happened to their powder. Come to think of it, they might not even believe him. Billy Joe thought for a few minutes and came up with what he figured was a pretty good plan to get himself out of this jam.

He set out for home at a jog. There was no time to waste. It was twilight and he was covered with sweat by the time he jogged into the yard. A few of the hounds barked halfheartedly at him. As he approached the house, he heard a low rumbling growl coming from under the front porch and he came to an abrupt halt.

"It's me, Boss. Good dog, good dog." Ignoring the hounds was one thing, but ignoring Boss was something nobody in his right mind did. Boss was Pa's catch dog, and Billy Joe along with half the surrounding county was scared spitless of him. Boss came out from under the porch and shook the dust from his short brindle coat. A massive brute, Boss was mean as a snake and feared neither man nor beast. A fact attested to by his tattered ears and the scars that decorated his muscular body. All the hounds gave Boss a wide berth.

Billy Joe stood without moving and let Boss sniff him to his heart's content. Boss had walked into the front yard two years ago, and while he acknowledged no owner, he showed no inclination to leave either. Visitors had to stand and be sniffed the same as Billy Joe. The only exception to this rule was Pa. And the only time Boss and Pa acknowledged each other's presence was when they hunted wild hogs together.

When Boss went back under the porch Billy Joe darted into the house and plundered through the cupboard until he found a brown paper bag like the one the coon had torn apart. But try as he might he couldn't find any of the large plastic storage bags.

He ran back outside, dragged his rusty old bicycle from behind the barn, and started pedaling down the road to town. Pa usually stopped off at Lonzo's for a drink after work or he could've probably borrowed his truck. It was just as well, Pa would've given him the third degree about why he wanted to borrow it. And if Billy Joe told Pa he needed to go into town to buy a box of gallon size storage bags, Pa would quite naturally want to know what he needed them for. It was not a discussion Billy Joe wanted to have.

Twenty minutes later and out of breath, Billy Joe dropped his bicycle outside Cutter's IGA Foodliner and rushed inside just as Mr. Cutter was getting ready to lock up. Fortunately, Mr. Cutter was in a hurry to get home to his supper and didn't bend Billy Joe's ear with stories of his youth as he normally did.

Billy Joe fidgeted while Mr. Cutter counted out his change and then, after what seemed like an eternity, he rushed back outside. With the storage bags clutched under his arm, he pedaled home by the light of the full moon. As he pulled up into the yard and stood for Boss's inspection, it dawned on him that he had forgotten to buy anything to replace the powder with.

Billy Joe tore through the house looking for something, anything, white and powdery, silently thanking God that Pa still wasn't home. Finally he found an unopened sack of flour in a cabinet and filled one of the plastic bags with it. The weight felt right. Maybe in the darkness, the two men wouldn't be able to tell the difference.

Pa still wasn't back at eleven when Billy Joe headed for Cedar Lake. Much to his dismay, Boss came out from under the porch and decided to tag along. Billy Joe didn't want to chance angering Boss by trying to shoo him back.

Billy Joe got to the lake about eleven thirty and got out of sight in the shadow of a large oak tree. The moon illuminated the clearing where the men would park their car, and from where he stood, Billy Joe had a good view of everything. Boss wandered off down by the lake sniffing the ground.

While he was waiting, Billy Joe had a disturbing thought. What was to keep the men from killing him and just taking the powder back? He racked his brain. How could he switch the powder for the money without getting himself killed?

The car topped the hill and pulled into the clearing. God! What could he do? Billy Joe could feel sweat trickling down his side. The two men got out and looked around for him. The tall one had a white cloth bag in one hand. Seeing the bag, Billy Joe decided to take his chances and stepped out of the shadows.

"Give me the stuff," said the tall one, pointing to the bag under Billy Joe's arm.

"The money first," said Billy Joe, trying to keep his voice from shaking.

"Guess again, kid," the short one said and pulled out a pistol. "Don't screw around with us if you know what's good for you."

"I'm-m-m not alone," said Billy Joe. "My friend is in the shadows. He's got a gun too!" Both men grinned and Billy Joe knew he hadn't fooled anyone.

The short one pointed the gun at Billy Joe. Billy Joe cursed himself for being such a fool and started praying.

Then from the shadows came a familiar low rumbling growl. Billy Joe stiffened. The two men turned toward the sound and the tall one said, "What the hell—"

Boss came out of the shadows running full speed, his hackles raised, his fangs glistening in the moonlight. He left the ground from ten feet away and hit the short man in the chest, knocking him into the tall one. Both men tumbled to the ground, and the cloth bag flew out of the tall man's hands.

Seizing the moment, Billy Joe dropped his brown paper bag, grabbed the cloth bag, and started running. He ran into the woods with the men's screams and Boss's snarls ringing in his ears. Billy Joe had no idea why Boss decided to attack and at that point he didn't care.

Billy Joe didn't stop running until he got home. Pa still wasn't there. He must really be tying one on at Lonzo's. In the security of his bedroom, Billy Joe opened the bag and breathed a sigh of relief. It was full of money. Ten thousand dollars just like they'd promised and all in brand new twenty dollar bills. They must have just drawn it out of the bank. Billy Joe hid the money under his mattress and fell asleep thinking about a certain redheaded fancy lady he knew who worked at Lonzo's.

The sun shining in his bedroom window awakened Billy Joe the next morning. He had a leisurely breakfast and took his second cup of coffee out on the front porch. Pa's truck was parked out front. Billy Joe hadn't heard him come in, but that wasn't unusual. Billy Joe was a sound sleeper.

About fifteen minutes later Boss came walking into the yard, no worse for the wear and tear. Ignoring Billy Joe, he went to his customary place under the porch to lie down.

Billy Joe got dressed and puttered around the house most of the day trying to figure out how to explain his new-found wealth. He knew Pa would want to know where he got the money when Billy Joe walked into Lonzo's that night. Billy Joe finally decided that since he turned eighteen today, and was legally an adult, he didn't have to explain anything to anybody.

About four that afternoon, Billy Joe showered, dressed, and put some of the money in his wallet. He had hoped to get a ride to town with Pa, but

Pa was still asleep. He figured that now that he was an adult it wouldn't look just right if he rode his bicycle into town. He decided he would hitchhike and was walking down the road when Sheriff Hamilton pulled off on the shoulder in front of him and stopped. The sheriff got out, the deputy stayed put. "Afternoon, Billy Joe," said Sheriff Hamilton, smiling.

The sheriff had never been nice to him before, and it made Billy Joe nervous. "Hello, sheriff."

"Got some news you might be interested in. You remember those two guys I stopped down by the lake yesterday, don't you? Well, it turns out they got killed by some drug dealers over in New Orleans. Seems they tried to sell them some flour. Imagine them trying something that stupid. Funny thing is, they were both covered with bite marks from a large animal. Isn't that odd?"

"Yeah, I guess so," said Billy Joe, wondering how much the sheriff knew.

"You know what else those guys were into? Counterfeiting. They made counterfeit twenties. Not very good ones. Not good enough to fool anyone who was paying attention."

Billy Joe's heart sank. Damn! All that money was counterfeit. There went his birthday celebration.

"Get in, Billy Joe," the sheriff said, smiling again and opening the car door.

"W-W-Why? What'd I do?" Billy Joe asked, trying to keep from panicking.

"Nothing. At least nothing I can prove. I saw you all dressed up and I just figured you were going to town to register to vote and needed a ride. I'm always available to assist my constituency, you know."

# Miz Sammy's Honor

### FLORENCE V. MAYBERRY

Every night at six I went for the milk. On the stroke of six. Miz Sammy was exact about this. Miz Sammy was exact about everything and everyone, with one exception. The exception was Old Drunk Tom Canady, her good-for-nothing husband. What she saw in him, only the Lord and Miz Sammy knew.

Except, maybe, me, only nobody ever asked me since I was only around nine years old. One time Miz Sammy was showing me her heirlooms in her parlor and she picked up this tinted photograph of the prettiest grown-up boy I ever saw. That boy had big blue eyes, curly black hair, pink cheeks, and a daredevil smile. I asked, "Is this your boy?" And Miz Sammy said, soft as silk whispering against silk, "No, no, I've got no children. This is Mr. Canady. Taken a long time ago, soon after I first met him."

Long time or not, it was hard to believe that pretty boy could turn into the bloated, whiskery giant I'd seen staggering around town. Some folks said he drank because he came out of white trash, was only a river boat cabin boy Miz Sammy had met up with that time she traveled by boat from St. Louis down the Mississippi to visit her folks in New Orleans. But along with that they did give a little sympathy for Old Drunk Tom, declared it could be a mite hard to live with high-handed quality like Miz Sammy, especially since her folks before they all died off never spoke a word to him after Miz Sammy married him. To Miz Sammy, they did, she was blood kin, but right in church one time her old daddy was heard praying out loud, "Thank You, Lord, for making my daughter barren."

Hard to blame the old man, my Grandma said afterwards, because Drunk Tom was just plain no good. If it hadn't been Miz Sammy was quality, and a scorcher when she was mad, Tom Canady might have been rode out of town on a rail. He was mean in a fight, all right, carried a big knife, but there were plenty of stout men in our Missouri River town could've handled him.

Persnickety as Miz Sammy was, once I got to her house on time and once she gave me to understand she had seen to it the milk was also ready on the dot, waiting in the cool downstairs in the cellar, she often took her time about telling Poncey, her Negro hired boy, to fill my pail. Miz Sammy liked to talk to me, and I liked to listen. Lots of times she showed me her heirlooms. She was mighty proud of being a Blair. "Good blood brings honor, and nothing's more important than honor. Mind that, Louisa. Honor. Pay your just debts, don't be beholden to nobody. I may have to sell milk by the pint to pay mine, but they're paid, once I know where they're at." She probably meant by this any stray debt she hadn't heard about, run up by Old Tom whenever he could talk some fool into trusting him. "Just remember, Louisa, always hold your head high by keeping yourself square with the world. We Blairs ended up poor as Job's turkeys, but we had honor. Or else."

"Or else what, Miz Sammy?"

"We disowned 'em," she said flatly.

I was known as a saucebox at home, and it was on the tip of my tongue to ask how this fitted in with Old Drunk Tom who didn't have anything, especially honor, what with charging up whiskey to Miz Sammy and getting her into debt she didn't know anything about. But maybe she figured if she finally found out and got them paid, why that kept Old Tom's head high.

I loved Miz Sammy's stories about the old days. About her granddaddy, Colonel Nelson Bedlington Blair, who had held a big chunk of the Missouri River country solid for the Confederacy. "He built this house, used to be a regular palace, parlor filled with fine furniture, handmade lace curtains on the windows, outside the lawn scythed smooth as velvet, parties with lanterns hanging from the trees, my mama decked out with real pearls, servants everywhere to take care of everything. And then that dratted war came. My granddaddy and daddy both fought in it."

She would sigh, and one night she said, "This house still has traces of that past time. In this very house, down cellar, there's a cell we never tore out, where granddaddy kept runaway slaves."

"Did your folks help 'em get free?" I asked.

"Land's sake, no! My granddaddy caught 'em, held 'em for their owners." Proudly, "We Blairs fought for the Confederacy, we were born and bred Southerners."

"I'm a Yankee," I said. "My grandpa freed the slaves. He did it in the Civil War when he was young. So if he'd been here then, he would have unlocked those slaves."

"Take your damned milk and scat home!" Miz Sammy shouted.

But that was just Miz Sammy's way. By the time Poncey got up the cellar stairs with the milk, she was feeding me sugar cookies and promising to show me the cell, iron bars and all, one of these days when she felt like climbing the stairs. Neither was I mad. All I cared about was getting a look at that cell. Imagine! Having your very own jail!

Miz Sammy was tall, close to six feet. She wasn't fat, but she was big. She had a proud lift to her head, and a figure that was all woman. Not that this meant anything to me back then. I was only nine and a girl besides.

Her blue eyes were wide-set. They could look deep into a person, but mostly they didn't. They just looked on Miz Sammy's own ideas. Her nose was straight and strong. And her mouth—I didn't like people hugging and kissing me, my mother said I was a "touch-me-not"—but I used to hope that sometime Miz Sammy would kiss me. Her mouth looked like if it kissed, the kiss would stay for keeps.

My mother said Miz Sammy would be handsome if she'd fix up. But lots of folks around town snickered about the men's clothes she wore when she worked in the cow barn or in the garden with Poncey. Behind her back, that is. Not to her face. When Miz Sammy got mad you could hear her cuss clear from her house surrounded by a two-acre lawn to the middle of town. Once when some white boys teased Poncey, she grabbed a couple and bounced their heads together. The fathers of the boys talked like they might join up and go have it out with Miz Sammy, but that never got farther than talk at the front stoop of the drugstore. Miz Sammy was the daughter of Judge Courtney Blair, who was the son of Colonel Nelson Bedlington Blair. Our town was named Blairsville.

I always liked it when Miz Sammy's stories concentrated on those days when she was still rich. Everybody knew Old Drunk Tom had used up the money her daddy left her. But some folks swore she still had the family's diamond rings, fine gold jewelry, even her mama's pearl necklace hid out in her cellar. That whetted me up to get down cellar, maybe find where the treasure was. But even more than that I wanted to see that slave cell.

On this particular late-afternoon, a hot summer evening when it hadn't rained for weeks, I ran to Miz Sammy's house, the milk bucket banging my bare legs. I stopped at the corner of the house and peeked around it to catch Poncey's signal. With Miz Sammy, it was as bad to be early as late. So Poncey always hung his red bandana on the outside knob of the back screen when it was exactly the time. Then, before I went inside, I would fold it up nice for him and hide it away.

The bandana was there, gently lifting in the breeze that was springing up. I tiptoed to the door, removed the bandana, and stuffed it down by the steps. Then I knocked on the porch screen and went inside.

The wooden striking clock on the shelf back of Miz Sammy's head said about a minute past six. Miz Sammy looked at the clock and then at me.

"Well, Louisa?" she said, then squinted her big blue eyes and leaned forward. "What's that blood doing on your hand, Miss? You fall and hurt yourself?"

Startled, I looked at my hand. Blood streaked the back of my fingers. "No," I said. "I didn't know it was there."

"No, *ma'am!*" Miz Sammy bawled. "What's the matter with your mother, not teaching you manners? Now that she's a widow, she ought to be learning how to be mother and father to you both and take you in hand."

"Don't you talk about my mother!" I said, banging the milk bucket on the table. I must have been a sight, skinny and freckled, my eyes glaring both mad and scared.

"I ought to blister you," Miz Sammy answered back, but very mild. "Go wash that blood off your hand. Poncey! Where did that dratted boy go? Poncey!"

I was standing by the window washing my hands and saw Poncey come out of his little cabin that was a few steps beyond the back porch of the big house. He had a white rag on his right hand with a big red splotch on it. Miz Sammy was hanging over my shoulder, looking too. When she spoke, no fight was in her voice. "I didn't know you were hurt, Poncey. You hurt bad?"

"No'm. Hit not deep, jist sprangled out."

"Come here and let me fix it. Right now, hear!" She turned to me with a curious, watchful expression. "How'd you get that blood on you, Louisa?"

I knew how. Off Poncey's red bandana. "I guess I got too hot running to be on time and my nose bled a little. I didn't carry a handkerchief."

She frowned. "Yes? Hum-m-m, well I'll pour out your milk and you better hike on home."

She took my bucket and opened the door which led to the cellar where the milk pans were kept in the cool. "Stay here, mind, don't follow me!" she ordered sharply and shut the door hard behind her. She was back up in a few minutes and came out on the back stoop to watch me go. I felt her watching me like it was a shove. She made me stiffen and get so knock-kneed I almost tripped.

That's why I noticed the blood, from watching how I stepped. Big scattered drops of it led from the stoop to the outside cellar door which slanted against the house foundation. The cellar door was padlocked. Beside the padlock there was a splat of blood on the white paint.

On the way home I had to pass the old brick church which had been built by the Blair family before the Civil War. It was so rundown, bricks at its corners sloughing away, that it was no longer used. In the early twilight it had a brooding, scary look, as though all the dead people who had once attended it were hiding inside in the dimness to grab anyone who intruded on their church. It didn't help to see the ancient slave cemetery in back of it, its few moss-grown grave markers sticking up like snaggle teeth.

I ran past the church. By the time I reached home, I was out of breath, and milk had trickled between the pail and its lid from being swung.

"Landamercy," Grandma said. "The Booger Man after you?"

My mother came out of our room, brushing her hair. I knew she and Grandma were fixing to go to a social. "That goose chase you again?" She meant the old gander who had staked out a bug patch at the end of our lane. "If you'd face up to that goose with a switch, you could drive him off. You can't go around all your life being afraid."

What I said next, I didn't mean to say. "You'd run too. Because somebody's just been killed in Miz Sammy's cellar."

"Law, law!" Grandpa said, and shook his head in mock wonder.

"Shame on you, making up such tales," Grandma said.

"If anybody got in Miz Sammy's way, I wouldn't put it past her," Mama put in. "But who'd be silly enough to do that? Except, of course, that good-for-nothing husband of hers."

"Hum-m-m." This was Grandma, a deep back-of-the-head look in her eyes. "I've not seen Tom Canady lollygaggin' around town for a spell. Wonder if he's been up to something?"

"Saw him three days ago," Grandpa said. "Was at the barbershop getting his face steamed and hair cut. Been on a bender."

"When ain't he on one?" Grandma asked. "Louisa, what's this about somebody killed in the cellar?"

"Well," I said, "not really killed. Poncey's the one who got cut and he's alive and Miz Sammy's fixing up his hand. But he came out of the cellar dripping blood. There's blood all over the yard."

"Did Miz Sammy act like something terrible happened, or just like Poncey cut his hand working around?"

"Well—"

"This child is an exaggerator," Mama said. "With her two things equal ten. And if a drop of blood was shed, it'd be all over the yard."

"Maybe yes, maybe no," Grandma said. "Wouldn't hurt a mite for us to stop on our way to the social and say howdy to Miz Sammy. She might like to come along with us."

"Miz Sammy! Go to a social!" This was Mama. "She'll likely be pitchforking hay to the cows in the barn."

"Then we'll just pass the time," Grandma persisted. "If we hurry there'll still be enough light to tell if blood's spattered around."

Then and there I gave up my idea of walking as far as town with them.

Maybe Poncey had washed away the blood. Maybe it wasn't his blood beside the cellar door, only browny-red spots of paint.

I hung around the front gate a few minutes after Grandma and Mama disappeared around a corner. Then I called to Grandpa that I was going up the street to play. He waved agreement.

I sauntered off, but once out of sight I ran. I cut back of the old church, had to slant across the edge of the slave graveyard, headed for Miz Sammy's cow lot near Poncey's cabin. The dark would help me hide if the grownups were standing around. And it was getting dark, faster than I liked. There was no moon and the stars only proved how dark the night was getting. At the corner of the church I ran blindly ahead. Next thing a murderous pain was in my foot and I was face down in soft spongy earth. I had tripped over a broken-off gravestone.

Fearful even to disturb the shadows, I didn't cry out. I lifted to one knee, hands crawling along the soft sod to gain support. My fingers fumbled over a soft cloth. I hung onto it for something to wipe off my feet and legs. Gone was my idea of eavesdropping back of Miz Sammy's house. I stood and stealthily retraced my steps. Still on the edge of the graveyard, back of the church, my bare feet stubbed on the hard, gritty ground.

As though it had waited for me to get near it, like a mean and clever dog at the end of a chain, a thought sprang at me. This earth I now walked over was hard and gritty, dry from lack of rain. But the sod around the gravestone I had tripped over was soft, loose. Why? WHY? Because that grave must have been dug up recently. Why? Nobody got buried there any more. So why would anybody want to dig up a scary old grave with a broken headstone?

Under the hanging street light near our house I brushed my arms and legs with the cloth I had picked up, froze in mid-action. It was Poncey's red bandana. Its blood was dry, didn't rub off on me. But what had Poncey been doing out in the graveyard after dark?

I threw the bandana into a gulley and ran home.

That night, late, it rained. Hard, with thunder and lightning. It puckered up again while we ate breakfast and rained more. I had been planning to tell Grandpa about that fresh-dug-up old grave and get him to go look at it. But with the ground everywhere a loblolly of mud and Mama insisting I was an exaggerator, not even Grandpa would pay attention.

At breakfast Grandpa asked Grandma and Mama, "You women find Miz Sammy last night?" He winked at me.

"The house was dark," Grandma said. "And so was the yard. We couldn't've seen blood splotches if they'd been there. We went around back because Miz Sammy sets in the kitchen most of the time, but if she was there, she never answered."

When the rain stopped I put on my overshoes and walked down to the old church to examine the grave I fell on. It and another smaller grave were straggled out of line with the main graveyard. A bunch of chopped-off weeds were strewed around it. But with the rain water running rivulets between the grave hummocks, everything muddy, the one I tripped over wasn't much softer than the others. I'd be called an exaggerator again. I should have kept that bloody bandana.

As I came down Miz Sammy's front walk early that evening, past the big scaly-white pillars of the veranda, around to the back door, my heart was beating fast. No red bandana was on the back doorknob. Poncey was even poorer than Miz Sammy. Likely had only one bandana, and I knew where that went.

"Come in, girl, don't let in the flies," Miz Sammy roared.

I went in. Poncey stuck his head from around the inside door to the cellar, said, "I gonna git it right now, Miz Sammy. Howdy, Miss Louizy."

I carried my bucket to the cellar doorway and stared past Poncey, trying to see below.

"All right, Louisa," Miz Sammy said sharply, "come sit right here at the table and wait. Hurry, Poncey."

Poncey vanished, shut the door solidly behind him.

The kitchen clock said ten to six. But for a wonder Miz Sammy paid no attention to the time. Just seemed in an almighty hurry to be done with me.

"Sit!" she repeated. "Now, don't bug those eyes out at me like a whipped pup. I baked some fresh buttermilk cookies, like to try a couple?" I nodded. Miz Sammy took two fat cookies out of a crock and handed them to me. I stared at her, and she stared at me. Then—I swear, it's the truth—she leaned over and lightly kissed my forehead.

"Well," she said, her cheeks real pink, which made her eyes look bluer than ever, "I'd like to know why I did that."

Before I had time to think up an answer, Poncey was back. He handed me my bucket, Miz Sammy took my money. With her other hand she pushed me out the back door. "I'll be right with you, Poncey," she said, and disappeared into the kitchen.

I stood on the steps, rubbing one foot on the other leg, thinking, dazedly, *Miz Sammy must like me, she must like me a lot.* Right after that I thought, *I sure would like to know what's in that cellar, I sure would.*

What pushed me into that second thought was, the outside cellar door wasn't locked. Its padlock lay on the ground beside it. Even a nine-year-old person might lift the door a crack, only a crack, and peek inside. And if that wasn't enough, the cellar was bound to be large enough to have hiding places. The door opening into the kitchen was at the middle of the house, the cellar entrance near one end. Even if Miz Sammy and Poncey came down to the cellar I could hunker down behind something.

I slipped around the corner of the house, hid my milk bucket in a shady flower bed. Whipped back, carefully lifted the slanted cellar door. Beneath it were shallow steps, a rough wall beside them blocking my view of the rest of the cellar. I raised the door higher, scooted under it, eased it down, tiptoed down the steps.

I was in a dim, hall-like corridor. Far down it, light from a high, narrow window revealed the corridor to be lined on each side with a series of alcoves. Odds and ends of furniture were stacked in one, boxes and trunks in another, a rake had fallen cattywise across the open side of another.

Where was the slave cell?

I tiptoed farther into the cellar, stopped as I saw a stair step angled into it, took a quick peek into the stair opening, and drew back. Miz Sammy stood at the top of the dim stairway. Poncey, a step down from her, his head blocking any view of me, was saying, "Hit's all right now, Miz Sammy, ever'thing quiet, hit's goan be fine for a spell."

I panicked, slipped across the corridor into an alcove, scrooged behind a ragged, busted-up sofa. Footsteps went up a step, the kitchen door shut.

A mouse skittered over a nearby board. I jumped into the middle of the corridor and was almost to the outside cellar door when I remembered I'd never have a better chance to see that old slave cell.

I tiptoed back. To left and right were the series of alcoves. Coal spilled from one. In another the faint light flickered on glass jars of canned fruit. The alcove with the rake held garden things, scythe, shovel, sacks of fertilizer.

And then I saw it. The alcove from which light filtered from the high, narrow window. This alcove was like the others, three heavy stone walls, no wall beside the corridor. But not open. Instead on that side were heavy iron bars, interrupted by an iron-barred door. The runaway slave cell.

I edged to it and stuck my nose between its first two iron bars. Inside was a cot, no other furnishing. A big man was lying on the cot. On his back, snoring, light from the high window touching his face. It was Old Drunk Tom Canady, Miz Sammy's no-good husband.

I said to myself, you better get out of here.

I ran back past the alcoves along the dim hallway and pushed against the slanted cellar door. It lifted slightly, then jerked against my thrust. It was now padlocked.

My breath whistled out. What would Miz Sammy, what would my folks do to me? What would I do if Old Tom woke up and saw me?

I took soft, sneaky steps halfway up the kitchen stairway and strained to hear movement. The kitchen was quiet. They had gone outside, found the cellar door unlocked, locked it. But maybe they would stay out awhile, give me time to slip through the kitchen, get outside, head for home.

A crack of light showed beside the door opening. Perhaps its catch was loose. I pushed it with my forefinger. The door swung open a few inches, and I almost jumped out of my skin.

There sat Miz Sammy at the table, her head on her arms, crying, her shoulders jerking. Horrifying, unreal. Like watching the Missouri River flood over its high bluffs to wash out the town. I caught the door's edge with my fingernails and closed it back to a crack.

Back down cellar I skittered to the alcove just short of the slave cell and across the corridor from it. This was beside the stairway, handy for escape. Also handy for Miz Sammy's milk pans, since a clean empty one sat on its broad shelf ready for morning's milk. I climbed up beside it so I could see better if Old Tom woke up. Too, I was hungry for the fading light from his window. I felt the cellar's dark creeping around me, ready to muffle me so not even a scream could be heard.

Whatever else could I do? I hated myself for being so little and stupid, with maybe no chance to grow up and get smart. Should I just stay hidden, wait for Grandpa and Mama to somehow find me? Or tiptoe right past Miz Sammy and take my chances on her skinning me alive?

Suddenly, from desperation, I saw what else I might do. I was small and skinny. The bars fronting the cell were about five inches apart. So were the three iron bars on the slave cell's window. I could slip through the cell's bars, shinny up the window wall, squeeze through the window bars.

But how climb about six feet to the window? The cellar walls were smoothed-off stone, no toeholds on them.

I recalled that board the mouse had scampered over, crept back to that first alcove I had explored, felt around until I found a stack of bed slats. I picked up one and went to the cell.

Old Drunk Tom still snored. I slipped the slat through the bars, sucked in my stomach, and turned sideways. My bottom snagged on one of the rusty bars and it rattled as I squeezed through. I didn't breathe for a minute, until a raucous snore released me.

The packed dirt floor of the cell was uneven, gouged out here and there. I found a handy rough spot beneath the window, braced the slat into it, put its other end against the window ledge. It formed a nice slanty climb.

On hands and feet, like a highbacked cat, I walked up the board until I touched the window ledge, steadied myself against its rough edge, reached with the other hand, and caught an iron bar. I let loose of the ledge and caught another bar. My full weight fell on them and I began to pull myself up.

Next thing I was sitting astraddle of the plank, two iron bars in my hands, splinters in my legs, and dried out, rotten concrete sprinkled over me.

A heavy movement came from the cot. I looked over my shoulder. Old Drunk Tom was sitting up, his figure shadowy and menacing. "Hey!" he said. He gargled and hawked in his throat. "Fetch me one a my bottles, young'un. Old Tom's dry."

Better Miz Sammy than him.

I jumped off the board and headed for the cell bars. Next thing I was muffled against Old Drunk Tom's chest, his sour filthy breath floating around my head. "Say, maybe you come here to steal my whiskey, huh? What you doin' in my house? No young'uns round here, you been stealin' I'm gonna thrash your—"

I screamed. A miserable nightmare scream, barely peeping out of my mouth. Old Tom grabbed my ear and twisted. "Shut up! Scream agin 'n I'll stuff it down your throat, cram it through your belly!" He took one arm from around me, grabbed my shoulder, and shook me like I was a puppy, then slung me on his cot.

"Whose young'un are you?" His voice was thick, like his tongue took up too much room.

I couldn't speak. "Whose young'un!"

"Myra Newport's," I whispered.

"Old Josh Clark's widowed girl Myra?"

The mention of my grandfather brought courage. "He's my grandpa. You better leave me be. My grandpa keeps a shotgun under his bed. Loaded. He'll shoot you!"

One hand snatched me up. With the other hand he fumbled under the thin mattress. I saw the flash of a knife. "Sass me, I'll cut out your tongue. Lyin' too, why would Josh Clark's girl be in my cellar? You're some gypsy girl sneaked in her to steal."

"Is too my gran'pa, my gran'pa, my gran'pa!" I babbled.

He hesitated. Straightened, swayed like a high wind had struck him. Steadied and shook me again, then slung me back. My head struck the wall. "Your ole gran'pap come after me, I'll cut him worse'n I cut Ponce! I got a belly full a being trounced around, locked up like some kinda animal. Looked down on like I ain't no man, just some kinda animal. I'm gonna slice my way outa this damn jail!" He began to yell, "Samantha! Samantha! Git here afore I kill this sneakin' young'un!"

A door above us banged against a wall. Steps pounded down the cellar stairs. And there Miz Sammy stood on the other side of the bars, holding a lamp high beside her face. "Louisa!" Her voice sounded like it was squeezed out.

Old Drunk Tom yanked me off the cot, pinioned my arms in front of him, put the tip of his knife against my throat. It pricked the skin. Stung.

"Tom, I'll let you out," Miz Sammy said quietly. "The key's in the kitchen, I'll get it. Set the child free."

Tom laughed. No fun in it. Deep, rough, like frogs inside him were trying to jump out. "No you ain't, you ain't gonna fool me no more. Onct this young'un's free, you'll take your time letting me out. You'll send Ponce for the constable, rouse up Josh Clark. Then I'll be nabbed onct I set foot outside. Neither you'll tell me where you had Ponce hide away my whiskey he stole, I won't git my whiskey. First you go bring me my whiskey, then mebbe I'll let go this young'un—"

"I'll get it," said Miz Sammy, turning toward the stairs. "There's a bottle in the pantry."

"Hold it!" he yelled. He laughed mean again, the frogs chunking up and down in his throat. The knife tip pressed at my skin. "Smart, ain't you? Allus been too smart, you and all them Blairs. But Tom's smarter. Thought you got all my whiskey outa that grave Ponce caught me scrabblin' in. Run off when I knifed him, but he come back later, dug up my bottles. Well, I got another hid back of you, over in them garden things. Got a bottle bedded down in a sack of fertilizer. Two more in that tub of shucked corn. You go git 'em, all three, or I'll slit this young'un's throat. Won't be my doin', it'll be yourn."

"Don't be a fool," Miz Sammy said coolly. "You do that, you'll end up not even drinking water. It's hard to swallow hanging from a rope."

"Woman, I got nowheres to go down, I already hit bottom. You reach me that whiskey or you'll have a murder in your hoity-toity damn house."

I felt squeezed into nothing as I saw Miz Sammy's broad shoulders droop like she just gave up. "Tom," she said. "Oh, Tom. What have we come to?"

This time his laugh lost its frog sound, sounded like a squawky trumpet. "Well, well. So I fin'ly got to show you who's boss."

"I reckon so," she said. "I'll go upstairs now and get the cell key. Then you bring out Louisa and get the whiskey yourself."

"No'm," said Old Tom, like licking on a stick of candy. "You'll not leave this cellar. You'll hand me them bottles. You'll poke 'em through these bars. This time I'm gonna drink in peace. I'm sick of drinkin' in jerks, scratching up a bottle at a time. Damn that Ponce anyway, spying, finding my grave hideout. Shoulda cut him for keeps."

"All right," Miz Sammy agreed. "But let Louisa go first. Louisa, how did you get in there?"

"I sc-scooted."

"Then scoot out. I'll fetch your bottles, Tom. When you have them, let the child go."

"Woman, I ain't crazy. This young'un's settin' right here 'til I drink my fill. Goin' no place, neither you. You kin set 'n watch."

"You're a fool! Josh Clark'll come looking for her. Any minute. She's expected home right after getting the milk."

"He comes messin' around 'n you call him in, me and this young'un'll both be outa here, her to Glory and me to hell," Tom said, mean. He flicked the knife's tip light and quick across my throat. It burned my skin in a fiery line.

Miz Sammy put the lamp nearer the bars, stared at me, her mouth tight in her white face. She turned, went swiftly toward the garden alcove just on the other side of the slave cell. There came the clatter of a spade or a hoe. She was out of our line of sight but now and again her shadow flickered on the corridor ceiling. I swiped at my neck, saw blood on my fingers. I was too scared to cry. I wondered if I could run fast enough, squeeze through the bars before Old Tom grabbed me. Knew I couldn't. Two of his big steps and he'd have me before I reached the bars.

In the alcove next door bottles clicked against each other. I thought I heard a splash, but wasn't sure: *Dear God, don't let Miz Sammy spill it all, he'll cut me sure if she does.*

"Git a move on!" Old Tom yelled.

And there came Miz Sammy against the bars, a bottle in her hand. She held it through the bars. "Where's t'other'n?" he demanded.

"Can't carry but one at a time with a lamp in my hand. And you can't drink but one at a time. Louisa's still with you, you've got what you asked for."

His laugh was almost a giggle. "Outsmarted by your ole man, huh? All that damn honor you brag your feisty folks left you with don't count for much tonight, does it? Set that bottle on the floor. Inside." She did. "Young'un, pick it up." I did.

Old Tom held the bottle in one hand, me with the other. "Uncork it," he ordered, then sniggered. "Maybe I oughta give her the first nip, Samantha, so she'll be more friendly." Miz Sammy drew a sharp breath, her face spooky in the lamplight. Nothing about her looked alive except her eyes.

I struggled with the cork, my fingers like rubber bands. Old Tom swore, shoved me toward the back of the cell. "Git in that corner and stay put. You run, I'll stick you."

He stood in the center of the cell. Uncorked the bottle, tipped it, took a long swallow. "Hell of a taste, musta turned on me. Been hid too long."

He grinned, said, "But a second swaller always kills the first." He drank again.

He spat. Strangled, coughed. Dropped the knife, grabbed his throat. Staggered to the cot and fell on it.

"Louisa! Scat out of there!" Miz Sammy's voice was like a whipcrack.

Tom groaned. "What's in this, what'd you gimme?" He croaked, gagged. The cell smelled awful, with sweat and sour stomach. I slipped through the bars.

"Run for Doctor Masters up the street! Hurry!" Miz Sammy ordered. "Tell Poncey come help me! Tell him Tom's poisoned, we got to pour salt water down him." She looked savage, as though she hated me. "Scat, you little meddling fool! He's dying!"

He did die. That night. Miz Sammy had put a dose of bug poison in his whiskey, figuring to give him just enough to get me free. She and Poncey washed him out quick as they could, and the doctor ran down with his stomach pump. Doctor Masters testified to the police that the dose was mild, ought only to have made him sick enough to let me free, he had such fast treatment. But according to the autopsy, Old Tom's stomach, already half eaten up with whiskey, had been in no shape for bug poison.

There was never any question about Miz Sammy being exonerated. It was barely considered even any kind of manslaughter, what with everybody in town trying to shake her hand for saving a child. As for the child, well, you better believe that's the last milk I was ever sent for. Only ones happy about that were me and the old gander.

Miz Sammy on her part wouldn't shake hands with anybody. Kept swearing she was guilty of murder, tried to get her lawyer to set up a trial. Said it wasn't honorable for her to go free, asked if it had been Old Tom poisoning her instead of the way it was, would he have gone free?

Weeks later, Poncey found Miz Sammy down in the slave cell. Dead. Lying on Old Tom's cot, a broken glass on the floor beside it. Bug poison again. This time a strong dose and nobody to rinse her out.

A sealed envelope addressed to Poncey was beside her. It read, "This is for Poncey Jones from Samantha Blair." Poncey was afraid to open it. He got Doctor Masters to do it. Inside was a heavy gold ring with a big diamond in it. A carat or more. Her daddy's ring.

That was all the Blair jewels ever found.

# First Week in September

### JEAN LESLIE

In Wyattsville the first week in September traditionally belongs to the Pioneer Society. Everyone dons a costume reminiscent of the early days when the town was the last wagon-train stop on the way to the gold fields, the men grow beards, and there is a kangaroo court held on the lawn in front of the courthouse. The real feature, though, is the rodeo. It draws such a big crowd that any one visitor goes unnoticed. No one paid any attention to a Mrs. John Metcalf who registered at the Californian on September third and checked out on the seventh, the day that Andy Wyatt put a gun in his mouth and blew off the top of his head.

Had he been questioned (which he wasn't) the desk clerk at the hotel might have remembered Mrs. Metcalf as a soft-spoken middle-aged woman who asked a lot of questions about the town's history. It is possible that old Mr. Pruitt, owner of the variety store, and Miss Tait, an elderly saleswoman in the Emporium, also would have recalled her. Both had given her a great deal of information about the leading citizens of the community, especially those who bore the Wyatt name. These seemingly casual conversations were forgotten in light of the shocking news of Andy Wyatt's suicide. No one—then, or later—associated her presence in Wyattsville with his death.

My first knowledge of Mrs. Metcalf came on the morning of September sixth when Velma put through a call to my desk. I heard her say, "Mr. Wyatt is out, ma'am. I will connect you with his secretary." A pleasant voice said, "Hello? Will Mr. Wyatt be in his office later today? I would like to make an appointment to see him."

Wyattsville isn't really "small town" any more, but most of us act as though it were, so it was quite natural for me to volunteer the information that Friday was Kid's Day at the rodeo and Mr. Wyatt would be staying for the whole program because he had two sons and five nephews entered in the various events. To make up for lost time, I said, he would be in his

office Saturday and could see her at five o'clock. She had to be content
with this, and I noted the time of her appointment on my desk pad and
on Andy's.

Those Wyatt boys took a total of eight firsts, three seconds, and five
thirds, and the biggest barbecue in town that night was at Andy and Laura
Lee's home where there were more than forty men, women, and children,
not one of whom wasn't a Wyatt by birth or marriage.

In spite of all the celebrating, Andy was in his office at nine o'clock on
Saturday morning and worked straight through until one, when John Bart-
lett came by to take him to the club for lunch and nine holes of golf. My
standing appointment at the Delta Beauty Salon always has been for three
o'clock on Saturday, so before I left the bank I went in and turned on
Andy's tape recorder. This is used at my discretion: when I'm not able to
be there to take notes, or when my presence in the room would be an
embarrassment. I listen to it later and decide what needs to be tran-
scribed. The recorder is in a lower desk drawer and the pickup is in the
desk lamp which always stands just about halfway between Andy's chair
and the one occupied by the person who has come to see him.

On this occasion, quite frankly, I wanted to know what Emil Sondergard would have to say about the route of the new freeway because of a
piece of property I own. His appointment was for four thirty and I was
afraid I wouldn't be back in time. As a matter of fact, my roots needed a
touchup and it was nearly five when I let myself into the bank. Emil's car
was in the parking lot and Andy's door was closed so I sat down and typed
a letter to the Chamber of Commerce saying Andy would be glad to pay
for three trees on the east side of Sacramento Avenue, "same to be spaced
evenly in the 150-foot strip north of Cabrillo Street and parallel with the
property owned by the Wyattsville Farmers and Merchants Bank."

The big clock over the entrance said exactly five o'clock when Mrs.
Metcalf tapped on the glass door and I went through the bank to admit
her. She was a trim, well-cared-for fifty or fifty-five; smartly, but not ex-
pensively, dressed in a lavender linen sheath, with matching pumps and
handbag, and a bandeau of violets which fitted snugly over her short grey
hair. What impressed me most was the fact that she looked cool, which is
quite a feat in Wyattsville in September. She seemed well at ease.

"Mrs. Metcalf?" I smiled and held out my hand. "I'm Sylvia Sommers,
Mr. Wyatt's secretary. You're new in town, aren't you?"

"I've been here a few days."

"One of our new teachers," I guessed.

"Yes. Is Mr. Wyatt ready to see me?" she asked.

"Not quite." I locked the door. "Come back where you can sit down.
He shouldn't be long." In my office we talked about Pioneer Week and

the marvelous record set by the Wyatt boys, and then the buzzer sounded. Emil Sondergard had left by the door to the parking area, the one we referred to as Andy's "escape hatch," so I took Mrs. Metcalf in and introduced her. "Unless you want anything else, Mr. Wyatt," I said, "I'll leave now."

"Nothing more, thank you." Andy smiled. "Will we see you at the Rodeo Ball?"

"No. Phil's in San Francisco this weekend." Phil Smart is the man who usually takes me to civic affairs.

"You can go with us," Andy suggested.

"Thanks, but no just the same. I'll see you Monday."

I stopped at the supermarket and bought a T-bone steak and a can of asparagus (you develop a thing about the fresh vegetable when you live where it grows and have to breathe the peat dust) and then walked on to the Delta Arms where I have lived all the years since I went to work as Andy's secretary. There are newer apartments, with pools and other attractions, but the Arms is within walking distance of the bank and it's air conditioned. More than anything else, it's sweet home to me.

After fixing a gin and tonic and leaving it to chill, I went in and took a shower and put on slacks and a shirt. It must have been seven thirty when Laura Lee called to ask if I knew where Andy was. They were already past due for the Bergens' cocktail party and had to be at the Lambertsons' for dinner at eight thirty. She reminded me (unnecessarily) that it was important they be on time because the dinner guests were all civic leaders whose appearance in time for the Grand March was obligatory. I promised her that I would go down to the bank and see if Andy were still there. I remember saying, "Wherever he is, Laura Lee, I'll find him and send him home."

I found him in his office, but I couldn't send him home. He was sprawled in his chair, staring open-mouthed at the acoustical tile ceiling. Bits of him adhered to the wall behind him and his gun lay on the carpet under his left hand.

Habits of efficiency are a great help in a crisis. The Wyattsville High School's marching band was to assemble in our parking lot, so I drew the curtains and made sure the "escape hatch" was locked. Then I picked up Andy's phone, which is left with an open line after Velma closes the switchboard, and dialed Chet Bergen's number. Someone answered and kept shouting "Hello? Hello?" over the background noise of a large and lively party. The answerer either closed a door or carried the telephone to another room because when he spoke again I could hear him distinctly and recognized his voice.

"Dr. Collins?" I said. "This is Sylvia Sommers. Can you come to the bank right away? Without saying anything to anyone? It's very important."

"Andy?"

"Yes. He's dead."

"I'll be there."

"He sure as hell did it himself," Corby Collins said. "Nobody gets a guy to open his mouth and take a slug like that." He looked down at the gun again. "I never knew Andy was left-handed."

"He was taught to write right-handed, but he attended so many service club luncheons that he had to learn to eat right-handed in self defense. Actually, he was a southpaw."

"That's right," Dr. Collins nodded. "He played golf and tennis left-handed." He gave a deep sigh. "You might as well call Bill," he said.

Bill Dean is our chief of police and one of Andy's oldest friends. I reached him at home. "Bill," I said, "this is Sylvia. I hate to be the one to tell you this, but Andy committed suicide. Dr. Collins and I are at the bank. Can you come down, alone, without saying anything to anyone?"

I hung up and fumbled in my purse for cigarettes and lighter. "You'd better talk to Laura Lee," I told Dr. Collins. "They already have missed the Bergens' cocktail party, and she's afraid they'll be late at the Lambertsons' dinner." Hearing my own words, I knew I was in a state of shock. "Well, somebody has to tell her *some*-thing!" I said desperately.

"You have to," he said gently. "If I call, she'll get the wind up and think he's had a heart attack. I wish it were only that!" He took a turn around the office and came back to stand in front of me. "Just say he isn't here, and that you'll phone around and see if you can locate him."

"But this just isn't like him!" Laura Lee wailed. "What should I do, Sylvia? Shall I go on or wait here?"

"You'd better wait," I advised. "I'm sure you'll hear something soon."

When I had cradled the phone, Dr. Collins said, "Indeed she will. Poor Laura Lee. I've coped with some heartbroken widows in my day, Mrs. Sommers, but I have a nasty feeling that tonight is going to set some sort of ghastly record."

"Shouldn't you get in touch with Mr. Tuttle?" I asked.

Corby Collins gave me a quick look of appraisal. "Very good thinking," he said dryly. "Who was it who said that behind every successful man was a clever woman, or words to that effect? Perhaps I'm just now learning what made Andy tick. I assume you know where Mr. Tuttle can be reached."

Incredibly, my watch showed that it was not yet eight. "They will still be at the Whitmans'." As I finished dialing the number there was a sharp, metallic rap on the front door. "That will be Bill," I said, and handed the phone to Dr. Collins.

The street light showed the comfortable bulk of Bill Dean's silhouette. When the door was opened he stepped inside and gripped my hands. "In heaven's name, why did he do it, Sylvia?" he asked.

"I don't know," I whispered. "That's what makes it so awful. I don't *know!*"

He asked the same questions of Corby Collins, and the doctor said, "It wasn't his health. You can rule that out. He had a physical every six months. So did Laura Lee. I checked them in July before they went on their vacation and they were in excellent shape."

There was a peremptory rattling of the big front doors and I went through to admit Mayor Tuttle. "Where's Corby?" he demanded. "What in hell is this all about? Why'd he call me away from—"

"Andrew Wyatt has committed suicide," I cut in coldly. "Come into his office, please." Addison Tuttle is ruthless and ambitious, qualities that make him a man to be reckoned with, but certainly endear him to no one.

Bill sat with his face in his hands, unashamedly weeping. By contrast, Ad Tuttle walked around Andy, apparently needing to assure himself that Wyattsville's favorite son was no longer a threat to his political future. Satisfied, he turned his long, thin-lipped face toward Corby Collins. "Incurably ill?" he asked.

"No. Nothing so convenient. I just told Bill and Mrs. Sommers that I had given him a complete physical in July and his health was fine."

The mayor's small, pale eyes swiveled around to me. "Anything here at the bank that could be considered—*irregular?*"

"Nothing," I said positively.

"Another woman?" he asked. "Anything like that?"

All of them looked toward me hopefully. "Of course not," I said. "I'm surprised you would even ask."

"But if there had been," he persisted, "you would have known, wouldn't you?"

"I suppose so. I was responsible for his deposits and withdrawals, and there was never a transaction which couldn't have been reported in the *Sentinel.*"

"An extramarital relationship doesn't have to involve money," Mayor Tuttle pointed out. "It could be someone we all know."

"In *Wyattsville?*" Dr. Collins' laugh was a short, derisive bark. "It would have been common gossip."

"I suppose you're right," Ad Tuttle conceded. He dragged at the lobe of his ear, then said, "See if there's a bottle in the desk drawer, Mrs. Sommers. All of us could use a drink."

Andy never would have a bar in his office, but he kept a fifth available. The bottle was about two thirds full. I got four paper cups from the dispenser beside the bottled water, and the mayor poured two or three ounces into each. There was an awkward pause after we picked them up, and then Bill Dean cleared his throat loudly and said, "To Andy. A really great guy."

"The greatest." Ad Tuttle took his whisky in one long swallow and dropped the empty cup into the wastebasket. "But dead. Why did he have to pick the first week in September?" He began to pace up and down the office, his long chin thrust out and up. "What we have to watch now is how this story breaks," he said. "If we can keep it under wraps for a few hours the Rodeo Ball will go off as scheduled. Then if it is in the morning papers, our final day should be terrific! I'll go to the Lambertsons' and talk to Drew," he decided. Drew owns the *Sentinel*. "Good thinking?" He tapped his temple and grinned at us.

"Very good," Corby Collins said. "We've been long on that tonight, if somewhat short on sentiment. I'm going to talk to Laura Lee."

"Do that," Ad urged. "And work out some plausible explanation for them missing the ball." He did not see the withering glance the doctor gave him because he had turned to Bill. "Ev Grant can be trusted, can't he?" he asked. "Call the mortuary and tell him to pick up the body after ten—*after ten*, mind—when everybody will be in the auditorium."

When I came back from letting Mayor Tuttle out of the building I was grateful to see that Bill had brought the bottle into my office. "You mustn't blame Ad," he said, filling two paper cups. "It's that kind of clear thinking that has made him what he is in Wyattsville. Here," he handed me my drink, "let's you and me drink to the Andy we knew. We can include the high school class of '42 and our first year at Cal, or we can just say the hell with it and drink to get drunk."

Bill and I had gone through school together from kindergarten on, just as Andy and Laura Lee had. The difference was that the two schools were on different sides of the track, so to speak, and we had to go to Wyattsville High before the four of us could rub elbows. Maybe we wouldn't have even then, except that Andy and Bill were outstanding football players and Laura Lee and I were pompom girls. Quite often we doubled after a game and went to a sock hop in the gym or had a hamburger and a malt somewhere. We became a regular foursome when we went to the University. All of us knew plenty of people on campus, but not as well as we knew each other.

Bill and I sat and talked about those days while we waited for ten o'clock and Ev Grant. "That first semester at Berkeley was really great," he recalled. "I guess I was the one that broke us up when I took the night job at the Dixie Diner. It was nice eating regularly, but it sure cut into our dating. And to this day," he added, "I can't stand ham or yams or corn-bread."

"Your working evenings was only part of it," I said. "Remember that Laura Lee spent Christmas vacation with that Tri-Delt from Piedmont and came back sure that she was in love with the girl's brother. How long did that last? Two months? Three?"

"I've forgotten. Long enough for Andy to get into the habit of coming around and crying on your shoulder." Bill finished his drink and stared into the empty cup. "I was jealous as hell. Did you know that? It took a lot of growing up before I could realize that you had been Andy's salvation."

"In what way?"

"If Andy hadn't had a real friend to turn to," Bill said slowly, "he could have dropped out of school, or he could have been snapped up by some smart girl who saw a chance to catch a rich rube on the rebound. You tided him over until Laura Lee came to her senses."

It was while I was consoling Andy that Bill had started dating Rosalie, who also worked the late shift at the diner. Rosie was the daughter of a Fresno farmer and had never been out of the San Joaquin Valley until she received a scholarship to the university. Unsophisticated she may have been, but she knew a good man when she saw one, and by June she was wearing a little garnet ring that had belonged to Bill's grandmother. By then, too, Andy and Laura Lee were pinned, and I had Sam Sommers' two-carat diamond and a wedding band.

Sam was the finest man I ever knew. We never met on campus because he was in his last year of law when I was a freshman. It took an afternoon during Easter Week at Carmel to bring us together. Neither of us cared much for jazz or the dates who had brought us there, so we got to talking and then took off on our own. We found a little coffee house in Monterey and, after that, a seafood place. Then we drove for hours through the Carmel Valley, each telling the other all there was to tell. It was dawn before we got back to the apartment where I was staying with five other girls from Cal. Standing beside his car he took my hands in his and asked me to marry him and I said I would and he kissed me for the first time. It was a wonderful marriage, but it didn't last long because Sam was one of the earlier casualties of the war. I stayed with his parents in San Francisco until 1948 when Father Sommers died. Mamma Sommers sold their wholesale grocery business then and went to live with a daughter in Santa Rosa. Having nothing to keep me in the city, I went back to Wyattsville on an exceptionally cold and foggy morning in February. Bill and Andy both had fine Navy records, both had been married for some years, and both had children. That was how things stood when I went to the bank and applied for a job. Luckily, the secretary Andy had inherited from his father was retiring and I took her place.

There was a discreet knock on the door that led from Andy's office to the parking area. "That will be Ev," Bill said heavily. "I'll take care of this part of it."

"Go with him, Bill," I asked.

"Sure? What about you?"

"I have some things to do so that tomorrow won't be too difficult for Laura Lee and the others."

"Don't stay here too long." His big hand closed on my shoulder, and then he dropped his keys on my desk. "Leave these over the sunvisor," he said. "I'll pick the car up later at your place."

I tried to close my ears to the macabre sound of Andy being wheeled out of the bank. Ev left by way of the alley, and then I went through to make sure Bill had locked the escape hatch. Andy wouldn't need it again. Not ever. The room had a terrible, unearthly stillness now that he was gone. It was then that I became aware of the faint hum of the tape recorder. I turned it off, and then something—cupidity, perhaps—made me wonder what Emil Sondergard had said about the freeway. I rewound the tape, turned up the volume, and heard Andy say, "Is this attempted blackmail, Mrs. Metcalf?"

I went back to the point where he asked me if I was going to the Rodeo Ball and I told him Phil was in San Francisco. There was the sound of a door closing as I left with nothing more on my mind than trying to remember which supermarket had the special on steaks.

Now I heard the faint squeak of Andy's swivel chair as he settled into it. "Well, Mrs. Metcalf," he said affably, "what can I do for you?"

"For me, Mr. Wyatt, nothing." She had a low-pitched voice and spoke in a manner which my mother would have described as "refined." "But for someone in whom we have a mutual interest there is a great deal you can do. What significance does this date have: November 22, 1941?"

After a long pause, Andy said, "None. Should it?"

"Yes. It is the birthdate of an illegitimate child which you fathered."

"That's nonsense," Andy stated flatly. "The most charitable view I can take of your allegation is that this is a case of mistaken identity."

She went on as though he had not spoken. "The mother's name was Mary Skouros. Six weeks after his birth she relinquished him, and my husband and I adopted him. We chose him for several reasons: he was healthy and handsome, we had confidence in the adoption agency, and paternity had been acknowledged. At that time, Mr. Wyatt, natural parents were not permitted to know where their child had been placed but adoptive parents were given full particulars, including the names of the mother and father. That child is an adult now, and in need of advantages which only you can give him."

"Is this attempted blackmail, Mrs. Metcalf?"

" 'Blackmail' is a very ugly word. I prefer to think of this as a mother's earnest effort to assure her son's future. My husband and I took a child you were willing to recognize as yours, but for whom you were unwilling, or unable, to assume responsibility. We had great plans for him, but Mr. Metcalf died when Jack was seven. On a schoolteacher's salary I could not give him many of the things my husband would have provided. I did, however, see to it that he made maximum use of his abilities and education so that he received an excellent scholarship at Berkeley. He graduated with honors and had a creditable service record."

"I congratulate you," Andy said, dryly. "Having done so well by this boy, why do you come to me now?"

"Because his incentive has been my promise that I had an old friend with money and prestige who would give him the kind of start which would carry him wherever he wanted to go."

"Does he know he is adopted?"

"No. Nor does he resemble you or any of the other Wyatts. I went to some pains to establish this fact. Here is his picture."

There was a considerable pause and then I heard Andy give a little grunt which might have been an expression of amusement. "No," he agreed, "he certainly doesn't resemble my family. His mother must have had the dominant genes. And now, Mrs. Metcalf . . ." his voice flattened and hardened ". . . suppose I call this blackmail, whether you like the word or not, and tell you to get the hell out of here. What would your next move be?"

"I would leave, of course," she said quietly, "but I would be back in a few days, with Jack. I have a teaching position at Wyattsville High School and I am certain Jack could find employment. He's very adaptable. Probably he could sell cars for your brother Conrad, or men's furnishings for Abner Wyatt. There are many possibilities."

"You've thought of everything, haven't you?" Andy said.

"I hope so. If, on the other hand, you elect to take him into the bank and advance him in every way possible in this community and this state, I believe he will be a credit to both of us."

"If—if—I give him a job in the bank, will you promise to stay out of Wyattsville, Mrs. Metcalf?" Andy's voice was harsh.

"No. Whatever you decide, I will be here to see that my son's best interests are served."

"Of course. I might have expected that." I could hear the little *thud,*

*thud, thud* that meant he was letting a pen or pencil run through between thumb and finger and then reversing it. "If I do anything for this boy," he said, "it will not constitute an admission of any sort."

"No admission is necessary," she reminded him. "Paternity is a matter of record in the form of a letter from the adoption agency which I have in my safe deposit box. Now, please write a letter to Jack which I have come prepared to dictate."

A drawer was opened and slammed shut, and as she talked I could hear the angry scratching of Andy's pen. " 'Dear Julia,' " Mrs. Metcalf said, " 'It was good to see you again after so many years. I was impressed with your son's records, academically and in the service. I feel sure he can go far in Wyattsville.' New paragraph. 'He is a very fortunate young man to have a mother so dedicated to his advancement.' Sign it, 'Cordially, Andrew Wyatt.' "

Andy laughed. It was a curiously light-hearted laugh. "I'm glad you've given his mother full credit," he said. "If he succeeds, I'm sure she will be on hand to take her bows. Now, how do I address this infamous document?"

"I resent that remark." For the first time her voice betrayed emotion. "My life has been devoted to this boy and I see nothing wrong in letting him know he is indebted to me. I intend to be a part of the success he will enjoy, and I expect him to feel that rightly I *should* be."

"The address, Mrs. Metcalf?"

"Send it to me: Mrs. John Metcalf, Box 1123, San Francisco. I'll mail it before my bus leaves at six fifty. I have a stamp."

"I was sure you would have."

"This," Mrs. Metcalf said, "I shall consider a guarantee of your good faith, and I will have no further worry about Jack's future."

"You need have none." Andy's voice had the deadly quality which he reserved for special occasions. "You have the boy's feet planted firmly on the economic ladder and he will be booted up it as high as he is capable of going, not because of any threats you have made, but because he is a Wyatt. Now, *get out!*"

There was some unidentifiable sound—an outraged gasp, perhaps—and then I heard a door close. I leaned over the tape, willing it to yield something more; but there were only small noises—the creaking of his chair, muted car horns from the street, something which might have been an epithet muttered through clenched teeth, and then the opening and closing of a drawer. Ten minutes later there was a sharp report of the gun and the muffled sound as it struck the floor.

I played it all back again and then I went to my typewriter and wrote:

*Dear Mr. Metcalf,*

*No doubt you will hear of Mr. Andrew Wyatt's death before learning that his last act was to assure you of a position with the Wyattsville Farmers' and Merchants' Bank. This is a commitment which the family will wish to honor. Please arrange to be here on Monday, September 14, at 3:00 P.M. for an interview.*

*There is an excellent opportunity for advancement in this community, and in the years to come I am sure your mother will have reason to be very proud of you.*

*Yours very truly,*
*Sylvia Sommers*

In the San Francisco directory I found a Mrs. John B. Metcalf and a John B. Metcalf, Jr., listed at the same address on Clay. This seemed appropriate for her income so I sent the letter there. It afforded me satisfaction to imagine her wondering how I knew of her conversation with Andy; how much, in fact, I knew about Jack.

In the safe in Andy's office there was a metal box for which he and I had the only keys. I took it out and went through the contents carefully. There was a considerable amount of cash, an exquisite diamond and emerald necklace which Laura Lee had seen and admired and which Andy had subsequently purchased as a surprise for her on her birthday in October, birth certificates for all of them, and two tape recordings which could bring Ad Tuttle's little political empire tumbling down in ruins. I took the tapes, and the things which were mine: the baby's identification bracelet, a larger one that read "Mary Sylvia Skouros Sommers," a plastic envelope that held a downy feather of dark hair, and the twenty-three stock certificates which had been Andy's penance candles.

He gave me the first seven of them on November 22, 1948. "Money's no substitute for a child," he said bluntly, "but it's one hell of a nice thing to have. These cost five thousand dollars each." He fanned them out on his desk. "They'll appreciate. Hang on to them, Sylvia, and one day you'll be a woman of property."

"You don't have to do this," I said.

"I know that. Let's say I do it for the same reason I give Laura Lee jewels. She's the only woman I've ever loved, and you're the only one I ever wholly trusted." And then he said, "There'll be another of these each year."

They had appreciated, and I am a woman of property. I put all of these things into my handbag together with the carbon of my letter to Jack, the carbon paper I had used, and the recording made that afternoon. What-

ever was left in Andy's office or mine was anybody's business, and would
be tomorrow.

I posted the letter to Jack Metcalf and drove on to my apartment. The
night was soft and still, and by contrast my apartment was too cool and
too quiet. I turned off the air conditioner and opened a window. The band
at the auditorium was playing a medley of old nostalgic tunes, and when
the clock struck twelve the musicians drifted into "September Song." I
hadn't cried in more than twenty years, but I cried now with noisy aban-
don. I wept for dear, good Sam who had begged me to keep Andy's child
and had given him a name which I refused to give to the adoption agency;
and for Andy, who did not love me but needed me, and who paid—finally
with his life—to keep the Wyatt escutcheon unblemished; and for my
son, whom I could not claim, and would not again disclaim; to whom I
would always be, as I had been to his father, just a trusted and loyal friend.

# The Witch
# of Wilton Falls

## GLORIA ERICSON

As I scanned the rest of my mail, I absentmindedly opened the one letter my secretary had left sealed, thinking it might be personal. Absorbed as I was, I failed to notice the return address, so its message came as rather a shock: *Since we could find no evidence of next-of-kin, and you seemed to be her only correspondent and visitor, we thought you would want to know that Miriam Winters passed away quietly in her sleep on the 25th.*

The sun pouring through the Venetian blinds of my office seemed suddenly chilled. I had been standing while I opened the letter, but now I sat, swung the big leather chair around, and gazed out the window. So she had died—at last. *Her only visitor.* I wasn't even that. When was the last time I had seen her—five years ago? Six? I remembered receiving a card from her this past Christmas and making sure Meg sent one in return. How lonely she must have been these last years. Suddenly I was filled with the worst kind of remorse—the kind you feel when someone's gone and it's too late to make up any neglect.

I was only a kid, no more than sixteen, when they let Old Man Winters out and, since I was the one responsible for his release, I went around that summer swaggering like a damn hero. It wasn't until later that I came to think differently of myself. I haven't been back to Wilton Falls in a good many years, and I wonder if they still tell their kids and their grandchildren about that summer. I wonder if they still tell it the wrong way, too—making Miriam Winters out to be some sort of witch. Well, they're wrong. She wasn't a witch. I talked to her enough later (*too* late) to know.

Swinging my chair back to the desk, I looked at the letter again. It was strange, but I was probably the only living person who had ever heard the full details of her side of the story. Certainly the newspapers had never given her her due. They were too busy making sensational copy out of the horror she had perpetrated—and it *was* horror. I have never denied that, or condoned what she did, but it was my fate to get a more rounded picture than anyone else, and so I always have felt differently about Miriam Winters. . . .

Miriam stopped to wipe the perspiration from her brow. There were two more shirts to iron. Harry was due home tonight, and he'd ask about them first thing. He had a lot of shirts, enough to last him four weeks on the road while an equal number were being done up at home. A salesman had to be well-groomed, Harry always said. Still, it seemed that he took more shirts than necessary. Miriam, after her first blunder, never mentioned it when she found lipstick or powder smudges on any of them.

She looked fearfully at the clock over the kitchen sink. Why had she waited until the last minute? Well, it had been a difficult month. Bobby had been sick, and then she'd had so many of those awful headaches. Ever since Harry had knocked her against the stove the last time he'd been home, she had been bothered by the headaches and that funny confused feeling that came over her from time to time. She put down the iron and rubbed her head. She didn't mind the headaches so much, but worried about the confused feeling. She wondered if she blacked out at such times and fervently hoped not. Bobby was pretty self-sufficient for a four-year-old, but who could tell what he would do if he found his mother unconscious someday?

Fortunately she had just put the final touches on the last shirt when she heard Harry's car drive into the old barn behind the house. He came banging in—a big man, a good twenty years older than Miriam—set down his luggage without an answer to her quavering "hello," and went out again. He returned with a couple of paper bags which he carefully placed on the kitchen table. Miriam's heart sank. It hadn't been a good trip, then. She could always tell by the amount of whisky he brought back with him to ease the few days' rest at home before he started off again.

"I have your supper all ready," said Miriam, poking at the pots on the stove.

Harry, fussing with the seal on one of the whisky bottles, stopped only long enough to glare at her. "My shirts done?"

"Yes—oh, yes—all of them. Now just you sit down and I'll dish out your supper."

He grunted and seated himself heavily at the wooden table.

Two hours later he was wildly drunk.

He would not allow her to go to bed, and although she was able to avoid his drunken lunges for a while, he finally had her backed into a corner. The whisky fumes of his breath and the feel of his fumbling hands at her clothes sickened her. "No, no, H-Harry . . ." Her voice involuntarily rose in a crescendo.

Then there were other hands plucking at her, and she looked down at Bobby. Aroused by the noise, he had come weeping into the kitchen. "Mama, Mama," he said, trying to pull her away.

Miriam swallowed and tried to speak calmly. "You must go back to bed, Bobby. Come, I'll take you."

But Harry held her firm. "You'll do no such thing. You can just stop being the damn mother for once. When a man comes home from the road he wants a little comfort—a little wifely comfort." Then to the child, who still clung, "G'wan, dammit. Get to bed."

But the weeping child did not move, and swift as lightning the big hand of the man swung out. The body of the small boy seemed to fly through the air before landing in a crumpled heap at the base of the sink. From the gash on the forehead blood spurted first, then flowed in a horrible red sheet down the face of the child. His mouth opened but no sound came out.

Even Harry seemed stunned by the sight and made no move to stop Miriam as she tore from his arms with a strange animal-like sound. The child's breath had come back, and his sobs mingled with hers as she rocked him in her arms and sponged at his face with a wet dish towel. There was no hope of outside help in this emergency, for there was no phone and Harry was too drunk to drive to a doctor. The house itself was isolated, situated as it was on the edge of a meadow. Beyond that stretched a wooded area. The nearest neighbor, Miriam knew, was at least a mile away.

Finally, thankfully, the flow of blood lessened and then stopped. As Miriam gently swabbed her son's head, she noted how wide the gash was and how frighteningly near his eye. Tomorrow morning she would have a doctor look at it, but now bed, probably, was the best therapy. She picked the child up and went past Harry, who had again settled himself at the table, silently drinking. She improvised a clumsy bandage, and tucked the still faintly sobbing child in bed. He did not want her to go, so she sat on the edge of the bed until, with a last convulsive shudder, he allowed himself to be overtaken by sleep.

She went quietly back to the kitchen. Harry had succumbed finally, and sat sprawled at the table, his head on his arms. Miriam shook him, but when he did not respond, she went to the knife drawer and selected the largest, sharpest knife she had. She shut the drawer and went and stood behind her husband, hefting the knife, gauging the angle of thrust that would be best . . .

It was odd. Her role in life up to this minute had been that of follower.

She was ever stumbling after some stronger-willed person, often hating it but never knowing how to break away; indecisive. That's why it was odd that suddenly she should know just what to do. She didn't have to agonize over her decision or consult someone else. Harry must be done away with. It was *right*. She *knew* it.

What stayed her hand, then?

A haunting phrase from her childhood Sunday school: *Thou shalt not kill?* An awareness of how difficult it would be to dispose of a dead body? Perhaps. But more probably it was the sudden image that flashed across her mind, an image of herself behind bars and Bobby alone. Murderers were always caught, weren't they? She had made no plans to cover her "crime," nor had she any belief that even if she did, the police wouldn't find out sooner or later. She was not *that* clever—merely right.

Slowly she lowered her hand. Perhaps she could not kill Harry, but he must be restrained in some way—the thing tonight was too close. Miriam shivered as she recalled the bloodied face of her child. No, just as wild beasts must be killed or locked up . . .

Locked up? She thought a moment. Of course. That was the answer. The big old house with its large expanse of fenced-in grounds had been purchased less than a year ago from former kennel owners. They had been breeders of Great Danes, as a matter of fact, and in the cavernous cellar one area had been sectioned off with sturdy cyclone fencing set in concrete. The area was about nine by nine feet, with the fencing extending even across the top. This "cage" had been used for whelping bitches and their puppies. Harry in such a cage would never be able to hurt Bobby or herself again.

She stared at Harry's bulk. Tomorrow she would wonder how she had been able to drag such a heavy man across the kitchen, down the cellar steps, and into the cage, but tonight she merely knew that it must be done.

Harry stirred and moaned once or twice in the tortuous journey but never fully awakened from his drunken stupor. Perspiration trickled down Miriam's back and between her breasts, and by the time she had hauled her unconscious husband into the caged area she was wringing wet. A wooden platform, raised a few inches from the floor, took up a portion of the cage. Apparently the dogs had slept on this. Miriam went upstairs and dragged two blankets from their bed and threw them in on the platform. Then she closed the cage door. There was a heavy padlock on the latch. She clicked it shut. She had no key for it, but that did not matter because she did not expect to open it again—ever.

The first few days were terribly noisy, of course. It was fortunate the house was so isolated or surely Harry's bellows of disbelief, anger, and frustration would have been heard. Miriam took Bobby to the doctor the next day to have his wound attended. The doctor was aghast and wanted to know why she hadn't come when it happened, and how *did* it happen?

"He fell against the latch of the sink cabinet last night and it would have been too difficult to come all this way on foot in the dark. My husband isn't home with the car," Miriam lied, confident that Bobby would not refute her story, and he did not. He was a quiet, obedient child, solemn beyond his years.

When they returned from the doctor's, they could hear Harry's shrieks of rage as they walked in the door. Bobby shrank against his mother. Miriam sat down on the straight chair near the door and took her son onto her lap. "Listen, Bobby, you mustn't let those noises in the cellar bother you. It's only . . ." She paused a moment, suddenly thinking of a different approach. "You remember those fairy tales we were reading the other night?"

Bobby nodded.

"Do you remember the one about the prince being turned into a frog?"

"Yes . . ."

"Well, something like that has happened, I think, to your father. He has been turned into a bear, a great shaggy bear, as punishment, I imagine, for not—for not being more kind. Well, anyway, he's in a cage in the cellar so he cannot hurt us."

Bobby's eyes were round. A particularly loud bellow rose from below at this point, and the child trembled. "He—he c-can't get out . . ." he quavered.

"No." Miriam's voice was firm. "He absolutely can't get out—and after a while he'll probably stop making so much noise." She slid the child from her lap and stood up. Then she added, "By the way, Bobby, you mustn't tell *anybody* at *all* about this, or they will make us let him out."

Glancing down at him, she saw his eyes widen with horror at the thought. She smoothed down her dress, satisfied. Bobby would never tell.

Miriam allowed three days to pass before she went down to Harry. He was lying down, seemingly exhausted by three days of shouting, but at her approach he sprang up and clutched with trembling fingers at the heavy cage meshing. Miriam stopped a few feet from the cage and set down on the floor the plate of food and shallow bowl of milk she was carrying. Then, as if repeating something she had rehearsed many times, she picked up a broom that lay nearby and shoved first the plate and then the bowl toward the "gate" of the cage, which cleared the floor by about three inches.

Harry's lips twitched. "All right, you, what's this all about?"

She did not answer but continued to shove the food toward him.

Harry's voice was shrill. "Dammit, Miriam, let me out! Miriam—Miriam, do you hear me . . ." His voice became uncertain. Her silence seemed to unnerve him. Was this the same woman whom he had browbeaten so long? The same woman who had heretofore quaked at his every command? He tried again, a conciliatory tone suddenly in his voice. "Listen, Miriam, I admit you may have a beef. Look, I know I had too much to drink, but you can't keep me locked up here forever, can you?"

She answered him then. She straightened up and looked with her unblinking clear blue eyes into his. "Yes," she said.

He was taken aback. "W-What?"

"Yes," she repeated. "I can keep you locked up forever. I can and I must." She indicated the food with her foot. The two dishes were half under the gate. "Here's some food. I'll bring you more tomorrow night." Then she turned and started up the stairs.

He was apparently shocked into silence for a moment, but then an outraged bellow of venomous anger escaped him. "You'll never be able to get away with it, Miriam!" he screamed. "People'll find out. Don't you realize, you idiot, you can't get away with something like this. You'll be arrested . . ."

The young woman on the stairs continued ascending as if she heard nothing. At the top she switched off the cellar light and shut the door carefully, quietly, behind her.

Every evening she took him food, seldom speaking herself, letting his increasingly hysterical screams of abuse cascade over her with no comment. When the stench in the cage became unbearable she employed the same means of cleaning it the former kennel owners apparently had used. She coupled a hose on a nearby spigot and hosed off the cage floor, the water and filth easily channeling themselves into the slight gully in the cement floor outside the cage. The gully led to an open drain in the floor, and this she kept sanitary by a periodic sprinkling with disinfecting powder. Several times a week she also slid a shallow basin of soapy water in to him so that he might clean himself if he wished.

As the weeks passed, Harry's vilification, his threats, became less. He tried a new tack. It was just a matter of time, he assured her. His company would be checking up soon. And, anyway, how long did she think she could hold out by herself? How would she live? How would she earn money? If his questions did not seem to disconcert her, it was only because she had given those same questions great thought herself.

For instance, Miriam had already telephoned Harry's company. She was sorry, she told them, but her husband had taken another job and wished to terminate his employment with them. As Harry had never been one of their better salesmen, they were not overly upset. Fine, they said, they wished him luck, but would he please send back his sample case and stock book. Miriam said she'd see that they were in the mail that day, and they were. Thus the company, which the man in the cage so desperately counted on to start a hullabaloo over his disappearance, quietly washed its hands of him.

The weeks immediately following Harry's incarceration were idyllic ones for Miriam and Bobby. They went to the nearby fields to pick wild strawberries, they frolicked in the woods. Never had Miriam been so happy. Her childhood had consisted of one indifferent foster home after another. Her marriage to Harry, which she had thought would be an escape, had merely had the effect of putting her in a new foster home with a new foster parent—and a more brutal one, at that. But now she was free —free for the first time in her life. Even her headaches and that confused feeling seemed to be bothering her less. In the fall Bobby would be starting school, and she must then consider her future. Harry's remarks about her inability to support herself were not lost on her, but there was enough money in the savings account for the present, and she was determined not to worry about anything until the fall.

In the fall her decision not to worry was completely justified because things fell into place beautifully for her. Old Mrs. Jenkins, the town librarian, died, and Miriam, ever a lover of books, applied for the position. There were few applicants for the job, and Miriam, although a comparative newcomer to town, made by far the best appearance. She was quiet, neat, and seemingly conscientious. Also, her implication that her salesman husband had abandoned her didn't hurt her chances. If anything, it aroused the town board's sympathies, and they gave her the job. The position didn't pay much, but Miriam's wants were few: merely enough money to maintain Bobby and herself and to feed the "Shaggy Bear" in the basement. The latter epithet had become particularly appropriate, for Harry had grown quite a beard and there were times when Miriam had difficulty recognizing the shaggy lumbering creature in the cage as her husband—so much difficulty that she soon stopped trying. He was merely the "Bear" who must be fed nightly and ignored as much as possible the rest of the time.

Ignoring him became more difficult during the winter months, for a change came over him. Until then he had been an abusive, vilifying creature, shaking the cage mesh violently, slamming his metal dishes around, screaming deprecations upon her head. But one night she went down with his food to find him holding onto the mesh and whimpering. He saw her, and a great tear rolled down his cheek and glistened on the rough beard. It was followed by others. The Bear was crying! "Miriam, Miriam," it sobbed.

How strange that a bear should know her name. But then, she must remember, it really was Harry in that bear suit.

"Miriam, please—please set me free. I know I haven't been good to you, but I promise I'll go away and never bother you again. Just set me free . . ." Great sobs shook the creature's frame.

Miriam felt tears well up in her own eyes. She was a sensitive person and could feel great sympathy for this caged creature. Carefully she set the dishes down for the Bear. "I'm sorry," she said softly before turning back to the stairs.

That night she had difficulty sleeping. What sadness there was in the world! How sorry she felt for that poor Bear. If only there were something she could do to ease his unrest, but of course there wasn't. Many was the time in the years to come that she had to remind herself that, sorry as she was for the Bear, there was nothing she could do about it, really.

Bobby, destined to grow up in such an unusual household, knew without asking that he must never bring boys home from school to play with him. His friends soon came to accept this eccentricity, just as the townspeople came to accept the fact that their sweet-faced librarian, although friendly enough at the library, lived a rather hermit-like existence with her son, and never asked anyone to visit.

Surely Bobby could not have long believed the father-turned-into-a-bear story. There must have come a day when curiosity overcame him and he peeked into one of the cellar windows. While still quite young, he may have been fooled by the sight of the shaggy creature, thinking it really was a bear, even as his mother had come to think of it as a bear. But as he grew older he must have looked again and known, and knowing, what could he do? Go to the police? Have his father, whom he only dimly remembered as a bellowing brute, freed? And where would his gentle mother be sent? To a jail—to a madhouse? No, no. He did not know—could not *afford* to know —what was in the cellar.

However slowly the years may have passed for the Bear, they passed quickly enough for Miriam and Bobby. Grammar school. High school. *War!* War was in the air. Hitler was marching through Czechoslovakia . . . Poland . . . Then Pearl Harbor. Bobby enlisted the next day in the navy. He kissed his mother's tearstained face and hugged her comfortingly. It would all be over soon, now that he was in it, he said to make her smile, but she did not smile. Her whole life was leaving.

Miriam told the Bear about it that evening. Over the years she had developed the habit of sitting outside the cage in an old rocking chair in the evenings when Bobby was at a basketball game or at some other school activity. She enjoyed chatting with the Bear—now that he had learned not to talk about the possibility of his freedom and instead quietly listened to her tell of things in the outside world: Bobby's athletic exploits, incidents at the library, and so on. It was quite cosy, really. She had placed an old floor lamp next to the rocker and sometimes she would read aloud from books she brought home from the library. The Bear seemed to appreciate that. This evening, when she told him of Bobby's leaving, he seemed most sympathetic.

"Miriam," he said, his voice rusty with disuse, "l-let me out now. Let me take care of you while Bobby's away."

She looked at him, stunned. After all this time and he still didn't understand—still could bring that up! Sorrowfully she got up from the rocker, snapped off the lamp, and started up the stairs. At the top she shut the door quietly but firmly on his pleadings. After all these years he still didn't understand that you don't let wild beasts loose. No matter how sorry you feel for the lions and tigers in the zoos, and no matter how tame they seem, you just don't go around letting them loose on society.

Soon there were long newsy letters from Bobby, which she read to the Bear at night. (He had apparently learned his lesson after his last outburst and had become more docile and quiet than ever.) It didn't seem long at all before Bobby was home on his first leave, healthy, bronzed, wonderful to look at. Miriam wished the Bear could see him.

Bobby used his leave to good advantage, too, by painting the house and making other repairs that were needed. The morning before he left he stood staring out the kitchen window. Miriam went over to him, and he looked down at her thoughtfully. "Mom, I noticed some kids cutting across the back lot yesterday. The fencing must be down back there."

Miriam nodded. "I dare say. After all, it's pretty old fencing."

Bobby shifted his weight and frowned. "I don't like it—kids cutting across the property. I'm going to town today and get some new posts and barbed wire."

He worked all that day and until it was time for him to leave the next evening. He came in hot and sweaty, but looking satisfied. "I put 'No Trespassing' signs up and strung the fencing real tight. I'd like to see any kid get through all those strands of barbed wire." He came over and put his arm around his mother. "It'll be good for years, Mom. Long after I come back . . ."

But he didn't come back. She was at the library when the telegram arrived. Everyone was terribly kind. There were offers of lifts home, but she refused them all, preferring to walk the two miles by herself—the last mile over the now overgrown private road that led to her house. She did not break down until she had sought out the Bear, and then she slumped down on the cold cement outside his cage and sobbed over and over, "Bobby's gone, Bear. Bobby's gone." Through the heavy wire mesh the claw-like fingers with the unclipped nails pushed, as if trying to stroke her. Tears rolled down the shaggy beard, but whether the Bear was shedding tears over the loss of his son or over the futility of his own life is not known.

Life goes on. By spring Miriam had come to accept with a kind of dull resignation Bobby's passing. She continued her job at the library, of course, for without Bobby's allotment check she was again the sole support of herself and the Bear. Bobby's insurance money she did not touch. Someday she might be unable to work and would need it.

The days in the old house at the end of the overgrown road established themselves in a seldom-varying pattern. The Bear had become quite trustworthy, and on weekends when the weather was nice Miriam even dared open from the outside the small window over his cage. It gave her much pleasure to see him rouse himself from his usual slump on the wooden platform and stand directly under the open window, inhaling great breaths of fresh air. Sometimes he would suddenly fling his arms up but then as suddenly drop them as they contacted the meshing on the top of his cage. Sometimes he rose on tiptoes as if straining to see out, but of course he could not. Often she brought him bouquets of flowers picked from the meadow, and he seemed to like that, burying his face in the blooms and sniffing hungrily. She was glad to do these things, for she had become quite fond of him, really, and more and more her prime concern in life became his comfort and contentment.

The years, one by one, passed slowly, quietly by. There were a few times of crisis, of course—the time the Bear was so sick, for instance. It was sheer torture for Miriam to listen to him call out hoarsely for a doctor and know that she could not possibly get one. She could do nothing but pray, and eventually her prayers were answered. The Bear stopped sweating and moaning, finally, and began to get better. Then there was the time she herself was sick. It was one summer during her vacation. She was too ill to go to the doctor and had no way to summon him to the house, nor would it have been advisable for her to do so even if she could for, as keeper, she was in a sense as much a prisoner as the Bear. The fever raged through her for several days and the only thing that kept her from succumbing was the distant sound of the Bear's plaintive calls. It would be so easy just to let go and die, but she could not. The Bear was hungry—needed her . . . So she fought, and lived to see the Bear fall upon the food she finally weakly brought to him. It was worth the fight.

Perhaps the worst time of all was when the pan of hot grease caught fire in the kitchen. With frantic efforts she managed to put it out, scorching her arms quite badly in the process. It was not the pain in her arms that left her trembling, though, but the thought of what might have happened had the fire spread. The Bear would have been trapped, burned alive. The thought left her weak. She wracked her brain for a solution to the possibility of such a thing's happening again, and suddenly remembered that Harry, her former husband (she had not thought of him in years), had owned a revolver. She went upstairs and found it in an old cupboard. She felt much better. This way the Bear was assured of a quick, merciful death.

The time the furnace broke down required even more ingenuity on her part, and the coffee she offered the Bear at that time was heavily laced with sleeping pills. When he fell into a deep, drugged sleep she threw dropcloths over the cage, ranged discarded furniture against it, and called the repairmen. The men worked for an hour over the furnace, completely unaware that within a few feet of them a creature, once-man, slept.

And the years ticked on . . .

I was kind of at loose ends that summer I was sixteen, anyway. Having lost my mother and father in an automobile accident only a few months before, I was spending some time with my grandfather in his "hunting shack" at Wilton Falls. My grandfather was a judge downstate and normally used the shack only once or twice in the fall for hunting, but this year he had taken time off in the early summer and come up with me. Guess he thought some fishing and general rambling in the woods would be good for me; get my mind off my loss.

I was out in the woods by myself that day, though, when I came across the rusted barbed wire that surrounded the Winters place. I tested it with my foot and it gave way. Nimbly I leaped over the broken strands and soon found myself in a choked meadow, on the edge of which perched a weatherbeaten Victorian house. I regarded the apparition with surprise. Was it occupied? Probably not; much too neglected-looking. I sauntered over to observe more closely, and then bent to peer through one of the cellar windows. The cellar was quite dark and it was a moment before my eyes accustomed themselves to the feeble light. Almost directly under the window there was a cagelike arrangement, with a hulking shape in one corner. A shadow? No, it seemed to move, and suddenly I was looking at a matted tangle of hair, out of which stared the deadest, most vacant eyes I had ever seen. My heart gave a sickening lurch. What I was seeing was impossible. I stayed a moment longer, as if riveted by those terrible dead-man eyes. Then the shaggy head turned away and I was released—released to run across the sunny unreal meadow, over the broken strands of barbed wire that tore at my clothes, through the adjoining woods. I had slowed down somewhat by the time I reached my grandfather's cabin and was a little ashamed of myself. After all, I was no kid—ye gods, I was *sixteen*—

and here I was running like a scared rabbit. Then the memory of those eyes returned in full force and I felt cold sweat pop out all over me.

My grandfather, looking strangely unjudgelike in his plaid shirt and denim pants, was fussing at the stove when I came in. "Hello there," he said. "I was wondering where you were. Lunch is almost ready."

I stood, my back against the door, still breathing hard. "Gramp," I said, and there was, despite myself, a quiver in my voice.

My grandfather looked up then. His glance sharpened. "Something the matter, son? You look upset."

I tried to wave my hand deprecatingly but failed in that gesture, too. "Gramp, who lives in that big old house at the edge of the meadow?"

My grandfather frowned. "At the edge of the meadow . . . Oh, you must mean Mrs. Winters' place. Why?"

"I was just over there now and I saw—"

"Over there? That place is posted. You shouldn't have gone there."

"But the fencing is all rusted and I didn't see any No Trespassing signs . . ."

"Well, maybe the signs *are* too weathered to read any more, but every-one around here knows it's posted."

"Well, I didn't know, and I looked in one of the cellar windows. Gramp, there's something in a big cage there. A—A man, I think it is . . ."

My grandfather pulled out a chair and seated himself at the table. "Now, let's hear this from the beginning. What are you talking about—a cage, and a man-you-think in it?"

I told him the whole thing, but I could see he wasn't convinced.

"You're sure your eyes, and imagination, weren't playing tricks on you, son? I mean, everyone knows Mrs. Winters lives there all by herself. She's had a very tragic life, actually. First her husband abandoned her and she had to bring up their son all alone. Then he was killed in the war. I wouldn't want any wild rumors circulated by a grandson of mine to hurt her."

"But it's no wild rumor, Gramp, it's *true*. Please, Gramp, you've got to go look yourself."

I guess the urgency in my voice decided him. He stood up. "Okay. Best to squelch this now. You'll see it was just your imagination . . ."

By nightfall all Wilton Falls was in a state of shock. The police had sawed off the old padlock and led a stumbling, half-blind Harry Winters into the fresh air of freedom, and the town's gentle middle-aged librarian had been taken into "protective custody." She did not seem to mind. Her only concern seemed to be that "The Bear" be taken care of. When assured that he would be, she went along docilely enough. Actually, both of them were taken to the county hospital for observation—but to different wings.

How the town did buzz the next couple of weeks. The story made even the downstate papers with a banner headline: HUSBAND KEPT IN CAGE 30 YEARS BY WIFE. Under my picture it said: *He dared to look in the Witch's dungeon.* Under Mr. Winters' picture it said: *Caged like a beast for 30 of his 75 years.* And under Mrs. Winters' picture: *The Witch of Wilton Falls— She turned her husband into a "Bear."* It was all pretty heady stuff for me, being hero-of-the-hour, as it were. But then I looked more closely at the pictures of Mr. and Mrs. Winters and suffered my first feeling of disquietude. They both had the look of puzzled children on their faces as they were led away.

Miriam Winters, of course, was sent to the state mental hospital, but deciding what to do with Harry Winters was more of a problem. The county psychiatrists had difficulty testing him due to his refusal (or was it *inability?*) to talk, and finally came to the frustrated conclusion that although his mind had undoubtedly been affected by his imprisonment, he was harmless enough, and could be released to proper care. But what was "proper care"? There was a great outcry against sending him to the county home, for it was felt that in the few years that were left to him he deserved to be "free." The public conscience was stirred on this point and it was finally arranged that the old man go back to his own house. A volunteer committee of townspeople was set up in which one member every day would check on the old man, bring him groceries, take away laundry, etc. Part of the volunteers' duties included "socializing"—but that aspect was dropped as soon as it became evident that Harry Winters had no desire to chat with *anybody.*

Just what did Harry Winters' freedom mean to him after all those years? I found out, unfortunately, one hot August night about six weeks after his reinstatement in his old home. I had been into town and decided to take a shortcut past the old Winters place on the way back. As I approached the house, I noted that it was unlighted except for a faint glow from the cellar windows. I recalled rumors I had heard in town. Nothing in the house ever seemed disturbed, they said—even the bed not slept in. Could it be that after all these years Harry Winters only felt comfortable sleeping in his cage and returned there each night?

Stealthily I crept up to a cellar window and peered in. In the dim light I could make out the outlines of the cage. Next to it was the rocking chair that Miriam Winters had used, but it was a moment before I realized that the hulking shape nearby was Harry Winters himself. He was sitting on the floor with his chin resting on one of the rocker's arms. There was a familiarity about the scene which I could not at first place, but then it came to me. In my grandfather's house there was a large painting in one of the bedrooms called *The Shepherd's Chief Mourner*. It showed a large dog mournfully resting his chin on the draped coffin of a deceased shepherd, his master. The sudden analogy between that painting and the tableau below sent a shaft of pain to my heart. I could not stand to see more, but as I prepared to rise, the mourning hulk suddenly moved. The shaggy head raised up, the throat arched, the mouth opened, and from it rose a cry of such utter anguish, such complete despair, that my hands flew instinctively to my ears to shut it out. But I could not shut it out. Again and again it came—a cry of longing—the longing of a tame bear for its gentle keeper.

I ran then. Even as I had once fled over a sun-choked meadow, now I flew over a moon-silvered one. This time, too, I was chased by horror, but this time the horror was of my own making and I knew I would never be able to outrun it.

They found Harry Winters the next morning in his cage—dead. His heart had given out, they said.

It was after my grandfather and I went downstate that I began to have the nightmares, though. Perhaps I cried out during them, because one morning at breakfast Grandfather remarked quietly, "I hope you don't feel guilty about reporting Miriam Winters, son. It *had* to be done."

I nodded my head. "Yes, I know . . ."

My lack of conviction must have shown, for my grandfather became emphatic. "It's time we laid this ghost away," he said. "You and I are going to the state mental hospital to see Miriam Winters."

Although I went reluctantly, the visit turned out to be surprisingly pleasant. Miriam was delighted to have company and chatted cheerfully. She had heard that the Bear was dead, which was sad, but then, she added philosophically, he was pretty old. She knew that if he became sick again she would have to put him to sleep permanently anyway.

My grandfather looked at me pointedly at this revelation. Surely I needed no more proof that we had done the right thing in reporting the Winters affair. From his standpoint the visit was a success, but in a way it backfired, for Miriam was a kindly, warmhearted woman. She said I made her think of her son Bobby, and she hoped I'd come to see her again. To my own amazement I found myself promising I would.

And I did, many times. Was it my way of assuaging the faint guilt I still felt over disrupting the Winters couple's strangely compatible life together? I don't know, but I do know that in chatting with her I gradually learned the full story of the events leading to Harry Winters' imprisonment.

I went to my grandfather. "She shouldn't be in a mental institution," I complained. "She's not really insane, except of course about the 'Bear,' and he probably caused that insanity, beating her and all . . ."

My grandfather stared at me and sighed. "That ghost is still not laid, hmmm?" He thought a moment. "The county home in Wilton Falls is a well-run place. I'll see what I can do."

Miriam was transferred to the county home three weeks later, and I felt more at peace than I had for a long time. I still went to see her, but less frequently, as it was a longer run up to Wilton Falls. Then I went away to college—later began working—got married—moved farther away. Visits became replaced by letters, letters by a Christmas card, and now . . .

I looked down at the letter in my hand. Now there would not even be any need for that. Miriam Winters had paid her debt to society, and presumably society was satisfied. But I knew that, for my part, could I but relive that long-ago summer day, this time I would stare into the almost-blind eyes of Harry Winters and go quietly on my way.

# The Perfect Victim

### WILLIAM BANKIER

**D**igby Staples looked into the kitchen where his landlady was watching porridge. "Mrs. Peterson, would it be all right for me to invite a friend next weekend? She'd stay in the front room." His heart was pounding. The decision was made, he was now embarked upon his campaign to murder Adelaide Dow.

"She pays, she stays." The tiny woman lifted a plug of boiled oats on the end of a wooden spoon. "Want some breakfast?"

"I'm due at the bank," Digby said, hitching his white linen cuffs, adjusting the knot in the Hawaiian tie. "I'll grab something on my way." A brick-orange cat was positioned like a cookie jar on the counter. It nuzzled toaster crumbs as the boarder tweaked its ear. "So long, Punkin." The cat acknowledged its name with a rasp of tongue on the back of Digby's hand.

"You were going to pick up a bottle of Van Holst," Mrs. Peterson called as he went out the door.

Having lived and worked most of his life in Albany, Digby Staples was still getting used to Algonquin Landing. Mrs. Peterson's house was on the east side of the lake. As he headed for the bridge, he could see a mile away across flat water the cluster of buildings that made up the town's commercial center. On the bridge, walking fast, he looked down the lake past the yacht mooring to the pier. Beyond, wooded hills threw a ragged profile against the sky. Not quite hidden by pines were colorful roofs indicating where the rich people lived. The pier was low to the water, a dark straight line, ending abruptly like an implied threat.

Digby went into The Corner and picked up a large coffee to go and two jelly donuts. The man behind the counter had once been a pro boxer. His name escaped the bank teller, but the face was familiar. Digby took one of the donuts from the bag and ate it on his way along the street to the brass-plated doors of Eastern Conglomerate Bank. What a relief to walk inside this establishment and not feel panic and depression. What a change from the bank in Albany, and the cruel supervision of Adelaide Dow.

Greeting his colleagues, unlocking his vault, getting his money in order for the day, Digby bit down on painful memories. Adelaide was paranoid. How did she ever gain and hold the Albany manager's job? How do all the emotional cripples of the business world scramble into positions of power and hold onto them?

It had to do with survival and evolution. In his mind's eye, Digby saw a primeval limpet, brainless and ugly, clamped onto a rock in some tidal pool.

Adelaide used people. They were no different to her, Digby believed, than the bank's computer consoles. You switched them on and off. When one broke down you replaced it. Now he would use this characteristic of hers to lure her to Algonquin Landing. He would offer Adelaide Dow a new pool of people to manipulate.

Digby remembered the way it used to be. Adelaide called a meeting almost every morning. The tellers and accountants sat in upholstered chairs while Adelaide went over procedures and grievances. Three pieces of ID needed on all checks cashed. Always refer to the file of signature cards. A siege mentality was fostered and maintained. Digby would swallow anger as he detected a half-hidden smile on Adelaide Dow's thin features. She was enjoying dishing out fear.

His own view of banking was so different. Of all the customers who came through the door on any day, 99 percent of them were law-abiding people. White, Chinese, black, or Hispanic, whether they had on a business suit or worker's clothing, or even if they were students, they were honest individuals just trying to cash a pay-check or withdraw their own funds. The teller's job was to greet these people with warmth and courtesy. Not to confront them as potential thieves.

Nor did Adelaide Dow's poison cease flowing when the bank closed its doors at four o'clock. Now she began heckling the tellers who were trying to balance their cash. "Come on, get it done! Ten minutes till the courier gets here! Digby, I need your tapes for the bag!"

He could not work under the conditions she imposed. Trying to get it right, he hit wrong keys on his calculator. The money-counter malfunctioned, it ate a five dollar bill. Elastic bands snapped as he secured packs of twenties. The courier was at the door! He was not ready!

Digby would walk out onto the street after five o'clock feeling like a survivor leaving a battlefield. His senses were shocked, his heart was beating too fast. Living alone, he had nobody to talk to. He tried self-hypnosis to calm himself down and that helped a little bit.

One Friday, as he was about to go home, Adelaide Dow asked him to come to her desk. He sat there while she made three telephone calls, her slate eyes on him all the while. She was tall, not an ounce of extra flesh on her bones; a long-beaked wading bird in a pin-striped suit.

"Now," she said, folding her hands on the clear glass surface, "it isn't working, is it. You can't seem to handle the pressure. We really must be able to meet company deadlines."

Digby felt his eyes filling up. This was terrible. All his life he had worked in jobs where he was praised for his aptitude and his attitude. Now here was this bitch about to cut him adrift! He heard himself saying, "Actually, I'm not staying. I'm leaving town. I was about to give in my notice."

Then he saw the tiny smile on her face. He was not mistaken. Adelaide Dow had spotted the tears in his eyes, she was registering his distress. And she was deriving satisfaction from it.

That must have been the moment, although he did not make the connection until some time later, when he realized Adelaide Dow would be the perfect victim.

EastCon Bank in Algonquin Landing opened its doors at ten. The flow of customers was steady but not heavy. The atmosphere behind the windows was free of tension because the manager was a civilized individual. Always a loner, Digby ate lunch out of the machines in the staff room upstairs, reading a movie magazine somebody had left behind on the sofa.

At closing, he went by the liquor store and bought a bottle of Van Holst, as instructed by Mrs. Peterson. She had a taste for the pungent Geneva-type gin and she had passed it on, heaven help his liver, to Digby Staples. Then he stopped at the shop on the east side of the bridge and picked up two orders of fish and chips, wrapped in newspaper. It was advertised as "English style," and for all Digby knew, never having been outside New York State, it was.

"When will your friend be coming?" the landlady asked. The table was cleared after their meal and she had provided two decks of cards. They were ready to start playing double solitaire and sipping gin from tiny glasses. Both activities were enhancements to idle conversation which would be, as always, the main feature of the evening.

"I haven't asked her yet."

"Sounds like you. Plenty of smoke, not much fire."

"I want to help her find a job."

"In this burg?"

"She's manager of the bank where I used to work. I read in the paper where they're closing a lot of branches." This was true. "The economy. Her branch is one. She'll have to relocate."

"She's lucky to have a friend like you."

Digby held his breath while the first taste of gin went down. It was a bit like drinking paint thinner. "She'd agree with you." He had never let on to Adelaide that he hated her. They had parted on good terms—that's the impression with which her ego and Digby's poker face had left her. He was pretty sure she would come when he invited her.

Laying out his cards as Mrs. Peterson laid out hers, playing the simple game, Digby had time to think. The hypnosis was the uncertain element in his plan. And there was no way to test it but to do it. Every subject was different. If Adelaide would not or could not cooperate, all bets were off. But he had certainly been able to make it work the last time.

It was when he was a senior in high school that Digby taught himself the art of hypnosis. He found a book on the subject in his father's library. His father died when Digby was fourteen. A lawyer and an avid fisherman, the senior Staples was struck by lightning while deep-water casting from a skiff on Lake Champlain.

Digby's mother remarried a year later. His stepfather, a minor-league second baseman, was on the road a lot. His new wife followed the team in her new Mercedes, a purchase which absorbed much of the insurance money. Digby had no quarrel with his stepfather. He found him to be a decent man, although he had trouble turning the double play. Digby shunned the ballpark, found the games endless. He preferred to spend his spare time in the musty room where his father's books slid and shifted like shale in a geological fault.

The hypnosis manual was easy to follow. When he had absorbed the technique, Digby tried it out with a friend after school. His aptitude was remarkable, blessed as he was with a sonorous baritone voice. Soon he was stretching his friend between two chairs and sitting on him.

Post-hypnotic suggestion came next. Digby's earliest experiment was the one he intended to repeat with Adelaide Dow. It was simplicity itself. "When you hear the word 'cradle,'" he had told his friend years ago, "you will begin to run forward in a straight line. You will run as fast as you can until you are tired. Then you will stop." These instructions were followed by the usual disclaimer that the subject would remember nothing about them when roused from the hypnotic trance.

It had been an exciting day. Digby and friend went for a walk on the playground. He was not sure whether the trick would work. But when he uttered the word "cradle," his friend took off across the field like an olympic sprinter. He covered half a mile before he wearied and pulled up.

The pier at Algonquin Landing was shorter than half a mile.

\*   \*   \*

Adelaide Dow's home number was in Digby's little book. It had been necessary to call her one time in the late evening in Albany when, overcome with fear, he decided he could not go to work on the following day.

Mrs. Peterson told him, "Dial direct." The telephone bill was to hand. She studied it. "This thing is beyond redemption anyway." She crumpled the pages into a ball and skipped it across the carpet in the direction of the cat. Punkin stared at her as if to say, "Why would you throw paper at me for no reason at all?"

Digby dialed and waited. She answered on the second ring.

"Yes?"

The irritation in her tone of voice was all the reassurance he needed to persuade him that he was about to take a giant step for mankind. "It's me, Adelaide. Digby Staples. How's it going?"

"Rotten. Where did you materialize from?"

"Algonquin Landing. I live here. I read something about the bank closing branches."

"It's a personal disaster. Tellers can always find a place. But I'm an executive. I really needed this."

"Would you consider moving?"

"Depends."

"I'm at Eastern Conglomerate here. This is the main bank in town. Our manager is about to retire. If you'd come down here, I could introduce you around."

"I wouldn't be caught dead in a place like that."

Digby was ready. "You don't understand. This branch needs shaking up. I've already told the owners what an efficiency expert you are. They want to meet you. If you come on board, you could really cut back the deadwood."

She hesitated. "Why are you doing this for me? I fired you."

"I'm doing it for myself. I've been seeing a shrink." Digby surprised himself with how easily his prepared story flowed. "I've got to come to terms with the past. What you did was not personal. It was for the good of the company. I see that now. I respect you for it."

"You're not just joking?"

"I would never joke with you, Adelaide."

She was intrigued. "It might be worth a visit."

They made arrangements for her to drive in on the following Friday night. Adelaide would spend the weekend getting to know Algonquin Landing with Digby as her guide. Then, on Monday morning, he would bring her in to meet management.

"What's going on?" Mrs. Peterson said after he put down the telephone.

"Sorry?"

"That woman could only hear your sugary words. But I could see your face. I was watching whatever it is in your eyes."

Digby experienced alarm. But the feeling passed quickly. He was safe. Mrs. Peterson knew nothing about the hypnotism. He and Adelaide would be alone when he planted the suggestion in her subconscious mind. So when she went for her long sprint on the short pier, it would be judged suicide. And why not? Her life was in a state of upheaval.

"You noticed some residual animosity," he confessed. "I've been trying to suppress it." He went on to explain how Adelaide Dow had spoiled his working life in the big town. There was no harm in letting the landlady know this. She would see for herself what a nasty piece of work Adelaide was when she arrived on Friday. "I truly hated her," he concluded. "I suppose on some level I still do. You noticed it. But I'm trying to do the right thing."

"Good for you. Revenge is a bad idea. You only end up hurting yourself. Better to forgive and forget. Put feelings of anger behind you."

"Easy to say."

"I know. Peterson was a bad example. It did him in."

"Your husband?"

"I told you he worked for the post office as a letter carrier. And he died. I never said how."

"What happened?"

"There are good routes and bad routes. He had the best route in town. Then it was taken away from him and given to the postmaster's nephew. Peterson never stopped hating that young man. He carried the grudge every day while he carried the mail. Even though it was the postmaster's doing, my husband went on hating the nephew. Until he got hold of this bomb."

"What?"

"Dynamite and a clock ticking inside a package. I never found out who it was to or from. But it was addressed to somebody on Peterson's route. He became suspicious, opened an end of the package, and saw the wires."

"He should have gone to the police."

"Of course. But my husband was consumed with hatred of the postmaster's nephew. So he taped up the package and re-addressed it to the nephew himself. And he took it to his home and carried it up the walk and onto the porch. He was putting it inside the screen door when it went off."

Digby sniffed his glass and set it down without drinking. "Did he die?"

"In a week."

"How do you know the story?"

"He confessed when I was sitting by his hospital bed. I told him what I'm telling you. Holding a grudge, seeking revenge, is self-defeating." The landlady capped the bottle. "Let it go, Digby, before you do yourself in."

On Friday, around seven in the evening, Adelaide Dow blew into town like a cold wind from Lake Ontario. Digby introduced her to Mrs. Peterson, then stood in the doorway of the front room while the visitor peered out the window at the street, the slice of lake between houses, the dark hills beyond. "I can't believe I'm doing this," she said.

"You'll like the bank on Monday."

"I hope so." She looked pensive. "Is there really a lot of deadwood on staff?"

"At least five people could go and never be missed," Digby said. "Let's get something to eat."

"Do they have a restaurant in this place?"

"Two. One has a license and the other doesn't."

They went where they could order wine. Adelaide mellowed. "Look at you," she said across the fettucini alfredo. "Trying so hard to get me to like you."

"I'm sorry we weren't better friends." He refilled her glass. "Perhaps it needed more effort."

"You make me nervous, you always did." An idea that pleased her entered Adelaide's mind. "What if you're one of the ones I cut adrift? Supposing I fire you again?"

"Never happen. I learned from experience. I'm a better teller now because of the way you shook me up."

The preposterous lie rang as true to Adelaide as a silver bell. "I'm beginning to be glad I came," she said.

He showed her the main street. He showed her the lake from the near end of the pier. "We'll walk out there tomorrow. The view from the far end is great." He guided her back to the boarding house, pointing out interesting homes and gardens on the way.

She was excited now. "I'm not sure I can sleep," she said. "I'm impatient for the Monday meeting with the EastCon people."

"You need your rest. I can help you sleep."

Standing in the doorway of the room, she gave him a look. "Don't even think of it, Digby."

"I didn't mean that. I can do hypnotism."

"Go on."

"I've been into it since high school. Nothing crazy, I don't make folks undress in public. Just a few words to calm you down."

"Are you serious?"

She almost went under right there. A very good subject indeed. She turned and he followed her into the room, closing the door behind them. "Sit there," he suggested and she settled obediently onto the edge of the bed. He pulled over a chair and sat facing her, close up. "Now, relax. Let go completely. You're very tired. You want to rest. Your eyelids are heavy. Your eyelids want to close. Let your eyelids close. That's right. Now . . . I am going to tell you a word. The word is 'cradle.' Say the word 'cradle.' "

"Cradle."

"The next time you hear the word 'cradle,' you will begin to run. You will run as fast as you can, straight ahead. Tell me, Adelaide, what will you do the next time you hear the word 'cradle'?"

"I will run as fast as I can. Straight ahead."

"Very good. Now, when I count to three, you will wake up. You will not remember anything of what we have just said. One, two, three."

Adelaide opened her eyes. She looked at Digby, she looked around the room. "Was I out?"

"You were in a trance."

"How long?"

"Less than a minute."

"Wow. I feel like I've been asleep for an hour."

"It works." He got up and went to the door. "You'll rest now. Good night."

Digby Staples was the one who had trouble sleeping. It occurred to him that he had already committed murder. The deed was done, the woman was as good as dead. Tomorrow, on the pier, he would utter the trigger word. Adelaide would sprint into eternity. The police would conclude (and why not?) that a troubled woman, about to lose her job, had decided to end her life. The perfect murder; the perfect victim.

Especially since she did not know how to swim. That fact had been established long ago in Centralia. Adelaide had boycotted a staff party at the beach for that very reason.

Had he said too much to Mrs. Peterson? Digby struggled with twisted sheets, pounded the comfortless pillow. The landlady's lecture on revenge suggested she had sensed what he might have in mind. What would she think when Adelaide turned up dead twenty-four hours later? Never mind, he was safe. There would be witnesses on the pier, strangers to testify the woman had jumped into the water by herself. And nobody knew about the hypnotism.

In the morning, Adelaide was up bright and early. She arrived at Digby's bedroom door with two cups of coffee on a tray. "You can put me to sleep any time." She raised his blind, dragged back the drapes. "It's a day and a half," was her assessment. As Digby sipped the strong brew and grudgingly admitted to himself that this was sort of neat, she went on, "I surprised our landlady in the kitchen. Does she always feed that cat on the table?"

"Punkin came aboard after her husband died. It's replaced the old man and then some."

"She's taking it in for booster shots today, I think she said. She was spelling everything so the cat wouldn't catch on."

"You can't tip your hand to a cat. If you do, it dematerializes and you see it next week."

Adelaide finished her coffee. "You promised to show me the lake."

"Right." The condemned woman was impatient to meet her fate. "Let me throw on some clothes and we'll go."

Ten minutes later, it became crowded in the vestibule. As Digby was about to open the front door for Adelaide, Mrs. Peterson appeared carrying a portapet box with Punkin inside—one angry eye at an airhole.

"Let me help you," the visitor said. She took the box from the landlady's hand. "He's heavier than I expected."

"Where's the vet's office?" Digby asked.

"Other side of the bridge."

"Can we go that way?" Adelaide asked. "I don't care if it's a longer walk."

The trio set out towards the main road, Adelaide in front because the box was bulky, Digby and Mrs. Peterson a pace behind. They were nearing the corner when the old lady called, "Be careful now with my precious. He's like a baby in his cradle."

Adelaide began to run. Holding the portapet firmly in her right hand, she sprinted straight ahead towards the intersection. Saturday morning traffic on the bridge road was heavy. There were vans, private cars, a bus, two lanes speeding in either direction.

Mrs. Peterson was screaming. She had no hope of catching the fleeting girl. Digby took off after her. Adelaide might get hit by a truck, she might die. Then again, she might not. But she was carrying Punkin. He could not bear the thought of that sweet animal, trapped in a box, being carried to its death.

"Stop her!" Mrs. Peterson's pleas drove him on. Adelaide was entering traffic, running fast. A car swerved. Horns began to blow. Digby was on her, grasping her shoulders, spinning her around, glimpsing the wild uncertainty in her eyes as she sensed the danger and wondered why this was happening. He managed to redirect her progress back towards the sidewalk and Mrs. Peterson, who seized her and held her, both of them sharing a grip on the cat-box handle.

Digby was not so fortunate. Physical reaction to the push that saved Adelaide sent him off balance into the road. A tractor-trailer could not stop in time. He was knocked a glancing blow, ending up prone on a grassy verge.

The paramedics were there in minutes. Digby was examined where he lay, then loaded onto a gurney and placed inside the ambulance with tubes already feeding life-saving substances into his veins.

His next view of the world was past the halo of light surrounding the curly blonde head of a sympathetic nurse. "You're going to be all right, Mr. Staples," she reassured him. "Just relax and leave everything to us."

Digby dozed. He awoke to find Adelaide Dow sitting by the bed on a straight-backed chair. She was pretending to read a magazine, narrow eyes focused far off. He cleared his throat.

"You're awake," she said. "They tell me you'll be okay."

Digby's sedated system managed to register alarm. He told himself she could not know anything of the posthypnotic suggestion. But he decided to test her memory. "Why did you race into the street?"

"I've been trying to figure that out. One minute we were walking and talking. Then I was off and running."

"It's one of those mysteries," Digby concluded, "that will never be understood."

"Whatever happened," she said, "you saved my life. They told me how you sacrificed yourself. I never knew you were the type. I've always put you down as a wimp. I mean, having me come here and finding me a job after what I did to you. I don't care what you said last night, your behavior shows zero backbone."

Righteous anger filled Digby to the limit. It felt good. "You're deluding yourself," he told her. He had no further use for her or for the pretense that he liked her. "I was saving the cat."

Adelaide went away. Mrs. Peterson came in. "What did you say to your friend? She told me she's leaving town."

"I'm letting her go. I've decided I don't need her to hate any more."

"That's healthy," the landlady said. "Reminds me of when I said good-bye to that husband of mine."

"When he was in the hospital?"

"Before that. When I bought the bomb that killed him."

"You said he discovered it. Addressed to somebody on his route."

"That's the story I told the police." Mrs. Peterson sat on the chair beside Digby's bed. "He was a bad husband. He hated cats. And there were other, lesser faults. I decided to be rid of him. So I saved my money and paid a man who used to live in your room. He was retired from the

CIA. I asked him one night when we were drinking our gin if he knew how to make an explosive device. He said he did."

"You'll give me a relapse," Digby said.

"The rest was easy. I told Peterson the timer was set for three o'clock. Then I set it for one-thirty."

Digby thought about what he had just heard. Then he said, "What about all that stuff you told me, the harm there is in hating somebody?"

"Q.E.D. I didn't waste my life hating my husband. I got rid of him." The old woman patted Digby's hand. "The best you could do is stop hating Adelaide. You're too much of a softy to kill anybody."

Mrs. Peterson decided it was time to end her visit. The patient was looking stressed. "Hurry up and get better and come home," she said from the doorway. "Punkin wants me to throw you a party for saving his life."

# Mercy's Killing

## BARBARA OWENS

O utside, rain fell cold and hard, what the locals called a gully washer. Dieter Francke was comfortably dozing through the 10 O'Clock News when his brother-in-law, Tim Shales, called from the sheriff's office.

"Hate to bother you on a night like this, Dieter, but you might want to come over. Sheriff's bringing in a woman claims she's killed her brother. You know the Webbs, live out east along Skinner's Creek?"

Dieter blinked, still half asleep. "I don't think so. What happened?"

"All we know now is she called in and said she shot him. If he's dead, this'll be one sorry case, Dieter. That's why I called."

"And she asked for me?"

"Naw, this particular woman won't know she even needs a lawyer. Come on over, see for yourself. Just keep it quiet I called you, okay?"

"Okay." Dieter's brain was starting to click. "Tell the sheriff I'm on my way, and that no one's to talk to her until I get there. Sorry case, you said? Hope I won't be sorry you called me, Tim."

He left a note for his sleeping wife and went out to brave the rain, adrenaline already pumping. If the guy was dead, this would be his first murder case. The town would have to take note of him. Peering through sheets of water at deserted streets, he tried to remember a family named Webb. In a place the size of Hadley, surely he'd heard it, but his memory was drawing a blank.

The county-jail building was squat and square. Tim looked up from his desk when Dieter came in, shaking rain from his coat.

"They just got in. Sheriff's waiting in his office. I told him you called, but I didn't say how you found out."

Dieter pitched his dripping coat across a chair. "Well, this had better be good. I had to swim part of the way here."

Tim's serious expression didn't change. "It's the real thing, Dieter. Cal Webb's dead. She got him with a double barrel to the head."

"Okay." Dieter was already on his way toward the sheriff's closed door. "What's her name?"

"Mercy. And she hasn't been around much. Go easy."

Sheriff Wes Parker answered Dieter's rap at the door. He looked faintly amused. "You picking up police calls now, Francke?" he asked in his deep bass drawl.

Dieter couldn't see past the bulky body blocking the doorway. "No, sir," he answered evenly, "but word manages to get around."

Parker's eyes flicked past him, settled on Tim Shales. "I expect it does. Well, come on in."

The woman was huddled in a wooden side chair, a thin cotton jail blanket drawn over her shoulders. A worn print housedress clung wetly to her. Dieter instinctively recorded the expression in her faded blue eyes—flat and frozen, like some small road animal trapped in the glare of on-coming headlights. Her body was slight and bony, as shapeless as a child's. Greying, limp wet hair. Stubby little hands with swollen knuckles, worked-hard hands. They clutched a thick coffee mug without knowing it. A ghostly, used-up woman, could be anywhere from forty to sixty-five. Mercy Webb didn't look strong enough to lift a shotgun, let alone fire it.

Dieter met the sheriff's eyes. "She been read her rights?"

Parker nodded. "She's already told me all about it, though. And she didn't ask for a lawyer first."

Dieter turned a smile on her. "Well, she's got one now if she wants me."

"How about it, Mercy?" Parker asked. "You want to talk to Mr. Francke here?"

For the first time, she stirred. "I don't know. You think I ought?" The voice was small and dry, scarcely audible.

"Might be a good idea," Parker said. "I'll just leave you two alone for a minute." He went out, closing the door behind him.

Dieter opened his case on the sheriff's desk, moving slowly, letting her get a good look at him. Her eyes followed his every move.

"You look cold," he said finally. "How'd you get so wet?"

Mercy set her coffee mug on the desk and folded her hands together in her lap. "Don't have a phone," she told him. "I walked to the neighbor's. That's more'n a mile."

He pulled a chair close to her, holding his friendly smile. "My name's Dieter. You don't know me, but you might know my wife Jan, Tim Shales' sister?" When she made no reply, he leaned toward her. "I'm here to help you, Mercy. We have to talk about what happened. It's all right for you to tell me. I'm on your side."

After a short moment, she sighed. "Well, what happened is, I killed Cal. But he said it would be all right." The hands in her lap knotted together. "I don't believe I need a lawyer. Don't see how I could pay for one, anyhow."

Dieter eyed her carefully. It looked like Tim was right—the woman had no understanding of her situation. "Look," he said, "don't worry about money now. Before the sheriff comes back in, we have to decide how to get you out of this. Now, who said it would be all right? Cal? Why would he say that?"

"The letter." She fumbled in a worn black purse on the chair beside her. "He said all I'd have to do was show it."

"Letter?" Dieter repeated.

She pulled out a crumpled sheet. "I already showed the sheriff. Cal said the letter would explain things. That's why he wrote it."

The paper she handed him was a page torn from a cheap tablet, undated, the few words scrawled across it in pencil by an unsteady hand. Dieter read it twice, a cold fist clenching in his gut: "Don't blame Mercy. I made her do it. A man shouldn't have to live this way." The signature was clear—Calvin Baxter Webb.

Dieter's mouth went dry. "Live what way?"

"Crippled like he was. His legs. Cal was in a car wreck about five years back. Out West somewhere—Nevada, I believe it was. Him and two other men. They was both killed. Anyhow, it made Cal one of those—" she sounded out the word carefully "—paraplegics. He's been going downhill ever since. Lately he just couldn't sleep or eat good, and he started pestering me to do it—you know, put him out of his misery."

Dieter looked at her with a sinking sensation. What had he gotten himself into? A mercy killing? As tough as cases get.

"But," he managed finally, "he had the use of his arms. He could have done it himself. Why involve you?"

Her gaze slid away from him. "He said he was scared. He might botch it and have more hurting. He worked it all out for me to give him a big dose of his sleep medicine and—" Mercy's eyes crept back to him "—and do it while he was asleep. So that's what I did."

Dieter's sinking sensation sank. Plain and simple, the woman didn't think she'd done anything wrong. His brain searched for a way out.

"Can we prove that Cal actually wrote the letter?"

Mercy looked surprised. "Well, I watched him write it. I was there."

Swell. Defendant backs up defendant's confession. He tried another tack. "Mercy, when Sheriff Parker read you your rights, did you understand that you didn't have to tell him anything without an attorney present?"

The hands in her lap twisted slowly. "He said that, but I didn't see any sense in lying. See, I'd already called and said I did it, hadn't I?"

"Well, think about this. Now that you look back on it, is it kind of a blur? Maybe you didn't really realize you were killing Cal. Think you could say that?"

Mercy thought for a minute, then shook her head. "I remember it clear. Cal and me went over and over it. He didn't want me to do it wrong."

"Mercy," Dieter said carefully, "what you did was commit a murder."

"No," she said quickly, "it wasn't. I just did what Cal wanted me to."

Dieter suppressed a sigh. "Why? Why did you do it if you didn't want to?"

"I just told you," she responded patiently. "Cal wanted me to. I was supposed to take care of him."

Dieter went out to summon the sheriff. "This won't take long," he reported grimly. "She's going to flat out admit it. I can't shake her."

Parker nodded. "You familiar with the family?"

"No."

"Well, you're going to learn some things. Most important is that Mercy there has always done what she's told." He laid a big hand on Dieter's shoulder. "Come on, let's go in and get it over with."

Over breakfast the next morning, Jan listened with sympathy and understanding. "Well, I'm glad you're going to defend her. That poor old thing deserves the best."

Dieter looked up, surprised. "You know her?"

"Nobody really knows her, but we all know about her."

"So, tell me."

"Well, she hardly ever steps foot off that place out there. She nursed her father for years, then Cal. Ask the guys who sit around the Drop-In drinking coffee. They'll know. And talk to Tim."

Dieter stared into his coffee. "How do I know they'll talk to me? I'm not the most popular guy in town."

Jan squeezed his hand. "Look, you're still the young hotshot lawyer who came down from Chicago and married the hometown girl. They don't dislike you, hon—they're just cautious, waiting to see what you're made of."

"I thought I'd like living in a small town," he groused. "Do some real good."

"And be a bigger fish," she said slyly.

He had to grin. "That, too."

"They'll talk because of Mercy," Jan said with confidence. "Trust me. She's one of us."

"Well, I've been here over a year. How many more before *I'm* one of us?"

Jan laughed. "Oh, about a hundred. Listen, you could wind up being the big man who gets her off. Go on now—get out and talk to people."

The president of the Hadley Bank, Hollis Graham, verified the letter's handwriting as Calvin Webb's. "I've been looking at that signature for a good many years. No question in my mind."

"I have to ask this," Dieter told him. "Tell me if you don't want to answer without proper authority. How will Mercy benefit financially from her brother's death?"

"Not a bit. Matter of fact, Cal's disability was mostly what they lived on, and that'll stop now. She'll get a few extra dollars in the bank and that old place where she lives. If you've seen it, you know what it's worth." Graham hesitated. "Mr. Francke, you let me know if I can be of any help. This town thinks a lot of Mercy Webb."

At the 10:00 A.M. bail hearing, Dieter got a firsthand look at the man who'd be prosecuting. In his day, Matthew Robbins had been a fiery opponent for any man, a high-power from Springfield. He was old now, but still firmly entrenched behind his tunnel view of the law. He reaffirmed this in their brief meeting.

"Don't even mention bargaining," he began before Dieter could mention it. "From my first look at the case, I feel sorry for the woman, but murder is murder and that's what we're going for. I'm asking for life."

"Have you met her?" Dieter queried with faint hope. "There's special circumstances here."

The old man flashed a sharp, lipless smile. "My position is inflexible on this, Mr. Francke."

The minister from the Methodist Church posted bail. He looked like a minister should, with a round, cherubic face, and he grasped Dieter's hand firmly before departing. "Mercy isn't a member, but the congregation volunteered this contribution. She's close to our hearts. Do right by her, Mr. Francke." Dieter assured him he would try.

Dieter drove Mercy home through a countryside fresh from the rain. In the daylight she looked even more worn, fine lines etched deeply into her featureless face. She kept her hands folded in her lap and her head turned away from him, issuing occasional soft directions as they drove.

"Do you understand there's going to be a trial?" he finally asked her. "I'll explain everything to you as we go along. If you have any questions, just ask."

She kept her face away from him. "Then I guess Cal was wrong, wasn't he?"

"I'm afraid he was. But don't worry. We're going in with a strong case." He wished he could believe it.

The car lurched and bumped down a narrow rutted lane, along ditches choked with weeds. At its end stood an aging, two-story house, weathered shingles feathering paint. The front porch leaned to one side, the yard was rough and unkempt. Not one flower or spot of color lightened the grimness. Dieter looked across to catch Mercy's gaze.

"Dad never saw much need in keeping things up smart," she said simply.

As she opened the door, he leaned toward her. "Are you going to be all right out here?"

"I've always been out here," she said.

He watched her through his rearview mirror as he started back up the lane. Looking neither right nor left, she marched through the yard, up the sagging steps, and vanished inside.

"Cal was older than me, but I remember him," Tim said. He had invited Dieter to the Drop-In Cafe for coffee. He seemed unaware that everyone in the narrow, converted railway car was watching surreptitiously. "There was only him and Mercy. Let's see, Cal must've been about fifty, Mercy's probably forty-five. The mother died when they were just kids. Cal took off the first time while Mercy was still in high school—she just stayed on and took care of things. Then old man Webb had a stroke about fifteen years ago. Bedridden and paralyzed—should've been in a home, but he wanted Mercy to take care of him, so she did."

Dieter glanced down at the big table near the door, holding maybe a dozen men, most in overalls, all talking quietly. Hard men, weathered from years of work in the outdoors. Several were watching him. He smiled, got a quick nod or two in return, and looked away. Tim was paying no attention.

"The family never had two nickels at the same time, but Cal didn't do a lick of work that I know of. He was gone for years. We heard he got into some trouble now and then, spent some time in jail. Don't know what for. Then he got hurt about a year before the old man died, and he came home for Mercy to take care of him, so she had the both of them for a while."

"Alone?" Dieter asked incredulously. "Wasn't there anyone to help her?"

Tim shook his head. "Some folks offered, but the old man and Cal didn't want anyone else around. I remember even as a kid I thought Mercy looked old and beat down. She never had a chance, Dieter. First one, then the other, kept a big foot on her, just squashed her spirit right out."

Without turning, Tim called over his shoulder, "Willis? You got a minute?"

A tall, sun-browned man detached himself from the group at the big table and came to stand silently at theirs.

"You know my brother-in-law, Dieter," Tim said. "Dieter, this is Willis Fry. We were just talking about Mercy, Willis. Wasn't it your brother wanted to marry her?"

Willis Fry nodded solemnly. "John. About broke his heart. Mercy wanted to, but old Herm wouldn't let her: she was to stay home and take care of him. She didn't have it in her to stand up to him. John went off to Vietnam and never come back."

Suddenly three more men were gathered at the table. "Heard you went to see the banker," one said. Dieter nodded. "He tell you Herm left everything to Cal when he died? Not a cent for Mercy. Cal could've done right and changed things, but he didn't."

"No," Dieter said. "I didn't hear that."

"Mercy can't even write a check," another volunteered. "Cal had it all in his name."

There was a short silence. Six men were now banked around the table.

"Nobody thought much of Cal," Willis said finally. His eyes fastened on Dieter. "It's too bad he got crippled up that way, but he sure was hard on her. We're hoping you intend to get her off."

Dieter felt a small fire flicker to life somewhere inside. Mercy deserved it—he was going to do just that. "I'll try like hell," he said.

First one, then several hands reached to grip his. Hard hands. Willis Fry's was last. "You need anything, you ask."

Then they were gone and Dieter was grinning across the table at Tim. "Thanks," he said. "Pretty smart, coming here with me. I owe you one."

Tim grinned back. "You need all the help you can get on this one, Dieter. A lot of people are counting on you."

Cal Webb's doctor confirmed Mercy's appraisal of her brother's physical condition. A gentleman of the old school, Sam Phillips had been Hadley's chief medical practitioner for more than thirty years.

"When he first got back home, Cal swore he'd walk again," he told Dieter. "Said he had to, to get out of this hellhole. I couldn't convince him otherwise. That poor girl waited on him hand and foot, both of them when their dad was still alive. There were plenty of things Cal could do for himself if he wanted, but he wouldn't try. I think finally accepting his condition only made him meaner. Cal wasn't much of a man, if you want my opinion."

"Mercy said he'd been going downhill lately," Dieter said. "Was he deteriorating?"

"More like quitting, I believe. Last spring he started having trouble sleeping, was losing weight, just letting himself atrophy. I tried to get him out of there into someplace where they'd force him into physical therapy. Let Mercy have a rest, too, but he wouldn't go."

Mercy's neighbor had lived on the next farm since she and Cal were born.

"Well, she looked a bit scared when she come to use the phone that night," he remembered. "But calm, like it was something she was supposed to do."

He told Dieter she'd always been a quiet girl, even when she was small. "After her mother died, Mercy just stepped in. Herm worked her like a mule. I don't believe she ever had one day of fun."

"Did they farm?"

"Some. Herm wasn't good at farming. After he got down, he rented out the land. The whole family was odd, Mr. Francke—never took much with neighbors." The man's eyes darkened. "When the creek flooded last spring, it come up in their basement. Me and my son went over to help clear it, but Mercy said Cal didn't want us on the place. Said he told *her* to do it, so I guess she did."

The fire inside Dieter was licking hotter. "I'm getting an angle," he told Jan. "I don't know if I can pull it off, but I'm convinced Mercy didn't understand the consequences when she put that double barrel against Cal's head. She was simply doing what she was told."

Jan looked thoughtful. "Are you talking some form of diminished capacity?"

"She did what she was told," Dieter repeated. "She had no resistance."

"Pretty tricky. Matt Robbins will jump all over you."

"I don't have to convince Matt Robbins. I have to convince the jury."

His biggest fear was that Robbins would ask for a change of venue, recognize the pulse of public sentiment. But something in his gut told him that Robbins was old, nearing the end of his career, and was out of his element in Hadley. Maybe he'd get careless, confident of his reputation and scornful of Dieter's inexperience. Although painfully aware of his shaky footing in the town, Dieter knew he was closer to being one of their own than Robbins was. He decided to gamble and do very little to rehearse Mercy for her trial.

"Tell the truth," he instructed her, "just the plain truth. Be yourself.

Matt Robbins will be hard on you. He'll try to fluster you, get you to say things you don't mean. Hang onto your head, Mercy. Tell what happened and why, that's all. A lot of other people will be on the stand backing you up. And I'll be right there with you."

They were sitting in the dark, cheerless living room of her house. Mercy listened carefully, her thin shoulders bowed. She had brewed him a cup of bitter black coffee and he sipped it while he surveyed the room's worn, spartan furnishings, the bare wooden floor. At the foot of the steep stairs to the second floor, the door to her brother's bedroom—the room where he died—was closed.

Mercy cleared her throat. "Well," she said in her dry little voice, "I never expected any of this. I was counting on Cal's letter to fix things."

"The letter will help," Dieter assured her. "We know what Cal wanted. Now we just have to show that to the jury."

Early-winter sunlight streamed through the wavy glass of the windows. "It was really tough on you, wasn't it, all the care you gave your father and Cal?" He was testing her. "Was Cal difficult to get along with?"

She looked away. "He needed a lot of things," she said finally, and that's all he got from her. All Matt Robbins would get, too, hopefully.

His inner fire was blazing. All he had to do was show the jury this woman had no ability to make decisions and he was home free. Finished with his coffee, he straightened. "What will you do when it's over?"

Mercy looked surprised. "What do you mean?"

"Maybe you could take a little vacation. Go away for a while."

Mercy ducked her head. "Mr. Francke, I've never been outside this county."

"Then it's time. Don't you have family? Someone to visit?"

"Well," she said after a minute, "I've got an aunt in Tulsa."

Dieter beamed. "There you are."

For a minute he thought she was going to smile, and he wanted to see that. Then her eyes clouded and the swollen fingers picked at the fabric of her dress.

"I don't know if there's enough money to pay for all this," she said. "I can't be thinking about going anywhere."

"Hey, we'll work it out," he assured her. "You think about it, okay?"

As the trial date neared, Dieter saw it coming together. Robbins had not requested a change of venue, so he'd been right in his assumptions. Robbins merely planned to shoot into town, blow away the local talent, and shoot back out again. Dieter smiled inside. He couldn't pretend to be unaware of his growing favor in town. People stopped him on the street to ask how things were going, and when he stopped by the Drop-In for coffee he was greeted and invited to join the men around the big table.

"I'm going to pull it off," he told Jan, exulting.

She eyed him with a grin. "Don't start running for senator yet," she warned. "First you've got to get her off. If you don't, we'll both have to leave town."

Dieter deliberately dressed down for court. Hair a little shaggy, top shirt-button open under his tie, he wanted the jury to remember he was no out-of-town attorney. Matt Robbins, in sharp creases and high polish on his shoes, was quick to take notice.

"Nice try," he murmured in passing. "But it's still murder. Reasons don't count."

From the first day, Dieter gave it everything he had—after all, he and Mercy were both on trial. Witness after witness testified that Cal Webb was pretty much worthless: he neglected his family and took advantage of them, he had bragged about his scrapes with the law. Several concerned citizens had tried to convince him to share his small inheritance with Mercy, but he refused. Dr. Sam Phillips was effective in picturing Mercy's caregiving.

"She lifted those men, bathed them, cleaned up after them, fed and medicated them, and in all the years I've known her I never heard her complain."

Voices rose to attest to Cal's refusal to allow a phone in the house or to maintain the upkeep of the farm. And he wouldn't let anyone help Mercy in any way.

Mercy was sensational on the stand. Small, faded, and forlorn, she looked bewildered by the proceedings, huddled into herself, but her story came out honest and true, her wispy voice mesmerizing the packed court-room as she described the details of her one violent act.

Only after Cal begged, cried, and offered to write the letter did she finally give in. Together, they rehearsed his plan. She put the sleeping medication in his supper—he asked for pork chops and sweet potatoes, and that's what she gave him—then when he was so deep asleep she couldn't rouse him, she put the double barrel to his head.

Matt Robbins was fierce in cross-examination, his scenario that she'd finally snapped after the years of sacrifice and simply wanted to be rid of him, but he couldn't sway her from her simple story: Cal wanted to die and she couldn't deny him. When she finished, looking exhausted but dry-eyed, there wasn't a sound in the courtroom.

Dieter's summation presented a woman who had always been in prison, a loveless place that had drained all the life and independence from her.

Yes, she helped plan it and, yes, she executed the plan. "But make no mistake," he told the jury, fixing them with his eyes. "Look at her. To this day, she doesn't fully understand what she's done. Mercy Webb didn't know that the law wouldn't recognize Calvin's letter exonerating her. She believed him. In her mind, Calvin Webb *was* the law."

When he looked behind the expressionless faces, he saw the outcome. He'd done it. Mercy was set free.

"Is it over?" was all she asked when the verdict was rendered, and at his answer he finally saw her smile, saw the sparkle light up her eyes. As people crowded in to congratulate him and comfort Mercy, Matt Robbins reached to shake his hand.

"You're lucky, Francke. You'd never have gotten away with that on my turf."

Dieter shrugged, smiled, and said nothing.

Robbins was already packing up, heading out. "I expect I'll be seeing you again."

Dieter grinned. "Who can say?"

Then Jan was hugging him, and there were people waiting—his people, wanting to shake his hand.

Mercy insisted that he accompany her to the bank to determine the amount of her assets, and she paid him the full token billing he had submitted as his fee. She was indeed planning to visit her aunt in Tulsa. When word got out, the Methodist Church took up a collection and presented her with luggage for the trip—one large suitcase and a hefty carry-on. Dieter himself saw her onto the bus.

"Don't be nervous," he assured her. "Just ask the driver if you get mixed up about anything. Is your aunt going to meet you?"

Mercy nodded. "I can't believe I'm going," she said, sounding breathless.

"Everything's different now. You have a good time. Come tell me about it when you get back."

He felt like a million dollars at least when she started up the steps and he handed her the heavy new carry-on bag . . .

Once settled in her seat, the bus moving under her, Mercy glanced at the heavyset woman beside her. The woman smiled and Mercy smiled back.

The carry-on was under her feet on the floor, supporting her short legs. A smile still lifting the corners of her mouth, Mercy turned her attention to the window and the scenery skimming by outside.

When you get back, Dieter Francke said. Not hardly.

If she wiggled her toes a bit, she thought she could feel the bundles of money stuffed inside the carry-on clear through the soles of her shoes. Almost a quarter mil, Cal bragged.

The bus picked up speed. The heavyset woman pulled out a magazine —Mercy was safe to stare through the window and have her little smile.

She thought it had gone pretty well. She'd gotten scared that night when Dieter told her the letter wasn't enough, but she'd managed to hold on and not give things away. After all the trouble she had getting Cal to write it, she was really counting on that letter.

"You won't get away with it," Cal had told her after she locked him in his bedroom and starved him for five whole days. "I'll tell somebody—the doc next time he comes."

By that time she was so mad she wasn't afraid of him any more. "Then I'll tell him about the money and they'll get you, Cal."

When he was finally so weak he could barely raise his head, he wrote what she told him to. Then she fed him—not much, just enough.

The mad started when he sent her down into the basement during the flood last spring to look for a little trunk he'd hidden there. She wasn't to look inside, he said, just bring it up so it wouldn't get wet. But when she lifted it, the top popped and she saw the money—stacks of it all wrapped in plastic. And the mad just jumped up and hit her, moved inside her like another person. Cal didn't want to tell her where it came from, but she starved him a bit and he finally did.

"Me and these two guys robbed an armored car in California. They almost caught us and we got separated. I made it away with most of the take. Remember the year I came back at Christmas? That's when I hid it down cellar—thought I'd wait a while, then come back and get it and go somewhere for a high old time. But those boys tracked me down in Nevada. They was taking me out in the desert to work me over till I told where it was. When we got to fighting in the car, that's when the wreck happened. Them boys didn't make it."

The mad had such a hold on her that she couldn't breathe. "And we've been living like this, not even a phone, while that money was down there all this time?"

Cal just looked back at her with his mean eyes. "I thought my legs would work again. Besides, it's not your money. It's mine."

Well, enough is enough. It took her awhile to figure out how to do it and get away with it. Once she hit on the idea of the letter, Cal begged her not to, said they'd take the money and go somewhere else, hire someone to take care of him. But the mad was telling her what to do. She could've just given him a heaping dose of the sleep medicine, but she wasn't sure how much to use. She might botch it and Cal would still be alive. Dad's old shotgun seemed like a sure thing.

The bus was crossing a river. Mercy watched with interest. Mr. Robbins had scared her again when he dug into her at the trial. Seemed like he was getting close to what really happened, but she remembered what Dieter told her—hang onto your head. She did, and here she was.

Mercy wiggled her toes against the money. Lucky she'd had Dieter. He'd really helped things. He never once asked flat out if she murdered Cal. She probably would have lied, but it was a comfort that she hadn't had to. It would have been a real shame to lie to such a nice man. His idea to take a vacation even helped her find an easy way to get out of town.

Of course, she didn't have an aunt in Tulsa. When she got there, she'd just take a bus to somewhere else, travel around as long as she wanted to, settle down if she found a nice place. Seems like all that money should last a while.

*When you get back.* It made her smile. She turned away from the window and the heavyset woman caught her eye.

"Got a long ways to go?" the woman asked.

"Seems like," Mercy said, wiggling her toes. "When you're just starting out."

# A Friend In Deed

## DON MARSHALL

An ornate hearse pulled by four ebony horses rolled along a dusty country road toward a weedy cemetery nestled in a cottonwood copse in Bear Valley, California. The matched quartet decorously bobbed their black-plumed heads in cadence with their clopping hooves and the gentle jingling of their brass-buckled traces. Two stiff-backed men, clad in formal black suits, top hats, and snow-white gloves, sat atop the driver's seat.

"Mr. Nickolas?" asked the younger of the two in hushed tones, a puzzled expression on his face.

"Yes, Andrew?"

"Mr. Nickolas," repeated young Andrew Clark to the middle-aged mortician sitting beside him, "you've always told me to be gentle with folks, just like you are, when someone in a family dies . . . even with the body. But this time you laid out Mrs. Harbinger in the box back there with an awful lot of extra special care. I know you and Mr. Harbinger's been close friends for years, but gee whiz, everyone in town hated Mrs. Harbinger. Nary a soul's sorry she died."

The mortician had been sitting lost in thought about his brand new, custom-made hearse, the finest money could buy. Four oaken posts spiraled to a gingerbread-bedecked tiered roof. Finely-etched ornate windows provided a view of the maroon, padded velvet interior and its contents, a plain pine coffin. Most people would have thought it a dark and foreboding carriage and would have taken little notice of the eloquent craftsmanship and luxurious comfort in which the hated occupant now rode her last mile. But the hearse was the pride and joy of Simon Nickolas, Bear Valley's friendly family mortician. A number of moments passed before the mortician answered his young apprentice.

"Andrew," Simon said, a hint of rebuke in his voice, "first, if I may correct you, that is not, nor should you ever refer to it as, a *box*. It's called a coffin, a casket, or even a sarcophagus, but *never* a box."

"Sorry, Mr. Nickolas," murmured Andrew, embarrassed by what he had said but grateful that his mentor corrected him on minor but essential secrets of the trade.

"Second," continued the mortician, "yes, Mr. Harbinger is my closest friend. I would be remiss if I didn't extend every possible courtesy during his time of crisis and sorrow. The least I can do is provide every possible consideration during these dark hours of his bereavement.

"Third, even though Mrs. Harbinger was the most hated, mean, rabid-mouthed, miserable individual in town, and in spite of what the townsfolk may think, the services of Simon Nickolas, Undertaker, will continue to bestow the epitome of respect upon the newly departed."

"Yes, sir, but it seems as though, in this case, you . . ."

". . . were more gentle than usual. Is that what you were going to say, Andrew?" Nickolas interrupted. "Well, yes, that's probably true. But it's all because of my long friendship with Henry, er . . . Mr. Harbinger.

"As long as we have some distance to go before reaching the cemetery, I'll explain why, in this particular instance, I am overly solicitous." The undertaker rose slightly from the cushioned seat and turned to check the funeral cortege.

The leading buggy carried the bereaved Mr. Harbinger and whitehaired Mr. Whorley, the old village parson. The second carriage held four dark-suited, somber-faced, grey-haired men recruited by the widower to assist in the delicate task of pallbearing. No others followed to pay their last respects to the deceased Mrs. Harbinger.

Simon Nickolas gently pulled the reins, reminding the horses to maintain their sedate cadence, then continued with his story. "It all began some twenty years ago in a little town called Zanesville . . . that's in Ohio. I first met Henry Harbinger in his general store there. I had recently graduated from undertaking school . . . not really a school, so to speak, but an apprenticeship such as you're taking now.

"I set out on my own to . . . I guess you could say conquer the world. Soon after I started my business, I needed to purchase an interment suit for a poor fellow who, after a hard-drinking session in town, had staggered across a field on his way home, fallen down an open cesspool, and drowned.

"In spite of his body's being fairly fresh, he hardly smelled like a bed of roses. I felt obliged to discard his soiled garments so that his inhumation might at least be bearable.

"Henry . . . Mr. Harbinger most generously gave me a very good price on a slightly moth-eaten suit with *two* pairs of pants. As a result, the services for the deceased procccdcd on schedule.

"That being my first interment, I and the family of the deceased, of course, owed a large debt of gratitude to Mr. Harbinger's timely generosity."

Nickolas leaned forward on the carriage seat and casually rested his elbows on his knees. It surprised Andrew that the normally stiff-backed undertaker was capable of relaxing in so easy a fashion. "The remaining set of trousers I used some months later for a pantsless gentleman who expired rather suddenly from bullet wounds as he was diving out a bedroom window, wearing only his coat. Apparently he forsook the opportunity to attire himself properly. No doubt due to the untimely appearance of the woman's husband."

The mortician reached down to his right and slowly applied pressure on the hearse's brake handle. The carriage eased down a grade, then rounded a slight bend in the road. Ahead lay the small, dried-grass covered valley with the cemetery situated on its far side.

"Since Mr. Harbinger's and my first business arrangement proved mutually profitable, we became fast friends." He let out a long sigh. "As you will learn in time, professional undertakers by necessity perform undertaking. This calling put quite a damper on my popularity in the community. But Henry's social life was suffering, too."

Andrew, encouraged by his patron's continued relaxed bearing and uncommon display of humor, ventured a cautious move with thumb and forefinger and pushed his hat top back to relieve the sweaty buildup trapped under the band.

"To go on with my story, Henry earned a comfortable living for his wife and himself, though his Mrs. constantly accused him of living beyond his means.

"If the two of us played chess at night, we burned too much coal oil. If we played checkers in the daytime, she called us lazy. One time, Henry committed the cardinal sin of donating some groceries and old clothes to a destitute widow and her three children. They lived in a shack down by the B & O railroad tracks. Winter was coming, and they faced a bleak future.

"Even I, in my own small way, had tried to help out when she got widowed by a train that ran over her husband. I arranged to bury him in a short grave for half price.

"Henry kept the little family supplied until the widow remarried. She and her new husband paid back every dime—not that Henry ever asked for or expected it."

The mortician clucked the horses, leaned back, and tilted his top hat a half-inch or so above his brow. Andrew noticed the gesture and sneaked a crooked forefinger inside his stiff celluloid collar to release some of the sweaty steam from his starched shirt.

"After that, Mrs. Harbinger never stopped reminding Henry that he had no business supporting anyone else's family and had better collect interest on the money the widow and her new husband paid back.

"I have to admit that any punishment the bard Dante described in his piece, the *Inferno*, didn't even come close to the harsh rasping of Mrs. Harbinger's vocal vehemence. It's been said . . . not by me, mind you . . . that her squawking, twangy, ear-bursting articulation soured the milk of every bovine within auditory range and withered and stripped every leaf off every tree in the valley, without even a faint hope for a wayward breeze to waft them out of earshot. Even the clams in the river's mud flats hightailed it to the sanctuary of the deep, hoping for a few precious moments of blessed silence."

With a slight shake of his head, mortician Nickolas mused half aloud, "How Henry endured those torments of the damned defies my understanding. But he did, and did it in silence to boot."

Leather harnesses creaked in muted rhythm with the horses' slow gait. A blazing sun beat down upon the parched road. Ahead, a small dust devil danced across the scorched earth. It picked up bits of dried grass and an occasional brown, crackly leaf, it darted under and between the horses' legs. Mischievously, it jumped in front of Andrew and deposited its burden of trash over his black suit, then merrily flitted across the field as if inviting a chase.

The young apprentice desperately longed to remove his white gloves, unbutton his coat, and cool his sweaty body. He resisted the impulse for fear of receiving a disapproving look from the mortician, whose sense of propriety never wavered, even under the most difficult of circumstances. Andrew felt a deepening confusion over his tutor's insistence that they handle the deceased Mrs. Harbinger with utmost caution.

"Yes, Andrew, that woman made life pretty miserable for Henry, his customers, their neighbors, and anyone else unfortunate enough to come within earshot of her.

"A rival store opened up in town and bestowed the final coup de grace. As much as his customers favored Henry, they just couldn't tolerate his Mrs. any longer. Soon, the whole town took their business to the new store.

"When the great rush to the California goldfields started, Henry decided to pull up stakes and head west. I, of course, always enjoyed a rather adventurous spirit and entertained a desire to visit the goldfields, too. So we both sold out and, ignoring her vitriolic prattle, caught the stage for

New York and boarded a steamer for Panama. All the way south, she carped about its leaky seams, the ill-mannered crew, and the bad food.

"We landed at Colón, engaged a canoe, and paddled upriver towards the staging point for the mule trains. All the while, she harangued our Indian guides to the point that four of them clamped their hands over their ears and leaped overboard. Apparently they preferred facing the caimans and poisonous snakes to enduring another minute of her caterwauling. Much the same thing happened later with the mules."

"But, Mr. Nickolas, if she were that obnoxious, how come *you* put up with it?"

"That, Andrew, is a very good question. The reason I 'put up with it,' as you say, is, first, that I, like old Parson Whorley, am a bit deaf. Second, and most important, as you will find out, is that men in our profession always enjoy the privilege of having the last word."

Andrew savored the words "men in our profession." A flood of pride surged through him when he realized that the mortician had referred to him as an equal.

Nickolas brushed off a bit of offending dust from his sleeve cuffs, scratched his nose, and continued his narration. "Eventually we arrived here in the Sierras, Henry to open his store, I to start this business, and Mrs. Harbinger to start trouble. In no time at all, she scolded, carped, rebuked, and chided every man, woman, and child in the county, and I don't believe she missed many of the horses, mules, chickens, dogs, cats, or Indians, either.

"Then one blessed day . . ." the older man paused. Andrew thought he glimpsed a hint of a smile flashing across the mortician's normally stoic face. "About five years ago, during one of her vein-popping tirades over some nonsense, she dropped dead."

Andrew forgot about an annoying bead of sweat trickling down his rib cage and sat bolt upright as though stung by a scorpion.

"Died? *Five* years ago! Mr. Nickolas, you're joshing me. She died *yesterday!*"

"Oh, yes, I know. But this is her second death. Let me explain. You see, there brews in the heads of some individuals a condition, a sort of nervous affliction, perhaps inherited. It occasionally subjects these poor souls to cataleptic fits, a suspension of the bodily senses and reflexes, and causes a muscular rigidity closely resembling death. It seems that unbeknownst to Mr. Harbinger or myself, his Mrs. suffered from this peculiar malady."

Nickolas took note of the cemetery gate just a few hundred yards ahead, straightened his back, adjusted his hat, and assumed a more professional position on the padded hearse seat.

"We gave her a proper funeral . . . up to a point. Henry, in spite of his most profound grief, seemed to enjoy the blissful respite from her wagging tongue."

"But you said, up to a point. What did you mean?" asked the puzzled apprentice.

"Ah, yes. Well . . . you see that fancy wrought-iron gateway up there ahead?" He pointed a bony finger toward the entrance to the cemetery, where two latticework columns supported an ornate arched span.

"Yes," Andrew nodded.

"Well, I drove the horses right up to the gate as I always do. The ride had been pretty bumpy, 'cause my old hearse wasn't smooth riding like this new one. It didn't have the modern C springs, the cross leather suspension, and the padded interior. This is the latest model, you know," he proudly added. "At any rate, the heat was oppressive, just like today. My attention wandered, and perhaps I drove a bit too close to the gate, because we felt quite a bump. We drove on in and unloaded the coffin in kind of a hurry, as we all were in a rush to get home out of the heat.

"One of the pallbearers with acute hearing abilities detected a muffled cry that came from the interior of the casket. Lo and behold! When we opened the lid to investigate, up popped Mrs. Harbinger, her eyes blinking like a frog's in a hailstorm and her mouth, as usual, working overtime."

"Golly, Mr. Nickolas, what a close call! Think of it—she almost got buried alive." The morbid thought sent shivers up and down Andrew's spine in spite of the blazing sun and his heat-absorbing dark suit. He imagined the horror of lying hopelessly trapped in a sealed coffin, listening to shovelfuls of earth thudding down overhead.

"Yes, indeed, it was a close call. I spoke to the doctor afterwards. He explained that the combination of the bumpy ride and the sharp rap on the gatepost jarred Mrs. Harbinger back to consciousness."

The plumed horses drew the hearse abreast of the burial ground. "Whoa, easy now," cautioned Nickolas as he pulled back the brake handle and cautiously locked it in place. "Now, Andrew, here we are, safe and sound. Remember, propriety is our stock in trade. When you climb down, do it slowly, quietly, and with dignity. Place yourself at the rear of the hearse, and gently open the door. I will direct the pallbearers. After services, remain with the horses while I fill in the grave."

Young Andrew performed exactly as instructed. Mr. Harbinger and old Parson Whorley alighted from their carriage and slowly walked in silence along the weed-lined path to Mrs. Harbinger's gravesite. The four men, hand-picked by Simon Nickolas, stepped down from their carriage and sedately assembled at the rear of the hearse. The lanky undertaker positioned himself to one side of the group. Andrew placed his hand on the door latch and, as cautioned, moved it gently downward. It made a slight click as the catch was released. He swung the door open. The four stone-faced men slowly pulled the pine coffin from the interior.

Andrew surveyed the length of the coffin. A sudden thought struck him; his eyes grew round. "Oh, Mr. Nickolas?" he called.

"Shhh! Not now, Andrew," whispered the funeral director, placing his index finger over his lips. "Remember . . . decorum's the word."

"But, sir," insisted Andrew with a hint of urgency in his hushed voice.

"Andrew, that is enough!" the mortician rasped in a hoarse whisper.

The young apprentice nodded. Gee whiz, he thought, I only wanted to ask if the same thing might not happen all over again . . . that "cataclysmic fit" or whatever he called it.

"Now, gentlemen, two of you to a side. Be careful to lift in unison," said Nickolas in hushed tones. "And please, boys . . . *don't bump that post.*"

# When God's in Town

## J. A. PAUL

When Grandma died, Jenny wasn't sad, though everyone thought she was because she cried. Jenny only cried because Mama cried, though why anyone would cry over losing Grandma, Jenny didn't know. After the funeral the church ladies came and patted Mama's hand. "Lucy," they said, "God knows best. Your mama was old and sickly and didn't enjoy life no more."

That's true, Jenny thought. Grandma yelled and hollered from the day she came to live with them after Jenny's father died. She just turned up on the porch one day saying she could help ease Mama's burden, so in she moved, dragging dusty hats and broken-heeled shoes. After that, everything got louder. The radio, the television, and everybody's voice.

If that wasn't enough, Grandma pestered Mama to ease her burden some more by remarrying. She pestered her so much that Mama believed Will when he sat on the porch saying he could ease her burden by tending the garden. Jenny liked their garden the way it was. It had apple and sour cherry trees and blueberries. Even so, Jenny didn't guess it was Will's primary reason for marrying Mama.

After a while Grandma started saying Will was the most selfish man Mama could of chose. Grandma was right, but Jenny discovered that being right don't mean being happy, because Grandma was purely miserable. If God only just got around to hearing about her, how long would it take Him to hear about Will? Nobody in town yelled more than Will. Nobody worked harder than him, his fruits didn't grow right, his joints hurt, and worst of all, Jenny's bike was always in his way. Those times he yelled first, and threw her bike second. The bike was the last present Jenny had received from her daddy, and she tried her best to protect it. It was hard, since Will wouldn't let her use the garage. Will was a collector of tools and "antique devices," and the garage held shelves and shelves and rows and rows of them, and still not enough to make him happy. Jenny wondered when God might be in town again. Will was sure to be next on His list, if "not enjoyin' life" was what counted. She thought about it for a while. Seeing as how God was the busiest Person alive, she really ought to save Him the work. She should find a way to kill Will herself.

Will liked to bake pies. It was the reason he liked Mama's mature fruit orchard so much. The parlor wall was covered with his plaques and ribbons, though he always grumbled about not getting cash or a collectible. Every weekend, all year long, Jenny and Mama had to taste a new mixture. Given Will's disposition, they always said it was delicious. Jenny still remembered pies flying through the kitchen window before they learned. Worse, Mama had to call somebody else to fix the window, and pay him, too.

But the pies gave Jenny an idea. Two years ago when Grandma was still tasting, Will had mixed a sourful combination of fruits and Grandma had spit it out.

"You tryin' to poison me?" she hollered. Will wouldn't let her taste after that, Grandma didn't want to anyway, but the memory of it gave Jenny her first plan. She'd poison one of Will's pies, and he would die.

When Jenny was small, Mama had taught her about poisonous plants. One of them was called nightshade. Its white droopy flowers made it easy to find, though it wasn't the flowers Jenny wanted. It was the clammy, wilted leaves. One hot afternoon she picked enough to fill a plastic sandwich bag and took them home to the stove. She tried to run the juice from them like Mama did with berries for jelly, but they only burned, so she improvised by boiling them in a little water. It gave her about an ounce of smelly brew, which she poured into a little jar and hid under her bed. She scrubbed everything she had touched and buried the cooked leaves in the back yard. The only thing left was to wait until Saturday morning.

An unbaked crust filled with apples was on the counter. Will faced the other way mixing orange juice with brown sugar. There were peels, rinds, and flour dust all over everything. Saturday mornings were a terrible mess in Mama's kitchen, thought Jenny. Will never cleaned a thing. Jenny took the jar from the pocket of her bathrobe and, quick as a flash, dumped its contents over the uncooked pie. She was sitting on the bottom step of the staircase when Mama came in from bagging the trash, another thing Will never did.

He must've heard the front door shut because right away he yelled to Mama, "Too much juice in these here apples! Didn't I tell you not to pick after a rain? Damn fool women." Mama glanced at Jenny on the step and gave a little shrug. Will picked his own fruit. It was the only thing he did, not trusting their judgment. The exception was at sour cherry time. Since it took him too long to pick what he needed, he made Jenny do it. Neither of them bothered to argue the lie. "Going to need more cornstarch on these here apples," he shouted to them.

This time Jenny was glad for his laziness. Someone else might've started over.

That night after supper Jenny remembered something that was just plain obvious. Will cut three pieces of pie. It was the only thing in his sorry life that he did polite, and she had forgotten it. He served her and Mama first. They were expected to take their bites before he took his. Jenny watched Mama's fork heading toward her mouth. This was no time to ponder her own poor planning.

"Aaaagh . . . !" Jenny yelled, swinging her milk glass across Mama's plate. Mama dropped her fork in astonishment. Jenny reached over to right her glass and her hand slipped into Mama's pie. Jenny flipped the dish and sent it crashing to the floor. She clutched her stomach. "Oh, I'm sick. I'm real sick!" she declared. If only she could throw up on purpose, the way some of the boys at school could. Instead, she swung her arms to demonstrate the size of her pain and managed to sweep Mama's coffee into the uncut pie in the center of the table. A "pain spasm" caught her as she reached to remove the cup, so she fell on it, pulverizing the remainder of the pastry. "I . . . I have a terrible pain," she said, falling back into her chair, allowing an elbow to land in her own wedge. Quickly surveying the destruction, she decided she couldn't have done much more. There was only one slice of pie left. A sputtering sound came from that end of the table. Will's face was purple and parts of it were pulsating.

"Get that kid outa here!" he roared.

The command was unnecessary, as Mama was already uttering soothing sounds, helping Jenny to her feet. They had reached the landing when Jenny heard a resounding spit. "Woman, where the hell you pick these apples? They taste like pig slop!"

So Will didn't die that night.

Jenny spent the next week thinking. She had almost killed Mama, then saved her. She hoped it was even. She'd have to be a lot more careful next time. She still liked the idea of poison, but she'd have to use a snake or something, placing it where it couldn't possibly get Mama. The most tempting place was the garage, where Will spent so much time admiring his collectibles. The problem was that Will often told Mama to clean the garage. Besides, Jenny didn't like the idea of hunting down a live, poisonous snake.

One day on her way home from school Jenny was kicking pebbles off the sidewalk. She spotted a daddy longlegs and carefully sidestepped it. It gave her an idea.

Later in the day she searched a rocky part of the woods, looking for the tangled web of a black widow spider. After finding it, she sat on a stump to wait. Sure enough, a shiny little black body with the telltale red dots soon appeared. She scooped it into the same jar used previously for the unsuccessful poisonous leaves and went directly to the one place Mama would be safe and Will would surely get bit. Will's sock drawer. Once Will's socks were washed and put in the drawer, Mama didn't touch them again until they were smelly and dirty and lying on the floor. Jenny picked the blue kind that Will wore every day and emptied the spider into one. She rolled them up the way Mama did and put them back with the rest. All that was left was for Will to die.

Meantime, Mama got a raise from Mr. Cooper's Appliance Store. She was real proud.

"I'm assistant manager now, right under Mr. Bickers," she said at supper.

Jenny began to say how great that was, but Will interrupted.

"How much more money you gettin'?" he asked, with his mouth still full of fried chicken.

"Fifteen dollars a week," said Mama. "And Mr. Cooper said he'd sell us a clothes dryer at cost. We could use the extra money to pay it off. Jenny's a big help hanging the wash, but when it rains . . ."

"Only fifteen dollars?" said Will. "Seems to me, a man gives up the comfort of havin' his wife at home alla the time, seems to me they oughta pay him more for it."

Jenny hoped he'd put on those socks real soon.

It was another two days before she heard the bellow from the bedroom. Mama was cooking breakfast. When she ran upstairs Jenny went with her. Will was standing in his underwear, hair sticking out all over, holding a dead spider.

"How'd this here get in my sock?" he demanded to know.

"What is it?" asked Mama.

"It's a black widow, is what it is. A dead one, lucky for me. What's it coming to when a man can't safely put on a pair of socks?"

"Maybe it crawled in from the clothesline," said Jenny. "If we had a clothes dryer . . ."

"From now on, you insecticide that clothesline, woman. You hear? And check every damn piece of my clothes!"

Time passed, but Jenny had no new ideas.

Then one day there was a talk at school. Jenny learned new information about accidents in the home. The best place was the bathtub, but that was downright unmanageable. Next best was falling downstairs, and that she could manage.

Mama had a big cedar chest along the wall at the top of the stairs where she kept sheets and blankets. It had little airholes in it that her daddy had put there when Jenny was a baby so that if she ever climbed in she wouldn't suffocate. All Jenny had to do was make a front hole bigger. She did this with one of Will's collectibles, a cordless drill. It was already charged because Will kept everything in the garage charged up even though he never used anything.

One evening when Mama and Will were downstairs, Jenny went up and emptied the cedar chest. She hid the pile of linens under her bed, hoping it wasn't too dusty.

The next morning Mama woke her as usual and went downstairs to make breakfast. While Will was dressing, Jenny hopped into the chest, letting the top close over herself. Mama's longest knitting needle lay waiting. Jenny pushed it into the hole she had enlarged, but not so far out that Will could see it. She waited. The chest was dark and cosy and smelled like the woods. She put her eyes to the other holes. The view wasn't great, but she would be able to see Will's legs approaching. When he got to the landing, she would shove out the needle and trip him down the stairs.

It didn't work quite right. Will moved faster than she expected, and because of it she wound up stabbing him instead of tripping him. He gave a great yowl, and in the end it worked out, for he went hurtling down the stairs just the same. After the thumping and banging stopped, it got quiet. Mama came running, then rushed to the telephone for help. While she was gone, Jenny jumped out of the chest, closed it, and went down to see what had happened. After Mama left with the ambulance, Jenny replaced the linens and needle and squeezed wet dust into the enlarged hole. With hopes high, she went off to school.

Mama wasn't there when Jenny got home, and she didn't take it as a good sign. When somebody died, people stayed home to make funeral plans. Sure enough, she learned that Will was only unconscious. It took another day for him to wake up. The good part was he didn't remember the fall, and nobody noticed the hole in his leg. The bad part, Jenny figured, was that there was no way to kill Will.

Will came home from the hospital full of news about the town fair. Naturally he expected to win the bake contest, but this year there was a new competition he was excited about. It was a three part race, and the prize was a brand new driving mower. At first Jenny thought it might come in handy to run him over with, but she guessed he would never let her or Mama drive it. She was right. The sound of hammering in the garage proved to be for a special platform to show it off. She and Mama would have to keep pushing the old mower even if Will won ten new ones. That being the case, Jenny vowed to prevent his winning.

It didn't take her long to find she could do nothing with the first two parts of the race. The swim across the creek was in the open where everyone would be watching. The second part was to throw a heavy disc close to a wooded path. The closer they got, the shorter and easier would be the third part, which was a blindfolded race through the woods to a clearing on the other side of the trees. Jenny liked the third part. If they were all blindfolded, it should be easy to stall Will.

Jenny spent the next week walking the wooded area looking for vines, which she tied together. She studied the path toward which they'd be throwing their discs. She made allowances for short throws, long throws, and the distance a blindfolded person might go astray. Then she laid the vine, tying one end to a tree and placing the remainder across and beyond the path. She would've used rope but thought it might be discovered before the race. The vine had a better chance of lying unnoticed, it being as natural to woods as squirrels. She carried the rest of it to the bottom of a strong tree, put a rock on it, and climbed up the tree holding on to the last ten feet of vine. This she wrapped loosely around a thick limb she would use as a perch on Fair Day. When she climbed down to remove the rock, the vine remained flat. Jenny covered the length of it with leaves, climbed back to her perch, and gave a tug. The leaves heaved slightly. It was ready to trip Will.

Everybody was in a good mood on Fair Day, especially Will, who laid claim to the blue ribbon in the pie contest as well as the big new mower.

Jenny ate popcorn, hot dogs, and cotton candy. She listened to the tinny fair music, went on a few rides with her friends, and slipped away in between to check her vine. Mama was selling chances on somebody's hand-made quilt, and Jenny saw Mr. Bickers stop to buy another ticket over and over instead of buying them all at once. Jenny grimaced. Mr. Bickers was married. When the afternoon was at its warmest, an announcement came to shut down the rides and lock up the booths. The race was on.

Up in the cool branches of her tree, Jenny couldn't see the swim part at all, and only saw a couple of the discs land. Either Will's swim was slow or his throw short, for he wasn't among the leaders. That would've made Jenny happy except that those ahead of him went so far astray she couldn't believe it. Some were walking the length of the woods instead of through it. Others moved too fast for being blindfolded, and either walked into trees or tripped and fell. By the time they got up, their sense of direction was gone. Some even went backwards to where they started, and had to begin all over again.

If just one of them could get to the other side, Jenny thought, the race would be over. How could it be that hard? She got so wrapped up in the cursing and shouting she almost missed Will. He was directly below her when she saw him and yanked the vine. His foot must've been on top of it because the vine didn't move, but the pressure exerted from her pulling at it caused her perch to crack. Quickly she grabbed a branch above her and swung her legs over it. Her original perch crashed to the ground, and she figured it must've been wormy. If she'd known before, she could've dropped it on his head. Below her, Will was using swear words that turned her ears red. Lucky for her, the tree was in full leaf in case a spotter came to check on him, or heaven help her, he should take his blindfold off and look up.

"What in hell you boys doin', makin' this here race under rotten timber! M'damn shoulder's dislocated!" he yelled. Jokes came back, and he cursed some more. Jenny wondered what made him think of rotten wood right off. She peeked through the leaves. Sure enough, his blindfold was askew. Good, thought Jenny. Now he'll have to forfeit. Her mouth dropped when she saw him glance around for spotters and, seeing none, replace his blindfold. The cheat, Jenny thought. He had seen the path and was heading straight for it. In a little while a whistle blew. Will had won.

Jenny went home early to clean herself up before Mama saw her so scratched and dirty. Afterwards, she sat alone on the porch, watching night fall and the lights of the fair flicker out. Pretty soon she heard a little parade coming down the street. Driving his new mower despite one arm in a sling, Will led the procession. Behind him, Mama was laughing and talking in a group that included Mr. Bickers. Mr. Bickers was holding the quilt Mama had sold the chances on. If there was doubt in Jenny's mind about Will's new mower, it was dispelled when someone asked if he would finally mow the lawn himself.

"And dirty this here?" said Will. "This here is both the maiden and farewell voyage of my latest collectible, which I'm gonna call Big Red. This here is my crownin' achievement. He's goin' to sit in a rightful place of honor in the center of m'other honorable collectibles."

He wore an extra ribbon on his chest, Jenny noticed. He'd won the pie contest, too.

As they arrived, Jenny went to sit under the maple tree not far from the garage. Her bike was there. It would start to rust any day now. Mr. Cooper opened the garage door. It was he who had donated the machine. "Will, those mowers aren't collectibles," he said. "They're pieces of equipment meant to make life easier."

"My life's easy enough," said Will as he drove up on the little platform and shifted gears. The mower lurched and kept going. It went over the far side and jolted Will into the overladen shelves at the rear. Down came old and new vises, chain saws, mallets, wheel trollies, and blacksmithing equipment. They learned later that it was a brand new, never used vise that hit him first.

Jenny remained under the maple tree. She heard the din. When the crashing stopped, she saw men run into the garage. She saw Mr. Bickers' arm go around Mama. She waited while the doctor and ambulance were summoned. She watched the doctor shake his head, and she saw Mama faint. A group of men were cleaning up the mess. There would soon be room for Jenny's bike. She wheeled it toward the garage, then stopped to kick the stand into place. She returned to the maple tree and peered up into its dark, whispering branches. God was back in town, and he was here, she was sure of it.

"I guess you just told me that in some things it's not my place to interfere," she whispered. She looked back over to where Mr. Bickers was wrapping his quilt around Mama. "But next time somebody climbs the porch to ease Mama's burden, would it be okay if I slam the door in his face?"

# Mrs. Mouse

## STANLEY ELLIN

The alarm clock had been set for six-thirty. Phil Yost woke three min-utes before it was scheduled to sound its chimes, cocked an eye at it, and depressed its Off button. Then he settled back to savor the three minutes he had thus earned. A sunshiny morning, pleasantly cool for a Massachusetts end of August. But before time was up he became aware of mysterious noises filtering through the venetian blinds from the direc-tion of the Chandler house next door.

He crossed the room and spread two slats of a blind to peer through them. The kitchen entrance to the Chandler house was visible from here, and beside it on the driveway was parked a beat-up station wagon with a woman and a child hauling stuff from it. Both were in just-as-beat-up T-shirts and jeans, the woman small and slight, her hair in a braid that fell almost to her waist, the boy at a guess close to Andy's age, Andy Yost having last month celebrated his twelfth birthday. There was no man in sight, no suggestion of any husband or male consort to help in the donkey work of unloading the heavy cartons, luggage, odd-shaped bundles.

Tenants? Phil wondered. For sure they weren't buyers. Judy Phelps, Linstead Township's leading real-estate lady and unofficial town crier, had said that the place was definitely not for sale. On the other hand, this certainly seemed a pair of ragamuffin tenants for a distinguished old house in the swankiest part of town. Mysterious all right, in line with the whole curious performance given by the Chandlers the past few months. The Chandlers were the colonel and his lady—Colonel Henry Chandler, U.S.A. retired, and Mrs. Maud Chandler—a partnership, so the word went, where he had the honors and she had the money, barrelfuls of it.

What they definitely hadn't had was any neighborly feeling, maintain-ing a chilly distance from all the prosperous young marrieds who had taken over the fine houses in the section, and, from the time Phil Yost and family had moved next door, coming on neighborly only once. That was the evening they had appeared at his door to tender their condolences on his wife's death. Even then they had refused any hospitality, just stood there in the foyer, the square-jawed colonel ramrod stiff, stately Maud murmuring, "How awful. Such a beautiful young woman. What can one say?"

What, indeed? Greta had been beautiful and young and the kind of challenging driver who invited disaster every time she got behind the wheel. It had been all her fault, her piling up the car, and the only thing to mitigate the horror had been her decision not to take Andy along on that shopping trip. Phil was consciously grateful for this several times a day, every day.

Anyhow, the colonel and his lady, who had hitherto lived by a precisely marked calendar—winters in some place they owned in the Sun Belt, summers in some place they rented in the Berkshires—this year had suddenly returned in mid-winter from the Sun Belt only to take off again a few days later, finally to show up once more right after Easter Week and oversee the loading of various furnishings into a small moving van. And that had been the last of them.

No goodbye to anyone, no nothing. Permanently relocating, said Judy Phelps, leaving a lot of their furnishings behind and with a landscaping outfit contracted to tend the grounds. And, Judy had added with some irritation, they had left instructions with her agency that the place was definitely not for sale.

And now, thought Phil, here in the Massachusetts dawn were this pair of shabby unknowns apparently taking occupancy. If nothing else, this information had to put him one up on Judy, the know-it-all lady. Last year he had finally come around to dating her—and, in fact, bedding her occasionally—but while she, with two divorces on the books, was making it plain she might be ready for yet another spouse, she was also too much the Greta type with that know-it-all quality, so that settled that.

Phil glanced at the clock and went into action. The breakfast meeting with Ray Hazen was set for eight o'clock in Boston, a half hour away, and since Hazen had said he'd be making the trip from the Coast just for this meeting—which might even be the truth—it would be courteous to show up on time. And when Hazen had said he was now prepared, blank contract in hand, to make a really sweet offer, that was undoubtedly the truth. Hazen-Wheeler was just one of the bigtime high-technology outfits who wanted Phil Yost very badly, but it was Ray Hazen who, by upping the ante with every phone call, had planted in Phil the idea that maybe the time had come to make the move from Silicon Strip, Massachusetts, to Silicon Valley, California, from Northeast Tektronics to Hazen-Wheeler. Goodbye, Route 128. Hello, San Jose.

Although the picture of uprooting Andy, finally over that nightmarish time getting used to being motherless—well, that was troublesome. And for sure there'd be no persuading Mrs. Walsh to make the trek west. Mrs. Walsh was the live-in housekeeper provided by a Boston agency after Greta's death. A widow of grandmotherly age, pure Boston Irish, she had soon become the affectionate, tough-minded woman in the house Andy needed. No chance of moving her to the Coast, not when she regarded Linstead Township itself as close to the limits of the known world.

Decisions, decisions, Phil thought, working the electric razor over his jaw. Life had been a lot simpler when they were all Greta's department— what the hell, he himself had been one of her decisions—but, on second thought, the simple life hadn't been all that sweet either.

Before going downstairs he tiptoed into Andy's room to look in on his son. Andy, sound asleep in an uncovered sprawl of arms and legs, was coming to look more and more like Greta, which, of course, was Andy's good luck. And a great kid, too, now, as the nightmare time was receding into the dim past, actually accepting his father as friend and trusted confidant. For which Mrs. Walsh was due all thanks. She had been the one to point out to Phil with acerbity that this motherless child needed a lot more in the way of a father than someone who worked at his job crazy hours day and night and came home, it seemed, just to use the facilities.

She had really handed Phil the rough side of that Boston Irish tongue, had, in the end, led him to reorder his priorities and nervously apply himself to the fatherhood role until he found, with some surprise, how gratifying it could be. The turning point was that as Andy came to comprehend his father's job—magic with all that dazzling micro-chip stuff— and as the basement of the house filled up with by-products of the magic, those handcrafted electronic games free of charge to any kids Andy chose to invite home, the boy had developed a mild case of hero-worship for the magician. Impossible to tell how long this might last with a kid approaching his teens, Phil sometimes warned himself, but while it lasted it was the best thing that had ever happened to him. There had certainly never been anything like it with Greta. Far from it.

Downstairs, having a quick orange juice at the kitchen window, he got another look at the couple moving in next door. This time the boy was on the tailgate of the station wagon futilely heaving against a heavily roped carton while the woman stood below hauling at it. Moved by conscience and a touch of the male imperative, Phil went outside and joined the party. "Let me," he said, and before there could be any protest he got a grip on the carton's ropes, dragged it clear of the wagon, and with that dead weight painfully banging his ankles every step of the way he managed it through the open door into the Chandlers' pantry, where he stacked it beside the other bundles there.

When he stepped outside the woman said in briefest explanation, "Books." Then very stiffly, "Thank you."

"No trouble at all," Phil lied. Close up, except for those extraordinarily large gray eyes, there was nothing prepossessing about her. The snub nose and wide mouth were almost clownish, in fact. And the grimy T-shirt and tight jeans plainly revealed a figure that was almost boyish. All in all a little disappointing, even allowing for those eyes. Not, Phil assured himself, that on his first look from upstairs he had developed any fantasies about himself and the girl next door. Besides, this was no girl. Definitely, from the web of fine lines at the corners of the eyes and the look of her, a woman well on his side of thirty. "I'm Phil Yost," he said. "I live right there next door."

"Sarah Chandler," the woman said. She motioned at the boy. "And that is Neil." She didn't have to add that Neil was her son. He was a small, pale, shaggy-haired replica of her.

"Pleased to meet you, Neil," Phil said. Chandler? Judy Phelps had once mentioned a Chandler son—the Chandler son—who had long ago left the nest, but there had been no mention of any daughter. Usually, when it came to ice-breaking chitchat with a stranger not in his line of work he was pretty much tongue-tied, but curiosity impelled him to ask the woman, "You're related to the Chandlers?"

"My husband's parents. He died a few months ago. They've given Neil and me this house."

"Oh." He had the sense of having clumsily poked into raw nerves. "I'm very sorry about your husband. Anyhow, if there's something you need in getting settled down, my housekeeper's in all day. Just ask her."

"Thank you." She hesitated. "And there is something, please. There weren't any stores open yet when we came through town, so if you'd have a bottle of milk to spare—"

He fetched her a carton of milk, and in bypassing the station wagon he observed that its license plate was Canadian. British Columbia. Sarah Chandler received the milk gratefully and came up with a handful of change, but Phil waved it aside. "Just let's call it a housewarming gift. Did you drive all the way here from B.C.?"

"Vancouver. Yes. No big deal. Nighttime driving only. And it took almost a week."

Nighttime driving from the Pacific to the Atlantic all on her own, no big deal. Quite a woman, Phil thought as he headed for his garage. A lot tougher than she looked. On the other hand, the same could have been said about Greta, so what did it prove?

The breakfast with Ray Hazen was held at the Ritz-Carlton, and the man, blunt-spoken and with a fanatic light in the eye, came to the point fast. Hazen-Wheeler had done well in the semiconductor trade with logic chips, calculation being a hot item. But this hot item was cooling now, so the company projected a big jump into the future. Memory chips, starting with the 64K RAM's. Not that calculation would be downgraded, simply that information storage would become *numero uno*. All of which was highly confidential, of course.

"The 64K RAM's?" Phil said. "But the Japanese—"

"Right," Hazen cut in. "And how far ahead would you say they are in the memory chip?"

"Oh, eight years. Going on ten."

"Right again. But what you will do, with Hazen-Wheeler backing you to the limit, is whittle down that eight years to zero in five years."

"Funny arithmetic," Phil said.

"Not really. You know what I mean."

"Yes. A super-crash program. Five years of it."

"And you've been through that with Northeast, and the idea doesn't make you too happy. But consider the positive. You write your own ticket, you set up the infrastructure, you give us five years, renewable at your request. We guarantee complete financing, and we all wind up happy. Except the Japs."

"Even so, Ray, I'm not too unhappy at Northeast. And I'm a widower with a kid who seems very happy where he is. Twelve years old and with a mind of his own. He happens to be my *numero uno*."

"Granted. And where both of you should be is right there in California. I know the California style takes some heavy kidding from you Easterners, but do I have to tell you there's a fat streak of envy in that?"

"I suppose not. But I still have to think it over, Ray."

"For how long?" Hazen's voice hardened a little. "We're making our move start of next year, so I need a firm date for the yes or no, Phil. Just in case I have to go looking for another Mister Right."

"Well, it'll take me about two months to finish the setup I'm on now. I can give you definite word by, say, November first."

Hazen looked disappointed, then said, "All right, if that's what it takes. Meanwhile, I'd like some idea which way the wind blows."

"It does seem to be toward California, doesn't it?"

Hazen raised his coffee cup. "I'll drink to that," he said.

But the fact was, Phil reflected on his way to the plant, that it would really be Andy's decision to make, just as hitherto all such decisions had been Greta's. That dated a long way back—fifteen years now—to the time when this tall, beautiful Greta Nilsen—she could have been the U. of

Minnesota campus queen if her father, a post-office clerk in St. Paul, had had the money to provide the necessary sorority style—attached herself to the socially low-rated, college whiz-kid Phil Yost, much to his own bewildered gratification, and took over his life. Married him, then promptly steered him out of post-grad work into that well paying job with Twin Cities Computer. And later had picked Northeast Tektronics with its top money offer as his base of operations. It had taken a while, but by then it hadn't come as any great shock, to realize that from the day Greta had first sized him up as a marital prospect what she had in mind was the big money he could bring in and all the nice things it could buy as soon as it was in her hand—the high-style clothes, the Mercedes, the too-large home in the best neighborhood, the gilt-edged country-club membership, the luxury trips to New York.

For which, patently uninterested in his work though passionately interested in its rewards, she played the devoted wife. Very good at it in company. More and more impatient with it in private. He bored her stiff, that was what it came down to. No line of communication there at all. But was that really all her fault when Andy, growing up, could rouse her ready interest by a tug of the hand?

Come to think of it, he didn't bore Andy. No, he did not. Irritated him sometimes when, usually at Mrs. Walsh's behest, he had to play the heavy father, but in their times together never—well, hardly ever—drew from his son Greta's kind of yawning, itchy response, the signal that she would like to cut this short. He talked to Andy man to man—at least, big man to little man—and, even more important, it seemed, had learned to listen patiently to whatever weird thoughts Andy was moved to air, gathering by way of contact with Andy's friends as well that almost all twelve-year-olds' thoughts are weird.

Anyhow, it meant a solid line of communication with his son. Certainly sufficient, Phil was sure, to have Andy deliver his honest opinion about a California move.

He came home winded after a frustrating day with some wilfully erring microprocessor circuits and found Mrs. Walsh at work preparing dinner while a noisy game of soccer went on in the back yard. Mrs. Walsh waited for him to mix himself a martini on the kitchen sideboard, then, addressing the pot she was stirring, she said, "Had a visitor this afternoon. New lady next door. A Mrs. Chandler."

"Oh?" said Phil.

"Brought a carton of milk to make up for what you gave her. Nice little thing, too. Got her to have a cup of tea while that little boy went out to play with Andy and his roughnecks. Neil. She tell you about her husband passing away?"

"Yes."

"Terrible thing, a young fellow like that. So that's what the colonel and his missus was up to with all that coming and going. Making arrangements and such. They're settled down in Arizona now for good, she says. Gave her this house here and they get the boy every summer and for Christmas and Easter and such. A lot better having her next door than them, I'll say that much. Freeze you out, their kind of people."

So they did, Phil thought. He went to the kitchen door to take in a view of the soccer game. Over the dividing hedge, the colonel had pointedly remarked how scruffy those games made what had once been a fine lawn. A real old sweetheart, the colonel, with all that West Point charm.

Phil said to Mrs. Walsh, "I don't see the kid out there. That Neil."

"Oh, he just played a little while, then went home with his mama. They're Canadian, did you know that? And while you're there you can tell that gang to go home and for Andy to come in and wash up. It's only ten minutes to supper."

Phil dutifully obliged, and as his scabby-kneed son passed by with a cheerful flip of the hand and a "Hi, Dad," he had the feeling that if Hazen's offer was explained to Andy right now, California would probably get voted down. A kid's decisions were based on the immediate, not the long view. So in fairness to all concerned, including Andy, the California style had to get some build-up. Some casual talk about it along the way.

As it turned out at the dinner table, there is no overestimating the twelve-year-old's capacity to see through adult guile. Phil brought up the subject of California, the Golden State, and after a little of this Andy said to him abruptly, "Are we moving out there?"

It took Phil a moment to right himself. "Suppose I said there's a chance we might?"

"Near Disneyland?"

"Not too far away, I guess."

"Well, all right," said Andy.

Go figure kids. "It's not happening tomorrow," Phil warned. "I'll let you know in plenty of time if and when it does."

"All right," said Andy. "Say, you know that Mrs. Chandler who moved in next door?"

"Yes."

"Well, her kid is really nothing."

The significance of this became clear a couple of days later. The new neighbors remained out of Phil's sight during this interim, but Mrs. Walsh kept him in touch with their goings-ons.

"She's still wearing them widow's weeds, so to speak," confided Mrs.

Walsh. "Do I have to tell you of all people how it feels to lose someone? Especially when you're that young?"

"There's other young mothers around," Phil pointed out. "Sooner or later she'll be making friends with them."

"Them?" Mrs. Walsh looked scornful. "Nice-looking young widows are not exactly what them ladies look to be friendly with. But," she said with obvious pride of possession, "she is kind of friendly with me. Comes in for a cup of tea. Went shopping with me today for school things for Neil. He's already registered for school when it opens next week. Sad little thing. Like Andy first day I walked in here. You remember?"

"Oh, I remember," said Phil.

The following day, Mrs. Walsh had a message for him. She waited until Andy was out of earshot before delivering it. "That Mrs. Chandler wants to have a talk with you."

"With me? About what?"

Mrs. Walsh looked knowing. "Not social. It's something she asked me to put to you, but I told her no, ma'am, that is her business. So she said any time after nine tonight when Neil's put to bed. She said don't let it bother you how late. She ain't much of a sleeper anyhow, the way she tells it."

That was likely true. Sarah Chandler must have taken for herself that front bedroom upstairs, the one directly facing his, and no matter how late he turned in, its light glimmered through his window-blinds. He could understand that. For a long time after Greta's death—her absence from the house had been almost palpable—he had gone through those sleepless nights.

At ten o'clock, after successfully defending his household chess championship against his son and seeing him off to the bathtub, he rang the Chandler doorbell, not without trepidation, and Sarah Chandler opened the door so promptly he had the feeling she must have been sitting on the edge of a chair poised for his arrival. She was in blouse and skirt now, the braided length of hair worked into a sort of coronet effect, and as she said primly, "It's kind of you to take the trouble," and led him inside, he saw that those legs in high heels were very shapely indeed. Still, she was a long way out of Judy Phelps's class and light years out of Greta's, as what woman he had ever encountered wasn't?

He had never been inside the house before. When he looked around at the living room—Federal in design and furnishings—Sarah Chandler read his thoughts correctly.

She said, "It is a little bare, isn't it, but they took the really valuable antique pieces with them. The Chandlers, I mean."

"I see," Phil said and felt himself freezing up with that same old self-consciousness—that miserable shyness—that had Greta privately despair over his performances in public. Especially her choice of public. And a solo housecall like this—

"Coffee?" said Sarah Chandler. "Or something else?"

"Well," Phil said with relief, "if you could whip up a tall Scotch and water—"

"I'm sorry. No makings for it on hand."

"Beer?" Phil said hopefully.

She shook her head. "I meant juice or soda."

"Coffee'll do fine," Phil said with a somber conviction that it would not.

"Coffee it is," said Sarah Chandler. "And would you mind if we used the kitchen? It's not quite as bare as this."

The kitchen was, in fact, almost fully furnished. Almost, because she brought his coffee to the table in a stoneware cup that suggested the Chandlers had removed their best china as well. She filled a cup for herself and sat down facing him. "This is a dreadful imposition in a way. I mean, involving you in Neil's problem."

"Neil's problem?"

She was taken aback. "Didn't Mrs. Walsh tell you anything about it?"

"Nope."

"Oh. Well, she told me so much about you. About what happened to your wife—I'm so sorry about that."

"It was a long time ago. Three years."

"Even so. And the way it affected Andy. At least, according to Mrs. Walsh. It made me feel you'd be especially understanding about Neil. Since Richard—since his father died, he's been going through the same kind of thing."

"They get over it," Phil said. "Anyhow, most of it. Andy did."

"I know. And he's such a capable and well balanced kid, isn't he? Neil idolizes him. He'd be happy just tagging after him all day. And I can see why Andy would be impatient about it. Two years' difference between children that age is an awful lot. And because it's so necessary for Neil to have someone like that, I thought, well, you might not mind helping out. Explaining it to Andy, that is. So he wouldn't just send Neil away every time he goes over there to play."

Phil said warily, "I could explain it to Andy. I couldn't guarantee results. There seems to be a whole gang of kids on the premises most of the time, and they'd have opinions too."

"Of course, but Neil wouldn't have to get into their games. Just be sort of a mascot, if you know what I mean. Just as long as he could be around them. Especially Andy."

"I know what you mean," said Phil. "All right, I'll talk to Andy about it."

"I was sure you'd understand," Sarah Chandler said. "And I'm so very grateful. I mean that."

It was pleasant, the way she said it and the way she looked when she said it. "Meanwhile," Phil heard himself say, "what will you be doing with yourself?" So there it was. Given the precisely right conditions, you didn't have to study the wallpaper and wonder what to say, you just said it.

"Well," said Sarah Chandler, "the main thing is Neil. Getting him through a bad time. Then someday I might go into teaching. I'm a licensed math teacher, but that's British Columbia, of course. I'd have to qualify here."

"You shouldn't have much trouble. You ever deal with computers?"

"Yes." Sarah Chandler smiled, the first time he had seen her smile. "But hardly on your level. Mrs. Walsh told me about your standing at Northeast. And she gave me that electronics magazine with your piece in it about microprocessor-controlled monitors. I'm working my way through it now."

"Make any sense of it?"

"Some. But there are still a lot of questions about their practical application, aren't there?"

It was after midnight, two more cups of coffee later, when with the magazine between them he cleared up the questions. It wasn't easy, because, as he discovered, she had a good scientific mind, an inquiring and challenging mind, that balked at generalities.

At the door she said with some embarrassment, "It's so funny. If you knew how I had to work up the courage to invite you here—"

"If you knew," Phil said, "how I had to work up the courage to push that doorbell."

Before he left for work next morning he woke his son, rubbing a thumb gently up and down a bony ankle, and when Andy had one comprehending eye focused on him, Phil delivered his message. Andy received it with dismay. "But he's just a baby."

"No, he's a ten-year-old whose father died only a few months ago and who now finds himself among total strangers. Get the picture? I'm not asking you to play big brother, just that you and the gang show him a little kindness. I have a feeling he'd be glad to just fetch and carry if you told him to."

"Mousie," said Andy. "And Mrs. Mouse."

"How's that?"

"Him. And his mother. That's what Mrs. Walsh says they are."

"Well, she shouldn't. As for you, sonny boy, a little kindness, that's the word. Understand?"

"Sure. If that's what you want."

"That is what I want," said Phil.

As he confided to Sarah a few weeks after this, omitting the Mrs. Mouse bit, that little passage with his son had been openers for the most manic-depressive day of his life.

"Starting right there," he remembered, "when it struck me that I might be explaining about Neil but it was Neil's mother I had on the brain. Then all that day, there you were. That was the high. Then logic kept getting in the way, and that made for the lows. I mean, you simply don't talk to an absolute stranger for a couple of hours and then think, my God, no woman ever made me feel like this, she is the one, she is what it's all about, and that settles it. After all, how do you know what she thinks about you?"

"How indeed?" Sarah murmured. Hair down, shoes off, she was seated on his lap, her legs comfortably extended on the sofa. They had long before given up those sessions at the kitchen table in favor of the living-room sofa—two upright chairs and the sofa were all the furniture the living room provided—where they could share a necessary, if frustrating, physical contact. Frustrating, because Sarah always had an ear cocked for any sound from her son in his room overhead. "Anyhow," she said, "you must have suspected that I thought of you very kindly, to say the least."

"Or that you were only being very polite. That's logic. Greta spent considerable time impressing on me how deficient I was in personal magnetism or whatever."

"Her mistake," Sarah said. "But it's good we can talk about it this way. Good for both of us."

True. Because his big breakthrough had come one strange evening when he suddenly found himself telling her about his childhood among four loud, totally extroverted brothers, where he, the middle one, was the inarticulate, dreamy misfit. And then, when Sarah was moved to reach across the table and squeeze his hand sympathetically, he had really popped his cork and come out with some painful details about his married life hitherto tightly bottled up in him.

Not that Sarah sat through this nodding wide-eyed agreement with him at every turn. She had some trenchant opinions to offer about, as she put it, his role in this Linstead Township version of an Ingmar Bergman film. His occasional failure—she had a feminist streak in her, all right—to recognize the unspoken needs of a bright and capable woman. Phil, without altogether agreeing, took such opinions with good grace. After all, he advised himself wryly, that compulsion of hers for truth-telling was not a compulsion to be scorned.

Her own breakthrough had come soon after this—by then they had made the move to the comforts of the living-room sofa—when he happened to ask about her plans to refurnish the house, or at least these ground-floor rooms, and she, after a long silence, came out with it and announced that there couldn't be any refurnishing because she was, not to mince words, a charity case.

"You're kidding," Phil said. "The market price of just this property—"

"A loan from the Chandlers. And they provide an allowance to go with it. As long as I stay here and prepare Neil to attend Linstead Academy when he's completed elementary school, and then on to Harvard. They're going to finance his education right up to Harvard graduation. First-class all the way."

"Must it be the Academy and Harvard?"

"Richard's schools," Sarah said. "It's obvious, isn't it? Their grandson is taking their son's place in their lives. And I don't have much choice, do I? I could never give Neil what they can."

"And Richard didn't leave you anything?"

"Just some debts that the Chandlers cleared up. He was the kind of extraordinarily idealistic man who never thinks of money."

The way she put it, with no hint of disapproval, depressed Phil. Surprise, surprise, he told himself, he was acutely jealous of the late Richard Chandler, or of his ghost or whatever you wanted to call it. In that case, wisdom dictated that henceforth the subject of Richard best be left off any agenda.

"I shouldn't have brought all this up," Phil said apologetically.

"Oh yes, you should," Sarah assured him. "It's time it was brought up."

Another troubling aspect of their affair, if that's what it could be called, came to weigh on them especially after Phil had taken to using their side doors for coming and going, out of regard for the sensibilities of the world close around them. Side doors or not, as Sarah pointed out, their neighbors must have strong, if inaccurate suspicions of what was going on in the Chandler house almost every evening. And that, said Sarah reflectively, had to include Mrs. Walsh, who had lately taken to spicing her conversation with some pretty heavyhanded teasing in that direction. Sort of a road-company Juliet's nurse, so to speak.

In the end, it was Andy Yost who abruptly brought the issue to a head one evening when Phil interrupted him at his homework to ask how Neil was making out as the gang's mascot.

Andy shrugged. "Sometimes he hangs around after school, sometimes he doesn't. We leave it up to him." He frowned at his father. "Say, are you going to marry Mrs. Chandler?"

Phil's stomach lurched. "Well," he said, trying to make it casual, "how does the idea strike you?"

"I don't know. All right, I guess. Anyhow, a lot better than having Mrs. Walsh around jumping on me fifty times a day for nothing."

So there it was. "Which," Phil said to Sarah later that evening after reporting on his son's judgment, "sort of leaves it up to you now, doesn't it?"

She was silent too long. Long and troublesome silences were not unusual for her. "There are problems," she finally said.

"None. We'll use my house, of course, and it has all the room we need. And since I'm already Big Daddy to one kid, another won't rock the boat. And you know I can give Neil everything his grandparents can without your being obligated to them."

Again a silence. But this time Phil said urgently, "No, don't take off by yourself. I'm still here. Keep talking."

"All right, but what about that California offer?"

"We write it off. Unless you want to try California."

"You must know by now," Sarah said, "that what I want is very much what you want."

"Oh? Then mark down two items. First, wedding bells in the very near future. A justice of the peace with his wife at the piano will do fine. Agreed?"

Sarah took a long time to say it, but, to his relief, she finally did say it. "Yes."

"And for the second item, I'd like Neil to sleep over tomorrow night at my place. It's time you and I had some total privacy for a little while. For obvious reasons."

"It is. And they are. But I don't know about his being away from home even for one night. He's still very—"

"No problem. I'll fit a cot into Andy's room for the night. It'll work out beautifully."

And, as he knew after their premature honeymoon when he eventually made his way to his own bed near dawn, it had worked out beautifully. If there were ever to be any incompatibility between them—he was sure she must share this conviction now—it would certainly not be a sexual incompatibility. His last waking thought was an unnerving one, the thought that it had been only sheer luck that had brought them together. And considering the predictable workings of such as the 64K RAM, this kind of celestial dice-throwing was no way to run the universe.

He came home from work that evening to find the dining table set for one and no Andy in sight.

"Didn't want any supper," Mrs. Walsh said. "Got home from school, went up to his room, and there he is. No TV, no phonograph. Just laying there."

"Is he sick?" Phil asked with apprehension.

"No. More like he got into some trouble in school."

Upstairs, Phil found Andy lying on his bed fully clothed. Still against the opposite wall was the folding cot taken from the attic for Neil's use the previous night. Phil sat down on the cot and surveyed his son. No question, the kid was in a state of misery. "What's wrong?"

"Nothing."

"Obviously, a lot more than that. Did something go wrong in school?"

"No. Anyhow, it's a secret. A big one. I don't want to talk about it."

"I think you do. And you know I'm good at keeping secrets."

"Even so. Neil told it to me last night, but nobody else in the world is supposed to know about it."

Andy went into a fetal position, shutting out the world, and out of experience Phil sat back and said nothing more. The minutes went by, and then, predictably, his son came to his feet. He closed the door and stood over Phil. "You swear you won't tell anybody else in the whole world about it?"

Phil held up a hand solemnly. "Yes. I swear it."

"All right then." Andy lowered his voice to a hoarse whisper. "Neil's mother killed his father."

"What?"

"She did. They were hassling and she had a gun and shot him right in the heart and Neil saw the whole thing. And now you can't tell anybody else in the world about it."

Phil found himself momentarily paralyzed, voiceless and immobile. Then he said angrily, "Oh, for God's sake, how long were you two kids watching shoot-'em-up shows on TV last night when you were supposed to be asleep?"

"It wasn't that! Neil was right there. He saw it."

"Did he? Now tell me the truth. Just before he came up with that story were you teasing him, maybe putting him down some way?"

"No," Andy said. Then he said uneasily, "Well, not exactly."

"Not exactly?"

"Well, he kept talking and talking while I was trying to read so I finally told him to quit it because he never said anything worth listening to. And he got mad."

"And then cooked up a nice gruesome story to impress you. And, if you'd only—"

"He said it happened. If you don't believe it, why don't you just ask Mrs. Chandler about it?"

"Matter of fact," Phil said grimly, "I will have to talk to her about it, because Neil can make big trouble for her with this nonsense. And, believe me, you'll only make it worse if you mention a word of it outside this room. Understand?"

He was using that tone intended to make clear that here was where he wanted the line to be drawn. It rarely failed, and judging from Andy's reaction, it didn't fail now.

"I know what you mean," Andy said placatingly, "but will you ask her?"

"Ask is not the word. But I will talk to her about it. Now let's both of us get back on the track and go down for supper."

Ten o'clock was the time he had come to set for his excursions next door, well after Neil's bedtime. He cut it short by half an hour this time, surprising Sarah. "Neil's probably still awake," she warned as she opened the kitchen door to him.

"Then we'll stay in here for a while. Sit down."

She frowned as she seated herself. "Trouble?"

He sat down opposite her. "Yes. Weird. And messy. It has to do with Neil."

"Last night?" She looked dismayed. "But I told him that any orders Mrs. Walsh gave him—"

"No problem there at all. But oh God, what these kids can come up with. You see, Andy got Neil pretty riled up with that 'You're only a baby' line, and so to score points—now hold on to your chair—Neil told him that you killed Richard. Shot him. And that he was there to see it. So when I say it's weird and messy—"

The silence hummed in Phil's ears. And that was not astonishment or outrage in those eyes fixed on him but desperate appeal. "My God," he said.

"Please listen to me." That desperate appeal was in her voice too. "I was going to tell you about it. Any day now. You have to believe that."

First, he found, he had to absorb it. He finally managed to say, "Then it really happened?"

"Yes."

"Some kind of accident?"

"No." She shook her head in anguish. "He was beating me. He did that sometimes when he was blind drunk. And this time I believed—I knew—

he was so out of control he might kill me. And his gun was right there on the dresser. Right behind me. I took it and shot him. Not accidentally."

Phil struggled for comprehension. "A wife-beater? And you lived with that?"

"You wouldn't understand. It was all so tangled up."

"No, don't start that. Just untangle it for me." He waited. "Now, Sarah."

She clasped her hands on the table, knuckles gleaming bloodless white. She said unsteadily, "After he graduated college here—"

"You mean it goes that far back?"

"Please, please, just listen. After he graduated he was going to be drafted into the Army. That was during the Viet war. But he became a draft-resister. He went to Canada instead. To Toronto first, then all across Canada, organizing American draft-resisters there. I was in college in Vancouver, we had a student group supporting your draft resisters, and that's how we met. We got married a little while later."

"Love at first sight," Phil said.

"You'd have to know him then. Very attractive, very fiery. He gave himself completely to the movement. But after the war ended he couldn't seem to find any other purpose in life. He lost every job he tried because all he had left in him was anger and frustration and somehow a sense of betrayal. Nothing that would help him live an ordinary life."

"So he started drinking. And instead of banging his own head against the wall, he banged yours."

"No, he did start drinking too much, but the first time he hit me—well, it could have been my fault. The one thing in the world he hated most was his father because of what happened between them when he said he wouldn't let himself be drafted. So when he got to Canada he would never even let his parents know where he was. But when Neil was born I felt they had to know that, at least, so I wrote them about it without telling Richard. He saw their answer in the mail and it drove him crazy. There was a check too—and we needed money so badly—but he tore it up and then he went out and got staggering drunk. When he came home, that was the first time. I mean, that he hit me."

"But not the last."

"No. Sometimes I had to go to the clinic because of it, it got that bad. I made up stories to tell them each time, but I know they never believed me. You can't imagine how ashamed you feel at times like that."

"What I still can't imagine is why you stayed with him. Out of love?" Jealousy, Phil knew, made it hard to say. He forced himself to say it. "Did you really love him that much?"

Sarah seemed bemused by this. "I'm not sure. I did come to see how

Neil adored him and was terrified of him at the same time, so you can live that way. I suppose I was living that way."

"And Neil? He told Andy he saw it happen. The shooting. Did he?"

"Yes." Her eyes dulled. "It was in our bedroom. I didn't know Neil was at the door until after it happened, and I saw him there. But I understood right then what I had done to him. Not so much to Richard or myself, but to him." She said, marveling, "And if you only knew how terrified I always was of that gun."

"Yes, the gun. Why did he have one, someone like that?"

"Because the only job he could get this time was being a security man. And they gave him a gun. Someone like that."

"And there was a trial?"

"Yes. And an acquittal. Self-defense. I think the only ones who didn't see it that way were the Chandlers."

"They weren't there, were they?"

"Oh, yes. They had to be told about Richard. So I had my lawyer locate them and phone them, and they came. And blamed me for everything that had ever happened to Richard. And then went to court and tried to get custody of Neil until I made them understand I'd just go off some-place where they'd never find him. So they finally offered this arrange-ment about the house and Neil's education and having him with them vacation times. But what I never dreamed would happen when I agreed to it—"

"Yes?"

"—was the miraculous thing that happened to me. Finding you. Find-ing what we have together." She drew a long breath. "Is that changed now? Is everything different for us now?"

"Not my feelings for you, no. Never."

She studied his face. "But there is something."

. "Yes. There's Andy. What would I be letting him in for? Do I make him a co-conspirator with Neil in a secret that can't possibly be kept? Lay that on him, knowing how cruel other kids can be—other people, too—when it comes out? If we get married—"

"If?"

"Sarah, I'm not saying we can't or won't. I'm just saying that first I have to get a handle on this, think it through, see if it can be made to work."

"But it can," she said intensely. "And kids grow up and go their own way so soon. When that happens I can't see us far apart from each other, thinking what we might have had."

"That, too. It's one of the things I have to work out." He stood up, almost knocking his chair over. "But I need time. Tonight, at least. I'll see you tomorrow morning first thing. Right after the kids have left for school."

"I'll be here," said Sarah.

Outside, he saw the light in Andy's window, so Andy would be up and waiting for him to report, and he certainly wasn't ready for that. Standing in the driveway, trying to organize the kaleidoscope of images in his head —Sarah, Neil, Andy, himself, past, present and future—he realized that he ached from head to foot as if he had just taken a physical beating. The worst of it was a dull hurt in the pit of the stomach, tension compressed into a lump of cold matter.

His workshop at the plant had always been his refuge when Greta got into one of her moods. He ran the car out of the garage as quietly as he could and headed that way, stopping briefly at the Linstead Inn for a tall double Scotch and water which, he found, provided neither antidote nor inspiration.

The plant at this hour was almost deserted, few cars remaining in the lot when he parked there. He signed in at the desk in the lobby, took the elevator up to the second floor, and walked the length of corridor to the XT room, the experimental test room, his territory.

He turned the lights on full. The room was vast, its floor a tangle of electric cables leading to the variety of machines ranged along three of the walls. With the machines silent like this, the muted humming of the air-conditioner and dehumidifier systems was an insistent presence in the ears.

Phil seated himself in the familiar rump-sprung swivelchair behind the horseshoe-shaped steel desk littered with incomplete circuits, charts, blueprints, and notebooks. He leaned back and closed his eyes, the better to concentrate on that kaleidoscope in his mind.

Faced squarely, the options were simple. Clear cut. Take the plunge or run for cover. Risk the marriage and its consequences because here at last is the woman for you. Or, because your son would be made to risk the consequences too, phone Hazen tomorrow and tell him that father and son, well ahead of schedule, would be on their way to California.

No, not so simple. Not clear cut at all. Agonizing was the word.

The lump in his stomach was now ice-cold and leaden. He opened his eyes despairingly to the machines around him—the wondrous world of the future, at least twenty million dollars' worth of it—waiting there for just a touch on the switch and the necessary input to have them work their magic, to answer any question you could come up with.

Except one.

# Just the Lady We're Looking For

## DONALD E. WESTLAKE

That morning Mary cleaned the kitchen, and after lunch she went shopping. It was a beautiful sunny day, but getting hot; the lawns and curbs and ranch-style houses of Pleasant Park Estates gleamed and sparkled in the sunlight, and in the distance the blacktop street shone like glittering water.

Mary had lived here barely five weeks now, but one development was very like another, and in her seven years of marriage to Geoff she'd seen plenty of them. Geoff transferred frequently, spending six months here, eight months there, never as much as a year in any one location. It was a gypsyish life, but Mary didn't mind: we're just part of the new mobile generation, she told herself, and let it go at that.

All the stores in the shopping center were air-conditioned, but that only made it worse when Mary finally walked back across the griddle of a parking lot to the car. She thought of poor Geoff, working outdoors 'way over at Rolling Rancheros, and she vowed to make him an extra-special dinner tonight: London broil, a huge green salad, and iced coffee. In fact, she'd make up a big pot of iced coffee as soon as she got home.

But she didn't get the chance. She'd barely finished putting the groceries away when the front doorbell sounded. She went to the living room, opened the door, and the man smiled, made a small bow, and said, "Mrs. Peters?"

He was about forty, very distinguished-looking, with a tiny Errol Flynn mustache and faint traces of gray at his temples. His dark suit fitted perfectly, and his black attaché case gleamed of expensive leather. He said, "I wonder if you could spare five minutes, or should I call back later?"

Mary frowned. "I'm sorry," she said, "I don't under—"

"Oh! You think I'm a salesman!" He laughed, but as though the joke were on himself, not on Mary. "I should have shown you my identification," he said, and from his inside coat pocket took a long flat wallet of black leather. From it he plucked a card, and extended it to Mary, saying, "Merriweather. Universal Electric."

The card was in laminated plastic, the printing in two colors. There was a photo of Mr. Merriweather, full face, and his signature underneath. The reverse side gave the office locations of Universal Electric in major cities.

Mr. Merriweather said, smiling, "You *have* heard of Universal Electric, I hope."

"Oh, of course. I've seen your ads on television."

Mr. Merriweather accepted his card back. "If you don't have time now—"

"Oh, I have time. Come on in."

"Thank you." He wiped his feet on the mat, and entered. "What a lovely home!"

"Oh, not really. We just moved in last month and it's still an awful mess."

"Not at all, not at all! You have charming taste."

They sat down, Mary in the armchair and Mr. Merriweather on the sofa, his attaché case beside him. He said, "May I ask what make of refrigerator you now have in your home?"

"It's a Universal."

"Wonderful." He smiled again. "And how old is it?"

"I really don't know—it came with the house."

"I see. And a home freezer unit, do you have one of those?"

"No, I don't."

"Well, fine. You may be just the lady we're looking for." Taking his attaché case onto his lap, he opened it and began removing brightly colored sheets of glossy paper. "A part of our advertising campaign for—"

Now she was sure. "Excuse me," she said, and got to her feet. Trying to smile normally and naturally, she said, "My groceries. I just got home from the store and nothing's put away yet. Your talking about the refrigerator reminded me."

"If you'd prefer that I come back la—"

"Oh, no." No, she didn't want to frighten him away. "This won't take a minute," she assured him. "I'll just put the perishables away, and I'll be right back."

He got to his feet and smiled and bowed as she left the room.

Her heart was pounding furiously and her legs didn't seem to want to work right. In the kitchen she went straight to the wall phone and dialed Operator, her hand trembling as she held the receiver to her ear. When the operator came on, Mary said, keeping her voice low, "I want the police, please. Hurry!"

It seemed to take forever, but finally a gruff male voice spoke, and Mary said, "My name is Mrs. Mary Peters, two-twelve Magnolia Court, Pleasant Park Estates. There's a confidence man in my house."

"A what?"

Didn't this policeman watch television? "A confidence man," she said. "He's trying to get money from me under false pretenses. I'll try to keep him here until you send somebody, but you'll have to hurry."

"In five minutes," the policeman promised.

Mary hung up, wishing there was some way to call Geoff. Well, she'd just have to handle it herself. Generally speaking, confidence men avoided violence whenever they could, so she probably wasn't in any direct physical danger; but you could never be sure. This one might be wanted for other more serious crimes as well, and in that case he might be very dangerous indeed.

Well, she'd started it, so she might as well see it through to the end. She took a deep breath, and went back to the living room.

Mr. Merriweather rose again, polite as ever. He now had the coffee table completely covered with glossy sheets of paper. She said, "I'm sorry I took so long, but I didn't want any of the food to spoil."

"Perfectly all right." He settled himself on the sofa again and said, "As I was saying, Universal Electric is about to introduce a revolutionary new type of refrigerator-freezer, with an advertising campaign built around the concept of the satisfied user. We are placing this refrigerator-freezer in specially selected homes for a six months' trial period, absolutely free, asking only that the housewife, *if* she loves this new product as much as we are convinced she will, give us an endorsement at the end of that time and permit us to use her statement and name and photograph in our advertising, both in magazines and on television."

What would a housewife say who hadn't seen through this fraud? Mary strove for a suitably astonished expression and said, "And you picked me?"

"Yes, we did. Now, here—" he pointed to one of the papers on the coffee table "—is the product. On the outside it looks like an ordinary refrigerator, but—"

"But how did you happen to pick me?" She knew it was a dangerous question to ask, but she couldn't resist seeing how he would handle it. Besides, if she acted sufficiently naive, there wouldn't be any reason for him to get suspicious.

He smiled again, not at all suspicious, and said, "Actually, *I* didn't pick you, Mrs. Peters. The names were chosen by an electronic computer at our home office. We are trying for a statistical cross-section of America."

It was time to leave that, and become gullibly enthusiastic. She said, "And you really want to *give* me a refrigerator for six months?"

"Six months is the trial period. After that, you can either keep the unit in payment for your endorsement, or return it and take cash instead."

"Well, it sounds absolutely fantastic! A brand-new refrigerator for nothing at all."

"I assure you, Mrs. Peters," he said, smiling, "we don't expect to lose on this proposition. Advertising based on satisfied customers is far more effective than any other sort of campaign." He flipped open a notebook. "May I put you down as willing?"

"Yes, of course. Who wouldn't be willing?" *And where in the world were the police?*

He started to write, then suddenly cried, "Oh!" and looked stricken. "I'm so sorry, there's something I forgot, something I should have told you before. As I explained, you have the option either to keep the unit or return it. Now, we want to be sure our trial users won't harm the units in any way, so we do request a small damage deposit before delivery. The deposit is automatically refunded after the six months, unless you wish to return the unit and we find that it has been mistreated."

Would the unsuspicious housewife become suspicious at this point? Mary wasn't sure. But if she seemed *too* gullible, that might be just as bad as seeming too wary. So she said, guardedly, "I see."

"I'll give you a receipt for the deposit now," he went on glibly, "and you show it when the unit is delivered. It's just as simple as that."

"How much is this damage deposit?"

"Ten dollars." He smiled, saying, "You can see it's merely an expression of good faith on your part. If the unit *is* mistreated, ten dollars will hardly cover its repair."

"I'm not sure," she said doubtfully. She *had* to act more wary now, if only to stall until the police got here. "Maybe I ought to talk it over with my husband first."

"Certainly. Could you phone him at work? I do have to have your answer today. If you elect not to take the unit, I'll have to contact our second choice in this area."

"No, my husband works outdoors. I wish I *could* phone him." There was nothing to do now but pay him the money and pray that the police would arrive in time. "All right," she said. "I'll do it."

"Fine!"

"I'll just get my purse."

Mary went back to the kitchen and looked longingly at the telephone. Call the police again? No, they were surely on the way by now. She got her purse and returned to the living room.

It seemed to take no time at all to give him the money and get the receipt. Then he was rising, saying, "The unit should be delivered within three weeks."

Desperately, she said, "Wouldn't you like a glass of iced coffee before you go? It's so hot out today."

He was moving toward the door. "Thank you, but I'd better be getting back to the office. There's still—"

The doorbell chimed.

Mary opened the door, and Mr. Merriweather walked into the arms of two uniformed policemen.

The next five minutes were hectic. Merriweather blustered and bluffed, but the policemen would have none of it. When Mary told them his line, they recognized it at once: complaints had been coming in from swindled housewives in the area for over a month. "There's always a couple of these short-con artists working the suburbs," one of the policemen said.

But Mr. Merriweather didn't give up until one of the policemen suggested that they phone the local office of Universal Electric and verify his identification. At that, he collapsed like a deflated balloon. Turning to Mary, he said, "How? How did you know?"

"Women's intuition," she told him. "You just didn't seem right to me."

"That's impossible," he said. "What did I do wrong? How did you tumble to it?"

"Just women's intuition," she said.

The policemen took him away, shaking his head, and Mary went back to the kitchen and got started on dinner. She could hardly wait for Geoff to get home—to tell him about her day.

Geoff came in a little after five, his suit and white shirt limp and wrinkled. "What a scorcher," he said. "If it keeps up like this, we'd better move north again."

He pulled a handful of bills from his pockets, fives and tens, and dumped them on the dining-room table. As he counted them, he said, "How was your day?"

"Got rid of some of the competition," she told him. "Guy working the Free Home Demonstration dodge. Get that grift off the table, I have to set it for dinner."

# The Hedge Between

## CHARLOTTE ARMSTRONG

The man named Russell, who happened to be a lawyer, sat full in the light of a solitary lamp. It shone upon the brown-covered composition book in his hands. A man named John Selby, a merchant in the small city, was seated in a low chair. He hung his head; his face was hidden; the light washed only his trembling head and the nervous struggle of his fingers. The Chief of Police, Barker, was seated in half shadow. And Doctor Coles loomed against the wall beside a white door that was ajar. It was 1:00 o'clock in the morning.

Doctor, Lawyer, Merchant, Chief . . .

"Well?" the Chief challenged. "Okay, Russell. You're smart, as Selby says you are. You come running when you're called, listen to five minutes' talk about this kid, and you predict there's got to be some such notebook around. Well? Now you've found it, why don't you see what it says?"

"I'm waiting for a direction," said the lawyer mildly. "It's not for me to turn this cover. Look at the big black letters. *Meredith Lee. Personal and Private.* It's not up to me to violate her privacy. But Selby's her kin. Coles is her doctor. And you are law and order in this town."

The doctor turned his head suddenly to the crack of the door.

"Any change?" the Chief asked eagerly.

"No. She's still unconscious. Go ahead, Russell. Don't be squeamish. She's a child, after all."

"See if there's anything helpful in there," the chief of police said. "See if that notebook can explain . . ."

"Explains," the lawyer mused, "how a fifteen-year-old girl solved a seven-year-old murder mystery in four days . . ."

"She didn't solve it all the way," said the Chief impatiently.

Russell ignored him. "What do you say, Selby? She's your niece. Shall we read her private notebook?"

Selby's hands came palms up, briefly. The policeman spoke again,

"Read it. I intend to, if you don't. I've got to get the straight of it. My prisoner won't talk."

The doctor said pompously, "After all, it may be best for the girl."

Russell said dryly, "I'm just as curious as the rest of you." He opened the book and began to read aloud.

Meredith Lee. New Notes and Jottings.

July 23rd.

Here I am at Uncle John's. The family has dumped me for two weeks while they go to New York. I don't complain. It is impossible for me to get bored, since I can always study human nature.

Uncle John looks much the same. Gray hairs show. He's thirty-seven. Why didn't he marry? Mama says he's practicing to stuff a shirt. He was very Uncle-ish and hearty when I got dumped last night, but he actually has no idea what to do with me, except tell the servants to keep me clean and fed. It's a good thing I've got resources.

Russell looked up. The Chief was chewing his lip. The doctor was frankly smiling. John Selby said, painfully, "She's right about that. Fool I was . . . I *didn't* know what to do with her." His head rolled in his hands.

"Go on," the Chief prodded.

Russell continued reading.

Went to the neighborhood drug store, first thing. Snooped down the street. I'd forgotten it, but my goodness, it's typical. Very settled. Not swank. Not poor, either. Very middle. No logic to that phrase. A thing can't be *very* middle, but it says what I feel. On the way home, a Discovery! There's a whopping big hedge between Uncle John's house and the house next door. The neighbor woman was out messing in her flower beds. Description: petite. Dark hair, with silver. Skillfully made up. Effect quite young. (N.B. Ooooh, what a bad paragraph! Choppy!)

So, filled with curiosity, I leaned over her gate and introduced myself. She's a Discovery! She's a Wicked Widow and she's *forbidden!* I didn't know that when I talked to her.

(N.B. Practice remembering dialogue accurately.)

*Wicked Widow:* Mr. Selby's niece, of course. I remember you, my dear. You were here as a little girl, weren't you? Wasn't the last time about seven years ago?

*Meredith Lee:* Yes, it was. But I don't remember you.

W.W.: Don't you? I am Josephine Corcoran. How old were you then, Meredith?

M.L.: Only eight.

W.W.: Only eight?

We came to a stop. *I* wasn't going to repeat. That's a horrible speech habit. You can waste hours trying to communicate. So I looked around and remembered something.

M.L.: I see my tree house has disintegrated.

W.W.: Your tree house? (N.B. She repeated everything I said, and with a question mark. Careless habit? Or just pace?) Oh, yes, of course. In that big maple, wasn't it?

M.L.: Mr. Jewell—you know, Uncle John's gardener?—he built it for me. I had a cot up there and a play ice-box and a million cushions. I wouldn't come down.

W.W.: Wouldn't come down? Yes, I remember. Eight years old and your Uncle used to let you spend the night—(N.B. She looked scared. Why? If I'd fallen out and killed myself seven years ago, I wouldn't be talking to her. Elders worry retroactively.)

M.L.: Oh, Uncle John had nothing to do with it. Mama's rational. She knew it was safe. Railings, and I always pulled up my rope ladder. Nobody could get up, or get me down without a lot of trouble. I was a tomboy in those days.

W.W.: Tomboy? Yes, seven years is a long time. (N.B. No snicker. She looked serious and thoughtful, just standing with the trowel in her hand, not even smiling. That's when I got the feeling I could really communicate and it's very unusual. She must be thirty. I get that feeling with really old people or people about eighteen, sometimes. But people in between, and especially thirty, usually act like Uncle John.)

Now I forget . . . her dialogue wasn't so sparkling, I guess, but she was understanding. Did I know any young people? I said No, and she politely hoped I wouldn't be lonely. I explained that I hoped to be a Writer, so I would probably always be lonely. And she said she supposed that was true. I liked that. It's not so often somebody listens. And while she may have looked surprised at a new thought, she didn't look *amused*. My object in life is not to *amuse*, and I get tired of those smiles. So I liked her.

But then, at dinner time, just as soon as I'd said I'd met her, she got forbidden.

*Uncle John:* (clearing his throat) Meredith, I don't think you had better . . . (He stuck. He sticks a lot.)

M.L.: Better what?

*Uncle John:* Er . . . (N.B. *English* spelling. Americans say uh. I am an American.) Uh . . . Mrs. Corcoran and I are not . . . uh . . . especially friendly and I'd rather you didn't . . . (Stuck again)

*M.L.:* Why not? Are you feuding?

*Uncle John:* No, no. I merely . . .

*M.L.:* Merely what? I think she's very nice.

*Uncle John:* Uh . . . (very stuffy) . . . You are hardly in a position to know anything about it. I'm afraid she is not the kind of woman your mother would . . .

*M.L.:* What kind is she? (You have to really pry at Uncle John.)

*Uncle John:* (finally) Not socially acceptable.

*M.L.:* What! Oh, for heaven's sakes, Uncle John! That's the stuffiest thing I *ever* heard! Why?

*Uncle John:* It's not stuffy, Meredith, and it's not easy to explain why. (Looks at me as if he wonders whether I understand English.) Maybe, if you knew that there was a strange business, years ago . . . Her husband was . . . uh . . . shot in rather mysterious circum. . . .

*M.L.:* Shot! Do you mean killed? Do you mean *murdered?* Really? Oh, boy! How? When? Who did it? What happened?

Now, why did Uncle John act so surprised? Did he think I'd be scared? Don't people who are thirty ever remember how they didn't used to be *scared* by interesting things? But he *was* surprised and also very sticky and stuffy for a while. But I kept prying.

And I think it's just pitiful. I don't know why Uncle John can't see how pitiful it is. Poor Mrs. Corcoran. Her husband came home late one night and as he was standing at his own front door, somebody shot him from behind. They found the gun but nothing else. He wasn't robbed. It's just a mystery. So, just because it is a mystery and nobody knows, they've treated her as if she were a murderess! I can just see how it's been and I'm ashamed of Uncle John. He sure is practicing to stuff a shirt. He lets the hedge grow, and he goes along with the stupid town. It sounds as if nobody has accepted her socially ever since. Fine thing! She is supposed to be a wicked widow, just because her husband got murdered by a person or persons unknown. Probably the town thinks such a thing couldn't happen to a respectable person. But it *could*. I'm very sorry for her.

The thing I'm saving for the bottom of this page is—it's my murder! I got that out of Uncle John. What do you know! What do you know! *I* was in my tree house that very night!

I'm just faintly remembering how I got whisked out of here so fast, that time. I never did know why. Holy cats! Eight years old. I'm asleep in a trcc and a murder takes place right under me! And I never even knew it! They didn't tell me! They didn't even ask me a single question! A fine thing! A real murder in my own life, and I can't remember even one thing about it!

The lawyer paused. The doctor stirred, looked through the door. Three raised heads queried him. He said, "Nothing. It may be a good while yet before she is conscious. Don't . . . worry."

Selby turned to stare blindly at the lamp. "My sister should never— should never have left her with me. I had no business—no business to tell her a word about it."

"You thought she'd be scared away from the widow?"

"I suppose so."

The Chief said, "Now, wait a minute. The girl puts down in there that she *couldn't remember even one thing* about the killing? But that makes no sense at all."

"That's the July twenty-third entry," said Russell. "Here is July twenty-fifth. Let's see."

I couldn't stand it—I just can't think about anything else but my murder. I had to find out more. This afternoon I had tea with the widow. I don't think she's wicked at all. She's very sad, actually. She was in the garden again. I just know she was conscious of me, on Uncle John's side of the hedge, all day yesterday. Today, finally, she spoke to me. So I went around and leeched onto her.

(N.B. Practice getting the "saids" in)

Nervously, she said, "I hope your Uncle won't be angry."

I said, pretending to blurt, "Oh, Mrs. Corcoran, Uncle John told me about the awful thing that happened to your husband. And to think I was right up in my tree house. I can't stop thinking about it."

"Don't think about it," she said, looking pretty tense. "It was long ago, and there is no need. I'm sorry he spoke of it."

"Oh, I made him," said I. "And now when I think that for all I know, I might have seen and heard exactly what happened, and the only trouble is, I was so little, I can't *remember*—it just about makes me wild!"

She looked at me in a funny way. I thought she was going to blurt, "Oh, if only you could remember . . ." But actually, she said, "If you would like more cake please help yourself."

"It's too bad it's a mystery," I said (cried). "Why couldn't they solve it? Don't you wish they could solve it? Maybe it's not too late."

She looked startled. (N.B. What happens to eyes, anyhow, to make the whites show more? Observe.)

"I wish you would tell me the details," I said. "Couldn't they find out *anything?*"

"No, no. My dear, I don't think we had better talk about it at all. It's not the sort of thing a sweet child ought to be brooding about," she said.

I was desperate. "Mrs. Corcoran, the other day I thought better of you. Because you didn't laugh, for instance, when I mentioned that I used to be a tomboy, years ago. Most older people would have laughed. I'll never understand why. Obviously, I'm quite different and seven years has made a big change, and why it's so *funny* if I *know* that, I cannot see." She was leaning back and feeling surprised, I judged. "So don't disappoint me, now, and think of me as an eight-year-old child," I said, "when I may have the freshest eye and be the open-mindedest person around."

She nibbled her lips. She wasn't offended. I think she's very intelligent and responding.

"I'm *going* to brood and you can't stop that," I told her. "I just wish I could help. I've been thinking that maybe if I tried I *could* remember."

"Oh, no. No, my dear. Thank you," she said. "I know you would like to help. But you were only eight at that time. I don't suppose, then or now, anyone would believe you."

"And now I'm *only* fifteen," I said crossly, "and nobody will *tell* me."

She said sweetly, "You're rather an extraordinary fifteen, my dear. If I tell you about it, Meredith, and you see how hopeless it is, do you think perhaps then you can let it rest?"

I said I thought so. (What a lie!)

"Harry, my husband, was often late getting home, so that night," she said, "I wasn't at all worried. I simply went to bed, as usual, and to sleep. Something woke me. I don't know what. My window was open. It was very warm, full summer. I lay in my bed, listening. There used to be a big elm out there beside my walk. It got the disease all the elms are getting, and it had to be cut down and taken away. But that night I could see its leaf patterns on the wall, that the moon always used to make at night, and the leaves moving gently. There was a full moon, I remember. A lovely quiet summer night." (N.B. She's pretty good with a mood.)

"I had been awakened, yet I could hear nothing, until I heard the shot. It paralyzed me. I lay back stiff and scared. Harry didn't . . .

cry out. I heard nothing more for a while. Then I thought I heard shrubs rustling. When I finally pulled myself to the window, your Uncle John was there." She stopped and I had to poke her up to go on.

"Your Uncle was forcing his way through the hedge, which was low, then. And I saw Harry lying on our little stoop. I ran to my bedroom door and my maid was standing in the hall, quite frightened, and we ran down. Your Uncle told me that Harry was . . . not alive. (N.B. Pretty delicate diction.) He was calling the doctor and the police from my phone. I sat down trembling on a chair in the hall. I remember, now, that as your Uncle started out of the house again, he seemed to recall where you were and went running to his garage for a ladder to get you down."

"Darn it," I said.

She knew what I meant, because she said right away, "You couldn't remember—you must have been sleepy. Perhaps you didn't really wake up."

"I suppose so," said I disgustedly. "Go on."

"Well, the police came very quickly—Chief Barker himself. And of course, Doctor Coles. They did find the gun, caught in the hedge. They never traced it. There weren't any fingerprints anywhere. And no footprints in that dry weather. So they never found out . . ." She pulled herself together. "And that, my dear, is all." She started drinking her tea, looking very severe with herself.

I said, "There never was a trial?"

"There was never anyone to try."

"Not you, Mrs. Corcoran?"

"No one accused me," she said, smiling faintly. But her eyes were so sad.

"They did, though," I said, kind of mad. "They sentenced you, too."

"Dear girl," she said very seriously, "You mustn't make a heroine of me. Chief Barker and Doctor Coles . . . and your Uncle John, too, I'm sure . . . tried as helpfully as they could to clear it all up, but they never could find out who, or even why. You see? So . . ." She was getting flustery.

"So the wind begins to blow against you," I said, mad as the dickens. "Or how come the hedge? Why does Uncle John tell me not to come here? What makes him think you're so wicked?"

"Does he?" she said, "I am not wicked, Meredith. Neither am I a saint. I'm human."

I always thought that was a corny saying. But it's effective. It makes you feel for whoever says it, as if they had admitted something just awful that you wouldn't admit, either—unless, of course, you were *trapped*.

"Harry and I were not always harmonious," she said. "Few couples are. He drank a good bit. Many men do. I suppose the neighbors noticed. Some of them, in fact, used to feel quite sorry for me. I . . ." Her face was real bitter, but she has a quick hunching way of pulling herself together. ". . . shouldn't be saying these things to you. Why do I forget you are so young? I shouldn't. Forgive me, and don't be upset."

"Not me," I told her. "I'm pretty detached. And don't forget my eye is fresh. I can see the trouble. There isn't anybody else to suspect. You need . . ."

"No, no. No more. I had no right to talk to you. And you'd better not come again. It is not I, my dear. I like you very much. I would love to see you often. But—"

I said, "I think Uncle John is a stuffy old stinker. To bend the way the wind blows. But *I* don't have to!"

"Yes, you do," she said, kind of fixing me with her eye. "It's not nice, Meredith, to be this side of the hedge. Now, please, never question your Uncle John's behavior." She was getting very upset. "You must . . . truly, you must . . . believe me . . . when I say . . . I think he meant . . . to be very kind . . . at that time." She spaced it like that, taking breaths in between.

"But that mean old hedge, for the whole town to see. It makes me mad!" I said.

She fixed me, again. She said very fast almost like whispering, "Perhaps it was I, Meredith, who let the hedge grow."

Naturally, my mouth opened, but before I got anything out she said, loudly, "It was best. There, now . . ."

(N.B. Yep. I was really disappointed. How I hate it when people say, "There, now." Implying that they know a million things more than me. And I better be comforted. I'm *not*. I'm irritated. It means they want to stop talking to me, and that's all.)

"It's all so old," she continued in that phony petting-the-kitty kind of way. "And nothing will change it. Let it rest. Thank you for coming and thank you for being open-minded. But go away now, Meredith, and promise me not to think about it any more."

I fixed her with *my* eye. I said, "Thank you very much for the lovely cake."

But I'm not angry. I feel too sorry for her. Besides, she let out hints enough and I should have caught on. Well, I didn't, then. But after the session I had with Uncle John . . . *Are they ever dumb!*

We had finished dinner when I decided to see what more I could pry out of *him.* I said, "If Harry Corcoran was a drinking man he was probably drunk the night he got shot."

Uncle John nearly knocked his coffee over. "How do you know he was a drinking man?" roared he. "Have you been gossiping with Mrs. Jewell?" (Mrs. Jewell is the housekeeper. Vocabulary about one hundred words.)

"Oh, no, I haven't. Was he?"

"Who?"

"Harry Corcoran?"

"What?"

"Drunk?"

"So they say," bites Uncle John, cracking his teeth together, "Now, Meredith—"

"Where were you at the time of the murder?" chirped I.

(N.B. Nope. Got to learn to use the "saids." They're neutraller.)

"Meredith, I wish you—"

"I know what you wish, but I wish you'd tell me. Aw, come on, Uncle John. My own murder! Maybe if I had all the facts, I'd stop thinking so much about it. Don't you see that?"

(N.B. False. The more you know about anything the more interesting it gets. But he didn't notice.)

"I told you the facts," he said (muttered?), "and I wish I had kept my big mouth shut. Your mother will skin me alive. How the devil did I get into this?"

(N.B. I thought this was an improvement. He's usually so darned stuffy when he talks to me.)

"You didn't tell me any details. Please, Uncle John . . ." I really nagged him. I don't think he's had much practice defending himself, because finally, stuffy as anything, he talked.

"Very well. I'll tell you the details as far as I know them. Then I shall expect to hear no more about it."

"I know," said I. True. I knew what he *expected.* I didn't really promise anything. But he's not very analytical. "Okay. Pretend you're on the witness stand. Where were you at the time?"

"I was, as it happened . . . (N.B. Stuffy! Phrase adds nothing. Of course it happened.) . . . in the library that night working late on some accounts. It was nearly 1:00 in the morning, I believe . . . (N.B. Of course he believes, or he would't say so) . . . when I heard Harry Corcoran whistling as he walked by in the street."

"What tune?"

"What?" (I started to repeat but he didn't need it. Lots of people make you repeat a question they heard quite well just so they can take a minute to figure out the answer.) "Oh, that Danny Boy song. Favorite of his. That's how I knew who it was. He was coming along from the end of town, past this house—"

"Was that usual?"

"It was neither usual nor unusual," said Uncle John crossly, "It's merely a detail."

"Okay. Go on."

"The next thing I noticed was the shot."

"You were paralyzed?"

"What?" He just about glared at me. "Yes, momentarily. Then I ran out my side door and pushed through the hedge and found him on his own doorstep . . . uh . . ."

"Not living," I said delicately.

He gave me another nasty look. "Now, that's all there was to it."

"That's not all! What did you do then? Didn't you even look for the murderer?"

"I saw nobody around. I realized there might be somebody concealed, of course. So I picked up his key from where it had fallen on the stoop—"

"The Corcorans' door was locked?"

"It was locked and I unlocked it and went inside to the phone. As I was phoning, Mrs. Corcoran and her maid came downstairs. I called Chief Barker and Doctor Coles."

"Yes, I know. And then you ran to get the ladder and pulled me down out of my tree. Okay. But you're leaving things out, Uncle John. You are deliberately being barren. You don't give any atmosphere at all. What was Mrs. Corcoran's emotional state?"

"I haven't the slightest idea," said Uncle John with his nose in a sniffing position, "and if I had, it would not be a fact."

I pounced. "You think she did it?"

He pulled his chin practically to the back of his neck. "I wish you would not say that. I have little right to speculate and none to make a judgment. There was no evidence."

"But you did pass judgment. You told me she was a certain kind of—"

"Meredith, I know only one fact. Your mother would not like this at all. In any case, I will not discuss Mrs. Corcoran's character with you. I must insist you take my word for it. There is no way. . . ." He kind of held his forehead.

"Uncle John, who let the hedge grow?"

"What? The hedge belongs to me."

"That ain't the way I heered it," said stupid I.

So *he* pounced. "Where have you been hearing things? Who told you Harry Corcoran was a drinking man? Where have you been, Meredith?"

So I confessed. No use writing down the blasting I got. It was the usual. Bunch of stuff about my elders wanting no harm to come to me, things not understood in my philosophy, mysterious evils that I wot not of, and all that sort of stuff. Why doesn't he tell me plain out that it's none of my business?

Well, I don't think it's evil. I think it's foolishness. I think that Uncle John's too sticky and stuffy to tell me . . . (Probably thinks I never heard of s-blank-x) . . . is that he used to be romantic about the pretty lady next door. Probably Uncle John saw a lot of Harry's drunken comings home and heard plenty of the disharmonizing. Probably he is one neighbor who felt sorry for her. Wonder if they were in love and said so. I doubt it. Probably they just cast glances at each other over the hedge and said nothing. That would be just like Uncle John.

Anyhow, when somebody shoots Harry Corcoran in the back, the widow gets it into her head that Uncle John did it. After all, she heard things—rustling bushes—looked out, and there he was. But gosh, even if she felt romantic about him too, she'd draw the line at murder! But of course, Uncle John didn't do it. He thinks *she* did. He knows she was unhappy with Harry. But he draws the line at murder, too. So, these dopes, what do they do? They have no "right" to pass "judgment" or "accuse" anybody. They pull themselves in, with the hedge between. All these years, with their very own suspicions proving that neither one could have done it . . . Probably if they'd had sense enough to speak out and have a big argument, they could have got married and been happy long ago.

Oh, how ridiculous! How pitiful! And oh, that I was born to put it right! (N.B. Who said that?)

The lawyer put the book down. John Selby groaned. "I had no idea . . . no idea what she had in her head. I knew she was bright . . ."

"Bright, yes," said Doctor Coles, "but that kid's so insufferably condescending!"

"You wouldn't like it even if she guessed right," said Russell thoughtfully. "The girl's got a hard way to go. She'll be lonely."

"Thought she was smart, all right," growled Barker. "Wasn't as smart as she thought she was. She was wrong, I take it?"

Selby didn't answer. His gaze was fixed on the lawyer's face.

"You shouldn't blame her for being wrong," Russell murmured. "She's not yet equipped to understand a lot of things. But she is compelled to try. There's her intelligent curiosity fighting a way past some clichés, but the phrase 'feel romantic' is flat, for her, and without shading."

"I still can't see what happened," Barker broke in to complain. "Never mind the shading. Go ahead—if there's more of it."

"Yes, there's more. We come to July twenty-sixth—yesterday." Russell began to read once more.

I've figured. I know exactly how to do it. I'll say *I can remember!* I'll tell them that when I was up in my tree that night the shot or something woke me, and I saw a stranger running away . . .

"So she made it up! Told a story!" Chief Barker slapped his thigh. "But . . . now wait a minute . . . you believed her, Selby?"

"I believed her," her uncle sighed.

"Go on. Go on," the doctor said.

I know how to make them believe me, too. This will be neat! I'll tell Uncle John first, and I'll mix into the story I tell him all the little bits I got from her that he doesn't know I've been told. So, since *they'll* be true, he'll be fooled, and think I really remember. Then I'll go to her, but in the story I tell her, all I have to do is mix in the bits I got from Uncle John that she doesn't know I've been told. It'll work! Ha, they'll never catch on to the trick of it. They'll believe me! Then they can get together, if they still want to. I'm not worried about telling a kind of lie about it. If anybody official starts asking questions I can always shudder, and be too young and tender, and clam up.

Get it exactly right. Make lists.

Russell looked up. "Meredith's good at math, I suppose?"

"A plus," her uncle groaned. "She scares me."

Russell nodded and began to read again.

List No. 1. For Uncle John. Things she told me.
  1. Warm night. Full moon.
  2. The elm tree that used to be there.
  3. The gun was found *in the hedge.*
  4. Harry didn't yell.

Now, put all these points in. Future dialogue.
By Meredith Lee.

*M.L.:* Oh, Uncle John, I do remember now!

*Uncle John:* What?

(Whoops! Since this is in the future, I better not write *his* dialogue. It might confuse me.)

*M.L.:* I was up in my room, thinking, and I began to hum that tune. That Danny Boy. It made the whole thing come back to me like a dream. Now I remember waking up on my cot and hearing that whistling. I peeked out between my railings. The moon was very bright that night. It was warm, too, real summer. I could see the elm tree by the Corcoran's walk. (Pause. Bewildered.) Which elm tree, Uncle John? There's none there now. *Was* there an elm tree, seven years ago?

(Ha, ha, that'll *do* it!)

I saw a man come up their walk. I must have heard the shot. I thought somebody had a firecracker left over from Fourth of July. I saw the man fall down but he didn't make any noise, so I didn't think he was hurt. I thought he fell asleep.

(What a touch! Whee!)

Then I saw there was another man, down there, and he threw something into the hedge. The hedge crackled where it landed. Then this man jumped through their gate and ran, and then you came out of this house . . .

(By this time the stuffing should be coming out of Uncle John.)

I'll say I don't know who the stranger was. "But it wasn't you, Uncle John," I'll say, "and the widow Corcoran's been thinking so for seven years and I'm going to tell her . . ."

Then I'll run out of the house as fast as I can.

He'll follow—he'll absolutely have to!

Russell looked up. "Was it anything like that?"

"It was almost exactly like that," said John Selby, lifting his tired, anxious face. "And I did follow. She was right about that. I absolutely had to."

"Smart," said Chief Barker, smacking his lips, "the way she worked that out."

"Too smart," the doctor said, and then, "Nurse? Yes?" He went quickly through the door.

"My sister will skin me alive," said John Selby, rousing himself. "Kid's had me jumping through hoops. Who am I to deal with the likes of her? Looks at me with those big brown eyes. Can't tell whether you're talking to a baby or a woman. I never had the least idea what she was thinking. You're smart about people, Russell—that's why I need you. I feel as if I'd been through a wind-tunnel. Help me with Meredith. I feel terrible about the whole thing, and if she's seriously hurt and I'm responsible . . ."

"You say you don't understand young people," began Russell, "but even if you did, this young person . . ."

"You take it too hard, John," said Chief Barker impatiently. "Doc doesn't think she's hurt too seriously. And she got herself into it, after all. Listen, go on. What did she say to the widow? That's what I need to know. Is it in there?"

"It must be," said Russell. "She made another list."

List No. 2. For the widow. Things Uncle John told me.
    1. Harry was whistling Danny Boy.
    2. He came in the direction that passed this house.
    3. He was drunk.
    4. He dropped his key.
Not so good. Yes it is, too. What woke her? She doesn't know, but I do! Future dialogue:

M.L.: Oh, Mrs.Corcoran, I think I'm beginning to remember! I really think so! Listen, I think I heard a man whistling. And it was that song about Danny Boy. And he was walking from the east, past our house. Would it have been your husband?

(Ha! She's going to *have* to say Yes!)

And he . . . it seems to me that he didn't walk right. He wobbled. He wobbled up your walk and he dropped something. Maybe a key. It must have been a key because I saw him bending over to hunt for it but . . .

(Artistic pause here? I think so.)

Oh, now I remember! He straightened up. He couldn't have found it because he called out something. It was a name! It must have been . . . Oh, Mrs. Corcoran, could it have been your name, being called in the night, that woke you up?

(Betcha! Betcha!)

Well, the rest of hers goes on the same. Stranger, throws gun, runs away, just as Uncle John comes out. "So it wasn't you," I'll say, "and I can prove it! But poor Uncle John has been afraid it *was*."

Then what? I guess maybe I'd better start to bawl.

Yep. I think that will do it. I think that's pretty good. They're bound to believe me. Of course, the two stories are not identical, but they can't be. *They'll* never notice the trick of it. They'll just have to be convinced that it wasn't either one of them who shot Harry Corcoran. I can't wait to see what will happen. What will they *do?* What will they *say?* Oh-ho-ho, is this ever research! I better cry soft enough so I can hear and memorize.

When shall I try it? I can't wait! Now is a good time. Uncle John is in the library and she's home. I can see a light upstairs in her house. Here goes, then.

(N.B. Would I rather be an actress? Consider this. M.L.)


The lawyer closed the book. "That's all." He put his hand to his eyes but his mouth was curving tenderly.

"Some scheme," said Barker in awe. "Went to a lot of trouble to work up all that plot . . ."

"She had a powerful motive," Russell murmured.

"My romance," said Selby bitterly.

"Oh, no. Research for her," the lawyer grinned.

"Whatever the motive, this remarkable kid went and faked those stories and she had it wrong," growled Barker. "But she must have got something right. Do you realize that?" He leaned into the light. "Selby, as far as you were concerned, you believed that rigmarole of hers. You thought she *did* remember the night of the killing and she *had* seen a stranger?"

"I did," John Selby said, sounding calmer. "I was considerably shaken. I had always suspected Josephine Corcoran, for reasons of my own."

"Lots of us suspected," the Chief said dryly, "for various reasons. But never could figure how she managed, with you rushing out to the scene so fast and the maid in the upstairs hall."

"What were your reasons, John?" Russell asked.

"In particular, there was a certain oblique conversation that took place in the course of a flirtation that appalls me, now. It seemed to me, one evening, that she was thinking that the death of her husband might be desirable—and might be arranged. I can't quote her exactly, you understand, but the hint was there. She thought him stupid and cruel and intolerable, and the hint was that if he were dead and gone she'd be *clean.* The shallow, callous, self-righteous . . . the *idea!* As if her life should rightfully be cleared of him with no more compunction that if he'd been . . . well, a wart on her hand." He held his head again. "Now, how is a man going to explain to his fifteen-year-old niece just what makes him think a woman is wicked? The feeling you get, that emanates from the brain and body?" He groaned. "That little talk pulled me out of my folly, believe me. That's when I shied off and began to let the hedge grow. When you realize that not long after that he *did* die, you'll see how I've lived with the memory of that conversation for seven years. Wondering. Was I right about what she had in mind and did I perhaps not recoil enough? Had I not sufficiently discouraged the . . . the idea? There was no evidence. There was nothing. But I've had a burden close to guilt and I've stayed on my side of the hedge, believe me, and begun to study to stuff a shirt." He groaned again and shifted in the chair. "When I thought the child had really seen a stranger with that gun, I was stunned. As soon as I realized where Meredith had gone . . .''

"You followed. You saw them through the widow's front door?" The Chief was reassembling this testimony.

"Yes. I could see them. At the top of the stairs. Mrs. Corcoran standing by the newel post and Meredith talking earnestly to her."

"You couldn't hear?"

"No, unfortunately. But if Meredith had rehearsed it, if she stuck to her script, then we must have it here."

"If it's there, I don't get it." Chief Barker passed his hand over his face. "Now, suddenly, you say—in the middle of the girl's story—the widow yelled something that you *could* hear?"

"She yelled, '*I told you to keep out of this, you nosy brat!*' And then she pushed Meredith violently enough to send her rolling down the stairs." Selby began to breathe heavily.

"And you got through the door . . .''

"By the time I got through the door, she was on the girl like a wildcat. She was frantic. She *meant* to hurt her." John Selby glared.

"So you plucked the widow off her prey and called us for help? Did Mrs. Corcoran try to explain at all?" Russell inquired.

"She put out hysterical cries. 'Poor dear! Poor darling!' But she meant to hurt Meredith. I heard. I saw. I know. And she knows that I know."

"Yes, the widow gave herself away," said Russell. "She was wicked, all right."

"So we've got her," the Chief growled, "for the assault on Meredith. Also, we know darned well she shot her husband seven years ago. But she won't talk. What I need," the Chief was anxious, "is to figure out what it was that set her off. What did the kid say that made her nerve crack? I can't see it. I just don't get it."

The doctor had been standing quietly in the door. Now he said, "Maybe Meredith can tell us. She's all right. Almost as good as new, I'd say."

John Selby was on his feet. So was Chief Barker. "Selby, you go first," the doctor advised. "No questions for the first minute or two."

The Chief turned and sighed. "Beats me."

Russell said, "One thing, Harry Corcoran never called out his wife's name in the night. Selby, who heard a whistle, would have heard such a cry."

"Do I see what you're getting at?" said Barker shrewdly. 'It shows the kid didn't get *that far* in the story or the widow would have known she was story-telling."

"She certainly didn't get as far as any guilty stranger, or the widow would have been delighted. Let's see."

"There was something. . . ."

"Was it the tune? No, that's been known. Selby told that long ago. Was it Harry's drunkenness? No, because medical evidence exists. Couldn't be that."

"For the Lord's sakes, let's *ask* her," the Chief said.

They went through the door. The nurse had effaced herself watchfully. Four men stood around the bed, Doctor, Lawyer, Merchant, Chief . . .

Young Meredith Lee looked very small, lying against the pillow with her brown hair pressed back by the bandages, her freckles sharpened by the pallor of her face, her big brown eyes round and shocked.

"How do you feel, honey?" rumbled the Chief.

"She pushed me down." Meredith's voice was a childish whimper.

Her Uncle John patted the bed and said compulsively, "There, Meredith. There now . . ."

"Don't say that," the Chief put in with a chuckle. "It just annoys her."

The girl saw her notebook in Russell's hands. She winced and for a flash her eyes narrowed and something behind the child face was busy reassessing the situation.

"Miss Lee," said the lawyer pleasantly, "My name is Russell. I'm a friend of your Uncle John's. I'm the one who ferreted out your notes. I hope you'll forgive us for reading them. Thanks to you, now we know how wicked the widow was seven years ago."

"I only pretended," said Meredith in a thin treble. "I was only eight. I don't really remember anything at all." She shrank in the bed, very young and tender.

Her uncle said, "We know how you pretended. I . . . I had no idea you were so smart."

"That was some stunt," the doctor said.

"Very clever," the lawyer said, "the two stories as you worked them out."

"You're quite a story-teller, honey," chimed in Chief Barker.

On the little girl's face something struggled and lost. Meredith gave them one wild indignant look of pure outraged intelligence before her face crumpled completely. "I am not either!" she bawled. "I'm not any good! I got it all wrong! Didn't get the plot right. Didn't get the characters right. I guess I don't know *anything!* I guess I might as well give up . . ." She flung herself over and sobbed bitterly.

Chief Barker said, "She's okay, isn't she? She's not in pain?"

The nurse rustled, muttering "shock." The doctor said stiffly, "Come now, Meredith. This isn't a bit good for you."

But Selby said, to the rest of them, "See? That's the way it goes. She's eight and she's eighty. She can cook up a complex stunt like that and then bawl like a baby. I give up! I don't know what you should do with her. I've wired my sister. She'll skin us both, no doubt. Meredith, *please*. . . ."

Meredith continued to howl.

The lawyer said sharply, "That's right, Meredith. You may as well give up trying to be a writer if you are going to cry over your first mistakes instead of trying to learn from them. Will you be grown-up for a minute and listen? We seriously want your help to convict a murderess."

"You do not," wailed Meredith. "I'm too stupid!"

"Don't be a hypocrite," snapped the lawyer. "You are not stupid. As a matter of fact, you are extremely stuffy—as this book proves to us."

Meredith choked on a sob. Then slowly she opened one brown eye.

"The average young person," hammered the lawyer, "has little or no respect for an elder's experience and nothing can make him see its value until he gets some himself. But even a *beginning* writer should have a less conventional point of view."

"Now wait a minute," bristled John Selby. "Don't scold her. She's had an awful time. Listen, she meant well . . ."

Meredith sat up and mopped her cheek with the sheet. The brown eyes withered him. "Pul-lease, Uncle John," said Meredith Lee.

So John Selby raised his head and settled his shoulders. "Okay." He forced a grin. "Maybe I'm not too old to learn. You want me to lay it on the line? All right, you *didn't* mean well. You were perfectly vain and selfish. You were going to fix up my life and Josephine Corcoran's life as a little exercise for your superior wisdom." His stern voice faltered. "Is that better?"

Meredith said, tartly, "At least, it's rational." She looked around and her voice was not a baby's. "You are all positive the widow is a murderess," she said flatly.

Chief Barker said, "Well, honey, we always did kind of think so."

"Don't talk down to her," snapped John Selby, "or she'll talk down to you. I . . . I get that much."

"Who are you, anyhow?" asked Meredith of the Chief.

He told her. "And I am here to get to the bottom of a crime. Now, young lady," the Chief was no longer speaking with any jovial look at all, "You jumped to a wrong conclusion, you know. She *was* guilty."

"I don't see *why* you've always thought so," said Meredith rebelliously.

"I guess you don't," said Barker. "Because it's a matter of experience.

Of a lot of things. In the first place, I know what my routine investigation can or cannot turn up. When it turns up *no* sign of any stranger whatsoever, I tend to believe that there wasn't one."

The Chief's jaw was thrust forward. The little girl did not wince. She listened gravely.

"In the second place, as you noticed yourself, there's nobody else around here to suspect. In the third place, nine times out of ten, only a wife is close enough to a man to have a strong enough motive."

"Nine times out of ten," said Meredith scornfully.

"That's experience," said Barker, "and you scoff at the nine times because you think we forget that there can be a tenth time. You are wrong, young lady. Now, somebody shot Harry Corcoran . . ."

"Why don't you suspect Uncle John?" flashed Meredith.

"No motive," snapped Barker.

"Meredith," began her Uncle, "I'm afraid you . . ."

"Speak up," said Russell.

"Yes. Right." Selby straightened again. "Well, then, listen. I'd no more murder a man as a favor to a neighbor than I'd jump over the moon. Your whole idea—that Josephine Corcoran would *think* I had—is ridiculous. Whatever she is, she's too mature for that. Furthermore, I never did want to marry her. And your mother may skin me for this but so help me you'd better know, men sometimes don't and women know it." Meredith blinked. "Also, even if I had," roared her Uncle John, "Barker knows it might occur to me that there is such a thing as divorce. Just as good a way to get rid of a husband, and a lot safer than murder."

Meredith's tongue came out and licked her lip.

"Now, as to her motive, she hated Harry Corcoran bitterly . . . bitterly. She's . . . well, she's wicked. To know that is . . . is a matter of experience. You spot it. Some cold and selfish, yet hot and reckless thing. That's the best I can do."

"It's not bad," said Meredith humbly, "I mean, thank you, Uncle John. Where is she now?"

"In the hospital," said Chief Barker, "with my men keeping their eye on her."

"Was she hurt?"

The doctor cleared his throat. "She's being hysterical. That is, you see, she was startled into making a terrible mistake when she pushed you, my dear. Now, all she can think to do is fake a physical or psychic collapse. But it's strictly a phony. I can't tell you exactly how I know that . . ."

"I suppose it's experience," said Meredith solemnly. She seemed to retreat deeper into the pillow. "I was all wrong about her. The town was *right!"* She looked as if she might cry, having been forced to this concession.

Russell said briskly, "That's not enough. No good simply saying you were wrong. You need to understand what happened to you, just how you were led."

"Led?" said Meredith distastefully.

"The widow was guilty," Russell said. "Begin with that. Now look back at the time you first hung over her gate. You couldn't know she was guilty or even suspect it, because you hadn't so much as heard about the murder yet. How could you guess the fright she got, remembering that little girl in the tree? You thought it was retroactive worry—that you might have fallen. Because that is a kind of fear in your experience. Do you see, now, when you turned up, so full of vigor and intelligence, that she never felt less like smiling in her life. *Of course* she took you seriously. And you were charmed."

"Naturally," said Meredith bravely.

"I can see, and now you should be able to see, how she tried to use your impulsive sympathy. Maybe she hoped that when you tried—as you were bound to try—to remember the night, long ago, that your imagination would be biased in her favor."

"I guess it was," said Meredith bleakly.

"Probably, she tried to put suspicion of your Uncle John into your head, not from innocence, but to supply a missing suspect to the keen and much too brainy curiosity that had her terrified. Now, don't be downcast," the lawyer added, his warm smile breaking. "I'd have been fooled, too. After all, this is hindsight."

"Probably you wouldn't have been fooled," said Meredith stolidly, "Experience, huh?"

"I've met a few murderers before," said Russell gently.

"Well, I've met a murderess now," said Meredith gravely. "Boy, was I ever dumb!" She sighed.

The Chief said, "All clear? Okay. Now, what do you say we find out where you were *smart?* What *did* it? Can't we get to that?"

"Smart?" said Meredith.

"This is our question to you, young lady. What cracked Mrs. Corcoran's nerve? Where were you in that story when she flew at you and pushed you down the stairs?"

The girl was motionless.

"You see, dear," began the doctor.

"She sees," said her Uncle John ferociously.

Meredith gave him a grateful lick of the eye. "Well, I was just past the

key . . ." she said. She frowned. "And *then* she yelled and pushed me."
The brown eyes turned, bewildered.

"What were the exact words?" said Barker briskly, "Russell, read that
part again."

But Russell repeated, lingeringly, "Just past the key . . . ?"

"I don't get it," Barker said. "Do you?"

"I just thought she'd be glad," said Meredith in a small groan. "But she
pushed me and hurt me. I got it *wrong*." She seemed to cower. She was
watching Russell.

"You got it right," said he. "Listen. And follow me. Harry Corcoran was
shot in the back."

"That's right," the Chief said.

"The key was on the doorstep." The lawyer was talking to the girl.

"I picked it up," said Selby.

"All this time we've been assuming that he dropped the key *because he
was shot*. But that isn't what you said, Meredith. You said that he dropped
the key *because he was drunk*. Now, all this time we have assumed that he
was shot from behind, from somewhere near the hedge. But if you got it
right, when he bent over to pick up the key . . . and was shot in the
back . . ." Russell waited. He didn't have to wait long.

"*She* shot him from above," said Meredith, quick as a rabbit. "*She* was
upstairs."

"From *above*," said Barker, sagging. "And the widow's been waiting for
seven years for some bright brain around here to think of that. Yep. Shot
from a screenless window. Threw the gun out, closed the window, opened
her door, faced her maid. Pretty cool. Pretty lucky. Pretty smart. And there
is nothing you could call evidence, even yet." But the Chief was not
discouraged or dismayed. He patted the bed covers. "Don't you worry,
honey. You got her, all right. And I've made out with less. By golly, I got
her method, now, and that's going to be leverage. And, by golly, one thing
she's going to have to tell me, and that is *why* she pushed you down the
stairs."

"She needn't have," said Meredith, in the same thin, woeful voice. "*I*
didn't know . . . *I* didn't understand." Then her face changed and something was clicking in her little head. "But she still *thinks* I saw him drop
the key. Couldn't I go where she is? Couldn't I . . . break her down? I
could *act*." The voice trailed off. They weren't going to let her go, the four
grown men.

"*I'm* going," said Selby grimly. "I'll break her down."

"Stay in bed," said the doctor, at the same time. "Nurse will be here. I
may be needed with the widow."

"And I," said Russell. But still he didn't move. "Miss Lee," he said to the little girl, "may I make a prophecy? You'll go on studying the whole world, you'll get experience, and acquire insight, and you will not give up until you become a writer." He saw the brown eyes clear; the misting threat dried away. He laid the notebook on the covers. "You won't need to be there," he said gently, "because you can imagine." He held out a pencil. "Maybe you'd like to be working on an ending?" She was biting her left thumb but her right hand twitched as she took the pencil.

"Meredith," said her Uncle John, "here's one thing you can put in. You sure took the stuffing out of me. And I don't care what your mother's going to say . . ."

Meredith said, as if she were in a trance, "When is Mama coming?"

"In the morning. I wish I hadn't wired—I wish I hadn't alarmed her . . . We're going to be in for it."

"Oh, I don't know, Uncle John," said Meredith. The face was elfin now, for a mocking second of time. Then it was sober. She put the pencil into her mouth and stared at the wall. The nurse moved closer. The four men cleared their throats. Nothing happened. Meredith was gone, imagining. Soon the four grown men tiptoed away.

Meredith Lee. New notes and Jottings. July 27th.

Early to bed. Supposed to be worn out. False, but convenient for all of us.

Everybody helped manage Mama. Doctor Coles put a small pink bandage on me. Chief Barker and Mr. Russell met her train and said gloating things about the widow confessing.

But, of course, Mama had to blast us some. She was just starting to rend Uncle John when I said, "Don't be so cross with him, Mama. He is the Hero. Saved my life." That took her aback. She was about to start on me, but Uncle John jumped in. "Meredith's the Heroine, sis. She broke the case."

Well, Mama got distracted. She forgot to be mad at us any more. "What's going on with you two?" she wanted to know. Well, I guess she could see that the stuffing was out of both of us.

(N.B. Men are interesting. M.L.)

# Mary, Mary, Quite Contrary

## GEORGE BAXT

A fter a restless, sleepless night, Mary Langtry got out of bed, put on a robe, and went to the kitchen where she got the coffee going. While the electric percolator chugged away, she went outside into her small, well kept garden at the rear of the cottage. She yawned and stretched her arms while staring at the sky, where the first light of dawn seemed to be having a struggle establishing itself. She wondered if today would be another scorcher. It was only mid-June and already the kind of hot uncomfortable weather that belonged to August. There was rarely weather like this where she came from. Where ah all comes from, she told herself in a southern accent.

Mr. Milkin, her boss, owner of the K-Zee Coffee Shoppe in the West Thirties off Seventh Avenue where Mary worked as a counter waitress, frequently commented, "Where did you get that accent? It's like no accent *I* ever heard Down South." During the war, Mr. Milkin had been stationed at an assortment of installations and camps in an assortment of southern states—always a cook but never a hero. And Mary continued to explain patiently, "I been talkin' this h'yeah way since I was a toddlah."

Lulu Dobson, Mary's friend and co-worker wisecracked, "That accent's straight out of *Gone With the Wind*." They had met three years earlier when Mary first arrived in New York, alone, friendless, and with no prospects. The girls struck up a conversation while standing in line to see a hit movie, and after the movie, over coffee, Lulu learned that Mary was perilously short of funds and in need of a job.

"Ever sling hash?" she asked Mary, who was hungrily slicing into a very damp melted cheese sandwich, her left hand holding the fork that she was swiftly piloting into her mouth.

"Suh-ling hay-ash?" she asked.

"Waitress," said Lulu, pouring sugar into her coffee. "That's what I do. Base pay is union and the tips are good." She described the K-Zee

Shoppe's location in the heart of the garment center, where the tips were abnormally generous.

"It wouldn't take me long to get the hang of it, do you think, love?"

"Love?" asked Lulu.

"Yes," said Mary with a warm smile. "Love. That's a term of endearment where ah comes from. My mammy and my pappy always called each other and everybody else 'love.' It's just an old habit."

"It's kind of nice," said Lulu. "I like it. Anyway, you look like you've got strong hands, I'm sure you can juggle dishes along with the best of us. The trick is to see if Milkin—that's the boss's name—is in the market for extra help."

As luck had it, Mr. Milkin *was* in the market for extra help, mostly because he was in the market for Mary. Mary was a handsome woman, though to Lulu it was obvious her hair was too heavily henna'd and her eye makeup was just a shade overdone. But Mary's figure was good and her legs were shapely and strong and in just a few days she was slinging hash like an expert.

She continued living at the Y.W.C.A. until Lulu told her about a bungalow that had become vacant down the street from where she lived with her mother in Canarsie.

"Canarsie? Where's Canarsie?" Mary's face was screwed up like a child having difficulty making a candy purchase.

Lulu laughed. "It's the tip of Brooklyn, honey, on Jamaica Bay. I've lived there since I was a kid. Mom and I have been together in the house for over five years now. We lost Dad six years ago and five years ago was when my rotten boy friend went back to his wife. So I moved back home because it was cheaper that way. Listen, come on home with me tonight after work. You can look at the bungalow and see if it suits you. It's on a not very nice street, but it's quiet."

"Does it have a garden?" The question was put softly, almost wistfully.

"Well, now," said Lulu, "I don't really know. It has a back yard and I suppose if you've got a green thumb you could fix it up real pretty." Then, as an afterthought: "You like gardening?"

"I love it," said Mary with a passion Lulu privately thought should be reserved for a lover, not a hobby. "I love growing things. I love pretty colors and eating my own vegetables."

That was three years ago and now Mary was in her garden examining the bush that had reached its full maturity of three feet. Its bell-shaped flowers were in full blossom, flowers of alternating blue-purple and dull red. Soon the berries would appear. Very black berries. Very lethal. Some unfortunate birds would peck at them and die and Mary would give them a haphazard interment in the garbage pail as she did with the birds of the previous two summers. Luckily, no neighbor children had invaded the garden and eaten the berries. She had taken the caution to warn some of her adjacent neighbors that the berries were dangerous.

It didn't matter to the neighbors one way or another, especially the women, who treated Mary as though she came from outer space, let alone the Deep South. Even Lulu had become somewhat remote and distant now that she had taken up with a new lover. That was fine by Mary. She treasured her privacy, and Lulu and her mother had had a habit, when Mary first moved into the bungalow, of dropping in on her unexpected and unannounced. Mary didn't like that. Soon they learned to phone first or wait for an invitation. Then after a while they ceased phoning and Mary rarely invited.

"Doesn't she have any men friends at *all?*" Mrs. Dobson asked Lulu shortly after Mary took possession of the bungalow.

"She could have plenty," said Lulu between sips of scalding coffee, "but she turns them all off. Even poor old Mr. Milkin's stopped pinching her backside. You know what, Ma, I think he's afraid of her."

"Oh, go on—not Milkin."

"Yes, he is. He says she said to him once through very narrow slitted eyes, 'Do that again, Mr. Milkin, and you'll lose those fingers.' "

"Oh, go on!"

"I swear on Poppa's grave."

Mrs. Dobson shook her head solemnly while contemplating Mary's celibacy. Then she inquired of her daughter gravely, "She's not queer or anything, is she?"

"Well, I've seen no signs," said Lulu with an authority she usually reserved for cab drivers. "It isn't a matter of her not liking men. She just doesn't like *anybody.*"

Mrs. Dobson folded her arms and leaned back. "She doesn't get any mail from Down South."

"How do you know that?"

"The mailman told me. He was in for a cup of coffee and we got to discussing Mary because he's interested in her and he told me she doesn't get anything but junk mail."

"How about that."

Now Mrs. Dobson was leaning forward conspiratorially. "Lulu—is it my imagination or is that accent of hers getting thicker?"

"Mama, I was wondering the same thing myself." Lulu sighed. "Yes, indeed, she's a very peculiar person. Still, she calls everybody 'love.' "

"But very insincerely, I'm sure," said Mrs. Dobson with a sniff as she helped herself to a third English muffin.

Now, three years later, Lulu was determined to get chummy with Mary again. The decision was due to no pressing urge of hers to revive the friendship—it had been pressed on her by Nick Abrams, one of the steady customers at the K-Zee Coffee Shoppe. Nick was a writer who lived in a reconverted loft just a few doors down from K-Zee. Nick's friend, Don Borelli, was Lulu's new lover. Nick had brought Don into the place for lunch and, as Don later explained to Lulu, "You bent over to serve me a salad and it was love at first sight." Lulu almost cried because Don had been trying to make time with Mary and of course was getting nowhere. Now it was Nick's turn to suffer that frustration.

"She's such a cold fish," Lulu insisted to Nick, "why bother?"

"I like a challenge. She fascinates me. Women of mystery always fascinate me."

"Oh go on," said Lulu with a disdainful wave of her hand. The only mystery she could see about Mary was why men were so interested in her.

And then one day came the dawn, and Lulu realized it was the mystery of unavailability that made Mary so desirable. Lulu herself had no patience with mystery and unavailability. Her hunger for men was earthy and honest.

Nick's pursuit of Mary never flagged. Every lunch hour he sat at her section of the counter, his eyes following her every move. His lunch diet never varied—a bowl of fresh fruit topped by a generous helping of cottage cheese. He flirted outrageously, but Mary never lost her cool. He tried to pique in her some interest in his writing, but she continued to reward him with a blank look and dull eyes. "I've got a very interesting new assignment," he told her one day between mouthfuls of cottage cheese as she was clearing dirty dishes from the counter. "I'm doing a series of articles on women killers." He winked at her. "Not people who *kill* women, but women who have killed. Are you interested in that sort of thing?"

"I like a good murder story sometimes."

"You mean you like to read them?"

"Sometimes I like to read them."

"I have a fine shelf of murder books up in the loft. Why don't you come up sometime and choose a few?"

"There's a bigger selection at the public library."

She walked away from him briskly with an armload of dirty dishes. Milkin, who had been watching them, said to Mary as she was about to enter the kitchen, "Can't you be a little nicer to the customers?"

Mary nailed his face with her eyes. "Do I do a good job?"

"Yes, Mary, you do a good job."

"Have I ever insulted a customer?"

"Never."

"Do I earn my money?"

Milkin shrugged. He knew when he was beaten. The uncertain smile on his face was all the answer Mary needed and she continued into the kitchen. Milkin walked down the aisle behind the counter until he reached Nick, whom he liked. "Nick baby," he said, "why do you waste your time?"

"What do you mean?"

"Mary. Why do you bother? In your line, you must meet plenty of interesting ladies who don't give you a hard time. Why do you bother?"

"It's hurting you?"

"No. I just hope it isn't hurting you."

"It's not hurting me. I'm enjoying it. Today I'm getting someplace." He smiled. "She spoke three sentences to me."

"Well, how about that," said Milkin.

After lunch, Nick went to the main branch of the public library to research his series of articles on women murderers. He'd been at it for weeks but he hadn't uncovered anything new or fascinating in the way of murderesses. Lizzie Borden, Winnie Ruth Judd, Ruth Snyder were all tried and trite. Mrs. Jacobs, an assistant librarian, was sympathetic to Nick's problem. "We have an excellent collection of foreign murderesses."

"They've been done to death, too," countered Nick, adding with a pixie grin, "No pun intended."

"No pun *detected*," said Mrs. Jacobs. "You just haven't been probing in the right places, Mr. Abrams. You've been digging around in the old files. Why don't you try some of the new files? We've some very interesting new material on a British murder case that shocked the English some three or four years ago. The murderer was never apprehended. It's a fascinating story. Come have a look."

The following Friday Lulu saw to it that she left the K-Zee with Mary and walked with her to Fifth Avenue, where they would get the bus to Canarsie. "Mary," said Lulu as they stood in line waiting to board the bus, "Mom and I miss the old closeness. I mean, we don't seem to see anything of you any more."

"I know," said Mary, pronouncing "know" so that it emerged "nay-ow." "It's all my fault. But you've been so busy with your boy friend—"

"Isn't Don cute?" Mary managed a smile. "I mean I know you showed him the back of your head when he tried to make time with you but, really, he's terrific."

"How come you're not out with him tonight?"

"He's helping Nick with his research. O.K., all right, now how come you don't like Nick?"

"I'm just not interested in getting involved with anybody."

"Nick isn't *anybody*. He's a *writer*."

"Big deal." *Bee-egg dee-yall.*

"He's doing this story on lady murderers—"

"He told me."

"That's right. He *said* he told you. Well, he's come across this case that nobody in this country has ever written about—" Mary was staring out the window "—this woman in England who was suspected of murdering her entire family. She poisoned them all with some kind of fruit. Can you imagine?"

Mary continued looking out the window.

"She murdered her husband and his mother and father and her *own* mother and father and her two sisters and both her brothers-in-law."

"Quite a haul," Mary said.

"And she got away with it! I mean she went on trial and everything like that and they couldn't prove she did it. Even though she was growing the poison berry bushes in her own garden, they couldn't prove a thing. And now she's disappeared without a trace. Nick said one of the articles he read in a British newspaper suggested she might have gone to Australia to continue her acting."

"She was an actress?" Mary's voice was dull and flat.

"An amateur actress. You know—local stuff. But the funny thing is, she'd made a big hit in some play about a Scottish poisoner named Madeline something who had poisoned her kid brother and got away with it, and they think it was this play that inspired her to do away with her family." Lulu sighed. "I don't tell it too good. When Nick tells it, I get goose pimples. Nick told me to tell you. He thought you'd be fascinated with the story."

Mary turned to Lulu, who was rummaging in her handbag. "Why would the story fascinate me?"

"Well, you being a gardener and all that." Lulu found her makeup and was lavishly rouging her lips. "I told him about how those berries you grew killed those poor little birds—"

"Making *me* a murderer too."

Lulu looked up and was surprised to see that Mary was smiling. "Oh no! Come on! I mean, like I told Nick about all the pretty things you grow besides the vegetables you eat and that the berry bush was the prettiest of all. I mean, you still grow that bush, don't you?"

"Oh, yes. As a matter of fact, thanks for reminding me. The berries are out. I must pick them and throw them away."

"Listen, Mary, I hope you don't think I'm getting out of line when I tell you this, but Nick's really got a case on you."

Mary echoed softly, "Nick's got a case on me."

"He and Don are coming out to dinner here with Mom and me tomorrow night. Why don't you join us?" Mary was staring out the window again. "I'll make him promise to behave."

"Oh, he always behaves."

"Well, you know what I mean. Not push too hard, that sort of thing. He's going to tell Mom all about this murderess. Now what was her name again?" Mary started to speak, but Lulu beat her to it. "Nancy Perkins, that was her name. I remember—they called her the bella-donna killer. And those berries were filled with arsenic or something like that." She fell silent and hummed under her breath for a few moments, then she resumed speaking. "Can you imagine anybody killing so much family?"

"They must have gotten on her nerves."

"The story hints she was in love with someone the family didn't like. I mean, she'd been cheating on her husband with just about everybody in the amateur acting company, and there was this guy—a butcher, I think—she was planning to run off with, but the husband was tipped off by a jealous woman and so he and the brothers-in-law got rid of him. I think he just sort of disappeared."

Mary coughed, reached into her handbag, found a handkerchief, and blew her nose. Lulu stared at her. "You catching a cold or something?"

When Lulu got home, she said to her mother, "You'll never believe this! You'll absolutely never believe this!"

Mrs. Dobson's eyes widened with joy as she clasped her hands together. "Don's asked you to marry him!"

"Oh, no—nothing like that. Mary's coming to dinner tomorrow."

Mrs. Dobson sat down. "I don't believe it."

"She is. And what's more, she said don't worry about dessert. She's going to bake something special. A real old-fashioned Down South pie filled with all sorts of fruits."

"Well, won't that be nice. I'm real glad she's coming, I really am. You say this Nick is sweet on her? Well, maybe she's loosening up at last. I mean, my God, living alone all these years without any companionship at all. I'm really glad she's coming. Now I know it'll be a real bang-up dinner."

In her garden, Mary was collecting berries into a mason jar. Softly she sang to herself, "Mary, Mary, quite contrary, how does your garden grow—" Then she chuckled and whispered to herself, "Why honeychile, it grows real useful, that's hay-ow it grows . . ."